WARNER
BOOKS

LARGE
PRINT

NELSON DEMILLE

★ UP ★
COUNTRY

— A NOVEL —

WARNER BOOKS

LARGE ⚅ PRINT

Copyright © 2002 by Nelson DeMille

All rights reserved.

Warner Books, Inc., 1271 Avenue of the Americas, New York, NY 10020

Visit our Web site at www.twbookmark.com.

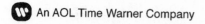 An AOL Time Warner Company

Printed in the United States of America

First Large Print Edition:
10   9   8   7   6   5   4   3   2   1

ISBN: 0-446-52993-1
LCCN: 2001093584

The Large Print Edition published in accord with the standards of the N.A.V.H.

Text Design: Stanley S. Drate / Folio Graphics Co. Inc.

FOR THOSE WHO ANSWERED THE CALL

Author's Note

Contemporary Vietnam, as represented in this book, is based partly on my experiences of January and February 1997, when I returned to Vietnam after a twenty-nine-year absence. Places such as restaurants, hotels, the former United States Embassy, and other locales were in existence and as described as of 1997, which is the time period of this story.

Truth exists; only falsehood has to be invented.
—GEORGES BRAQUE

— B O O K I —

★

Washington, D.C.

CHAPTER ONE

---★---

Bad things come in threes.

The first bad thing was a voice mail from Cynthia Sunhill, my former partner in the army's Criminal Investigation Division. Cynthia is still with the CID, and she is also my significant other, though we were having some difficulties with that job description.

The message said, "Paul, I need to talk to you. Call me tonight, no matter how late. I just got called on a case, and I have to leave tomorrow morning. We need to talk."

"Okay." I looked at the mantel clock in my small den. It was just 10 P.M., or twenty-two hundred hours, as I used to say when I was in the army not so long ago.

I live in a stone farmhouse outside Falls Church, Virginia, less than a half-hour drive to CID Headquarters. The commute time is actually irrelevant because I don't work for the CID any longer. In fact, I don't work for anyone. I'm retired, or maybe fired.

In any case, it had been about six months since my separation from the army, and I was getting bored, and I had twenty or thirty years to go.

As for Ms. Sunhill, she was stationed at Fort

Benning, Georgia, about a fourteen-hour drive from Falls Church, or twelve if I'm very excited. Her caseload is heavy, and weekends in the army are often normal duty days. The last six months had not been easy on our relatively new relationship, and with her interesting career and my growing addiction to afternoon talk shows, we don't have a lot to talk about.

Anyway, bad thing number two. I checked my e-mail, and there was a message that said simply, *1600 hrs, tomorrow, the Wall*. It was signed, *K*.

K is Colonel Karl Hellmann, my former boss at Headquarters, and Cynthia's present commanding officer. That much was clear. What wasn't clear was why Hellmann wanted to meet me at the Vietnam War Memorial. But instinctively, I put this under the category of "bad things."

I considered several equally terse replies, none of them very positive. Of course, I didn't *have* to respond at all; I was retired. But, in contrast to civilian careers, a military career does not completely end. The expression is, "Once an officer, always an officer." And I had been a warrant officer by rank, and a criminal investigator by occupation.

Fact is, they still have some kind of legal hold on you, though I'm not really sure what it is. If nothing else, they can screw up your PX privileges for a year.

I stared at Karl's message again and noticed it was addressed to Mr. Brenner. Warrant officers are addressed as Mister, so this salutation was a reminder of my past—or perhaps present—army rank, not a celebration of my civilian status. Karl is not subtle. I held off on my reply.

And, last but not least, the third bad thing. I'd apparently forgotten to send in my response to my book club, and in my mail was a Danielle Steel novel. Should I return it? Or give it to my mother next Christmas? Maybe she had a birthday coming up.

Okay, I couldn't postpone the Cynthia call any longer, so I sat at my desk and dialed. I looked out the window as the phone rang at the other end. It was a cold January night in northern Virginia, and a light snow was falling.

Cynthia answered, "Hello."

"Hi," I said.

A half-second of silence, then, "Hi, Paul. How are you?"

We were off on the wrong foot already, so I said, "Let's cut to the chase, Cynthia."

She hesitated, then said, "Well . . . Can I first ask you how your day was?"

"I had a great day. An old mess sergeant gave me his recipe for chili—I didn't realize it fed two hundred, and I made it all. I froze it in Ziploc bags. I'll send you some. Then I went to the gym, played a basketball game against a wheelchair team—beat them big time—then off to the local tavern for beer and hamburgers with the boys. How about your day?"

"Well . . . I just wrapped up the rape case I told you about. But instead of time off, I have to go to Fort Rucker for a sexual harassment investigation, which looks tricky. I'll be there until it's concluded. Maybe a few weeks. I'll be in Bachelor Officers Quarters if you want to call me."

I didn't reply.

She said, "Hey, I still think about Christmas."

"Me, too." That was a month ago, and I hadn't seen her since. "How's Easter look?"

"You know, Paul . . . you could move here."

"But you could be reassigned anytime. Then I'd wind up following your career moves. Didn't we discuss this?"

"Yes, but . . ."

"I like it here. You could get stationed here."

"Is that an offer?"

Whoops. I replied, "It would be good for your career. Headquarters."

"Let me worry about my career. And I really don't want a staff job. I'm an investigator. Just like you were. I want to go where I can be useful."

I said, "Well, I can't be following you around like a puppy dog, or hanging around your apartment when you're away on assignment. It's not good for my ego."

"You could get a job here in law enforcement."

"I'm working on that. Here in Virginia."

And so on. It's tough when the guy's not

working and the woman has a traveling career. To make matters worse, the army likes to change your permanent duty station as soon as you're comfortable, which calls into question the army's definition of permanent. On top of that, there are a lot of temporary duty assignments these days—places like Bosnia, Somalia, South America—where you could be gone for up to a year, which pushes the definition of temporary. Bottom line, Cynthia and I were what's called these days GU—geographically unsuitable.

The military, as I've always said, is tough on relationships; it's not a job, it's a calling, a commitment that makes other commitments really difficult. Sometimes impossible.

"Are you there?" she asked.

"I'm here."

"We can't go on like this, Paul. It hurts."

"I know."

"What should we do?"

I think she was willing to resign and forfeit a lot of her pension, in exchange for the M word. Then we'd decide where to live, find jobs, and live happily ever after. And why not? We were in love.

"Paul?"

"Yeah . . . I'm thinking."

"You should have already thought about all of this."

"Right. Look, I think we should talk about this in person. Face-to-face."

"The only thing we do face-to-face is fuck."

"That's not . . . well, we'll talk over dinner. In a restaurant."

"Okay. I'll call you when I get back from Rucker. I'll come there, or you come here."

"Okay. Hey, how's your divorce coming?"

"It's almost final."

"Good." Regarding her loving husband, I asked, "Do you see much of Major Nut Case?"

"Not much. At the O Club once in a while. Can't avoid those situations."

"Does he still want you back?"

"Don't try to complicate a simple situation."

"I'm not. I'm just concerned that he might try to kill me again."

"He never tried to kill you, Paul."

"I must have misinterpreted his reason for pointing a loaded pistol at me."

"Can we change the subject?"

"Sure. Hey, do you read Danielle Steel?"

"No, why?"

"I bought her latest book. I'll send it to you."

"Maybe your mother would like it. It's her birthday, February 10. Don't forget."

"I have it memorized. By the way, I got an e-mail from Karl. He wants to meet me tomorrow."

"Why?"

"I thought maybe you knew."

"No, I don't," she said. "Maybe he just wants to have a drink, talk about old times."

"He wants me to meet him at the Vietnam Memorial."

"Really? That's odd."

"Yeah. And he never mentioned anything to you?"

"No," she replied. "Why should he?"

"I don't know. I can't figure out what he's up to."

"Why do you think he's up to anything? You two worked together for years. He likes you."

"No, he doesn't," I said. "He hates me."

"He does not hate you. But you're a difficult man to work with. Actually, you're difficult to love."

"My mother loves me."

"You should re-check that. Regarding Karl, he respects you, and he knows just how brilliant you are. He either needs some advice, or he needs some information about an old case."

"Why the Wall?"

"Well . . . I don't know. You'll find out when you meet him."

"It's cold here. How's it there?"

"Sixties."

"It's snowing here."

"Be careful driving."

"Yeah." We both stayed silent for a while, during which time I thought of our history. We'd met at NATO Headquarters in Brussels. She was engaged to Major What's-His-Name, a Special Forces guy, we got involved, he got pissed, pulled the aforementioned gun on me, I backed off, they got married, and a year later Cynthia and I bumped into each other again.

It was in the Officers Club at Fort Hadley, Georgia, and we were both on assignment. I was undercover, investigating the theft and sale of army weapons, she was wrapping up a rape case. That's her specialty. Sexual crimes. I'd rather be in combat again than have that job. But someone's got to do it, and she's good at it. More important, she can compartmental- ize, and she seems to be unaffected by her work, though sometimes I wonder.

But back to Fort Hadley, last summer. While we were both there, the post commander's daughter, Captain Ann Campbell, was found on a rifle range, staked out, naked, strangled, and apparently raped. So, I'm asked to drop my lit- tle arms deal case, and Cynthia is asked to assist me. We solved the murder case, then tried to solve our own case, which is proving more diffi- cult. At least she got rid of Major Nut Job.

"Paul, why don't we put this on hold until we can meet? Is that okay?"

"Sounds okay." In fact, it was my suggestion. But why point that out? "Good idea."

"We both need to think about how much we have to give up and how much we stand to gain."

"Did you rehearse that line?"

"Yes. But it's true. Look, I love you—"

"And I love you."

"I know. That's why this is difficult." Neither of us spoke for a while, then she said, "I'm younger than you—"

"But I'm more immature."

"Please shut up. And I like what I do, I like my life, my career, my independence. But . . . I'd give it up if I thought . . ."

"I hear you. That's a big responsibility for me."

"I'm not pressuring you, Paul. I'm not even sure I want what I think I want."

I'm a bright guy, but I get confused when I talk to women. Rather than ask for a clarification, I said, "I understand."

"Do you?"

"Absolutely." Totally clueless.

"Do you miss me?"

"Every day," I said.

"I miss you. I really do. I'm looking forward to seeing you again. I'll take some leave time. I promise."

"I'll take some leave time, too."

"You're not working."

"Right. But if I was, I'd take a leave to be with you. I'll come to you this time. It's warmer there."

"Okay. That would be nice."

"You like chili?"

"No."

"I thought you liked chili. Okay, good luck

with the case. Give me a day's notice, and I'll be there."

"It'll be about two weeks. Maybe three. I'll let you know when I get into the case."

"Okay."

"Say hello to Karl for me. Let me know what he wanted."

"Maybe he wants to tell me about his alien abduction."

She laughed.

So, just as we were about to end on a happy note, she said, "You know, Paul, you didn't have to resign."

"Is that a fact?" The case of the general's daughter had been trouble from minute one, a political, emotional, and professional minefield, and I stepped right into it. I would have been better off not solving the case because the solution turned out to be about things no one wanted to know. I said to Cynthia, "A letter of reprimand in my file is the army's way of saying, 'Call your pension officer.' A little subtle, perhaps, but—"

"I think you misinterpreted what was happening. You were scolded, you got all huffy, and you acted impulsively because your ego was bruised."

"Is that so? Well, thank you for informing me that I threw away a thirty-year career because I had a temper tantrum."

"You should come to terms with that. I'll tell

you something else—unless you find something equally important and challenging to do, you're going to get depressed—"

"I'm depressed now. You just made me depressed. Thanks."

"Sorry, but I know you. You were not as burned out as you thought you were. The Campbell case just got to you. That's okay. It got to everyone. Even me. It was the saddest, most depressing case—"

"I don't want to talk about that."

"Okay. But what you needed was a thirty-day leave, not a permanent vacation. You're still young—"

"You're younger."

"You've got a lot of energy left, a lot to give, but you need to write a second act, Paul."

"Thank you. I'm exploring my options." It had gotten noticeably cooler in the room and on the phone.

"Are you angry?"

"No. If you were here, you'd see me smiling. I'm smiling."

"Well, if I didn't love you, I wouldn't be saying these things."

"I'm still smiling."

"See you in a few weeks." She said, "Take care of yourself."

"You, too."

Silence, then, "Good night."

"'Bye."

We both hung up. I stood, went to the bar, and made a drink. Scotch, splash of soda, ice.

I sat in my den, my feet on the desk, watching the snow outside. The Scotch smelled good.

So, there I was with a Danielle Steel novel on my desk, an unpleasant phone call still ringing in my ears, and an ominous message from Karl Hellmann on my computer screen.

Sometimes things that seem unconnected are actually part of a larger plan. Not your plan, to be sure, but someone else's plan. I was supposed to believe that Karl and Cynthia were not talking about me, but Mrs. Brenner didn't raise an idiot.

I should be pissed off when people underestimate my intelligence, though in truth, I affect a certain macho idiocy that encourages people to underestimate my brilliance. I've put a lot of people in jail that way.

I looked at the message again. *1600 hrs, tomorrow, the Wall*. Not even "please." Colonel Karl Gustav Hellmann can be a bit arrogant. He's German-born, as the name suggests, whereas Paul Xavier Brenner is a typical Irish lad, from South Boston, charmingly irresponsible, and delightfully smart-assed. Herr Hellmann is quite the opposite. Yet, on some strange level, we got along. He was a good commander, strict but fair, and highly motivated. I just never trusted his motives.

Anyway, I sat up and banged out an e-mail to Karl: *See you there and then*. I signed it, *Paul Brenner, PFC*, which, in this case, did not mean Private First Class, but meant, as Karl and I both knew, Private F-ing Civilian.

CHAPTER TWO

———————— ★ ————————

I t was three o'clock, and I was at the National Mall, a park in Washington, D.C., a rectangular strip of grass and trees, running from the U.S. Capitol in the east to the Lincoln Memorial in the west, a distance of about two miles.

The Mall is a good place to jog, with nice vistas, so rather than waste a trip into the city just to see Karl Hellmann, I came dressed in a sweat suit and running shoes, and I wore a knit cap pulled over my ears.

I began my run around the Capitol reflecting pool and paced myself to arrive at the Wall at the appointed hour of 4 P.M., my time, 1600 hours, Karl's time.

It was cold, but the sun was still above the horizon, and there was no wind. The trees were all bare, and the grass was dusted with last night's snow.

I set off at a good pace, keeping to the south side of the Mall, past the National Air and Space Museum, the Smithsonian, and other museums in between.

This is, as I said, officially a park, but it's also where everyone wants to erect something important; monuments, museums, memorials, and statues, and if this marble mania keeps up, the Mall will someday resemble the Roman Forum, packed full of temples to this and that. I'm not being judgmental—important people and events need a memorial or a monument. I've got my memorial: the Wall. It's a very good memorial because it doesn't have my name on it.

The sun was lower, the shadows were longer, and it was very still and quiet, except for the snow crunching under my feet.

I glanced at my watch and saw it was ten minutes to the appointed hour. Herr Hellmann, like many of his ethnic group, is fanatical about punctuality. I mean, I don't like to generalize about races, religions, and all that, but the Irish and the Germans don't share the same concept of time.

I picked up my pace and headed north around the reflecting pool. My butt was starting to drag, and the cold air was making my lungs ache.

As I crossed the landscape of Constitution Gardens, the Vietnam Women's Memorial statues came into view: three nurses clad in jungle fatigues, around some wounded guy I couldn't yet see.

About a hundred yards farther toward the Wall was the statue of the three servicemen— three bronze guys in jungle fatigues near a flagstaff.

Beyond the two groupings of bronze statues

was the black wall itself, highly contrasted against the white snow.

The Wall is probably the most visited monument in Washington, but there weren't many people around on this cold weekday. As I got closer, I had the sense that the people who were there, staring hard at the Wall, were people who needed to be there.

A solitary man stood out from the sparse crowd; it was Colonel Karl Hellmann, dressed in a civilian trench coat, wearing a snap-brim hat, and, of course, looking at his watch, probably mumbling to himself in his slightly accented English, "Vhere is dis guy?"

I slowed my pace so as not to alarm my former boss with the sight of me running full tilt toward him, and when I was on the path that runs parallel to the Wall, about twenty yards from Herr Hellmann, a church bell chimed somewhere, then a second chime, and a third. I slowed to a walk and came up behind Karl Gustav Hellmann, just as the fourth bell chimed the hour.

He sensed my presence, or perhaps saw me in the reflection of the black wall, and without turning, he said, "Hello, Paul."

He seemed delighted to see me—or sense me—though you couldn't tell how thrilled he was. If nothing else, I was right on time, and this puts him in a good mood.

I didn't reply to his greeting, and we both stood, side by side, looking at the Wall. I really wanted to walk off the run, but I remained standing, trying to catch my breath, clouds of fog coming out of my nostrils like a horse, and the sweat starting to get cold on my face.

So, we stood there, silently getting to know each other again after a six-month separation, sort of like dogs sniffing each other to see who's top dog.

I noticed that the section of the Wall before which we were standing was marked *1968*. This is the largest expanse of the Wall, 1968 being the unhappy year of the highest American casualties: the Tet Offensive, the Siege of Khe Sanh, the Battle of the A Shau Valley, and other lesser-known but no less terrifying engagements. Karl Hellmann, like me, was there in 1968, and he knew of some of these places and events first-hand.

The homefront wasn't so terrific in 1968 either: the assassinations of Martin Luther King Jr. and Bobby Kennedy, the campus riots, the urban riots, and so forth. Bad year all around. I understood why Hellmann had put himself in front of 1968, though I didn't understand why we were here in the first place. But, old army guy that I am, I never speak to a superior officer until spoken to. Sometimes not even after I'm spoken to, like now. For all I gave a shit, we could stand there in complete silence until midnight.

Finally, Karl said, "Thank you for coming."

I replied, "It sounded like an order."

"But you're retired."

"Actually, I resigned."

"I don't care what *you* did. I made it a retirement. That's much more pleasant for everyone."

"I really wanted to resign."

"Then we couldn't have had that nice party— the one where you read your letter of reprimand to everyone."

"You asked me to say a few words."

Hellmann didn't respond, but said, "So, you look very fit."

"I should. I've been jogging all over Washington, meeting people at monuments. You're the third today."

Hellmann lit a cigarette and observed, "Your sarcasm and bad sense of humor haven't changed."

"Good. So, if I may ask, what's up?"

"First, we need to exchange pleasantries and news. How have you been?"

"Terrific. Catching up on a lot of reading. Hey, do you read Danielle Steel?"

"Who?"

"I'm going to send you a book. You like chili?"

Hellmann drew on his cigarette, probably wondering what possessed him to contact me.

"Let me ask you, Paul, do you think you've been unfairly treated by the army?"

"No more so than a few million other guys, Colonel."

"I think the pleasantries are finished."

"Good."

"Two administrative things. First, your letter of reprimand. This can be removed from your file. Second, your retirement pay. This can be computed differently, which could be a considerable amount of money over your expected life span."

"Actually, my expected life span got longer when I left the army, so the smaller amount works out okay."

"Do you want to know more about these two items?"

"No. I smell trouble."

So, we both stood there in the cold, sniffing the air, thinking five or six moves ahead. I'm good at this, but Karl is better. He's not quite as bright as I am, certainly not as glib, but he thinks deep and long.

I actually like the guy. I really do. In fact, to be honest, I was a little hurt when I never heard from him. Maybe he was annoyed over my silliness at the retirement party. I'd had a couple, but I vaguely remember doing an impression of a Prussian field marshal named, I think, von Hellmann.

Finally, Karl said, "There is a name on this wall of a man who was not killed in action. A man, who was, in fact, murdered."

I did not reply to that startling statement.

Karl asked me, "How many men do you know on this wall?"

I stayed silent for a moment, then replied, "Too many." I asked him, "How many guys do you know here?"

"The same. You had two tours of duty in Vietnam. Correct?"

"Correct. The '68 tour, then again in '72, but by that time, I was an MP, and most of my fighting was with drunken soldiers outside Bien Hoa Airbase."

"But the first time . . . you were a frontline infantryman . . . You saw a good deal of combat. Did you enjoy it?"

This is the kind of question that only combat veterans could understand. It occurred to me that in all the years I've known Karl, we never spoke much about our combat experiences. This is not unusual. I looked at him and said, "It was the ultimate high. The first few times. Then . . . I became used to it, accepted it as the norm . . . then, in the last few months before I went home, I got very paranoid, like they were trying to kill me personally, like they weren't going to let me go home. I don't think I slept the last two months in-country." We made eye contact.

Karl nodded. "That was my experience as well." He stepped closer to the Wall, focusing on individual names. "We were young then, Paul.

These men are forever young." He touched one of the names. "I knew this man."

Hellmann seemed unusually pensive, almost morose. I guess it had something to do with where we were, the season, the twilight and all that. I wasn't particularly chipper myself.

He took out a gold cigarette case and matching lighter. "Would you like one?"

"No, thanks. You just had one."

He ignored me, the way smokers do, and lit up another.

Karl Gustav Hellmann. I didn't know much about his personal life, but I knew that he grew up in the ruins of postwar Germany. I've known a few other German-American soldiers over the years, and they were mostly officers, and mostly retired by now. The usual biography of these galvanized Yankees was that they were fatherless or orphaned, and they did chores for the American Army of Occupation to survive. At eighteen, they enlisted in the U.S. Army at some military post in Germany, as a way out of the squalor of the defeated nation. There were a good number of such men in the army once, and Karl was probably one of the last.

I wasn't sure how much of this specific biography applied to Karl Hellmann, but he must be very close to mandatory retirement, unless there was a general's star in his immediate future, in which case he could stay on. I had the thought that this meeting had something to do with that.

He said to me, or maybe to himself, "It's been a long time. Yet sometimes it seems like yesterday." He looked at the Wall, then at me. "Do you agree?"

"Yes, 1968 is as clear as a slide show, a progression of bright silent images, frozen in time . . ." We looked at each other, and he nodded.

So, where was this headed?

It helps to know where it started. As I mentioned, I'm Boston Irish, South, which means working-class. My father was a World War II vet, like everybody else's father in that place and time. He did three years in the army infantry, came home, married, had three sons, and worked thirty years for the City of Boston, maintaining municipal buses. He once admitted to me that this job was not as exciting as the Normandy invasion, but the hours were better.

Not too long after my eighteenth birthday, I received my draft notice. I called Harvard regarding a spot in their freshman class, and a student deferment, but they pointed out, rightly, that I'd never applied. Same with Boston University, and even Boston College, where a lot of my co-religionists had found asylum from the draft.

So, I packed an overnight bag, Dad shook my hand, my younger brothers thought I was cool,

Mom cried, and off I went by troop train to Fort Hadley, Georgia, for Basic Training and Advanced Infantry Training. For some idiotic reason, I applied for and was accepted to Airborne School—that's parachute training—at Fort Benning, also in Georgia. To complete my higher education in the field of killing, I applied for Special Forces Training, thinking maybe the war would run out before I ran out of crazy schools, but the army said, "Enough. You're good to go, boy." And soon after Airborne School, I found myself in a frontline infantry company in a place called Bong Son, which is not in California.

I glanced at Karl, knowing that we'd been over there at about the same time, having traveled very different roads to that war. But maybe not so different after all.

Karl said, "I thought it would be good if we met here."

I didn't reply.

After Vietnam, we both remained in the army, I think because the army wanted us, and no one else probably did. I became an MP and served a partial second tour in Vietnam. Over the years, I took advantage of the army college extension program and received a B.S. in Criminal Justice, then got into the Criminal Investigation Division, mostly because they wore civilian clothes.

I became what's known as a warrant officer: a quasi-officer with no command responsibility, but with an important job, in this case, a homi-cide detective.

Karl took a slightly different and more gen-teel route, and went to a real college full-time on the army's nickel, getting some half-assed degree in philosophy while taking four years of Reserve Officers Training, then re-entering ac-tive duty as a lieutenant.

At some point, our lives nearly touched in Vietnam, then converged at Falls Church. And here we were now, literally and figuratively in the twilight, no longer warriors, but middle-aged men looking at the dead of our generation spread out in front of us; 58,000 names carved into the black stone, and I suddenly saw these men as kids, carefully carving their names into trees, into school desks, into wooden fences. I realized that for every name in the granite, there was a matching name still carved somewhere in America. And these names, too, were carved in the hearts of their families, and in the heart of the nation.

We began walking, Karl and I, along the Wall, our breaths misting in the cold air. At the base of the wall were flowers, left by friends and family, and I recalled that the last time I'd been here, many years ago, someone had left a base-ball glove, and when I saw it, before I knew what was happening, tears were rolling down my face.

In the early years of the memorial, there had

been a lot of such things left at the Wall: photos, hats, toys, even favorite foods, like a box of Nabisco graham crackers, which I saw that time. Today, I noticed, there weren't any personal items, just flowers, and a few folded notes stuck in the seams of the Wall.

The years have passed, the parents die, the wives move on, the brothers and sisters don't forget, but they've already been here and don't need to return. The dead, young as they were for the most part, didn't leave many children, but the last time I was here, I met a daughter, a lady in her early twenties, who never knew her father. I never knew a daughter, so for about ten minutes, we filled a little of the emptiness in each other, the missing parts, then we went our separate ways.

For some reason, this made me think of Cynthia, of marriage, children, home and hearth, and all sorts of warm and fuzzy things. If Cynthia were here, I might have proposed marriage, but she wasn't here, and I knew I'd be myself again by morning.

Karl, who had probably been thinking similar thoughts about war and peace, mortality and immortality, said, "I try to come here once a year, on August 17, the anniversary of a battle I was in." He stayed silent a while, then continued, "The battle of Highway 13 . . . Eleventh Armored Cavalry, the Michelin rubber plantation. You may have heard of it. A lot of people around me were dying. So, I come here on August 17, and say a prayer for them, and a prayer of thanks for myself. It's the only time I pray."

"I thought you used to go to church every Sunday."

"One goes to church with the wife and children."

He didn't elaborate, and I didn't ask. We turned and walked back the way we came.

He said, in a different tone of voice, "So, are you curious about the man who was murdered?"

"I may be curious. But I really don't want to know."

"If that were the case, you'd leave."

"I'm being polite, Colonel."

"I would have enjoyed that politeness when you worked for me. But as long as you're being polite, hear me out."

"If I listen, I can be subpoenaed at some future judicial proceeding. Says so in the manual."

"Believe me, this meeting and this conversation never took place. That's why we're here, not in Falls Church."

"I already figured that out."

"May I begin?"

I was on solid ground now; the next step was a greased slope. There was not a single good reason in the world that I could think of for me to listen to this man. But I wasn't thinking hard enough. *Cynthia*. Get a job, get a life, or whatever she said.

Karl asked, "May I begin?"

"Can I stop you anytime I want?"

"No. If I begin, you listen, I end."

"Is this a criminal case?"

"I believe homicide is criminal, yes. Do you have any other stupid questions?"

I smiled, not because of the insult, but because I was getting on his nerves. "You know what? To prove how stupid I really am, I'll listen."

"Thank you."

Karl had walked away from the Wall toward the Women's Memorial, and I walked with him. He said, "It has come to the attention of the CID that a young lieutenant, who is listed as killed, or perhaps missing in action, was in fact murdered in the city of Quang Tri, on 7 February 1968, during the Tet Offensive battle for that city." He added, "I believe you were in Quang Tri Province at that time."

"Yes, but I have an alibi for that day."

"I only mention that as a coincidence. In fact, your unit was some kilometers away from the provincial capital of Quang Tri City on that day. But you can appreciate the background, and visualize the time and place."

"You bet. I also appreciate you checking my service records."

Hellmann ignored this and continued, "I was, as I said, with the Eleventh Armored Cavalry, stationed at Xuan Loc, but operating around Cu Chi at about that time. I don't remember that particular day, but that whole month during the Tet Offensive was unpleasant."

"It sucked."

"Yes, it sucked." He stopped walking and looked at me. "Regarding this American lieutenant, we have evidence that he was murdered by an American army captain."

Karl let that sink in, but I didn't react. Now, I'd heard what I didn't want to hear, and now I was in possession of a Secret. Details to follow.

We stared at the Vietnam Women's Memorial, the three nurses, one tending to the wounded guy lying on sandbags, one kneeling close by, and the other looking up at the sky for the medevac chopper. The four figures were in light clothing, and I felt cold just looking at them.

I said to Karl, "These statues should be closer to the Wall. The last person a lot of those guys over there saw or talked to before they died was a military nurse."

"Yes, but perhaps that juxtaposition would be too morbid. This man here looks to me as though he will live."

"Yeah . . . he's going to make it."

So we stayed silent awhile, lost in our thoughts. I mean, these are statues, but they bring the whole thing back again.

Karl broke the silence, and continued, "We don't know the name of the alleged murderer, nor do we know the alleged murder victim. We know only that this captain murdered this lieutenant in cold blood. We have no corpse—or I should say, we have many corpses, all killed by the enemy, except the one in question. We do know that the murder victim was killed by a single pistol shot to the forehead, and that may narrow down the name of the victim based on battlefield death certificates issued at that time. Unless, of course, the body was never found, and the victim is listed as missing in action. Are you following me?"

"I am. A United States Army captain pulls his pistol and shoots a United States Army lieutenant in the forehead. This is presumably a fatal wound. This happened in the heat of battle nearly thirty years ago. But let me play defense counsel—maybe it wasn't murder. Maybe it was one of those unfortunate instances where a superior officer shot a lower-ranking officer for cowardice in the face of the enemy. It happens, and it's not necessarily murder, or even illegal. Maybe it was self-defense, or an accident. You shouldn't jump to conclusions." I added, "But of course, you have a witness. So I shouldn't speculate."

We turned and began walking back toward the Wall. The light was fading, people came and went, a middle-aged man placed a floral wreath at the base of the black granite and wiped his eyes with a handkerchief.

Hellmann watched the man a moment, then said, "Yes, there was a witness. And the witness described a cold-blooded murder."

"And this is a reliable witness?"

"I don't know."

"Who and where is this witness?"

"We don't know where he is, but we have his name."

"And you want me to find him."

"Correct."

"How did you first hear from this witness?"

"He wrote a letter."

"I see . . . so, you have a missing witness to a thirty-year-old murder, no suspect, no corpse, no murder weapon, no motive, no forensic evidence, and the murder took place in a godforsaken country very far from here. And you want me to solve this homicide."

"That's correct."

"Sounds easy. Can I ask you why? Who cares after thirty years?"

"I care. The army cares. A murder was committed. There is no statute of limitations on murder."

"Right. You realize that this lieutenant who was killed, or is missing, is believed by his family to have died honorably in battle. So what is gained by proving that he was murdered? Don't you think his family has suffered enough?" I nodded toward the man at the Wall.

"That is not a consideration," said Karl Hellmann, true to form.

"It is to me," I informed him.

"It's not that you think too much, Paul, it's
that you think of the wrong things."

"No, I don't. I think that there is a name on
this wall that is best left alone."

"There's a murderer at large."

"Maybe, maybe not. For all we know, the alleged murderer was later killed in action. That
was a nasty time, and odds are that this captain
got killed in battle."

"Then his name doesn't belong on this wall
with those men who died honorably."

"I knew you'd say that."

"I knew you'd understand."

"I think we worked together too long."

"We worked well together."

This was news to me. Maybe he meant we got
the job done together, which was true, despite
our big differences in personalities, and the fact
that one of us was a stickler for rules, while the
other was definitely not.

We walked away from the Vietnam Women's
Memorial and stopped at the three bronze male
statues: two white guys and a black guy, who
were supposed to represent a marine, an army
guy, and a sailor, but they were all dressed in
jungle fatigues, so it was hard to tell. They were
staring at the Wall, as if they were contemplating

the names of the dead, but in a creepy sort of way, these guys looked dead themselves.

Karl turned toward the wall and said, "At first, I didn't like that Wall. I preferred these heroic bronze statues because the Wall, for all its abstractness and metaphorical nuances, was in reality just a massive tombstone, a common grave with everyone's name on it. That's what disturbed me. Then . . . then I accepted it. What do you think?"

"I think we have to accept it for what it is. A tombstone."

"Do you ever feel survivor's guilt?"

"I might have, if I hadn't been there. Can we change the subject?"

"No. You once told me that you bear no ill will toward the men who didn't serve. Is that true?"

"It's still true. Why?"

"You said you were more angry at the men who did go to Vietnam, but who didn't do their job—men who let the others down, men who engaged in dishonorable acts, such as rape and robbery. Men who carelessly killed civilians. Is that still true?"

"Finish the briefing."

"Yes. So, we have this captain, who most likely murdered a junior officer. I want to know the name of this captain and the name of the murdered lieutenant."

I noticed that the obvious question of why—

the motive—hadn't specifically come up. Maybe, as with most cases of murder in wartime, the motive was petty, illogical, and unimportant. But maybe it was the central reason for digging up a thirty-year-old crime. And if it was, and if Karl wasn't mentioning it, then I wasn't going to mention it. I stuck to the facts at hand and said, "All right, if you want some reality checks, consider that this captain—this alleged murderer—if he didn't die in combat could be dead of natural causes by now. It's been thirty years."

"I'm alive. You're alive. We have to find out if *he's* alive."

"Okay. How about the witness? Do we know if *he's* alive?"

"No, we don't. But if he's not, we want to know that, too."

"When is the last time this witness showed signs of life?"

"Eight February 1968. That's the date on the letter."

"I know the army post office is slow, but this is a record."

"In fact, the witness was not an American soldier. He was a soldier in the North Vietnamese army, named Tran Van Vinh. He was wounded during the battle of Quang Tri City, and was in hiding among the ruins. He witnessed these two Americans arguing and witnessed the captain pulling his pistol and shooting the lieutenant.

In his letter, which he wrote to his brother, he referred to the murderer as dai-uy—captain— and the murder victim as trung-uy—lieutenant."

"There were some marines around Quang Tri at that time. Maybe this is not a case for the army."

Hellmann replied, "Tran Van Vinh, in his letter, mentioned that these two men were ky-binh—cavalry. So obviously he saw their U.S. Army First Cavalry shoulder patches, which he knew."

I pointed out, "The First Cavalry Division, of which I was a member, had over twenty thousand men in it."

"That's correct. But it does narrow it down."

I thought about all this for a moment, then asked Karl, "And you have this letter?"

"Of course. That's why we're here."

"Right. And the letter was addressed to this guy's brother. How did you get it?"

"In a very interesting way. The brother was also a North Vietnamese soldier, named Tran Quan Lee. The letter was found on Tran Quan Lee's body in the A Shau Valley in mid-May of the same year by an American soldier named Victor Ort, who took it as a souvenir. The letter was sent home by Ort and lay in this man's steamer trunk full of other war memorabilia for almost thirty years. Very recently, Ort sent the letter to the Vietnam Veterans of America, based here in Washington. This organization asks its members to return found and captured enemy documents and artifacts, and to provide information that these veterans might have concerning enemy dead. This information is then turned over to the Vietnamese government in Hanoi to help the Vietnamese discover the fate of their missing soldiers."

"Why?"

"They are no longer the enemy. They have McDonald's and Kentucky Fried Chicken in Saigon. In any case, we want them to help us find *our* missing in action. We still have about two thousand MIAs unaccounted for. They have an astounding three hundred thousand missing."

"I think they're all in San Diego."

"No, they're all dead. Including Tran Quan Lee, killed in the A Shau Valley, possibly by Mr. Ort, though he was vague about that." Hellmann continued, "So, this American veteran, Victor Ort, sent the letter he found on the body of Tran Quan Lee to the Vietnam Veterans of America, with a note saying how, where, and when he found the letter and the body. The VVA, as a courtesy to the men who are sending such letters, had the letter translated, and was about to send the translation to Mr. Ort, but someone at the VVA—a retired army officer—read the translation and realized that what he was reading was an eyewitness account to a murder. This man then contacted us. A civilian would have contacted the FBI."

"It was our lucky day. And did anyone send the translation to Mr. Ort?"

"Mr. Ort was sent a translation of a love letter, and a note of thanks."

"Right. And you have the original of this letter?"

"Yes, and we've had it authenticated regarding paper and ink, and we've had three different translators work on it. They all came up with nearly the same wording. There's no mistaking that what Tran Van Vinh is describing to his brother, Tran Quan Lee, is a murder. It's a very compelling and disturbing letter." He added, "I'll show you a translated copy of it, of course."

"Do I need it?"

Hellmann replied, "There's not much in the way of clues in the letter other than what I told you, but it might motivate you."

"To do what?"

"To find the author of the letter. Tran Van Vinh."

"And what are the chances of Tran Van Vinh being alive? I mean, really, Karl, that whole generation of Vietnamese was nearly wiped out."

"Nearly is the operative word."

"Not to mention a short natural life expectancy."

"We have to try to find this witness, Sergeant

Tran Van Vinh." Hellmann added, "Unfortunately, there are only about three hundred
family names in Vietnam, and the Vietnamese
population is about eighty million."

"So the phone book won't be much help."

"There are no phone books. But we're lucky
this man's family name wasn't Nguyen. Half the
Vietnamese family names are Nguyen. Fortunately, the family name Tran is not as common,
and the middle and first names of Van Vinh and
Quan Lee narrow it down."

"Do you have a hometown and date of birth?"

"No date of birth, but an approximate age, of
course—our age group. The envelope was addressed to the brother via an army unit designation, and also on the envelope was Tran Van
Vinh's return army address. We know from
these addresses that these two men were in the
North Vietnamese army, not the local South
Vietnamese Viet Cong, so they're northerners.
In fact, in the letter there is a mention of their
village or hamlet, a place called Tam Ki, but we
find no such village on any of our maps of Vietnam, North or South. This is not unusual, as
you might remember—the locals often referred
to their hamlets or villages by one name, and
the official maps had another for the same
place. But we're working on that. The village of
Tam Ki will be an important clue in finding this
man, Tran Van Vinh."

"And if you find him? What's he going to tell you that he hasn't already put in the letter?"

"He could possibly identify the murderer from old army ID photos."

"After thirty years?"

"It's possible."

"So, you have suspects?"

"Not at the moment. But we're going through army records now, trying to discover the names of all First Cavalry Division United States Army captains who were in or near the city of Quang Tri on or about 7 February 1968. Also, of course, we're looking at the First Cav lieutenants who were killed or missing in action at the same time and place. That's all we have—two ranks, a captain and a lieutenant, their division, the First Cav, a place, Quang Tri City, and the date of 7 February 1968, the actual date of the murder that was described in the letter written the following day."

Karl and I walked away from the statues, and I thought about all of this. I saw where this was going, but I didn't want to go there.

Karl continued, "We can narrow this down and come up with a list of possible suspects based on army records. Then, we will ask the FBI to question these former captains if they are civilians, and we will question any who are still in the army. At the same time, we will be looking for the only witness to this homicide. It sounds like a long shot, Paul, but crimes have been solved with even less to go on, as you well know."

"What do you want from me?"

"I want you to go to Vietnam, Paul."

"Oh, I don't think so, Karl. Been there, done that. Got the medals to prove it."

"Vietnam in January is actually quite pleasant, weatherwise."

"So is Aruba. That's where I'm headed next week," I lied.

"A return trip might do you some good."

"I don't think so. The place sucked then, it sucks now."

"Veterans who've returned report a cathartic experience."

"It's a totalitarian Commie police state with two hundred thousand tons of unexploded mines, booby traps, and artillery shells buried all over, waiting to blow me up."

"Well, you need to be careful."

"Are you coming with me?"

"Of course not. The place sucks."

I laughed. "Colonel, with all due respect, you can take this case and shove it up someone else's butt."

"Listen to me, Paul—we cannot send an active duty man to Vietnam. This is . . . well, an unofficial investigation. You'll go over as a tourist, a returning veteran, like thousands of other men—"

"You mean I wouldn't have any official status or diplomatic immunity?"

"We would come to your aid, if you got into trouble."

I asked, "What kind of aid? Like smuggling poison into my cell?"

"No, like having an embassy person visit you if you were detained, plus, of course, we'd lodge an official protest."

"That's very reassuring, but I don't think I want to see the inside of a Communist prison, Karl. I have two friends who spent a lot of years in the Hanoi Hilton. They didn't like it."

"If you ran afoul of the authorities, they'd just kick you out."

"Can I tell them you said that?"

Hellmann didn't reply.

I thought a moment and said, "I'm assuming that the Vietnam Veterans of America has sent the original of this letter to Hanoi as part of their humanitarian program to help the North Vietnamese learn the fate of their dead and missing. Therefore, Hanoi will locate the family of the deceased Tran Quan Lee, and they will know if his brother, Tran Van Vinh, is alive and where he is. Correct? So, why don't you go through normal diplomatic channels, and let the Hanoi government do what it does best— keep track of its miserable citizens."

Hellmann informed me, "Actually, we've asked the VVA not to send that letter to Hanoi."

I knew that, but I asked, "Why?"

"Well . . . There are a number of reasons we thought it best that Hanoi didn't see the letter at this time."

"Give me one of those reasons."

"The less they know, the better. The same is true for you."

We made eye contact, and I realized that there was more to this than a thirty-year-old murder. There had to be, or none of this would make any sense. But I didn't ask anything further. I said, "Okay, I've heard too much already. Thanks for your confidence in me, but no thanks."

"What are you afraid of?"

"Don't try that on me, Karl. I've put my life on the line for this country many times. But this is not worth my life, or anyone's life. It's history. Let it be."

"It's a matter of justice."

"This has nothing to do with justice. It's something else, and since I don't know what it is, I'm not putting my ass into Vietnam for a reason that no one's telling me. The last two times I was there, I knew why."

"We thought we knew why. They lied to us. No one's lying to you this time. We're just not telling you why. But trust me that this is very important."

"That's what they said then, too."

"I won't argue with that."

The sun had almost set, and a cold wind was

starting to blow. We were nearly alone, and both of us stood silently with our thoughts. Finally, Karl Hellmann said in a soft voice, "It is twilight. The shadows are long." He looked at me. "The shadows stretch from there to here, Paul. That's all I can tell you."

I didn't reply.

A man appeared dressed in an old fatigue jacket, wearing a bush hat. He was about our age, but looked older because of a full gray beard. He put a bugle to his lips and played taps. As the last mournful note died away in the wind, the man faced the Wall, saluted, and moved off.

Karl and I lingered a moment longer, then Hellmann said, "All right, I understand. It could be a bit risky, and middle-aged men don't risk their lives for something that could be foolish or useless. To tell you the truth, this man Tran Van Vinh is most likely dead, or even if he were alive, he probably wouldn't be helpful. Come on, let me buy you a drink. There's that place you like on Twenty-third Street."

We walked in silence through the Mall, and Hellmann asked, "May I at least show you the letter?"

"Which one do I see? The love letter or the real one?"

"The translation of Tran Van Vinh's letter."

"A true and complete translation?"

Karl didn't reply.

I said to him, "Give me the original letter in Vietnamese, and I'll have it translated."

"That's not necessary."

I smiled. "So, there's something in the letter that is not for my eyes. But you want my help, and you're holding a lot back."

"It's for your own good. Whatever I'm not telling you is irrelevant to the mission of finding Tran Van Vinh."

"It's relevant to *something*, or you wouldn't be so cloak-and-dagger about it."

Karl said nothing.

I asked, "How long ago did you get this letter from the VVA?"

"Two days ago."

"And I assume you've begun the search of army records?"

"Yes, but that's going to take a week or two. Also, there was that record storage fire—"

"Karl, that 1973 fire has been used to cover up more crap than any fire in history."

"That may be, but there *are* missing files. Yet, I think that in a few weeks, we'll be able to come up with a list of First Cavalry army captains who may have been in that place at that time. The list of army lieutenants who were actually killed in action in Quang Tri City on or around 7 February will be much shorter and more detailed. I can't imagine more than two or three names on that KIA list. There is a presumption that the captain and the lieutenant were in the same unit, so that could narrow down the names of the captains who could be suspects. That's why I think this is not such a long shot."

I replied, "Well, you may come up with a prime suspect, but you'll never get a conviction."

Karl replied, "Let's find the witness and the suspect and worry about the consequences later."

I thought a minute, then said to Karl, "As you mentioned, I was there at the time. And, FYI, the city itself was garrisoned by the South Vietnamese army, not Americans. Our guys were at firebases around the city. Are you sure these two Cav officers were *in* the city?"

"The letter strongly indicates that. Why?"

"Well, then maybe these two Americans were attached to the South Vietnamese army as advisors—Military Assistance Command, Vietnam. MACV. Right?"

"That's a possibility."

"So, that narrows it down even more. Do some desk work here before you go sending somebody into 'Nam."

"We want parallel and concurrent investigations."

"It's your show." In fact, I strongly suspected that the CID had been working on this much longer than Karl was indicating. I also suspected that the CID had already narrowed down the list of possible suspects and the possible victim, and maybe they already had their prime suspect. But they were not telling Paul Brenner about that. What the CID wanted now was for me to find the only eyewitness to this crime. I said to Colonel Hellmann, "An interesting case, and my bloodhound instincts are aroused. But I don't need the frequent flier miles to Southeast Asia. I can think of a few other guys who'd love to go."

"No problem." Hellmann changed the subject and asked, "Are you still seeing Ms. Sunhill?"

I love it when people ask you questions about things they already know. I replied, "Why don't you ask her?"

"To be honest, I already have. She indicates that there seems to be some problem with the relationship, which is why I thought you might be open to an overseas assignment."

"I am. Aruba. And stay out of my personal life, please."

"Ms. Sunhill is still CID, and as her commanding officer, I have a right to ask certain personal questions."

"That's what I miss about the army."

Karl ignored this and asked, "By the way, are you looking for a civilian job in law enforcement?"

"I might be."

"I can't imagine you doing nothing in retirement."

"I've got plenty to do."

"I might be able to help you with a government job. The FBI hires a lot of former CID. This overseas assignment would look very good on your résumé."

"Not to mention my obituary."

"It would look good there, too."

Karl doesn't make too many jokes, so to be polite, I chuckled.

This encouraged him, I think, to press on. He said, "Did I mention that the Department of the Army will retroactively promote you to Chief Warrant Officer Five and recompute your retirement pay?"

"Tell them thanks."

"In exchange for about two or three weeks of your time."

"There's always a catch."

Hellmann stopped and lit another cigarette. We faced each other under a lamplight. Hellmann exhaled a stream of smoke and said, "We can get someone else, but your name came up first, second, and third. I've never asked a favor of you—"

"Of course you have."

"And I've gotten you out of some very messy situations, Paul."

"That you put me in, Karl."

"You put yourself in most of them. Be honest with yourself."

"It's cold out here. I need a drink. You smoke too much." I turned and walked off.

End of meeting. End of Karl. I continued walking, picturing Karl standing under the lamplight, smoking his cigarette, watching me. Well, that was one bad thing resolved.

For some reason, I found that my pace was slowing. All sorts of thoughts suddenly filled my frozen brain. Cynthia was one of them, of course. Write a second act, Paul. Was I set up, or what?

Certainly I needed to do something to get my juices flowing again. But I couldn't believe that Cynthia would want me to risk my life to perk up our relationship. Probably, she didn't know exactly what Karl had in mind.

As I walked, I thought about my favorite subject—me. What was best for Paul Brenner? Suddenly, I had this image of me going to Vietnam and returning a hero; that hadn't happened the last two times, but maybe it would this time. Then, I had this other image of me coming home in a box.

I found myself in a circle of light under a lamp pole, and I wasn't walking. I turned back toward Karl Hellmann. We stared at each other across the darkness, each of us visible in a pool of light. I called out to him, "Would I have any contacts in 'Nam?"

"Of course," he called out. "You'll have a contact in Saigon, and one in Hanoi. Plus, there may be someone in Hue who can help. The mission is in place. It lacks only a person to fulfill it."

"How long would this person need to fulfill it?"

"You have a twenty-one-day tourist visa. Any longer would arouse suspicion. With luck, you'll be home sooner."

"With bad luck, I'll be home even sooner."

"Think positive. You must visualize success."

In fact, I visualized a lot of people gathered in my honor, everyone drinking whiskey; a homecoming party, or an Irish wake.

I don't mind dangerous assignments. I thrived on them once. But it was the 'Nam thing . . . the idea that I escaped my destiny and that destiny was stalking me. It was creepy.

I asked Karl, "If I don't make it this time, do I get my name on the Wall?"

"I'll look into that. But think positive."

"Are you sure you don't want to come with me?"

"I'm positive."

We both laughed.

"When do I leave?"

"Tomorrow morning. Be at Dulles at eight hundred hours. I will e-mail you instructions for a rendezvous at the airport."

"My own passport?"

"Yes. We want light cover. Your friend at the airport will have your visa, tickets, and hotel reservations, money, and a few things to memorize. You need to go in clean."

"That's it?"

"That's it. Can I buy you a drink?"

"When I get home. See you later."

Karl said, "Oh, one more thing. I assume you will let Cynthia know you're away. Don't be too specific. Would you like me to speak with her after you're gone?"

"Do you mean gone, dead, or gone to Asia?"

"I'll speak with her after you take off."

I didn't reply.

Karl said, "Well, then, good luck and thank you."

If we were closer, we'd have shaken hands, but we both just gave half-assed salutes by touching our caps. We turned away from each other and walked off.

CHAPTER THREE

———★———

After my meeting with Karl, I had a few drinks by myself at home, then sent an e-mail to Cynthia. You should never drink when you have access to any form of communication—e-mail, cell phone, telephone, or fax machine. I printed out my message to her and put it in my overnight bag, intending to re-read it in the morning to see how drunk I'd been. I erased the message on my computer, in case CID Internal Security were the next people to go into my computer.

There was an e-mail from Karl with my airport rendezvous instructions, as he'd promised. His short message ended with "Thanks again. Good luck. See you later."

I noticed he didn't invite either a phone call or a reply to his e-mail. In fact, there was nothing left to say. I deleted his message.

I left a note for my housekeeper, informing her I'd be away for about three weeks and to look after things. In fact, I tidied up a bit, in case the CID arrived before the housekeeper to look for sensitive materials that may have been left behind by the deceased. I always tidy up; I want to be remembered as a man who didn't leave his dirty underwear on the floor.

At 7 A.M. the next morning, I checked my e-mail, but there was no reply from Cynthia to last night's message. Maybe she hadn't accessed her mail yet.

A horn honked outside, and I gathered my small suitcase and overnight bag and went out into the cold, dark morning, sans overcoat, as instructed by Karl. In Saigon, it was eighty-one degrees and sunny, according to the efficient Herr Hellmann.

I got into the waiting taxi, exchanged greetings with the driver, and off we went to Dulles Airport, a half-hour drive at this time of the morning. Normally, I would drive myself to Dulles, but long-term airport parking might not be long enough for this trip.

It was a gloomy morning, which may have accounted for my morbid thoughts.

I recalled a similar dawn trip to the airport, many years ago. The airport was Boston's Logan, and the driver was my father in his '56 Chevy, which has since become a classic, but which was then a jalopy.

My thirty-day pre-Vietnam leave had come to an end, and it was time to fly to San Francisco, and points west.

We'd left Mom at home, crying, too upset to even scramble eggs. My brothers were sleeping.

Pop was pretty quiet during the trip, and it was only years later that I thought about what he must have been thinking. I wondered how his own father had seen him off to war.

We had arrived at the airport, parked, and went into the terminal together. There were a lot of guys in uniforms with duffel bags and overnight bags, a lot of mothers and fathers, wives or maybe girlfriends, and even kids, probably siblings.

Sharply dressed military police strode in pairs through the terminal, an unusual sight just a year before. The homefront during wartime is a study of extreme contrasts: sorrow and joy, partings and reunions, patriotism and cynicism, parades and funerals.

I was flying American Airlines to San Francisco, and I got in the appropriate line, which was comprised of mostly soldiers, sailors, marines, and airmen, and some civilians, who looked uncomfortable being in the same line.

My father wanted to wait, but it looked like most of the families had left, so I talked him out of it. He took my hand and said, "Come home, son."

For a moment, I thought he was ordering me to leave with him and forget this idiocy. Then I realized he meant come home alive. I looked him in the eye and said, "I will. Take care of Mom."

"Yup. Good luck, Paul." And he was gone. A few minutes later, I caught a glimpse of him through the glass doors, watching me. We made eye contact, he turned, and was again gone.

I checked in at the ticket counter and went to the gate, where I discovered that this was where most of the families had disappeared to. You could go right to the gate in those days to see people off. I thought maybe my father might re-appear, or even my girlfriend, Peggy, who I insisted not come to the airport. I realized that I really wanted to see her one more time.

Despite the large number of guys my own age from the Boston area, I didn't see anyone I knew. This was to be the beginning of my year of looking for familiar faces, and imagining them on other people.

So, I stood there by myself while people around me stood quietly, or talked or cried softly. I've never seen so many people make so little noise.

A few MPs stood at the edge of the crowd, looking for signs of problems among the young men who were about to leave for ports of embarkation and war.

In retrospect, this whole scene had made me uncomfortable: the MPs, the mostly unwilling soldiers, the quiet families; the sum total of which was this very un-American feeling of government control and coercion. But it was wartime—though not my father's war, which was about as popular as any war could get—and in wartime, even the most benevolent governments get a little pushy.

This was November 1967, and the anti-war movement wasn't yet in full swing, and thus there were no protesters or demonstrators at Logan, though there were a bunch of them around when I landed in San Francisco, and a lot of them a few days later at Oakland Army Base, urging the soldiers not to go, or better yet, to make love, not war.

On that subject, my high school girlfriend, Peggy Walsh, was a pretty but rather repressed young lady, who went to confession on Saturday and took communion on Sunday. At a confraternity dance in St. Brigid's High School gym, we were all made to raise our right hands while Father Bennett led us in renouncing Satan, temptation, and the sins of the flesh.

The chance of Peggy and me having sex in peacetime were about as good as my father's chances of winning the Irish Sweepstakes.

I smiled at that thought and came back to the present. The taxi was making good time, just as my father had done so many years before. I remember thinking then, *When you're going to war, what's the hurry?*

I closed my eyes and let my mind drift back

to the months before I was waiting to board that airplane at Logan.

I'd gone into the army a virgin, but during advanced infantry training at Fort Hadley, I and some adventurous barracks mates discovered the young ladies of the cotton mills—lint heads, we called them, because they had cotton fibers in their hair from working in these hellish mills, doing whatever they did. The hourly pay was bad, but there were plenty of hours available because of the war. There was, however, a better way to make more money for less work. These girls were not prostitutes, and they'd make sure you understood that; they were mill workers, patriotic young women, and they charged twenty bucks. I was making about eighty-five dollars a month, so this was not as good a deal as it sounds.

In any case, I spent all my off-duty Sunday afternoons in a cheap motel, drinking cheap wine, and picking lint out of the hair of a girl named Jenny, who told her parents she had a double shift in the mill. She also had a boyfriend, a local guy, who sounded like a total loser.

Predictably, I fell in love with Jenny, but we had a few things going against the relationship, like my eighty-hour training week, her sixty-hour workweek, our bad-paying jobs, and me always being broke (because I paid her twenty bucks a pop), her other dates, which caused me some jealousy, my impending orders to Vietnam, and last but not least, her strong dislike of Yankees and her love for her loser boyfriend.

Other than those things, I think we could have made a go of it.

Also, there was Peggy, who insisted that our love remain pure. In other words, I wasn't getting laid. Having discovered the forbidden pleasures of the flesh, however, I was obsessed with the idea of showing Peggy what Jenny had taught me.

So, after infantry training and airborne training, back in Boston for my thirty-day pre-Vietnam leave, I worked on poor Peggy day and night.

Bottom line here, my infantry training had taught me how to storm a fortified hill, but storming the defenses of Peggy Walsh's virginity was more difficult.

In a stupid moment of honesty, I told her about Jenny. Peggy was really pissed, but it also got her hormones going, so instead of giving me the heave-ho, she gave me absolution, along with a punch in the face.

She informed me that she understood that men couldn't control their animal urges, and acknowledged the fact that I was about to ship out for Vietnam, and there was the possibility that I'd never return, or might get my dick shot off, or something.

And so the last seven days of my leave were spent in intimate hours with Peggy in her bedroom while her parents were at work. I was surprised—shocked, actually—to discover that Peggy Walsh was about ten times hotter than Jenny, whose last name I never knew. Better yet, I didn't have to pick lint out of Peggy's hair.

Back to the present, I noticed my cabdriver looking at me in the rearview mirror. He asked me, "What airline?"

I looked out the window and saw we were at Dulles. I replied, "Asiana."

"Where you heading?"

"Vietnam."

"Yeah? Thought you were heading for someplace nice. Saw you smiling."

"I just came back from someplace nice."

As per my e-mail instructions from Herr Hellmann, I went directly to the Asiana Airlines lounge, known as the Morning Calm Club.

I was buzzed in, and as instructed, showed my passport to the pretty East Asian lady behind the desk, whose nametag said Rita Chang. Normally, you need to be a club member, or need to show First or Business Class tickets to use an airline lounge, but Ms. Chang looked at my passport and said, "Ah, yes, Mr. Brenner. Conference Room B."

I went into the cloak room and left my suitcase there, then checked myself out in a full-length mirror and combed my hair. I was wearing khaki trousers, a blue button-down shirt with no tie, a blue blazer, and loafers; suitable travel attire for Business Class, and for the check-in at the Rex Hotel in Saigon, according to Karl.

I took my overnight bag, went into the lounge, and got myself a coffee. There was a breakfast buffet that included rice, octopus, seaweed, and salted fish, but no chili. I took three bags of salted peanuts and put them in my pocket.

I went to Conference Room B, which was a small, paneled room with a round table and chairs. The room was empty.

I put down my overnight bag, sat, and sipped my black coffee. I opened a bag of nuts and popped a few in my mouth, waiting for whomever.

I'd obviously come up in life since my last departure to Vietnam, but what I was feeling in my gut wasn't much different.

I thought again of Peggy Walsh.

She had insisted that we go to confession before I left for Vietnam. Well, I'd rather get a punch in the jaw from Peggy Walsh than face Father Bennett's wrath when he listened to me telling him I'd been screwing his second favorite virgin.

But what the hell—I needed absolution, so I went with Peggy to Saturday confession at St. Brigid's. Thank God Father Bennett wasn't one of the priests hearing confession that day. Peggy went to one confessional booth, and I went to another. I can't remember the priest's name, and I didn't know him, but he sounded young behind the black screen. Anyway, I started off easy, with stuff like lying and swearing, then got down to the big one. He didn't totally freak out, but he wasn't real happy with me. He asked me who the young lady was, and I told him it was Sheila O'Connor, who I always wanted to screw, but never did. Sheila had a wild reputation anyway, so I didn't feel too bad about substituting her for Peggy. I'm a real gentleman.

This priest was probably going to hand me about a million Hail Marys and Our Fathers, but I said to him, "Father, I'm leaving for Vietnam in two days."

There was a long silence, then he said, "Say a Hail Mary and an Our Father for penance. Good luck, my son, and God bless you. I'll pray for you."

I went to the communion rail, happy that I'd gotten off easy, but halfway through my Hail Mary, I realized that saying you were going to

Vietnam was like saying "Father, have mercy on me," and a cold chill ran down my spine.

Poor Peggy spent about an hour on her knees reciting the rosary while I passed around a football with some guys at St. Brigid's High School playing field.

Afterward, we'd both sworn to be sexually faithful for the year I was gone. There were probably about a half-million such vows made that year between parting couples, and maybe some of those promises were kept.

Peggy and I talked about getting married before I shipped out, but she'd defended her virtue for so long that by the time I discovered she was a hottie, it was too late to get the marriage license.

In any case, we were unofficially engaged, and I hoped officially not pregnant.

This story could have had a happy ending, I think, because we wrote to each other regularly, and she continued living at home and working at her father's little hardware store where her mother also worked. More important, she didn't go weird like most of the country did in '68, and her letters were filled with patriotic and positive feelings about the war, which I myself did not share.

I came home, in one piece, ready to pick up where I left off. I had a thirty-day leave, and I was looking forward to every minute of it.

But something had changed in my absence. The country had changed, my friends were either in the military, or were in college, or were not interested in talking to returning soldiers. Even South Boston, bastion of working-class patriotism, was divided like the rest of the country.

In truth, the biggest change was within me, and I couldn't get my head together during that long leave.

Peggy had somehow regained her virginity and refused to have sex until after we were married. This at a time when people were fucking their brains out with total strangers.

Peggy Walsh was as pretty and sweet as ever, but Paul Brenner had become cold, distant, and distracted. I knew that, and she knew that. In fact, she said something to me that I've never forgotten. She said, "You've become like the others who have come back." Translation: *You're dead. Why are you still walking?*

I told her I just needed some time, and we decided to give it another half year until I was out of the army. She wrote to me at Fort Hadley, but I never wrote back, and her letters stopped.

When my time in the army was up, I made the fateful decision to re-enlist for three years, which eventually became almost thirty years. I have no regrets, but I often wonder what my life would have been like if there was no war, and if I'd married Peggy Walsh.

Peggy and I never saw each other again, and I learned from friends that she'd married a local guy who had a football scholarship to Iowa State. They settled there for some reason, two Boston kids in the middle of nowhere, and I hope they've had a good life. Obviously, I still think about her now and then. Especially now, as I was about to return to the place that had separated us, and changed our lives.

My contact still hadn't shown up, and I was finished with my coffee and two bags of peanuts. The clock on the wall said ten after eight. I considered doing this time what I should have done last time—getting the hell out of that airport and going home.

But I sat there and thought about this and that: Vietnam, Peggy Walsh, Vietnam, Cynthia Sunhill.

I took my e-mail to Cynthia out of my overnight bag and read:

Dear Cynthia,
As Karl has told you, I've taken an assignment in Southeast Asia. I should return in about two or three weeks. Of course, there's the possibility that I may run into some problems. If I do, it's important for you to know that it was my decision to take this assignment, and it had nothing to do with you; it has to do with me.

As for us, this has been what's called a stormy relationship from day one in Brussels. In fact, fate, jobs, and life have conspired to keep us apart and keep us from really knowing each other.

Here's a plan to get us together, to meet each other halfway, literally and figuratively: During the war, the single guys would take their one-week R&R in exotic places where they could loosen up a little. The married guys, and the guys in serious relationships, would meet their ladies in Honolulu. So, meet me in Honolulu twenty-one days from today, the Royal Hawaiian Hotel, reservations under both our names. Plan on a two-week R&R in one of the remote islands.

If you decide not to come, I understand, and I know you've made your decision. Please don't reply to this, just come or don't come.

> Love,
> Paul

Well, that wasn't too embarrassingly sloppy and sentimental, and I didn't regret sending it. Everything was spelled right, rare for an e-mail.

As of this morning, as I said, there was no reply, which could mean she hadn't opened her e-mail, or she took me at my word when I said, *Please don't reply to this*, as Peggy Walsh had taken me at my word when I told her not to come to the airport.

The door opened, and a well-dressed man about my age entered, carrying two cups of coffee and a plastic gift store bag. He put the bag and the coffees on the table, then put out his hand and said, "Hi, I'm Doug Conway. Sorry I'm late."

"I'm sorry you're here at all."

Doug Conway smiled and sat opposite me. "Here, this coffee's for you. Black, correct?"

"Thanks. You want peanuts?"

"I've had breakfast. First, I've been instructed to thank you for taking this assignment."

"Who's thanking me?"

"Everybody. Don't worry about that."

I sipped the coffee and studied Mr. Conway. He looked pretty bright and sounded pretty sharp so far. He was wearing a dark blue suit, subdued blue tie, and looked sort of honest, so he wasn't CIA. Also, I can spot CID a mile away, and he wasn't that either, so I asked, "FBI?"

"Yes. This case, if it has any resolution, will be a domestic matter. No CIA involved, no military intelligence, no State Department intelligence. Just FBI and army CID. It sounds like a murder, so we'll handle it like a murder."

Well, he did *look* honest, but he wasn't. I asked him, "Will anyone in the Hanoi embassy know of my presence there?"

"We've decided to limit this information."

"To whom?"

"To those who need to know, which is practically nobody. The embassy and consulate people are about as useful as tits on a bull. I didn't say that. But fortunately, we've got an FBI guy in the Hanoi embassy, who's on assignment to give classes to the Vietnamese police on the drug trade. His name is John Eagan, and he's been briefed on your trip. He's your guy if you're in trouble and need to contact the U.S. embassy."

"Why doesn't John Eagan go find this guy I'm supposed to find?"

"He's busy giving classes. Also, he has less ability to travel around than does a tourist."

"Also, you don't want any direct U.S. government involvement in this case. Correct?"

Mr. Conway, of course, did not reply. He said instead, "Do you have any threshold questions to ask before I begin my briefing?"

"I thought I just asked one."

"All right, then I'll begin. First, your mission is clear, but not simple. You have to locate a Vietnamese national named Tran Van Vinh—you know that. He is an eyewitness in a possible murder case."

Mr. Conway went on a while, doing the FBI thing, as though this was just another murder that needed to be worked and packaged up for a U.S. attorney general. I sipped my coffee and opened my last bag of peanuts.

I interrupted his legal spiel and said, "All right. So if I find Tran Van Vinh, I tell him he's won an all-expense-paid trip to Washington, D.C. Right?"

"Well . . . I don't know."

"Well, neither do I. What do you want me to do with this guy if I find him alive?"

"We're not sure yet. In the meantime, we're trying to come up with some possible suspects, and/or the possible murder victim. If we do, we'll get photos to you of these guys from when they were in the army. If that happens, and if you find Tran, you'll show him a series of photos— just like in any criminal case, and see if he can ID the suspected murderer and/or the victim."

"Yeah. I think I've done that a few thousand times. But my Vietnamese is a little rusty."

"You can hire an interpreter anywhere."

"Okay. Why don't I take a video camera or tape recorder with me?"

"We thought about that. But that sometimes causes problems at Customs. We might have your contact in Saigon give you a video camera or tape recorder. Did you bring a regular camera?"

"Yes, as instructed. I'm a tourist. How about an international cell phone?"

"Same problem. They're very paranoid at the airport, and if they search your luggage and find things like that, they get nosy. Visa or no visa, they can turn you around and boot you out for almost no reason. We need you *in* the country."

"Okay."

"But we may get you a cell phone in Saigon. Be advised, however, that their cell phone system is very primitive, and they have more dead zones than a cemetery."

"Okay, so if you decide you want this guy in Washington, then what?"

"Then we might go to the Vietnamese government and explain the situation. They'll cooperate."

"If you don't want their cooperation now in finding this guy, why do you think they're going to cooperate after you tell them you've been snooping around their little police state and found one of their citizens who you need for a murder trial?"

Doug Conway looked at me a moment and said, "Karl was right about you."

"Karl is right about everything. Please, answer my question."

Conway stirred his coffee a few seconds and said, "Okay, Mr. Brenner, here's the answer to your questions, past, present, and future. The answer is, We are bullshitting you. You know that, we know that. Every time we bullshit you, you find little inconsistencies, so you ask another question. Then we give you more bullshit, and you have more questions on the new bullshit. This is really annoying and time consuming. So, I'll tell you a few things right now that aren't bullshit. Ready?"

I nodded.

"One, there is more to this than a thirty-year-old murder, but you know that. Two, it's in your best interest that you don't know what this is about. Three, it's really very important to our country. Four, we need you because you're good, but also because if you get in trouble, you're not working for the government. And if you get busted over there, you don't know anything, and that's what you tell them because it's true. Just stick to your story—you're on a nostalgia trip to 'Nam. Okay? You still want to go?"

"I never wanted to go."

"Hey, I don't blame you. But you know you're going, and I know you're going. By now, you're bored with retirement, you've got a deep-rooted sense of duty, and you like living on the edge. You were an infantryman once, you were decorated for bravery, then you became a military policeman, then a criminal investigator. You were never an accountant or a ladies' hairdresser. And you're here talking to me. Therefore, we both know that you're not going home this morning."

"Are we done with the psychobabble?"

"Sure. Okay, I have your tickets, Asiana Airlines to Seoul, Korea, then Vietnam Airlines to Ho Chi Minh City, known to us old guys as Saigon. You are booked at the Rex Hotel—upscale, but Saigon is cheap, so it's affordable for Mr. Paul Brenner, retired chief warrant officer."

Conway took a piece of paper out of the plastic bag and said to me, "This is your visa, which we secured from the Vietnamese embassy with an authorized copy of your passport that the State Department was kind enough to provide."

He handed me a sheet of cheap paper printed with red ink, and I glanced at it.

"And here is a new passport, an exact copy of yours, which you'll give me now. On this passport is the Vietnamese embassy stamp for your entry into the country, and the other pages are clean because the Vietnamese get suspicious of people who have too many entry and exit stamps on their passports, as you do."

He handed me my new passport, and I gave Conway my old one. I looked at the one he'd given me. I noticed that even the photo was the same as my old one, plus, an expert FBI forger had been nice enough to sign it for me. I commented, "It's amazing that you were able to get a copy of my passport made, use it to apply to the Vietnamese embassy for a visa, and have everything ready for me less than twelve hours after I knew about this assignment."

"It is amazing," agreed Mr. Conway. He handed me a pencil and said, "Fill out the emergency contact information the way it was on your old passport—your lawyer, I believe."

"Right." Actually a CID lawyer, but why bring that up? I filled out the information, handed him back his pencil, and put the passport in my breast pocket.

Mr. Conway said, "Make a few photocopies of your passport and visa when you get to Seoul. In 'Nam, everyone wants to hold your passport and visa—hotels, motor scooter rentals, and sometimes the police. You can usually satisfy them with a photocopy."

"Why don't we send a photocopy of me to Vietnam?"

He ignored that and continued, "You'll arrange your own ground transportation in Vietnam. You'll stay in Saigon three days, and that's how long you're booked at the Rex—Friday night, which is your arrival night, Saturday, and Sunday. You'll leave Saigon Monday. Do whatever you please in Saigon, except don't get kicked out for smoking funny cigarettes, or bringing a prostitute up to your room, or anything like that."

"I don't need a morals lecture from the FBI."

"I understand, but I have to brief you, as per my instructions from my people. I was already briefed by Karl, and I know you're a pro. Okay? Next, you will be contacted in Saigon by an American resident of Saigon. This person will have no U.S. government connections—just a businessperson who's doing a little favor for Uncle Sam. The meeting will take place at the rooftop restaurant of the Rex, at or about 7 P.M. on Saturday, your second night there. That's all you have to know. The more unplanned it is, the more unplanned it will look. Okay?"

"So far."

"This person will give you a number. That number will correspond to a map key in your guidebook." Mr. Conway reached into the plastic bag and put a book on the table. "This is the Lonely Planet Guide to Vietnam, third edition. It's the most widely used book over there, so if for some reason it gets taken by the customs idiots at Tan Son Nhat Airport, or you lose it, or somebody lifts it, you can usually get another one by buying it from a backpacker, or your Saigon contact can get one for you. You're going to need this book a few times. Okay?"

"Okay."

"I'll explain this number further in a few minutes. After you leave Saigon on Monday, you have until Saturday to look and act like a tourist. Do what you want, but you should visit some of your old battlefields." He added, "I believe you served part of your tour in the Bong Son area."

I said, "If that's not part of this mission, I'll skip that."

He looked at me a long time and said, "Well, that's not an order, but it is a strong suggestion."

I didn't reply.

Mr. Conway leaned toward me and said, "FYI, I was there in '70—Fourth Infantry Division, Central Highlands and the Cambodian invasion—and I went back last year to come to terms with some stuff. That's why they sent me to brief you. We're bonding. Right?"

"Not quite, but go on."

Mr. Conway continued, "During these five days of travel, you will determine if you're being watched or followed. But even if you are, don't presume anything. Often, they just follow and watch Westerners for no good reason."

"Especially Americans."

"Correct. Okay, after five days on the road, you arrive in Hue on Saturday, which is Lunar New Year's Eve—Tet—where you are booked at the Century Riverside Hotel. At this time, regarding the number you got from your contact in Saigon, you look at the city map of Hue in your guidebook, which has a numbered key to various sites around the city, and that's where you go at noon the following day, Sunday, which will be New Year's Day, a holiday with lots of crowds and few police. Okay?"

"Got it."

"There are alternative rendezvous points, and I'll explain that now." Conway gave me the details of my meeting in Hue and concluded, "This person you meet in Hue will be a Vietnamese national. He will find you. There's a sign and countersign. He will say, 'I am a very good guide.' You will reply, 'How much do you charge?,' and he will reply, 'Whatever you wish to pay.'"

I asked, "Didn't I see this in a movie once?"

Mr. Conway smiled and said, "I know you're not used to this kind of stuff, and to tell you the truth, neither am I. We're both cops, Mr. Brenner, and this is something else. But you're a bright guy, you grew up during the Cold War, we all read James Bond, watched spy movies, and all that stuff. So this isn't totally alien to people of our generation. Right?"

"Right. Tell me why I need a contact in Saigon if all I need is a number? You can fax me a number."

"We decided you might need a friend in Saigon, and we need someone there we can be in touch with in case you fall off the radar screen."

"Gotcha. Do we have a consulate in Saigon yet?"

"I was about to get to that. As you know, we've just re-established diplomatic relations with Vietnam, and we have a new embassy building and a new ambassador in Hanoi. The embassy will not contact you directly, either in Hanoi or during your trip. But, as an American citizen, you can contact them if you need to, and you will ask for John Eagan, and no one else. Regarding Saigon, aka Ho Chi Minh City, we've recently sent a consular mission there, and they're located in some temporary, non-secure rented space. You'll have no contact with the Saigon consulate, except through your contact person in Saigon."

I said, "So I can't run into the American consulate in Saigon and ask for asylum?"

He forced a smile and replied, "They don't have much office space, and you'll be in the way." He added, apropos of something, "Vietnam is becoming important to us again."

I didn't ask him why, but important to the

American government always meant oil, sometimes drugs, and now and then strategic military planning. Take your pick.

Mr. Conway was looking at me, anticipating a question about "important," but I said, "Okay. What else?"

He said, "Another thing to keep in mind, as I said, it's the Tet holiday season, Lunar New Year—you remember Tet '68. Right? So, the whole country is visiting graves in their native villages, and whatever else they do. Transportation, communication, and accommodations are a nightmare, half the population is not at work, and the normal inefficiency is worse. You'll need to be resourceful and patient. But don't be late."

"Understood. Tell me more about the guy in Hue."

Doug Conway explained, "The contact in Hue will tell you where to go next, if he knows. Tran Van Vinh, if he's alive, is most probably in the north, so you can expect to travel north from Hue. Foreigners, especially Americans, are not particularly welcome in the rural areas of the former North Vietnam. There'll be a lot of travel restrictions, not to mention non-existent transportation. But you have to overcome this if your destination is a rural area. Okay?"

"No problem."

"Well, it is. First of all, it's illegal for foreigners to rent cars, but you can get an official government-licensed car and driver through the state-run travel agency called Vidotour—but you don't want that for the secret part of your mission. Right?"

"Makes sense to me."

"There are private travel agencies, and private cars and drivers, but the government does not officially recognize them, and sometimes in some places they don't exist, or you can't use them. Understand?"

"Can I rent a bicycle?"

"Sure. The country is run by the local Party chiefs, like old-time warlords, and they make up the rules, plus the central government in Hanoi keeps changing the rules for foreigners. It's chaos, but you can usually get around some of the restrictions by making donations to key individuals. When I was there, five bucks usually did the trick. Okay?"

"Okay."

"There are also intercity buses—torture buses, they call them, and you'll see why if you need to get on one. And there's the old French railroad along the coast, which is now up and running. There will be no tickets available on any public transportation during the Tet holiday, but a fiver will get you on board anything that moves, except an aircraft. You should avoid local airports in any case. Too much security there."

"Did I mention that I had plans to go to Aruba?"

"This is much more meaningful, and the weather will be just as nice."

"Right. Please continue."

"Thank you." He continued, "Regarding travel, bribes, and so forth, you may ask your Saigon contact for advice. This person should know the ropes. But don't be too specific."

"All right."

"By the time you get to Hue, with luck, we'll have for you at least the location of Tran Van Vinh's native village of Tam Ki. Because it is the Tet holiday, the chances are very good that you will find many people of the family of Tran in that village." He looked at me. "Right?"

I replied, "It occurs to me, Mr. Conway, that the information about this murder didn't come to light a few days ago, but perhaps a few weeks or months ago, and you've waited until the Tet holiday to send me to Vietnam because that's, as you say, when people return to their native villages, and that's also when the security forces and police are least effective."

Mr. Conway smiled at me and said, "I don't know when we got this information, and what your bosses know that you—and perhaps I— don't know. But it is fortunate that you'll be in Vietnam at this holiday time." He added, "During Tet of '68, the Communists caught you guys with your pants down. Maybe you can return the favor."

"An interesting thought. Sort of symmetrical,

like the balanced Scales of Justice. But I really
don't give a rat's ass about revenge, or any of
that. The fucking war is over. If I'm going to do
this, I don't need or want a personal motive. I'm
just doing the job I said I'd do. Understood?"

"Don't rule out some personal motivation
once you get there."

I didn't reply.

"Okay, you make your rendezvous in Hue on
the Sunday, but if it's a no-go for any reason,
then Monday is the backup day, and you'll be
contacted in some way at your hotel. If you're
not contacted, then it's time to get out of the
country, quickly. Understand?"

I nodded.

Mr. Conway said, "All right, assuming all is
going well, you leave Hue on Tuesday. This is
the difficult part of the trip. You need to get to
Tam Ki by any means possible, and to be there
within two days, three latest. Why? Because the
Tet holiday lasts for four days after New Year's
Day, so everyone who has returned to their ancestral homes should still be there before heading back to wherever they live at the moment.
This guy Tran Van Vinh may live full-time in Tam
Ki, but we don't know that. Best to be there
when you know he'll be there. Understand?"

Again, I nodded.

Mr. Conway continued, "In any case, win,
lose, or draw, you need to be in Hanoi no later
than the following Saturday, which is the fif-

teenth day of your trip. You are booked into the
Sofitel Metropole, and I have a voucher for you
for one night." He tapped his plastic bag and
said, "You may or may not be contacted in
Hanoi. More importantly, you will leave the next
day, Sunday, the sixteenth day of your trip, well
before your standard twenty-one-day visa expires. Okay?"

"I wanted to sightsee in Hanoi."

"No, you want to get out of there as soon as
possible."

"Sounds even better."

He said, "You are booked on Cathay Pacific
from Hanoi to Bangkok on Sunday. You'll be
met in Bangkok and be debriefed there."

"What if I'm in jail? Do I need an extension
on my visa?"

Mr. Conway smiled, ignored me, and said,
"Okay, money. There's an envelope in this bag
with one thousand American dollars, in singles,
fives, and tens, all non-accountable. You may
legally use greenbacks in the Socialist Republic
of Vietnam. In fact, they prefer it. Also in the bag
is a million dong, about a buck-fifty—just kidding. About a hundred bucks, to get you started.
The average Vietnamese makes about three or
four hundred dollars a year, so you're rich. And
there's another thousand in American Express
traveler's checks, which better hotels and restaurants will accept, and which some banks on
some days will exchange for dong, depending

on their mood. There is an American Express office in Saigon, Hue, and Hanoi. That's all in your
guidebook. Use your own credit card whenever
you can. You'll be reimbursed. The army has authorized you temporary duty pay of five hundred
dollars a day, so you should see a nice check
when you return." He added, "Jail time is double
pay."

I looked at Conway and saw he wasn't joking. I asked, "For how many days?"

"I don't know. I never asked. Do you want
me to find out?"

"No. What else?"

"A couple of things—like getting you out of
the country. As I said, Cathay Pacific from Hanoi,
but as I also said, it may develop that you need
to leave earlier and more quickly from some
other place. We have a few contingency plans
for that. Want to hear them?"

"On this subject, you have my undivided attention."

Mr. Conway outlined some other methods of
leaving Vietnam, via Laos, Cambodia, China, by
boat, and even by cargo plane out of Da Nang. I
didn't particularly like or believe in any of them,
but I said nothing.

Conway said, "Okay, Tam Ki. That is your destination before Hanoi. One way or the other, we
will locate this place, and get the information to
you in Hue, at the latest. Once in Tam Ki, you
will, as I said, probably find many people whose

family names are Tran. You might need an interpreter before you get to Tam Ki because they
won't be speaking much English there. Okay?"

"Okay."

"You know a little French, correct?"

"A real little."

"Sometimes the older folks and the Catholic
clergy speak some French. But try to get an
English-speaking guide or interpreter. Now, I
don't have to tell you that an American asking
around about a guy named Tran Van Vinh in a
tiny village of Trans might draw some attention.
So think about how you're going to handle that.
You're a cop. You've done this before. Get a feeling for the situation, the people—"

"I understand. Go on."

Mr. Conway went on, "Okay, my personal belief is that Tran Van Vinh is dead. Got to be.
Right? The war, his age, and so forth. If he was
killed in the war, chances are his body is someplace else, like his brother's was in the A Shau
Valley. But there will be a family altar in his memory. We need you to make an absolute confirma-
tion and verification of death. Sergeant Tran Van
Vinh, age between fifty and sixty, served in the
People's Army, saw action at Quang Tri, deceased brother named Tran Quan Lee—"

"Got it."

"Okay. On the other hand, he may be alive—
in Tam Ki or elsewhere."

"Right. This is where I'm a little unclear

about my mission and my goal. What am I supposed to do with Mr. Tran Van Vinh if I find him alive?"

Conway made eye contact with me and said, "What if I told you to kill him?"

We maintained eye contact. I said, "Tell you what—I'll find him, *you* kill him. But you'd better have a good reason."

"I think when you talk to him, you might discover the reason."

"Then someone whacks me."

"Don't be melodramatic."

"Sorry, I thought we were being melodramatic."

"No, we're being realistic. Here's the mission in clear English—you first determine if this guy is dead or alive. If dead, we'd like some proof; if alive, establish if he lives in Tam Ki or elsewhere, then talk to him about this incident of February 1968 and see what he remembers, and see if he can identify the murderer from a photo pack that we'll try to get to you. Also, as you will read in the letter, Tran Van Vinh took a few things from the murder victim. We took souvenirs from the dead, they took souvenirs. He probably still has these items, or if he's dead, his family will have them—dog tags, wallet, whatever. This will identify the murdered lieutenant for us, and it will also connect Tran Van Vinh to the murder scene, and if he's alive, make him a credible witness."

"And we don't want a live credible witness."

Mr. Conway did not answer.

I finished my coffee and said, "So, if I find Tran Van Vinh alive, I see if he can ID some photos that maybe I'll get along the way, and see if I can look at his souvenirs, and maybe buy them from him, or his family if he's dead, and maybe get this guy out of the country, maybe videotape him, and/or leave him where he is, or maybe give Mr. Eagan in the Hanoi embassy this guy's address and whatever happens to Tran Van Vinh happens. And if he's dead, you want proof."

"That's about it. We're playing it by ear. We'll get in touch with you over there, in Saigon or Hue latest. There's still some debate here about the best course of action."

"Be sure to let me know what you decide."

"We will. Any further questions?"

"No."

Mr. Conway asked me, in an official tone, "Mr. Brenner, do you understand everything I've told you so far?"

"Not only that, I understand some stuff you're not telling me."

He ignored that and continued, "And you remember all of these verbal instructions I've given you?"

"I do."

"Do you have any further questions for me at this time?"

"Can I ask you why you want this guy whacked?"

"I don't understand the question. Anything else?"

"Nope."

Doug Conway stood, and I also stood.

Conway said, "Your flight leaves in an hour, you're traveling Business Class, which isn't too extravagant for your station in life. The occupation on your visa says 'Retired,' the purpose of your visit says 'Tourism.' Understand, there's some chance of a man your age traveling alone getting stopped at Tan Son Nhat and being questioned. I spent half an hour with a paranoid little gent in an interrogation room when I went back. Keep cool, don't get hostile, stick to your story, and if the war comes up, give him some bullshit about how terrible it was for *his* country. Express remorse or something. They love that. Okay?"

"So, I shouldn't mention that I killed North Vietnamese soldiers."

"I wouldn't. That might get you off on the wrong foot. But be honest about being a Vietnam veteran and wanting to visit some of the places you saw as a young soldier. Tell the interrogator you were a cook or a company clerk or something. Not a combat soldier. They don't like that, as I found out the hard way. Okay?"

"Got it."

Conway continued, "When you get to your hotel, do not contact us. The hotels sometimes keep copies of faxes that you send, and the local police sometimes look at these faxes. Same with phone calls. All dialed numbers are recorded for billing purposes, like anywhere else in the world, but they're also available to the police. Plus, the phones may be tapped."

I already knew all of this, but Conway had a mental checklist he needed to go through.

He informed me, "Regarding your arrival, your contact in Saigon will verify that you checked in at the Rex. It won't arouse any suspicion if the call comes in locally. The contact will then notify us via a secure fax or e-mail from an American-owned business. So, if somehow you don't check in at the Rex, we'll know."

"And do what?"

"Make inquiries."

"Thanks."

"Okay, in this plastic bag is a twenty-one-day supply of anti-malarial pills. You were supposed to start taking them four days ago, but not to worry—you'll be in Saigon for three days, where there aren't many malaria mosquitoes. Take a pill now. There's also an antibiotic, which I hope you don't need. Basically, don't drink the water and be careful of uncooked food. You could pick up hepatitis A, but by the time you experience symptoms, you'll be back home. If we knew sooner that you were leaving, we'd have gotten you a hepatitis vaccine—"

"You knew some time ago that I was leaving—I'm the one who didn't know."

"Whatever. Read your Lonely Planet Guide on the flight. There's also a copy of the translated letter in this bag. Read it, but get rid of it on your layover in Seoul."

"Oh . . . I planned to have it on me at Tan Son Nhat."

Mr. Conway said to me, "I'm sorry if at any time in this briefing I've insulted your intelligence or professional ability, Mr. Brenner. I'm just following orders." He looked at me and said, "Karl said I might not like you, but I do like you. So, here's some friendly advice—the chances are that you're going to find out more than you need to know. How you deal with these discoveries will determine how you are dealt with."

Mr. Doug Conway and I stared at each other for a really long time. A sane man would have left right then and there. But Mr. Conway had calculated, correctly, that Paul Brenner was not frightened by that threat; Mr. Paul Brenner was more curious than ever, and highly motivated to find out what this was all about. Paul Brenner is an idiot.

Mr. Conway cleared his throat and said, "Okay, you have a long layover in Seoul. Spend

it in the Asiana lounge. There may be a person
or a message there for you, with more information. And if this turns out to be a no-go, this is
where you will be turned around. Understood?"

"Understood."

Mr. Conway asked me, "Is there anything I
can do for you at this time? Any last-minute messages, instructions, personal matters that I can
help you with?"

"Actually, yes." I took an envelope out of my
pocket and said, "I need an airline ticket from
Bangkok to Honolulu, and a hotel reservation in
Honolulu for a few days, then Maui. Here's the
itinerary, and my American Express number."

Mr. Conway took the envelope, but said, "I
think they'll want you back in Washington."

"I don't care what they want. I want two
weeks in paradise. We'll debrief in Bangkok."

"All right." He put the envelope in his pocket.
"Anything else?"

"Nope."

"All right, then, good luck and be careful."

I didn't reply.

"You know . . . believe me when I tell you
that, aside from your mission, this trip will do
you more good than harm."

"Hey, my first two trips there would have
been great except for the war."

Mr. Conway did not smile. "I hope I've done
a good job of briefing you. That always concerns me."

"You've done an excellent job, Mr. Conway. Sleep well tonight."

"Thank you."

He put out his hand, but I said, "Hold on. I almost forgot." I opened my overnight bag and handed Mr. Conway my Danielle Steel book.

He looked at it curiously, as though there were some special significance or meaning to the book.

I said, "I don't want that found at home if I don't make it back. Understand? Give it to somebody. You don't have to read it yourself."

Mr. Conway looked at me with some concern, then again put out his hand, and we shook. He left without even thanking me for the book.

I opened the plastic bag left on the table, putting the money, tickets, hotel vouchers, letter, and visa in my breast pocket. I put the malaria pills, antibiotic, and *The Lonely Planet Guide* in my overnight bag.

At the bottom of the plastic bag was something wrapped in tissue paper. I unwrapped it and saw it was one of those stupid snow globes. Inside the globe was a model of the Wall, black against the falling snow.

★

CHAPTER FOUR

──────★──────

The Asiana Air 747 began its descent into Kimpo International Airport, Seoul, Korea. After fifteen hours in the air, I wasn't sure of the local time, or even what day it was. The sun was about forty-five degrees off the horizon, so it was either mid-morning or mid-afternoon, depending on where east and west were. When you're circling the globe, none of this matters, anyway, unless you're the pilot.

I noticed that the landscape below was covered with snow. I listened to the hydraulic sounds of the aircraft as it made its initial approach.

The seat next to me was empty, and I hoped I was as lucky on the final leg of the trip.

Then again, there might not be a final leg if I was turned around in Seoul. Of course, the chances of that happening were near zero, but they always put that in your mind as a happy possibility. I had a similar experience the first two times I was headed to Vietnam. My orders said "Southeast Asia," instead of the V word, as if I might be headed to Bangkok or Bali. Right.

It was time to read the letter that had started this whole thing. I took a plain envelope from my pocket, opened it, and drew out several sheets of folded paper. The first sheet was a photocopy of the original envelope, addressed to Tran Quan Lee, followed by an abbreviation, which I supposed was his rank, then a series of numbers and letters that was his North Vietnamese army unit designation.

The return address was Tran Van Vinh, followed by his rank and Army unit. In neither address was there a geographical location, of course, because armies move, and the mail follows the soldiers.

I put the envelope aside and looked at the letter itself. It was a typed, three-page translation, and there was no photocopy of the original letter in Vietnamese, making me again wonder what was missing or altered.

Regarding the provenance of this letter, I tried to imagine the North Vietnamese army postal system during the war, which must have been as primitive as a nineteenth-century postal system; letters handed from person to person, to couriers, making their way slowly from civilians to their soldiers, or from soldiers to family, or soldiers to soldiers, as in this case, and very often, the recipient, the sender, or both were dead before the letter was delivered.

In any case, it must have taken months for letters to reach their recipients, if at all. I thought of the three hundred thousand missing North Vietnamese soldiers, and the million known dead, many of them vaporized by thousand-pound bombs from B-52 strikes along the infiltration routes.

It was a miracle, I realized, that this letter ever got out of the besieged city of Quang Tri, another miracle that the letter found its recipient, Tran Quan Lee in the A Shau Valley, nearly a hundred kilometers away, and a further miracle that the letter was found on Lee's body by an American soldier. The final miracle, perhaps, was that this American soldier, Victor Ort, survived the war himself, saved the letter for almost thirty years, and then made an attempt to get the letter to Hanoi via the Vietnam Veterans of America.

The letter, however, had been rerouted to Army CID Headquarters in Falls Church, Virginia, because of some sharp-eyed person at VVA, an army veteran, whose instinct would be to go to Army CID instead of the FBI. If the FBI had gotten it first, I knew, the CID would never have heard about it, and neither would I. But as it turned out, it was a CID case with FBI help, an arrangement that probably satisfied no one, myself included.

I looked again at the typed translation, not quite ready to read it until I'd come to fully understand how this thing landed in my lap.

And then there was the question of *why* I was doing this. Aside from Cynthia, there was duty, honor, country, not to mention boredom, curiosity, and a little macho posturing. In fact, my separation from active duty had not ended on just the right note, and this assignment would certainly be the final note, high or low.

I looked at the letter and saw it was dated 8 February 1968. I read Tran Van Vinh's words to his about-to-be deceased brother:

> My beloved brother Lee,
>   As I write this letter, which I hope finds you well and in good spirits, I lay wounded with several of my comrades in the city of Quang Tri. Do not worry, I am not badly injured, but have received some shrapnel wounds to my back and legs which I know will heal. We are being tended to by a captured doctor from the Catholic Hospital, and by medics of our own People's Army.
>   The battle for the city rages around us, and the American bombers come day and night, and their artillery falls without end. But we are safe in a deep cellar of the Buddhist high school outside the walls of the Citadel. We have food and water, and I hope to return to duty soon.

I looked up from the letter and recalled those days around the city of Quang Tri. My battalion was to the west of the city, and we never saw any of the fighting within the city, but we did see North Vietnamese soldiers straggling out of Quang Tri, which they'd held for only a week or so before the South Vietnamese army rooted them out. The enemy began exfiltrating in small groups, trying to reach the relative safety of the hills and jungle to the west, and my battalion's mission was to intercept them. We'd managed to find, kill, or capture some of them, but not all of them. Statistically, Tran Van Vinh's chances of making it out of the city were small, and his chances of having survived the final seven years of the war were even smaller. And if he had survived, would he be alive almost thirty years later? Not likely, but this case already had a few miracles in the equation.

I went back to the letter and read:

I must tell you of a strange and interesting occurrence that I witnessed yesterday. I was lying on the second floor of a government building within the Citadel, having been wounded by the shrapnel of an exploding artillery shell which killed two comrades who were with me. There was a hole in the floor, and I was looking down through the hole, hoping to see some of my comrades. At this moment, two American soldiers entered the building. My first thought was to kill them with my rifle, but I didn't know how many others were close by, so I held my fire.

These two Americans did not make a search of the building that was half destroyed. Instead, they began talking. I could see from the rank insignia on their helmets that one was a captain and the other a lieutenant—two officers! What a good kill I could make! But I held my fire. I could also see that both men had the shoulder insignia of the helicopter cavalry, who are numerous in this area, though I had not seen them in the city before.

As I watched, ready to kill them if they saw me, they began to argue with each other. The lieutenant was being disrespectful of the higher ranking officer, and the captain was very angry with him. This continued for perhaps two or three minutes, then the lieutenant turned his back on the captain, and walked toward the opening through which they had entered.

I then saw the captain draw his pistol and shout something to the lieutenant, who turned back toward the captain. Nothing more was said, and the captain shot the lieutenant in the front of his head. The lieutenant's helmet flew into the air, and the man was thrown back and lay dead on the floor among the rubble.

I was so surprised at this that I failed to react as the captain ran out of the building. I waited to see if the sound of the pistol would bring enemy soldiers, but there was much gunfire and explosions around the city, and this single shot was not heard above the others.

I lay there and looked down through the hole until nightfall. Then I descended the staircase and went to the body of the dead American. I took his canteen of water, some cans of food, his rifle and pistol, his wallet, and other items from his body. He had a fine watch, which I took, but as you know, if I were captured by the Americans with this watch, or any other American items, I would be shot. So, I will have to decide what to do with the things I have taken.

I thought you would be interested in this occurrence, though I can attach no meaning to it.

Have you heard from our parents and sister? I have heard from no one in Tam Ki for two months. Our cousin, Liem, has written to me and said that they see trucks filled with our wounded comrades passing through each week, and long columns of healthy comrades marching south to liberate our country from the American invaders, and from their Saigon puppet soldiers. Liem says the American bombers have increased their activity in the area, so, of course, I am worried about our family. He says the food in Tam Ki is sufficient but not plentiful. The harvest in April should provide ample rice for the village.

I have not heard from Mai, but I know she has gone to Hanoi to nurse the sick and wounded. I hope she will be safe there from the American bombs. I would have liked her to remain in Tam Ki, but she is very patriotic, and goes where she is needed.

My brother, may you be safe and well, and may this letter find its way to you, and then to our family. If mother, father, and sister read this, I send my greetings and my love. I have much faith that I will be out of Quang Tri in a day or two, in a safe place so that I may fully recover, and continue with my duty to free our

country. Write to me and tell me how it goes
with you and your comrades.

> (Signed) Your loving
> brother, Vinh

I refolded the letter and thought about what
I'd read. This letter, written to a soon-to-be-
dead brother certainly gave me a different perspective of the war. Yet, despite the stilted
translation, and the patriotic tag-ons, I thought
this was the kind of letter that could have been
written by an American GI; the subtext of loneliness, homesickness, fear, concern about family, and, of course, the barely hidden anxiety
about Mai, who I guessed was a girlfriend. Girlfriends working in military hospitals in the big
city were certainly subject to some temptations
and pressures the world over. I smiled.

I felt that I could relate a little to Tran Van
Vinh, and I realized that we'd once shared the
common experience of war at the same time
and place. I might even like the guy, if I actually
met him. Of course, if I'd met him in 1968, I
would have killed him.

As for Lee, remarkably our paths may also
have crossed. My battalion of the First Cavalry
Division, after the action at Quang Tri in February, was airlifted to Khe Sanh in April to relieve
the siege there, then airlifted into the A Shau
Valley in May. We were an air mobile unit,
meaning that wherever the shit was hitting the

fan, we'd go in by helicopter. How lucky can a guy get?

Well, enough pleasant reverie. I re-read the letter, concentrating on the details and circumstances of the alleged murder. First, it certainly *did* look like murder, though that might depend on what the argument was about. Second, it *was* a strange and interesting occurrence, as Sergeant Tran Van Vinh said.

I began from the beginning of the letter—a government building within the Citadel. Many Vietnamese cities had citadels, built by the French in most cases. The Citadel was the walled and fortified center of the city that contained government buildings, schools, hospitals, military headquarters, and even residential sections. I knew the Citadel at Quang Tri because I was ordered to an awards ceremony there in July '68, out on the parade ground, where the Vietnamese government was handing out medals to American soldiers for various battles. The Citadel was half in ruins, and I realized now that I must have been standing somewhere in the vicinity of where this incident had taken place six months earlier. I received the Vietnamese Cross of Gallantry, and the Vietnamese colonel who pinned it on me had, unfortunately for me, been trained by the French, and he gave me a kiss on both cheeks. I should have told him to kiss my ass, but it wasn't his fault I was there.

In any case, I could sort of picture where this incident took place. I tried to picture, also, these two American officers coming into the half-ruined building within the Citadel, while the battle raged around them, and Tran Van Vinh lying there with his itchy trigger finger on his AK-47, bleeding from an American artillery shell burst.

The American officers were definitely not combat infantrymen, or they'd have their troops all around them; these guys were undoubtedly rear echelon types, most probably MACV advisors, and, as I recalled, they had their headquarters somewhere in the Citadel. Somehow they'd gotten separated from whatever South Vietnamese army unit they were attached to, or the South Viets had taken a powder, which they sometimes did. This was partly speculation on my part, but it was the most logical explanation of how two American officers wound up alone, without troops, in a city that was garrisoned solely by the South Vietnamese army.

So, these two guys are caught in the middle of a slugfest between the North and South Viets, the city is a killing zone, and these two find the time to go off on their own and have an argument about something that leads to one guy blowing away the other guy. Strange. And I agreed with Tran Van Vinh—"I can attach no meaning to it." But I had a feeling that whatever that argument was about was what this whole thing was about.

I glanced at the letter again: *the captain ran out of the building*. Tran Van Vinh, smart survivor that he is, doesn't move until nightfall, then he goes down to the body of the lieutenant, has some water, which is his first priority, then takes the dead American's C rations, and rifle, and also his pistol—probably a Colt .45—his wallet, and "other items from his body." Such as what? The dog tags undoubtedly. This was a big prize for the enemy and was proof that you'd killed an American, and it got you a piece of fish or something. But as Sergeant Tran Van Vinh noted, if he were captured with any American military items, he'd be shot, Geneva Convention notwithstanding. So, he had to decide what to do with these items, these war trophies.

Maybe he kept them, and maybe, whether or not he was still alive, they were proudly displayed in his little family hut somewhere. Maybe.

So, what was missing from the translation of this letter? The phrase *and other items from his body* may have been substituted for Vinh's actual words.

But I could be reading too much into this, and maybe I was more suspicious than I needed to be. A little suspicion and speculating are good; too much and you start to outsmart yourself.

I realized that we were almost on the ground. A few seconds later, the 747 touched down, rolled out, and taxied toward the terminal.

Inside Terminal Two of Seoul's Kimpo Airport, I passed quickly through Passport Control and Customs.

I'd actually been stationed in Korea over twenty years before: six months at the DMZ, six months in Seoul. It was okay duty, the Koreans seemed to like their American allies, and the American soldiers in return behaved reasonably well. I had only a single homicide case involving a Korean citizen, three rapes, and a bunch of drunk and disorderly cases. Not bad, really, for fifty thousand guys in a place they didn't want to be.

I passed into the Main Terminal, which was huge and cavernous, with a mezzanine level that ran around all four sides.

I had a four-hour layover, and my baggage was checked through to Ho Chi Minh City, or so they said at Dulles.

There seemed to be a lot of noodle shops and snack bars around, and the whole place smelled of fish and cabbage, which brought back a lot of memories of twenty years ago.

I noticed a big digital clock on the wall and saw it was 15:26, and the day, in English, said

Friday. In fact, almost everything was subtitled in English, so I followed a sign that said *Airline Clubs*.

The Morning Calm Club was on the mezzanine level, and once inside, I gave my ticket to the young lady behind the counter. She smiled and said, "Welcome to the club. Please to sign book."

I signed the register, and I noticed she was staring at my ticket. She said, as I expected, "Oh, Mr. Brenner, there is a message for you." She rummaged around behind the counter and handed me a sealed envelope with my name on it.

"Thank you." I picked up my overnight bag and went into a big, well-appointed lounge. I got myself a coffee, sat in a club chair, and looked at my message. It was a telex from Karl, and it said: *It's a go—All instructions from Mr. C. remain—Narrowing down names in personnel files here—I may see you in Bangkok—Honolulu a possibility—Have a safe and successful trip—K.*

I put the telex in my pocket and sipped my coffee. *It's a go*—great news. *Honolulu a possibility*. What the hell did that mean?

I went to the club's business center and used the shredder to destroy Karl's telex, my e-mail to Cynthia, and the Tran Van Vinh letter. I then made two photocopies of my visa and passport, put them in my overnight bag, and went back to the lounge. I found a day-old *Washington Post* and skimmed through it.

I guess I was a little annoyed about Karl's *Honolulu a possibility*, and the vagueness of that remark. Had he spoken to Cynthia? Did he mean Honolulu was okay with him, but Cynthia was undecided? Or did he mean Honolulu was a possibility depending on what happened in Bangkok? And what the hell was going on with Cynthia? Karl is so fucking insensitive he didn't even mention if he'd spoken to her.

I was getting myself pissed off, which was not the way to go into an assignment.

I found myself drifting in and out of a sort of half-sleep, and these unexpected images passed through my mind: Peggy, Jenny, Father Bennett, my parents, the shadow of the priest behind the confessional curtain, St. Brigid's, my old neighborhood and childhood friends, my mother's kitchen and the smell of cabbage boiling in a pot. It was all very sad, for some reason.

CHAPTER FIVE

———— ★ ————

The Vietnam Airlines flight from Seoul through two time zones to Saigon was uneventful, unless you counted the events that were going on in my head.

In any case, the food, service, and drinks were good, and it seemed strange to be sitting in Business Class of a modern Boeing 767 owned and operated by Vietnam Airlines. People I knew who'd gone back to Vietnam in the 1970s and '80s reported that the Vietnam Airlines equipment was all Russian Ilyushins and Tupelovs, scary aircraft, and the pilots, too, were mostly Russian, plus the food and service sucked. This seemed to be an improvement, but we weren't on the ground yet. In fact, there seemed to be a problem regarding the weather, specifically a typical Southeast Asian tropical rain squall.

It was about 11 P.M., and we were already an hour late, which was the least of our problems at the moment.

I was in the window seat, and I could see the lights of Saigon through the breaks in the weather, and it seemed to me that if you could see the ground, you should land the damned airplane.

Again, I recalled my first government-paid trip to Vietnam in November 1967. I was flying Braniff that time—a military-chartered, psyche-delic yellow Boeing 707, out of Oakland Army Base, complete with pretty Braniff stewardesses wearing wild outfits. The stewardesses were a little wild, too, specifically one named Eliza-beth, a patriotic young lady, whom I'd met at a USO dance in San Francisco a few days before I flew to 'Nam.

Regarding my vow to Peggy to be chaste for a year, I guess I didn't get off to a very good start with Elizabeth. The future then was looking a little uncertain for me, and I was able to justify nearly anything. But maybe I shouldn't try to justify any of it three decades later. You had to be there.

Regarding the Braniff flight, who but the Americans could send their armed forces into war on a luxury jetliner? It was bizarre, and it was ultimately cruel. I think I'd have preferred a troopship, which was a slower transition from peace to war, and which at least got you into the habit of being miserable.

I don't know what happened to Elizabeth, or to Braniff for that matter, but I realized that a lot of long-forgotten stuff was starting to come back, and there was a lot more to come, most of it much less pleasant than Elizabeth.

The guy next to me, a Frenchman, had been ignoring me since we boarded, which was fine, but now he decided to talk and said in passable English, "Do you think there is a problem?"

I took my time answering, then said, "I think the pilots or the airport are making a problem."

He nodded. "Yes, I think that is the case." He added, "Perhaps we have to go to another airport."

I didn't think there was another airport around that could accommodate a 767. Thirty years ago, there were any number of military airfields with runways that stretched forever, and the military pilots then had beaucoup balls, as we used to say. On the downside, you had to dive in fast to avoid the little guys with the machine guns who wanted to win an extra bowl of rice for smearing you across the landscape.

Despite the turbulence, and our proximity to the airport, and despite FAA regulations that didn't apply here anyway, two flight attendants came by, one holding a champagne bottle, the other holding fluted champagne glasses between her fingers.

"Champagne?" asked the bottle holder with a nice French pronunciation. Cham-pan-ya.

"Oui," I said.

"S'il vous plaît," said my French friend.

The two flight attendants were impossibly young and pretty with straight, jet black hair to their shoulders. Both wore the traditional ao dai: silk floor-length dresses with high Mandarin collars. The yellow dresses had slits up the sides to their waists, but, alas, the young ladies also wore the modest white pantaloons to distinguish themselves from the bar girls on the ground.

The Frenchman and I each took a glass from the fingers of the second flight attendant, and the first poured half-glasses of bubbly as the aircraft bounced. "Merci," we both said.

Unexpectedly, the Frenchman touched his glass to mine and said, "Santé."

"Cheers."

The Frenchman asked me, "You are here on business?"

"No, tourism."

"Yes? I have a business in Saigon. I buy teak and other rare woods. Michelin is also back for the rubber. And there is oil exploration off the coast. The West is again raping the country."

"Well, somebody has to do it."

He laughed, then added, "In fact, the Japanese and Koreans are also raping the country. There are a lot of natural resources in Vietnam that have never been exploited, and the labor is very cheap."

"Good. I'm on a tight budget."

He continued, "The Communists, however, are a problem. They don't understand capitalism."

"Maybe they understand it too well."

Again, he laughed. "Yes, I think you are correct. In any case, be careful. The police and the party officials can be a problem."

"I'm just on vacation."

"Bon. Do you prefer girls or boys?"

"Pardon?"

He pulled out a notebook from his breast pocket and began writing. He said, "Here are some names, addresses, and phone numbers. One bar, one brothel, one exquisite lady, and the name of a good French-Indochine restaurant." He handed the note page to me.

"Merci," I said. "Where should I start?"

"One should always begin with a good meal, but it's very late, so go to the bar. Don't take any of the prostitutes—choose one of the bar maids or cocktail waitresses. This shows a degree of savoir faire."

"'Savoir faire' is my middle name."

"Don't pay more than five dollars American in the bar, five in the brothel, and twenty for Mademoiselle Dieu-Kiem—she's part French and speaks several languages. She's an excellent dinner companion and can help you with shopping and sightseeing."

"Not bad for twenty bucks." That's what Jenny got thirty years ago in Georgia, and she only spoke English.

"But be advised, prostitution is officially illegal in the Socialist Republic of Vietnam."

"Same in Virginia."

"Vietnam is a series of contradictions—the government is Communist, totalitarian, atheist, and xenophobic. The people are capitalists, free-spirited, Buddhists, Catholics, and friendly to foreigners. I am speaking of the south—in the north, it is quite different. In the north, the people and the government are one. You need to be more careful if you go to the north."

"I'm just hanging around Saigon. See a few museums, catch some shows, buy a few trinkets for the folks back home."

The Frenchman stared at me a moment, then sort of blew me off by picking up a newspaper.

The PA came on, and the pilot said something in Vietnamese, then French. Then the co-pilot, who was a round-eye, said in English, "Please return to your seats and fasten your seat belts. We'll be landing shortly." The flight attendants collected the champagne glasses.

I looked out the window and saw arcs of green and red tracer rounds cutting through the night sky around Saigon. I saw incandescent flashes of outgoing artillery and rockets, and red-orange bursts where the shells and missiles landed in the rice paddies. I saw these things with my eyes closed, thirty-year-old images burned into my memory.

I opened my eyes and saw Ho Chi Minh City, twice the size of old Saigon and more brightly lit than the besieged wartime capital.

I sensed the Frenchman looking at me. He said, "You have been here before." It was more of a statement than a question.

I replied, "Yes, I have."

"During the war—yes?"

"Yes." Maybe it showed.

"You will find it very different."

"I hope so."

He laughed, then added, "Plus ça change, plus c'est la même chose."

I listened to the hydraulic sounds of the aircraft as it made its approach into Tan Son Nhat Airport. This was going to be, I knew, a strange journey back into time and place.

—BOOK II—

SAIGON

CHAPTER SIX

--- ★ ---

We came in through the clouds, and I looked down at Tan Son Nhat Airport for the third time in my life.

Strangely, it looked the same as it did almost thirty years before; the sandbagged revetments hadn't been removed after the war, and there was still a military side to the airport where I could see Russian-made MiG fighters around the old American hangars. I also caught a glimpse of an American C-130 cargo plane, and I wondered if it was operational, or if it was some sort of war trophy.

I recalled that Military Advisory Command, Vietnam had been headquartered at Tan Son Nhat, which turned out to be convenient when, in April 1975, the victorious Communist troops approached the airport; the MACV guys, among the last American soldiers in Vietnam, blew up their headquarters and flew off on Air America planes. I had seen it on TV, and now I saw some rubble that might have been the old MACV Headquarters, known then as Pentagon East.

As we approached the runway, I saw that the civilian terminal, too, was the same old piece of crap I remembered. I had this weird feeling that

I'd passed through the Twilight Zone, and I was going back for my third tour. Actually, I *was*.

We came down on the wet runway with barely a bounce, so the round-eye was flying. The tarmac, however, must still have had shell holes in it or something because the rollout was a mile of bad road.

The aircraft turned onto a taxiway and for some reason stopped. On the approach, I hadn't seen a single aircraft around, so it wasn't like we were backed up waiting for a gate at this nowhere airport. When the Americans ran it during the war, Tan Son Nhat was the third busiest airport in the world, and it ran fine. But that's another story. I knew I needed to get my head into the reality of this time and place, and I tried. But as we waited on the taxiway, my mind kept pulling me back to 1972, and the events that led up to my second visit to this place.

I was stationed at Fort Hadley, where I had re-enlisted after my first tour, after Peggy Walsh and I had stopped writing to each other, or I had stopped writing to her, to be more honest.

After about six months at Hadley, for some reason known only to God and Sigmund Freud, I married a local Midland girl named Patty.

Patty was very pretty, had a cute Georgia accent, didn't hate Yankees, loved sex and bourbon, was poorer than me, and always wanted to marry a soldier, though I never found out why. We had absolutely nothing in common and never would, but getting married young and for no good reason seemed to be part of the local culture. I really don't know what I was thinking.

Housing for married people was tight during the war, and there was nothing available on the fort, so we lived in this squalid trailer park called Whispering Pines, along with hundreds of other soldiers, their wives, and kids.

We watched guys go off to war and some of them came back, some didn't, and worse, some came back to the army base hospital, missing parts. We drank too much, there was too much fooling around with spouses not one's own, and the war dragged on with no end in sight.

So, there I was, a kid from Boston living in a trailer park with a wife whose accent and outlook made her incomprehensible half the time, and I had a few years to go in the army, and guys around me were getting their second and even third sets of orders for 'Nam. Don't think I didn't miss Peggy and Boston, and my friends and family. Especially when Patty would turn on the country western station, and I had to listen to songs titled "Get Your Tongue Outta My Mouth 'Cause I'm Kissing You Goodbye." Or "How Can I Miss You if You Won't Go Away?"

Mom and Pop and my brothers had not yet

had the pleasure of meeting the new Mrs. Brenner; I kept avoiding a trip north, or them coming south.

I never thought I'd see Whispering Pines Trailer Park again, but I did, last summer, when I was on undercover assignment at Fort Hadley investigating the arms deal case that turned into the case of the general's daughter. I could have lived anywhere while undercover, but I chose Whispering Pines, which by that time was nearly deserted and filled with ghosts.

As I get older, I'm starting to make weird choices and decisions, and it seems that consciously or unconsciously I'm revisiting things and places from long ago. Like now, sitting on the taxiway at Tan Son Nhat Airport. I need to talk to a mental health professional.

But back to 1971, Fort Hadley, Georgia. By this time, I was a four-stripe sergeant—we made rank fast in those days—and as a combat veteran, I was assigned to the Infantry Training School, teaching young draftees how to stay alive and kill other young guys. The infantry sucks, by the way, but training new infantrymen was better than being one in Vietnam.

The country was in open rebellion by this time, the quality of the draftees was pretty low, and morale and discipline were in the toilet.

But all good things must come to an end, and I knew I was on the verge of getting orders for Vietnam, Part Two.

I really wanted to avoid this exciting opportunity, but I also had to get out of that hellhole I
was in, including, I'm sorry to admit, my marriage. I wouldn't be the first soldier who chose
war over garrison duty and marriage, and I
wouldn't be the first to regret it either.

And there were other considerations; my
brother Benny was now draft age. Benny was
and is today a great guy, very bright and easygoing. Unfortunately, he spends a good deal of
time with his head up his ass, and his chances of
surviving a combat tour were not good.

The army had a sort of semi-official policy of
not sending brothers, fathers, and sons to 'Nam
at the same time, so I knew if I went back,
Benny would probably not go until I returned,
or might never go if I didn't come back. The war
was starting to wind down, and the name of the
game was buying time.

I had a plan, and I'm a clever, take-charge
kind of guy, and I managed to get accepted to
Military Police School at Fort Gordon, Georgia.
This was temporary duty, so Patty stayed at
Whispering Pines Trailer Park in Midland, while
I went to MP school at Gordon.

Under the conditions that prevailed at that
time, if a soldier left his young wife alone for
more than twenty-four hours around a military
base, some guy named Jodie was helping her
get over her loneliness. I wasn't sure that's what
happened with Patty, but something happened.

Or, as the country western song says "She's Out Doin' What I'm Here Doin' Without."

So, I returned from Fort Gordon after three months with a new MOS—military occupation skill. My old MOS had been Eleven-Bravo, meaning infantry, meaning a second tour in Vietnam from which I had no reasonable expectation of returning home alive this time. My new military occupation skill was Military Police, and Vietnam was a possibility, but not a sure thing. And even if I went to 'Nam as an MP, my chances of getting killed or maimed by the enemy were less than the chances of that happening breaking up a brawl in the Enlisted Men's Club.

While I was at MP school, Benny got drafted, completed Basic Training, and was at that time in Advanced Infantry Training with a high probability of going to Vietnam, despite the troop reductions. We all knew that within the next year or so, someone was going to be the last guy in 'Nam to turn off the lights when he left, and someone was going to be the last man killed there. No one knew exactly when that was going to happen, but everyone knew they didn't want to be one of those guys.

In any case, my marriage was heading south, so I decided to do the same and volunteered for 'Nam.

Quicker than you can say bye-bye, and with no leave time, I was at Tan Son Nhat Airport in January of 1972, where I got orders for Bien Hoa, the big replacement center nearby. Bien Hoa was where some of the fresh meat arrived from the States, awaiting further orders to join their units up country. It was also where a lot of the guys heading home waited for the freedom flight. It was a crazy place, made more so by the juxtaposition of the damned and the saved. They didn't share the same barracks, but they mingled. They had little in common except two things: Those who were going home wanted to get drunk and get laid, and those who were about to go to the front wanted to get drunk and get laid. I, an MP sergeant, got caught in the middle.

As I said, morale and discipline had gone to hell, and I barely recognized the army that I had entered only about four years earlier. In fact, I barely recognized my own country anymore. So 'Nam was not that bad a place to be.

The war was winding down, at least for the Americans who were pulling out, but it would go on for another three terrible years for the poor bastards who had the misfortune of being born Vietnamese.

In fact, my second Vietnam tour lasted only six months before my MP company got orders to go home.

I hadn't heard much from Patty in those six months, and what I did hear through her brief, but neatly written letters didn't sound too positive. In fact, one letter said, "I'm sitting here listening to 'I'm So Miserable Without You, It's

Like Havin' You Here,' which is how I'm feeling now."

Some men returning unexpectedly from overseas call ahead, so that the loving wife can make preparations, or the unfaithful wife can get rid of the cigars in the ashtray. I called from San Francisco in June '72, saying I'd be home in three days. This news was met with some ambivalence.

When I finally got out of the taxi that had taken me from Midland Airfield to Whispering Pines Trailer Park, I was somewhat ambivalent myself about what I wanted to find.

I threw my duffel bag on the ground and went to the door of the trailer. Coming home after a long absence in a war zone is a strange experience, like you just re-entered the earth's atmosphere from outer space, and you know that things on earth have changed.

I tried the doorknob, and it was unlocked. I stepped inside my trailer and stood in the small living room. I knew she wasn't there, so I didn't even call out.

I went to the refrigerator for a beer and saw the note: *Paul—I'm sorry, but it's over. I filed for divorce. There's no one else, but I just don't want to be married no more. I guess I should say Welcome Home. Have a good life. Patty. P.S. I took Pal.* Pal was the dog.

The grammatical error of the double negative annoyed me, and I could hear her drawl in the written words. The title of another country western song ran through my head—"Thank God and Greyhound She's Gone."

I threw the note in the trash and found one beer left in the refrigerator, which wasn't my brand, but it was cold.

I walked around the place that had been my home for a few years and saw that she'd taken all of her things, but she hadn't taken the furniture because it belonged to the trailer and was mostly bolted down. She did, however, take all the linens, meaning a trip to the PX that evening. Actually, I didn't even have a car because she didn't take Greyhound; she took our '68 Mustang, which I still miss. I also miss Pal. I had anticipated him knocking me to the floor and licking my face, which I think he learned from Patty in the early days of our marriage.

This was not what homecomings were supposed to look like.

I spent a few days at Whispering Pines and Fort Hadley, getting my paperwork in order and all that, then I went back to Boston for my leave, where I was welcomed more warmly. My brother Benny was still in the service, so he wasn't home—in fact, he was in Germany, holding the line against the Red Hordes on the Eastern Front. I'd like to think my second 'Nam tour kept him out of Southeast Asia.

My brother Davey was just eighteen, and had drawn a low number in the new lottery draft system and was looking forward to being called.

He liked my uniform. The war really was coming to an end, so I didn't try to talk him out of the army or into college, and he, too, served his country, mostly at Fort Hadley. When he got to Hadley, I tipped him off about the lint heads and told him to look up a strawberry blonde named Jenny, but he never ran into her.

Regarding my homecoming to South Boston, the neighborhood seemed different somehow, more so than the last time I'd returned. I realized my boyhood was over, and yes, you can't go home again.

After my leave, I returned to Fort Hadley and Whispering Pines, and I discovered from a neighbor that Patty had lied about there not being anyone else—surprise! It turned out to be another soldier, and she's probably on her fourth or fifth by now. There's something about a man in uniform.

But things work out, and within a few months, I was back into a work routine on post and bought a nice yellow VW bug from a guy who was heading to 'Nam. The army doesn't give you a lot of time to sulk or contemplate the meaning of life, and they don't encourage you to talk about your personal problems. The army expression is "Got a personal problem? Go see the chaplain, and he'll punch your tough-shit ticket."

That was the old army, of course. The new army has trained counselors who'll talk to you before punching your tough-shit ticket.

But it makes a man out of you, and you learn to keep shit to yourself. And that's the way it should be if you've picked this life.

I was drawn back to the present by the sight of an open truck approaching the aircraft. This was our escort vehicle, a variation on the little truck with the revolving light that you see at most airports.

We followed the truck to the terminal, but we didn't actually get right to a gate. We stopped on the apron, and the engines shut down. We had arrived.

It was still raining, and below I saw a line of young ladies holding umbrellas, which I guess is cheaper than a mobile jetway. I also saw a few soldiers standing under a corrugated steel canopy, carrying AK-47s. Two men rolled a stairway toward the aircraft.

As I stared out the window, my mind flashed back to Tan Son Nhat Airport, November 1967, my first tour.

We had landed just before dawn, and as I stepped out of the air-conditioned Braniff 707, a blast of hot, humid air hit me, which was surprising at that predawn hour in November, and I recalled thinking it was going to be a long year for a guy who liked autumn and winter in Boston.

A few hundred American soldiers had been standing on the tarmac behind a rope, wearing short-sleeve khakis, carrying overnight bags, and staring up at the aircraft. The Braniff 707 that had brought me to Vietnam would be quickly refueled, and without even changing the crew, the aircraft would take these guys home.

When I came down the stairway into the predawn light, I had to pass the guys behind the rope. I could clearly recall the looks on their faces; most appeared anxious, like this wasn't going to come off like it should, but there were a few optimists who looked happy or excited.

A few of these homeward-bound men shouted out words of encouragement to the fresh meat, others shouted things like "You're gonna be sorreee!" or "It's a *long* year, suckers!"

As I looked closer at these guys, I noticed that some of them—who I realized later were the combat vets who'd seen too much—had this strange, faraway stare that I'd never seen before, but which I got familiar with later; this was my first clue that this place was worse than I'd imagined it from stories I'd heard, or from what I'd seen on the TV news.

My French companion brought me back to the present by saying, "What is so interesting out there?"

I turned away from the window and replied,

"Nothing." Then I said, "I was just recalling my first landing here."

"Yes? This time should be more pleasant. No one is trying to kill you."

I wasn't completely sure of that, but I smiled.

A bell chimed, and everyone stood to deplane. I got my overnight bag from the overhead compartment, and within a few minutes I was on the aluminum staircase where the smiling young ladies held umbrellas over everyone's heads. At the bottom of the staircase, I was handed an open umbrella, and I followed the line of passengers in front of me to the terminal, under the watchful eyes of the soldiers under the corrugated canopy.

My first sense of the place was the long forgotten smell of the rain, which did not smell like the rain in Virginia. A soft breeze carried the odor of burning charcoal, along with the rich and pungent smell of the surrounding rice paddies, a mixture of dung, mud, and rotting vegetation, a thousand layered years of cultivation.

I had returned to Southeast Asia, not in a dream or a nightmare, but in reality.

Inside the terminal, a lady took my umbrella, and motioned me to follow the others, as if I might have other plans.

I passed through a doorway into the International Arrival Terminal, a cavernous space that had the air of neglect and a sense of abandonment. The place was completely empty, except for my fellow passengers. Half the lights were out, and there was not one single electronic information screen, or any signs at all, for that matter. I was also struck by how quiet it was— no one speaking, and no PA system. Compared to the aircraft, the terminal was very humid, and I realized there was no air-conditioning, which wasn't a problem in January, but must be interesting in August.

As it turned out, however, this primitive facility was going to be the least of my problems.

Directly in front of me was a line of Passport Control booths, and beyond the booths I could see a single luggage carousel, motionless and empty. There were no porters visible, no luggage carts, and strangely, no Customs stations. More strangely, no one was waiting for any of the arriving passengers, most of whom were Vietnamese and should have had people eagerly expecting their arrival. Then I noticed that there were soldiers at the glass exit doors, and beyond the doors were crowds of people peering through the glass. Apparently, no visitors were allowed in the Arrival Terminal, which was weird. In fact, this whole place was weird.

I walked up to one of the passport booths and handed the uniformed guy my passport and visa. I looked at him, but he never made eye contact with me. He seemed interested in my passport and visa.

I looked again into the cavernous terminal beyond the booths and saw, hanging from the ceiling at the far end of the terminal, a huge red flag with a yellow star in the center—the flag of the victorious North Vietnamese Communists. The full reality of the Communist victory struck me, a quarter century late, but with unmistakable clarity.

When I landed at Tan Son Nhat in '67 and '72, soldiers didn't go through the civilian terminal, but I recalled that outside the terminal was the Stars and Stripes flying alongside the old red, green, and yellow South Vietnamese flag. No one had seen either of those flags around here in over two decades.

I had a creepy feeling, which was reinforced by the Passport Control guy, who kept staring at my passport and visa. I realized he was taking too long, and people in the other booths were passing through more quickly. At first, I just put this down to my usual bad luck of getting in a supermarket checkout line where the cashier was the village idiot.

But then the passport guy picked up a phone and began talking to someone. I could only remember a few words of Vietnamese, but I clearly heard him say the word My—American. This is not in and of itself a negative word, but you had to consider the context. I affected a look of bored impatience, which was lost on the passport guy.

Finally, another uniformed Vietnamese appeared, a short, stocky guy who took my passport and visa from the guy in the booth, and motioned me through. I picked up my overnight bag and followed him.

Standing on the other side of the line of passport booths was my French friend, who had passed through at least five minutes before with no problem. He seemed to be waiting for me, then noticed that I had an escort. He raised his eyebrows and said something in Vietnamese to my escort. The uniformed guy answered back sharply. The Frenchman, too, raised his voice, and they had a little argument, but the Frenchman didn't seem cowed by the Commie in uniform.

The Frenchman said to me, in English, "I think this is only a random questioning. Be polite, but firm. If you have nothing to hide, it will go well."

Actually, I had something to hide. I said to my new friend, "See you at Mademoiselle Dieu-Kiem's."

The short, tubby Viet guy gave me a push, which pissed me off so much I almost clocked him. But I got myself under control. The mission comes first. Clocking Commies was not part of the mission this time.

As I turned to follow the Viet, I heard the Frenchman say, "It is quite different now that neither your country nor mine is the power here. *They* have the power."

So off I went with this little guy in uniform, whose hat had a big red Commie star on the peak. Last time I was here, I had an M-16, and *I* had the power, and if I'd seen this guy then, I'd have painted him as red as that star.

I realized I was getting myself wound up, so as I walked with this guy through the nearly deserted terminal, I calmed myself down with a mental image of me with my hands around Karl's throat.

It occurred to me that there were three possibilities at the end of this walk. One, whoever it was I was going to talk to would kick me out of the country. Two, I'd be free to visit the Socialist Republic and do my sightseeing. Three, I'd wind up in the slammer.

I realized I might have some control over these possibilities, depending on what I said. I'm pretty good at bullshit.

We got to the far end of the terminal and came to a closed door, which my Commie companion opened, and which led to a long hallway lined with doors. The hallway was narrow, so my friend got behind me and prodded me again with a push. I could have broken his fat neck in a heartbeat, but then I wouldn't know what door I was supposed to go through.

He grabbed my arm halfway down the hall,

then knocked on a door. The voice behind the door barked, "Di Vao."

My pushy friend opened the door, thumped his hand on my shoulder, and I entered the room. The door closed behind me.

CHAPTER SEVEN

———————★———————

I found myself in a hot, dimly lit room whose stucco walls were the color of nicotine. In fact, the air smelled of cigarette smoke. The room was small and windowless, and a paddle fan hung motionless from the ceiling.

As my eyes adjusted to the dim light, I saw on the far wall a portrait of Ho Chi Minh and a small red flag with a yellow star in the center. I could also see a photo of a guy in uniform, who I thought might be General Giap, and a few photos of unsmiling civilians, who were undoubtedly government or Party officials. I concluded that this was not the Travelers' Aid Office.

There was a desk to my right and behind the desk was a middle-aged man in uniform. He said to me, "Sit."

I sat in an olive drab chair that I recognized as an American army camp chair. The desk, too, was American; the standard gray steel that hasn't changed since about World War II. On the wall above the desk was a big ventilation louver, and I could hear the rain falling outside.

The guy who had shown me into the office, who I'd nicknamed Pushy, deposited my passport and visa on the desk, then, without a word, he took my overnight bag and left.

The middle-aged guy in uniform studied my passport and visa by the light of a gooseneck lamp. I studied the guy.

He had on an olive-colored short-sleeve shirt with shoulder boards, and on the boards, he wore the rank of a major or colonel—I never could get the foreign insignia straight. Also, he had three rows of colored ribbons on his left breast pocket, and I assumed some of those dated back to the American War, as they called the Vietnam War here.

He had one of those faces that you instinctively don't like—pinched and perpetually frowning, with high, prominent cheekbones. His eyes were narrow, and his eyeballs seemed fixed in their sockets.

He looked older than me, but I knew he wasn't. In any case, he was the right age to be a veteran of the American War, and if he was, he had no positive feelings about Americans. I assumed, too, he was a North Vietnamese because he looked a little bigger and heavier than the southerners, who were slight of build. Also, it was mostly the North Viets who staffed the positions of power in the defeated south. My instincts told me this was not going to be a pleasant interview.

The guy looked up from my passport and said to me, "I am Colonel Mang."

I didn't reply. But the fact that he was indeed

a full colonel led me to believe this wasn't a simple passport and visa check.

Colonel Mang, in good English, asked me, "What is the purpose of your visit to the Socialist Republic of Vietnam?" He had a kind of high, staccato voice that was irritating.

I replied, "Tourism," which was the lie from which all future lies would spring. And if this guy knew it was a lie, then he'd let me keep lying until he had enough lies to make a noose.

"Tourism," said Colonel Mang. He stared at me. "Why?"

I replied, "I was a soldier here."

Suddenly Colonel Mang's demeanor changed from unpleasant to overly interested. Maybe I should have ignored my instructions and lied about that, but it's really important to stick close to the truth.

Colonel Mang asked me, "When were you here?"

"In 1968, then again in 1972."

"Two times. So you were a career military man."

"I became a career military man."

He tapped my visa and said, "Now you are retired."

"That's right."

Colonel Mang thought a moment and asked me, "And what were your duties in Vietnam?"

I hesitated a half-second too long, then replied, "I was a cook. An army cook."

Colonel Mang seemed to mull this over. He asked, "And where were you stationed?"

"In 1968 I was stationed at An Khe. In 1972 at Bien Hoa."

"Yes? An Khe. The First Cavalry Division."

"That's right."

"And Bien Hoa. What division?"

"I was a cook at the replacement center mess hall."

"Yes?" Colonel Mang lit a cigarette and drew thoughtfully on it. Finally, he informed me, "I was a lieutenant with Division 325 of the People's Army of Vietnam."

I didn't reply.

Colonel Mang continued, "I was an infantry platoon commander. In 1968, my regiment operated around Hue and Quang Tri. There were units of your division there as well. Were you ever stationed in that area?"

Again, sticking to the truth, but against my better judgment, I replied, "I was near Hue and Quang Tri a few times."

"Yes? Cooking?"

"That's right." I thought that this could be a pleasant conversation between two veterans, except for the fact that we had once been trying to kill each other.

Colonel Mang smiled for the first time and said, "Since our time there coincided, perhaps we once met."

Somewhat intemperately, I replied, "If we

had met, Colonel, only one of us would be here now."

Colonel Mang smiled again, but it was not a nice smile. He said, "Yes, that is true." He stared at me awhile, then remarked, "You don't seem to me like a cook."

I considered offering him my recipe for two hundred servings of chili, but instead I said, "I'm not sure what you mean, Colonel."

Colonel Mang puffed on his cigarette and seemed to be staring into the past. I had to assume he was used to questioning American veterans. I assumed, too, he enjoyed his job. What he was after, and what he knew, was another matter.

Colonel Mang said to me, "Many American soldiers have returned."

"I know."

We both sat quietly as Colonel Mang enjoyed his cigarette. I wasn't particularly uneasy, and so far this seemed like just a random stop and question, a case of profiling, but I really didn't like being on the answering side of an interrogation desk.

Colonel Mang asked me, "And what is this interest in coming back to Vietnam?"

I replied, "I'm sure each man has his own reason."

"Yes? And what is *your* reason?"

Well, I was working undercover for the United States government to investigate a strange murder case. But Colonel Mang didn't need to know that. In fact, this question had Zen overtones to it, so I replied, "I think after my visit here, I'll know the answer to that question."

He nodded appreciatively, as though this was the only possible answer.

Colonel Mang now got down to specific questions that needed non-Zen answers. He asked me, "Are you staying in Ho Chi Minh City?"

I replied, "I'm staying in Saigon."

This honked him off, and he informed me, "There is no Saigon."

"I saw it from the air." Why do I piss people off? What is wrong with me?

Colonel Mang fixed me with a cold stare and said, "Ho Chi Minh City."

I recalled Mr. Conway's and the Frenchman's advice to be firm but polite. How can you be both? But I backed off and said, "Right. Ho Chi Minh City."

"Correct. And how long are you staying there?"

"Three days."

"Where are you staying?"

"The Rex."

"Yes? The American Generals' Hotel."

"I always wanted to see where the generals stayed."

Mang gave me a little sneer and said, "They lived in luxury while their soldiers lived and died in the jungles and rice paddies."

I didn't reply.

He continued his political education lesson and said, "Our generals lived with us and shared the hardships. My general had no more rice than I did. He lived in a simple peasant's hut. Your generals at An Khe base camp had air-conditioned house trailers from America. I saw these with my own eyes when we liberated the south. Did you not see these at An Khe?"

"I did."

"And there was a golf course for the officers."

"Only nine holes," I reminded him. "And your snipers and mortar guys made it a tough course."

He actually laughed, then got himself under control and said, "And I am sure you cooked better food for the officers."

"No, everyone got the same food."

"I do not believe that."

"Well, it's true. Ask the next veteran you speak to."

Colonel Mang didn't want any of his preju-dices upset, so he changed the subject and asked me, "What rank did you retire with?"

"Warrant officer."

"Yes? So, how much did they pay you?"

Recalling that Mr. Conway said the average Vietnamese made three or four hundred dollars a year, I was a little embarrassed to reply, "About forty-five hundred dollars."

"A month. Correct?"

"Right. You already know this, so why are

you asking? And what is the purpose of these questions?"

Colonel Mang did not like my retort, but like most Vietnamese, he kept his cool.

He hit an intercom button and said something in Vietnamese. A few seconds later, the door opened and Pushy came in.

Colonel Mang and Pushy exchanged a few words, and Pushy handed Mang the stupid snow globe, that being the only thing in my overnight bag that had obviously confused him.

Mang examined the snow globe, and Pushy said something, so Mang shook it and watched it snow on the Vietnam Memorial. He looked up and asked me, "What is this?"

"It's the Vietnam War Memorial. A souvenir."

"Why do you have this with you?"

"It was a gift at the airport."

"Yes?" He stared at the globe and shook it again. I would have laughed, but Mang might think I was laughing at him.

Mang said, "Yes, I recognize this. The names of your dead are carved on this wall. Fifty-eight thousand. Correct?"

"That's right."

He informed me, "We have one million dead."

I replied, "The north and the south each had one million dead. That's two million."

He said, "I do not count the enemy."

"Why not? They were also Vietnamese."

"They were American puppets." Colonel

Mang put the globe on his desk and said to me, "Please empty all your pockets on my desk. Everything."

I had no choice but to comply, so I put my wallet on his desk, along with the envelopes in my jacket pocket, and also my pen, comb, handkerchief, and Tic Tacs. I held on to the addresses the Frenchman had given me.

Colonel Mang first went through my wallet, which held some American currency, credit cards, retired military ID card, with rank but no occupation, medical card, and my Virginia driver's license.

Next, he went through the things from my jacket, giving the pen, comb, handkerchief, and Tic Tacs a cursory inspection. Then he opened the envelopes with American money, Vietnamese money, and traveler's checks. Next he opened the envelope that held my airline tickets, then the envelope with my hotel vouchers. He studied everything and made notes on a piece of paper. As he was writing, he said something in Vietnamese, and Pushy replied. They both seemed interested in the amount of money I had, which represented a few years' salary for both of them. Obviously, there is no justice in the world when the defeated enemy could return to the scene of his defeat loaded down with cash.

Anyway, Pushy said something sharply to me in Vietnamese, then repeated it, which made him laugh. The Vietnamese are worse than Americans in regard to their impatience with people who don't speak their language. I tried to remember a Vietnamese word or two, like "Fuck you," but I was tired, and it wasn't coming back to me.

Finally, Pushy left the room and forgot to take the snow globe with him. Mang continued working on his notes, then looked up at me and said, "You have reservations at the Century Riverside Hotel in Hue, and the Metropole in Hanoi."

I didn't reply, and this seemed to tick him off.

He lit another cigarette and said, "Please take your things off my desk," as though I had annoyed him by depositing everything there.

I gathered my wallet and envelopes, odds and ends, and put them in my pockets. I noticed that Mang held on to my passport and visa. I said, "If that's all, Colonel, I'd like to get to my hotel."

"I will tell you when and if we are finished, Mr. Brenner."

That was the first time he'd used my name, and he wasn't being polite; he was telling me he knew my name, my addresses in Vietnam, my departure date, and the contents of my wallet, and so forth.

He said to me, "You have some days between your hotel reservation in Ho Chi Minh City and Hue."

"That's right."

"Where are you going?"

"I'm not sure."

"Certainly you will go to An Khe."

I might have, but not now. I said, "If it's possible."

"It is not a problem. However, part of your old base camp is a restricted area, used now by the People's Army."

"Including the air-conditioned house trailers?"

He didn't respond to that, but said, "The town of An Khe is not restricted. However, the brothels and massage parlors are all closed as are the bars and opium dens."

"Well, that's good news."

"Yes? You are happy that Dodge City is closed? That is what you called that district—correct? Built by your own engineers."

"Never heard of it."

Colonel Mang all of a sudden turned nasty and said to me, "Moral pollution. Degeneracy. That's why you lost the war."

I wasn't going to let him bait me, so I didn't reply.

Colonel Mang went on awhile about American imperialism, Agent Orange, the My Lai massacre, the bombing of Hanoi, and a few other things that even I wasn't familiar with.

This was a very angry man, and I couldn't even take any personal pleasure in getting him angry because he hated me before I walked through his door.

I recalled Mr. Conway's advice to express remorse for the war, and I realized this wasn't just
a suggestion, but a requirement. I said, "The
war was a terrible time for both our people, but
especially for the Vietnamese, who suffered so
much. I regret my country's involvement in the
war, and especially my own involvement. I've
come here to see how the Vietnamese people
are living now in peace. I think it's good that so
many American veterans are returning, and I
know that many of them have contributed time
and money to help heal the wounds of war. I
hope to be able to do the same."

Colonel Mang seemed pleased with my little
speech and nodded approvingly. This could be
the beginning of a beautiful friendship, but I
doubted it.

He asked me, "And where do you go between
Hue and Hanoi?"

Actually, on a secret mission, but I replied,
"I don't know. Any suggestions?"

"Surely you will visit some of your old battlefields?"

"I was a cook."

He gave me a conspiratorial smile, like we
both knew that was bullshit. He said in a flatter-
ing tone, "You seem to me like a man who
would not be satisfied stirring a pot."

"Well, I was a real sensitive kid. The sight of
blood on the pork chops used to make me sick."

Colonel Mang leaned across his desk and

said, "I killed many Americans. How many Vietnamese did you kill?"

I kind of lost it right then and there, and I stood and replied, "This conversation has become harassment. I'm going to report this incident to my consulate in Saigon and to my embassy in Hanoi." I looked at my watch and said, "I've been here half an hour, and if you delay me one more minute, I'm going to demand that you let me call the consulate."

Colonel Mang, too, lost his cool, stood and slammed his hand on the desk. He shouted for the first time, "You will make no demands on me! I will demand of you! I demand from you a full itinerary of your travels in the Socialist Republic!"

"I *told* you, I *have* no specific plans. I was told I could travel freely."

"I am telling you, you must give me an itinerary!"

"Well, then, I'll think about it. Please give me my passport and visa."

Colonel Mang got himself under control and sat. He said in a calm, matter-of-fact voice, "Please be seated, Mr. Brenner."

I remained standing long enough to piss him off, then sat.

He informed me, "I will hold your passport and return it to you before you leave Ho Chi Minh City. At that time, you will provide me with a full and accurate itinerary of your time between Ho Chi Minh City and Hue, and between Hue and Hanoi."

"I'd like my passport now."

"I do not care what you like." He looked at his watch and said, "You have been here ten minutes, this was a routine passport and visa check, and you are now free to leave." He pushed my visa across the desk and said, "You may take this."

I stood and took my visa, leaving the snow globe on Mang's desk, and walked toward the door.

Colonel Mang needed a parting shot and said, "This is my country, Mr. Brenner, and you are not the one with the guns any longer."

I had no intention of responding, but then I started to think about this guy's anger, his obviously traumatic war years as a combat platoon leader. I'm not a very empathetic guy, but because we were both combat veterans, I tried to put myself in his place.

But even if Mang was partly entitled to his anger, it wasn't doing him any good. I asked him, "Don't you think it's time to make peace with the past?"

Colonel Mang stared at me, then stood. He said in a soft tone that I could barely hear, "Mr. Brenner, I have lost most of my family and most of my friends to American bombs and bullets. My high school class are nearly all dead. I don't have a living male cousin, and only one of my four brothers survived the war, and he is an amputee. Now, if that happened to you, would you be able to forgive and forget?"

"Probably not. But history and memory should serve to inform the next generation not to perpetuate the hatred."

He thought about that for a few seconds, then said, "You can do whatever you wish in your country. I hope you learn something here. I suggest adding to your itinerary a visit to the Museum of American War Crimes."

I opened the door and left.

Standing outside was Pushy, who motioned me to walk in front of him. I re-traced my route down the narrow corridor and into the main terminal. Pushy gave me a little shove toward the baggage carousel. I walked across the deserted terminal and saw my suitcase and overnight bag, sitting at the feet of an armed soldier.

I reached for my suitcase, but Pushy grabbed my arm. He thrust a piece of paper toward me. I took it and read the handwritten words in English: *$20—Arrival Tax*.

My little guidebook had mentioned a departure tax, but I had the feeling that Pushy invented the arrival tax. I don't like being shaken down, and it was time to push back. I crumpled up the blackmail note and threw it on the ground. "No."

This sent Pushy into a frenzy, and he began

shouting in Vietnamese and waving his arms around. The soldier stood by impassively.

I picked up my bags, and Pushy didn't try to stop me. In fact, he shouted, "Di di! Di di mau!" which means get moving, and is not very polite.

I started to turn away, then I had a good idea that would make everyone happy. I put my bags down, reached into my breast pocket, and took a twenty-dollar bill from the envelope. I showed it to Pushy and gestured toward my bags. He wrestled with this temptation for a minute, weighing about three weeks' pay against his dignity. He looked around, then shouted at me to walk to the door as he picked up my bags. If he'd been nicer, I would have pointed out the retractable handle and wheels on the suitcase.

Anyway, I went out into the hot, humid air, which smelled heavily of exhaust fumes. The rain was now a drizzle, and there was a covered walkway that led to a line of taxicabs. A few people did double takes at the sight of a uniformed guy carrying my baggage, and they probably thought I was a big-shot American.

We got to the lead taxi, and the driver wanted to put the bags in the trunk, but Pushy had the drill by now and threw both bags in the trunk.

I held out the twenty, and Pushy snatched it rudely. I really wanted to knee him in the balls, but that might have cost me another twenty. Pushy said something to me in a nasty tone of voice, then yelled at the taxi driver and stomped off.

The driver closed the trunk, opened the passenger door, and I got inside the small Honda, not much bigger than a Civic. It stank of cigarette smoke and mildew.

The driver jumped in the car, started it up, and sped off.

We got clear of the airport in a few minutes, and the driver said, in passable English, "You American? Yes?"

"Yes."

"Come from Seoul?"

"That's right."

"Why take you so long?"

"The moving walkway was stuck."

"They ask you questions?"

"Yes."

"Communists eat shit."

This took me by surprise and I laughed.

The driver took a pack of cigarettes out of his shirt pocket and held the pack over his shoulder. "Smoke?"

"No, thanks."

He lit his cigarette with a match and steered with his knees.

I looked out the window and saw that the city had crept out to the airport. In place of the ramshackle bamboo huts and concession stands that I remembered on this road, I saw stucco structures. I noticed electric lines strung everywhere, and I saw TV antennas, and even a few satellite dishes. There were also a lot of small trucks and motor scooters on the road in place of the ox-drawn carts I'd remembered. Now, as then, there were a lot of bicycles. Something else new was a lot of plastic and paper trash along the road.

I didn't expect to see the old Vietnam, which in many ways was picturesque and pristine, but this horn honking and the TV antennas were a little jarring.

I thought about Colonel Mang for a moment and decided that the whole incident was, indeed, random. Unfortunately, as luck would have it, my run-in with the authorities had compromised the mission. I had to decide whether to push on or abort.

The driver said, "Hotel?"

"The Rex."

"American General Hotel."

"Really?"

"You a soldier in Vietnam. Yes?"

"Yes."

"I know. I drive many soldiers."

"Do they all get stopped and questioned?"

"No. Not many. They come out of building . . . you know? They come . . . how you say?"

"Alone? Late?"

"Yes. Late. Communists eat shit." He broke into loud laughter, warming to his subject. "Communists eat dog shit."

"Thank you. I get the picture."

"Mister, why the soldier carry your bag?"

"I don't know. What did he say?"

"He say you are American important person, but you are imperialist dog."

"That's not nice."

"You important person?"

"I'm the leader of the American Communist Party."

He got real quiet and shot some glances at me in the rearview mirror. He said, "Joke. Right? Joke?"

"Yes, joke."

"No Communists in America."

The conversation had a little entertainment value, but I was jet-lagged, tired, and cranky. I looked out the window. We were in old Saigon now, on a wide, well-lit boulevard whose street sign said Phan Dinh Phung. I seemed to recall that this boulevard passed the Catholic cathedral and in fact, I caught a glimpse of the cathedral spires over the low, French-style buildings.

My new friend said, "My father a soldier. He was American ami. You understand?"

"Biet," I replied, in one of my few remembered Vietnamese words.

He glanced back at me, and we made eye contact. He nodded, turned back to his driving, and said, "He prisoner. Never see him again."

"Sorry."

"Yes. Fucking Communists. Yes?"

I didn't reply. I was, I realized, more than tired. I was back. Thank you, Karl.

We turned onto Le Loi Street, Saigon's main drag, and approached the Rex Hotel.

I never saw any of Saigon when I was an infantryman. It was off limits, except for official business, and the average grunt had no official business in Saigon. But during my brief tour as an MP, I got to know the city a little. It was, then, a lively place, but it was a besieged capital, and the lights were always dimmed, and the motor traffic was mostly military. Sandbags were piled up at strategic locations where Vietnamese police and soldiers kept an eye on things. Every restaurant and café had steel gratings in front of the windows to discourage the local Viet Cong on motor scooters from tossing satchel charges and grenades at the paying customers. Yet despite the war, there was a frenetic energy about the city, a sort of joie de vivre that you see, ironically, when death is right outside the walls, and the end is near.

This Saigon, this Ho Chi Minh City, looked frenetic, too, but without the wartime psychosis that used to grip the town each night. And, surprisingly, there were lighted advertisements all over the place—Sony, Mitsubishi, Coca-Cola, Peugeot, Hyundai—mostly Japanese, Korean, American, and French products. The Commies might eat shit, but they drank Coke.

The taxi stopped in front of the Rex, and my friend popped the trunk and got out.

A doorman opened my door while a bellboy grabbed the bags from the trunk. The doorman said in good English, "Welcome to the Rex, sir."

My driver said to me, "Here my card. Mr. Yen. You call me. I show you all city. Good tour guide. Mr. Yen."

The ride was four dollars, and I tipped Mr. Yen a buck.

Yen looked around to make sure no one was listening, and he said, "That man in airport is security police. He say he will see you again." He jumped back in his taxi.

I entered the Rex Hotel.

The lobby of the Rex was a big, polished marble affair, with vaguely French architecture, and hanging crystal chandeliers. There were potted plants all over, and the air-conditioning worked. This was much nicer than Colonel Mang's office.

I also noticed that the lobby was decorated for the Tet holiday, which I was here for in '68 and '72. There were lots of flowering fruit branches stuck in big vases, and a big kumquat tree in the center of the floor.

There were a few people in the lobby, but at this hour—it was after midnight—it was pretty quiet.

I went to the check-in desk where a nice young Vietnamese lady, whose nametag said *Lan*, greeted me, took my voucher, and asked for my passport. I gave her my visa, she smiled, and again asked for my passport.

I informed her, "The police have taken it."

Her nice smile faded. She said, "I'm sorry, we need a passport to check you in."

"If you don't check me in, how will the police know where I am? I gave them this address."

The logic of this impressed her, and she got on the horn and jabbered awhile, then came back to me and said, "We will need to hold your visa until you check out."

"Fine. Don't lose it."

Lan began playing with her Japanese computer terminal. She said, "This is a busy season. It is the Tet holiday, and the weather is good for tourists."

"It's hot and sticky."

"You must come from a cold climate. You will get used to it. Have you stayed with us before?"

"I walked past the place a few times in 1972."

She glanced up at me, but didn't reply. Lan found me a deluxe suite for my hundred and fifty bucks a night and handed the key to the bellboy. She said, "Have a pleasant stay, Mr. Brenner. Please let the concierge know if there is anything you need."

I needed my passport, and to have my head examined, but I said, "Thank you." I was not supposed to call or fax anyone regarding my safe arrival. Someone would call here, which they'd probably done already, and they were wondering why I hadn't yet checked in.

Lan said to me, "Chuc Mung Nam Moi. Happy New Year."

My Vietnamese was mostly forgotten, but my pronunciation was once good, and I was able to parrot her. "Chuc Mung Nam Moi."

She smiled. "Very good."

So, off I went toward the elevators with the bellboy. The Viets are basically pleasant people, polite, good-natured, and helpful. But beneath the placid, smiling Buddhist exterior lay a very short fuse.

Anyway, up the elevator to the sixth floor, down the wide hallway to a big door. The bell-hop showed me into a nice suite with a sitting area, a view of Le Loi Street, and, thank God, a room bar. I gave him a buck and he left.

I hit the bar first and made myself a Chivas and soda with ice. This was just like a vacation, except for the bullshit at the airport and the fact that I could get arrested any minute for no reason, or for a good reason.

The room was decorated in what I call French Whorehouse, but it was big, and the bathroom had a stall shower. I examined my suitcase on the luggage stand and saw that everything was a mess. Same with my overnight bag.

Also, the bastards had taken the photocopies of my passport and visa. I guess they didn't have their own copy machine. Yet nothing else had been taken, and I gave Colonel Mang and his stooge credit for honesty and professionalism, despite Pushy trying to shake me down for twenty bucks. In fact, I would have been more comfortable if Colonel Mang was just a cop on the take—but he was something else, and that gave me a little worry.

I hung my clothes, straightened things out, peeled off my clothes, and got into the shower. That silly song "Secret Agent Man" kept running through my jet-lagged brain, then a few tunes from the James Bond movies.

I got out of the shower and dried off. I'd planned to check out the city, but I was barely conscious. I fell into bed and blacked out before I could turn off the lamp.

For the first time in many years, I had a war dream, a combat dream, complete with the sounds of M-16s, AK-47s, and the terrible chatter of a machine gun.

I awoke in the middle of the night in a cold sweat. I made myself a double Scotch and sat in a chair, naked and cold, and watched the sun rise over the Saigon River.

CHAPTER 8

─────★─────

I went to a late breakfast in the hotel's coffee lounge, and the hostess gave me a copy of the *Viet Nam News,* a local English-language publication. I sat, ordered a coffee, and looked at the headline, which read, "When U.S. Confidence Received a Major Blow." I had the feeling this newspaper might have a slant.

The headline story was written by a Colonel Nguyen Van Minh, a military historian. It said, "On this day in 1968, our army and people launched an attack against enemy strongholds at Khe Sanh. The attack shocked the United States and forced President Lyndon Johnson and the Pentagon to focus on coping with us at Khe Sanh."

I seemed to recall the incident because I was there. I read on and learned that the U.S. forces "suffered a severe and humiliating defeat." I didn't remember that part of it, but whoever controls the present, controls the past, and they're welcome to it.

I had trouble following the bad translation as well as the logic in this article, but I was interested to see a mention of my division, the First Air Cavalry, that was translated as "The Flying

Cavalry Division Number One." More interest-
ingly, the war was still news here, as I already
discovered from Colonel Mang.

I looked around. The other guests seemed to
be mostly Japanese and Korean, but there were
a number of Westerners, and I heard French and
English spoken. Saigon, it seemed, was making
a comeback.

I checked out the menu, which was in a variety of languages and came with photos, just in
case. None of the photos showed dogs or cats,
or half-formed chick embryos, as I remembered
from last time. I ordered the American breakfast
and hoped for the best.

I finished breakfast and went to the front
desk where I inquired about my passport. The
clerk looked and said, "No, sir." Neither were
there any messages. I suppose I half expected a
fax from Cynthia. I went out onto Le Loi Street.

Coming out of the cool, dimly lit lobby of the
Rex into the hot sunlight was a bit of a shock:
the sudden roar of the motor scooters, the con-
tinuous horn honking, the exhaust fumes, and
the mass of people, bicycles, and motor vehicles. Wartime Saigon had been somehow quieter, except for the occasional explosion.

I began walking the streets of Saigon, and
within ten minutes, I was sweating like a pig. I
had a map from the front desk, and I had my
camera slung over my shoulder. I wore cotton
khakis, a green golf shirt, and running shoes. In

fact, I looked like a dopey American tourist, except that most American tourists wear shorts wherever they go.

Saigon did not seem overly dirty, but neither was it real clean. The buildings were still mostly two to five stories high, but I noticed that a few skyscrapers had sprung up. Some of the architecture in the center was old French Colonial, as I recalled, but most of the city remained nondescript stucco with perpetually peeling paint. The city had some charm by day, but I remembered it mostly for its sinister and dangerous nights.

Traffic was heavy, but moved well, like choreographed chaos. The only vehicles that weren't playing by the rules were military vehicles, and yellow, open jeep-like police vehicles, all bullying their way through the streets, scattering everything in front of them. This hadn't changed much since last time, only the markings on the vehicles were different. You can always tell a police state, or a country at war, by how government vehicles move through the streets.

The most predominant form of transportation now, as well as then, were the motor scooters, whose riders were almost all young, men and women, driving in a predictably insane manner. The biggest difference now was that nearly everyone was talking on their cell phones.

I recalled when any of these men or women

could suddenly produce a grenade or a satchel, and chuck it at a café without screening, a military truck, a police booth, or a bunch of drunken soldiers, American or Vietnamese. These new cell phone cyclists seemed a danger only to themselves.

The city was bustling because of the approaching Tet holidays, which to the Viets is like Christmas, New Year's Eve, and the Fourth of July all rolled into one, plus they all celebrate their birthdays on New Year's Day, and everyone is a year older, like thoroughbred horses, no matter when they were born.

The streets were jammed with vendors selling flowers, branches of peach and apricot buds, and miniature kumquat trees. A lot of the vendors thought I needed these things for some reason, and they tried to entice me into buying fruit branches to carry around.

Some streets were crowded with stalls where vendors sold greeting cards saying Chuc Mung Nam Moi, and I thought about buying one for Karl and adding the words Phuc Yu.

The streets were also packed with cyclos, a uniquely Vietnamese form of transportation, a sort of bicycle with a one-seat passenger compartment up front. The driver pedals and steers from the rear, which is exciting. The cyclo drivers really wanted a Western fare, and they were bugging me to hop in and relax as they followed me through traffic and masses of people.

There were also swarms of kids circling me like piranha, pulling on my arms and clothes, begging for a thousand dong. I kept saying, "Di di! Di di mau! Mau len!," and so forth. But my pronunciation must have been bad because they acted like I was saying, "Come closer, children. Come bother the big My for dong." You could get people fatigue real fast here.

I found a street that I recalled from 1972, a narrow lane near the Cholan district, the city's Chinatown. This street was once lined with bars, brothels, and massage parlors, but now it was quiet, and I guessed that all the nice girls had spent a little time in re-education camps, atoning for their sins, and now they were all real estate brokers. I'd been on this street as an MP, of course, not as a customer.

I took a few photos as I walked, but I'd determined that I wasn't being followed, so all this tourist stuff was kind of wasted, unless I got Karl to sit through five hours of slides back in Virginia.

I got my bearings and headed toward the Museum of American War Crimes, which Colonel Mang had urged me to visit.

Within fifteen minutes, I found the place on the grounds of a former French villa that had once housed, ironically, the United States Information Service during the war. I paid a buck and went into the compound, where a big, rusting American M-48 tank sat on the grass. It was quieter here, there were no beggars or hawkers, and I found myself actually happy to be at the Museum of American War Crimes.

I looked around at the displays, which were mostly photos housed in various stucco buildings, and it was all pretty depressing and sickening: photos of the My Lai massacre, horribly mutilated women and children, deformed infants who were victims of Agent Orange, the famous photo of the naked girl running down the road burned by American napalm, the photo of the South Vietnamese officer blowing out the brains of a captured Viet Cong in Saigon during the '68 Offensive, a child sucking at the breast of his dead mother, and so on.

There was also a rogues gallery: Lyndon Johnson, Richard Nixon, American generals including my division commander, John Tolson, and pro-war politicians, plus photos of anti-war protesters all over the world, and policemen and soldiers knocking college kids around, the Kent State shootings, and on and on. The captions in English didn't say much, but they didn't have to.

There were a lot of photos of the major American anti-war figures of the day: Senator John Kerry from my home state, who'd served in 'Nam at the same time I did in '68, Eugene McCarthy, Jane Fonda, manning a North Vietnamese anti-aircraft gun, and so forth.

There was also a display of American war medals sent to Hanoi by the recipients as a protest against the war.

I could hear the Sixties screaming in my head.

I found a particularly disturbing photographic collection with an accompanying text. The photos showed hundreds of men being lined up, shot by a firing squad, then getting the coup de grâce with a pistol. But this wasn't another American or South Vietnamese war crime. The text explained that the victims were South Vietnamese soldiers, and pro-American hill tribespeople, the Montagnards, who'd continued the fight against the victorious Communists after the surrender of Saigon.

The text described the Montagnards as belonging to the FULRO, the Front Unitié de Lutte des Races Opprimées—the United Front for the Struggle of the Oppressed Races, a CIA-sponsored group of bandits and criminals, according to the caption. These photographs of the cold-blooded executions were supposed to serve as a lesson to anyone who had any thoughts about opposing the government. Actually, these photographs were not much different than the others showing American atrocities. The Hanoi government was obviously clueless about how these photographs would play to a Western audience. In fact, an American woman standing next to me seemed pale and shocked into silence.

As I looked at all this stuff, I wasn't sure what I felt. This was obviously an unbalanced presentation, omitting, for instance, the Communist massacres at Hue, and the one at Quang Tri City that I saw with my own eyes.

I'd seen enough and went out into the sunlight.

The people around the museum were mostly American, and they were divided by generation; the older men, obviously veterans, were angry, and some of them were swearing about the "one-sided, propaganda bullshit," to use one overheard phrase. Some of the veterans were with wives and children, and they were a little quieter.

Well, enough fun for one afternoon. I walked toward the exit, and noticed souvenir stands selling pieces of army munitions, flower vases made out of shell casings, old American dog tags, and models of Huey helicopters made from scrap aluminum, like works of origami. I saw old Zippo lighters, engraved with the names of their previous GI owners, along with mottoes, unit crests, and so forth. I spotted a lighter that was engraved with the same thing that mine was engraved with: *Death is my business, and business has been good.* I still owned the lighter, but I'd left it home.

I went out through the gate onto Vo Van Tan Street and turned back toward the center of the city.

Now and then, out of the corner of my eye, and the corner of my mind, I'd see the remnants of the once proud ARVN—the Army of the Republic of Vietnam; middle-aged men who looked ancient, missing legs and arms, blind, lame, scarred, stooped and broken. Some begged from fixed spots in the shade. Some just sat and didn't bother to beg.

Now and then, one of them would notice me, and he'd call out, "Hey, you GI? Me ARVN!"

These were men of my own generation, my former allies, and I felt guilty ignoring them.

It was a short walk back to the Rex, and when I entered the lobby, the air-conditioning hit me like a Canadian cold front.

I inquired at the desk for my passport, but no luck; no messages either. I got my key, went to the health club on the sixth floor, and scheduled a massage. In the men's locker room, I undressed, got a towel, robe, and shower clogs, and took a shower, sweating Saigon out of my pores, but not out of my mind.

I lay on a tatami mat in a quiet room, easy listening music coming out of a speaker. An attendant brought me a cup of sake.

By sake number three, I was feeling a little buzz, and an instrumental of "Nights in White Satin" was coming out of the speakers, and it was 1972; I was puffing on a big, fat joint in a lady's apartment off Tu Do Street not far from here, and she was lying next to me wearing nothing more than a cannabis smile, and we passed the joint back and forth, her long, black silky hair on my shoulder.

But then the lady began to fade, and it started to come to me that part of what I was feeling, being back here, was a sense of nostalgia for a time that was past; I was not young anymore, but I had been young once, in this place, which for me had been frozen in time. And as long as this place remained frozen in time, then so did my youth.

I must have drifted off because a guy was shaking me gently by the shoulder and saying I had a message, which turned out to be actually a massage appointment.

A receptionist at the health club desk directed me to Room C. Inside Room C was a massage table covered by a clean white sheet. I hung my robe, slipped off my shower clogs, and lay on the table, wearing my towel, stretching and yawning.

The door opened, and an attractive young woman wearing a short white skirt and sleeveless white blouse entered and smiled. "Hello."

Without too much more conversation, she motioned me to turn over on my stomach, loosened my towel around my waist, and jumped up on the table with me.

She was really strong for a small woman and cracked every bone and joint in my body. She grabbed an overhead bar and walked on my back and butt with her bare feet, kneading her toes into my muscles. I could get used to this.

There were mirrors on each of the walls, but this didn't seem too unusual, though I noticed that the young lady and I could look at one another in the mirrors, and she was smiling a lot.

Finally, she turned me over on my back and somehow I'd lost my towel. She was kneeling between my legs, and she pointed to a place she hadn't massaged yet. I had a feeling the shiatsu part of the massage was over.

She said, "Ten dollar—Okay?"

"Uhh . . ."

She smiled and nodded encouragingly. "Yes?"

Give this hotel another star.

Moral considerations aside, the words "sexual entrapment" popped into my head. That's just what I needed—Colonel Mang coming through the door taking a video of me getting a blow job in the massage room of the Rex Hotel.

I sat up and found myself face-to-face with my new friend. I said, "Sorry, no can do."

She made a big pout with her lips. "Yes, yes."

"No, no. Gotta go." I slid off the table and slipped into my shower clogs.

Miss Massage sat on the table and kept looking at me, pouting.

I took my robe from the hook and said, "Great massage. Give you big tip. Biet?"

She was still pouting.

I put on my robe, left the massage room, and went to the reception desk where I signed a hotel chit for the ten-dollar massage, then added another ten for a tip. The reception lady smiled at me and inquired, "You feel good now?"

"Very good." I would have felt even better if I'd gotten the CID to pay for a blow job.

Anyway, that little Southeast Asian interlude over, I went back to the locker room, got dressed, and left the health club, realizing that Colonel Mang wasn't part of that deal. I recalled that M never instructed James Bond to steer clear of sexual entrapments. The Americans, on the other hand, especially the FBI, were very puritanical about sex on the job. Maybe I should look into a foreign intelligence service for my next career. I mean, I was having so much fun already.

I went to my room, got a cold Coke, and collapsed into an armchair. As I sipped my Coke with my eyes closed, an image of Cynthia materialized. She seemed to be staring at me as if I'd done something wrong. I am basically monogamous, but there are times that try men's souls.

So, I sat there, deciding what I should wear to my seven o'clock rendezvous on the rooftop restaurant.

Then I noticed something. At the head of the bed near the pillow was the snow globe.

★

CHAPTER NINE

———★———

I took the elevator up to the rooftop restaurant and exited into a large enclosed area that held a bar and cocktail lounge. Mr. Conway hadn't been specific about where to meet my contact—the more unplanned it is, the more unplanned it will look. Right. But this was a big place, and through a glass wall, I could see a wide expanse of tables out on the roof itself.

I gave the bar and cocktail lounge a once-over, then went out to the roof, and a maître d' asked me in English if I was alone. I said I was, and he showed me to a small table. Service people all over the world address me in English before I even open my mouth. Maybe it's how I dress. Tonight I wore a blue blazer, a yellow golf shirt, khakis, and docksiders with no socks.

I looked around at the rooftop garden. There were enough potted plants to simulate a jungle, and I wondered how anyone was going to find me. The roof was paved in marble tiles, surrounded on three sides by a wrought iron railing, and the fourth side by the rooftop structure I'd just come out of. About half the tables were full, from what I could see, and the crowd looked divided about evenly between East and West. The men were dressed well, though no one wore a tie, and the ladies looked a bit overdressed in light evening gowns, mostly floor length. I hadn't seen much leg since I'd arrived, unless you count Miss Massage. There was, however, one middle-aged American couple in shorts, T-shirts, and running shoes. The State Department should issue a dress code.

There were hurricane lamps on each table with lit candles, and colored paper lanterns were strung around the garden.

Toward the far end of the rooftop was a huge metal sculpture of a king's crown with the word *Rex* in lights. Not a very socialist symbol. On either side of the crown stood a big sculpture of an elephant rearing up on its hind legs, and beneath the crown, a four-piece combo was starting to set up.

A waiter came by with a menu, but I told him I just wanted a beer. I inquired, "Do you have 333?"

"Yes, sir." And off he went.

I was glad they were still making Triple Three in the Socialist Republic—in Vietnamese, it's Ba Ba Ba, and it's a good luck number, like 777 in the West. I needed a little good luck.

The beer came in the bottle that I remembered, and I poured it into a glass, which I'd never done before. I noticed for the first time that the beer had a yellowish cast to it. Maybe that's why some of the guys used to call it Tiger Piss. I sipped it, but I couldn't recall the taste.

I looked out into the city. The sun was setting in the southwest and a nice breeze had come up. The lights of Saigon were coming on, and I saw that they stretched nearly to the horizon. Beyond the lights had been the war, sometimes close to Saigon, other times not so close, but always there.

The four-piece band started playing, and I could hear the mellow notes of "Stardust." There was a small dance floor near the band, and a few couples got up and tried to dance to this somnolent tune.

I don't know what I expected to find here, and I guess I was prepared for anything, but maybe I wasn't prepared for "Stardust" on the rooftop garden of the Rex Hotel. I tried to imagine the American generals and colonels and staff sitting here each night, and I wondered if they looked out to the horizon as they were dining. From this height, no matter how far off the war was, at night you could see the artillery and rockets in the distance, and maybe you could even see the tracer rounds and illumination flares. Certainly you could hear the thousand-pound bombs, unless the band was playing too loudly, and you surely couldn't miss the napalm strikes whose incandescent fire lit up the universe.

I sipped my beer, felt the breeze against my

face, listened to the band, which had segued into "Moonlight Serenade," and I suddenly felt very out of place, like I shouldn't be here, like this was somehow disrespectful toward the men who had died out there in the black night. What was worse was that no one on this roof knew what I was feeling, and I wished Conway, or even Karl, was with me right then. I looked around to see if I was alone, then I spotted a guy my age with a woman, and I could tell by how they were talking and by how he looked that he had been here before.

I was halfway into my second beer, and the band was halfway into "Old Cape Cod"—how did they know these songs?—and it was twenty past the appointed hour, and still no contact. I fantasized about a waiter giving me a fax message saying, "The murderer has confessed— Tickets to Honolulu at the front desk." But what about my passport?

While I was lost in my reverie, a young Caucasian woman had approached my table. She was dressed in a beige silk blouse, dark skirt, and sandals, and she was carrying an attaché case, but no handbag. She seemed to be looking for someone, then came over to my table and asked me, "Are you Mr. Ellis?"

"No."

"Oh, I'm sorry. I was supposed to meet a Mr. Earl E. Ellis here."

"You're welcome to join me until he arrives."

"Well . . . if you don't mind."

"Not at all." I stood and pulled a chair out for her. She sat.

She was about thirty, give or take a few years, with brown hair, which she wore long and straight, parted in the middle, like the Viet women. Her eyes, too, were brown and very big, and her face was lightly tanned, as you'd expect in this climate. She wore no jewelry, just a sensible plain watch, and almost no makeup, except a light pink lipstick, and no nail polish. Despite the Vietnamese hairstyle, she gave the impression of a business lady who you'd see in Washington, a lawyer or maybe a banker or stockbroker. The attaché case reinforced the image. And did I mention that she was well built and pretty? Irrelevant, of course, but hard not to notice.

She placed her attaché case on the empty chair, then reached her hand across the table and said, "Hi, I'm Susan Weber."

I took her hand, and thinking this was a James Bondian moment, I looked her in the eye and said, "Brenner. Paul Brenner." I thought I heard the band playing "Goldfinger."

"Thank you for letting me intrude. Are you waiting for someone?"

"I was. But let me buy you a drink while we both wait for our parties."

"Well . . . all right. I'll have a gin and tonic."

I signaled a waiter and ordered a gin and tonic and another beer.

Ms. Weber said something to the waiter in Vietnamese, and he smiled, bowed, and moved off.

I inquired, "You speak Vietnamese?"

"A little." She smiled. "How about you?"

"A little. Things like, 'Show me your ID card' and 'Put your hands up.'"

She smiled again, but didn't reply.

The drinks came, and she said, "I think they use real quinine. Something to do with malaria. I hate the malaria pills. They give me . . . well, the runs. I don't take them."

"You live here?"

"Yes. Almost three years now. I work for an American investment company. Are you here on business?"

"Tourism."

"Just arrived?"

"Last night. I'm staying here."

She raised her glass and said, "Welcome to Saigon, Mr. . . . ?"

"Brenner." We touched glasses.

Her accent, I noticed, had a touch of New England in it, and I asked her, "Where are you from?"

"I was born in Lenox—western Massachusetts."

"I know where it is." Lenox was one of those picture-perfect postcard towns in the Berkshire hills. I said, "I drove through Lenox once. Lots of big mansions."

She didn't respond to that, but said, "Summer home of the Boston Symphony—Tanglewood. Did you ever go to Tanglewood?"

"I usually summer in Monte Carlo."

She looked at me to see if I was jerking her around, couldn't seem to decide, then asked me, "How about you? I think I hear a little Boston."

"Very good. I thought I'd lost that."

"You never do. So, we're both Bay Staters. Small world and all that." She looked around. "It's nice up here, except in the summer when it's too hot. Do you like the hotel?"

"So far. Got a great massage this afternoon."

She caught this right away, smiled, and replied, "Did you now? And what kind of massage?"

"Shiatsu."

She informed me, "I love a good massage, but the girls only make about a dollar from the hotel—they make more by offering extras, which is why they don't like to massage women."

"You could tip."

"I do. A dollar. They like men."

"Well, FYI, I just got the massage. But this is a loose place."

"You need to be careful."

"I'm doing better than that. I'm being good."

"That's very commendable. How did we get on this topic?"

"I think it was me."

She smiled, then said, "About the hotel—it was once owned by a wealthy Vietnamese couple who bought it from a French company. During the American involvement here, it housed mostly American military."

"So I've heard."

"Yes. Then when the Communists came to power in 1975, it was taken over by the government. It remained a hotel, but it housed mostly North Vietnamese party officials, Russians, and Communists from other countries."

"Nothing but the best for the winners."

"Well, I understand it became a pigsty. But sometime in the mid-1980s, the government sold an interest in it to an international company, who managed to get rid of the Communist guests. It was completely renovated and became an international hotel. I always book this place for American and European businesspeople." She looked at me. "I'm glad you like it."

We made eye contact, and I nodded.

She looked at her watch. "I can't imagine where this Mr. Ellis is."

"Try the massage room."

She laughed.

I said, "Have another drink."

"Well . . . why not?" She said something to a passing waiter, then reached into her attaché case and took out a pack of Marlboros. She offered the pack to me.

I said, "No, thanks. But you go ahead."

She lit her cigarette and while lighting it, she said softly, "I have something for you." She exhaled a stream of smoke.

I didn't reply. I hadn't expected a woman, but I realized it was less conspicuous.

She said, "I received a fax from your firm. I marked what you need in a newspaper, which is in my attaché case. The crossword puzzle. They said you'd understand."

"Offer the newspaper to me when you leave."

She nodded, then said, "I faxed your firm last night that you'd checked in here. I told them your flight was delayed because of weather, but that you'd checked in an hour and a half after you'd landed." She asked me, "Was there a problem at the airport?"

"They misplaced my luggage."

"Really? There are not many flights arriving, and there's only one baggage carousel. How could they misplace your luggage?"

"I have no idea."

Her gin and tonic came along with another beer. The band was playing "Stella by Starlight." There seemed to be a sky theme in these selections.

I asked Ms. Weber, "Do you really work for an American company?"

"Yes. Why?"

"Have you ever done anything like this before?"

"I don't know—what am I doing?"

Clever reply, but I needed an answer, so I asked her again.

She replied, "No. I was just asked to do this favor. First time."

"Who asked you?"

"A man I know here. An American."

"What does this man do for a living?"

"He works for Bank of America."

"How well do you know him?"

"Well enough. He's my boyfriend of the moment. About six months. Why are you asking these questions?"

"I'd like to be sure you're not on the watch list of the local KGB."

She nodded, then said, "Everyone here is under surveillance by the Security Police. Especially Americans. But the Viets are not very efficient about it."

I didn't reply.

She added, "Three fourths of the Vietnamese police force are in plainclothes. These guys at the next table could all be police, but unless I light a joint and blow smoke in their faces, they're more interested in their beers than in me. It's all very random. I get stopped and fined two dollars about once a month for some stupid traffic violation."

I didn't reply.

She continued, "It's all about money. This city is full of high-priced imported consumer goods, and the average Nguyen makes about three hundred a year, but he wants everything he sees, so if he's a civilian, he works close to Western tourists for the tips, his kid brother begs in the streets, his sister turns tricks, and his brother, who's a cop, extorts money from the tourists and the expats."

"I think I've met them all."

She smiled and informed me, "It's a corrupt country, but the bribes are pretty reasonable, the people are basically nice, street crime is rare, and the electricity works in Saigon, even if the plumbing is a little unreliable. I wouldn't worry too much about police state efficiency here. It's the inefficiency, the government paranoia, and xenophobia concerning Westerners, trying to convince them you're just here to make a buck, or take pictures of pagodas, or have cheap sex, and that you're not here to overthrow the government. I'm no hero, Mr. Brenner, and not a patriot, so if I thought there was any danger to me in doing this little favor, I'd say no."

I thought about all this and concluded that Ms. Weber was a little cynical, though she didn't strike me that way at first. But maybe 'Nam got to her. I asked her, "So why did you agree to do this little favor?"

"I told you—my stupid boyfriend. Bill. Now that we have consulate people here, he thinks they can help his business. The government knows as much about business as I know about government."

"So someone in the consulate asked Bill to—what?"

"They asked Bill to ask me to meet you. The consulate wanted a woman. The police don't pay much attention to women, and I guess this is less conspicuous."

"Can I check out this guy Bill?"

She shrugged. "I'll give you his card. I have a stack of them."

"You're a very loyal girlfriend."

She laughed, then said, "You're very suspicious."

"Also, paranoid. And there's a possibility I'm being watched, so don't be completely surprised if you're questioned later."

Again, she shrugged. "I don't know a thing."

I informed her, "I'm a veteran, and I'm here to reminisce, and to see some of the places where I served."

"That's what I was told."

"And that's all you know. Your business date didn't show up, and you're about to leave."

She nodded.

I asked her, "Aside from the newspaper, is there anything else you're supposed to give me?"

"No. Like what?"

"Like a cell phone."

"No. But you can have mine. It doesn't work well between cities. But it's good for Saigon. You want it?"

"Not if it can be traced to you."

"It's up to you. Is there anything else I can do for you?"

"What were you told you could do?"

"Take and deliver a message."

"What's the deal on me faxing a message out of here?"

"You mean in the hotel? You just fax it."

"Do they look at it? Make a copy?"

She thought a moment, then replied, "They do. They won't give your sheet back until they've made a copy. But I can send a secure fax or e-mail from my office." She added, "That's what I did last night."

"Are you also supposed to fax someone regarding this meeting?"

She nodded. "A 703 area code. Virginia."

"Right. Okay, along with your rendezvous report, say that I was stopped at the airport, and they took my passport, but I think it was a random stop, and I'll be leaving Saigon on time, if I have my passport. Okay?"

She looked at me, then repeated the message, and said, "I'm not supposed to ask you any questions, but—"

"Don't ask any questions. And if you get a reply to the fax, memorize it. Do not carry it with you to this hotel. Contact me and we'll meet somewhere. Okay?"

"Whatever you say."

"Thanks."

"No problem. So, they stopped you at the airport? That's why you were late."

"Right."

"I'm not surprised. You look shifty." She laughed and asked, "Did they want an arrival tax?"

"Twenty bucks."

"Did you give it to them?"

"I did."

"You shouldn't have. They understand no if you're firm about it."

"I made this little security guy carry my luggage to the cab."

She laughed. "That's great. I love it." She added, "You know, the passport guy and everyone split the loot. That's the scam."

I asked her, "So, you think it was just a random shakedown?"

"Sure . . . except they hardly ever take a passport." She thought a moment, then said, "You'll hear from them again."

"I hope so. They have my passport."

She lit another cigarette, and I had the impression she wasn't in a hurry to leave. I said, "Offer me the newspaper, and then you can take off for your next appointment. I need your business card and Bill's."

She looked at me, and we held eye contact awhile, then she put out her cigarette and said, "My business card is in the newspaper. I'm not sure you're supposed to know anything about Bill. Call me, and I'll let you know about that."

"Okay."

She stood and picked up her attaché case from the chair. She said, "Thank you for the drinks."

I stood. "My pleasure."

She said, "I have an English language newspaper I'm finished with. Do you want it?"

"Sure. I can use something to read."

She took her *International Herald Tribune* from her attaché case and put it on the table. "It's a day old, but it's the weekend edition. You won't see another one until Monday night."

"Thanks."

She put out her hand and we shook. She said, "Good luck."

I replied, "Chuc Mung Nam Moi."

She smiled and said, "Chuc Mung Nam Moi." She turned and left.

I sat down and left the newspaper where it was, waiting for something unpleasant to happen as I sipped my beer.

I waited a full minute, nothing happened, and I picked up the newspaper and unfolded it. I palmed her business card and slipped it in my jacket pocket as I extracted my handkerchief and wiped my forehead. I sat sideways to the table and read the front page by the light of the table candle.

Well, so far, so good. I've never worked a case in a hostile country, though to be truthful I've worked cases in friendly countries that I've made hostile. In any case, I thought my spy craft was pretty good, considering I was just a cop. Mr. Conway was right—it's in the blood of my generation. Too many spy novels and movies. What would James Bond do now?

Well, James wouldn't have let Ms. Weber get away, for starters. But when you're working for the CID or the FBI, as I'd done a few times, you keep your cork in your shorts. And then, of course, there was Cynthia. And Bill, whoever he was. Plus, Ms. Weber didn't need any more trouble than she might already be in.

I looked up and noticed that Susan Weber had returned to the table. She sat down. She said, "Mr. Ellis has canceled our appointment. Also, I was supposed to tell you not to hesitate to call me if you need anything and to let me know when you're about to leave Saigon on Monday morning. But the phones in most foreign business offices are presumed to be tapped—not necessarily for security reasons, but in hopes they can hear something that will give them a business advantage. Still, you have to be careful what you say on the landline phones. My cell number is on my card, but you'll need a cell phone to call me, if you don't want the conversation monitored. If you call me from a landline, and you need to say something important, I can meet you. I've been asked to stay in Saigon all weekend. Okay?"

"You forgot all that?"

"Well, I said you could call me, if you need anything. I'm just elaborating."

"Okay. Thanks."

"It's Saturday night and I don't have a date."

"Where's Bill?"

"I told him I might be busy, depending on what happened tonight."

"Am I missing something?"

"I wanted to see if you were interesting or not."

"Well, then, I guess this is good-bye."

She smiled. "Come on. Don't give me a hard time."

"Look . . . Susan . . . my instructions were—"

"I have new instructions. They want me to brief you about the country so you don't get totally lost and confused after you leave Saigon."

"Is that true?"

"Would I lie to someone from my home state?"

"Well . . ."

"I'm not used to no."

"I don't imagine you are. Will you join me for dinner?"

"I'd be delighted. How nice of you to ask."

I signaled a waiter and asked for menus. I said to my new friend, "How's the food here?"

"Actually, not bad. They have Japanese,

French, Chinese, and, of course, Vietnamese. This is the Tet holidays, so there'll be a lot of specialty holiday foods offered."

The menus came, and I asked her, "What's the word for dog meat?"

"Thit cho." She smiled and picked up her menu. "What do you want? Chinese, Vietnamese, or French?"

"I want a cheeseburger and fries."

"I'll order for us from the holiday menu."

The maître d' appeared, and they had a conversation about the menu, punctuated by some laughs and glances toward me. I said, "No thit cho."

The maître d' laughed again and said something to Susan. To show I understood the language, I told him in Vietnamese to put his hands up.

The guy left and Susan said, "I ordered a lot of little things so you could taste everything and eat what you like." She asked me, "Why did you tell him to put his hands up?"

"Just practicing."

She asked, "Don't they have lots of Vietnamese restaurants in Washington?"

"Why do you think I live in Washington?"

"I assume you work *for* Washington."

"I live in Virginia. I'm retired."

"Did you have Vietnamese food when you were here in the army?"

"I had C rations. You weren't allowed to eat

the local stuff. Army regulations. Some guys got very sick on the food."

"Well, you still have to be careful. Drink lots of gin and tonics, bottled water, beer, and Coca-Cola. I was really sick when I first got here. We call it Ho Chi Minh's revenge. But I haven't been sick since then. You build up immunities."

"I won't be here that long."

The food came, course after course. Ms. Weber ate like a Vietnamese with the bowl up to her face, shoveling in everything with chopsticks. I used my knife and fork.

We made small talk, mostly about Saigon and her job. She explained what she did, but I being a government employee with no business background, none of it made sense to me. It had to do with giving advice and arranging loans for mostly American investors who wanted to do business in Vietnam. Even though it made no sense to me, it made sense to her, and I concluded that she really was an investment advisor. I can usually tell when someone's faking it because many of my assignments require me to take on an undercover role and pretend I'm a clerk, or an armory sergeant, or anything that will get me close to the suspect.

After a while, I think we felt comfortable with each other. She said to me, "I know I'm not supposed to ask you questions, so I don't know what to ask you to make conversation."

"Ask me anything you'd like."

"Okay. Where did you go to school?"

"I can't answer that."

She smiled. "You think you're funny."

"I *am* funny. Where did *you* go to school?"

"Amherst. Then Harvard for my MBA."

"And then?"

"I worked in New York with an investment bank."

"For how long?"

"If you're trying to figure out my age, I'm thirty-one."

"And you've been here three years."

"Three years next month."

"Why?"

"Why not? It's a good résumé builder, and no one bothers you here."

"You like it here?"

"Actually, I do."

"Why?"

She shrugged, thought a moment, then said, "I guess . . . being an expat is who I am. You understand?"

"No."

"Well . . . it's part of my identity. In New York, I was nobody. Just another pretty face with an Ivy League MBA. Here, I stand out. I'm exotic to the Vietnamese and interesting to Westerners."

I nodded. "I think I understand. When are you going home?"

"I don't know. I don't think about it."

"Why not? Don't you get homesick? Family?

Friends? Fourth of July? Christmas? Ground
Hog Day?"

She played with her chopsticks awhile, then
said, "My parents and my sister and brother
come and visit at least once a year. We get along
very well now because I'm here and they're
there. They're all very successful and competi-
tive. Here I can be my own person. A few good
friends have visited, too. Also, the American
community here goes out of its way to celebrate
holidays, and somehow the holidays are more
special and more meaningful. You understand?"

"I think so."

"Also, this isn't just a Third World country. It's
a semi-totalitarian state, and the Westerners
here feel like they're living on the edge, so every
day is interesting, especially when you beat
these idiots at their own game." She looked at
me. "Am I making any sense, or have I had too
much to drink?"

"Both. But I understand."

"You should. You're a spy."

I informed her, "I'm a retired army person, I
served two tours here in '68 and '72, and I'm
back here as a tourist."

"Whatever. Does this place bum you out?"

"No."

"Did you have a bad time when you were
here?"

"I've had better times."

"Were you wounded?" she asked.

"No."

"Did you ever have any post-traumatic stress?"

"I have enough everyday stress to keep me happy."

"Where were you when you were here?"

"Mostly up north."

"You mean Hanoi?" she asked.

"No. Hanoi was in North Vietnam. We never fought there."

"You said north."

"The northern part of the old South Vietnam. The DMZ. Did they teach you any of this in school?"

"In high school. I didn't take history in college. So, where were you stationed?"

"In '72, I was at Bien Hoa. In '68, I was mostly in Quang Tri Province."

"I've been as far north as Hue. Beautiful city. You should try to get there. I've never been to the Central Highlands. I did fly to Hanoi once. They hate us in Hanoi."

"Can't imagine why."

"Well, whatever you did, they still hate us." She looked at me. "Sorry. That came out wrong."

"Don't worry about it."

"So, are you going to visit those places?"

"Maybe."

"You should. Why else would you come here? Oh . . . I forgot, you're . . ." She put her finger to her lips and said, "Shhh," then laughed.

I changed the subject. "Do you live in central Saigon?"

"I do. Most Westerners do. The surrounding districts can be a little too native." She changed the subject back and asked me, "What did you do here in Vietnam?"

I said, "I'd rather not talk about the war."

"Do you *think* about it?"

"Sometimes."

"Then you should talk about it."

"Why? Because I think about it?"

"Yes. The point is, men keep things to themselves."

"Women talk about *everything*."

"That's healthy. You need to talk things out."

"I talk to myself, and when I do that, I know I'm talking to an intelligent person."

"You're a tough guy. Old school."

I looked pointedly at my watch. Somehow, Ms. Weber and I had become familiar, which may have been a result of too many beers. I said, "It's been a long day."

"I'm having dessert and coffee. Don't run off."

"I'm jet-lagged."

She lit a cigarette, ignored me, and said, "I never smoked before I got here. These people smoke like chimneys, and I got hooked. But I don't do grass or opium. I haven't gone completely native yet."

I watched her in the flickering light of the candle. This was a somewhat complex woman, but she seemed to be a straight shooter. I never compare Woman A to Woman B, but Susan reminded me a little of Cynthia—the straightforwardness, I think. But whereas Cynthia was formed by the army, as I was, Susan came from another world, Lenox, Amherst, Harvard. I recognized the upper-middle-class accent and bearing, the *other* Massachusetts that Southies used to laugh at, but also envied.

She signaled a waiter and asked me, "Coffee or tea?"

"Coffee."

She said something to the waiter, and he left. She said to me, "The native coffee is good. It's from the highlands. You want dessert?"

"I'm stuffed."

"I ordered fruit. The fruit here is out of this world."

She seemed to be enjoying my company, or enjoying herself, and that's not always the same thing with women. In any case, she was kind of fun, except she'd had a beer too many and was starting to get silly.

It was cooler now, a beautiful, star-filled evening, and I could see the last sliver of the waning moon. I said to her, "New Year's Eve is next Saturday night. Correct?"

"Yes. You should try to be in a major city that night. It could be fun."

"Like New Year's Eve at home?"

"More like Chinese New Year in Chinatown in New York. Fireworks, noisemakers, dragon dancing, puppet shows, and all that. But it's also very solemn, and a lot of people go to pagodas to pray for a good year and honor their ancestors. The party ends before midnight because everyone goes home to be with their families at midnight. Except that the Catholics go to midnight mass. Are you Catholic?"

"Sometimes."

She smiled. "Well, then go to midnight mass if you're near a church. Someone will invite you to come home with them and share a meal. But the first visitor who crosses the threshold of a Vietnamese home after midnight must be of good character, or the family will have an unlucky year. Are you of good character?"

"No."

"Well, you can lie." She laughed.

I said, "And I understand that the celebration lasts for a week afterward."

"Officially four more days, but in reality about a week. It's a tough week to get anything done because just about everything is closed. The good news is that all the pre-holiday traffic and congestion come to an end, and most places look like ghost towns. The restaurants and bars are usually open only at night, and people party hard every night. But each city and region has some differences in how they celebrate. Where do you think you'll be for Tet?"

I thought, *Probably in jail.* I said, "I'm not sure about my itinerary."

"Of course." She thought a moment, then said, "You must have been here for a Tet holiday if you were here twice."

"I was here for Tet '72 and '68."

She nodded. "I know about Tet '68. I'm historically challenged, but that I know about. Where were you?"

"Outside Quang Tri City."

She said, "I understand it was very bad in Quang Tri and Hue. Maybe you can be in Hue for Tet. That's a very big celebration."

I replied, "I'm not sure where I'll be."

"Do you at least know what you're doing tomorrow?"

"I'm sightseeing tomorrow."

"Good. You need a guide and I'm available."

"Bill might be annoyed."

"He'll get over it." She laughed again and lit another cigarette. "Look, if you're going up country, you need some tips. I'll give you some good advice."

"You've been helpful enough." I asked her, "Do you use that expression? Up country?"

"I guess so. I heard it here. Why?"

"I thought it was only a military expression."

"The Westerners use it here. Up country.

Means someplace out of Saigon or any major city—usually someplace that you'd rather not be—like in the wilds. Right?"

"Right."

"So, if you'd like, I'll show you the real Saigon tomorrow."

"That's above and beyond the call of duty."

She looked at me through her cigarette smoke, then said, "Look, Paul, I'm not . . . I mean, I'm not coming on to you."

"That never crossed my mind."

"Right. Are you married? Am I allowed to ask that?"

"I'm not married, but I'm in a . . . what's it called these days?"

"A committed relationship."

"That's it. I'm in one of those."

"Good. Me, too. The man's an idiot, but that's another story. Princeton. Need I say more?"

"I guess that says it all."

"I hope you're not Princeton."

"God forbid. I'm army college extension program, cum laude."

"Oh . . . anyway, here's where I'm coming from. I'm not—"

The fruit and coffee came.

The band was playing some Sixties stuff now and swung into "For Once in My Life," Stevie Wonder, 1968.

She picked at some fruit, then patted her lips

with her napkin. I thought she was getting ready to leave, but she asked me, "Would you like to dance?"

This took me by surprise, but I replied, "Sure."

We both stood and moved to the small dance floor, which was crowded. I took her in my arms and there was a lot of woman there. We danced. I was a little uncertain about where this was going, but maybe I was reading this wrong. She was bored with Bill and wanted a little kick by having dinner with Super Spy.

The band was playing "Can't Take My Eyes Off You." Her body was warm, she danced well, and her breasts were firm against my chest. She had her chin on my shoulder, but our cheeks were not touching. She said, "This is nice."

"Yes, it is."

We danced on the roof of the Rex Hotel, with the lighted rotating crown above us, the stars overhead, a warm tropical breeze blowing, and the band playing slow dance music. I thought of Cynthia, though I was holding Susan. I thought of our few, short times together, and the fact that we'd never shared a moment like this. I found myself looking forward to Hawaii.

After a few minutes of silent dancing, Susan asked me, "So, do you want company tomorrow?"

"I do, but . . ."

"Here's where I'm coming from. I'm not political, I'm strictly business. But I'm not real
thrilled with these idiots who run this place.
They're bullies, anti-business, and anti-fun. The
people are nice. I like the people. I guess what
I'm trying to say is that I've never in my life done
anything for my country, so if this is for my
country—"

"It isn't."

"Okay, but I'd like to do something for you because I have a feeling you might need more tips
about this place than anyone has given you. And
I'd like you to succeed at whatever you're doing
here. And I don't want you to get in trouble
when you leave Saigon. The rest of this place is
not Saigon. It can get a little rough out there. I
know you're a tough guy, and you can handle
this place—you did it twice. But I'd feel better if
I gave you a day of my time and gave you the benefit of my extensive knowledge of Vietnam.
How's that?"

"Good pitch. Are you doing this for me, or
because you like to live dangerously, or because
you like to do things that the government here
doesn't like you to do?"

"All of the above. Plus, for my country, no
matter what you say."

I mulled this over as we continued to dance.
There was no good reason why I shouldn't
spend the day with this woman, but something

told me this was trouble. I said to her, "I expect to be called to some government office to answer some questions. You don't want to be around for that."

"They don't frighten me. I can trade insults with the best of them. In fact, if we're together, you won't look so suspicious."

"I don't look suspicious."

"You do. You need a companion for the day. Let me do this."

"Okay. As long as you understand why you're doing it, and that I'm just a tourist, but a tourist who's come to the attention of the authorities for some reason."

"I understand." The band took a break, and she took my hand and led me back to the table.

She found a pen in her attaché case and wrote on a cocktail napkin. "This is my home number if you need it. I'll meet you tomorrow in the lobby at 8 A.M."

"That's a little early."

"Not for an 8:30 mass at the cathedral."

"I don't go to church."

"I go every Sunday, and I'm not even Catholic. It's part of the expat thing." She stood and said, "If you're not in the lobby, I'll try the breakfast room. If you're not there, I'll ring your room. And if you're not there, I know who to contact."

I stood. "Thanks." I added, "I had a really nice evening."

"Me, too." She picked up her attaché case. "Thanks for dinner. You'll let me buy you dinner tomorrow."

"Sure."

She hesitated, then looked me in the eye and said, "I know a few men your age who work here, and a few men who I've met here who have returned to find something, or maybe lose something. So, I know it's tough, and I can understand. But for people my age, Vietnam is a country, not a war."

I didn't reply.

"Good night, Paul."

"Good night, Susan."

I watched her disappear into the enclosed restaurant.

I looked at the cocktail napkin, memorized her home phone number, and crumpled the napkin into my coffee cup.

It was, as I say, a beautiful evening with a warm breeze rustling the plants. The band was playing "MacArthur Park." I closed my eyes.

A long time ago, when Vietnam was a war and not a country, I could recall nights like this out under the stars, the tropical breeze moving through the vegetation. And there were other nights without a breeze, when the vegetation moved, and you could hear the tapping of the bamboo sticks that they used to signal one another. The tree frogs stopped croaking and even the insects became still and the night birds flew off. And you waited in the deathly silence, and even your breathing stopped, but your heart thumped so loudly you were sure everyone could hear it. And the sound of the tapping bamboo came closer, and the vegetation swayed in the breezeless night.

I opened my eyes and sat there awhile. Susan had left a half bottle of beer, and I drank from the bottle to moisten my dry mouth.

I took a deep breath, and the war went away. I found myself looking forward to tomorrow.

I went to my room carrying the newspaper. There was no message light on, no message envelopes anywhere, and the snow globe had been moved by the maid who turned down the bed. It was now on the desk.

I sat at the desk and opened my *International Herald Tribune* to the crossword puzzle, which was the *New York Times* puzzle and was half finished. I studied the puzzle a moment, then I noticed that next to number 32 down was a tick mark.

I opened my *Lonely Planet Guide* to the section on Hue. There was a map of the city and a numbered key that showed points of interest. Number 32 was the Halls of the Mandarins, located, I saw, in the Imperial Enclosure, which was a walled section within the Citadel walls of the Old City.

This was where I was supposed to meet my contact on the appointed day at noon. He—or she—was a Vietnamese, and that's all I knew.

If I somehow missed the hour, or if no one was there to meet me, I was to go to the alternate rendezvous at 2 P.M. The alternate was identified by the reverse of the digits 32, according to Mr. Conway. I looked at the map of Hue and saw that number 23 was the Royal Library, which was located in the inner sanctum of the Imperial Enclosure, called the Forbidden Purple City.

The third alternate at 4 P.M. was the sum of 3 and 2, which on the map was an historic temple called Chua Ba, outside the Citadel walls of the city.

If my contact didn't show up at any of these rendezvous, then I was to go back to the hotel and wait for a message. I was supposed to be prepared to leave at a moment's notice.

I thought this was all a little melodramatic, but probably necessary. Also, I didn't like the idea of having to trust a Viet, but I had to assume the people in Washington knew what they were doing. I mean, they'd been so successful here before.

I put a few more tick marks against the numbers in the crossword puzzle and did more of the puzzle, noticing that Ms. Weber got some really difficult clues right. Obviously a bright lady, and obviously, too, she had her own agenda—or someone else's agenda.

Tomorrow should be interesting.

CHAPTER TEN

---★---

I got off the elevator and walked into the hotel lobby at ten aftereight.

Sitting in a chair under a palm tree was Susan Weber, reading a magazine. Her legs were crossed, and she was wearing black slacks and walking shoes. As I got closer, I could see that the magazine was in English and was called the Vietnam Economic Times.

She put down the magazine and stood. I could see now she was also wearing a tightly tailored red silk shirt with half sleeves and a high mandarin collar. She had sunglasses on a cord around her neck, and one of those nylon fanny packs around her waist. She said, "Good morning. I was just about to start calling around for you."

"I'm alive and well."

She said, "I may have had a little too much to drink last night. If so, I apologize."

"I certainly wasn't in a position to judge. I hope I was a good dinner companion."

She replied, "I enjoy talking to people from home."

Ms. Weber was a little cooler this morning than she'd been last night, which was understandable. Remove the alcohol, the music, the candlelight, and the starry night, and people get a little more reserved around last night's date, even if they've wound up in the same bed.

I was wearing my standard khaki slacks, and instead of a golf shirt, I wore a short-sleeve dress shirt. I replied, "Am I dressed all right for church?"

"You're fine. Ready?"

"Let me get rid of my room key." I went to the front desk and gave the clerk my key. "Any messages?"

He checked my box and said, "No, sir."

I walked toward the front doors where Susan was standing. This was really annoying about the passport. Mang knew I was leaving tomorrow, and I needed my passport to travel.

I joined Susan, who said, "I see you didn't get your passport back. But I'm sure they'll return it today if they know you're leaving tomorrow."

"I think I'll be picking it up at Gestapo Headquarters."

"They usually just return it to the hotel. Or they'll tell you to pick it up at the airport. But that usually means you're going home sooner than you thought."

Fine with me, though I didn't say that.

She asked, "Do you have your visa?"

"The hotel has my visa."

She thought a moment and said, "You should

always have photocopies of your passport and visa with you."

"I did. The police stole them from my overnight bag at the airport."

"Oh . . ." She said, "I'll get a copy of your visa made." She walked to the front desk and spoke to the clerk, who checked a file box. He pulled out a piece of paper, read it, and said something to Susan. Susan came back to me and said, "The police have taken your visa."

I didn't reply.

She said, "Well, don't worry about it."

"Why not?"

"No one's going to stop us. Ready?"

We walked outside, and it was hotter than the day before. Motor traffic on Le Loi was a little lighter on a Sunday, but there were as many bicycles and cyclos as on Saturday.

Susan gave the doorman a dollar, and we walked toward a red motor scooter parked on the sidewalk. She stopped beside the motor scooter, took a pack of cigarettes from her fanny pack, and lit one. "I need a cigarette before we go." She smiled. "You might need one after we get on the road."

"Can we take a taxi?"

"Boring." She patted the motor scooter. "This is a Minsk, 175cc's. Russian made. A good machine for around town. I also own a motorcycle, a 750cc Ural, a real beast. Great for the open road, and a very good crossover bike in the mud." She took a drag on her cigarette and said, "The Russians make decent bikes, and for some reason, there are always parts available."

"Are there helmets available?"

"You don't need helmets in Vietnam. Do you ride?"

"When I was your age."

"There were no helmet laws in the States when you were my age. Did you wear a helmet?"

"I suppose not."

She drew on her cigarette and asked me, "Did you get your number?"

"Couldn't find it."

"Couldn't find it? I ticked off number 32 on the crossword puzzle. Didn't you notice that?"

"I'm not that bright. Took a few spills when I had my motorcycle."

She laughed and said, "Thirty-two. I'll remember it for you." She asked me, "What's it mean?"

"Thirty-two down? I think the word was rotisserie."

She didn't think that was funny, but left it alone.

I looked at her as she finished her cigarette. She passed the direct sunlight test—in fact, she looked better than last night, with a nice tan, and bigger and brighter eyes than I'd noticed in the candlelight. Also, the shirt and slacks fit well.

She took a final drag on her cigarette and said, "Okay. I *have* to stop smoking." She threw the cigarette in the gutter and said, "I went to my office this morning and sent that fax."

"Thanks."

"It was about 7 P.M., Saturday, their time, but someone replied. They work long hours there, wherever and whoever they are."

"What was the reply?"

"Just acknowledged receipt, said to keep them informed. They wanted me to give them a time when you and I could be near the fax for a confidential response later. I said I'd come back to the office at 8 P.M. my time for the fax. Is that okay?"

"Well . . . considering that you're not being paid to go in on a Sunday, that's fine."

She replied, "Whatever they have to say can wait twelve hours." She added, "You might have your passport by then, or your exit visa. Ready to roll?"

She put on her sunglasses, jumped on the motor scooter, started the engine, and revved it a few times. "Hop on." She took an elastic band out of her pocket and tied her long, flowing hair back so it wouldn't blow in my face.

I got on the saddle seat, which was a little small, and held on to the C-strap. Susan pushed off the center stand and drove down the sidewalk, then cut onto Le Loi Street. I put my feet on the footpegs just as we made a sharp U-turn.

Within five terrifying minutes, we were at the Cathedral of Notre Dame, an out-of-place Gothic structure with twin spires, but made of brick instead of stone. There was a small grassy square out front where we dismounted. Susan chained the motor scooter to a bike rack. I remembered this square from 1972, and nothing much had changed. Even the big statue of the Virgin Mary had survived the war and the Communist takeover. On that subject, I asked Susan, "How are the Commies with religion?"

"Depends on the program of the moment. They seem okay with the Buddhists, but not thrilled with the Catholics, who they view as subversive."

We walked toward the cathedral, and I said, "And therefore, you go to church."

She didn't reply, but continued, "They give the Protestants a really hard time. They harass the missionaries, kick them out, and close their mission schools and churches. There are no Protestant churches in Saigon, only some private services in homes." We got to the steps of the cathedral, and she asked me, "Did you ever come here during the war?"

"Actually, I did, twice, when I got into Saigon on a Sunday."

"So, you were a good Catholic then."

"There are no bad Catholics in a foxhole."

We climbed the steps of the cathedral, and Susan said hello to a few Americans, and people who sounded like Australians. I noticed there weren't many Vietnamese, and I commented on that.

She replied, "Father Tuan says this mass in English—the next is in French, then the rest are in Vietnamese."

"Are we staying for all of them?"

She ignored me, and we went into the narthex, and here, too, Susan chatted with some people and introduced me to a few of them. One woman looked at me, then asked Susan how Bill was. There's always one.

We walked into this big Gothic monster that could have been in France, except that I noticed that the place was decorated with blossoms and kumquat trees for the Tet holiday, which I vaguely recalled that even the Catholics celebrated here.

As I was looking up at the vaulted ceiling, Susan said, "Are you afraid it might fall on you?"

"I told you I needed a helmet."

We walked up the center aisle. The place was cool and dark and about half full. We sat in a pew toward the front. Susan said, "There's a chance Bill may show up. I spoke to him last night."

"Was he happy that you got home after midnight?"

"He's not the jealous type, and there's nothing to be jealous of." She added, "If he seems a bit unfriendly, that's just his manner."

"Right. Look, why don't I go back to the hotel after mass?"

"Shhh. It's starting."

The organ cranked up, and the processional started up the aisle. The priest and all the altar boys and everyone else in the processional was a Viet, except the man on the processional cross who was Jewish. It's all pretty amazing, if you think about it.

Anyway, the mass started, and Father Tuan's English was something else. I think I would have understood the French better. Like the mass, the hymns were in English, and I discovered that Susan had a beautiful singing voice. I faked the hymns, though I can really belt out "The Rose of Tralee" when I'm drunk.

The sermon had to do with sins of the flesh and the many temptations in the city. Then there was something about the souls of the impoverished girls who sold their bodies, and so forth. The priest made the point that without sinners, there'd be no sin—no opium, no prostitution, gambling, pornography, and massage parlors.

I had the impression he was looking at me. I started feeling like a character in a Graham Greene novel, sweating in some godforsaken tropical climate, wracked with Catholic guilt over some sexual transgression, which, in the final analysis, was not that big a deal.

Anyway, the mass went on for an hour and five minutes, though I wasn't timing it.

The organ cranked up again, and the recessional moved out. I followed down the center aisle and lost Susan somewhere.

I stood near her motor scooter, out in the sunlight of the square. I actually felt good about having gone to church.

I saw Susan at the bottom of the steps where Father Tuan and a lot of parishioners were chatting.

Maybe there was something to this expat thing. I mean, if you're expatting in London, Paris, or Rome, it's no big deal. You have to pick some totally fucked up place like this where you're six inches taller and ten shades lighter than everyone, and where you stand out like a sore thumb; and if that thumb is in the eye of the local government, so much the better. And all the other pale round-eyes were your friends, and you got together for cocktails and bitched about the country. People back home thought you were cool, and they were secretly envious of you, and you celebrated American holidays that back home were just a three-day weekend and a sale at the shopping mall. You even voted, for a change, with absentee ballots.

Of course, there was the other type of expat, people who hated their own countries, and there were also those who were running away from something or someone, and those who were running away from themselves.

Susan, by her own admission, fell into the category of expat who thought it was neat to be an American in a place where she stood out, where her family and peers back home had to use a different and actually unknown standard to judge her success and her life.

Well, I didn't want to be too cynical or analytical, especially since I liked Susan, and she was self-aware enough to figure herself out.

Susan walked toward me, accompanied by a man of about her age. He wore a light, tropical sport jacket, wasn't bad looking, tall and very thin, with sandy-colored hair. He looked like a Princeton man, so it must be Bill.

Susan stopped and said to me, "Paul, this is my friend, Bill Stanley. Bill, this is Paul Brenner."

We shook hands, but neither of us voiced a greeting.

Susan picked up the ball and said to Bill, "Paul was here in '68 and . . . when?"

"Seventy-two."

"Yes. It must have been very different then," she prompted.

"It was."

Susan said to me, "I was just telling Bill that you had some problems at the airport."

I didn't reply.

Susan then said to Bill, "I think Jim Chapman

might be around this weekend. I'll call him at home." She said to me, "He's with the new consulate delegation. Friend of Bill's."

Bill didn't have much to say about that, and neither did I.

This conversation was not approaching liftoff, so I said, "I think I'll go back to the hotel and make some inquiries from there. Susan, thanks for accompanying me to church. I never like to miss mass when I travel. Bill, great meeting you." I turned and left.

I have a good sense of direction, and within fifteen minutes, I was back on Le Loi Street, and the hotel was in front of me. I noticed I wasn't sweating as much as yesterday, so I must be acclimating.

I heard a motor scooter behind me on the sidewalk, and I moved to the right. She pulled up next to me and said, "Get on."

"Susan—"

"Get on."

I got on.

She gunned it, and we jumped the curb onto the street.

We didn't speak, and she was tearing up and down the streets, making sharp unexpected turns. She called out, "It's fun to open it up on Sunday when the streets are clear."

The streets looked pretty crowded to me.

Susan took her cell phone out of her fanny

pack and handed it to me. She shouted, "Give it to me if you hear it ring. Or vibrate. It's got a vibrator."

Having just come from church, I resisted an off-color remark and put the phone in my shirt pocket.

Her cell phone rang and vibrated, and I handed it to her. She held it to her ear with her left hand while she steered with her right hand on the throttle. If we had to make a sudden stop, she wouldn't be able to squeeze the front brake grip, but that didn't seem to bother her or any of the other scooter drivers with cell phones.

She was obviously speaking to Bill, or listening to Bill—she wasn't saying much. Finally she said loudly, "I can't hear you. I'll call you tonight." She listened and said, "I don't know what time." She hit the end button and handed the phone back to me. "You answer it if it rings again."

I put the flip phone back in my shirt pocket.

She continued her death-defying motor scooter run, which was actually, of course, just her venting a little anger at Bill. But *I* wasn't angry at Bill, and there was no reason for me to get splattered across the pavement. "Susan, slow down."

"No backseat driving."

A cop was standing in a traffic circle, and he held up his hand as we approached. Susan swerved around him and when I looked back over my shoulder, the cop was flapping his arms and shouting. I said to her, "You almost ran over that cop."

"You stop, you get a ticket for something, and it costs you two dollars on the spot." She added, "Also, it could be a major hassle because you don't have any ID."

"What if he got your license plate number?"

"I was going too fast. But next time, put your hand over the plate."

"What next time?"

"I have an NN plate. That's the prefix on the plate, and it tells them I'm a foreign resident— nguoi nuoc ngoia. Foreigner, and not a tourist. The tourists get hit with a ten-dollar fine because they think that's cheap, and they're frightened anyway. It's not the money, it's the principle."

"I think you've been here too long."

"Maybe."

We approached the fenced-in gardens that held Reunification Palace, formerly the home of the South Vietnamese presidents, when it was called Independence Palace. I remembered this place from '72, and then I saw it again in April of 1975 on television in the now famous videotape of a Communist tank breaking through the massive wrought iron gates.

We turned into a side street and drove through a gate into the grounds of the presidential palace, then pulled into a small parking lot and dismounted. Susan chained the motor scooter to a bike rack and took off her sunglasses. She said, "I thought you'd like to see the old presidential palace."

"Are we expected?"

"It's open to the public."

She opened one of her saddlebags and took out a camera and slung it over her shoulder. She said, "I can guarantee you we weren't followed, but if they radioed ahead or something, and they know you're here, then you're just sightseeing with some local chick who you picked up somewhere. Right?"

"Let me worry about my cover."

"I'm here to help. Plus, I like showing out-of-towners around. Follow me."

We walked on a garden path around the palace and came to the front of the big building, which was not a traditional ornate palace, but a precast concrete structure whose architecture can be described as tropical modern mortarproof. About a hundred meters across a wide lawn were the wrought iron gates, now looking in better shape than when the North Vietnamese tank crashed through them. In fact, to the left side of the gates was a big Russian T-59 tank sitting on a concrete platform, and I assumed this was *the* tank.

Susan asked me, "Do you know what this place is?"

"I do. Is that the tank?"

"It is. I was very young when all this happened, but I've seen the videotape. You can see it inside for a dollar."

"I saw it on TV when it happened."

I noticed a lot of Westerners around the tank taking photos. But unlike the rusting American tank in the war crimes museum, this Russian-made tank was chained off, with flags all around it. This was a very important tank.

She said, "I've taken a lot of Americans here, including my parents, and I've memorized the guide's tour. You want to hear it?"

"Sure."

"Follow me." We climbed the palace steps and stood at the top. She said, "So, it's April 30, 1975, and the Communists have entered Saigon. That tank is barreling up Le Duan Street and bursts through those gates. It continues on across the lawn and stops right here in front of the palace. That's what you saw on the videotape, taken by a photojournalist who happened to be in the right place at the right time."

She continued, "A minute or so later, a truck comes through the gates, drives across the lawn, and stops near the tank. A North Vietnamese officer jumps out and walks up these steps. Okay, standing right here is General Minh, who had become President of South Vietnam about forty-eight hours earlier, after President Thieu beat it.

Minh is surrounded by his new cabinet, and they're probably very nervous, wondering if they're going to be shot on the spot. The Communist officer climbs the steps, and Minh says, 'I have been waiting since early this morning to transfer power to you.' The Communist officer replies, 'You cannot give up what you do not have.' End of story, end of war, end of South Vietnam."

And, I thought, End of Nightmare. When I saw the tank bursting through the gates on television, I recalled feeling that all those American lives that had been lost trying to defend South Vietnam had been wasted.

I tried to remember what happened to General Minh, but like everyone else in America, after April 30, 1975, I turned off the Vietnam Show.

She asked me, "Do you want a picture of you with the tank in the background?"

"No."

Near the front doors of the palace was a ticket booth, and in English, a sign said *Foreigner: four dollar—Vietnamese: free*.

Susan had an argument with the guy in the booth, and I guessed it was the principle and not the money.

I said to her, "Tell them I want a senior citizen's discount."

"Today is on me," she said.

Finally, they settled on six dollars, we each got a paper ticket, and went inside.

She said, "Shut off the phone. They go nuts if a cell phone rings in one of their shrines."

The palace wasn't air-conditioned, but it was cooler than out in the sun. We walked into the big, ornate reception hall, and through the massive four-story palace. The place looked better inside than it did outside, and the modern architecture had an open, airy feeling. Most of the furnishings were time capsule Sixties Western modern, but there were a lot of traditional Vietnamese touches, including a collection of severed elephant feet.

There were a large number of people touring the palace, mostly Americans, if I went by the number of shorts. Each section of the palace had a Vietnamese guide, who kept telling Susan in English to stay with the group. Susan would reply in Vietnamese, and there'd be a little argument, which Susan always won.

She really pushed the envelope, and I guess this was part of her persona; she wanted to be recognized as an American, but not as a tourist. Also, she was a bit of a bitch, to be truthful. I think Bill would back me on that.

We went up to the roof of the palace where dozens of tourists stood around taking photos of the city. It was a nice view, except for the pall of smog. A female Vietnamese guide stood on a helipad next to an old American Huey helicopter, and said in English, "This is where the American puppet and number one criminal President

Thieu and his family and friends get on helicopter and fly away to American warship as the victorious People's Army approach Saigon."

The rooftop helipad was a good place to smoke, and Susan lit up. She said, "I've learned a lot of history since I've been here. It's interesting to be with someone who actually lived some of this."

"Are you suggesting that I'm a relic?"

She seemed a little embarrassed for a change and said, "No, I just mean . . . well, you were probably *very* young when you were here." She smiled. "You're still young."

In fact, Cynthia and Susan were about the same age, so I guess I was still in the game. It must be my immature personality that fooled women.

Susan finished her cigarette, and we went back into the palace. On the second floor, we entered the presidential receiving room. Susan gave the guard a dollar and said to me, "You can sit in the president's chair. I'll take a picture of you."

I really don't like my picture taken when I'm on assignment, and I said, "That's all right—"

"I already paid a buck. Sit."

So, I sat in the silly chair of the former president of South Vietnam, and Susan took a photo. This was too much fun, and I said, "Have we seen it all?"

"No, I've saved the best for last. Follow me."

We went down several staircases into a dimly lit hallway off of which were many doors. Susan said, "This was the air raid shelter, and also the war rooms."

She led me into a big room that was lit with old fluorescent fixtures. We seemed to be the only people there. The walls were cheap luan mahogany plywood, the kind of stuff Americans once used to finish basement rec rooms.

On the walls were dozens of maps of South Vietnam in various scales, maps of the individual provinces, and some closer detailed maps of towns and cities. On all the maps were colored symbols showing the locations of American, South Vietnamese, and enemy military units deployed around the country.

The maps were dated, and some of them went back to the Tet Offensive of January and February 1968, and I saw the location of my infantry battalion, marked by a pin with a flag, outside Quang Tri City, which was eerie. Some maps were dated April 1972, the time of the Easter Offensive, which I was also here for.

Susan asked me, "Does this interest you?"

"It does."

"Show me where you were stationed."

I showed her my little flag outside of Quang Tri City. "This was my base camp in 1968, called LZ Sharon."

She said, "LZ is Landing Zone—another vet told me that, and all the camps were named after women."

"Most, but not all." I showed her another pin. "This was LZ Betty, which was actually an old French fort, also outside Quang Tri City. That was brigade Headquarters, where the colonel lived."

"Are you going to visit these places?"

"Maybe."

"I think you should. And where were you in '72?"

"Bien Hoa. Right outside Saigon. You must know it."

"Sure. But I didn't know it was an American base."

One map was dated April 1975. I can still read military symbols, and I recognized the positions of the South Vietnamese forces and the progression of the North Vietnamese army, represented by red arrows, as they swept over the country. It appeared that at some point, no one bothered to make any further marks, or move any more pins on the map. Whoever kept the map updated must have realized that the end had come.

You could hear the ghosts if you listened, and if you had a good imagination, you could picture the military men and politicians here each and every day and night through the month of April 1975, as it became clear that the red arrows on the map were not abstract, but were hundreds of thousands of enemy troops and tanks, coming toward Saigon—toward them.

We looked around the underground war rooms: conference rooms, a communications room with vintage radios and telephones, a nicely furnished bedroom and sitting room for the president, and so forth, all frozen in time.

We left the underground war rooms and went outside into the sunlight, behind the palace, where President Thieu's old Mercedes-Benz still sat; another piece of frozen time that made this place eerie.

We walked through the gardens of the former presidential palace, which were quite nice.

She asked me, "Was that all right?"

"Interesting. Thank you."

"I'm never sure what people want to see, but as a vet, I thought you'd appreciate that little piece of history. I have a few more places in the standard tour, then you get to pick."

"You really don't have to show me around Saigon."

"I enjoy it. When I lived in New York, I never got to see the Statue of Liberty and the Empire State Building unless out-of-towners were in."

"I have the same deal in Washington."

"You know, I've never been to Washington."

"Sometimes I wish *I'd* never been to Washington."

She glanced at me, then said, "If I ever get to Washington, you owe me a tour."

"Deal."

We continued our walk around the grounds. The air was fragrant with blossoms, which was nice in January. We stopped at a refreshment stand, and we each bought a half-liter bottle of water.

We drank as we walked, and I asked her, "When your parents first visited, what was their reaction?"

"They were appalled. They wanted me to pick up and leave right then and there." She laughed and added, "They couldn't picture their coddled little girl living in a Third World city. They were really bummed out by the prostitutes, the Communists, the beggars, the food, the heat, disease, me smoking, me going to a Catholic church—you name it, they were bummed out." She laughed again.

I asked, "Did you take them on your motor scooter?"

"Heavens, no. They wouldn't even get in a cyclo. We took taxis." She added, "My brother and sister came once on their own, and they loved it. My brother disappeared one night and came back with a smile."

"I'm sure he went to a puppet show. How old is he?"

"He was in college then."

"What do your parents do?"

"My father is a surgeon, and my mother is a high school teacher. How's that for perfect?"

"My father was a mechanic, my mother was a housewife. I grew up in South Boston."

She didn't reply to that, but she made a mental note of it.

She seemed to be heading for a particular destination, and we took a path that led through a line of flowering shrubs. In front of us was a small slope of grass, and she walked halfway up it and sat down. She took off her shoes and socks, and wiggled her toes, then unbuttoned the top few buttons of her silk shirt.

I sat a few feet from her.

She took off her fanny pack, fished out a cigarette, and lit up.

I took the cell phone out of my pocket and said, "Maybe I should call the hotel."

She took the cell phone from me and put it in her fanny pack. "No rush. I'll call for you later. They respond better when you speak to them in Vietnamese."

She finished her cigarette, rolled up her sleeves, lay back on the grass, and closed her eyes. "Ah, that feels good. You should take off your shirt and get some sun."

I took off my shirt and lay down beside her, but not too close. I put my shirt and empty water bottle under my head.

The sun felt good on my skin, and there was a little breeze blowing now.

She said, "You looked too pale."

"I just came from winter."

"I actually miss winter. I miss the fall in the Berkshires."

We made small talk for a while, then I said to her, "This may be none of my business, but I feel a little guilty if you and Bill had an argument about you spending your Sunday with me." I didn't feel at all guilty, but I wanted a response from her.

She didn't reply for a while, obviously considering the right response. Finally she said, "I explained to him that you were going up country Monday morning and needed to be briefed—that this was part of the stupid favor he was asked to ask me to do." She added, "He wanted to come along. I told him no."

"Why?"

"In Vietnam, three is an unlucky number, and three people together bring bad luck."

I replied, "I thought three was a lucky number in Vietnam. You know—Ba Ba Ba—lucky beer."

She stayed quiet a moment, then said, "Maybe I got it wrong." She laughed, but didn't really answer my question.

It was getting hot in the sun, and I was sweating, but she looked cool as a pomegranate. I said, "So, brief me."

"Where are you headed next?"

"I'm not sure."

"Then how can I brief you? And why don't you know where you're going?"

"I'm just supposed to travel around, maybe visit some battlefields, then I have an appointment about a week from now."

"Where?"

"I can't say."

"You're not helping me."

"Just give me a general rundown of transportation, communication, how the hotels work, customs, currency, and all that."

"Okay. It's the Tet holiday, as you know, and it's hard to get transportation for the next week. Then, from New Year's Day on, everything's shut down, or on a very light schedule—the train service actually shuts down for four days. The roads, planes, and buses are empty because everybody stays close to home, and they eat and sleep. Nine months from now, there'll be a baby boom, but that's not your problem."

"And most people are in their native towns and villages?"

"That's right. I'd say ninety percent of the population manages to get home. The big towns and cities that are full of formerly rural people really empty out—and the villagers and peasants have the pleasure of houseguests in their little huts for a week."

I remembered the weeks leading up to Tet '68, and the sight of thousands of people walking, bicycling, riding in ox carts on the rural roads. The army had put out a communication telling the troops what this was all about, and we were told not to interfere with this mass movement of people, but to keep an eye out for Viet Cong, who might have infiltrated these pilgrimages. Viet Cong meant any male of military age who had two arms and two legs and wasn't wearing a South Vietnamese army uniform and wasn't carrying an ID card.

I didn't recall finding any VC, but in retrospect, these throngs of civilians must have been filled with VC infiltrators, on the move and getting into place for what was to come. And to make matters worse, a good portion of the South Vietnamese army was either on leave, or were going AWOL to be home. General Giap, in Hanoi, who had planned this surprise attack on Tet Eve, the most sacred and most militarily defenseless day of the year, was a smart guy. I hoped that Colonel Hellmann in Washington, who had planned my Tet operation, was at least as smart.

Susan went on about the general conditions in the countryside and reinforced some of what Conway had told me.

She said, "The people are generally friendly, and they won't rat you out to the police. They don't like their government, but they love their country. Be respectful of their customs and traditions, and show an interest in their way of life."

"I don't know any of their customs."

"Neither do I. I know Saigon, but it's very different out there. Don't pat anyone's head. The head is sacred. The feet are the lowest part of the body. Don't get your feet above their head. That's disrespectful."

"How would my feet get above someone's head?"

"I can think of a few ways."

So, we lay there, and Susan went on about customs, pitfalls, police, health matters, food, guest houses where they didn't report your presence to the police, and so on.

I asked her, "Is there still a danger of land mines?"

"There seems to be. Every once in a while you read about some kid getting blown up. If you're really out in the boondocks, stay on the well-trodden paths." She added, "You wouldn't want to find what you missed last time."

"No, I wouldn't."

She asked me, "Are you going into the former North Vietnam?"

"Maybe."

"Well, if you are, then the situation changes. The Communists have been in power there since the 1950s, and they're pretty well organized. According to my company booklet, which I had to read, the secret police in the north have an extensive network of government informers. The people in the north are not particularly friendly to Americans, as I discovered on my first business trip to Hanoi. We killed about a

million of them. Right? These people *will* rat
you out to the police." She glanced at me and
said, "If you're going to the north, be prepared
for a more efficient police state."

"I've heard."

"Pass yourself off as an Australian. They'll be
friendlier to you. But that doesn't work with the
cops, of course, who can look at your passport."

"How does an Australian act?"

"Always have a can of beer in your hand."

"Right."

"You might hear the words Lien Xo spoken
regarding yourself. Kids in rural areas, who
don't see many Caucasians, will yell out, 'Lien
Xo!' This just means foreigner, or Westerner, but
the literal translation is Soviet Union."

"Run that by me again."

"Okay. When the Russians were here from
1975 to the 1980s, there were no other Westerners here, and the term Lien Xo came to mean
Westerner. In the north, Lien Xo is not derogatory—the Soviets were their allies. In the south,
it once had derogatory connotations because
the southerners hated the Russian military and
civilian advisors. Now it just means Westerner.
Follow?"

"Sort of. In the south, I'm an American, in the
north, I'm Australian. But people will call me
Soviet."

"That just means Westerner. Don't get confused."

"Why can't I be a New Zealander, or a Brit, or how about a Canadian?"

"I don't know. Try it. Okay, up north, the people are not as materialistic as they are in the south."

"That's good."

"No, that's bad. They're real Reds, and are not as bribable as in the south. Maybe it's a philosophical or political thing, but it's also because there aren't as many consumer goods in the north, so American money isn't God. So, you can't give a cop a tenner and expect him to turn the other way. Understand?"

"How about a twenty?"

She sat up suddenly and said, "You know . . . my office is closed the week after next for the holiday. And this week is very slow. You want company?"

I sat up.

She said, "I'd love to travel around the country. I've hardly been out of Saigon in a year. It might be interesting to see some of the war stuff with a veteran."

"Thanks, but—"

"You're going to need an interpreter. They don't speak a lot of English outside the cities. I wouldn't mind taking a vacation."

"I'm sure there are other places you could go. Winter in the Berkshires."

"I always go out of the country on vacation, but I'd like to take an in-country vacation."

"I'm sure Bill would be happy to join you."

"He doesn't like Vietnam. Can't get him out of Saigon."

"I'm sure he'd make an exception if he was looking for us."

She laughed and then said, "We can travel together as friends. People do it all the time. I trust you. You work for the government."

"I don't think the people who sent me here would approve of me taking on a traveling companion."

"They would if they understood what this place is about. Aside from the language problem, men traveling on their own are hassled unmercifully by pimps and prostitutes. That doesn't happen if you have a woman with you. Also, the police are less likely to bother you. A guy by himself is presumed to be up to no good. I don't know why they sent you here alone."

Neither did I, now that I thought about it. I suppose it had to do with the strong desire to limit the knowledge of this murder investigation that wasn't a murder investigation. I smiled and said to Susan, "How do I know you're not a double agent?"

She smiled in return. "I'm a boring investment advisor. I need a little excitement."

"Drive your motor scooter."

"Done that. Think about my offer. I can leave a message in the office tonight, pack, and be at the Rex at 10 A.M., latest."

I asked, "And Bill?"

"What's your obsession with Bill?"

"It's a guy thing. Does he have a gun?"

She laughed. "No. Of course not." She added, "Having a gun here is a capital offense."

"Good."

She said, "I'll send him a telegram from our first stop. Wherever that is."

"Let me think about this."

"Okay, but if you decide you'd like me along, I'd like you to understand this is strictly platonic. I mean it. I'll pay for my own room, and you're free to sample the local ladies, except I want a dinner companion."

"Who pays for dinner?"

"You, of course. I order, you pay. And when you need to go off on some secret meeting, I'll disappear."

I thought about all of this, sitting there on a grassy slope with the presidential palace in the distance, the buildings of Saigon all around the park, the scent of flowers in my nostrils, and the sun on my face. I glanced over at her and our eyes met.

Susan lit another cigarette, but didn't say anything.

I'm used to working alone, and, in fact, I prefer it. If I screwed up on my own, my friends in Washington would be disappointed, and maybe sympathetic, depending on the circumstances. If I screwed up while traveling around with a woman, they'd hang me by my balls. James Bond never had this problem.

Also, I wasn't at all sure what she was up to. She made a reasonable case for wanting to take an in-country vacation, and then there was the excitement and adventure thing, and this might be her prime motive. Then there was moi. I *am* charming. But not that charming.

In any case, her motives were completely irrelevant to the mission at hand. When I'm on a case, I'm totally focused, and I don't even *think* about women. Hardly ever. Now and then, but only on my own time.

And then, of course, there was Cynthia. Cynthia was a pro, who worked with a lot of men herself, and I'm sure she'd understand. Maybe not.

"Are you thinking?"

"I was watching that dragonfly."

"Well, let me know by 6 A.M. tomorrow. Then, as we say in business, the offer is off the table." She put on her shoes and socks, buttoned her shirt, stood and put on her sunglasses.

I stood and put on my shirt as she fastened her belt pouch. "Ready to roll?"

We walked down the slope to the parking lot. She unchained the motor scooter, then took her cell phone out and dialed. She said, "I'm calling the Rex." She said something in Vietnamese into the phone, and I heard her use my name. She didn't seem satisfied with the answer and got a little sharp. *Bitch*. After a lot of monosyllables and consonants, she hung up and said to me, "Nothing there for you. But I gave them my cell phone number and told them to call as soon as your passport or anything else arrives for you."

She handed me the cell phone, started the motor scooter, and I hopped on the back. She said, "I'm sorry. I should have asked you if you wanted to drive."

"Later."

We rode through the streets of Saigon, and Susan was taking it easy. She asked me, "Do you remember this guy's name at the airport?"

"Why? Do you know the bad guys by name?"

"Some of them. The names get around."

"His name was Mang. A colonel in uniform."

She informed me, "Mang is his first name. Do you have the whole name?"

I replied, "He called himself Colonel Mang. How could that be his first name?"

"I thought you spent some time here. The Viets use their first names—which are actually at the end—with their titles. So you would be Mr. Paul, and I'm Miss Susan."

"Why do they do that?"

"I don't know. It's their country. They can do what they want. Didn't you know that from when you were here?"

"To be honest with you, the American soldiers knew very little about the Vietnamese. Maybe that was one of the problems."

She didn't respond to that, but said, "They're very careful about forms of address. You always use a title—Mr., Miss, Mrs., Colonel, Professor, whatever—followed by their first names. They love it if you know the Vietnamese word. Dai-Ta Mang. Colonel Mang. Ong Paul. Grandpa Paul." She laughed.

I wondered what the word was for bitch.

She said, "I'll check around for a Colonel Mang, but find out his last name, if you see him again."

"I'm sure I'll see him again."

"Did you tell this guy where you were heading?"

"He has part of my itinerary from my hotel vouchers. He wants to know the rest of my itinerary before he gives me my passport."

"Do you want him to know where you're going?"

"Not particularly."

"Then make it up. This is not an efficient police state. You want to see another famous place?"

"Sure."

"Are you having fun?"

"I have fun at this speed."

She reached back and patted my knee. She said, "I'm going to get the beast later, and we'll

drive out toward the Michelin rubber plantation. I want to get out of the city. Okay?"

"Maybe I should stay close to the hotel in
case this Commie colonel needs to see me."

"It's Sunday. He's home reading the biography of Ho Chi Minh while his wife cooks the
family dog." She laughed.

I, too, laughed. I mean, you have to laugh.

For some guys, Susan Weber would be pure
male fantasy. But I had this thought that Susan
Weber was like the country she was living in:
beautiful and exotic, seductive like a tropical
breeze on a starry night. But somewhere in the
back of my mind I heard the clicking of bamboo
sticks getting closer.

CHAPTER ELEVEN

──────── ★ ────────

We went up Le Duan Street, a wide leafy boulevard, and Susan pulled over onto the sidewalk and pointed across the street. "Do you recognize that place?"

Beyond a high concrete wall with guard turrets was a massive stark-white building about six stories high; another Sixties-type structure of preformed bombproof concrete. It took me a few seconds to recognize the former American embassy.

Susan said, "I've seen that news footage of the Viet Cong breaking into the embassy during the Tet Offensive."

I nodded. That was February 1968, the beginning of the end; the end itself came seven years later in 1975 when the embassy became the Fat Lady, singing the last aria in an overlong tragic opera.

I looked up at the roof and saw the smaller structure where the last Americans had left the city by helicopter on April 30, 1975, as the Communist troops approached. It was yet another of those famous or infamous video scenes that were emblematic of the whole sorry mess; the marine guards fighting with screaming and crying Vietnamese civilians and soldiers, who had overrun the compound and wanted to escape, the embassy staff trying to look cool as they made their way to the helicopters, embassy files burning in the courtyard, the city of Saigon in chaos, and the Ambassador carrying the folded American flag home.

I'd seen this on the TV news with a bunch of other soldiers, as I recalled, on a television in the NCO club at Fort Hadley, where I was still stationed. I recalled, too, that no one around me said much, but now and then someone would say softly, "Shit" or "Oh, my God." One guy actually wept. I would have left the room, but I was mesmerized by the image of this real-life drama, and further fascinated by the fact that I'd actually been to the embassy a few times, which made what I was watching even more surreal than it looked to most people.

Susan broke into my time trip and said, "The building is used by the Vietnamese government oil company, but the American government is negotiating to get it back."

"Why?"

"They want to level it. It's a bad image."

I didn't reply.

"It's American property. They may build a new consulate building there. But I think the Communists might want to make it another tourist attraction. Six bucks at least. Free to Viet-namese."

Again, I didn't reply.

Susan said, "The Americans are back, the people want them back, and the government is trying to figure out how to get their money without getting *them*. I live this every day on my job."

I thought about my own reason for being in this country, but there were still big gaps in my understanding of this mission, which is not the usual way to send a man on a dangerous assignment. This only made sense if I put Susan Weber into the equation.

Susan asked, "Do you want a picture of you with the embassy in the background?"

"No. Let's go."

We drove through central Saigon, crossed a small bridge over a muddy stream, and she said, "We're on Khanh Hoi Island, mostly residential."

This was a low-lying piece of land, swampy in areas, with clusters of wood shacks near the wetlands, and more substantial residential blocks on the higher ground. I asked, "Where are we going?"

"I need to get my motorcycle."

We drove through a warren of wooden houses with gardens, then a cluster of multistory stucco buildings. Susan turned down an alley and into a parking area that was actually an open space beneath a stucco building, elevated on concrete pillars. The parking space was jammed with bicycles, motorbikes, and assorted odds and ends.

We dismounted, and she chained her motor scooter to a rack.

She walked over to a big black motorcycle and said, "This is my beast. The Ural 750. It's illegal for foreigners to own anything over 175cc's, so I keep it here."

"To look at?"

"No, to drive. The police check up on what foreigners have around their house. Friends of mine, the Nguyens, live in this building."

"What happens when you take it on the road?"

"You move fast." She added, "It's not a huge problem once you're out in the country. From here, Khanh Hoi Island, I can head south over a small bridge and be out of town in another fifteen minutes. The motorcycle has Vietnamese citizen plates, and is actually registered to a Vietnamese national—another friend of mine—and the police, when they stop you, have no way to check who actually owns it. And if you give them five bucks, they don't care."

"You *have* been here too long."

She unchained the big bike with a key from her pocket and said to me, "Ready for adventure?"

"I'm trying to keep a low profile. Do we need to take the illegal bike?"

"We need the muscle on the hills. You weigh too much." She patted my stomach, which sort of surprised me.

I said, "You should wear a helmet for highway driving."

She lit a cigarette. "You sound like my father."

I looked at her and said, "It's a long way from Lenox, isn't it?"

She thought about that, then said, "Indulge me in my petty acts of rebellion." She took a drag on her cigarette. "You wouldn't have recognized me three years ago."

"Just don't get yourself killed over here."

"You, too."

"Hey, I'm on my third tour. I'm a pro."

"You're a babe in the woods is what you are."

She took out her cell phone, and still smoking, she dialed someone, spoke in Vietnamese, listened, spoke sharply, then hung up. She said, "A message for you that they didn't call me about."

"Would you like to share it with me, or are you not finished complaining about the desk clerk?"

"The message was from Colonel Mang. He said you are to report to the Immigration Police headquarters tomorrow morning at eight, and ask for him." She added, "I'll help you make out an itinerary."

"I can study a map." I pointed out, "I may be going home, and I know the way."

She asked me, "Did you say or do anything to get this guy angry with you?"

"I was firm but polite. However, I may have said something to honk him off."

She nodded, then asked me, "Do you think he knows something?"

"There's nothing to know. Thanks for your concern, but this is not your problem."

"Of course it is. You're from Massachusetts. Plus, I like you."

"Well, I like you, too. That's why I want you to stay out of this."

"It's your show." She jumped on the big Ural, and I got on the back, which was much roomier and more comfortable than the motor scooter. She had a backrest, which had a grip for me to hold on to. She started the engine, and the roar echoed off the low ceiling.

Susan pulled out of the parking area, and we headed south and crossed another small bridge over a stream, and off the island. To my left I could see the wide expanse of the Saigon River, filled with pleasure boats on this Sunday afternoon.

Susan pulled off to the side of the road, turned to me and said, "If they think you're up to something, they won't kick you out. They'll watch you."

I didn't reply.

"If they arrest you, they'll do it in some small town where they can do what they want with you. That's why it would be good if you had someone with you."

"Why wouldn't they arrest you, too?"

"Because I'm an important member of the American business community, and it would cause a real stink if I were arrested for no reason."

I replied, "Well, if I need a nanny along, I'll let you know."

She said, "You're a cool customer, Mr. Brenner."

"I've been in worse situations."

"You don't know that yet."

She gunned the motorcycle and bounced back onto the road.

CHAPTER TWELVE

─────── ★ ───────

We headed west through a mixed landscape of rural and urban: rice paddies, new industrial parks, primitive villages, and high-rise apartments.

Within twenty minutes, we had left the urban sprawl behind us, and we were into the open country. Motor traffic was light on a Sunday afternoon, but there were lots of ox carts, bicycles, and pedestrians, which Susan wove through without slowing down, horn honking almost continuously.

The countryside had gone from low-lying rice paddies to rolling terrain; vegetable plots, pasture, and clusters of small trees.

Now and then, I'd see a pond, which I could identify as a bomb crater. From the air, they used to come in three colors: clear blue water, muddy brown water, and red water. The red water indicated a direct hit on a bunker with lots of people in it. People soup, we called them.

Susan shouted above the noise of the engine, "Isn't this beautiful country?"

I didn't reply.

We passed four wrecked American-made M-48 tanks, which all had the faded markings of the former South Vietnamese army on them, and I assumed they had been destroyed in April 1975 by the North Vietnamese as they drove toward the final battle of Saigon, which mercifully never took place.

A huge cemetery appeared around a curve in the road, and I said to Susan, "Stop here."

She pulled off the road, and we dismounted. I went through an opening in a low wall and stood among the thousands of lichen-covered stone slabs lying flat on the ground. Stuck in the ground beside some of the slabs were red flags with a yellow star in the center. On each of the slabs was a ceramic bowl that held joss sticks, some of which were smoking.

An old man walked up to us, and he and Susan had a short conversation.

Susan said to me, "This cemetery is mostly for the local Viet Cong and their families. That part of the cemetery is for the North Vietnamese who died liberating the South—well, he said liberating. I guess you—we would say invading."

"Ask him if there's a South Vietnamese military cemetery around here."

They conversed, and Susan said, "Such cemeteries are forbidden. He says that the North Vietnamese bulldozed all the South Vietnamese military cemeteries. This makes him sad and angry because he cannot honor the grave of his son, who was killed while serving with the

South Vietnamese army. His other son was a Viet
Cong and is buried here."

I thought about that, and about our own
Civil War cemeteries that honored the North
and the South. But here, all memory of the defeated nation seemed to have been obliterated,
or displayed in a dishonorable way, like the
wrecked tanks that had been left as reminders
of the Communist victory.

I saw an old lady sitting against the wall selling joss sticks. I gave her a dollar and took a
joss stick. I walked to the closest grave and read
the inscription: *Hoang Van Ngoc, trung-uy,*
1949–1975. He was born the same year as me,
but thankfully that's all we had in common. Susan came up beside me and lit the joss stick
with her lighter. The smoke and smell of incense rose into the air.

I don't pray, unless I'm being directly shot at,
but I put the stick in the bowl, thinking about
the 300,000 North Vietnamese missing who had
no grave markers, our two thousand who were
missing, and the hundreds of thousands of
South Vietnamese soldiers who I'd just discovered lay underground in bulldozed cemeteries.
I thought about the Wall, about Karl and me
standing there, then about Tran Van Vinh.

One part of me said that Tran Van Vinh could
not possibly be alive, while another part of me
was convinced that he was. My conviction was

based partly on my own ego; Paul Brenner had not come this far to find a dead man. Partly, too, there was that almost miraculous set of circumstances that had led me here, and which, as a rational person, I wanted to discount, but couldn't. And finally, there was this suspicion that Karl and his friends knew something I didn't know.

I turned away from the grave, and we walked back to the motorcycle.

We continued on. I remembered this area west of Saigon because I had ridden shotgun a few times with convoys to Tay Ninh near the Cambodian border. In those days, the rural population lived mostly in strategic hamlets, meaning guarded compounds, and the ones who didn't were Viet Cong who lived in the Cu Chi tunnels. Then there were the part-time VC— pro-Saigon government by day, dinner with the family, then off to the night shift with the AK-47.

This area between the Cambo border and the outskirts of Saigon had been heavily contested throughout the war, and I recalled reading somewhere that it was the most bombed and shelled piece of real estate in the history of warfare. That could be true, from what I remembered.

I also recalled a lot of defoliation with Agent Orange, and when the vegetation was all dead and brown, the American bombers would drop napalm and set the countryside on fire. The pall of black smoke would hang for days until a rain came and deposited wet soot on everything.

This is what the generals could see from the rooftop of the Rex, if they looked west during dinner.

I saw that the vegetation had come back, but it didn't look right; it looked scrawny and sparse, the result no doubt of the residual defoliants in the soil.

The Ural 750 made a lot more noise than an equivalent American or Japanese motorcycle, so we didn't talk much.

We'd been on the road about an hour, and now we were heading northwest toward Cu Chi and Tay Ninh, which was where Route 22 went. Funny, I still get lost in northern Virginia, but I knew this road. Obviously, it was important to me once.

We entered Cu Chi, which I remembered as a small heavily fortified provincial town, but which was now a bustling place of new buildings, paved streets, and karaoke parlors. It was hard to imagine the intense fighting that had gone on in and around this town for thirty years, beginning with the French Indochina War in 1946, through the American War, and ending with the Vietnamese themselves in a fight to the finish.

Red flags flew everywhere, and in the center of a traffic circle was yet another North Vietnamese tank on a concrete platform surrounded by flags and flowers.

Susan turned into what looked like the main street, then she pulled over and stopped. We dismounted, and I chained the motorcycle to a rack as Susan took her camera out of the saddlebag.

We stretched and beat the red dust off our clothes. She asked me, "Have you ever been here?"

"A few times. On my way to Tay Ninh."

"Really? What were you doing in Tay Ninh?"

"Nothing. Part of a convoy escort, as I recall. Bien Hoa to Cu Chi to Tay Ninh, then back before dark."

"Amazing."

I wasn't quite sure what was amazing, and I didn't ask. My butt was sore, my legs ached, and I had dust in all my body orifices.

We took a walk along the main street, and I was surprised to see groups of Westerners. I asked Susan, "Are these people lost?"

"You mean the Americans? They're here to see the famous Cu Chi tunnels. They're a big tourist attraction."

"Are you kidding?"

"No. Do you want to see the tunnels?"

"I want to see a cold beer."

We turned into an open café and sat at a small table.

A young boy hurried over, and Susan ordered two beers, which materialized in a few seconds, sans glasses. So we sat there, covered with dust, chugging beer from bottles without labels, Susan smoking, still wearing her sunglasses.

The sinking sun was angled below the café's canopy, and it was hot. I commented, "I forgot how warm it is here in February."

"It's cooler up north. As soon as you go over Cloudy Pass, the weather changes. It's rainy season up there."

"I remember that from '68."

Susan seemed to be staring off in space, then said, as if to herself, "Even all these years after the last shot was fired, the war hangs over this place . . . like that guy across the street."

I looked across the street and saw an old man swinging on crutches, one leg missing, and part of one arm also gone.

She said, "And those tanks on the sides of the road, the Cu Chi tunnels, military cemeteries all over the place, battlefield monuments, and war museums in every town, young men and women with no living parents . . . I kind of ignored all this when I first got here, but you can't ignore it. It's everywhere, and I don't even see half of it."

I didn't respond.

Susan continued, "It's also part of the economy, the reason for a lot of the tourism here. The young expats sort of make fun of all this war nostalgia—you know, the vets coming back to see this and that. They . . . we call it visiting Cong World. That's pretty awful. Very insensitive. That must piss you off."

I didn't reply.

She said, "That was nice of you—the joss stick."

Again, I didn't reply, so we sat in silence. Finally, I said, "It's very strange being back here . . . I'm seeing something you're not seeing . . . recalling things you never experienced . . . and I don't want to get weird on you . . . but now and then . . ."

"It's okay. Really. I just wish you'd talk about it."

"I don't think I have the words for how I feel."

"Do you want to go back to Saigon?"

"No. I'm actually enjoying this more than not enjoying it. Must be the company."

"Must be. It's sure not the heat and the dust."

"Or your driving."

She called the boy over, gave him a dollar, said something to him, and he ran off into the street. A few minutes later, he was back with a pair of sunglasses and a wad of dong in his hand, which Susan told him to keep. She opened the sunglasses and put them on me. She said, "There, you look like Dennis Hopper in Easy Rider."

I smiled.

Susan picked up her camera and said, "Look tough."

"I *am* tough."

She snapped a picture of me.

Susan gave the camera to the boy, then pulled her chair next to mine, and threw her arm around me. The kid took a shot of us with our heads together and bottles touching. I said, "Get a few extras for Bill."

Susan took the camera from the boy and said, "Can I send these to your house, or will that cause a problem?"

I recognized the question for what it was and replied, "I live alone."

"Me, too."

We used the single WC in the rear and washed off the road dust. Susan gave the proprietor a dollar for both beers and exchanged New Year's greetings with him. We went out to the street and walked back to the motorcycle. Susan asked me, "Would you like to drive?"

"Sure."

She slung the camera over her shoulder, gave me the keys, and we mounted up. I started the engine, and Susan gave me a quick course on driving a Russian Ural. She said, "The gears are a little sticky, the front brakes are soft, and the back brakes grab. The acceleration may be a little faster than you're used to, and the front tends to climb. Otherwise, it's a dream to drive."

"Right. Hold on." I found myself going too fast down the main street. I passed two cops sitting on their bicycles, and they yelled something at me. "Do they want me to stop?"

"No. They said have a nice day. Keep going."

Within ten minutes, we left the town of Cu Chi behind, and I was getting the hang of the machine, but the congestion on the narrow road was giving me some problems.

"Use your horn. You have to warn people. That's the way they do it here."

I found the button and blasted the horn as I swerved through bicycles, pedestrians, motor scooters, Lambrettas, pigs, and ox carts.

Susan leaned forward and put her right arm around my waist and her left hand on my shoulder. She said, "You're doing fine."

"They don't think so."

She gave me directions, and within a few minutes, we were off on a narrow road that was barely paved.

I asked, "Where are we going?"

"Cu Chi tunnels straight ahead."

After a few more kilometers, I could see ahead to a flat open area where a half dozen buses were parked in a field. Susan said, "Pull into that parking field."

I pulled into the dirt field partially shaded by scraggly trees.

Susan said, "This is one of the entrances to the tunnels."

"Is this part of Cong World?"

"This is the ultimate Cong World. Over two hundred kilometers of underground tunnels, one of them going all the way to Saigon."

"Have you been here?"

She replied, "I've been this way, but never actually in the tunnels. No one wants to go in with me, and I figured you'd have no problem with it."

That sounded like a challenge to my manhood. I said, "I love tunnels."

We dismounted, chained the motorcycle to a tree, and walked to the entrance of the tunnels.

It was a buck-fifty to enter, which Susan paid for in American dollars without an argument.

We joined some people under a thatched roof whose sign said *English*. The crowd was mostly Americans, but I heard some Aussie accents as well. There were also thatched pavilions for other languages. Apparently, someone in the People's Ministry of Tourism had been to Disney World.

A female guide handed out brochures to the crowd of about thirty English speakers.

The guide said, "Please to be quiet."

Everyone shut up, and she began her spiel. I wasn't too familiar with the Cu Chi tunnels, and I had the feeling I wasn't going to learn much more from our guide, whose English was somewhat unusual.

I read the brochure, whose English was also a little off.

Anyway, between the guide and the brochure, I learned that the tunnels were begun in 1948 during the Communist fight against the French. They started at the Ho Chi Minh Trail in Cambodia, and zigzagged all over the place, including underneath former American base camps. The original tunnels were only wide enough for a small VC to crawl through, and we should be careful of insects, bats, rats, and snakes.

The lady guide informed us that the tunnels could hold up to sixteen thousand freedom fighters, and that people actually got married in the tunnels, and women had babies down there. There were kitchens and full surgical hospitals in the tunnel complex, sleeping rooms, storage rooms once filled with weapons and explosives, drinking wells, ventilation shafts, false tunnels, and booby-trapped passages. The guide smiled and joked, "But no more booby traps for you."

I said to Susan, "I hope not, for a buck-fifty."

The lady also informed us that the Americans had dropped hundreds of thousands of tons of bombs on the tunnels, had entered them with flamethrowers, had flooded them, gassed them, and sent in teams of men called tunnel rats with miners' helmets and dogs to go hand-to-hand with the inhabitants of the tunnels. Over the twenty-seven years of the tunnels' use, ten thousand of the sixteen thousand men, women, and children who'd occupied the tunnels had died, and many were entombed below.

"So," said our guide, "we are ready now to go in the tunnels. Yes?"

No one seemed too eager, and about ten people suddenly remembered other appointments. No refunds.

As we walked to the entrance, the guy beside me asked, "You a vet?"

I looked at him and replied, "Yeah."

He said to me, "You look too big to be a tunnel rat."

"I hope I look too smart to be a tunnel rat."

He laughed and said, "I did it for three months. That's all you can do." He added, "You got to give it to these bastards. I mean, they had balls." He noticed Susan and said, "Sorry."

She said, "It's okay. I swear, too."

I said to the guy—who was short, but no longer thin—to make him feel good, "You guys did a hell of a job, too."

"Yeah . . . I don't know what the hell I was thinking when I volunteered for that job. I mean, meeting Mr. Charles face-to-face crawling in a small space is not fun."

We got to the entrance of the tunnel, and the guy said, "I have the worst fucking nightmares about these tunnels . . . you know, I'm crawling in the dark, and I can hear somebody else breathing, and I got bugs crawling under my uniform, biting the shit out of me, bats in my hair, snakes moving over my hands, and the fucking ceiling is about three inches over my ass and dripping water, and I can't even turn around, and I know Chuck is right in front of me, but I don't want to turn the miner's lamp on, and—"

I interrupted and said, "Maybe you shouldn't go in there."

"I gotta go. You know? If I go in there, my nightmares will disappear."

"What genius told you that?"

"Another guy who did it."

"It worked for him?"

"I guess so. Why else would he tell me to do this?"

"His name isn't Karl, is it?"

"No . . . Jerry."

Anyway, the lady guide stopped at the mouth of the tunnel that was covered by a wooden shed. She asked, "Is any person here who has been in this tunnels in the war?"

My buddy raised his hand quickly, and everyone looked at him.

The guide said, "Ah . . . so, you fight in tunnel. Come to talk with me."

The former tunnel rat moved to the front of the group and stood beside the guide. I thought we were about to get a lecture on American imperialism, but she said, "Please to tell everyone to stay together and to be not frightened. It is very safe."

The tunnel rat repeated the guide's instruction and advice, and added a few tips of his own, becoming an unpaid assistant guide. Really bizarre, if you thought about it.

We filed into the tunnel, and the tunnel rat was asked by the guide to bring up the rear.

The entrance to the tunnel was wide, but very low, and everyone had to stoop. The incline started out easy, then got steeper, and the passage got narrower. The tunnel was barely lit by a string of dim light bulbs.

There were about twenty of us, including some young Australian couples, about six middle-aged American couples, some with kids, and the rest young guys, mostly backpackers.

The guide made a little commentary now and then, waited for a Japanese group to move on, then continued deeper into the labyrinth.

It was a lot cooler in the tunnels, but very damp. I heard a bat chirping somewhere. I said to Susan, "This is a good second date place."

So, we zigged and we zagged, and the tunnels got narrower and lower, and soon we were crawling over reed mats and sheets of wet, slimy plastic in the dark. I mean, do I need this shit?

We finally came into a space the size of a small room, lit by a single bulb, and everyone stood. The guide turned on a flashlight and pointed it around the underground chamber. She said, "Here is cooking place. You see there place where cooking, and up on ceiling hole where goes smoke. Smoke goes into farmer house, and farmer cooks so American think it is farmer cooking. Yes?"

A lot of flashbulbs started to go off, and Susan said, "Smile" and blinded me with a photo flash.

The guide passed the flashlight beam over the group and said, "Where is American who fight in tunnel? Where?"

We all looked around, but the guy was gone. AWOL. The guide seemed concerned, but considering the limited liability exposure of the Cu Chi Tunnel Corporation, not overly worried.

We moved on for about another half-hour, and I was getting cold, wet, tired, claustrophobic, and filthy. Something bit me on the leg. This had stopped being fun a while ago, and I dubbed this tour "Charlie's Revenge."

Eventually, we got into the same tunnel through which we'd entered, and within five minutes, we were out into the sunlight. Everyone looked like crap, but in a few seconds, people started to smile. Was this worth a postcard home or what?

The guide thanked us for our courage and our attention, and everyone gave her a buck, which explained her fondness for what had to be the worst fucking job on the planet.

As we moved off, I saw her washing herself in a basin of water. I said to Susan, "Thank you for suggesting that."

"I'm glad you enjoyed it." She looked around

and asked, "Hey, what happened to the tunnel rat guy?"

"I don't know. But if that group of Vietnamese behind us doesn't come out, you have your answer."

"Be serious. The guy may be lost, or freaked out in there. Shouldn't we do something?"

"The guide knows she lost someone. She'll take care of it. He owes her a buck."

We walked over to an area of vendor stalls. Souvenir shops were selling more war junk like in the Museum of American War Crimes, and a guy tried to sell us a pair of Ho Chi Minh sandals, made of old tires, that he swore were once worn on the Ho Chi Minh Trail by Viet Cong. All the vendors, I noticed, were dressed in black pajamas and sandals, and wore conical straw hats, just like the VC. This was totally surreal at first, then I decided it was idiotic.

Susan asked me, "Are you okay with this?"

"Sure. Cong World."

We each got a liter of bottled water and used half to wash off and half to drink.

She said, "I can't imagine how people lived in there for years. And I can't imagine how you guys must have lived out in the jungle day and night."

"Neither can I."

We spotted our tunnel rat friend sitting in a plastic chair with a bottle of beer in his hand. We went over to him, and I said, "We thought you got lost."

He looked up at me with no recognition.

I asked him, "You with anyone?"

"Bus."

"Good. Maybe you should get back on the bus."

He didn't reply for a few seconds, then said, "I'm going back in."

Susan suggested, "That might not be a good idea today."

He looked at her—through her, actually. He stood and said, "I'm going back." He began walking toward the tunnel entrance where the pavilions were.

Susan said to me, "Maybe you should try to talk him out of it."

"No. Let him go. He's got to try it again. He's come a long way."

We got back to the motorcycle, and Susan said, "I'll drive. We need to be in Saigon before dark, and I know the roads."

We mounted up and drove out of the parking field. Susan continued north on the back road, which was now barely more than a dirt trail. She called out, "This is usually okay as a dirt bike, but you've got to hold on."

We were bumping wildly, and the bike skidded a few times, but she was a very good driver, and I started to feel more confident that we weren't going to wind up alongside the road kill.

She said, "This road goes to Route 13, which

goes through the Michelin rubber plantation. Thirteen will take us back to Saigon, and it's a very lightly traveled road, so we'll make good time."

We traveled north over the worst road in the hemisphere, and I thought my kidneys were going to pop out of my ears.

Finally, we reached a two-lane paved highway, and Susan cut to the right. She said, "This is the rubber plantation. Those are rubber trees."

The road seemed nearly deserted, and she opened the throttle. We were clipping along at about sixty miles an hour, but it was a good road. The sun, however, was sinking fast, and the shadows of the rubber trees were long and dark.

I remembered that Karl said he'd seen action here with the Eleventh Armored Cavalry, and I knew from other veterans of that unit that there had been a number of running battles within the Michelin plantation, and along Highway 13.

I pictured Karl here, manning a machine gun atop an armored vehicle, puffing away on a cigarette, scanning the spooky forest with field glasses, and probably pretending he was Field Marshal Guderian leading a panzer army into Russia. I'd have to tell him I was here—if we ever spoke again.

Within twenty minutes, we were out of the spooky rubber forest and into an area of scrub brush. It was dark now, and the only traffic on the road was some scooters and small cars. As we got closer to Saigon, the traffic became heavier, and Susan had to keep slowing down.

Wartime Saigon at night was like a sea of light in a vast ocean of darkness. Within the city, life went on; on the outskirts of the city, barbed wire and roadblocks sprang up and soldiers became alert. Nothing outside the city moved after dark, and if it did move, you killed it. And beyond the barbed wire were the military bases, smaller islands unto themselves, like Bien Hoa and Tan Son Nhat, where soldiers and airmen drank beer and gambled, watched movies from home, wrote letters, cleaned their equipment, cursed the war, stood guard duty, and slept fitfully. And if you were unlucky enough to be assigned to a night patrol, you sometimes met the men and women of the Cu Chi tunnels.

We were approaching the city from the north now, and I saw the lights of Tan Son Nhat Airport. Farther to the east would be my old base at Bien Hoa, which also had runways, but only for military aviation. I asked Susan, "Do you know what happened to the American military base at Bien Hoa?"

"I think it's a Viet military airfield. Jet fighters. I didn't know it had been an American base until you told me."

"I guess I can't visit my old barracks."

"Not unless you want to get shot."

"Not this trip."

We crossed a muddy canal and got on Khanh Hoi Island from the same bridge we'd left from. The streets of Khanh Hoi were dark, but Susan knew the way. We passed a yellow police jeep, and the guy in the passenger seat looked at us and looked at the motorcycle. He began to follow, and I said to Susan, "We have company."

"I know." She shut off her lights and drove into a narrow alley where the cop car couldn't follow. She seemed to know the alleys and passageways, and within a few minutes, we were pulling up to the parking lot beneath the Nguyen apartment.

We transferred everything from the Ural saddlebags to the Minsk saddlebags, and switched mounts like a pony express rider. Within a few minutes we were on our way with the small Minsk, which seemed even more uncomfortable than I remembered it.

Susan looked at her watch as she headed toward the center of the city. She said, "Good timing. It's twenty to eight, and we should be in my office by eight."

"Where's your office?"

"On Dien Bien Phu Street. Near the Jade Emperor Pagoda."

"Is that a restaurant?"

"No, it's the Jade Emperor Pagoda."

"Sounds like a restaurant on M Street in Georgetown."

"I can't believe I spent a whole day with you."

"Neither can I."

"Just kidding. You're fun. Did you have fun today?"

I replied, "I did. I don't know which I liked the best—meeting Bill, the heat, your driving, wartime memories of Saigon, the road from hell to the Cu Chi tunnels, or giving that cop back there the slip."

"Didn't I buy you a beer, and a pair of sunglasses, and pay for all the tickets?"

"Yes. Thank you."

We crossed the muddy stream into central Saigon and followed the embankment road along the Saigon River. The city was incredibly crowded for a Sunday night, and I remarked on this.

Susan said, "It's called Sunday Night Saigon Fever. Sunday night is a bigger night than Saturday for some reason. It's totally crazy. We'll go out after dinner and have a few drinks, maybe some dancing, and a karaoke place, if you're game."

"I'm really exhausted."

"You'll get your second wind."

We headed up a narrow street that crossed a few heavily traveled boulevards. As we waited at a stoplight, I asked Susan, "Do you ever ride alone? I mean out in the country."

"Sometimes. Bill is not a big motorcycle buff. Sometimes I go with a girlfriend. Viet or American. Why?"

"Is it safe for a woman alone?"

"Sure. The thing about most Buddhist countries is that women aren't hassled. It's a cultural thing more than religious, I think. Of course if you're young and pretty, like me, and you're in a bar, a Viet guy might try to pick you up, but they don't have great lines."

"Give me an example."

She laughed. "Well, first they tell you how beautiful you are and how they've noticed you on the street many times."

"What's wrong with that? I use that line a lot."

"Did it ever work?"

"No."

She laughed again, and accelerated through the intersection. A few minutes later, we turned right onto Dien Bien Phu Street.

Within a minute, we passed a very impressive pagoda, which would make a great restaurant some day, then Susan pulled onto the sidewalk in front of a modern glass and steel building that was cantilevered over the sidewalk. We got off the Minsk, and she walked it to the front door. A guard opened the door, smiled and said something in Vietnamese.

Susan opened the saddlebag and retrieved her camera. She left the motor scooter in the marble lobby of the office building, and I followed her to the elevators.

The elevator doors opened, and we got on. Susan used a key to activate the seventh floor button. She said, "Don't let Washington talk you into something dangerous."

It was a little late for that advice.

CHAPTER THIRTEEN

———————★———————

The elevator doors opened onto a large reception area decorated with black lacquered furniture, rice paper prints, and a pink marble floor. The brass letters over the reception desk read *American-Asian Investment Corporation, Limited.*

Susan said, "Welcome to AAIC, Mr. Brenner. Would you like to buy half of a fish canning factory?"

"I'll settle for a whole Scotch and soda."

Beneath the corporate sign hung a banner in gold metallic letters that read *Chuc Mung Nam Moi*, and beneath that, in English, *Happy New Year*.

A small kumquat tree sat on the floor, and a few twigs of blossoms were stuck in what looked like an umbrella stand. Most of the petals had fallen to the floor.

To the right of the desk was a set of red lacquered double doors, and Susan put her hand on a scanner. A chime sounded, and she opened one of the doors.

I noticed a security camera sweeping the lighted reception area.

I followed her into a large open space filled with desks and cubicles; a typically modern office that could have been anywhere in the world.

The place was deserted, but the fluorescent lights were all on, and again I noticed cameras scanning the room. The air reeked of stale cigarette smoke, which I hadn't smelled in an American office in two decades.

She said as we walked, "We have the whole top floor with a terrace. The AC is turned off, so it's a little stuffy in here."

We came to the rear of the floor where three widely spaced doors indicated large enclosed offices. She went to the door on the left whose brass plaque read *Susan Weber*, with no title. There was a combination lock pad on the door, and she punched in a series of numbers, then opened the door to her office.

The office was dark, and she turned on the overhead lights, revealing a big corner office with windows on two walls. I glanced around for a video scanner, but I didn't see one. "Nice office."

"Thank you." She put her camera on the desk along with the exposed roll of film. She opened the top drawer and got a carton of cigarettes from which she took a pack of Marlboros. She lit up with a chrome desk lighter and took a long drag. "Ah . . ." She informed me, "I get strung out and bitchy if I don't get my fix."

"What's your excuse the rest of the time?"

She laughed and took another pull on her cigarette. She said, "I went to New York six months ago for a meeting. Four hours in a no-smoking building, and I was also having PMS. I almost freaked out. How can I go back to the States to live and work?"

It was a rhetorical question, but I answered it. "Maybe you can't. Maybe this is it."

She looked at me, and our eyes met. She put out her cigarette and said, "I'll send you copies of the photos we took if you give me your address."

I inquired, "Is your mail secure?"

She replied, "We have a company pouch that goes out every day by FedEx, and the mail is sorted in New York and sent on. If you ever want to send anything to me, mail it to New York." She gave me a business card with the New York address of American-Asian Investment Corporation. I memorized the address and gave the card back to her, saying, "It's best if I'm not carrying this."

She looked at me. "We're in the Manhattan directory, if you forget."

Susan sat at her desk, put on a headset, and called up her voice mail. She said, "Ice and mix-ers under that sideboard. I'll have a gin and tonic."

I opened the cabinet, which revealed a small refrigerator, and I took out an ice tray and mix-ers. The glasses and liquor decanters were on the sideboard, and I made the drinks while she listened to her messages.

On the wall above the sideboard were her two framed diplomas—Amherst and Harvard. Also hanging on the wall was a commendation from the American Chamber of Commerce—Ho Chi Minh City branch. This was mind-boggling, but my mind had been so boggled in the last twenty-four hours that if I'd seen she'd been awarded the Order of Lenin for increased profits, I wouldn't have been surprised. Somehow I'd entered an alternate universe where we had won the war.

On the sideboard itself were four framed photographs. The closest was one of Susan in a graduation cap and gown—crimson, so it must be Harvard, if my Boston memory served me right. In the photo, Susan looked younger, of course, but also . . . I guess you'd say not yet burned up by the corporate world in New York, or toughened by the years in Saigon. I have a high school graduation picture like that of myself, before *I* went to Vietnam.

I glanced at her, and beautiful though she was, she looked a bit world-weary for her age. To be more charitable, her face revealed some character.

The second photograph was a studio shot of a handsome well-dressed couple in their early fifties; her parents, obviously. Dad looked like an okay guy, and Mom was a looker.

The third photo was a family shot, a Christmas tree and a fireplace in the background. There was Mom and Dad, Susan, her younger brother, and a sister who looked a little younger than Susan. They were all good looking, wore turtleneck sweaters and tweeds and were about as Protestant as they come; old line Yankees from West Waspshire.

The fourth photo was taken outdoors, and it could have been a summer wedding—the entire clan was gathered, grandmas and grandpas, couples, kids and babies. I found Susan wearing a long white summer dress and short hair. Standing beside her, with his arm around her bare shoulder, was Harry Handsome, wearing a white dinner jacket and a bronze face. He could be a relative, but he didn't look related, so it must be the boyfriend, or maybe even her fiancé since he was in a family shot.

I noticed there was no photo of Beau Bill.

I turned away from the sideboard and saw that Susan was now checking her e-mail. She glanced up at me and said, "That's my family, obviously. They're perfect in every way, except for some interesting eccentricities and undiagnosed mental disorders." She laughed. "But I love them all. I really do. You'd like them."

We made eye contact, and she said, "They'd

probably like you. Except for Grandpa Burt who thinks the Irish should be deported."

I smiled.

She went back to her e-mail and said, "Have a seat over there. I'll be with you in a minute."

I sat in a swivel chair near the windows at an oval table with a black granite top. I watched Susan at her desk, clicking away at her keyboard. She'd shifted into a different personality almost as soon as we'd entered the lobby of the building.

I looked around at the office as I sipped my Scotch and soda. The carpet was a plush jade green, the furniture was burled wood, and the walls were covered in yellow silk with a subtle pattern of bamboo.

Through the east-facing windows, I could see the waning moon. In less than a week, there would be no moonlight, which, if I was in open country, might serve me as well as it did the enemy at Tet 1968.

In a large alcove, I noticed a fax machine, a photocopier, a shredder, and a floor safe. To have your own items like this was not just a status symbol, but an obvious sign of security consciousness. Nothing important had to leave or come into this office from the cubicle farm. I recognized the setup.

Susan got up from her desk and sat in a chair across from me. She picked up her gin and tonic and said, "Cheers."

We touched glasses and drank. She lit another cigarette and left it burning in the chrome ashtray, which I noticed was half full of butts. The trash can, too, was half full, and there had been petals on the rug in the reception area. No cleaning or maintenance was done here before or after business hours. They had obviously hired a security advisor. Or maybe they didn't need any outside advice.

Susan said, "Do you have any wallet photos?"

"Of what?"

"Your family."

"If I don't carry business cards into enemy territory, why would I carry pictures of my family?"

"Right. You're in enemy territory. I'm not." She smiled and said, "I thought you were a tourist."

"I'm not."

"Now we're getting somewhere."

I changed the subject and said, "Your parents must have at least approved of your office."

"How could they not? I have arrived in the corner office years before I would have in the States."

In that respect, Susan and I had similar Vietnam experiences. When I was in the infantry in '68, you made rank fast, mostly because of sudden personnel losses. 'Nam was a good career builder, but you needed to go home to get back into the mainstream of army life—the real world. Susan Weber hadn't yet made that transition.

American-Asian Investment Corporation aroused my curiosity, and I asked her, "Who has the other two offices?"

"My boss, Jack Swanson, and a Viet. We have three other Americans—two guys and a young woman, Lisa Klose, with a new MBA."

"Ivy League, I hope."

"Of course. Columbia. Plus there's a Canadian woman, Janice Stanton, who is our financial officer. Also, we have two Viet-Kieus with us. Do you know Viet-Kieu?"

"Nope."

"Former Vietnamese refugees who've returned. Some of them are so homesick, they'd rather be here in a poor, totalitarian country than wherever it was they'd escaped to. Our Viet-Kieus are a man and a woman, both from California, both speak perfect English and Vietnamese. They're an important part of a lot of multinational businesses here, a cultural bridge between East and West."

I asked, "How are they treated here?"

She replied, "The Communists used to harass them, called them traitors and American lackeys and all that. But for the last five or six years, the Viet-Kieus have been officially welcomed back."

"And how about next year?"

"Who the hell knows? Every time the politburo or the National Assembly meet, I hold my breath. They're just totally unpredictable. Business doesn't like unpredictability."

"Maybe you should address the politburo and tell them that the business of Vietnam is business. Screw this Marxist stuff."

"I detect a little anti-capitalism in you, Mr. Brenner."

"Not me. But there *are* more important things in life than making money."

"I know that. I'm not that shallow. And the reason I'm here doesn't have a lot to do with money."

I didn't ask her what it had to do with; I already knew some of it, and the rest of it she probably wasn't sure of herself, though it might have to do with a guy. Maybe Harry Handsome in the photo.

Ms. Weber got back to the subject of staff and said, "We also have about fifteen Viets working for us, mostly female secretarial. We pay them twice the average wage."

"And you don't trust any of them."

She didn't reply for a moment, took another drag on her cigarette, and said, "They're under a lot of pressure to take things out of here that shouldn't be taken. We help them by removing the temptation."

"And the phones are monitored, the doors can only be opened by the round-eyes, maintenance and cleaning are done only during business hours under round-eye supervision, and the cameras record everything."

She looked at me awhile, then said, "That's right." She added, "But there are no cameras or bugs in this office. I am a member of the Inner Party." She smiled. "You can speak freely."

I observed, "This place could be a CIA front." I added, jokingly, "AAIC backward is CIA."

"How about the other A?"

"That's the disguise."

She smiled. "You're nuts." She stirred her drink and said, "Anyway, the Americans, Europeans, and Asians are here just to make a fair profit, not to corrupt or undermine the government or the country. If that's what's happening, it's because of *their* greed, not ours."

"Was that in your company handbook?"

"You bet. And I wrote it."

I looked out the window and saw the huge lighted advertising signs all over Saigon. If someone had told me thirty years ago that I'd be sitting here like this in the plush office of an American woman with an MBA from Harvard, I'd have recommended them for a psychiatric discharge.

I hated to admit it, but in some ways, I liked the old Saigon better; for sure, I liked the image of the younger Paul Brenner with an MP uniform patrolling the streets of Saigon instead of the older Paul Brenner looking over his shoulder for the fuzz.

Susan broke into my thoughts and said, "So, you can see why I'm here. I mean, from a career point of view. I'm in charge of charming the foreign investors, private and corporate. Do you have any money? I could double your money."

"You could triple it, and it still wouldn't amount to anything." I asked, "Do you have an office in Hanoi?"

"We have a small office there. You have to be where the political power is. Also, an office in Da Nang. The Americans left a great port facility there, plus a great airfield and other infrastructure."

"I actually left the country in 1968 from Da Nang."

"Really? Are you going there?"

"Maybe."

"Did you get to China Beach?"

"No, I was anxious to get to Boston."

"Right. If you get to Da Nang, don't miss China Beach this time."

"I won't. So what about the Viet guy in the corner office?"

"You guess."

"He's the son of an important government official, and he comes in only on Wednesdays in time for lunch."

"Close. But he does have the contacts. Everything in this country has to be a joint venture, which means buying part of a company that the government confiscated from the rightful owners in 1975, or starting a new company and giving the government a share for peanuts. I mean, it's more complex than that, but there's nothing that can happen here without some government involvement."

"Is it worth it?"

"It could be. Lots of natural resources, a hardworking, low-paid population, mostly all literate, thanks to the Reds. The harbors are terrific—Haiphong, Da Nang, Cam Ranh Bay, and Saigon—but the rest of the infrastructure is a mess. The American military put in some good infrastructure during the war, but whenever an area was contested, the bridges, roads, rail lines, and everything else got blown up again."

"It's sort of like playing Monopoly, but everyone gets a hammer."

She didn't reply, and in fact looked a little impatient with my sarcasm.

I thought about all of this, about Vietnam Incorporated. To the best of my knowledge, this was the only country in Asia where the Americans had a distinct business advantage over anyone else, including the Japanese, who the Viets were not fond of. The Soviets who were here after 1975 screwed things up, the Red Chinese weren't welcome, the Europeans were mostly indifferent except for the French, and the other East Asians either weren't trusted or were disliked.

So, in some ironic way, for reasons that were

partly historical and nostalgic, and mostly financial and technical, the Americans were back. Ms.
Weber and her compatriots, armed with MBAs,
engineering degrees, letters of credit, and lots
of hustle, were racing around Saigon on their
motor scooters, carrying satchels of money instead of satchel charges of plastique. Swords
into market shares. And what did this have to do
with me? Maybe nothing. Maybe everything.

Susan said, "Are you sulking about something?"

"No. I'm just processing. There's a lot to
take in."

She observed, "If you'd never been here, this
wouldn't seem so strange to you."

"Good point."

She looked at me and said, "We won the war."

I wasn't going to reply to that statement,
then I said, "Fifty-eight thousand dead men
would be happy to know that."

We sat in silence while I thought about AAIC.
The place looked legit, and Susan sounded legit,
but . . . But stay awake, Brenner. The bamboo
was clicking in my brain again, and the vegetation swayed without a breeze. I looked at my
watch. It was ten after eight. "Time to fax," I said.

"We'll finish our drinks and relax. They're
not going anywhere."

Ms. Weber seemed indifferent to my fate, but
she was right; they weren't going anywhere. I
asked her, "Where's your apartment from here?"

"On Dong Khoi Street. South of Notre Dame, not far from the Rex."

"Don't think I know it."

"Sure you do. It was once Tu Do Street, heart of the red-light district." She smiled. "You may have seen it once or twice."

In fact, I had, of course. My Vietnamese lady friend had lived in a little cul-de-sac, right off Tu Do. I couldn't, for the life of me, remember her name, but like a lot of the Viet ladies, she'd adopted an Anglo name. I knew it wasn't Peggy, Patty, or Jenny, or I'd have remembered it. In any case, I remembered what she looked like, and our times together, so I wasn't senile yet.

"Are you remembering Tu Do Street?"

"Actually, I was there a few times. Professionally. I was an MP on my tour of duty in '72."

"Really? And how about the other time? Sixty-eight, right?"

"Right. I was a cook."

"Oh . . . I thought you did something dangerous."

"I did. I cooked." I asked her, "So you live in a red-light district?"

"No, it's quite nice now. According to the guy I rented it from, it was once called Rue Catinet, during the French time. It was fashionable then, but very sinister, with spies, double agents, murky bistros, high-priced courtesans, and private opium dens. It went downhill from there during the American period, then the Commu-

nists cleaned it up and named it Dong Khoi—
General Uprising Street. I love their stupid
names."

"I vote for Rue Catinet."

"Me, too. You can still call it that, or Tu Do,
and most people know what you're talking
about." She added, "My apartment was built by
the French—high ceilings, louvered windows,
ceiling fans, and beautiful plaster moldings that
are crumbling, and no air-conditioning. It's very
charming. I'll show it to you if we have the time."

"Speaking of time . . ."

"Okay." She stood. "Let's fax."

She went to the fax machine in the alcove,
and I followed. She wrote something on a sheet
of company letterhead, then handed it to me. It
said, "Weber—64301." She informed me, "That's
my code so they know it's me, and that I'm . . .
something . . ."

"Not under anyone else's control."

"Right. If the number has a nine in it, it
means I'm under duress. Am I under duress?"

"No comment. Now I'm supposed to sign it,
right?"

"Right. I guess somebody there knows your
signature."

"I guess so." She gave me a pen, and I signed
the sheet.

She said, "This is exciting."

"You're easily excited."

She fed the paper into the fax machine, and I

watched her dial the 703 area code for northern Virginia, then the number, which I didn't recognize. The fax rang, then started to grind away. She said, "Not bad. First try."

The fax went through, and Susan said, "That calls for a drink."

She left the alcove and went to the sideboard where she made two fresh drinks. As she returned, the fax rang. She handed me my drink, then took the fax she'd sent and put it through the shredder.

The return fax came through, and I took it out of the tray. The familiar handwriting said: Hello, Paul—You had us worried for the last fifteen minutes. Glad to hear from you and hope all is well. We can continue this communication via e-mail. Ms. W has instructions. Regards, K.

I stared at the message, words from another galaxy, as though I'd been contacted by aliens, or by God. But it was only Karl; I'd recognize his tight, anal handwriting anywhere.

Susan was already sitting at her desk and was going online. I shredded Karl's message.

I left the alcove and wheeled a chair beside Susan. She said, "Okay, we've made contact. He wants you to go first. What do you want to say?"

"Tell him I have an appointment at the Immigration Police headquarters tomorrow at oh-eight-hundred—purpose unknown."

She typed and sent, waited and got his reply, which said: Do they still have your passport?

"Yes, and my visa." She typed the reply, and I said to her, "Let me sit there, Susan. You'll have to move away from the screen."

She glanced at me, then stood, took her drink, and sat in the chair opposite her desk.

Karl replied: Tell us what happened at the airport.

I took another swallow of Scotch and began typing, relating the encounter fully, but succinctly. It took me ten minutes to type all of this, and I ended with: I believe this was a random stop and question. But it may have compromised the mission. Your call.

The reply was some time in coming, and I could picture Karl in an office with a few other people: Conway, maybe, some other FBI types, and CID people, and people who I could only guess at.

Finally, his reply came, a lot shorter than the conversation in Virginia that led up to it. It said: Your call, Paul.

I tapped my fingers on the desk and took another swig of Scotch. I didn't want to let too much time go by, as if I was hesitating. Yes or no? Simple. I replied: It may be Colonel Mang's call. I realized that was a bit of a cop-out, so I added: If I get my passport back, I'll go forward with the assignment. I pushed send.

The reply came quickly: Good. If you're expelled, we know you did your best.

I replied: There is a third possibility.

They thought about that in Virginia, then Karl

replied: Be sure to have Ms. Weber in a position to know if you are detained. Set up a meeting time or phone call with her, and tell her to contact us if you don't make your contact with her at the scheduled time or place.

I replied: I know how to set up a failure-to-show alert. Thank you.

Karl, true to form, wasn't going to be baited, and he replied: Is Ms. Weber under any surveillance? Has she been seen with you other than at the Rex rooftop?

I glanced at Susan and said to her, "They want to know if you think you're under surveillance."

"How do I know? I don't think so. It's not my turn this month."

I typed: She doesn't believe she is. Because I'm a pro, and I don't ignore sticky parts of multiple part questions, I typed: We spent the day sightseeing. Saigon, Cu Chi.

I could hear Karl's voice, "What? You did what? Are you insane?"

His actual response was: I hope you had a pleasant day, but I know Karl. He was pissed.

I don't like having to explain myself, but I typed: It was good cover, and an opportunity for me to take advantage of her knowledge of conditions up country. I added: I don't have my platoon with me this time.

Karl's reply was terse: Roger.

There was nothing further on that subject, so

I typed: Ms. Weber's boyfriend has contacted or will contact the consulate on my behalf.

Karl replied: We've already done that, obviously. Are you forming an entire spy ring there?

My, my. We were becoming a little snippy. In conversation, I wouldn't even reply to that, but with e-mail, you had to reply, so I typed: :).

Karl, obviously in a jocular mood and with an audience, replied: :(.

I asked Susan, "Can this keyboard give the finger?"

She laughed and said, "Are they giving you a hard time?"

"They're working at it." I mean, my ass is on the line here, and they're busting my balloons. I typed: Do you have any further information for me regarding my assignment?

Karl replied: Not at this time.

I asked specifically: Haven't you located that stupid village yet?

Herr Hellmann replied: That's irrelevant if you're not at liberty to travel, and that is information you shouldn't have before you meet Colonel Mang. We'll let you know when and if you get to Hue.

I thought about that and concluded that they had located the village, or always knew its location. Also, the name of the village was not and had never been Tam Ki. They'd changed that in the letter, of course, so if anyone here were squeezing my nuts, and if I gave it up, it wasn't my actual destination. In fact, Tam Ki might not exist. Fairly certain of my conclusion, I asked Susan, "Does Tam Ki mean anything in Vietnamese?"

"Spell it."

I spelled it.

She said, "The whole language is based on accent marks, diphthongs, and stuff like that— compliments of the French who gave them the Roman alphabet. Unless you pronounce it right, or know the accent marks, I can't translate it."

"Can it be a village? A place name?"

"Could be, but for instance, T-A-M can mean to bathe, or a heart, depending on the pronunciation, which is based on the accent marks. Tam cai is a toothpick, tam loi is an air bubble. See what I mean?"

"Yeah . . . how about K-I?"

"K-I is usually a prefix—ki-cop is stingy, ki-cang is carefully, ki-keo is to bargain or complain."

"Could this just be a made-up name?"

"Could be. Doesn't sound like a place name."

I looked back at the screen and saw: Acknowledge.

I replied in the military style: Affirmative, which has different shades of meaning, depending on who's talking to whom, and how the conversation is going. In this case, it meant: Yeah. I added, to see what he'd say: Do you want me to research the location of this village?

The reply was immediate: Negative. Do not ask

and do not look at maps. Maps are inaccurate and many villages have the same name. We will contact you if and when you get to Hue.

I replied: Roger. How are you making out with names of suspects and name of victim?

Karl replied: Narrowing list. Then: If at liberty, where will you go tomorrow?

I replied: Narrowing list.

He answered me: Colonel Mang wants an itinerary and so do we.

I looked up at Susan and asked her, "Where would be a good place to go from here tomorrow to kill a few days?"

"Paris."

"How about a little closer to Saigon? Someplace where Westerners go."

"Well, Dalat, the French mountain resort. The rail line is still blown up, but you can get there by car or bus."

"Okay, any place else?"

"There's the old French beach resort of Vung Tau."

"So, I have my choice of the mountains or the beach. Where's Vung Tau?"

"A little south of here. I can take you with my motorcycle. I go there on weekends."

"I need to head north."

"Why don't you call your travel agent?"

"Come on. Help me out."

"You didn't want my help."

"I apologize."

"Say please."

"Please." I couldn't believe I'd gotten myself in this situation; hounded by a Vietnamese version of Lieutenant Colombo, apologizing to a sulky upper-middle-class snot, and Karl shoveling shit at me over the Internet. Where is my M-16 when I need it?

I calmed down and asked Susan, "How about Nha Trang?"

She nodded. "Not bad. Not too far, nice beach, and lots of places to stay. Do you know it?"

"Yeah. I actually had a three-day in-country R&R there in '68." I asked her, "Are there any Western tourists there?"

"Usually. It's still warm enough to swim there. You won't stand out, if that's what you mean."

"That's what I mean." I also meant I didn't want to wind up in some godforsaken place where the fuzz could pick me up without any of my compatriots around to witness it. But that was negative thinking. *Visualize success.* I asked Susan, "Can I get there easily?"

"I can get you there, and I can find you a place to stay. Money talks, and I have a good travel agent who does business with the firm."

"Okay. Nha Trang. Thanks."

I started typing, and she said, "Tell them I'm going with you."

"Yeah. Right." I typed: My intended destination is

Nha Trang—unless transportation or accommodations are not available. If it changes, Ms. W will let you know ASAP.

Karl replied: Understand. Suggest you stay in Nha Trang or alternate until Hue rendezvous. The less movement, the better. Fax Ms. W your Nha Trang or alternate address when you arrive. Instruct her to give it to the consulate.

Susan said to me, "Did you tell them?"

"I did. They said flat out no."

"You didn't ask them. Tell them you need a guide and interpreter."

I typed: I will attempt to keep to the itinerary I give to Mang until the time I leave Hue for Tam Ki. The missing days between Hue and Hanoi may cause some problems when I show up in Hanoi.

Karl replied: If you're still having a police problem when you get to Hanoi, contact Mr. Eagan at embassy. But do not go to embassy unless instructed. Acknowledge.

Roger. I pictured myself living in the American embassy for five years while the State Department negotiated my safe departure from the Socialist Republic. This really sucked. I asked: Should I contact you from Hue—directly or through Ms. W?

The reply came: Negative. If you don't check in at the designated hotel in Hue, we will know and will assume a problem. When you do check in, you'll be instructed regarding further communication.

Instructed by whom?, I asked.

Karl replied: You'll be contacted.

I typed: Anything further regarding my Hue contact?

Karl responded: Negative. Do you understand your rendezvous times and places?

I answered: Affirmative. 32 down. The word was rotisserie.

Karl replied: The word had nothing to do with it. Do you understand your instructions?

I replied: I do. :). I added: Hey, I saw the Cu Chi tunnels, Highway 13, the Michelin plantation. Good tank country. Did you have fun?

Karl replied: :(.

I typed: We should come back together.

He replied: I'll think about that. Remember, we need to know what happens tomorrow re Mang. Are you confident in Ms. Weber's understanding of what she needs to do?

I replied: She's very savvy, resourceful, motivated. Give her a raise.

He replied: I have nothing further. You?

Yeah. What the hell is this all about? But I typed: Cynthia? Honolulu?

I waited for the reply, and it seemed a long time before it came up on the screen. It said: We have not been in contact with her. But your travel arrangements are made from Bangkok to Honolulu, then Maui.

I typed: Contact her.

Karl's reply was: She's on a case. But if she intends to meet you in Honolulu, the army will approve her leave quickly, and get her to Hawaii. He added: Focus on mission.

I typed: Let me know by Hanoi.

He replied: By Bangkok, latest.

I replied: Roger.

Karl sent me an early valentine: Good luck, Paul, God speed, and safe home.

I sat at the keyboard a long moment, knowing this might be the last message from home for a long time. I knew that feeling, from the last two times, when I spoke to my parents on a special radiophone that the GIs could use about twice a year. I typed: I'm glad I came back. I'm confident I'll be successful and home on time. Love to Cynthia.

Karl replied: Roger. Further?

Negative.

Out.

I signed off, deleted everything, and sat there awhile, then stood and went to the sideboard. I made myself a Scotch on the rocks and skipped the soda.

Susan asked me, "Is everything okay?"

"Yes."

She thought a moment and said to me, "If you're not able to travel tomorrow . . . if they keep you here for a few days, I can make a business trip for you. Meet someone, or whatever."

I looked at her and smiled. "Thank you. That's a very nice offer, but it's a lot more complex than that. Okay, how do I get to Nha Trang?"

"I'll e-mail the company's travel agent and see what I can do." She sat down at her desk. "Do you want me to try to book you a room somewhere, or do you want to wing it?"

"I'll need to give Mang an address."

"Not necessarily. Every major town has an Immigration Police office. Basically, they watch foreigners. So, if you tell Mang you have no address in Nha Trang, he will tell you to report to the Immigration Police either on your arrival, or after you've found a place to stay."

I thought about that, then said to Susan, "I'll find a place to stay when I get there." I added, "In fact, I'll try to find the R&R hotel on the beach that the army took over during the war. That should be a nostalgia trip."

"Should be. What was the name of it?"

"Don't remember. An old French place. But I'll recognize it. In any case, I'll fax you here after I check in to someplace. If I don't contact you within twenty-four hours of my departure from Saigon, contact my firm."

"I'm here to help." She turned her attention to her computer and started typing. She said, "I'm asking my travel agent about a train or mini-bus reservation to Nha Trang for tomorrow. Planes have been booked for months. I'm offering twice the ticket price, which is already quadrupled for foreigners. Okay?"

"It's not my money."

"Good." She continued typing and said, "I'm also asking her about a private car. There's also a hydrofoil to Nha Trang, though I'm sure everything's booked. But we'll get you to Nha Trang, even if I have to put you on the torture bus."

"A private car sounds like the way to go. Money is no object. Will this travel agent get back to you ASAP?"

"She's in at 8 A.M.—Saigon starts early. You'll be seeing Colonel Mang at about that time. I will meet you in the lobby of the Rex, and we'll see if you need to go to Nha Trang, or the airport and home." She added, "And if you're not at the Rex by, say, noon, then I know who to contact."

"Do you mind if I give the instructions?"

She looked up from her keyboard and said, "Mr. Brenner, this is not rocket science, and I learn fast. I've taken the responsibility of getting you out of Saigon, or reporting your detention or expulsion. Let's do this my way."

My goodness. Ms. Weber really was a different lady in her office. Or maybe she was a little miffed at me for not wanting her along on the trip.

She continued banging away at the keyboard and said, "I'm now e-mailing my boss,

Jack Swanson, saying I won't be in until tomorrow afternoon."

It seemed to me that there was a lot of typing
going on for these relatively simple messages.

Ms. Weber shut down her computer, stood,
finished her drink, and said to me, "Let me take
you to dinner."

"That's very nice of you. But I do have an expense account."

"So do I. And I'm going to tell you why you
should invest in Vietnam. It's the Pacific Rim
country with the most potential for growth."

I replied, "I've already invested enough in
Vietnam."

She didn't reply, walked toward the door,
and put her hand on the light switch. "Ready?"

I said, "Please print out the fax report and
shred it."

"Oh . . . you're a real pro." She went to the alcove, printed out the fax activity report, and ran
it through the shredder.

I took the camera and the exposed roll of
film from her desk and said, "Please put this in
your safe."

She punched the keypad on her safe, and I
gave her the film and the camera, which she put
in the safe and closed the door.

We left the office and walked around the
perimeter of the suite. Susan pointed out the library, the conference room, and a lunch room
that looked like a French café.

She said, "We treat ourselves well here. It's cheap, and it's a mental health perk. Here's the workout room and the showers." We entered a room with a few exercise machines. Through an open door, I saw a massage table.

I thought we were going to our respective places of residence to clean up, but Susan indicated a door that said *Men*, and informed me, "There's everything you need in there. I'll be in the ladies' shower."

"If I need anything."

"Behave. See you here in the exercise room."

I went into the men's locker room, got undressed, and stepped into a big shower stall. I turned on the water, got a handful of soap from a liquid dispenser, and washed off the grime of the last twelve hours.

Some men sing in the shower; I think. And what I thought was that no one and nothing here in Saigon or in Washington was as it seemed.

CHAPTER FOURTEEN

——★——

I went into the exercise room, found Friday's *Wall Street Journal* Asian edition on a chair, sat, and read.

It was quiet in the empty building, and from behind the door of the ladies' locker room, I could hear a muffled voice, and I was fairly sure it was Susan making her promised phone call to Bill.

About ten minutes later, Susan came out of the locker room wearing a long yellow sleeveless silk dress, and slung over her shoulder was a small leather pouch. The dust was off her face, and she was very tan. Her hair was neatly parted in the middle and hung over her shoulders. A little lip gloss completed the makeover. I stood and said, "You look lovely."

She didn't reply to my rare compliment, and I had the impression she'd had a little tiff with Bill. I said, "Maybe I should go back to the Rex and change."

"You're fine."

We went into the reception area, the elevator came, and we got off in the lobby. She said to me, "I've had enough driving. We'll take cyclos."

I followed her out the doors and onto the

sidewalk. We walked for about ten seconds before a flock of cyclos descended on us.

Susan haggled with the cyclo drivers, and I
looked at them. They were poorly dressed,
scrawny, and not young. A guy I knew who'd
been here told me the cyclo guys were mostly
former ARVN, and this was one of the few jobs
open to them as former enemies of the state.

Susan cut a deal with two of them, and we
each hopped into a cyclo and off we went up
Dien Bien Phu Street. Susan called over to me,
"It cost me double for you because of your
weight."

I looked at her and saw that she wasn't kidding. I said, "You're lucky they don't charge by
IQ."

"You'd ride for free."

Dien Bien Phu Street was a wide boulevard,
heavy with motor traffic, bicycles, and cyclos,
and it was a little unnerving sitting in an open
compartment with the driver in the rear and
cars and scooters cutting in and out.

The city was very lively on a Sunday night,
horns honking, boom boxes blasting, and pedestrians crossing in mid-block and against red lights.

Susan pointed out a few sights as we made
our way along the boulevard. She said, "This
street, Dien Bien Phu, was named after the final
battle between the French and the Viet Minh—
the predecessors of the Viet Cong. The Viet
Minh won."

"Whoever wins gets to name the streets."

"That's right," she said. "In ten years, this will be called Avenue of the Multinational Corporations."

Susan took out a pack of cigarettes and offered one to her driver, who took it, then the two cyclos came close so she could hand the pack to my driver. She said to me, "My guy wants to know if you're a veteran."

I hesitated, then said, "Tell him First Cavalry, Quang Tri, '68."

She relayed this, and they both said something to her. Susan said to me, "They are both veterans. My driver was a jet fighter pilot, yours was an infantry captain. They say, good to see you again."

I looked at her driver and made the V for victory sign. He returned the sign, half-smiled, then stared straight ahead.

We rode around central Saigon, and Susan pointed out the sights, but mostly we just watched the street show.

She said, "See those apartment blocks? They were built by the Americans in the '60s for CIA and embassy people. They now house Communist party officials."

The apartment blocks were drab gray concrete, without the usual balconies, and they looked like a penal institution. I said, "Serves them right."

We passed Notre Dame, and I noticed that

the small square was filled with people prome-
nading. The uniformed cops seemed to have
disappeared, and I assumed the plainclothes
cops took over after dark. And yet, by outward
appearances, Saigon did not look like a police
state. In fact, it looked like everyone was going
out of the way to break some law or another—
public drinking, prostitution, sleeping on the
sidewalks, running traffic lights, jaywalking, and
whatever else they did that I couldn't see.

On one level, the South Viets were second-
class citizens in their own country, ruled like an
occupied nation by the cadres of Communist
carpetbaggers from the north, and exploited by
the Asian and American capitalists. Yet, on another level, they seemed happier and more free
than the Communists, like Colonel Mang, or the
capitalists, like Susan Weber.

We were at the northern end of Dong Khoi
Street now, and it was as if we'd entered Times
Square or Piccadilly Circus. The brightly lit
street was choked with pedestrians, cyclos, bicycles, and motor scooters, all heading south toward the river.

The facades of the old French-style buildings
were nearly covered with neon advertisements,
and names of places like Good Morning Vietnam, Ice Blue, and the Cyclo Bar. There were
also a number of upscale French and East Asian
restaurants and a few grand hotels from another
era. I recognized the Continental, where the

war correspondents used to stay and make up news stories in the bar.

The metamorphoses from Rue Catinet to Tu Do to Dong Khoi had not been complete, and it seemed like all three versions of the same street co-existed as one. I did remember Tu Do, and I saw a building now and then that I thought I recalled, but too much time had passed and all the names were changed. I called out to Susan over the noise, "Is there still a place called Bluebird? Or Papillon?"

She shook her head. "Never heard of them." She added, "I understand that the Communists shut everything down in 1975."

"They're not fun guys."

"No, they're not. A lot of places started to reopen in the late '80s. Then in '93, the Communists got annoyed with all the bars and karaoke places and pulled a raid all over the city and shut everything down again. Some places were allowed to re-open, but only if they used Vietnamese names and cleaned up their acts. Little by little, it all came back, bigger, brighter, and crazier than ever, and with Western names again." She said, "I think, this time, it's all here to stay. But you never know. They're unpredictable. No respect for private property and business."

I pointed out, "They could kick *you* out."

"They could."

"Where would you go?"

She replied, "I have a book called The Worst

Places in the World to Live. One of those." She laughed.

I tried to locate the little alleyway that led to the cul-de-sac where my friend used to live. It was on the left side as we headed down to the river, but I didn't see it. I said to Susan, "You *live* on this street?"

"I do. It's not so bad five nights out of the week. And I'm on the fifth floor and closer to the river. I'll show you."

The throngs on the street were mostly young; boys and girls in T-shirts and jeans, the guys chatting up the girls, the girls mostly in groups.

I could see the end of Dong Khoi, and the moonlight on the Saigon River in the distance. Susan called out, "That's my building."

She was pointing to the left at a stately old French-style building on the last corner before the river. On the ground floor was a Thai restaurant, and next door was another old hotel called the Lotus, which Susan informed me was once the Miramar, and which I remembered.

She said, "Top floor. Corner apartment, river view."

Sounded like a real estate ad in the *Washington Post*. I looked up at the corner apartment and noticed lights in the window. I said, "Someone's home."

She replied, "Housekeeper."

"Of course. You like those corner locations, don't you?"

The cyclos swung onto the river road where a nice breeze was blowing across the moonlit water. The nice breeze smelled of God knows what, but if you held your nose, it was beautiful. The shore across the river, I noticed, was almost totally black, which I recalled from last time, and there seemed to be not a single bridge over the river. I said to Susan, "That's still undeveloped over there."

"I know. There are thousands of acres of flower farms there—orchids, exotic plants, and all that. When I go to sleep at night, I dream about subdivisions and shopping malls, then when I wake up and look out my window, it's all flowers—a waste of prime property."

I looked at her and realized she was putting me on. I smiled to show her I was a good sport.

The cyclos went a short block, then swung north onto Nguyen Hue Street, which ran up to the Rex and was parallel to Dong Khoi. This was a wider street, and it, too, was filled with humanity and vehicles.

Susan said to me, "It's a clockwise circuit—down Dong Khoi, then along the river, and up Nguyen Hue, then right at the Rex on Le Loi, and right again on Dong Khoi. An all-night parade."

"You mean I have to listen to this from my hotel?"

"Only until about dawn. Then it gets quiet until rush hour starts ten minutes later."

"Did you pick the Rex for me?"

"I did. It's close to my apartment, as you can see."

"I see."

"I like the rooftop restaurant. I like slow dancing."

We turned right on Le Loi and continued east. Susan said, "The kids call this circular parade chay long rong—means living fast."

"We never got above walking speed."

"I don't make up the language—I just translate it. It's like cruising, living in the fast lane; it's metaphor, not physical speed."

"I have problems with metaphors. Time for dinner."

She said something to her driver, and we continued on.

Within five minutes, the cyclos pulled up alongside a big building that looked like an old French opera house, and which Susan said was now a people's theater, whatever that means. Along one side of the theater was an outdoor café whose tables were filled with Westerners and a few well-dressed Viets, male and female.

We got out of the cyclos, and Susan insisted on paying the drivers—a buck for hers and two bucks for mine. She was being uncharacteristically generous, but I wasn't comfortable with that, so I gave each of the guys another dollar.

They wanted to shake my hand, so we all shook, then Susan's driver—the guy who in another life had flown jet fighters—said something and Susan translated. "He says his wife and children were allowed to emigrate to America four years ago. But he wasn't allowed to leave because he was an officer in the South Vietnamese air force. But under the . . . what we call the Orderly Departure Program that the Americans have negotiated with Hanoi, he hopes to be allowed to leave next year."

I said, "Tell him I wish him good luck."

She translated, he said something, and she said to me, "He thanks America for taking his family. They are doing well and send him money. They live in Los Angeles."

"Well . . . I hope they wind up someplace nice."

My driver, the infantry captain, didn't have anything to say, and I had the impression he was well beyond any hope for anything.

We walked into the outdoor café whose name, according to a small sign, was the Q-Bar. It seemed to occupy a piece of this theater building and was very minimalist, sort of like a trendy Washington yuppie hangout.

There was an inside section with tables and a bar, and on the walls were murals of what looked like Caravaggio paintings, but it was hard to tell through the cigarette smoke.

A young Vietnamese waitress in a black and white uniform greeted Susan in English, "Good evening, Miss Susan, and where is Mr. Bill tonight?"

I was happy for the opportunity to speak English and replied, "He's washing his Princeton sweater, but he'll be along shortly."

"Ah . . . good. Table for three?"

"Two."

Susan didn't clear up the confusion.

The waitress showed us to a table near the railing, lit by an oil lamp. Susan ordered a California Chardonnay, and I asked for a Dewar's and soda, which didn't seem to be a problem.

The waitress moved off, and Susan lit a cigarette. She said, as if to herself, "Washing his Princeton sweater."

"Excuse me?"

"Was that the best you could do?"

"It was short notice. It's late."

We let that go, and I checked out the patrons. They dressed like they made more than a buck a day, and on the street, I saw a few Japanese luxury cars—Lexus and Infiniti, which I hadn't noticed during the day.

The drinks came. I would have raised my glass to my hostess and said something nice, but I had the feeling she'd heard enough from me. In fact, she said, "Probably I should have taken you someplace else."

I said, "Of all the gin joints in Saigon, she takes me here."

She smiled.

I said, "What if Bill shows up?"

"He won't." She raised her wine glass. We

clinked and drank. "You can get a great burger and fries here. I thought you might be in the mood for that."

"I am. Good choice."

Susan said, "This place is owned by an American from California, and his Vietnamese-born wife, who's also a Californian. The Q is a play on the word kieu—a Viet expat who's returned. Viet-Kieu. Get it?"

"Got it."

She said, "This place is popular with the American community and Viet-Kieu high rollers. It's expensive."

"Keeps out the riffraff."

"Right. But you're with me."

To show her I wasn't completely at the mercy of her hospitality and to show some savoir faire, I said to her, "A Frenchman on the flight in gave me the names of a lot of good restaurants and bars."

"Such as?"

"The Monkey Bar."

She laughed. "Wall-to-wall whores. And very aggressive. They put their hands down your pants at the bar. You can go to the Monkey Bar after we leave here."

"I was just checking up on what this guy said."

"Well, he wasn't doing you any favors."

"He recommended a restaurant called Maxim's—like the one in Paris."

"It's a ripoff. Bad food, bad service, over-priced, just like in Paris."

My French friend was batting zero for two. I asked Susan, "Do you know a woman named Mademoiselle Dieu-Kiem?"

"No. Who is she?"

"A courtesan."

She rolled her eyes and didn't reply.

I said, "But I'd rather be with you."

"So would ninety percent of the men in Saigon. Don't push your luck, Brenner."

"Yes, ma'am." So, my attempt at independence and suavity was squashed like the ugly little bug that it was. "Thank you for bringing me to one of your special places."

"You're welcome."

The waitress brought over tiny menus. Susan ordered fruit and cheese for herself and another wine. I got my burger and fries and ordered a Corona, which they had.

It was cooler than last evening, but I had a film of moisture on my face. I remembered Saigon as hot and unhealthy when I'd left here in June of '72. I asked Susan, "Do you have a summer house or a weekend place?"

She replied, "That concept hasn't developed here yet. There's no running water in the countryside. If you go into the country, you step into the nineteenth century."

"So, what do you do on weekends in the summer?"

"I sometimes go up to Dalat where it's cooler, or to Vung Tau, formerly known as Cap Saint Jacques."

"Not to Nha Trang?"

"No. Never been there. It's a hike." She added, "But I'd love to see it. I'm sorry I can't go with you."

I let that one alone and asked her, "How difficult is it to travel into the interior of the former North Vietnam?"

She thought about that a moment, then said, "Generally speaking, anywhere along the coast is relatively easy. Highway One, for instance, goes from the Delta all the way to Hanoi, and it's being improved every year. The Reunification Express—that's the train—also links the north and south now. But if you mean heading west toward Laos, it's difficult. I mean, the Viets do it, but they have a lot more tolerance for washed-out roads and bridges, landslides caused by overlogging, steep mountain passes, and vehicle breakdowns. And it's the winter rainy season up there—a persistent drizzle called crachin—rain dust." She asked, "Are you headed that way?"

"I'm awaiting further instructions. Have you gone into the interior?"

"No, I'm just reporting what I hear. A lot of Western scientists go there—biologists, mostly. They've actually discovered previously unknown species of mammals in the northern interior. They just found an ox that no one knew existed. Plus, there are still tigers in the interior. Have a good trip."

I smiled. "I actually saw a tiger here once. And an elephant. And they weren't in the Saigon Zoo where they belonged."

"Well, be careful. You really can get hurt or get sick out there, and the conditions are very primitive."

I nodded. At least with the army, the medics were good, and the helicopters got you out of anywhere within half an hour, and onto a hospital ship. This time, I was on my own.

Susan said, "If you're going into the interior, you may want to pass yourself off as a biologist or naturalist."

I looked at her. I'd had the same thought as she was telling me about the unknown species. And now I had a new thought: I was getting the briefing I never got in Washington. In fact, a lot of what had seemed like Viet trivia today may have had a purpose.

The food came, and the burger and fries were terrific, and the Corona was ice cold with a lime in it.

She asked me, "Where do you live?"

I replied, "I live outside Falls Church, Virginia."

"And this is your last assignment?"

"Yes. I retired last year, but they thought I should press my luck and do Vietnam, Part Three."

"Who are they?"

"Can't say."

"And what are you going to do after this?"

"I haven't thought about it."

"You're too young to retire."

"So I've been told."

"By your significant other?"

"She's very supportive of whatever I want to do."

"Does she work?"

"Yes."

"What does she do?"

"Same as what I did."

"Oh, so you met on the job?"

"Right."

"Is she ready to retire?"

I cleared my throat and said, "She's younger than I am."

"Was she supportive of you going to Vietnam for this last assignment?"

"Very. Can I get you another beer?"

"I'm drinking wine. See the glass?"

"Right. Wine." I signaled the waitress and ordered another round.

Susan said, "I hope you don't think I'm prying."

"Why would I think that?"

"I'm just trying to get an image of you, your life, where you live, what you do. Stuff like that."

"Why?"

"I don't know. My favorite subject is usually

me." She thought a moment, then said, "Maybe you're interesting because you're not here on business."

"I am here on business."

"I mean, money business. There's no money in this for you. You're doing what you're doing for some other reason. I mean, it's not even because of your career. What is your motivation?"

I thought about that and replied, "I honestly think I'm stupid."

"Maybe it's a personal reason, something you're doing for your country, but really for yourself."

"Have you considered a radio talk show? Good Morning, Expats."

"Be serious. I'm trying to help you. You need to know why you're here, or you won't be successful."

"You know, you're probably right. I'll think about that."

"You should."

To change the subject again, and because I needed some information, I asked her, "How good is your travel agent?"

"Very good. She's a Viet-Kieu—understands Americans and Vietnamese. Can-do attitude." She added, "Bottom line, money talks."

"Good."

Susan reminded me, "But Colonel Mang might kick you out."

Maybe I had one beer too many, but I said to

her, "What if I didn't go to see Colonel Mang to find out? What if I just went up country? Would I be able to do that?"

She stared directly into my eyes and said, "Even if you were able to get around the country without anyone asking for your passport or visa, you'll never get *out* of this country without one. You know that."

I replied, "What I had in mind was going to the consulate first thing tomorrow and getting an emergency passport issued."

She shook her head and said, "They are not yet an official delegation and have no passport-issuing capabilities. That won't happen for at least six months. So, if you don't have a passport or a visa, or even photocopies, you won't get far."

I replied, "If I get to the American embassy in Hanoi, it becomes their problem."

"Look, Paul, don't compound the problem. See Colonel Mang tomorrow."

"Okay. Tell me about the Immigration Police. Who are these clowns?"

"Well, their business is foreigners. The police in this country were organized by the KGB when the Russians were here, along KGB lines. There are six sections, A to F. Section A is the Security Police, like our CIA. Section B is the National Police, like our FBI, and Section C is the Immigration Police. Sections D, E, and F are respectively Municipal Police, Provincial Police, and Border and Port Police." She added, "The Immigration Police usually just handle visa and passport violations, so I wouldn't be too concerned about this."

"Right." But I had the thought that Colonel Mang could be an A or B guy in C clothing. That was a fairly common ruse. The other thought I had was that Ms. Weber knew a lot about the Vietnamese fuzz, but maybe all expats had a handle on that.

It was pushing 11 P.M., and I said, "I think I'll call it a night. Got an early A.M."

I called for the check, but Susan insisted on paying for it with her company credit card, and I wasn't going to argue with that.

She wrote something on her copy of the charge slip and said, "Paul Brenner—company unknown—discussed fish cannery investment, dangerous missions, and life." She smiled and put the slip in her little bag.

We stood and went out in the street. I said, "I'll walk you home."

"Thank you. Sort of on the way is one last place I want to show you. Just two blocks from here. We'll have a nightcap, and you'll be back to your hotel by midnight."

Famous last words. I said, "Fine."

"Unless you'd rather go to the Monkey Bar."

"I'd much rather have a nightcap with you."

"Good choice."

We walked a few blocks to a quiet street that

wasn't particularly well lit. At the end of the street was a big, illuminated building whose sign said *Apocalypse Now*. I thought I was seeing things, but Susan said, "That's where we're going. Have you heard of this place?"

"I saw the movie. Actually, I lived the movie."

"Did you? I thought you were a cook."

"I guess I wasn't a cook."

"I didn't think so."

"Neither did Colonel Mang," I said.

"You told him that?"

"Sounded better than combat infantryman. He may have gotten the idea I killed one of his relatives."

"Did you kill anyone?"

I didn't answer that, but said, "The army unit portrayed in that movie was the First Cavalry Division. My division."

"Really? I saw the movie. Helicopters, rockets, machine guns—Ride of the Valkyries. Unreal. That's what you did?"

"Yup. Don't remember the Ride of the Valkyries, but sometimes they'd play cavalry charges from a helicopter on a loudspeaker."

"Weird."

"I think you had to be there."

We had arrived at the front door to a long, low yellow building in front of which were about twenty cyclo drivers, hanging around, smoking.

I said to Susan, "Come here often?"

She laughed. "Actually, no. Just when I have

out-of-towners in. I brought my parents here. They were uncomfortably amused."

A Caucasian man opened the door, and we stepped into Apocalypse Now.

The first thing I saw was a cloud of smoke, like someone had popped about a dozen smoke canisters to mark a landing zone in the jungle. But it was only cigarette smoke.

The place was hopping, and a four-piece combo of Viets was playing Jimi Hendrix. Against the left side of the place was a wall of sandbags and barbed wire, like firebase chic. A big poster from the movie of the same name hung on a wall, and Susan said it was autographed by Martin Sheen, if I wanted to look. I didn't.

The overhead paddle fans were helicopter blades, and the light globes had red paint splattered on them to look, I guess, like blood.

We went to the long bar against the back wall, which was packed with mostly middle-aged guys, black and white, and they definitely had the look of former military about them. I had this sense of déjà vu, Americans again on the prowl in Saigon.

I got two bottles of San Miguel from the American bartender, who said to me, "Where you from, buddy?"

"Australia."

"You sound like a Yank."

"I'm trying to fit in."

Susan and I sidled up to the bar and sucked

up the suds. The place was absolutely fogged in with cigarette and cigar smoke, and Susan lit up. She said to me, "So, GI, you lonely tonight?"

"I'm with someone."

"Yes? Where she go? She go away with general. She butterfly. I stay with you. Show you good time. I number one girl. Make you very happy."

I didn't know whether to be amused or to freak out. I said, "What's a girl like you doing in a nice place like this?"

She smiled and said, "Need money to go to Harvard."

I changed the subject and said, "This is the opposite of Cong World."

"It's R&R World. Does this offend you?"

"I think that anything that trivializes war is offensive."

"Want to leave?"

"We'll finish our beers." I asked, "When does the shooting start?"

But it wasn't so easy to leave. There were four couples next to us, all middle-aged, and they struck up a conversation. The men were all former American air force officers, and they had their wives with them to show the ladies where they'd served and all that. They were okay people, and we chewed the fat awhile. They'd all been stationed up north at Da Nang, Chu Lai, and Hue–Phu Bai Airbase, and they'd bombed targets around the DMZ, and that was their ultimate destination. They asked me about my wartime service without asking me if I was a vet. I said, "First Cav, Quang Tri, '68."

"No shit?" said one. "We blew the crap out of a lot of targets for you guys."

"I remember."

"You going up country?"

"I think we're already there," I said.

This got a big chuckle, and one of the guys said, "Is this place unreal, or what?"

"It's unreal," I agreed.

The wives didn't seem overly interested in any of this war stuff for some reason, but when they learned that Susan lived in Saigon, they descended on her, and the five ladies talked shopping and restaurants, while the five guys, myself included, told war stories until the shell casings and bullshit were knee deep. They seemed fascinated about the life of an infantryman and wanted all the gory details.

I obliged, partly because they bought me another beer, but also because this was part of their nostalgia trip, and I guess mine as well. I never get into this stuff at home, but here, in this place, and with a little buzz on, it seemed okay to talk about it.

They told me about dodging surface-to-air missiles and anti-aircraft fire, and blowing the living shit out of everything that moved in the DMZ. They used empty beer bottles to demonstrate all of this, and I realized that these guys

had totally removed any moral or ethical considerations from the stories, and saw aerial combat
as nothing more than a series of technical and
logistical problems that needed to be dealt with.
I found myself caught up in these narratives of
bombing and strafing, which was kind of scary. It
doesn't take much to stir the heart of old warriors, myself included. It was 1968 again.

Midnight came and midnight went. The band
was playing the Doors now, and my grip on reality and chronology was slipping.

Now and then, when the band stopped for a
few minutes, a loudspeaker would blast a cavalry charge, followed by Wagner's "Ride of the
Valkyries."

As far as theme bars went, this was right up
there with Planet Hollywood.

Somewhere in the conversation, we got
around to places to see and where we'd already
gone. I said to them, "You've got to get out to
the Cu Chi tunnels."

"Yeah? What's there?"

"These really big tunnels, the size of train
tunnels, where the VC had hospitals, dormito-
ries, supply rooms, kitchens. You go in with
electric golf carts. It's a great tour, and you can
have lunch and cocktails in one of the VC dining
halls. I think they have ladies silk shops in there,
too. The wives will love it." Why do I do things
like this?

The guys made a note of it.

The four airmen came to a belated realization that my First Cavalry Division and the First Cavalry Division in the movie and the theme bar were one and the same, and this called for another round of beers and more war stories.

We ran out of ammunition, and one of the guys asked me, "Who's the lady?"

"What lady?"

"The lady you're with."

"Oh . . . just somebody I met last night. She lives here."

"Yeah. So she said. That's some good-looking woman."

I'm never sure what to say when someone says that, but I said, "Your wives are very attractive."

They all agreed that their wives were wonderful and were saints to put up with them. I agreed with this, too, but they wanted to get back to Susan. One guy asked me, "You on top of that?"

"We're negotiating."

They all got a big laugh out of that, and that in turn led them to the subject of hookers. We all got a little closer for this conversation, and one guy said, "We're trying to get them to go shopping on their own."

"The hookers?"

"No. The wives. All we need is a few hours, but they won't go by themselves. The city scares them."

"Get them a female English-speaking guide from the hotel."

"Yeah. That's what I said. See, Phil? He agrees. Get them a guide, and we're on our own."

I recommended the Monkey Bar. "Wall-to-wall whores—don't pay more than five bucks for the prostitutes, but the waitresses and bar-maids can be had for a few bucks more. Then take the wives to Maxim's for a late dinner."

They hatched the plot right then and there and did high fives. I thought army guys were bad, but flyboys were worse. I remembered an old army joke and told it. I said, "What's the difference between an air force pilot and a pig?"

"What?"

"A pig won't stay up all night trying to fuck a pilot."

They roared. Good one. Were we having fun, or what?

One o'clock came, and one o'clock went. I needed to take a leak, and I excused myself.

I found the men's room in a passage that led to another crowded room in the back. When I got out of the men's room, Susan was waiting for me. She said, "There's a garden in the back. It's quiet, and I need some fresh air."

"Why don't we leave?"

"We will. I just want to sit down a minute."

Susan led me to an enclosed garden with lit-tle café tables that had candles on them. The garden was strung with paper lanterns, and it was quiet here, and the air smelled better.

We sat at an empty table, and I looked around at couples holding hands. I guess this was sort of like post-Apocalypse, where you went after you died or something.

I also noticed the smell of incense in the air, and the smell of cannabis burning. In fact, I saw little glowing fireflies dancing around the tables as the Js were passed, inhaled, and passed again. I had a sudden urge for a joint, something I hadn't felt in twenty years.

Susan said to me, "You seemed to be having fun."

"Good guys."

"The wives were nice, too. They wanted to know if we were a couple."

"Is that all women talk about? Sex, sex, sex."

"We weren't talking about sex. We were talking about men."

"It's the same thing."

"Do you want some tea?"

"What kind of tea?"

"Real tea. The other tea is BYO."

She called over a waitress and ordered tea.

We sat there in the dark garden, and neither of us spoke. A pot of tea came with two little teacups, and I poured. I don't even like tea.

We sipped the hot, flavorless tea for a while. I inhaled the steam, and my lungs started working again.

I was exhausted and even Susan yawned, but it was beyond the hour that would have mattered in regard to a good night's sleep, so we sat there and sipped this horrible tea. After about ten minutes, I realized this was quite pleasant.

Finally, Susan said, "You know what would make me happy?"

"What?"

"If you went home tomorrow."

For some reason, I told her, "It would make me happy if *you* went home."

This was a somewhat intimate exchange between two people who hadn't yet been intimate. I said, "You need to get out of here before something happens to you . . . I mean mentally." I heard myself saying, "You're worried about me, but I'm worried about you."

She stared at the flickering candle for a long time, and I saw tears running down her face, which surprised me.

We were both a little drunk, and this moment wasn't real, or even rational. With that in mind, I said softly, "When I was here . . . there was this story going around among the troops . . . the story of Gordon's Kingdom. Gordon was supposed to be this Special Forces colonel, who went off into the jungle to organize a tribe of Montagnards to fight the VC, but Gordon went around the bend, went native, and got really messed up in the head . . . you know the story. It was a version of Conrad's Heart of Darkness, but somehow the story got transferred to Vietnam . . . this apocalyptic story that they made into this movie . . . but apocalyptic or not, it was a warning . . . a fear that we all had, that we would stop wanting to go home, that we would get really messed up in the head, and we couldn't go home anymore . . . Susan?"

She nodded and let the tears keep flowing.

I gave her my handkerchief, and we sat there, listening to the night insects, and the muffled sound of sexy Janis Joplin from the bar, punctuated by "Ride of the Valkyries." I couldn't even guess at what caused her to weep.

I held her hand, and we sat there awhile longer.

Finally, she took a deep breath and said, "Sorry." She stood. "It's time to go."

We left Apocalypse Now and went out to the street. We got into a taxi, and I told the driver, "Dong Khoi."

Susan shook her head. "We need to go to the Rex." She said something to the driver, and he pulled away.

As the taxi moved through the streets, Susan said, "I get weepy when I drink too much. I'm okay now."

I said, "You must have Irish blood. My whole family and all my Boston friends get drunk, sing Danny Boy, and cry."

She laughed and blew her nose into my handkerchief.

Within a few minutes, we were at my hotel. Susan and I got out, and she said, "Let's check that message and see if there's anything else."

"That's okay. I'll call you at home if there's anything new."

"Let's check."

So, we entered the hotel and went to the front desk. I got my room key and an envelope. The message inside, in barely readable English, said: You to meet Colonel Mang at Immigration Police headquarters, 0800, Monday. You to bring all travel documents and to bring travel itinerary.

It would appear that I was going to get my visa and passport back in exchange for an itinerary. That's what I would do if I were Colonel Mang. I had aroused his curiosity, and also pissed him off. He wanted me around.

Susan looked at the message, then got businesslike again and said, "I'll see you here in the morning when you return from your appointment. I suggest you pack and check out before you leave to see Colonel Mang, and have the hotel hold your bags in the lobby. You may not have a lot of time to spare. I'll have tickets with me for something by the time I get here, or I'll have the tickets delivered here. I'll go with you to the train or bus station, or wherever you need to go. In any case, I'll be here at nine, waiting."

"If I'm later than noon, do not wait. Leave the tickets here and contact my firm."

She took her cell phone out of her bag and

gave it to me. She said, "I'll call you from my apartment in the morning with some tips for your meeting, and I don't trust the hotel phones."

I asked, "Is your apartment phone secure?"

"It's another cell phone. I have a landline, but that's only for long distance." She added, "Call me if you need anything, or if something comes up." She looked at me and said, "Sorry if I kept you out too late."

"I enjoyed my day. Thank you."

She smiled, and we gave each other a friendly little hug and kiss on the cheek, and she turned and left the hotel.

I stood in the lobby another few minutes, waiting, I guess, to see if she came back, the way she'd done on the Rex roof. The door opened, but it was just the doorman, who said to me, "Lady in taxi. Okay."

I walked to the elevators.

★

CHAPTER FIFTEEN

———————★———————

I woke before dawn and took two aspirin and one malaria pill.

I'd decided to wear what I wore when I first met Colonel Mang: khaki slacks, blue blazer, and a blue button-down shirt. Cops like to see suspects in the same clothes each time—it's a psychological thing, having to do with a cop's negative knee-jerk response to people who change their appearance. This outfit would be fixed in Colonel Mang's little brain, and with any luck, we'd never see each other again.

I put the snow globe in my overnight bag to give to Susan as a thank-you present. As I was making a final check of the room, Susan's cell phone rang in my pocket. I answered it and said, "Weber residence."

She laughed and said, "Good morning. Did you sleep well?"

"I did, except for the chay long rong parade outside my window, and the Ride of the Valkyries running through my head."

"Same here. I'm a little hungover." She added, "Sorry if I got weepy."

"Don't apologize."

She got down to business. "Okay, any taxi knows where the Immigration Police headquarters is. It's actually in the Ministry of Public Security. Give yourself fifteen minutes because of rush hour. Don't hold your taxi—they don't like to hang around that building."

"Maybe Colonel Mang will offer me a ride back to the Rex."

"He may actually do that if he wants to see some kind of ticket to Nha Trang. But most likely he'll instruct you to report to the Nha Trang Immigration Police."

"If he does come back to the Rex, make yourself scarce."

"Let's see how it plays."

I asked her, "Are you glad you got involved with this?"

"Beats going to work. All right, I have an e-mail from my travel agent, and she's working on transportation to Nha Trang. Leave my cell phone with the front desk, and I'll pick it up when I get there."

"Okay."

"Now, regarding Colonel Mang—try not to piss him off. Tell him you saw the Cu Chi tunnels, and you've earned a new respect for the people's anti-imperialist struggle."

"Screw him."

"When you get to the Ministry of Public Security, you want Section C—that's the Immigration Police. Stay away from A and B, or we may never see you again." She chuckled, but she wasn't kidding.

She continued, "You'll be directed to a waiting room, then you'll be called, but not by name. It's random, but old people go first in Vietnam, so you'll be called first. You then go into another room, and the guy there asks what you want. He's nasty. Most people are there because they've been stopped with an expired visa, or they need visa extensions, or work or residence permits. Low-level stuff."

That didn't explain why I was told to go there, but I didn't point this out.

She continued, "You have an appointment, so ask the nasty guy for Colonel Mang. The word for colonel is dai-ta. You ask for Dai-ta Mang. Give the nasty guy something with your name on it."

"They've got everything with my name on it."

"Give them your driver's license or your hotel bill or something. They're supposed to speak foreign languages for their job, but they don't, and they don't want to look stupid. So make it easy for them."

"You've been to this place?"

"Three times after I first got here. Then, somebody in my office told me to stop answering their summonses. So I did, and now they come to my office or my apartment every few months."

"Why?"

"Paperwork, questions, and a tip. They call it a tip, like they just did me a service. Usually takes me about ten minutes and ten bucks to get rid of them. But don't offer Colonel Mang any money. He's a colonel, and maybe a pure and true Party member. You could get arrested for bribery, which is the biggest joke in this country because you usually get arrested for non-bribery."

"Right."

"But if he *asks* for money, give it to him. The going rate to ransom your passport and visa is fifty bucks. Don't ask for a receipt."

I thought about this and about my conversation with Colonel Mang at the airport, and I was fairly certain that money was not what Colonel Mang was after.

She continued, "Some of these guys are nothing more than corrupt former South Vietnamese police who've managed to stay on the job with the Reds. But some of them are northerners, trained by the KGB, and they still have KGB heads. Also, the higher the rank, the less corrupt. Be careful with Colonel Mang."

"Right." And this raised the question of how I got lucky enough to meet Colonel Mang in the first place.

Susan asked me, "Did he seem old enough to have fought in the war?"

"He remembers the war quite well."

She stayed silent for a few seconds, then said,

"Maybe you can turn your shared experiences into something positive."

"Yeah. Look, I'm not going there to bond with the guy—I just want my papers, and I want out of there."

"But you don't want him to kick you out of the country."

"No, and he has no intention of doing that. I'm not going home today—I'm going to Nha Trang, or to jail—so be prepared to fax my firm either way."

"I understand."

"Anything else?"

"No, that's about it. See you later."

"Okay . . . look, Susan . . . if I don't see you later . . . thanks—"

"See you later. 'Bye."

I hung up, turned off the cell phone, and put it in my jacket pocket.

I gathered my bags and took them down to the lobby. I went to the front desk and saw that one of the clerks was Lan, the same woman who had checked me in. I gave her my room key and said, "Checking out."

She played with her computer and said, "Ah, yes, Mr. Brenner. I check you in."

"You did."

"Did you enjoy your stay?"

"I really did. Saw the Cu Chi tunnels."

Lan made a face and didn't reply. As the bill

printed out, she asked me, "Can we assist you in any way with your travel plans?"

"Yes, you can. I need to go now to the Immigration Police to get my passport. You remember all that."

She nodded, but said nothing.

"So, I'll leave my luggage here and with luck—ba ba ba—I'll be back shortly to collect it."

Again, she nodded, then handed me my bill. She said, "Your room has been pre-paid. How would you like to settle the extra charges?"

I scanned my bill and felt I needed to explain that I hadn't gotten a blow job in the spa, despite the big charge. But I replied instead, "I'll settle it when I return with my passport and visa, and collect my luggage."

Lan thought about that a moment and replied, "As you wish."

It's got to be tough running a four-star hotel in a totalitarian state. I mean, your guests disappear without a trace, the police come to search the rooms and upset the maids, and there are so many phone taps that you can't make a dinner reservation without getting a cop on the line.

I gave Lan Susan's cell phone and said, "A young lady, an American, will be along shortly to pick this up. Please see that she gets it."

"Certainly."

I took the snow globe out of my overnight

bag and gave it to Lan. "Also, please give this to her and tell her I said thank you."

Lan examined the snow globe, but didn't comment on it. To a Vietnamese, it may have looked like a layer of rubble around a partially destroyed building.

Lan called over a bellboy, who gave me two receipts for my luggage and who got a dollar in return. Lan said to me, "Thank you for staying with us. The doorman will call a taxi for you."

I went out to the sidewalk and a taxi appeared. I said to the doorman, "Tell the driver I need to go to police headquarters. Ministry of Public Security. Biet?"

The doorman hesitated for a beat, then said something to the taxi driver as I got in.

We pulled away from the curb and headed west on Le Loi Street.

We drove through a section of the city that looked as if it held every cheap hotel and guest house in Saigon, and between the cheap lodgings were cheap eateries. The area was filled with young backpackers of all races and colors, boys and girls on a great adventure; a far different Vietnam experience than my own at that age, when I, too, carried a backpack.

The taxi turned into a street named Nguyen Trai, and continued on. I looked at my watch: It was five minutes to eight.

We pulled over and stopped near a three-story building of dirty yellow stucco, set back from the street behind a wall. The driver motioned to the building, and I paid him and got out. He sped off.

The structure was big and seemed to be part of a larger compound. There was a flagpole out front that flew a red flag with a yellow star.

There were two armed policemen at the open gate in the wall, but they didn't challenge me as I passed through. I guess no one tries to break *into* this place.

I crossed the small forecourt and entered the building into a sparse lobby.

In front of me was a high, ornate wooden desk, like a judge's bench, which looked very Western, like it had been left over from the French. A uniformed guy sat there, and I said to him, "Immigration Police."

He stared at me awhile, then handed me a small square of green paper that had the letter C on it. He pointed to my left and said, "Go."

So, off I went, thinking, "Go directly to jail. Do not pass Go."

I walked down a wide corridor that had offices on either side, and through the window of an open office I could see a large interior courtyard. The Ministry of Public Security was obviously a big and important place with much work to do. I had no doubt that the courtyard was used for executions under the French, and maybe under the South Vietnamese, and the Communists.

I passed a few uniformed cops, and a lot of

badly dressed bureaucratic types with attaché cases. They all eyed me, but the little green pass got me to the end of the corridor to a door marked C. Above the door was a sign that said *Phong Quan Ly Nguoi Nuoc Ngoai*. Nuoc, I know, means water, and Ngoai is foreign, according to Susan's license plates—so this was either the ministry that imported foreign water, or it was the place where foreigners from overseas had to report. Betting on the latter, I walked through the open door and entered a medium-sized waiting room. The room held about two dozen plastic chairs and nothing else. There were no windows, only louvers near the ceiling, and no fans. Also, there were no ashtrays, judging by the cigarette butts all over the tile floor.

Four of the chairs were occupied by young backpackers, with their packs on the floor. They were chatting with one another—three guys and a girl. They looked up at me, then went back to their conversation.

I took a seat. On one wall was a big poster showing a condom. The condom had a face, two feet, two arms, and was carrying a sword and a shield. Dangling from the sword was the word *AIDS*, and written on the condom was the word *OK*. Some comedian had written on the condom in English, *Vietnamese Fighting Meat Puppet Show—People's Theater*.

On another wall was a poster of a Vietnamese

woman and a Western gent embracing, and the words in English said *AIDS Can Kill You*.

On the far wall was a poster of Ho Chi Minh surrounded by happy peasants and workers, and next to that was a sign in English that said *Not to cause big disturbances and not with radio*. This enigmatic message was repeated in several languages, and I hoped that at least one of them made sense.

A few more people entered the room, mostly young people, but then a middle-aged Vietnamese couple entered, and I guessed they must be Viet-Kieus with a visa problem.

The young people were all chatting with one another in English, and with various accents ranging from American to Australian to several European-sounding accents. I heard the word "fuck" pronounced six different ways.

Also, from what I could overhear, most of these kids were looking for a visa extension, but some of them were looking for their visas and passports that had been officially stolen by the police. None of them seemed particularly concerned. The Viet couple, however, looked frightened, and also astounded at the backpackers who didn't. Interesting.

It was ten after eight, and I decided to give it ten more minutes before I caused big disturbances not with radio.

A few minutes later, a guy in a khaki uniform entered the room and looked around. He saw me and motioned for me to come with him. It's a pretty good deal being old in a Buddhist country.

I followed the guy out into the hallway, then into another room, an office, across the hall.

A uniformed officer in khakis with shoulder boards sat behind a desk, smoking. He said to me, "Who you? Why you here?"

This must be the nasty guy. I looked him in the eye and said in slow, simple English, "I—" I tapped my chest, "here to see Dai-ta Mang." I tapped my watch, "Appointment," then gave him my hotel bill. I didn't want to give him my driver's license because these clowns had enough of my official identification, and I pictured myself out in the street with no ID, except my monogrammed handkerchief.

In any case, the guy seemed okay with the bill, which he examined for some seconds. He then looked at a sheet of paper and seemed to be trying to match names. His cigarette ash broke off and landed on my hotel bill. I looked around for a fire extinguisher, or an exit sign.

Finally, Nasty looked up and said something to the guy who'd brought me in, waved the hotel bill around as if he was an unsatisfied hotel guest, and the other guy took the bill and motioned me to follow him. And we complain about rude civil servants.

So, I followed this guy down the long, straight hallway, wondering if I'd gotten my message across, or if they thought I was a bill collector from the Rex looking for a deadbeat named Mang. I hadn't realized how useful it was to have Susan with me.

Anyway, this guy stopped and knocked on a door numbered 6. The guy opened the door, but motioned me to stand back. He entered, I could hear talking, then the guy came out and pointed inside.

I entered a small windowless room. Sitting at a wooden table was Colonel Mang, and on the table was the hotel bill, a newspaper, his attaché case, a teapot and cup, and an ashtray overflowing with butts. This was obviously not his office, which I suspected was in Section A; this was an interrogation room.

Colonel Mang said, "Sit."

I sat in a wooden chair across from him.

Colonel Mang looked as unpleasant as I remembered him at the airport. The narrow eyes, high cheekbones, sneering, thin lips, and taut skin made him look like he'd had six facelifts. His voice also still annoyed me.

Colonel Mang pretended to be looking at the papers on his desk, then looked up at me and said, "So, you have brought for me your itinerary."

"Yes, I have. And you've brought for me my passport, and my visa, which you took from the hotel."

Colonel Mang looked at me a long time, then said, "Your itinerary."

I replied, "I leave for Nha Trang today. I will stay there for four or five days, then I go to Hue."

"Yes? And how do you travel to Nha Trang?"

"I've asked a travel agent to find me transportation. My ticket will be waiting for me at the Rex."

"And you have no ticket to show me?"

"No."

"So, you may go by automobile."

"I may."

"If this is the case, you must go through Vidotour, the official tour agency. This is the authorized way to travel by automobile and driver in Vietnam. You may not hire a private car and driver."

"I'm sure my travel agent knows that."

"They know. But they do not always follow this procedure. If you travel by automobile, you must book through Vidotour, and you must tell Vidotour office to call this office and report the name of your driver and the automobile license plate number."

"Sounds very reasonable." The good news seemed to be that I was free to go to Nha Trang. The bad news was that I was free to go to Nha Trang.

Colonel Mang asked me, "Who is this travel agent?"

"I don't know."

"Why do you not know?"

"I asked an American acquaintance in Ho Chi Minh City to assist me."

"Yes? And who is this American acquaintance?"

"Bill Stanley. Bank of America."

Colonel Mang hesitated a moment, then made a note of this. Bill Stanley now had something in common with Sheila O'Connor, who I'd ratted out to Father Bennett in another lifetime. Sometimes you've got to rat someone out, but never rat out a friend. Pick an Ivy League grad whenever you can.

Colonel Mang asked me, "How do you know this man?"

"We went to Princeton together. College."

"Ah . . . and you say he is with the Bank of America?"

I was getting a bad vibe about this for some reason. I replied, "I believe that's what he said."

Colonel Mang nodded, then said to me, "Inform your travel agent that he or she must telephone this office this morning and ask for me."

"Why?"

"You ask too many questions, Mr. Brenner."

"*You* ask too many questions, Colonel Mang."

This pissed him off, but he kept his cool. He looked at me and said, "You are the one who is raising questions in my mind."

"I have been completely truthful and cooperative with you."

"That remains to be seen."

I didn't reply.

He repeated, "Tell your travel agent to call me. Where are you staying in Nha Trang?"

"I have no reservations at this time."

"You must have an address."

"I'll get an address when I get there."

"Why do you wish to go to Nha Trang?"

"It was recommended as the best beach in Southeast Asia."

This seemed to please the little shit, and he said, "It is. But you did not come all this way to go to the beach."

"I was there in 1968."

"Ah, yes, where the combat soldiers would go for rest."

I didn't reply.

Meanwhile, the guy was chain-smoking, and the air was thick with smoke, not to mention humidity and the smell of sweat, which may have been my own.

Colonel Mang made another note on a piece of paper and said to me, "When you arrive at Nha Trang, you will report to the Immigration Police and give them your address. If you do not find accommodations, inform them of this." He looked at me and said, "They will see to it that you have a place to sleep."

I thought he meant jail, but he continued, "They have some influence with the hotels." He smiled.

"I'm sure they have. I thank you, Colonel

Mang, for your assistance, and I won't keep you any longer."

He gave me a nasty look and informed me, "It is I, Mr. Brenner, who am keeping you longer." He took a sip of tea and said to me, "How do you propose to travel from Nha Trang to Hue?"

"By whatever means are available."

"You must inform the Immigration Police in Nha Trang of your means of travel."

"Can they help me with transportation?"

He seemed to miss my sarcasm and said, "No." He looked at me and asked the big question. "You have five days between the time you leave your hotel in Hue and the time you are to check into the Metropole in Hanoi. What do you intend to do with those days?"

Well, I had to go to Tam Ki on a secret mission, but I really wanted to go to Washington and break Karl's neck.

"Mr. Brenner?"

"I'm going to travel up the coast, by train or by bus, to Hanoi."

"The trains do not run for four days after Sunday. The bus is unsuitable for Westerners."

"Really? Well, I'll hire a car and driver. Through Vidotour, of course."

"Why do you wish to travel by land and not aircraft?"

"I thought it would be educational to see the former North Vietnam on my way to Hanoi."

"What do you wish to learn?"

"How the people live. Their customs and way of life."

He thought about that a moment, then informed me, "For ten years, the people in the north suffered and died under American bombs, and shells from your battleships. I recommend to you the Vinh Moc tunnels where the residents of that coastal town lived for seven years during the American bombardment. You may not find those people as friendly to you as you may have found them here in the former American puppet state."

Colonel Mang might make a good Cong World tour guide. I said, "Well, then, I want to learn from that experience."

He seemed to be mulling this over. If I was Colonel Mang, I wouldn't press Paul Brenner about this loose itinerary from Hue to Hanoi. Because if Paul Brenner was up to something, then most likely what he was up to was going to transpire during those days.

Mang looked at me and said, "You are free to travel north from Hue to Hanoi by any legal means at your disposal."

We made eye contact. We both knew we were both full of shit.

Colonel Mang made a few more notes on his piece of paper, and though I'm trained to read upside down, I can't even read Vietnamese right side up. Colonel Mang said to me, "And when you are in Hue, you will visit the places in the vicinity where you were stationed. Correct?"

I replied, "I intend to take a day trip to Quang Tri City and see my former base camp."

"Well," said Colonel Mang, "you will be disappointed. There is no city of Quang Tri any longer. Only a village, and no evidence of the former American bases in the area. Everything was completely destroyed by American bombs in 1972."

I didn't reply.

He said, "You will report to the Immigration Police in Hue." Colonel Mang sat back, lit yet another cigarette, and stared at me through the smoke. "So, how have you spent your days in Ho Chi Minh City?"

Not wanting to piss him off again about place names, I said, "In Ho Chi Minh City, I saw many excellent places. I took your advice and went to the Museum of American War Crimes."

He didn't seem overly surprised at this, making me wonder if I'd been followed.

I continued, "I saw photographs of what happened to the South Vietnamese soldiers and the Montagnard hill people who didn't lay down their arms after the surrender. They paid a high price, but they should have just gone into the re-education camps like a few million other people, and they would have come out happier and better citizens of the Socialist Republic."

Colonel Mang seemed uncertain of my enthusiasm and conversion. Maybe I was laying it on too thick, but there was no reason to stop. "That evening, I had dinner at the rooftop restaurant of the Rex where the American generals dined while their troops fought and died in the rice paddies and jungles."

I made eye contact again with Colonel Mang. If he was sharp, he already knew from my hotel bill where I had dinner, and that I hadn't dined alone, unless I ate a lot. But he just stared at me.

I said, "On Sunday, I saw the former presidential palace where Diem and Thieu lived like emperors while their soldiers and the people suffered and died."

Again, I couldn't tell if he already knew this. I decided that I was giving him too much credit for police state efficiency. I said to Mang, "I'm very impressed with all I've seen and learned." I elaborated a bit, as though I was an inmate in a re-education camp looking to get out.

Colonel Mang listened as I related my many moments of epiphany, and he nodded. He seemed to be buying it. If I'd bought those Ho Chi Minh sandals, I would have put my feet on his desk, but I seemed to be doing okay without the props.

I said, "On Sunday, I went out to the Cu Chi tunnels."

He leaned forward. "Yes? You traveled to the Cu Chi tunnels?"

Colonel Mang realized he'd shown genuine surprise instead of inscrutability. He asked, "How did you get to Cu Chi?"

"I took a tour bus. It was absolutely amazing. Two hundred kilometers of tunnels, dug right under the nose of the South Vietnamese and American armies. How in the world did they hide all that dirt?"

Colonel Mang answered my rhetorical question. "The soil was thrown into streams and bomb craters by thousands of loyal peasants, a kilo at a time. When the people work as one, anything is possible."

"I see that. Well, it was all very educational, and it certainly changed my thinking about the war." So, let's get the fuck out of here.

Colonel Mang stayed silent for some time, then asked me, "Why do you travel alone?"

"Why? Because I couldn't find anyone to go with me."

"Why did you not join a veterans' group? There are groups of men who shared the same experience and who return with organized tours."

"I've heard about that, but I wanted to come here during Tet, and I made a last-minute decision to just come."

He looked at my visa again and said, "This is dated ten days ago."

"Right. Last-minute decision."

"Americans usually plan for months in advance."

Obviously, this is what first caught the eye of the guy at the Passport Control booth. I owed Karl a kick in the nuts. I said, "I'm retired. I just go where I want, when I want."

"Yes? And yet your passport was issued several years ago, and there are no visa stamps or entry and exit stamps on the pages."

"I travel in the United States and Canada."

"I see. So this is your first overseas trip?"

"Since that passport was issued."

"Ah."

Colonel Mang gave me one of those looks that suggested he was somewhat confused by an inconsistency in my responses. He changed the subject and asked me, "Are you married?"

I replied, "That is a personal question, Colonel Mang."

"There are no personal questions."

"There are, where I come from."

"Yes? And you can refuse to answer the question of a policeman?"

"That's right."

"And what happens to you when you refuse to answer?"

"Nothing."

He said to me, "I have heard this, but I do not believe it."

I replied, "Well, go to the U.S. and get yourself arrested."

He didn't think that was funny. He played around with the papers on his desk, and I didn't see my passport. "You have seen many prostitutes in Ho Chi Minh City. Correct?"

"I may have."

"They service the foreigners. Vietnamese men do not go to prostitutes. Prostitution is not legal in Vietnam. You have seen karaoke bars and massage parlors. You have seen drugs for sale, and you have seen a great deal of Western-influenced decadence in Ho Chi Minh City. You are thinking that the police have lost control, that the revolution has been corrupted. Correct?"

"Correct."

He informed me, "There are two cities that occupy the same time and space. Saigon and Ho Chi Minh City. We let Saigon exist because it is useful for the moment. But one day, Saigon will no longer exist."

"I think, Colonel Mang, the foreign capitalists may disagree with you."

"They may. But they, too, are here only as long as we want them here. When the time comes, we will shake them off, the way a dog shakes off his fleas."

"Don't be so sure of that."

He didn't like that at all and stared at me a long time. He changed the subject and said, "As you travel, Mr. Brenner, you can see the destruction your military caused, which is still not repaired."

I said, "I think both sides caused the destruction. It's called war."

"Do not lecture me, Mr. Brenner."

"Don't insult my intelligence, Colonel Mang. I know what war looks like."

He ignored that and continued his lecture. "Now you will see a country at peace, ruled for the first time in a hundred years by the Vietnamese people."

Poor Colonel Mang. He was a real patriot, and he was trying to come to grips with the guys in Hanoi who were selling the country to Coca-Cola, Sony, and Credit Lyonnaise. This must really be a bitter pill to swallow for this old soldier who gave his youth and his family for a cause. Like most soldiers, myself included, he didn't understand how the politicians could give away what had been bought in blood. I almost felt some empathy with the guy, and I wanted to tell him, "Hey, buddy, we all got screwed—you, me, and the dead guys we know, we all got the shaft. But get over it. The new world order has arrived." Instead, I said to him, "I'm very much looking forward to seeing the new Vietnam."

"Yes? And when you visit your old battlefields, what will you feel?"

I replied, "I was a cook. But if I was a combat soldier, I have no idea what I'd feel until I stood on the battlefield."

He nodded. After a few seconds, he said to me, "When you arrive in Hanoi, you will again report to the Immigration Police."

"Why? I'm leaving the next day."

"Perhaps. Perhaps not."

I leaned toward Colonel Mang and said, "My first stop in Hanoi will be the American embassy."

"Yes? And for what purpose?"

"I'll leave that for you to figure out."

Colonel Mang thought about that and said to me, "Did you contact your consulate here?"

I replied, "Through my acquaintance here, I registered my presence in Ho Chi Minh City, my problem at the airport, my passport being taken, and my arrival date in Hanoi." I added, "My acquaintance here will or has already contacted the American embassy in Hanoi."

Colonel Mang did not reply.

I liked the subject of the American embassy, so I said, "I think it's a very good thing that Washington and Hanoi have established diplomatic relations."

"Do you? I do not."

"Well, I do. It's time to bury the past."

"We have not even buried all the dead yet, Mr. Brenner."

I wanted to tell him I knew about the Communists bulldozing the cemeteries of the South Vietnamese military, but I was already a pain in his ass. I said, "If America had no diplomats here, who could I complain to about your behavior?"

He actually smiled, then informed me, "I liked it much better the way it was after 1975."

"I'm sure you did. But it's a new world, and a new year."

He ignored this and asked me, "Did you give your acquaintance, Mr. Stanley, your travel itinerary?"

"I did."

He smiled. "Good. So if you met with a misadventure along the way, and if no one hears from you in Nha Trang or Hue or at the Metropole in Hanoi, your embassy and the police can join in making inquiries."

I said, "I don't intend to meet with any misadventures, but if I do, my embassy will know where to make the first inquiry."

Colonel Mang seemed to enjoy exchanging subtle threats and counter-threats. I think he appreciated me on one level. Also, by this time, he was starting to suspect that he and I were in a similar business. And I was fairly sure that Colonel Mang was several steps up from an Immigration police officer; he'd borrowed this ratty office in Section C, full of backpackers and condom posters. Colonel Mang's real home was in Section A or maybe B. Section C put the suspect at ease and off his guard. And regarding my notifying the embassy, or Karl, they weren't as concerned about the Immigration Police as they would have been about the Security Police or the National Police.

Also, I thought, there was some irony and symmetry at work here—I wasn't a former cook or a tourist, and Colonel Mang was not an Immigration cop. And neither of us was going to get nominated for Best Actor Award.

I said, "Colonel, I need to get back to the Rex Hotel, or I might miss my transportation. Thank you for your time and advice."

He pretended he didn't hear me and looked at my hotel bill. He said, "A very expensive dinner. Did you dine alone?"

"I did not."

He didn't ask any further questions and didn't ask for money. He took a piece of cheap paper and wrote something on it, then took a rubber stamp off the desk, and pressed it onto the paper. Colonel Mang said, "You will show this to the Immigration Police wherever you report to them." He handed me the stamped paper, my hotel bill, my passport, visa, and another square of paper with a C on it, though this one was yellow. "You will take this pass directly to the desk where you entered the building and give it to the man there." He smiled and added, "Do not lose your pass, Mr. Brenner, or you will never get out of this building."

Colonel Mang had a little sense of humor; warped, but at least he was trying. I stood and said, "I had an interesting visit, but I don't want to overstay my welcome."

He ignored this and informed me, "If you deviate from your itinerary, notify the closest Immigration Police. Good day."

I said to him, "And thank you for returning my souvenir to my room."

"That is all, Mr. Brenner."

I couldn't resist and said, "Chuc Mung Nam Moi."

"Leave, before I change my mind."

Well, we didn't want that, so I left.

Outside in the hallway, there was no one to escort me, so I just walked down the hall by myself.

I got to the front lobby and gave the guy there my yellow pass, and he pointed to the front doors and said, "Go."

I walked toward the front doors. The Ministry of Public Security was sort of a bad imitation of Orwell's Ministry of Love, but there was a palpable presence of police power in this building, a feeling of accumulated decades of fear, intimidation, interrogations, blood, sweat, and tears.

I left the building and walked out into the sunlight. As Susan said, there were no taxis around, and I walked a block before a cab pulled alongside me. I got in and said, "Rex Hotel."

And off we went. I glanced at the note that Colonel Mang had given me. It was a long sentence in Vietnamese, except for the words *Paul Brenner*. I also recognized the word *My*—American. Colonel Mang had signed the note with his full name, which was Nguyen Qui Mang, followed by his rank, *dai-ta*. These Nguyens got around. Anyway, the stamp on the note was a red star with a few words, including *phong quan ly nguoi nuoc ngoai*. I put the paper in my pocket, pretty pissed off about having to carry around a note from the fuzz.

It was a few minutes after nine, and within ten minutes, I was back at the Rex.

I walked into the lobby, and there was Susan Weber, sitting in a chair facing the door, wearing navy blue slacks, walking shoes, and a tan cotton shirt with the sleeves rolled up. She saw me, stood, and moved quickly toward me, as though we were lovers meeting for a tryst.

Neither of us wanted to be overdramatic, so we just took each other's hand without any hugging or smooching. She said, "How did it go?"

"Fine. I'm free to roam. How'd you do with the ticket?"

"I've got you booked on the train to Nha Trang."

"Great. You're terrific."

"But the ticket isn't here yet, and it's a 10:15 departure."

"How far is the station?"

"About twenty minutes, this time of day. So, what did Colonel Mang say?"

"I'm re-educated."

She smiled. "Did you keep your smart mouth shut?"

"I tried. He said the prostitutes, the drugs, the karaoke bars, and you would soon be history." I added, "Not you by name, of course."

"You know, it doesn't have to be one or the other."

"It does, if you're Colonel Mang. He's got a serious double-think problem going in his head, and I'm afraid he may have a nervous breakdown. Meanwhile, when is my ticket going to arrive?"

"Any moment. And thank you for that snow globe. Is that for me?"

"Yes. It's not much, but you don't need much."

"It's the thought that counts."

"Precisely." I said, "I've got to settle my bill here—"

"It's done."

"That wasn't necessary."

"It could have been, and now you have time to tell me about the twenty-dollar massage charge." She smiled.

"I overtipped." We let that one go, and I said, "Colonel Mang wants your travel agent to call him tout de suite and report in." I added, "Sorry if that causes a problem. He insisted."

"That's okay. Vidotour reports everything, but the private travel agents don't, unless they're specifically told to. I'll call her."

"Does Bill use the same travel agent?"

"Sometimes. Why?"

"Because he was the one who called the travel agent on my behalf. I didn't want to use your name."

"Oh . . . well . . . it doesn't matter. I'll call him and straighten it out."

"Tell him I thank him for getting me out of Saigon. That will make him happy."

She didn't respond to that and said, "Did Colonel Mang give you any sort of note, or anything in writing?"

I showed her my note from Colonel Mang and asked, "What's it say?"

She looked at it and gave it back to me. "It says, 'Register the address of Paul Brenner, American, and his arrival and departure, and means of transportation to and from your location.'"

I nodded. What the note didn't say was, "Report this to the Security Police," but that was understood.

Susan said, "It used to be common for Westerners to register with the Immigration Police. You used to need a travel permit in addition to your passport and visa. Travel has become less restrictive in the last few years."

"Not for me."

"Apparently not. Let me make a few calls." She added, "Maybe someone can get a fix on Colonel Nguyen Qui Mang."

She walked off toward the door where the

signal would be better and made a few calls. I hate to leave other people holding the bag for me, and I never do that in my private life, but when I'm on an assignment, Rule Number One is the mission comes first, and Paul Brenner comes second, and everyone else is last. That didn't include Susan, of course, and probably shouldn't have included Bill Stanley. It was no big deal, anyway, though I noticed that Susan seemed a little concerned or maybe annoyed.

Susan returned from her cell phone calls and said, "It's all straightened out."

"And Bill was pleased that I gave his name to Colonel Mang?"

She said, "You could have used my name."

"No, I couldn't have. I don't want Colonel Mang questioning you and finding inconsistencies in my conversation with him."

"I thought you were being chivalrous."

"Spell that."

I noticed a kid of about twelve coming through the door. Susan walked over to him and said something. He gave her an envelope, she gave him a tip, then said something to my friend Lan, and motioned me toward the door.

Things started to move fast now, and Susan and I were out on the sidewalk. She said, "That's my taxi, and your bags are in the trunk. Let's move."

We got into the taxi, and Susan spoke to the driver, and off we went.

I said to her, "You don't have to come to the station—"

"It will go much faster if I'm with you, unless you've learned to read and speak Vietnamese in the last few hours."

"Okay. Thanks. I'll take the ticket."

"I'll hold it. I need to show it at the station. You don't actually have a seat, but I got you a car number. It's a second-class coach and will be filled with Viets, any one of whom will give up his seat for five bucks, and stand. You can't do that in First Class because they're mostly Westerners, and they'll tell you to fuck off. Okay?"

I said to Susan, "When you get back to your office, I need you to fax or e-mail my firm and tell them I'm off to Nha Trang. Tell them Colonel Mang wants me to report to the Immigration Police there, but I don't believe the mission is compromised, though I may be under surveillance. Okay?"

She stayed quiet a moment, then said, "I thought they'd be on pins and needles waiting to hear the outcome of your meeting, so I called the consulate when I made those other calls. I kept it short, in case the call was monitored. I got hold of the guy there who knows about this. I think he's the resident CIA guy. I just said, 'He's free to travel. Wire his firm.' Okay?"

I thought about this and said, "Okay. But you e-mail or fax them with a full report when you get to the office."

"Will do."

The train station was north of the center, and within fifteen minutes we pulled up near the entrance amid dozens of taxis, buses, and swarms of people.

Susan gave the driver a five, and we got out as he popped the trunk. I pulled my bags out of the trunk and noticed a big yellow backpack in the trunk. Susan pulled it out and slammed the trunk closed, then put on the backpack. She said, "Okay, let's move."

"Uh . . . hold on."

"Come on, Paul. We'll miss the train."

We? I followed her into the station, pulling my suitcase through the big central terminal. Susan looked at the display board and said, "Track 5. That's this way. Let's move."

We hurried across the open area crowded with travelers, and I said, "We can say good-bye here."

She replied, "I hate good-byes."

"Susan—"

"I feel responsible for getting you to Nha Trang. Then you're on your own. Okay?"

I didn't reply.

We got to the track, and Susan showed the woman at the gate two tickets. They exchanged some words, Susan gave her a dollar, and the woman waved us through.

We hurried along the platform, and Susan said, "Car 9. That's at the far end, of course."

My watch said 10:12, and the conductor was calling all aboard in Vietnamese, which could have been funny if I was in a better mood.

We got to Car 9, and I hefted my suitcase on board, then jumped on and pulled Susan up after me. We stood there in the end vestibule compartment, and I was huffing, puffing, and sweating.

The conductor gave the last all-aboard, the doors closed, and the train started to move. We stood there and looked at each other as the train began gaining speed, moving away from the station.

I asked, "How much do I owe you for the ticket?"

She smiled. "We'll settle later."

I said, "I really didn't see this coming."

"Of course, you did. You're a spy. You saw that I wasn't dressed for the office. I held the tickets. I already called the consulate. I stopped mentioning that I wanted to go with you. I came to the station. I held a taxi with your luggage in the trunk—along with mine. So what was your first clue?"

"All of the above, I guess."

"So, stop acting surprised."

"Right."

"Do you want me along?"

"Yes."

"Good. I'll only stay in Nha Trang a few days, then I'm going back to Saigon."

"Did you get a hotel?"

"No, we'll find that hotel you stayed at on your R&R—if it's still standing."

I looked through the window of the vestibule door and saw that the coach was packed with people, luggage, crates, and just about everything except farm animals. I said, "We may be better off standing."

She said, "It's five or six hours to Nha Trang. We'll buy two seats."

The train was passing through the northern outskirts of Saigon, and I saw a jet fighter, a Russian-made MiG, coming in to land at what must have been Bien Hoa Airbase, my former home away from home.

A conductor came into the small vestibule, and Susan and he spoke. She counted out twelve singles, and he left. She said to me, "He'll do the deal. He keeps the change."

The tracks swung east now, toward the coast, and the Saigon sprawl rolled on with the train. I could see houses that were little more than shacks, and I remembered these from 1972, when almost a million refugees from the countryside had crowded into the relative safety of Saigon.

Susan said to me, "I really love the beach. Do you have a bathing suit?"

"Yes. Bathing suits in your luggage look touristy to government snoops going through your things."

"You spies are really clever."

"I'm not a spy."

"That's right." She smiled. "I packed light, as you can see. Just a few days. I brought my swimsuit. The beach is supposed to be magnificent."

"Is the beach topless?"

She smiled. "Always thinking. No, you can't do that here. They go nuts. But at Vung Tau there are secluded spots where the French go to swim and sunbathe in the nude. But if you get caught by the local fuzz, you've got a problem."

"Did you ever get caught?"

"I never went topless or nude. I'd love to, but I'm a resident, so I can't claim ignorance." She asked, "So you had an R&R in Nha Trang?"

"Yes. May 1968. The weather was good."

"I thought you went someplace out of the country for R&R."

"There were three-day in-country R&Rs available to people who did something to deserve it."

"I see. And what did you do to deserve an in-country R&R?"

"I invented a new recipe for chili."

She didn't reply for a few seconds, then said, "I hope in the next few days you'll feel comfortable enough to tell me about your experiences here."

I replied, "And maybe you'll tell me why you're here and why you stay."

She didn't reply.

The train moved on, east across the Saigon

River, through a landscape of rice paddies and villages.

I looked at Susan and saw that she was looking at me. We both smiled. She said, "What would you have done without me?"

I replied, "I don't know, but I'll find out after you go back to Saigon."

She said, "After three days with me, you'll be good to go."

"After three days with you, I'll need a three-day R&R."

She smiled. "You keep up pretty good for an old guy. Do you swim?"

"Like a fish."

"Hike?"

"Like a mountain goat."

"Dance?"

"Like John Travolta."

"Snore?"

I smiled.

She said, "Sorry. Just teasing."

The train moved on, away from old Saigon, away from the new Ho Chi Minh City, north toward Nha Trang, and back to May 1968.

★

—BOOK III—

Nha Trang

CHAPTER SIXTEEN

———★———

The conductor led us through the crowded coach to seats vacated by two young Viet guys. I threw my suitcase on the overhead luggage rack, then sat with my overnight bag stuffed under my seat. Susan sat beside me on the aisle and squeezed her backpack under her legs.

The seat was wood, and it had enough legroom for an amputee. The width was okay for the two of us, but almost all the other seats had three people sitting in them, plus babies and kids riding laps.

We were on the right, so we'd have a view of the South China Sea at some point as we traveled north. There was no air-conditioning, but a few of the windows were open, and small fans mounted in the corners kept the cigarette smoke circulating.

I said, "Maybe we should have taken a car and driver."

"Highway One can be a problem. Also, this is a good experience for you."

"Thanks for your interest in my character development."

"You're quite welcome."

I asked her, "What is the fascination here for all these young backpackers?"

"Well, Vietnam is cheap. Then you have sex and drugs. That's pretty fascinating."

"Right."

"Kids talk to one another via e-mail, and this has become a hot place."

"It was pretty hot when I was here." I added, "It just seems a little incongruous for a totalitarian state to be so attractive to all these young tourists."

"They don't think like you do. Half of them don't know this place is run by Communists, and the other half don't care. *You* care. That's your generation. That was your big boogeyman. These kids are into world peace through pot. International understanding through intercourse."

"And your generation? What's your take on Vietnam?"

"Money."

"Do you ever feel that there's something missing in your life? Like something to believe in or to live for beyond yourself?"

"That sounds like an antagonistic question, though maybe I need to think more about that." She added, "We live in incredibly dull times. I think I would like to have been a college student in the Sixties. But I wasn't. So, a lot of this emptiness and shallowness is not my fault, or the fault of my generation."

"Do the times make the generation, or does the generation make the times?"

"I have a hangover. Can we make idle chit-chat?"

We chatted about the landscape.

A cloud of cigarette smoke hung in the hot, humid air, and the rail felt as though it had been torn up by the Viet Cong and never repaired. How bad could Highway One be?

About sixty kilometers out of Saigon, the train made its first stop at a place called Xuan Loc, which I knew had been the location of the Black Horse Base Camp, headquarters of the Eleventh Armored Cavalry. I said to Susan, "The gentleman called K, whom we communicated with in your office, was stationed here in '68."

"Really? Why didn't he come back here with you?"

"That's a good question. He would have enjoyed Colonel Mang. They're cast from the same mold."

People got off at Xuan Loc, and people got on. Balance and harmony were achieved, and the train moved on. I said, "Xuan Loc was the site of the last stand of the South Vietnamese army before the fall of Saigon."

Susan yawned and replied, "I'm too vapid and self-centered to care."

I think I'd pissed her off. Or maybe it was the generation gap. I suddenly felt middle-aged.

It had been a long night and an early morning for both of us, and Susan fell asleep with her head on my shoulder. Within a few minutes, I, too, was asleep.

We both awoke as the train approached Cam Ranh Bay, about four hours from Saigon. I could see the huge bay, and also part of the former American naval installation, and some gray warships at anchor. Farther north on a peninsula that formed the bay had been the big American airbase. Susan was awake now, and I asked her, "Have you ever been here?"

She said, "No, no one comes here. It's mostly off-limits." She asked me, "Were you ever here?"

"Once. Briefly in '72. I was on a military police detail to pick up a couple of soldiers who'd gotten into some trouble. We had to take them down to LBJ—that's Long Binh Jail—outside Bien Hoa. Back in '68, when Johnson was still President, we used to say about guys going to jail, 'LBJ got you once, now LBJ got you again.' Get it?"

"Is this in the history books?"

"Probably not."

I looked out the window again. The American naval and air installations at Cam Ranh Bay were considered among the best in the Pacific at that time. After 1975, the Soviets were handed the whole complex by the new regime. I asked Susan, "Any Russians still here?"

"I'm told there are some left. But mostly the Vietnamese navy uses the place." She added,

"It's a deepwater port, and it would make a great commercial port for container ships and oil tankers, but Hanoi has pretty much banned all development in the area. I don't think you'd be allowed to visit the base unless you want to get shot."

"That's okay." That was two places now—Bien Hoa and Cam Ranh Bay—where I couldn't go home again.

The train stopped at Cam Ranh Bay station. Only a few people got off, and the people getting on were mostly Vietnamese sailors and airmen, and most of them jammed into the vestibule.

Susan took a half-liter bottle of water out of her backpack, opened it, and drank, then passed it on to me.

The train moved out and continued north.

Now and then I could see a bomb crater, a derelict tank, a few dilapidated sandbag bunkers, or a French watchtower. But mostly the war seemed to have been erased from the land-scape, though probably not from the minds of the people who had lived through it, myself included.

Susan took a container of yogurt out of her bag and a plastic spoon. "Want some?"

I hadn't eaten since the hamburger in the Q-Bar, but I'd rather starve to death than eat yo-gurt. I said, "No, thanks."

She spooned the stuff into her mouth.

I asked, "Does this train have a dining car?"

"Of course. You go through the bar car, then the panoramic observation car, and you get to the dining car."

I was hungry and light-headed enough to believe that. I noticed that everyone around us had brought lots of food and drink. I said to Susan, "I'll have some yogurt."

She put a spoonful of this white goo in my mouth. It wasn't all that bad.

We finished the water and yogurt, and Susan wanted to switch places, but there was no room in the aisle, so she squeezed onto my lap, then I slid across to the aisle seat. I said, "Let's do that again."

She smiled.

Susan lit up an after-dinner cigarette and blew the smoke out a crack in the window. She had a copy of the London *Economist* with her, which she read.

A half-hour after we'd left Cam Ranh Bay, and about six hours after we'd left Saigon, the train began slowing down as we approached Nha Trang.

We came in from the west, and the landscape was spectacular with mountains running down toward the sea. Picturesque brick towers—which Susan said were Cham Towers, whatever that is—dotted the foothills. There was a huge Buddha statue in the hills to our left, and on a small hill ahead, overlooking the train station, was a Gothic-style Catholic cathedral, which I remembered.

The train slowed down and stopped at the station.

This was the last stop, and people grabbed kids, luggage, and packages, and headed for the doors as the mob on the platform fought to get in.

As we pushed toward the door, Susan said, "Just keep pushing. You're the biggest guy on the train, and everyone behind us is counting on you."

We finally popped out the door onto the platform.

It was cooler here than in Saigon, and the air was about a thousand times cleaner. The sky was blue and wispy clouds floated by.

Susan and I walked along the platform into the small station house, then outside where dozens of taxis waited for fares.

We got into a taxi, and Susan said something to the driver, who did a double take at her Vietnamese, then pulled away from the station. Susan asked me, "What do you remember about that R&R hotel?"

"It was toward the south end of the beach. It was a French colonial structure, maybe three stories. It could have been white, or maybe pale blue."

She said, "Not bad for an old guy." Susan

spoke to the driver. He listened as he drove and nodded.

We passed through Nha Trang, which looked like many other seaside resort towns—white stucco buildings and red tiled roofs, palm trees, and climbing bougainvillea. The town was in better shape than I remembered it, when it was filled with military vehicles and soldiers. It had been a generally safe haven from the war, and I didn't recall any major war damage, though now and then Charles would lob in a few mortar rounds from the surrounding hills. Also, the CIA had a big sub-station in Nha Trang, a sure sign that the place was safe and had good restaurants and bars.

Within a few minutes, the taxi turned south along the beach road. The beachside buildings to our right ranged from ramshackle to bright new hotels and resorts. To our left was the beach, miles of white sand, palm trees, beach restaurants, and turquoise water under a bright sunlit sky. The beach was crescent-shaped, and two headlands jutted out into the South China Sea from the north and south. Across the water were several intriguing-looking islands of dark green vegetation. Susan said, "Oh, this is beautiful."

"It is."

"Is this how you remember it?"

"I was here only three days, and I believe I was drunk the entire time."

The taxi stopped, and the driver pointed and spoke to Susan. About a hundred meters beyond a concrete balustrade that ran along the road was a big, white, three-story stucco building with two wings jutting out from the main section. A blue and white sign read *Grand Hotel*.

Susan said, "The driver says this was one of the hotels used by the Americans during the war. It was called the Grand then, got a Communist name change to Nha Khach 44—which just means Hotel Number 44—and it's now the Grand again. Look familiar?"

"Could be. Ask him if there's a waitress named Lucy in the bar."

Susan smiled, said something to the driver, and he drove in between two tall pillars, into a circular driveway, in the center of which was an ornamental pool.

The place did look familiar, including the veranda out front where people were sitting and drinking. I could almost picture Lucy waiting on tables. I said, "This has to be the place."

The driver let us off at the front steps, we collected our bags from the trunk, and I paid him.

As the taxi pulled away, I said to Susan, "They might not have any rooms."

"Money talks."

We carried our bags up the wide steps, through a set of screen doors, and into the lobby.

The lobby was very run-down and sparse, but had fifteen-foot ceilings with crumbling plaster moldings, and an air of having once been elegant. Along the right-hand wall was a long counter with a keyboard on the wall, and behind the counter sat a young clerk, asleep in a chair. Susan asked me, "So, is this it?"

I looked through an arched opening off the left side of the lobby and saw the dining room, more faded elegance, and open French doors that led to the veranda. I nodded. "This is it."

"Great."

Susan hit the desk bell, and the clerk jumped like he'd just heard the whistle of an incoming round.

He composed himself, and he and Susan began the negotiations. Susan turned to me and said, "Okay, he says he has only expensive rooms left. He has two on the third floor. Each room has its own bath, and hot water in the morning. They're big rooms, but big is relative here. He wants seventy-five bucks a night for each room, which is a joke, and I offered him two hundred each for the week. Okay?"

Last time I was here, the army paid, and this time, the army was still paying. I said, "Fine. You staying the week?"

"No, but I made a better deal for the two weekly rates. He wants dollars."

I took out my wallet and began counting out

four hundred dollars, but Susan said, "I'm paying for my own room."

"Tell this guy I was here during the war, and
they had hot water 24/7, and the place was a lot
cleaner when the American army ran it."

Susan informed me, "I don't think he cares."

We filled out registration cards and showed
our passports and visas, which the guy absolutely insisted he had to hold on to by law. Susan gave him ten dollars instead.

We each gave him two hundred dollars, and
he gave us receipts for a hundred dollars,
which was interesting math. He gave us each a
key, then hit his bell, and a bellboy appeared.
The kid looked about ten, but he managed to
get Susan's backpack on and carry my suitcase
up three flights of stairs. As we climbed the
stairs, Susan asked, "Is the elevator broken?"

"The elevator runs fine, but it's not in this
building. It's in that nice new place next door."
I added, "You can stay there, if you'd like. I
have to stay here."

"I know. I didn't mean to complain. This is
actually quite . . . charming. Quaint."

We got up to the third floor. The hallways
were wide, and the ceiling was high. Above
each door was a screened transom to provide
for cross-ventilation.

We came to my room, Number 308, and the
kid went in with the luggage.

Susan and I followed. The room was actually big and held three single beds, as though it were still an R&R hotel for soldiers. Each bed had a wooden frame around it, from which hung mosquito netting. I remembered the mosquito netting from last time. Nostalgia is basically the ability to forget the things that sucked.

The plain stucco walls were painted a strange sky blue, and there was an odd assortment of floor fans, lamps, and cheap modern furniture arranged haphazardly around the large floor space. A paddle fan hung from the high ceiling, which was also painted blue.

The evidence that the Americans had once been here was a lot of electrical wiring in metal channels running along the walls to standard American electrical outlets, which now had adapters plugged into them to accept Asian-made appliances. Yes, this was definitely the place.

I said, "Well . . . not bad."

Susan, trying to be a sport, said, "Great mosquito netting."

I opened the louvered doors to the balcony, letting in a nice sea breeze.

We stood on the balcony, looking out across the front lawn, the circular drive, and the ornamental pool, to the palm-lined white beach across the road. I could see a lot of chaise lounges on the beach, but not a lot of people around.

Susan said, "Look at that water and that beach and those mountains and those islands out there. This was a good idea to come to Nha Trang. Okay, I'll go to my room and unpack and get cleaned up." She looked at her watch. "Let's say drinks on the veranda at six. Is that okay?"

I said, "Make it six-thirty. I have to drop by the Immigration police station, and tell them where I'm staying."

"Oh . . . do you want me to come with you?"

"No. I'll see you on the veranda at six-thirty. If I'm late, don't be overly concerned, but if I'm very late, then make inquiries."

"Let them know you're traveling with someone. They're not as likely to try anything if they know you aren't alone."

"I'll see how it plays. You may have noticed that there's no telephone in the room. So, if I need to call you, I'll have the front desk look for you. Let them know where you'll be."

"Okay." She looked at her key and said, "I'm in 304."

"I need to get some photocopies made."

"Post office. Buu dien."

"See you later."

She left with the bellboy, and I stayed on the balcony, looking at the sea.

It was hard to believe that not so many days ago, I was on the other side of that water and across a wide continent.

Somewhere in the back of my mind, I think I

always knew I would come back to Vietnam. And here I was.

The sleepy desk clerk called a taxi for me. I went outside and within a minute one pulled into the circular driveway. I got in and said, "Buu dien. Le Bureau de poste. Post office. Biet?"

He nodded and off we went to the buu dien in the center of town, about a ten-minute drive. I told the cab driver to wait, and I went inside. For a thousand dong, about ten cents, I had three copies each made of my passport and visa, and three copies of Colonel Mang's note.

I got back into my taxi and told the driver, "Phong Quan Ly Nguoi Nuoc Ngoi." I guess I got that right because a few minutes later, we pulled up to the Immigration police station, instead of a bottled water vendor. The cabbie pantomimed that he'd wait down the block.

The police station was a modest stucco building with an open archway instead of a door. The waiting room was light and airy, and was populated with the usual suspects—backpackers and Viet-Kieus, trying to deal with bureaucratic stupidity and laziness.

This little police facility seemed a lot more informal than the forbidding Ministry of Public Security in Saigon, and there were bicycles in the waiting room as well as sand on the floor from the beach.

I presented photocopies of my visa and passport to a bored-looking policeman sitting at a desk in a small alcove, and showed him a copy of my note from Colonel Mang. He read it, picked up his phone, and called someone. He said to me, "Sit."

I stood.

A minute later, another uniformed guy came into the room, ignored me, and took the note from the desk guy and read it. Then he looked at me, and said in passable English, "Where you stay?"

"Grand Hotel."

He nodded, as though the Grand Hotel had already called and reported my presence, and most probably the presence of my traveling companion as well. I was also sure that Mang had alerted the Immigration Police to my expected visit.

The guy asked me, "You here with lady?"

"Meet lady on train. Not my lady."

"Yes?" He seemed to buy this, probably because of the separate rooms.

The cop said to me, "You stay one week."

"Maybe."

"Where you go leave Nha Trang?"

"Hue."

All this was going on in the waiting room with an interested audience of Aussies, Americans, and others.

The cop asked, "Lady go with you?"

"Maybe."

"Okay, you leave passport and visa. Give you later."

I was prepared for this and knowing first-hand that cops don't like negative responses, I said, "Okay." I took the photocopy of my passport and visa from the other cop's desk and gave them to him, along with a five-dollar bill, which he quickly pocketed.

I said, "Have a good day." I turned and headed for the door.

"Stop."

I looked back at the cop.

He asked, "How you go to Hue?"

"Bus or train."

"Yes? You come here and show ticket. You need travel stamp."

"Okay." I left.

The taxi was waiting down the block, and I got in. "Grand Hotel."

The taxi headed south along the beach road. I recalled spending a lot of time on the beach when I was here, along with the other two guys in my room, both of whom were combat vets, but not from my unit. All of us had done something really brave and stupid to get this three-day R&R, and all of us had varying degrees of jungle rot, which was helped by the sun and salt water.

There were maybe a hundred guys in the Grand Hotel, and the place resembled a home for burnouts during the day. We slept too much, and we drank too much beer on the beach.

At night, the walking wounded came alive, and we'd stay out until dawn, hitting every bar, whorehouse, and massage parlor in town until the sun came up. Then we'd sleep on the beach or in the hotel, and do it all over again on night two, then again on the last night. Men came and went, and not everyone's three days coincided, but you could tell the first-day guys from the third-day guys: Day One was sort of culture shock—you couldn't believe you were here. Day Two, you drank and fucked your brains out. Day Three, with what was left of your brain, you drank and fucked even more because you were going back to hell.

Aside from some improvement in my jungle sores, crotch rot, and immersion foot, I rejoined my unit in much worse shape than when I'd left. Everyone did, but that's what rest and recuperation is all about.

The taxi pulled into the driveway of the Grand and deposited me at the front steps.

Inside my room, I unpacked and showered in cold water. There was no soap or shampoo, but there was a towel, and I left the bathroom and dried off in the bedroom where there was some ventilation from the fan and the open balcony.

There was a knock at the door. I went to the

door, but there was no peephole. I said, "Who is it?"

"Me."

"Okay . . ." I wrapped my towel around me and opened the door.

Susan said, "Oh . . . did I catch you at a bad moment?"

"Come in."

She came in and closed the door behind her. "How did it go?"

"It went fine." She was wearing white slacks, a gray T-shirt that said *Q-Bar, Saigon*, and sandals. I said, "Don't peek, and I'll get dressed."

She went out on the balcony while I put on a pair of black chinos and a white golf shirt. As I dressed, I related my brief meeting with the Immigration Police, mentioning that they knew we'd checked in together. I said, "Okay. I'm decent."

She came back into the room, and I slipped into a pair of docksiders and said, "Let's go have a drink."

We got down to the lobby, walked through the empty dining room that had a service bar in the corner, and went out onto the veranda.

Only about half the café tables were filled, and we seated ourselves near the railing.

The sun was behind the hotel now, and the veranda was in the shade. A sea breeze blew across the lawn and rustled the palms.

The other guests were all Westerners, mostly

middle-aged. The Grand Hotel was a bit upscale for backpackers, not quaint or charming to Japanese and Koreans who had money, and absolutely unacceptable to any class of middle-aged Americans, except maybe schoolteachers. I concluded that everyone there, except us, were Europeans.

It was very nice on this old-fashioned white stucco veranda with paddle fans overhead, the smell of salt water, the wide lawn, and the turquoise waters stretching out to the green islands. It would have been perfect if I had a drink, but there were no serving people around. I said, "I think we have to get our own drinks."

"I'll go. What do you want?"

"I'll go," I said, as I sat on my ass. Women understand that this is total bullshit, and Susan stood. "What do you want?"

"A cold beer. And see if they have any snacks. I'm starving. Thanks."

She went through the French doors into the dining room.

I recalled sitting here almost thirty years ago, and I remembered when the female staff were plentiful and very attentive, thrilled out of their minds to be working here for the Americans while out there, their country was disintegrating, and their fathers, brothers, and husbands were bleeding and dying alongside the Americans who were so far from home; but here in

Nha Trang, there was a sign outside the barbed wire that said *Off-Limits to Death*. Not a literal sign, of course, but an unspoken understanding that you were not going to meet a violent end in this place.

And for the infantrymen and the helicopter door gunners and the chopper pilots and the long-range patrol guys and the tunnel rats and the combat medics, and for all the guys who had seen what the insides of people looked like, Nha Trang was more than a haven; it was a reaffirmation that somewhere amid all this shooting and dying, a place existed where people didn't carry guns, and where the day ended with a sunset that you knew you'd live to see, and the night held no terror, and the morning sun rose over the South China Sea and illuminated a beach of sleeping, not dead, bodies.

Susan came back without the drinks and said, "The waitress will bring our drinks." She sat. "You're in luck. The waitress is Lucy."

"Great."

An elderly woman came through the French doors carrying a tray. She looked about eighty, with a weathered face and betel-nut-stained teeth and lips, but she was probably closer to my age.

Susan said, "Paul, this is your old friend, Lucy."

The woman cackled and put down the tray.

Susan said something to the woman, and they

chatted. Susan turned to me and said, "She was a chambermaid here when she was a young girl, and this place was a resort for the French plantation owners. She stayed on when the Americans took it over as an R&R hotel, then in 1975 it became a Communist Party hotel, and now that it's a public hotel again." Susan added, "In 1968, she was a young cocktail waitress, and she says she remembers an American who looks like you who used to chase her around the tables, trying to pinch her ass."

The old lady cackled again.

I suspected the last part of Susan's story was not true. But to be a sport, I said, "Tell her she's still beautiful—co-dep. And I'd still like to pinch her ass."

The old lady laughed at co-dep before Susan could translate the English, and when Susan got to the ass-pinching part, the woman broke into a girlish laugh, said something, smacked me on the shoulder playfully, and trotted off.

Susan smiled and said, "She says you're an old goat." She added, "She also said, 'Welcome back.'"

I nodded. Welcome back, indeed.

Nha Trang and the Grand Hotel and the old woman had escaped most of the war, but in the end, nothing escaped.

Susan had a gin and tonic, and I poured a bottle of Tiger beer into a plastic cup. There was a bowl of something on the table that looked like trail mix, but I couldn't identify what trail it came from.

I raised my glass and said, "Thanks for your help and your company."

We touched glasses, and she said, "Thanks for inviting me."

We both got a laugh out of that.

We sipped our drinks and watched the sea. It was one of those perfect times when sun, sea, and wind were just right, the beer is cold, the hard day's journey has ended, and the woman is beautiful.

Susan asked me, "What did you do when you were here besides get drunk?"

"Mostly lay in the sun and had some good food." I added, "A lot of the guys were stressed out, of course, so we played a lot of cards, and most of us had jungle sores, so the sun and sea were good for the skin."

She lit a cigarette and asked, "How about women?"

I replied, "Women, except for employees, were not allowed in the hotel."

"Were you allowed *out* of the hotel?"

"Yes."

"Ah, ha. And were you involved with anyone from home when you were here?"

"I was. Her name was Peggy, a good Irish Catholic Southie."

She drew on her cigarette and looked out to

sea. "And how about in '72? Were you involved with anyone then?"

"I was married. It was a brief marriage, and it ended when I returned. In fact, before I returned."

She thought about that awhile and asked, "And since then?"

"Since then I made two promises to myself—never go back to Vietnam and never get married again."

She smiled. "Which was worse? Combat or marriage?"

"They were both fun in their own way." I asked her, "And how about you? You're on."

She sipped her drink, lit another cigarette, and said, "I've never been married."

"That's it?"

"That's it. Do you want a sexual history?"

I wanted to get to dinner before eight, so I said, "No."

The old woman came by, and I looked at her as Susan ordered another round and chatted with her. She *could* have been Lucy, but Lucy existed in my mind as a happy, funny girl, who traded mock insults with the soldiers who were all in love with her, but she wasn't for sale. Guys always want what they can't have, and Lucy was the grand prize at the Grand Hotel. Assuming this old crone was not Lucy, I hoped Lucy had survived the war, married her

Viet soldier boyfriend, and that they were happy somewhere.

Susan asked me, "What are you thinking about?"

"I was thinking that the last time I was here, you weren't even born."

"I was born, but not toilet-trained."

The second round came, and we sat watching the sky darken. I could see lights in the thatched cafés and souvenir stands down on the beach. The breeze picked up, and it got cooler, but was still pleasant.

About halfway through our third round, Susan asked me, "Don't you need to contact someone back in the States?"

"I was supposed to contact you in Saigon and say I'd arrived. But you're here."

She replied, "The hotel has a fax machine, and I faxed Bill at his office and his home and told him we'd arrived, and where we were staying. He knows to contact the consulate, who will contact your people." She added, "I stood over the clerk while he faxed, got my original back, and ate it. Okay?"

"Good tradecraft. Was Bill surprised to get a message from you in Nha Trang? Or did you tell him about your trip when you called him from the Rex?"

"I still wasn't sure I wanted to go with you at that point." She added, "I haven't gotten his reply yet."

"If I'd gotten a message from my girlfriend that she went to a beach resort with a guy, I might not bother to reply."

She thought about that and said, "I asked him to acknowledge receipt." She added, "When Westerners who live here travel, they always tell someone where they're going . . . in case there's a problem. Also, this is official business. Right? So he needs to reply."

"Or at least acknowledge receipt."

"Actually . . . I was feeling a little . . . guilty. So I asked him to join us here."

This sort of took me by surprise, and I guess my face betrayed that surprise, and maybe something else. I said, "That's nice," which was pretty lame.

She stared at me in the dim light. She said, "What I really told him was that it was over between us."

I didn't know what to say, so I just sat there.

She went on. "He knows that, anyway. I didn't want to do it that way, but I had to. This has nothing to do with you, so don't get an inflated ego."

I started to say something, but she said, "Just listen. I realized that I was having more fun . . . that I'd rather be in the Q-Bar with you than him."

"High praise, indeed."

I saw that I'd interrupted a moment of true confession with my big mouth and said, "Sorry. I just sometimes get . . . uncomfortable—"

"Okay. Let me finish. You're an interesting man, but you're very conflicted about life and probably love. And part of your problem is that you don't read yourself very well." She looked at me closely and said, "Look at me, Paul."

I looked at her.

She asked, "How did you feel when I told you I'd asked Bill to join me?"

"Lousy." I added, "My face dropped. Did you see that?"

"It fell in your beer." She informed me, "You've been giving me a hard time, and I don't like that. You could have blown me off anytime you wanted, if you really wanted me gone. But instead, you—"

"Okay. Point made. I apologize, and I promise to be nice. Not only that . . . I want you to know I not only enjoy your company, I look forward to your company."

"Keep going."

"Right. Well, I'm extremely fond of you, I like you a lot, I miss you when you're not around, I know if I let myself go—"

"Good enough. Look, Paul, this is an artificial situation, you've got someone back home, you're here on important business, and this place is silently freaking you out. I understand all this. So, we'll just compartmentalize these few days. Fun in the sun, and whatever happens, happens. You go to Hue, and I go back to Saigon. And, God willing, we'll both find our way home."

I nodded.

So we held hands and watched the night turn from purple to black. The stars over the water were brilliant, and the waning moon cast a sliver of light on the South China Sea. A boy brought oil lamps to each of the tables, and the veranda shimmered in lights and shadow.

I paid the bill, and we walked across the lawn, across the road, and down to the beach, where Private First Class Paul Brenner had walked a long time ago.

We picked an outdoor restaurant called Coconut Grove, set among palm trees and trellises.

We sat at a small wooden table lit with a red oil lamp and ordered Tiger beers. The breeze was stronger here, and I could hear the surf fifty yards away.

The menus came, and they were in Vietnamese, English, and French, but the prices were in American.

Most of the selections were seafood, as you'd expect in a fishing town, but for ten dollars, I could experience bird's nest soup, which seemed to be an addition to the menu, since it was harvested only twice a year, and lucky for me, this was a harvest month. The nest was made of red grass and sparrow saliva, but the real selling point was that this delicacy was also an aphrodisiac. I said to Susan, "I'll have the bird's nest soup."

She smiled. "Do you need it?"

We ordered a huge plate of mixed seafood and vegetables, which the waiter grilled at tableside over a charcoal brazier.

The people around us seemed to be mostly northern Europeans, escaping the winter. Nha Trang, which had been founded by the French, had once been called the Côte d'Azur of Southeast Asia, and it seemed to be making a comeback, though it had a long way to go.

We kept ordering more seafood, and the waiter was kidding Susan about getting fat. This was a very pleasant place, and there was magic in the night air.

Susan and I kept the conversation light, the way people do who have just had an intense talk that pushed the table limits higher.

We skipped dessert and took a barefoot walk on the beach, carrying our shoes. The tide was going out, and the beach was covered with seashells and stranded marine life. A few people were surf-casting, backpackers had lit fires on the beach, and couples strolled hand in hand, including Susan and me.

The sky was crystal clear, and you could see the Milky Way, and a number of constellations. We walked south, away from the center of town, along a widening beach where new hotels sat along the coast.

About half a mile down the beach, we came upon the Nha Trang Sailing Club, an upscale place where a dance was going on inside. We

went in, ordered two beers, and danced along
with a lot of Europeans to some terrible, loud
Seventies music played by the worst band anywhere along the Pacific Rim—maybe the world.
But it was fun, and we chatted with some Europeans and even switched partners now and
then. A few of the men pegged me for a Vietnam
veteran, but that's as far as it went; no one, myself included, wanted to talk about it.

I don't know if I was drunk, mellowed out,
or just happy about something, but for the first
time in a long time, I felt at peace with myself
and my surroundings.

We left the Nha Trang Sailing Club after one
A.M. and as we walked back toward the colored
lights of the cafés on the beach, Susan asked
me, "Is what you're doing here dangerous?"

"I just need to find someone and question
him, then go to Hanoi and fly home."

"Where is this person? Tam Ki?"

"I don't know yet." I changed the subject and
asked her, "Susan, why are you here?"

She took her hand out of mine and lit a cigarette. She said, "Well . . . it's not as important or
. dramatic as why you're here."

"It's important to you, or you wouldn't be
here. What was his name?"

She took a long draw on her cigarette and
said, "Sam. We were childhood sweethearts,
dated through college—he went to Dart-
mouth. We went to B-school together—you

may have seen his picture in my office, the group shot."

Harry Handsome, but I didn't say that.

"We lived together in New York . . . I was totally crazy about him, and couldn't imagine a world without him. We got engaged, and we were going to get married, buy a house in Connecticut, have children, and live happily ever after." She stayed silent for a while, then continued, "I was in love with him since we were kids, and right up to the time he came home one day and told me he was involved with another woman. A woman at work. He packed his bags and left."

"I'm sorry."

"Well . . . these things happen. But I couldn't believe it was happening to *me*. I never saw it coming, which made me wonder about myself. Anyway, I couldn't get over it, and I quit my job in New York and went home to Lenox for a while. Everyone there was totally stunned. Sam Thorpe was the boy next door, and the wedding was all planned. My father wanted to do an autopsy on him while he was still alive." She laughed.

We continued walking, and she said, "Well, I tried to get over it, but there were too many memories in Lenox. I was crying too much, and everyone around me was starting to lose patience with me, but I missed him, and I just couldn't get myself together. Long story short, I

looked around for an overseas job that no one
else wanted, and six months after Sam left, I
was in Saigon."

"Did you ever hear from him again?"

"I sure did. A few months after I got to
Saigon, he wrote me a long letter, saying he'd
made the biggest mistake of his life, and would
I come home and marry him. He reminded me
of all the good times we had as kids—school
dances, our first kiss, family parties, and all that.
He said we were part of each other's lives, and
we should be married and have children and
grow old together."

"I guess the other thing didn't work out for
him."

"I guess not."

"And what did you reply to him?"

"I didn't." She took a deep breath. "He broke
my heart, and I knew it could never be the same
again. So, to save us both a lot of misery, I just
didn't answer his letter. He wrote a few more
times, then stopped writing." She threw her cigarette in the surf. "I heard from mutual friends
that he got married to a girl in New York."

We walked along the water's edge, and the
wet sand and surf felt good on my feet. I
thought about Susan and Sam, and while I was
at it, about Cynthia and Paul. In a perfect world,
people would be like penguins and mate for
life and stay close to the iceberg where they
were born. But men and women get restless,

they stray, and they break each other's hearts. When I was younger, I thought too much with my dick. Still do. But not as much.

I asked Susan, "Would it have made a difference if he had come to Saigon, instead of asking you to come home?"

"That's a good question. I went home once on leave, and I think he knew I was home, though by that time, I guess we both knew we couldn't see each other again. But I don't know what I would have done if he'd shown up on my doorstep on Dong Khoi Street."

"What do you think?"

"I think that a man who did what he did, and who was truly sorry, would not have written a letter. He would have come to Saigon and taken me home."

"And you would have gone with him?"

"I would have gone with a man who had the courage and conviction to come and get me. But that wasn't Sam. I think he was exploring his options by mail." She glanced at me. "Someone like you would have just come to Saigon without the stupid letters."

I didn't respond directly to that, but I found myself saying, "Cynthia and I live a few hundred miles from each other, and I'm not making the move, though I think she would."

"Women will usually go to where the man is. You should think about why you're not going to where she is."

I changed the subject back to her and said, "You got away from what you were running from. Time to move on."

She didn't reply, and we kept walking along the wet sand. She threw her sandals onto the beach and walked into the water up to her knees. I waded in beside her.

She said, "So, that's my sad story. But you know what? The move to Saigon was one of the best decisions of my life."

"That's a little scary."

She laughed and said, "No, I mean it. I grew up real fast here. I was spoiled, coddled, and totally clueless. I was Daddy's girl, and Sam's sweetheart, and Mommy's perfect daughter. I belonged to the Junior League, for God's sake. But it was okay. I was happy." She added, "I think I was dull and boring."

"You certainly fixed that problem."

"Right. I realized that Sam was bored with me. I never even flirted with other guys. So, when he said he was screwing this woman at work, I felt so betrayed . . . I should have gone out and fucked his best friend." She laughed, then said, "Are you sorry you asked?"

"No. Now I understand."

"Yeah. So, anyway, when I first got here, I was terrified, and I almost turned around and went home."

"I know the feeling."

She laughed. "My tour here can't possibly

compare to yours, but for me, this was a big step toward growing up. I knew if I went home, I'd . . . well, who knows?" She said, "I told you, you wouldn't have recognized me three years ago. If you'd met me in New York, you wouldn't have spoken to me for five minutes."

"I'm not sure about that. But I hear you. So, is your character development nearly complete?"

"You tell me."

"I told you. It's time to go home. There comes a point of diminishing returns."

"How do you know when that is?"

"*You* have to know." I said to her, "During the war, the military limited the tour of duty here to twelve or thirteen months. The first year, if you survived it, made a man out of you. If you volunteered to stay, the second year made something else out of you." I added, "At some point, as I mentioned in Apocalypse Now, you couldn't go home, unless you were ordered to leave, or you went home in a body bag."

She didn't respond.

I said, "Look, this place isn't so bad now, and I see the attraction, but you've got your Ph.D. in life, so go home and use it for something."

"I'll think about it." She changed the subject and said, "We should take a boat out to those islands."

We stood there in the water, and I took her

hand, and we looked out at the sea and the night sky.

It was pushing 2 A.M. by the time we got to the hotel, and a guard let us in. There was no one at the front desk, so we couldn't check for messages, and we walked up the stairs to the third floor.

We got to my room first, and I opened the door and checked for a fax message. There was none, and we walked to Susan's room.

She opened the door, and there was a single sheet of paper on the floor. She went into the bedroom, turned on a lamp, and read the fax. She handed it to me, and I read: Your message received and transmitted to proper authorities. I am very hurt and angry, but it's your decision. Not mine. I think you're making a terrible mistake, and if you hadn't gone to Nha Trang with someone, we could have discussed this. Now, I think it's too late. It was signed Bill.

I gave the fax sheet back to her and said, "You didn't have to show that to me."

"He's such a romantic." She added, "Notice he didn't bother to come to Nha Trang."

"You're tough on men. God knows what you're going to say about me over drinks in the Q-Bar."

She looked at me and said, "Anything I have to say about you, I'll say to you."

There was this awkward moment, and I looked around the room, which was much like my own. I noticed the snow globe on her night table and a few things hung in the open alcove. I said, "Did they give you any soap or shampoo?"

"No. But I brought my own. I should have told you."

"I'll buy some tomorrow."

"You can have half my soap bar now."

That wasn't what I had in mind when I brought up the soap problem, and we both knew it. I said, "That's okay. Well . . ."

She gave me a big hug and buried her face on my chest. She said, "Maybe before I leave. I have to think about it. Is that all right?"

"Sure."

We kissed, and for a moment, I thought she already thought about it, but she broke away and said, "Okay . . . good night. Breakfast? Ten?"

"Fine." I don't like lingering good-byes, so I turned and left.

Back in my room, I took off my shirt and peeled off my wet pants and threw them on one of the beds.

I pulled a chair out to the balcony and sat with my feet on the wrought iron railing. I looked up at the starlit sky and yawned.

I could hear music from the beach and voices carried on the night breeze, and the surf hitting the sand. I listened for a knock on my door, but there was no knock.

My mind drifted back to May 1968, when I was here in Nha Trang, with only one worry in

the world—staying alive. Like a lot of middle-
aged men who have been to war, there were
times when I felt that war had a stark and honest simplicity to it, an almost transcendental
quality that focused the mind and the body as
nothing else had done before, or would do
again.

And yet, for all the adrenaline rushes, and
the out-of-body experiences, and the incandescent flashes of truth and light, war, like a drug,
took its toll on the body, the mind, and the
soul. There *was* a point of diminishing returns,
and a price to pay for spitting in the eye of
Death, and getting away with it.

I stared at the stars and thought of Cynthia,
of Susan, and of Paul Brenner, and of Vietnam,
Part Three.

I got into bed and pulled down the mosquito
netting, but I couldn't sleep, so I played taps in
my head: *Day is done, gone the sun, from the
lakes, from the hills, from the sky, all is well,
safely rest, God is nigh . . .*

★

CHAPTER SEVENTEEN

───────★───────

I got to the veranda at 10 a.m., and Susan was already sitting at a table with a pot of coffee, reading her Economist.

There were a few other people having breakfast, all Westerners, so I concluded I wasn't under the eye of the Ministry of Public Security. I kind of wished I was because I had no anti-government activities planned for the day.

The great minds in Washington had scheduled this as a down week, the week in which Mr. Paul Brenner, Vietnam veteran, established his innocence as a tourist. This was standard tradecraft. Very short trips to faraway places always look suspicious to immigration and customs people. Similarly, visas applied for shortly before a major trip also look suspicious, as Colonel Mang indicated. But it was too late to worry about that.

I sat and said to Susan, "Good morning."

She put down the magazine and said, "Good morning. How did you sleep?"

"Alone."

She smiled and poured me a cup of coffee.

Susan was wearing khaki slacks, as was I, and a sleeveless navy blue pullover.

It was a beautiful morning, the temperature was in the mid-seventies, and there wasn't a cloud in the sky.

The waiter came, and Susan informed me, "They have only two breakfasts—Viet and Western. Pho soup or fried eggs. They don't know scrambled, so don't ask."

"Eggs."

Susan ordered in Vietnamese.

I asked her, "Did you have hot water?"

"Oh, I forgot to tell you. There's an electric hot water tank above the toilet. Didn't you see it?"

"I thought it was part of the toilet."

"No. There's a switch you turn on, and it heats about twenty gallons of water. Takes awhile. They turn off the electric to the tanks at 10 A.M."

"I didn't have any soap anyway."

"We'll go to the market later and get a few things."

I asked her, "Do you think that when Bill contacted the consulate, he mentioned to them that you'd come along to Nha Trang?"

She lit a cigarette and replied, "I thought about that. On the one hand, he should have told them, if he's serious about being useful to the consulate. On the other hand, they all know he and I are—were—dating, so maybe he's embarrassed to tell them I took off with you."

I nodded.

She asked, "Do you think you'd be in trouble with your firm if they discovered we'd made this trip together?"

I replied, "They would not be happy, but what are they going to do about it? Send me to Vietnam?"

She smiled. "Sounds like something you guys said when you were here."

"Every day."

"Well . . . I'm sorry if this winds up causing you a problem."

"No problem." As long as Karl didn't rat me out to Cynthia. But he wouldn't do that—unless it served a purpose for him.

The eggs came. Susan said to me, "I was thinking about what I told you about Sam, and why I'm here and all that. I didn't want you to think that a man was the cause of me being here."

"That's exactly what I thought."

"I mean, he was not the *cause* of me being here. *I* made that decision. He was the catalyst."

"Got it."

"I needed to prove something to myself, not to Sam. Now I think I'm the person I want to be, and I'm ready to find the right person to be with."

"Good."

"Tell me what you think. Be honest."

"Okay. I think you got it right last night when you were drunk. I also think that you came to Vietnam with the intention of staying only as long as it took for you to make Sam interested in you again. If he'd come here to get you, you'd have gone back with him long before you proved anything to yourself. But it was important for you that he come and see that you *could* make it on your own. So, bottom line, this was all for a guy. But I think you're beyond that now."

She didn't say anything, and I wondered if she was annoyed, embarrassed, or stunned by my blinding insights. Finally, she said, "That's about it. You're a pretty sharp guy."

"I do this for a living. Not advice to the lovelorn, but I analyze bullshit all day. I don't have a lot of patience for bullshit, or self-justification. Everybody knows what they did and why they did it. You either keep it to yourself, or you tell it like it is."

She nodded. "I knew I could trust you to tell me what you thought."

"The question remains, What are you going to do next? If you stay here, stay for the right reasons. Same if you go home. My concern for you, Ms. Weber, is the same concern I had for the guys I knew who couldn't leave here."

"How about guys who stay in the army all their lives?"

"You mean me?"

"Yes, you."

"Point made. So maybe I know what I'm talking about."

"Why did you come back?"

"They said it was important. They said they needed me. And I was bored."

"What's so important?"

"I don't know. But I'll tell you what—when I'm out of here, we'll meet someday for a drink in New York, Washington, or Massachusetts, and I'll tell you what I discovered."

She replied, "Make it Washington. You owe me a tour of the city. But first, make sure you get out of here."

"Did it twice already."

"Good. Ready to go?"

"First, tell me how you knew I was working for the army."

"Oh . . . I guess someone told me. I guess it was Bill."

"He had no need to know that."

"Then I guess it was someone in the consulate. What difference does it make?"

I didn't reply.

She looked at me and said, "Actually, I wasn't asked by Bill to do a favor for the consulate. They asked me directly. The CIA guy there. He gave me a very sketchy briefing. Mostly your bio. Nothing about the mission. I don't know anything about that. Only a few details about you." She added, "The CIA guy said you were army Criminal Investigation Division, and this was about a criminal matter, not a spy thing."

"Who's the CIA guy?"

"You know I can't tell you that." She smiled

and said, "He gave me your photo, and I took the job right there on the spot."

I asked her, "When did this take place?"

"Oh . . . about four days before you got here."

The first time they sent me here, they at least gave me sixty days' notice, a thirty-day leave, and recommended I make out a will.

I stood. "Is breakfast included?"

"If they don't include soap, why would they include breakfast?"

"Good observation." I called over the waiter and paid for breakfast, which came to two bucks.

We walked out to the beach road where about two dozen cyclo drivers were parked. They descended on us, and Susan picked two drivers, one of whom had an arm missing. We got in the cyclos, and Susan said, "Cho Dam."

Her guy had the missing arm, and I said to Susan, "Ask him if he's a veteran."

She asked him, and he seemed first surprised at her Vietnamese, then surprised that anyone cared if he was a veteran. She said to me, "He says he is."

As we rode up the beach road, Susan conversed with her driver, and I knew she was telling him that I was a veteran.

As our cyclos came side by side, she said, "He was a soldier here in Nha Trang, and he was captured when the Communists took the city. His entire regiment was imprisoned in the soccer stadium here, without food or water for many days. He had a wound on his arm that turned gangrenous." She paused. "His comrades removed his arm without anesthesia."

I looked at the driver, and our eyes met.

Susan continued, "He was so sick that he wasn't sent to a re-education camp, so he was able to stay in Nha Trang with his family, and he recovered."

I guess that's the Viet equivalent of a story with a happy ending. Maybe I should stop taking cyclos, or at least stop asking these wraiths about their war service. I said to Susan, "Tell him I was proud to serve alongside the Army of South Vietnam."

Susan relayed this to the guy, and he took his one hand off the handle bar and snapped a quick salute.

My driver was listening to all this, and he began talking to Susan.

Susan listened and translated, "He says he was a sailor at Cam Ranh Bay and had the chance to escape by boat as the Communists approached, but he left his ship to make his way back to his village outside Nha Trang. He was captured along the way by North Vietnamese troops and spent four years in a re-education camp."

I said to Susan, "Tell him . . . America still remembers its South Vietnamese allies," which was total bullshit, but sounded good.

So, we rode along the nice beach road under

an azure sky, the smell of the sea in my nostrils, and the human wreckage of a lost cause propelling us on.

The street we were on dead-ended at a gated marketplace. We dismounted, and I gave each of the drivers a fiver, which made them very happy. At this rate, I'd be broke by next week, but I'm a sucker for a sad story. Also, I think, I was feeling some survivor's guilt, which I'd never felt before.

We wandered through the market, and I got a chunk of mystery soap wrapped in tissue paper, and a bottle of American shampoo, whose brand, I think, they stopped making in '68. Susan bought me a pair of Ho Chi Minh sandals, made out of tire treads, and I bought Susan a T-shirt that said *Nha Trang is the lovely beach— Tell the dears at home.*

Who writes this stuff?

Susan also picked up two silk blouses. She said, "This is cheaper than in Saigon. The silkworm farms and factories are in this area. I should come here to shop."

"For the factories?"

She laughed.

We wandered around the outdoor stalls for about an hour, and Susan picked up a scented candle, a bottle of rice wine, and a cheap vinyl tote to carry the junk. Women love to shop.

We went to the flower section, and Susan bought branches of Tet blossoms tied with twine. She said, "For your room. Chuc Mung Nam Moi."

We took cyclos back to the hotel, checked for messages, but there were none, then went to my room.

Susan tied the Tet blossoms to the mosquito net frame of my bed. She said, "This will bring you good luck and keep the evil spirits away."

"I like evil spirits."

She smiled, and we stood there a few seconds, looking at each other.

She asked me, "Do you want to go to the beach?"

"Sure."

She took my soap and shampoo out of her tote and gave them to me. "I'll knock on your door when I'm ready." She hesitated, then left.

I got into my bathing suit, pulled on a gym shirt, and slipped into my brand-new Ho Chi Minh sandals.

I put my wallet, passport, visa, vouchers, and airline tickets in a plastic bag, wondering if the desk clerk would hold this stuff, or go to America with it.

I sat in a chair and watched a gecko crawl up the wall. I ran some stuff through my mind as I watched the gecko and waited for Susan.

Susan Weber. Probably she was what she said she was: an American expat businesswoman. But there were signs that she had a second job. In a country where our intelligence assets were limited, but our needs were big and getting bigger, it was common practice to recruit friends in the American business or expat community to do a little something for Uncle Sam on the side.

There were at least three agencies who did this kind of recruiting overseas—State Department Intelligence, Military Intelligence, or the Central Intelligence Agency.

And then there was American-Asian itself. The whole operation looked legit, but it also had all the bells and whistles of a CIA front.

The other question was Susan Weber's fondness for Paul Brenner. You can fake a lot of things in life—women fake orgasms, and men fake whole relationships—but unless I was really losing my ability to read people, Susan was honestly taken with me. It wouldn't be the first time something like this happened, which was why intelligence agencies instinctively distrusted their human employees and loved their spy satellites.

In any case, Susan Weber and Paul Brenner were on the brink of a sexual liaison that wasn't part of the original script and could only lead to disaster.

There was a knock on the door, and I called out, "It's open."

Susan came in, and I stood.

She was wearing the Nha Trang T-shirt I

bought her—*tell the dears at home*—and it came down to her knees. She had on sandals and was carrying her new tote.

She smiled and said, "Love your sandals." She took a plastic cup out of her tote, filled with white powder. She said, "This is boric acid. You sprinkle it around your bed and luggage."

"Then what? Pray for rain?"

"It keeps the bugs away. Specifically, cockroaches."

I put the cup on my night table and we left the room. On the way down the stairs, I said, "I have all my valuables in this plastic bag. Can I trust these with the front desk?"

"Sure. I'll take care of it."

We got down to the lobby, and Susan spoke to the desk clerk. The deal was that we had to inventory everything, including Susan's money and passport as well as my own stuff. As all this was going on, I said to her, "Mind if I snoop through your passport?"

She hesitated a second, then said, "No. Terrible photo."

I looked at her photo, which, of course, was not that terrible, and I noticed that the passport had been issued from the General Passport Office a little over three years before, which was consistent with her arrival here. I looked at her photo and saw that her hair was much shorter then, and there was something very sad and innocent about her expression—but maybe I was just projecting because of what she'd told me. In any case, the woman standing beside me looked a lot more confident and assured than the woman in the passport photo.

I flipped the pages and saw that she had three entry stamps for the U.S., two for New York and one for Washington. That was not totally consistent with her claim that she'd never been to Washington—but it could have just been an entry point for a connecting flight to somewhere else, like Boston.

Her Viet visa stamp was different from mine, and was probably a work visa rather than a tourist visa. It had been renewed once, a year ago, and I pictured her at Section C of the Ministry for Public Security, two years into her tour, and giving everyone a hard time.

She'd also been to Hong Kong, Sydney, Bangkok, and Tokyo, which was either for R&R or business. Nothing tricky there. But the Washington thing stuck out.

I put the passport back on the counter, and the clerk gave us the handwritten receipt, which we all had to sign, and Susan gave him a dollar.

We walked across the road, and the beach was fairly empty. We picked two chaise lounges, and a hundred kids descended on us, carrying everything in the world we'd ever need. We took two chaise mattresses and towels, two peeled pineapples on sticks, and two Cokes. Susan passed out dong and chased off the kids.

I pulled off my gym shirt and Susan removed her T-shirt. She was wearing a skimpy two-piece, flesh-colored number, and she had an absolutely voluptuous body, all tanned and nicely toned.

She noticed I was glancing at her—staring, actually. I looked at the water. "Nice beach."

We sat at the edge of our lounges and ate the pineapple on a stick.

As we ate, vendors came by, selling food, beverages, maps, silk paintings, Viet Cong flags, beach hats, and things I couldn't identify. I bought a tourist map of Nha Trang.

We went down to the water, and Susan left her tote on the chaise lounge, which she said would be safe.

We waded out until we were standing up to our necks, and I could see brilliant tropical fish in the clear water. I said, "I remember big jelly-fish all along the coast. Portuguese man-of-war."

"Same at Vung Tau. You have to keep an eye out. They can paralyze you."

"We used to throw concussion grenades in the water. It stunned the jellyfish, and hundreds of other fish would float to the surface. The kids would gather them up. They'd eat the squids alive. We thought it was gross. Now I pay twenty bucks in a sushi restaurant for raw squid."

She thought about that and said, "Concussion grenades?"

"Yeah. They're not fragmentation grenades.

You throw them in bunkers or any confined space, like tunnels. Causes concussion. Somebody figured out that you can fish with them. They cost Uncle Sam about twenty bucks apiece. But it was one of the perks of the job." I added, "Feeding people through high explosives."

"What if you needed the grenades later?"

"You order more. Munitions is one thing we never ran out of. We ran out of will."

We swam. Susan was a good, strong swimmer, and so am I, so we stayed out about an hour, and it felt great.

Back on the chaise lounge, as we dried off, the vendors returned. They could pester the hell out of you, but they didn't steal anything because within a short time, they had all your money anyway.

Several young ladies approached with bottles of oil and hand towels. Susan said to me, "You haven't had a massage since the Rex Hotel. Let me treat."

"Thanks."

We both got massages on the beach. I was feeling more like James Bond again.

We lay there on the chaise lounges; Susan read a business magazine with her sunglasses on, and I contemplated the sea and the sky.

I thought, someday I should come back here without any government involvement. Maybe Cynthia would like to join me, and we'd take a month and explore the country. But that pre-supposed that when I got out of here, I was not persona non grata, or persona in a box.

I looked over at Susan and watched her reading. She sensed me looking at her and turned to me. She said, "Isn't this nice?"

"It really is."

"Are you glad I came along?"

"I am."

"I can stay a few more days."

I replied, "If you go back to Saigon tomorrow, I think you can smooth it over with Bill."

"Who?"

"Let me ask you a personal question. Why did you get involved with him if you think so little of him?"

She put down her magazine. "Good question. Obviously, the pickings are a little slim in Saigon. A lot of the guys are married, the rest are fucking their brains out with Vietnamese women. Bill, at least, was faithful. No mistress, no prostitutes, no drugs, no bad habits—except me."

In retrospect, Bill Stanley didn't seem to me, in my brief meeting with him, to be quite such a Boy Scout. There was more to Bill Stanley, and I needed to keep that in mind.

At 6 P.M., we packed it up.

Back in the hotel, we got our stuff from the desk clerk, and we arranged to meet on the veranda at seven.

I went to my room, showered in cold water and orange soap, and took a little siesta in the raw. I woke myself up at quarter to seven, got dressed, and went down to the veranda. Susan wasn't there, but Lucy was, and she got me a cold beer.

Susan appeared a few minutes later, dressed in one of her new silk blouses, a pink one, with a little black skirt. I stood and said, "The blouse looks good on you."

She sat and said, "Well, thank you, sir. You look all tanned and rested."

"I'm on R&R."

"I'm glad this is the R&R part of your visit." She added, "I'm going to worry about you."

I didn't reply.

"I was thinking . . . I need to take a business trip to Hanoi. Maybe I can meet you there. Metropole. Saturday after next. Right?"

"How did you know that?"

"I snooped through your papers while you were snooping through my passport."

"You should forget what you saw."

"I will, except the Metropole, Saturday after next."

"I'll only be there one night."

"That's okay. I just want to be there when you arrive."

This woman knew all the right words, and she was starting to get to me. I said, "Metropole, Hanoi, Saturday after next."

"I'll be there."

We had a few beers until it got dark, then took cyclos into town.

We found a restaurant with a garden out back; a pretty hostess in an ao dai showed us to a table.

The air was fragrant with blossoms, and the cigarette smoke was carried away by a nice breeze.

We ordered fish because it was the only thing on the menu, and we talked about this and that. Susan brought up the subject of Colonel Mang, and I mentioned that I had reminded him that this was a new era of Vietnamese-American relations, and that he should get with the program.

Susan looked thoughtful, then said, "The last time we had an embassy in this country, it was in Saigon, and it was April 30, 1975. The U.S. Ambassador was on the roof of the embassy, carrying the American flag home, and General Minh was in the palace, waiting to surrender South Vietnam to the Communists. Now we have a new ambassador, this time in Hanoi, and we have some consulate staff in Saigon, including economic development people, looking for a nice building to set up shop when Hanoi gives us the go-ahead. This will be an important country for us again, and no one wants to see this new relationship screwed up. I'm talking billions of dollars in investments, oil, and raw materials. So, I don't know why you're here, or who actually sent you, but please tread lightly."

I looked at Susan Weber. She had a better grasp of geopolitics than she'd led me to believe. I said to her, "Well, I know who sent me, though I'm not sure why. But believe me when I say that it's not important enough, and I'm not important enough, to affect anything that's already been accomplished."

She replied, "Don't be so sure of that. There are lots of people in Hanoi and in Washington who don't want the two countries to have normal relations. Some of these are men of your generation, the veterans and the politicians on both sides, who will neither forgive nor forget. And many of these people are now in positions of power."

"Do you know something I don't?"

She looked at me and said, "No, but I sense something . . . we have a history here, and we've learned nothing from that history."

"I think we have. But that's not to say we're not going to make new mistakes."

She dropped the subject, and I didn't press it. It seemed to me that her concerns were those of a businessperson. But there was more to this than business; if it was just business, and an unsolved murder, then our new ambassador in Hanoi would now be talking to the Vietnamese government asking their help in finding the witness to an American homicide case. So, this was about something else, and whatever it was, Washington wasn't telling Hanoi; they weren't even telling me.

After dinner, we took a stroll down to the beach and walked the beach back to the hotel. The subject of Vietnam did not come up again.

Upstairs, I walked Susan to her room and went in. There were no messages left on the floor, and no clear signals to me from Ms. Weber. I said, "I had a nice day."

"Me, too. I'm looking forward to tomorrow."

We arranged to meet again for breakfast at 8 A.M.

She said, "Don't forget boric acid and the hot water heater."

Back in my room, I sprinkled the boric acid around my bed and my luggage. A really first-rate hotel would do that for you.

The sun and sea had knocked me out, and I was half asleep as soon as I hit the bed.

My last thought was that I didn't recall seeing the snow globe on Susan's night table.

★

CHAPTER EIGHTEEN

—————★—————

I got to the veranda before Susan, found a table, and ordered a pot of coffee.

It was another perfect day in Nha Trang.

Susan appeared, dressed in yet another pair of cotton pants, green, this time, with a white boat-neck pullover. That backpack must have been bigger than it looked.

I stood, pulled out her chair, and said, "Good morning."

"Good morning." She poured herself some coffee and said, "Last night I dreamt of you."

I didn't reply.

"We were in the Metropole in Hanoi. I've stayed there, so I could visualize it. It was very real." She laughed at me. "We had cocktails, dinner, and danced in the hotel lounge."

I said, "Let's try to do that."

The waiter came by, and we ordered Breakfast Number One, pho.

She said, "I could turn this place into at least a two-star hotel for American servicemen who stayed here. The R&R Grand. Hooker Night in the Full Metal Jacket lounge. I'll make Lucy the hostess. What do you think?"

I didn't reply.

She said, "That was a little insensitive. Whatever you did to get here wasn't funny. I do apologize."

"Forget it." In fact, it wasn't funny, and I couldn't forget it. I said, "Battle of the A Shau Valley, May '68. You should look it up someday."

"I will. But I'd rather you tell me about it."

Again, I didn't reply.

The pho came, and I sipped it with my coffee spoon. I asked Susan, "What exactly is in this?"

She was sipping out of her bowl, and replied, "Well, it's the national dish. It's basically noodles, veggies, and broth seasoned with ginger and pepper. You can add a little uncooked chicken, or pork if you're rich. The hot broth cooks the meat and veggies." She added, "When in doubt about the sanitation, order pho because they have to get the water hot enough to cook the meat, so you know the water is sterilized."

"Good tip."

She said, "Hey, I make a mean pho. I'd love to cook it for you someday."

I said, "That would be nice. I make chili."

"Love chili. I miss chili."

We had another cup of coffee. I said to Susan, "I didn't see the snow globe on your night table."

She thought a moment, then said, "I didn't notice . . . I'll check when I get back to the room."

"You didn't move it?"

"No . . . the maids are usually trustworthy, if you put a few dong on the bed for them."

"Right. So, what's the plan for today?"

She said, "Well, I had the desk guy book us a boat, and we're going to explore the islands. I thought it would be nice for our last day together. Bring a bathing suit."

I paid for breakfast. Still two bucks.

We went up the stairs, and when I got to my room, I said to Susan, "Check for that snow globe."

I went into my room and put my swimsuit on under my last pair of clean khakis. I decided to go with my Ho Chi Minhs instead of my docksiders. As I was ready to leave the room, I noticed, on my nightstand, the snow globe.

This thing gets around.

I went down to the lobby, and a few minutes later, Susan appeared with her tote. She said, "I can't find the snow globe."

"That's okay. It's in my room."

"How did it get there?"

"Maybe the maid got confused. Let's go."

We went outside where a taxi was waiting for us. Susan said to the driver, "Cang Nha Trang."

The taxi drove out to the beach road and turned south. Susan said to me, "That's not possible."

"What?"

"How the snow globe got in your room."

"Well, the thing gets around." As we drove, I told her the story of the snow globe from Dulles Airport, to Colonel Mang's office at Tan Son Nhat, then to my room at the Rex.

She didn't say anything for a long time, then said, "That's . . . I can't believe that. Someone was in my room."

"Why do you find that hard to believe? Do you think you're in Lenox? It's a police state. You may have noticed." I added, "If we had phones, they'd be tapped. And there may be bugs in the rooms, and the boric acid won't help."

She stayed silent, then nodded. She asked me, "But what's the point of the snow globe?"

"I guess it's just Colonel Mang playing mind games. He should be keeping a low profile, so we don't think about things like bugs in the room. But he's amusing himself."

"That's a little sick."

"Maybe it's a slow week at the Ministry of Public Security."

The road followed the long, crescent-shaped beach, and we passed the Nha Trang Sailing Club, then a few kilometers farther, there was a sprawling new resort of red tiled villas, whose sign said Ana Mandara. It looked as if it had been floated in from Hawaii.

A lot of money was pouring into this country, not only in Saigon, but also the hinterlands, from what I could see from the train, and here in Nha Trang.

As we got closer to the docks, I saw a cluster of nice old villas, set on three lush hills right on the beach. "Look at that."

Susan asked the driver about the villas, and she translated, "Those are the Bao Dai Villas, built by the last emperor of Vietnam and named after his humble self. It was his summer home. Then, it was used by the South Vietnamese presidents— Diem and Thieu. The driver says you can rent a room there, but a lot of Party officials use the place, and Westerners are not always welcome."

"Hey, I can party with the Party."

"Is that head injury bothering you today?"

We continued on the beach road toward the southern headland, which ended at a big squat hill. At the base of the hill was a picturesque village, and across the road, I could see boats around a long wharf that jutted out into the South China Sea.

We pulled up to the foot of the wharf, I paid the driver, and we got out. It wasn't much of a facility, and most of the boats looked like pleasure craft, if your idea of pleasure isn't too well defined. There were also a few fishing boats, all painted a midnight blue with red trim, like all the fishing boats I'd seen in Nha Trang. It must be a local custom, or the only paint available.

We walked onto the wharf where about twenty guys were offering to take us anywhere we wanted to go. How about the Potomac River?

Susan was looking for a particular guy, and she called out, "Captain Vu? Captain Vu?"

Amazingly, everyone there was named Captain Vu. We finally found the real Captain Vu, and he led us to his boat, which was not a pleasure craft, but actually one of the blue and red fishing boats. It looked like a sturdy craft, about twenty-five feet long, with a low stern, a high bow, and a wide beam. Sort of like a cartoon tugboat. We all got aboard.

There was a small wheelhouse set amidship, made mostly of glass windows, and a fishnet hung along the port side of the boat.

Captain Vu spoke a little English and said, "Welcome on board man and lady."

The boat smelled a little fishy because it was a fishing boat, and what else was fishy was why the desk clerk hadn't gotten us a pleasure boat. Obviously the clerk and Captain Vu were related, or in business together. I said to Susan, "This is a fishing boat."

"Isn't it great? A real Nha Trang fishing boat."

"Right." Some people need to experience everything. At my age, I try to experience as little as possible. Been there. Six times. Done that. Twelve times.

Captain Vu showed us a chest of ice, beer, water, and soft drinks. He said, "For you."

Captain Vu smoked and was delighted that Susan smoked, too, and they fired up a couple of Marlboros. The captain spread a nautical chart on the engine housing, and he and Susan looked over the chart and chatted for a while.

Susan turned to me and said, "We can probably visit four or five islands."

"Let's make it four."

"Okay. The last island I wanted to visit is called Pyramide—still has a French name. It also has a nude beach."

"Make that five islands."

"I figured." She spoke to Captain Vu, and he chuckled.

I suggested, "Make Pyramide the first island."

He understood this and laughed louder.

Anyway, a kid of about fourteen was on the wharf, and he helped us cast off, then jumped on board. The kid said he was named Minh, after the great leader, Ho Chi Minh. I showed the kid my sandals, and he approved.

Captain Vu went into the wheelhouse, and a minute later, the engine kicked over, coughed, and caught. Minh and I shoved off, and we were on our way.

There were two plastic chairs in the stern, and Susan and I sat. I looked in the cooler beside me and found a liter of bottled water, which we shared.

The sea was calm, and Captain Vu opened the throttle a little. We headed southeast, toward a small island.

428 N E L S O N D E M I L L E

Susan had the chart on her lap and said to me, "That island there is Hon Mieu—South Island. There's a fish farm there. Want to see it?"

"No. Where's Pyramide Island?"

"The next island is Hon Tam, then Hon Mot, then we'll go to Hon Cu Loa—Monkey Island, then the big mountain island of Hon Tre, which means Bamboo Island." She gave me the chart. "Take a look."

"Where's Pyramide Island?"

"It's on the map, Paul."

"It's called a chart. Where's that island?"

"North."

"Right. I see it." Of course, it was the farthest away. I folded the chart. Well, something to look forward to.

Our first port of call was Hon Tam, where there was a small resort. We rented two kayaks and paddled around awhile. We also had a beer at the resort and made a pit stop.

Then, on Hon Mot, we rented some snorkeling gear and spent an hour looking at brightly colored tropical fish and incredible coral reefs in crystal clear water. I also watched Susan Weber underwater, who had on another skimpy bathing suit, this one white.

Then on to Monkey Island, where these obnoxious monkeys harassed a lot of stupid tourists. One of them—the monkeys—tried to lift my wallet, and I thought I was back in Saigon. Another one, obviously an alpha male, hung by his toes from a branch and grabbed Susan's boob. And he hadn't even bought her dinner.

These disgusting monkeys had absolutely no fear of people, and that was because no one had ever broken one of their necks. You only had to break one neck, and the others would get the message.

Anyway, we bid adieu to Monkey Island, and I insisted that we skip Bamboo Island because I didn't want to miss Pyramide Island, though I didn't say that. I said, "There's bubonic plague on Bamboo Island. Read about it this morning."

Ms. Weber didn't seem to believe me. She said something to Captain Vu, and he took a new heading.

I asked, "Where are we going?"

"Oh, I thought we'd call it a day. It's pushing 3 P.M."

"What happened to Pyramide Island?"

"Oh . . . right. Do you still want to go there?"

"Yes. Now."

She smiled. "That's where we're headed. You're so basic."

Susan sat back in her chair and lit a cigarette. The wind was blowing through her long hair, and she looked very good. She said to me, "When I first met you, I had the initial impression you were a little repressed."

"I was."

"Then I realized you were just putting on a cool act."

"I was being professional."

"Me, too."

That, I thought, depended on her profession.

Within half an hour, I spotted land dead ahead. Captain Vu turned to us from the open wheelhouse. He pointed and said, "Hon Pyramide."

We approached this tiny island from the west, and Captain Vu pulled back the throttle while the kid got out on the bow to look for coral reef and sandbars. I could see a long dock extending out from the shore, and there were about a dozen boats of all types and sizes tied up there.

Pyramide Island indeed looked like a pyramid with steep rocky sides that sloped up to a blunt point at the top. There were people rappelling down the rocks for some reason.

Captain Vu pulled alongside the dock, and cut the engine while Minh and I jumped out and tied the boat.

Captain Vu came out of the wheelhouse, and I said to Susan, "Ask him what those people are doing on the rocks."

Susan asked him and said to me, "This is one of the islands where they collect the sparrow nests for bird's nest soup." She added, "The higher the nest, the bigger erection you'll get."

"You made that up." I said to Susan, apropos of nothing that was being discussed, but something that was on my mind, "Ask Captain Vu if he's seen any Russian warships while he's been out fishing."

She hesitated a moment, then asked him. He replied, and she said to me, "Not so much anymore. But they still come into Cam Ranh Bay now and then. Maybe once a month."

"Ask him if he's seen any American warships."

She asked, he replied, and she said to me, "Lately he's seen a few. Why are you asking?"

"Just curious."

Captain Vu gave us directions to the nude beach and said to me, in English, "You like."

We took a few Cokes, put them in the tote, and told Captain Vu we'd be back at sunset. The kid wanted to come along, but Captain Vu wanted to fish, and he needed the kid for the nets. Minh didn't look happy.

Susan and I walked along the dock to the shore and turned onto a trail that cut through the brush along the shoreline.

We didn't say much as we walked, and I think we were both a little tense about this. I mean, swimming in the raw is not that big a deal, but with someone you've not seen naked before, it could be a little awkward.

After about fifteen minutes, the trail curved around a rock formation, and on the other side of the rocks, about fifty yards away, was a beautiful sandy cove beach nestled in the cliffs of the pyramid. There were about fifteen women on the beach and in the water, all naked.

Well, there were men, too, but who cares? Susan and I stopped a moment, and she said, "I guess my information was correct."

"Who told you about this place?"

"An expat in Saigon. I thought he was kidding, but I checked with the desk clerk, who said yes, though nude swimming is forbidden." She looked around at the cliffs, the sky, the sandy beach, the turquoise water, and the trees near the shoreline. She said, "This is beautiful."

We walked down the sandy path to the beach where people were swimming and sunning. There were about thirty of them, all Caucasians, except for one young Vietnamese couple.

The beach was only about fifty meters long and about that wide. The rocks formed a sort of amphitheater around it, making it very private, except for the guys on the ropes way up on top of the rock pile who were looking for bird's nests.

Susan and I found a flat rock on the sand where she put her tote.

The closest couple was about twenty feet away, lying face up on a blanket.

I said, "Well, time for a swim." I took off my shirt and kicked off my sandals.

Susan pulled off her shirt and sandals, too, and took her slacks off and laid them on the rock.

I peeled off my bathing trunks, and Susan took off her bikini top. Then she slid her bottom off and threw it in the tote bag.

We stood there a moment, naked in the sunlight, and it felt good.

Her bathing suit hadn't left too much to my imagination, but my imagination wasn't as good as the real thing. She had a well-trimmed bikini cut.

We walked across the beach, down to the shoreline. The women ranged in age from about twenty to fifty, and there was not a bad body among them. I wondered if I should include any of this in my post-mission report.

We stood at the edge of the beach and the gentle surf washed over our feet. The sun was to our front, hovering over the hills behind Nha Trang, whose shoreline we could see about twenty kilometers away. The sun sparkled on the water, and the sky was filled with gulls.

We just stood there and took this all in—nature at its most beautiful, surrounded by total strangers who, like us, were naked and without a sign of worldly goods, and whose station in life was completely irrelevant and totally unknown on this one sunny afternoon.

A very nice-looking woman of about forty was coming out of the water, and she walked toward us, clearing her eyes and nose of water. She said to us in accented English, "Good temperature. No jellyfish. Very safe."

Susan said, "Thank you."

"Americans?"

"Yes."

"Not many here. Mostly Europeans and Australians. I am from Sweden."

Even stark naked, we looked like Americans.
Must be my circumcision.

So, we stood there and chatted with this nice
lady, and her husband joined us, and we talked
about where we were staying, about restaurants, Nha Trang, and Vietnam in general. The
funny thing is that after a few minutes, you forget that everyone is naked. Well, maybe not forget, but you keep good eye contact.

The guy said to me, "May I ask if you were
here during the war?"

I replied, "I was."

"How does it seem to you?"

"Pleasant. Peaceful."

"War is so terrible."

"I know that."

He waved his arm to take in the beach and
sky and said, "The whole world should be like
this."

"It was," I reminded him. "Garden of Eden.
We blew it."

They both laughed. The woman said, "Well,
have a pleasant stay." And off they went.

Susan said, "They were nice."

I replied, "Yours are nicer."

She laughed.

We dove into the water, then swam along the
beach and explored the rocky cliffs. There's
something very different about swimming in the

nude. We swam for about half an hour, then came back toward the shore.

We walked in the water until we were up to our chests, then stopped. I turned Susan toward me, and we put our hands on each other's shoulders and stood looking at each other. We wrapped our arms around each other and kissed. Our hands slid down to each other's butts, and I pulled her close and felt her pubic hair against my penis.

She broke away and took a deep breath. She said, "Let's go lie on the beach."

I replied, "You go. I need some time to let down the periscope."

She smiled, turned, and walked onto the beach.

I watched her as she strode across the sand, and she had a beautiful walk.

She stopped along the way to talk to the Vietnamese couple, who were sitting on a rock under a tree. They were smiling and nodding away.

Periscope down, I walked onto the beach toward Susan, who was now lying on the sand with her head on the tote.

I knelt beside her, and she looked up at me and smiled.

She flipped over and handed me a tube of suntan lotion from her tote. "Can you do my back?"

"Sure." I spread the lotion on her back, then over her buttocks and down her legs.

She said, "Oooh, that feels good."

I massaged her neck, shoulders, back, and butt.

She said to me, "I'll do your back."

I lay on my stomach, and she sat on my butt with her knees straddling me as she massaged the lotion into my back.

She said, "Hey, do you want to take some pictures?"

"I don't think that's a good idea."

"I want to remember this day. I have an idea. We'll get someone to take our picture together, and we'll hide our faces."

She stood and walked over to the Vietnamese couple and spoke to them. The guy came back with her, but the girl seemed shy and stayed on the rock under the tree. Susan introduced me to Mr. Hanh, and I stood and shook hands with the young man. She gave Mr. Hanh her camera, and Susan and I stood close together with our arms on each other's shoulders, and our hands covering each other's faces. Mr. Hanh thought that was funny and took a picture while he giggled. For the next shot, our other hands covered each other's pubic area. This was all a little silly and maybe a little kinky. I'm from South Boston.

We thanked Mr. Hanh, who bowed and went back to his companion. I asked Susan, "Will they develop these in Saigon?"

"No, they won't develop nude shots here, and if they do, they'd be all over Saigon in two days. I'll send the film to my sister in Boston. Is that okay?"

"Sure. If I ever meet her, we'll have something to talk about."

Susan laughed.

We sat cross-legged in the sand and cracked open the Coke cans. I said, "And what will you tell your sister about the pictures?"

She replied, "I'll tell her I met a wonderful man who was here on business, and we spent some beautiful days in Saigon and Nha Trang, and he went home to Virginia and I miss him."

I didn't know what to say, but I managed, "I wish things weren't this complicated."

She nodded.

The sun was behind the Nha Trang Mountains now, and the dying light silhouetted the land against the dark blue sky. The water, too, had become darker and no longer sparkled. A fleet of blue and red fishing boats were making their way through the twilight back to Nha Trang. I looked around and saw people getting dressed and leaving the beach.

There were a number of places out there on the mainland, not too far from here, where I came close to death. And if I'd died here, I wouldn't be on this beach with this woman, and I would not have lived long enough to see this country at peace. If there was a heaven for the men who died here, it should look like this.

We got dressed and walked back to the boat.

We arrived at Cang Nha Trang after dark, and I gave Captain Vu his fee and a nice tip, plus a fiver for Minh as compensation for missing the nude beach.

There were a few taxis at the wharf, and we took one back to the hotel.

Upstairs, we went to Susan's room, opened the French doors, and let in the sea breeze.

She turned off the lamp and lit the candle she'd bought at the market. I opened the bottle of rice wine, and we poured some into two plastic cups. We touched cups and drank. There was music coming from the beach café across the road, Fats Domino's "Blueberry Hill," which would not have been my first selection for this moment, but my CD player was in Virginia.

Susan said, "Let's dance."

We put down our wine, kicked off our sandals, and danced to "Blueberry Hill."

This was fun, and I like some non-sexual foreplay, but I was a little tense, and very worked up.

The music changed to Johnny Mathis's "The Twelfth of Never," and this is my all-time favorite slow dance song.

We danced close, and I could feel her breath on my neck. She put her hands under my shirt and caressed my back. I did the same on her back, and unhooked her bikini top.

We pulled up our shirts and danced, bare chest to breasts. She slid her hands down the back of my pants, and I did the same, cupping her buttocks tightly.

We didn't finish the dance because suddenly we were into each other's clothes, which were all over the room in about five seconds.

We practically dove into the bed, and she pulled the mosquito netting down around us.

We kissed hard, and our hands were all over, and our bodies were thrashing around in the small bed.

Finally, we got it under control, and we lay side by side and held each other for a while, then our hands started to roam. She was very wet and I was very hard.

I got on top of her and slid in easily.

We made love, then fell asleep exhausted in each other's arms.

I woke in the middle of the night with Cynthia on my mind and Susan in my bed. I also thought about Karl, what lay ahead, and what awaited me back home.

This mission had gotten off to a bad start at Tan Son Nhat Airport, and when that happens, you're supposed to abort before you crash and burn. But this mission had become a personal journey, and if that included an unhappy ending, I was prepared for that, too.

★

CHAPTER NINETEEN

———— ★ ————

In the morning, with the sun rising over the South China Sea and a breeze coming in through the open French doors, we made love again.

We showered together and lay naked in bed until about ten, then got dressed, went down to the veranda and had coffee.

Everything looked the same as the last two mornings, but the world had changed for me, and for her, I think.

We both understood that she wasn't going back to Saigon while I was still in Nha Trang, but I was very firm about her not accompanying me to Hue. I said to her, over coffee, "Hue is the start of my official business here. We got away with this, but if you went with me to Hue, Washington would go ballistic."

She replied, "I understand that. But I will see you in Hanoi."

Susan wanted to sightsee, so we hired a car and driver and went to the Oceanographic Institute. We saw a bunch of fish in an aquarium, and thousands of dead sea creatures preserved in glass jars. It's places like this that could use a direct hit from an artillery shell.

In the afternoon, we visited the Cham Towers in the area, slightly more interesting than the pickled fish in the jars. Susan had a brochure, and informed me, "The Cham people were Hindus, and they occupied this area from the seventh to the twelfth centuries before they were conquered by the ethnic Vietnamese coming down from the north."

"Fascinating." Would I be doing this if I hadn't gotten laid?

There was a Cham Temple complex called Po Nagar where the statues of the Hindu gods and goddesses were very erotic, and this place was kind of interesting. There were sculptures of these huge penises called lingas, and vaginas called yonis, and one of the yonis had a water fountain gushing out of it. You don't see stuff like this in a Catholic church.

We spent part of the afternoon exploring the countryside, including an enchanted spot called Ba Ho where three waterfalls fell into three pools in a secluded forest. As we sat by the waterfalls with our feet in the water, Susan studied my guidebook and said to me, "I know you like nude beaches, so I've found another."

I replied, "I hope you don't think that's all I want to do. I loved the Oceanographic Institute."

"I know you did. But you can also learn something at a nude beach. Let's go."

We got into our car, and Susan directed the driver to a place called Hon Chong, which is a big stone promontory jutting out into the South China Sea.

From the top, we had a spectacular view of the headlands to the north, and Nha Trang to the south. The sun was over the mountains to the west, and the South China Sea was blue and gold. "Very nice," I said.

She led me to what appeared to be a huge handprint in a big boulder. She said, "This handprint was made by a drunken giant male fairy as he fell on these rocks."

"Takes a lot of rice wine to get a giant fairy drunk," I said.

Susan continued, "He was ogling a female fairy bathing in the nude, down there on Fairy Beach."

I looked down the mountain and saw the beach, but I didn't see any female fairies, nude or otherwise.

Susan said, "The giant got up, ran down to the beach, and captured the female fairy. Sort of like what happened to me yesterday."

That wasn't the way I remembered it, but I know when to keep my mouth shut.

"Despite his aggressive behavior, they fell in love and began a life together."

"That's nice. And lived happily ever after?"

"No. The gods were angry at them for what they had done."

"Did the gods live in Washington?"

"Some place like that. The gods sent the male fairy off to a re-education camp."

"Bummer."

"Right. But the female fairy waited for him for centuries."

"Good lady."

"Yes. But she was heartbroken, and thought he would never return. So she lay down and turned into stone. See that mountain?" She pointed to the northwest. "That's called Nui Co Tien—Fairy Mountain. That peak on the right is her face, gazing up at the sky. The middle peaks are her breasts, and the peaks on the left are her crossed legs."

I looked, and yes, you could imagine a reclining female with her legs crossed.

Susan said, "One day, the male fairy returned to this spot and seeing what had become of his lover, he slammed his hand down over his old handprint, where he'd first seen her bathing on the beach. He was so grief-stricken, he died, and he, too, turned to stone."

I didn't say anything for a while, then commented, "Sad story."

"Almost all love stories have a sad ending." She asked, "Why is that?"

I replied, "I think when the affair begins illicitly, and when everyone around the lovers is hurt or angry . . . then the affair is going to have an unhappy and probably tragic ending."

Susan looked off at Fairy Mountain. She said, "More importantly, though, the lovers stayed true to each other."

"You're a romantic."

She asked, "Are you the practical type?"

"No one ever accused me of being practical."

"Would you give up your life for love?"

"Why not? I've risked my life for less important things."

She gave me a kiss on the cheek, took my hand, and we walked down the mountain.

That night, we went to the new resort called Ana Mandara that we'd seen on the way down to the Nha Trang docks, and we had a first-rate dinner of Westernized Vietnamese food. The place was owned by a Dutch concern, and the clientele was mostly European, but there were a few Americans as well.

A nice combo was playing at poolside, and we had a few drinks, danced, talked, and held hands.

Susan said, "After dinner at the Rex, I went home that night floating on a cloud."

I replied, "I think I felt the same way."

"You sent me away. What if I hadn't come back?"

"Weren't you told to stick close to me?"

She replied, "Only if you wanted my company, or needed something. If not, I was supposed to disappear. But I wasn't going to do that. I was going to phone you. Then, I decided to just come back and join you for dinner."

"I'm glad you did," I said, but I recalled thinking at the time that it wasn't as spontaneous as Susan was suggesting. Then there were the inconsistencies in the Bill Stanley story, and a few other things that didn't quite add up. The elephant grass swayed, but there was no breeze; the bamboo clicked, a little closer now.

We left the Ana Mandara, and walked back to the Grand Hotel. We'd kept both rooms, but Susan's room was the one where I slept.

We made love and lay close together on our backs in the bed, surrounded by the cocoon of the mosquito netting, the bed garlanded with branches of Tet blossoms, the orange-scented candle flickering, and the boric acid on the floor.

We watched the paddle fan spin lazily overhead. A breeze blew in from the open balcony, and I could smell the sea. The next day, Friday, was to be our last full day in Nha Trang, so I said to her, "Have you arranged transportation back to Saigon?"

She was running her foot over my leg. "What?"

"Saigon. Saturday."

"Oh. The trains stop running Saturday. That's Lunar New Year's Eve."

"How about a car and driver?"

"I'll try to arrange that tomorrow."

This didn't sound like a definite plan. I asked, "Will that be a problem?"

"Maybe. Maybe not. I've never tried to travel around Tet."

"Then maybe you should leave tomorrow."

"I'm not leaving early. I want to spend as much time with you as possible."

"Well, me, too, but—"

"How are you getting to Hue?"

"I don't know. But I need to be there."

She said, "Every plane and train has been booked for months."

"Well . . . maybe I should also leave tomorrow."

"You should if you want to try to buy yourself a place on the train."

"Could I get a car and driver tomorrow?"

"We'll try. If all else fails, there's always the torture bus. No reservation required. Just buy a ticket at the terminal, and jam yourself in. All you need are elbows and dong."

"What do I do with my dong?"

"Dong. Money. Stop being an idiot." She said, "I took a bus once, Saigon to Hue, just for the experience, and it *was* an experience."

"Maybe we should see about getting out of here tomorrow."

"Yes, that's what we should do first thing to-morrow."

Part Two. She informed me, "I was supposed to go to a Tet Eve house party with Bill."

I didn't reply.

She said, "Everyone we know will be there. Americans, Brits, Aussies, and some Catholic Viets."

"Sounds like fun."

"Well, I'm certainly not going now. I'll just stay home and watch the dragon dances from my window."

"You'll thank yourself in the morning."

"My housekeeper will be with her family, of course, and most of the bars and restaurants are closed, or open only by invitation. So, maybe I'll just warm up some pho and get a bottle of rice wine, put on a Barbra Streisand album, and get to sleep early."

"Sounds horrible. How about the Beach Boys?"

"I suppose I could go to the party, but it would be awkward."

"Would you like to go to Hue with me?"

"Oh . . . that's an idea." She crawled on top of me and said, "You're such a sweetheart."

"And you're trouble."

"What are they going to do to you? Send you to Vietnam?"

She kissed me, my linga got longer, and we made love again. It was less than an hour since we'd done this, and I hadn't had my bird's nest soup today. This was fast becoming like my last R&R in Nha Trang, except then, I was a lot younger. I pictured myself meeting Karl in Bangkok on crutches. At least I was tanned.

She fell asleep in my arms. A strong wind had come up, and I could hear the surf crashing. I couldn't get to sleep, realizing that I was up to my tanned butt in official trouble, and getting in deeper.

I thought about the cautionary fable I'd learned on Hon Chong Mountain. No one could say I hadn't been warned.

The world is not always kind to lovers, and in the case of Paul Brenner and Susan Weber, we had really pissed off the gods.

Susan was right that we had to leave tomorrow rather than Saturday, which was Lunar New Year's Eve. But she knew that all week.

I was certain that Susan Weber was ready to go home, if I took her home. But she never once said, "Let's get out of here." She said, "Let me go with you wherever you have to go."

And that brought me to three possible conclusions: One, she was bored, finished with Bill, and was looking for an adventure and challenge; two, she was madly in love with me and didn't want to leave my side; three, she and I were on the same assignment.

One, all, or any combination was possible.

That aside, I think we both understood that if

we parted here in Nha Trang, we might never meet in Hanoi, or anywhere; and if we did meet in Hanoi, it wouldn't be the same. My journey had become her journey, and her way home had become my way home.

CHAPTER TWENTY

———— ★ ————

Early Friday morning, we went to the government travel agency, Vidotour, but like most government agencies, they were closed for the holiday. In fact, aside from food and flower shops, the town was starting to shut down.

We went next to the train station, but this being the last day that any trains were running until the following Friday, we couldn't even buy a standby ticket. To make matters worse, even if we bribed our way on a train, the ticket or bribe was only good to Da Nang where we'd have to go through the process again, or get stranded in Da Nang.

As we left the train station, Susan asked me, "Why did they send you here during the Tet holiday?"

I replied, "It's not as stupid as it seems. I need to find someone in his native town or village."

"Oh. Well, he should be there."

"I hope so. That's the only address we have."

"Tam Ki? Is that the village?"

"I don't think that place exists. It's another place whose name I'll get in Hue. After Hue, I need to go to this place. But you will *not*—repeat not—go with me."

"I know that. I'll stay in Hue. Then I'll get my-self up to Hanoi and meet you."

"Fine. Meanwhile, we need to get to Hue."

"Money talks. I'll get us to Hue."

We walked around town with the tourist map that I'd bought on the beach, but the two pri-vate travel agencies were closed.

As we walked, I looked for a tail, but I was fairly certain we were alone. After some in-quiries on the street, we found a mini-bus-tour office that was open near the central market. The guy behind the counter was a slicky boy with dark glasses and the instincts of a vulture. He smelled money and desperation the way a carrion-eating bird smells impending death. Su-san and he slugged it out for ten minutes, then she said to me, "He's got a tour group leaving here at 7 A.M. tomorrow. They arrive in Hue about 6 P.M., in time for Tet Eve. When do you have to meet your person?"

"Not until noon the next day—New Year's Day. Sunday."

"Okay. He says there are no actual seats left on the mini-bus, but we can sit in the doorwell or someplace. Plenty of room for our luggage. Fifty bucks each."

"What kind of tour group?"

She asked Slicky Boy, then said to me, "They're French."

"Let's walk."

She laughed.

"Tell him he has to pay *us*."

She actually translated this to Slicky, and he laughed and slapped my shoulder.

I said, "Ask him if he has a car and driver available today."

She spoke to him, and he looked doubtful, which meant, "Yes, and it's going to cost you a fortune."

Susan said to me, "He has a man who can drive us to Hue, but because of the holiday, it will cost us five hundred dollars."

I said, "It's not my holiday. Two hundred."

She spoke to Slicky, and we settled on three hundred. Susan said to me, "He says the driver and the car aren't available until about 6 P.M." She added, "By car, we can make it in seven or eight hours if we leave about six when traffic gets light. That will get us in at one or two in the morning. Is that okay?"

"Sure. We can sleep in the hotel lobby if there isn't a room available."

"All right . . . you understand that night driving isn't that safe?"

"Neither is day driving around here."

"Right. I'll tell him to pick us up about six at the hotel."

I took her aside and said to her, "No. Tell him we'll come here. And tell him we're going to Hue–Phu Bai Airport."

She nodded and passed this on to Slicky Boy.

We left Slicky Boy Tours and found an outdoor café where we got coffee.

I said to Susan, "You did a great job. I was
getting a little concerned about getting out of
here."

"For that kind of money—about a year's
salary—you can get what you want. As my father
used to say, 'The poor suffer, the rich are slightly
inconvenienced.'" She looked at me and said, "If
we have three hundred dollars, we must have
more. And it's a night drive. So don't fall asleep."

"I already figured that out. That's why I'm
still alive." I added, "If we don't like the looks of
this tonight, we have the mini-bus in the morning as a backup."

She sipped her coffee and asked me, "Why
didn't you want the driver to pick us up at the
hotel?"

"Because Colonel Mang doesn't want me using private transportation."

"Why not?"

"Because Colonel Mang is a paranoid asshole. I need to go to the Immigration Police
and show them a ticket to Hue. You said I
could get a bus ticket."

"Yes. The ticket is good for any time, Nha
Trang to Hue. So the police won't ask what bus
you intend to take. Hue is about 550 kilometers
from here, and that could take ten to twelve
hours by bus, so my guess is the last bus for Hue

will leave here about 1 P.M., to arrive in Hue about midnight."

"So, if I was really taking the bus, I'd need to leave soon."

"That's right. And you'd have to check out of the hotel soon."

"Okay." I stood. "Bus station."

We paid the bill, left, and walked to the main bus terminal.

The bus terminal was a mass of impoverished humanity, and I didn't see a single Westerner there, not even a backpacker or a schoolteacher.

The lines were long, but Susan went to the front of the line and gave a guy a few bucks to buy my ticket. Susan asked me, "One way, or round-trip?"

"One way, observation deck, window seat."

"One ticket for the roof." The Viet guy bought the ticket, and we left the teeming bus terminal.

Susan said, "The ticket agent said there's a noon bus, and a one P.M. bus."

We walked toward the police station, and I said to Susan, "You stay here. By now, they know you speak Vietnamese. I do better with pidgin English."

She said, "More importantly, if you don't come out of there, I'll contact the embassy."

I didn't reply and walked to the Immigration police station.

Inside was a different guy behind the desk,

and I presented him with Colonel Mang's letter, which he read.

The waiting room was nearly empty this time, except for two backpackers sleeping on benches.

The Immigration cop said to me in passable English, "Where you go now?"

"Hue."

"How you go Hue?"

I showed him my bus ticket.

He seemed a little surprised, but I had the five-dollar ticket so I must be telling the truth. He asked me, "When you go?"

"Now."

"Yes? You leave hotel?"

The guy knew I was checked in until tomorrow. I said, "Yes, leave hotel today."

"Why you leave today?"

"No train to Hue tomorrow. No plane. Go bus. Today."

"Yes. Okay. You go to police in Hue."

I said sharply, "I know that."

"Lady go with you?"

"Maybe. Maybe not. We talk."

He asked, "Where lady now?"

"Lady shop." I looked at my watch and said, "I go now."

"No. You need stamp." He produced the photocopies I'd given to them when I arrived, and he said, "I stamp. Ten dollars."

I gave him a ten. He stamped my photocopies,

and wrote something on the stamps. I think they make this up as they go along.

I left before he thought of anything else.

I looked at the stamps and saw that the guy had handwritten *Hue—Century* over the red ink, so he already knew where I was staying. He'd also written the time, 11:15, and dated it.

I met Susan down the street, and she asked me, "Any problems?"

"No. Just another round-eye tax." I showed her the photocopies with the red stamps on them and asked, "What are these?"

She looked at them and said, "These are the old internal travel stamps you used to need years ago."

"Cost me ten bucks."

"I buy my own rubber stamps for five bucks."

"Bring them next time."

She said to me, "So, you're staying at the Century Riverside. That's where I stayed when I was in Hue."

"Well, that's where you're staying this time. But we'll try to get separate rooms."

We took a taxi back to the Grand Hotel. As we drove along the road, Susan asked me, "If I weren't here, would you have gotten a Viet girl to stay with you at the hotel all week, or had a different one every night, or picked up a Western woman at the Nha Trang Sailing Club?"

There didn't seem to be a correct answer

among the choices. I said, "I would have spent more time at the Oceanographic Institute and continued with the cold showers."

"No, I mean really."

"I'm involved at home."

Silence.

I'm good at this stuff, so I said, "Even if I wasn't involved with anyone, when I'm on an assignment, I never do *anything* that can complicate or compromise the mission. But in this case, you're sort of part of the team—as I very recently found out—and therefore I felt I could make an exception."

She replied, "I'm not part of the team, and you didn't know anything about that in Saigon when we decided to come to Nha Trang together."

I didn't recall making that decision, but again, I know when to shut up.

She continued, "So, if you're on an assignment with a female co-worker, then you might consider a sexual or romantic involvement. That's how you met what's-her-name."

"Can we stop at the marketplace for a leash?"

"Sorry."

We arrived at the Grand without any further conversation.

At the front desk, there was a fax for Susan on Bank of America letterhead. I said, "Maybe your cyclo loan has been approved."

She read the fax and handed it to me. It was from Bill, of course, and it read: Washington firm absolutely insists that you return to Saigon as soon as possible. They need to talk with you via e-mail. On a personal note, I would have no objection if you wanted to come to the Vincents' party, Tet Eve. We can be civilized about this, and perhaps discuss our relationship, if any. Need a full response.

I handed the fax back to her.

She said to me, "It's your decision now, Paul. These are your bosses."

I said, "This is directed to you, not me."

"Oh. Well, I have no bosses in Washington. I did the favor for the American consulate in Saigon. End of story."

I wasn't so sure of that, but I said, "Fax Bill that you're going with me to Hue."

She got a piece of fax paper from the desk clerk and wrote on it. She handed it to me, and I read: Mr. Brenner and I are headed to Hue. Inform his firm of same. Will return to Saigon sometime week after next. Regards to the Vincents from me, and my regrets.

Susan went into a small back room with the desk clerk and came out a few minutes later. She said to me, "I told the desk clerk we were checking out today, and we needed a taxi in half an hour to take you to the bus station and me to the train station."

We climbed the stairs, and I said, "Dress for adventure."

*   *   *

We were downstairs in the lobby at noon, both dressed in blue jeans, polo shirts, and walking shoes. We checked out, and Susan led me into the dining room. We found Lucy waiting on tables on the veranda, and Susan pressed some money into her hands. The old woman thanked us profusely. She said something to Susan, who said to me, "She said she doesn't remember you, but she remembers the American soldiers who were . . . very high-spirited and . . . crazy, but who were always kind to her. She wishes us a safe journey."

"Tell her I will always remember the kindness and the patience of the young ladies here who made our time away from the war so pleasant."

Susan translated, the old woman bowed, then we held each other's shoulders and kissed, French-style, both cheeks.

We went back to the lobby, got our bags, and went outside, where a taxi was waiting for us.

Susan said, "That was very nice. What you said to each other."

"We're old friends. We went through a war together."

The driver put our bags in the trunk and off we went.

★

—BOOK IV—

Highway One

CHAPTER TWENTY-ONE

———————— ★ ————————

The taxi from the hotel dropped Susan off at the train station first, then me at the bus terminal.

I went into the terminal, then back outside and took a taxi to the Thong Nhat Hotel on the beach. I left my luggage with the bell captain, and went to the terrace and got a table. Within five minutes, Susan joined me.

We had some hours to kill before we needed to be at Slicky Boy Tours, and this was as good a place as any and wouldn't attract attention. The clientele was all Western, and no one from the Ministry of Public Security was dining there.

Susan and I had lunch.

I asked her, "Why are you taking this trip with me?"

"I don't want to go back to Saigon."

"Why not?"

"I'd rather be with you."

"Why?"

"Well . . . you might think it's because I'm supposed to keep an eye on you, or you might think it's because I'm bored and I want some excitement, or you might think it's because I'm crazy about you."

"I had all three thoughts."

She smiled and said, "Pick the ones that suit you best. But no more than two."

I thought about that and said, "The ones that suit me best are the first two because if something happened to you because of the last one, I'd never forgive myself."

She lit a cigarette and stared out at the fishing boats coming out of the river into the sea. She said, "I don't want you to feel responsible for my safety. I can take care of myself."

"Okay. But even in the infantry, we had the buddy system. Two guys who looked out for each other."

"Did you ever lose a buddy?"

"Two of them."

She didn't reply for a long time, then asked, "Did you ever save a buddy's life?"

"A few times."

"Anyone ever save your life?"

"A few times."

She said, "So, we'll look out for each other, and we'll do the best we can."

I didn't reply.

She said, "But if you're going into the interior after you leave Hue, a male Caucasian traveling alone attracts attention."

"I understand that. And I will be traveling alone."

She continued, "As I said in the Q-Bar, you should try to pass yourself off as a naturalist, or an amateur biologist. If you were being watched here in Nha Trang, you've already shown some interest in biology at the Oceanographic Institute."

I looked at her, but didn't say anything.

"And you'll really need an interpreter. It's very difficult without an interpreter once you get away from the coast."

I said, "I didn't have an interpreter the last two times I was here. I'm good at making myself understood."

"I'm sure you were when you had a rifle."

"Point made. I'll get an interpreter. They may have someone for me in Hue."

She didn't reply for a while, then said, "They haven't given you much backup so far."

"That's because they have complete trust and confidence in me. I'm very resourceful."

"I see that. But you can't be sleeping with bilingual women all the way up country."

I smiled and said, "You're not coming with me past Hue."

At 5:30, I left the hotel terrace and walked to Slicky Boy Tours on Van Hoa Street, a few blocks away. Susan stayed to settle the bill and was to follow within ten minutes.

Slicky Boy was still wearing his wraparound shades, and a phony smile. His front teeth were rimmed in gold, and he had a diamond stud in his ear. The only thing missing was a T-shirt that said *Con Artist*.

Susan had informed me that his real name was Mr. Thuc, and I greeted him by this name. He spoke a little English and asked me, "Where you lady?"

I replied, "Not my lady. Maybe she come. Maybe not."

He said, "Same price."

"Where's my car?"

"Come. I show you."

We went outside. Parked in his little mini-bus lot was a dark blue Nissan rice burner with four-wheel drive and four doors. I didn't recognize the model, but Mr. Thuc assured me, "Good car."

I examined good car and saw that it had no seat belts, but the tires looked okay, and there was a spare.

It was almost six hundred kilometers to Hue, according to Susan. This should take less than six hours on a decent road, but if the estimated drive time was seven or eight hours on Highway One, then Highway One was in much worse shape then I remembered it in 1968, when the Army Corps of Engineers was in charge of the roadwork.

There were no keys in the ignition, so I asked Slicky for the keys, and he gave them to me reluctantly. I sat in the driver's seat and started the engine, which sounded all right, but there was only a quarter tank of fuel. That may not mean anything, but might mean that Slicky Boy had a shorter trip planned for us.

I popped the hood, got out, and checked the engine, which was a small four-cylinder, but seemed okay. I asked Slicky, "Where's the driver?"

"He come."

I shut off the engine and kept the keys. I looked at my watch and saw that fifteen minutes had already passed since I left Susan. Just as I was starting to worry about her, she showed up in a cyclo. She was wearing her backpack and carrying her new tote.

She exchanged greetings with Slicky Boy, and shook my hand as if we were recent acquaintances who had arranged to share a ride. This had been my idea, and even I was impressed by my tradecraft. James Bond would be proud of me.

Susan asked, "Is that our car?"

"That's it." I took her aside and said, "Quarter tank of gas. And check the radio antenna."

She glanced at the antenna, where an orange plastic strip had been tied. "Sort of makes it stand out from all the other dark blue Nissan four-wheels."

She looked into the rear compartment and said to me, "No gas cans, which are standard for a long drive, and no ice chest, which is a common courtesy in 'Nam."

Slicky Boy was looking our way, but with the wraparound shades, I couldn't tell if he was getting as suspicious of us as we were of him. This was not Hertz.

The driver showed up, on foot, a guy of about forty. He wore black cotton pants and a white short-sleeve shirt, like half the men in this country. He also wore sandals and needed a pedicure. He was a little hefty for a Viet, and seemed to me a bit nervous.

Mr. Thuc introduced us to Mr. Cam, and we all shook hands. Mr. Thuc said to us, "Mr. Cam speak no English, and I tell him lady speak good Vietnamese." Mr. Thuc checked his watch and said, "Okay? You pay now."

I counted out a hundred and fifty dollars and said to Slicky Boy, "Half now, half to Mr. Cam when we arrive in Hue." I put the money in his shirt pocket.

"No, no. All now."

"Am I in Hue? Is this Hue?" I opened the rear hatch of the Nissan and threw my bags inside. Susan put her backpack in, and I closed the hatch.

Slicky Boy was pissed, but he calmed himself down. He said, conversationally, "So, where Mr. Cam take you in Hue?"

I replied, "I think we told you. Hue–Phu Bai Airport."

"Yes? Where you go?"

"Hanoi."

"Ah." He looked around, the way people do

in a police state, and informed me, "Too many Communists in Hanoi."

"Too many capitalists here."

"Yes?" He said to Susan and me, "Need you passport and visa. I make copies."

Well, we really didn't want Slicky Boy to know our names, so I said to him, "No."

Slicky started complaining about us not showing identification, and not paying in full, and not trusting him.

I said to him, "You want to make three hundred bucks, or do you want to be an asshole?"

"Please?"

Susan translated, and I wondered what the word was for asshole. She said to me, "Calm down."

I said to Susan, "Let's go. We'll find another car and driver." I plucked the cash out of Slicky's pocket and opened the rear hatch.

He looked shocked, and his mouth dropped open. He said, "Okay. Okay. No passport. No visa."

I put the money back in his pocket.

He said something to the driver, and they went inside the office.

Susan and I made eye contact. She said, "Mr. Cam is not dressed for a night drive up north."

"The car has a heater."

"They rarely use the heater because they think it wastes gas. Same with headlights, if you can believe that. Also, if the car breaks down, they'd freeze to death."

"How cold is it up north?"

"Probably in the fifties at night. That's very cold for someone from Nha Trang."

I nodded and said, "We must look stupid."

"Speak for yourself. Also, Mr. Cam may speak some English. So watch what you say."

"I know that."

She looked at me and said, "Are you sure you don't want to take the mini-bus tomorrow?"

I replied, "I can handle Mr. Cam."

"Can you handle getting robbed on the road?"

"I'm driving."

"Paul, you aren't allowed to drive."

"Don't worry about it."

She informed me, "Sometimes they're in cahoots with the police. They'll pull over the chauffeured car and fine the Westerners in the car big bucks. If you're driving, you'll get arrested."

"If they catch me."

She looked at me and said, "I guess the R&R is over."

"You bet."

She forced a smile and said, "So we outrun the police or speed through the ambush."

"Right. Mr. Cam wouldn't be so accommodating." I asked, "Is there an alternate route?"

"No. At night, it's Highway One, or stay

home. The other roads aren't drivable at night, unless you want to go about ten miles an hour."

"Okay. This is a challenge. I like challenges."

She didn't reply.

I realized that Susan might not share my enthusiasm for irrational behavior. I said, "Look, I'm the one who needs to make a rendezvous. I'll go, and you follow with the Frenchmen tomorrow."

"Oh, so I have to ride with a busload of Frenchmen, and all you have to do is stay awake eight hours and watch out for highway robbers. I thought you were a gentleman."

"Be serious."

"Look, Paul, chances are nothing is going to happen. And if it does, the nice thing about this country is that they don't kill you. And the women aren't raped. It's only about money. You just hand over everything you own, and they're gone." She added, "We can hitchhike the rest of the way in the morning."

"I'm not getting a good image of us standing in our underwear on Highway One, trying to flag down an ox cart."

She handed me her tote bag, which was heavy. I said, "What do you have in here?"

She replied, "Some American companies keep a little protection locked in the safe."

I didn't say anything.

She continued, "In the Binh Tay Market in

Cholan, you can buy pieces of American military hardware under the counter. You put the pieces together, and voilà, you have something. In this case, a Colt .45 automatic, American military issue. You're familiar with this weapon."

I looked at her and reminded her, "You said this was a capital offense."

"Only if you get caught."

"Susan . . . where did you hide this?"

She replied, "In the hot water tank. There's always an access panel."

My mind was reeling, and I started to say something, but Mr. Thuc and Mr. Cam had come out of the office.

I looked at them and had the impression that they'd gone over the final details of their plan, as Susan and I had gone over the details of our plan to screw up their plan.

Mr. Thuc was smiling again, and he said, "Mr. Cam ready. You ready. Have good journey to Hue." He added, "Chuc Mung Nam Moi," then reminded us, "Pay Mr. Cam when you get to Hue."

Not wanting to seem as jumpy as Mr. Cam, we shook hands with Slicky Boy and wished him a Happy New Year. Mr. Thuc and Mr. Cam each opened a rear door for us, and we both got in the back.

We pulled out of the lot and halfway down Van Hoa Street, Susan said something to Mr.

Cam. He replied, and she got a little sharp with him. I put my hand on his shoulder and said in English, "Do what lady say."

He realized we weren't going to be that easy. Within a few minutes, he pulled into a gas station.

He filled the tank, and I stood near him. Susan went into the service station office, and came out a few minutes later with a guy who was carrying two ten-liter cans of gasoline. Susan had a plastic bag that contained two liters of bottled water, a lot of cellophane bags filled with snacks, and a road map.

I made Mr. Cam pay for the gas, and as he did, I took my Nha Trang map and guidebook out of my overnight bag. We all got in the car, me in the front this time, and off we went.

We headed north, and on the map I could see we were going in the right direction, toward the Xam Bong Bridge.

The long bridge passed over a few small islands where the Nha Trang River widened and emptied into the South China Sea. The sea had turned from blue to gold as the sun began to set above the hills to our west. It would be dark within half an hour.

We continued north on a fairly decent road that cut through the high hills north of Nha Trang.

I recognized this road and looked to my

right. I said to Susan, "That's where the giant fairy fell down drunk and put his handprint in the rock."

"Glad you were paying attention. And up there, on the next mountain, is where his lover turned to stone." Susan said, "This is sad. Leaving Nha Trang. I had the best week I've had since I've been here."

I looked back at her, and we made eye contact. I said, "Thanks for a great R&R."

Within fifteen minutes, the road intersected Highway One, which ran straight to Hue, about six hundred kilometers due north.

The so-called highway had one lane in each direction, but widened now and then to three lanes for passing. Motor traffic was moderate, but there were still a lot of ox carts and bicycles on the road. Mr. Cam's driving would not get him a Highway Safety Award, but he was no worse than anyone else on the road.

Highway One ran along the coast, and up ahead I could see another mountainous promontory jutting into the sea. To our left, rice paddies and villages stretched along the highway, and beyond them were more mountains which now blocked the sun. It was getting to that time of day that in the military we called EENT, the end of evening nautical twilight, with enough light left to dig in for the night.

This was going to be the first time since 1972 that I was in the Vietnamese countryside after dark, and I wasn't looking forward to it. The night belonged to Charlie, and to Charlie's son, Mr. Cam.

But unbeknownst to Mr. Cam, Susan Weber had an old, but I hoped, well-oiled Colt .45 ready to point at his head.

In fact, as the sun set, I was less angry at her for bringing the gun, and I hoped it was assembled and loaded. I could assemble and disassemble a Colt .45 literally blindfolded, and do it in under fifteen seconds, including slapping in the magazine, chambering a round, and taking it off safety. But I didn't want to try to break my record.

It was dark now, and the traffic had all but disappeared, except for a few trucks wasting gasoline with their lights on. We passed through a small town, which my map said was called Ninh Hoa. A mountainous headland blocked the view of the sea to the right, and up ahead was a stretch of desolate road. I could see a few peasants' huts with lights in the windows, and water buffalo being led in from the fields. It was dinner time, and perhaps ambush time.

I said to Mr. Cam in English, "I need to pee. Biet? Take a leak. Make nuoc."

He looked at me. "Nuoc?"

Susan translated, and Mr. Cam pulled over to the side of the road.

I reached over, shut off the ignition, and took the keys. I got out of the car and closed my door.

I came around to the driver's side and took the orange streamer off the antenna. I opened the driver's door, gave Mr. Cam a little push, and said, "Move."

He was not happy, but he slid across the seat. I'm sure he had thoughts about making a break, but before he considered this option, I was behind the wheel, and the car was moving. I shifted through the gears and cruised along Highway One at about a hundred kilometers an hour. The Nissan drove well, but with two Caucasians and one Viet, and a full tank, it was a bit underpowered.

I didn't really want Mr. Cam along, but neither did I want him going to a police station. So, I kidnapped him. I said to Susan, "Tell him he looked tired, and I'll drive. He can go to sleep."

She translated.

Mr. Cam looked anything but tired. He looked agitated. He said something, which Susan translated as, "He says you will be in big trouble if the police see you driving."

"So will he. Tell him." She told him.

I got the Nissan up to 120 KPH, and without traffic, it wasn't too bad. But now and then we hit a pothole, and I almost lost control. The springs and shocks weren't the greatest, and I was relying on the spare if I had a blowout. I certainly wasn't relying on my membership in the AAA.

About ten minutes later, I noticed in my

rearview mirror the headlights of a car, and as it got closer, I saw that it was a small open jeep. I said, "We have company."

Susan looked out the back window and said, "It could be a police jeep. I think there're two people in it."

I floored the Nissan.

The road was straight and flat as it passed through the rice paddies, and I eased the Nissan to the center of the road where I hoped the blacktop was better. The vehicle behind me was keeping up, but not gaining.

Mr. Cam was looking in his sideview mirror, but said nothing.

I asked Susan, "Do the police have radios?"

She said, "Sometimes."

Mr. Cam said something to Susan, and she said to me, "Mr. Cam believes there's a police car behind us, and he suggests we pull over."

I replied, "If it was a police car, he'd have his lights and siren on."

She said to me, "They don't have lights and sirens here."

"I know. Just being funny."

"This isn't funny. Can we outrun them?"

"I'm trying."

I was maxed out at 160 KPH, and I knew if I hit a major pothole at this speed, I'd have a blowout, or I'd lose control, or both. The police knew the same would happen to them, but they seemed uncommonly dedicated to the chase, and I figured they had more in mind than a two-dollar ticket. In fact, if Mr. Thuc had set us up, the cops had also figured out by now that Mr. Cam wasn't driving.

The Nissan held the speed, but this was a total crap shoot regarding who was going to hit the first big pothole.

There was a big truck in front of me, and I came up behind it like it was standing still. I swung onto the oncoming lane and saw another truck coming head-on. I passed the truck, then at about two seconds before I would have collided with the oncoming one I swung back into the right lane. A minute later, I saw the headlights of the jeep behind me, and he'd lost some ground.

Mr. Cam was getting increasingly agitated, and he kept trying to reason with Susan, who kept telling him, "Im lang," which I recalled meant be quiet or shut up.

The vehicle behind us was about a hundred meters away, and maybe a little closer than last time I looked. I asked Susan, "Do the cops carry rifles or just pistols?"

"Both."

"Do they shoot at speeding cars?"

"Why don't we assume that they do?"

"Let's assume they want to rob the stage-coach, and they don't want everything incinerated in a ball of fire."

"Sounds right."

I said to Susan, "Get ready to toss that thing in your tote. We don't want to face a firing squad."

She said, "I've got it in my hand. Tell me when."

"How about now? Before I flip this car, and they find it on us."

She didn't reply.

"Susan?"

"Let's wait."

"Okay, we'll wait."

I tried to remember the map, and if I recalled correctly, there was another small town a few minutes ahead. If there was another cop in the area, that's where he'd be.

Mr. Cam was quiet, the way people are when they have accepted their fate. In fact, I thought I saw his lips moving in prayer. I didn't expect him to do anything stupid at this speed, like grab the wheel or try to jump out, but I said to Susan, "Tell Mr. Cam that I'll stop at the next town and let him out."

She told him, and he seemed to buy this. Why, I don't know, but he bought it.

Meanwhile, I was hitting potholes, and we were all bouncing wildly.

Up ahead was a small car, stopped right in the middle of the road. I could see a woman in my headlights waving for assistance. This, I figured, was the ambush where we'd be relieved of what the cops hadn't gotten in fines. But the law hadn't caught me yet, and Mr. Cam was not behind the wheel. He said, however, in rehearsed English, "I stop. Car need help. I stop."

"You're not driving. I no stop."

I swung into the oncoming lane where I could better judge the distance to the drainage ditch on my left, and shot past the lady in distress and her car.

I tried to divide my attention between the road outside my windshield, and the headlights behind me. I saw the lights swing around the stopped car in the road, and the jeep almost veered off into the ditch, but then it got back on the road.

Susan was watching out the back window.

I said to her, "Sorry about this."

"Don't worry about it. Drive."

"Right. That guy's not a bad driver."

She asked me, "Do you know how to blind a Vietnamese driver?"

"No. How?"

"Put a windshield in front of his face."

I smiled.

What wasn't so funny is what happened next. I heard what sounded like a muffled backfire, and it took me about half a second to recognize the hollow popping sound of an AK-47. My blood froze for a moment. I took a deep breath and said, "Did you hear that?"

She replied, "I saw the muzzle flash."

I had my foot all the way down to the floor,

plus some, but the Nissan was maxed. I said, "Okay, ditch the gun. We're going to stop."

"No! Keep going. It's too late to stop now."

I kept going and again I heard a gunshot. But was he firing *at* us? Or just trying to get our attention? In any case, if his four-wheel drive was bouncing as badly as mine, the guy with the rifle couldn't get a good shot at this distance, which was about two hundred meters now. I swung the Nissan into the oncoming lane so that the shooter would have to stand and fire over his windshield, but the police jeep also swung into the oncoming lane behind us. So, I swung back into the right lane.

I heard another shot, but this time, his bullet was a tracer round, and I saw the green streak off to my right and high. *My God.* I hadn't seen a green tracer round since 1972, and it made my heart stop for a second. We used red, they used green, and I started seeing these green and red streaks in front of my eyes.

I brought myself back from that nightmare to this one.

Mr. Cam was sobbing now, which was fine, except he started beating his fists on the dashboard. Next it would be my head. I recognized the little signs of hysteria. I let go of the wheel with my right hand, and gave him a backhand slap across the face. This seemed to work, and he put his face in his hands and wept.

I had this crazy idea that all of this had been

a misunderstanding and a coincidence—the police car just wanted to check our registration, the car in the middle of the road really was broken down, and Mr. Cam was pure of heart. Boy, wouldn't he have a story to tell around the Tet dinner table?

We'd whizzed through a few small villages that straddled Highway One, and I saw within the villages people on bicycles and kids on the road. This was dangerous, and so were the potholes and the guys shooting at us. It all came down to luck—one of us was going to make a fatal mistake.

I threw my map and guidebook back to Susan and said, "Can you tell how far the next town is?"

She used her lighter to see the page and said, "I see a place called Van Gia. Is that the one?"

"Yeah. That's it. How far?"

"I don't know. Where are we now?"

"We're about thirty kilometers from Ninh Hoa."

"Well . . . then Van Gia is right here."

And sure enough, I could see the lights of a town ahead.

Susan said, "You can't go through that town at this speed, Paul. There will be trucks, cars, and people on the road."

"I know." I needed to do something fast.

A truck was right in front of us now, and his brake lights were going on and off as he slowed down for the town. I swung out into the on-coming lane, passed him, and got back into my lane. I slammed on my brakes and discovered they were not antilock. The Nissan fishtailed, and I fought to keep it under control. The truck was right on my tail now, and I killed my lights. I kept about five meters in front of the truck, hidden from the police car.

I had no idea how close the police car was, but he should be alongside me in a few seconds. I waited and saw his headlights on the road to my left, then the yellow jeep was right beside me. In a split second, the guy in the passenger seat with the AK-47 saw me, and our eyes met. He looked surprised, then aimed his rifle as I ac-celerated and sideswiped the jeep. I didn't have to hit him hard because the driver, who was looking for me up ahead, wasn't expecting it, and the yellow jeep went off the road and skid-ded on the soft shoulder. In my sideview mirror, I saw the jeep hit the drainage ditch and flip over. I heard a muffled crash and saw flames, then an explosion.

I had the accelerator to the floor, and I was still in the oncoming lane. I pulled back into my lane and saw in my mirror that the truck had come to a stop on the road. I put my headlights back on.

I pumped the brakes and got the speed down to sixty KPH as we entered the town of Van Gia.

It was very quiet in the car, and I could hear my breathing. Mr. Cam was actually on the floor, curled into a fetal position. I glanced in my rearview mirror and saw Susan staring straight ahead.

I was doing about forty KPH now down the main street, which was Highway One.

There weren't any streetlights, but most of the one-story stucco buildings were lit, and this illuminated the road. I saw a karaoke parlor to my left, and dozens of kids were hanging out in front of it. Bicycles and motor scooters were parked everywhere, and people were crossing the street. I said to Susan, "You should get down."

Susan slumped down in the rear.

Up ahead on the right, a yellow police jeep was parked in front of the police station, and a few men in uniform were outside. If the cops back there had radioed ahead, then this was the end of the road, and we'd be lucky if we got a firing squad.

I literally held my breath as I approached the police station. There was not a single car moving on the road because at night there weren't many places you'd want to go, and the town was small enough to walk or bicycle. So, the dark blue Nissan stood out. I slumped down in the seat to try to look like I was five feet tall, and I put my right hand over my face as though I was scratching lice or something. Mr. Cam made a movement, and I took my hand away from my face, grabbed his hair, and pushed him down. "Im lang!" I said, even though he wasn't talking, but I couldn't remember how to say, "Don't move!"

We were abreast of the police station now, and I was trying to keep my head turned to the side, and my eyeballs on the cops, while holding Mr. Cam by his hair. I know you're not supposed to touch a Vietnamese's head, but he was in the fetal position, and I couldn't get my hand on his balls.

The policemen glanced at the dark blue Nissan, and I realized I was about to pull Mr. Cam's hair out. I slid my hand down to his neck and held it.

We were past the police station now, and I looked in the right sideview mirror. The cops were looking at the car, but I could tell they weren't looking for me. Still, the car held their interest. I kept moving in first gear up the main street.

A kid on a bicycle passed right in front of me, and we made eye contact. He yelled out, "Lien Xo! Lien Xo!" which I recently learned meant Soviet, or sometimes foreigner, meaning me.

It was time to go. I accelerated and soon we had passed through the town of Van Gia and were back on the dark highway.

I shifted through the gears and in a few minutes we were sailing along at a hundred KPH. I kept looking in the rearview mirror to see if the kid tipped off the cops to the Lien Xo, but I saw no headlights.

I breathed for the first time in about ten minutes. I said to Susan, "How about some nuoc?"

She already had the bottle open and passed it to me. I took a long swig and offered the bottle to Mr. Cam on the floor by tapping it on his head. I figured he was dehydrated by now, but he didn't want any water, so I passed the bottle back to Susan, who took a long drink.

She drew a deep breath and said, "I'm still shaking, and I have to take a pee."

I pulled off to the side of the road, and all three of us took a well-deserved pee. Mr. Cam tried to make a break for it, but it was a half-hearted attempt, and I pushed him back in the car.

I checked the tires, then I examined the car for bullet holes, but I couldn't find any. They either weren't shooting at us, or their aim was off because of the bouncing. It really didn't matter.

I looked at the driver's side and saw that it was scraped, and the left front fender was bent, but basically I just kissed the jeep, which is all it took.

Back in the car, I accelerated to a hundred and maintained that speed. I said to Susan, "I really am sorry about that."

"Nothing to apologize for. We were running from bandits. You did a great job." She asked, "Do you drive like that at home?"

"I actually took an FBI course in offensive driving. I passed the course."

She didn't reply, but she did light a cigarette. She offered one to Mr. Cam, who was sitting in his seat now, and he took it. She lit it for him, and between her shaking hand and his trembling lips, I'm surprised it got lit.

The sea was on our right again, and the last sliver of the moon reflected just enough light off the water to make it not totally black. I passed a truck heading north, but there were no vehicles heading south. This was a totally desolate road at night, which was good for making time, but not good for much else. Now and then I could see a pothole, and I swerved to avoid it. Sometimes I didn't see the pothole and hit it, putting the Nissan into a jarring bounce.

Susan asked, "Do you think anyone is looking for us?"

"The only people looking for us are dead."

She didn't reply.

I said to her, "Mr. Thuc, however, may be looking for Mr. Cam by now."

She thought about that and said, "Mr. Thuc will have heard from his lady-in-distress by now that we were running from the cops, so he's thinking we're either dead or continuing on to Hue."

"Why won't he call the cops?"

"Because the cops would want about a thousand dollars just to look for the car, and thousands more if they found it." She added, "Mr. Thuc is just hoping for the best by now. He'll worry about it tomorrow if he hasn't heard from Mr. Cam. When you think of cops here, don't think of helpful boys in blue who call you sir when you ask for help. They're the biggest thieves in the country."

"I understand."

Susan spoke with Mr. Cam, who seemed a little better after his cigarette. Susan said to me, "He denies that we were being set up to be robbed. He says we are very untrusting. He wants to get out."

"Tell him he has to drive the car back from Hue–Phu Bai Airport, or Mr. Thuc will kill him."

Susan told him, and I recognized the word giet, which means murder or kill. Funny how I remembered some unpleasant words. I said to Susan, "Tell him he'll be home with his family tomorrow, if he behaves."

She told him, he said something, and Susan said to me, "I doubt very much if he'll go to the police. There's nothing in that for him but trouble."

"Good. Because I really don't want to have to kill him."

She didn't reply for a long time, then asked me, "Are you serious?"

"Very."

She sat back in her seat and lit another cigarette. "I see why they sent you."

"They didn't send me. I volunteered."

Mr. Cam seemed to be trying to follow the conversation, probably wondering if we were talking about killing him. To cool him down, I patted his shoulder and said, "Xin loi," which sort of means "Sorry about that."

Susan asked me, "Is your Vietnamese coming back?"

"I think so. Xin loi. When we wasted somebody, we'd say, 'Xin loi, Charlie.' Like, sorry about that, Charlie. Get it?"

She stayed quiet for a while, wondering, I'm sure, if she was with a psychopath. I wondered about that, too. I said to her, "My adrenaline is pumped. I'll be all right."

Again, she said nothing. I think she was a little frightened of me, and to be honest, so was I.

I said to Susan, "You wanted to come along."

"I know. I'm not saying anything."

I put my hand over my shoulder, and she took it and squeezed.

I went back to my driving. The flatland narrowed here to a strip between the mountains on our left, and the sea on our right. Traffic had totally disappeared, and I was making a steady hundred KPH.

Susan asked, "Do you want me to drive?"

"No."

She began massaging my neck and shoulders. "How you doing?"

"Fine. There's a place a few hundred klicks up

ahead called Bong Son where I served for a few months. Look for the Chamber of Commerce sign."

"I'll keep an eye on the map. Why don't you tell me how you got your R&R in Nha Trang."

"Tell you what. We'll go to the A Shau Valley outside Hue, and I'll tell it to you where it happened."

"All right." She massaged my temples and said, "I told you at the Rex that it's good to talk about these things."

"Tell me that after you hear this story."

She stayed silent awhile, then said, "Maybe when you leave here this time, you'll leave the war here, too."

I didn't reply, then said, "I think that's why I'm here."

★

CHAPTER TWENTY-TWO

———————★———————

We continued north, up Highway One, through Vung Ro, a beach resort with a few guesthouses and a small hotel with an outdoor café. If Mr. Cam hadn't been along, we'd have stopped for a coffee or a drink, which I needed.

After Vung Ro, the road swung away from the coast and became desolate again, a dark expanse of rice paddies and dikes, and an occasional peasant's hut.

Mr. Cam was sitting silently. He'd realized, I guess, that if we were going to kill him, we'd have done so already. This realization makes some captives relax and go along peacefully; others get the idea that it might be safe to make a break.

I kept glancing in my rearview mirror, looking for headlights. Headlights meant trouble. I said to Susan, "There is not one single vehicle on the main national highway."

"People really don't travel in the countryside at night, except for the occasional bus. During the day, Highway One is so crowded, you barely make thirty miles an hour." She added, "I'm told that the police stop patrolling the highways about an hour after dark."

"That's a break."

"Not really. The army patrols the highways until dawn. The cops stay in the towns." She added, "The army patrols will stop anyone on the highway."

"What's the next major town?"

She looked at the map and said, "A place called Qui Nhon. But Highway One passes to the west of it, so we don't have to go through the town."

I said, "That was a big American hospital town."

"You remember it?"

"Yes. Qui Nhon got the cases that the hospital ships didn't get. We also did a lot of Vietnamese military and civilian cases there. Plus, there was a big leper hospital outside town."

"Oh . . . I've heard of that place. There's still a leper hospital there."

"We had a combat medic who got so burned out in the field, he volunteered to work in the leper hospital. We made a joke of it. You know? Whenever things got really bad, we'd all volunteer for the leper hospital at Qui Nhon." Susan didn't laugh. I said, "I guess you had to be there." I asked her, "How far?"

"I think just up ahead a few kilometers."

"Can you read a map, or are you faking it?"

"That's a sexist remark."

"Xin loi."

She gave me a punch in the shoulder, which

surprised Mr. Cam. I said, "Mr. Cam's wife never punches him. I'm going to marry a Vietnamese woman."

"They're so docile, you'd be bored out of your mind."

"Sounds good."

She said, "I'm glad you're feeling better."

I said to her, "I'm a little concerned about the truck driver."

She thought about that, then said, "Well . . . the truck driver didn't know we were foreigners. He assumed we were Vietnamese, who were being chased by the cops. He didn't see a thing."

"Good point."

We passed the Qui Nhon road that intersected Highway One, and there were a scattering of buildings at the intersection, including a gas station, but it was closed. I asked Susan, "Do you think any gas stations are open?"

"Why would they be?"

"Right. I don't think we're going to make it to Hue on one tank of gas, even with the spare gas cans."

"Turn off your headlights. Saves gas. Ask Mr. Cam."

I looked at the gas gauge and did a little arithmetic in my head. I figured we could go another two hundred to two hundred and fifty kilometers, depending obviously on the size of the tank and our gas mileage. The extra ten liters in the cans would add maybe another fifty or sixty Ks to our range. I said to Susan, "Ask Mr. Cam where he would get gasoline at night."

She asked him, he replied, and she said to me, "He doesn't know. He's never driven this far north, and rarely drives at night."

I laughed. "Well, where was he going to refuel?"

Susan replied, "Obviously, he had no intention of driving us to Hue."

"I know that. Tell him that."

She told him, and Mr. Cam looked a little sheepish.

Susan said, "I remember some late night gas stations in Da Nang."

"How far is Da Nang?"

She looked down at her map and said, "About three hundred kilometers."

I looked at my fuel gauge again and said, "I hope it's downhill, or we're not going to make it. Maybe we should get chubby here out of the car."

"We need him to pump gas. Paul? What were we thinking?"

"I thought we'd have a bigger gas tank or get better mileage. If worse comes to worse, we'll pull over, wait until light, and get to an open gas station."

I looked up ahead, and on the flat horizon, I could see the glow of lights. I asked Susan, "Is that Bong Son?"

"It should be."

I began decelerating and looked around at the sparse landscape, which seemed familiar. I said, more to myself than to Susan, "This is where I saw the elephant."

"What elephant?"

I didn't reply for a few seconds, then I said, "It's an expression. Men who have seen combat for the first time say, 'I have seen the elephant.'" I looked at the road and the terrain on either side where I'd had my first firefight, on an early morning in November 1967, the day after Thanksgiving.

Susan asked, "What's it mean?"

"Don't know. But I know it's old—not 'Nam related. Maybe it goes back to Roman times when Hannibal crossed the Alps with elephants." I repeated, "I have seen the elephant."

Susan remarked, "It sounds almost mystical."

I nodded. "There is no one on this earth more mystical, superstitious, and ultimately religious than a combat soldier. I've seen men kiss their crucifix and make the sign of the cross before battle . . . then they'd put an AK-47 round in their helmet band, which represented the enemy bullet that had been meant for them. And they'd stick an ace of spades in their helmet because the Vietnamese regarded it as a symbol of death. And there were all sorts of other talismans, and rituals that men would go through before battle . . . bottom line, you pray."

Susan stayed quiet awhile, then said, "And this is where you saw the elephant?"

"This is where I saw the elephant."

She thought awhile, then said, "When we were being shot at back there . . . I think I caught a glimpse of the elephant."

"Did you go ice cold with fear and feel your mouth go dry and your heart trying to burst through your chest?"

"I did."

"Then you caught a glimpse of the elephant."

Up ahead, I could see a bridge that I recalled, and which passed over the An Lao River, on the other side of which was the town of Bong Son.

Susan put on her sunglasses and asked, "Do I look like a co-dep?"

I looked at her in the rearview mirror. With her long, straight hair parted down the middle, and with the shades, she could pass for a Vietnamese woman in a dark moving car. I looked at Mr. Cam. He could pass for a Vietnamese, too, because he was Vietnamese. The problem was me.

I looked at Mr. Cam again, and I had the impression he was going to make a break for it when we hit the town.

I pulled onto the shoulder and said to Susan, "Get the shoelace from one of my docksiders in my suitcase."

She got out of the car, opened the rear hatch,

and took a few things out of the luggage. She called out to me, "It's getting cold out here."

I lowered my window, and it seemed to me that it was still warm, but I hadn't lived here for three years. I remembered the smell of the wet night earth and the river.

Susan closed the hatch and got back into the car. She handed me a leather lace from one of my deck shoes. She also had one of her high-necked silk blouses, which she put on over her polo shirt.

I took the strip of leather and motioned for Mr. Cam to lean forward and put his hands behind his back. He seemed happier about being tied up than being strangled, and he cooperated fully.

I tied his thumbs together, then tied the loose ends of the leather lace to his belt.

Susan handed me my sunglasses and said, "Slicky boys wear these day and night. You won't look too weird."

I put the glasses on, but as far as I was concerned, I still looked like a six-foot Caucasian with wavy hair and a prominent nose.

I put the Nissan into gear, and we drove toward the bridge. I said to Susan, "See those concrete bunkers on the corners of the bridge? They were built by the French. American platoons took turns manning the bunkers. It was good duty—better than out in the boondocks.

There used to be barbed wire all over and mine-fields. Every few weeks, Charlie would come around to see if we were awake. They really wanted to blow that bridge, but they never got past the barbed wire and the minefields. The minefields were laid by the French, and we didn't have a map of the mines, so when Charles blew himself up out there, we couldn't go in to retrieve the bodies. They'd lay out there and feed the buzzards and maggots for weeks. This place used to stink a lot. Smells okay now." I raised my window.

Susan had no comment.

We drove onto the bridge across the An Lao, which flowed into the South China Sea. I put the Nissan into second gear and slid down in my seat.

We came off the bridge into the main street of the town of Bong Son. The town seemed to be as I remembered it. The stucco buildings were fairly nice, and there were palm trees planted here and there. Bong Son had apparently not been hit hard by the war.

There were a few restaurants on the street, and I remembered that a lot of ethnic Indians and Chinese once lived here, who owned most of the shops and restaurants, but I saw no evidence of them now. The GI bars, massage parlors, and whorehouses had been on a side street, away from the good citizens.

Back to the present, I saw that there were a

lot of motor scooters and bicycles on the street, and more important, there were a few cars moving around, so we didn't look too out of place.

I said, "Up ahead, at the end of town, used to be the headquarters of the National Police. They were mostly guys from well-connected families, and police service kept them out of the army. They were also sadistic. See that stone wall over on the right? And those big wrought iron gates?"

"Yes."

"Inside the wall is a French colonial building. I think it was the town hall or something. One night, a bunch of VC infiltrated the town and attacked the building. The National Police killed and captured about a dozen of them. A few days later, I came into town with a bunch of guys in a Jeep to see what we could buy or barter on the black market. The National Police had hanged a dozen VC bodies from those gates. Most of them were full of holes, but some had been hanged alive, and not by the neck— but by their thumbs. The bodies were rotting in the sun." I added, "The ARVN would just shoot captured VC in the head. The National Police were not so nice."

I looked at Susan in the rearview mirror. She was not looking at the gates, but I looked at them as we passed by, and I could see those bodies hanging there. "I still remember the stench."

She had no comment.

"We reported it to our company commander,

and he passed it up the line. The National Police were pissed at us for interfering in their object lesson. Don't get me wrong—we were no angels, either, but you have to draw the line somewhere. War is one thing, but this wasn't war. On the other hand, the Vietnamese had been at it so long, and they'd lost so many friends and family, that they'd gone around the bend long before we got here."

I continued, "The First Cavalry was moved out of Bong Son after the new year, and we went up to Quang Tri, which turned out to be a lot worse than this place."

Again, I looked in my rearview mirror and saw that Susan was sitting very still. I said, "I was eighteen years old."

The National Police headquarters came up on our left, and I saw a red flag with a yellow star hanging from the building. There were four yellow jeeps parked out front, and about six policemen, smoking and chatting. I turned my head away as we passed close by and kept going.

I said, "After the Communist victory, the big bloodbath that everyone had predicted turned out to be not too bad. The executions were selective, and most enemies of the state wound up in re-education camps. But the National Police, who were hated by just about everyone, were systematically hunted down and executed by the new National Police." I added, "What you sow, you reap."

Susan, I saw, had a pack of cigarettes in one hand, a lighter in the other, but she just sat there. Finally, she said, "I never understood any of this in Saigon."

"It was a very dirty war in the countryside. But it's history. Memories fade, and life goes on. The next generation might be okay." I looked at Mr. Cam and wondered about his own history. Maybe I'd ask him later.

The town of Bong Son stretched on along Highway One for a hundred more meters, then we were out in the countryside again. I said, "The big American camp, called Landing Zone English, was a few kilometers from here to the left. There's a valley there called An Lao, where the river starts in the hills. We cleared out all the population of the valley, and resettled the people in strategic hamlets so that they couldn't aid the local VC or North Vietnamese army with food or labor. The An Lao Valley became a free-fire zone, and anything in the valley that moved was shot— including farm animals left behind and wildlife. We even went bird hunting with Browning automatic shotguns. We burned every structure, killed every fruit-bearing tree, oiled the rice paddies, and leveled the forest with these things called Rome Plows. Then we air-dropped cardboard barrels filled with crystals that produced noxious, choking gas. We renamed the An Lao Valley the Valley of Death." I paused. "I wonder if anyone lives there now."

Susan said nothing.

I got the Nissan up to a hundred KPH as we continued north.

Highway One swung east toward the sea again, and there were white sand beaches along the coast, and white sand hills to our left, covered with scrub brush. I said to Susan, "This is where I spent Christmas 1967. The white sands of Bong Son. We made believe it was snow." I added, "There was a forty-eight-hour truce. We got a lot of Christmas packages from the Red Cross, and from private organizations and individuals. At that time, before Tet, people still supported the troops, if not the war itself."

I recalled that Christmas was a particularly hot day, and the white sands had no shade trees. Christmas dinner had been delivered by helicopter, and we were sitting in the sand, eating turkey with all the trimmings, trying to keep the sand flies away, and the sand out of the food.

A kid from Brooklyn named Savino saw a long bamboo pole in the sand and decided to use it to make a shelter with his rubber poncho to keep the sun off him. He reached for the pole, someone shouted for him to stop, he pulled the pole, which was attached by a wire to a very large explosive device, and he blew himself back to Brooklyn in a body bag.

A bunch of other guys got hurt, half the platoon was deaf, and pieces of the kid were everywhere, including everyone's mess tins and canteen cups. Merry Christmas.

I said, "A guy in my platoon was killed by a booby trap on Christmas day."

"Was he a friend?"

"He . . . he wasn't here long enough." I added, "It was sort of a waste of time to make friends with the new guys. They had a bad survival rate, and they got people around them killed. If they were still alive after thirty days, then you'd shake their hand or something."

We left my old area of operations, and I didn't recognize this terrain.

Mr. Cam appeared to be getting uncomfortable with his arms behind his back. Susan noticed and asked me, "Should we untie him?"

"No."

"He can't get away when we're moving this fast."

"No."

Susan finally lit her cigarette. I actually wanted a cigarette myself, probably because my head was still back in the Bong Son area of operations, where I used to do a pack a day. I said, "Let's hear from Mr. Cam. Ask him if he remembers the war."

She asked him, and he didn't seem to want to answer. Finally, he spoke, and Susan translated. She said, "He was thirteen when the war ended. He lived in a village west of Nha Trang, and he remembers when the Communists arrived. He says that thousands of South Vietnamese troops had been passing through his village as they retreated from the highlands, and everyone knew the war was ending. Many people fled to Nha Trang, but he stayed in his village with his mother and his two sisters."

"And what happened?"

She prodded him a little, he spoke in a quiet tone, and Susan translated. "He says everyone was very frightened, but when the North Vietnamese troops came, they behaved well. There were only women and children left in the village, and the women were not molested. But the Communists found a young army officer who had a leg amputated, and they took him away. Later, political cadres came and questioned everyone. They found two government officials disguised as peasants, and they were taken away. But no one was shot in the village."

I nodded. "And his father? Brothers?"

Susan asked him, and he replied. She said to me, "His father had been killed in battle many years before. He had an older brother serving with the ARVN in the highlands, but he never returned home. He says his mother still waits for her son to return."

I looked at Mr. Cam and saw he was upset. Susan, too, seemed disturbed by Mr. Cam's story. My own memories of that time were starting to fill my head.

When you begin a journey like this, you have to expect the worst, and you won't be disappointed.

We continued on along the black highway, through the night, and back in time.

CHAPTER TWENTY-THREE

─────── ★ ───────

We had come about three hundred kilometers from Nha Trang, and it was close to 10 p.m. I was keeping the speed down to conserve fuel, and we weren't in any particular hurry, anyway. I looked at the fuel gauge, and the needle was hovering around a quarter full.

I asked her, "How far to Da Nang?"

She'd already figured it out and said, "About a hundred fifty kilometers. How's the fuel?"

"We burned some fuel back there running the fuzz. We may be able to reach Da Nang with the extra ten liters. Or maybe we'll see an all-night station on the way."

"In the last three hundred kilometers, we've passed only four gas stations, all closed."

"Don't we pass through Quang Ngai?"

"Yes. It's right on Highway One. Provincial capital. It's about seventy-five kilometers from here."

"Take out my guidebook and see if they mention a gas station."

She opened the guidebook and said, "Well, there's a small map of the town . . . there's a hotel, a pagoda, a church, a post office, a place

called Rice Restaurant Thirty-four, a bus station—"

"These cars can run on rice."

"I hope so. This map doesn't show a gas station. But there has to be a few in a town that
size. Maybe one is open. If not," she added,
"there's one more town after Quang Ngai and
before Da Nang that we may be able to make.
It's called Hoi An, an old Chinese seaport. Very
touristy and charming. I took a trip there the
time I was in Hue. There are a lot of accommodations in Hoi An, and maybe a gas station that
will be open late. We may be able to make it
that far. There's nothing between Hoi An and
Da Nang."

"Okay. Let's see how it goes."

Mr. Cam figured out that we were discussing
fuel, and he said something to Susan.

She said to me, "Mr. Cam, who is now our
friend, said that we can sometimes buy gasoline
from private vendors. He says they sell it in stalls
along the road. We should look for a painted
sign that says et-xang, which means gasoline."

"And they're open all night?"

"Sort of. You go to the house near the sign,
and they'll sell you gasoline. I've done that on
my motorcycle. The gasoline is usually sold in
soft drink bottles, and it's expensive."

"How many Coke bottles do we need to fill a
tank?"

"I don't have my calculator. Look for a sign that says et-xang."

I said to Susan, "Tell me again why Mr. Cam won't do his civic duty and go to the police. Make believe Mr. Cam's life depends on your answer."

She stayed silent for some time, then replied, "I couldn't even translate the concept of civic duty. If he gets his car back and about a hundred bucks for himself, two for Mr. Thuc, and a few hundred to fix the damage, he is not going to the police. When there's an accident in Saigon, the last thing they want is for the police to show up."

"Good. Case closed."

Mr. Cam wanted a cigarette, and he deserved it. Susan lit it for him and held it while he puffed away.

We came to a place called Sa Huynh, a picturesque village on the coast surrounded by salt marshes. Before you could say "quaint," we were out in the country again.

We continued on, and the highway swung inland through an area of small villages and rice paddies.

I glanced at my fuel gauge and saw that it was below a quarter of a tank. The road was flat, and I was keeping the speed down to eighty KPH, so I figured I'd be able to squeeze out enough fuel to reach Quang Ngai. If not, we had twenty liters in the gas cans.

I had not seen a single sign that showed distances between cities, or even a sign that showed the name of a city. We were doing this all by map. The road itself was alternately good and terrible, mostly terrible. This place had a long way to go, but in fairness, after thirty years of war, they'd come a long way.

Susan said, "We should be approaching Quang Ngai. It's on this side of the Tra Khuc River, and Highway One becomes the main street. Maybe we shouldn't try to get through the town at this hour. And even if we found an open station, you'd have to change places with Mr. Cam."

"So, what's your suggestion?"

"I suggest we pull the car into some trees and wait until dawn. We can go into Quang Ngai in the morning and fill up."

"All right. Look for a place to pull over."

I slowed down, and we looked for a place where the car would be out of sight.

We were only a few kilometers from Quang Ngai, and I could see the lights of the town on the horizon. It was amazing, I thought, how distinct the towns were from the surrounding countryside, with no urban or suburban sprawl, no shopping malls, and obviously no gas stations. On the plus side, I hadn't seen a cop on the highway since we started, except the two I ran into a ditch. But according to Susan, the military patrolled the highway after dark, and if there was one single military vehicle on the road, and one civilian car—this one—we'd be pulled over for no reason. The ace in the hole, of course, was the Colt .45. They wouldn't expect that.

Quang Ngai was right up the road, about a kilometer, but I didn't see any place to pull over. It was mostly rice paddies and villages, and the land was open, except for small stands of palm trees which didn't offer any concealment.

I spotted a rise of land in the middle of a rice paddy that was connected to the highway by a dirt causeway or dike. I knew what this was, but it took a few seconds before it came to me. I said, "That's a burial mound over there. We can park on the far side of it, and no one will see us."

I slowed down and cut the wheels onto the dirt causeway that ran through the flooded rice paddies.

All of a sudden, Mr. Cam started going nuts. "What's his problem?"

"He says that's a burial mound."

"I know what it is. We used to dig our night positions into burial mounds. Soft earth, good elevation, fields of fire—"

"He wants to know why you're driving to the burial mound. You should stop."

I stopped halfway to the big mound, and Mr. Cam calmed down. "What's he saying?"

Susan spoke to him, and he got agitated again. She said to me, "I told him we were going to spend the night there. He's not too thrilled about that."

"Come on. They're all dead. Tell him we'll be very respectful, and we'll pray all night."

"Paul, he won't spend the night on a burial mound. You'd have to hog-tie him. They're very superstitious, and it's also disrespectful."

"I'm not superstitious or culturally sensitive."

"Paul."

"Okay." I threw the Nissan into reverse and backed it down the narrow dirt dike. I got on the highway, threw the car into gear, and we continued on. As soon as you do something nice, your luck runs out.

And sure enough, coming up the highway toward us was a pair of headlights, about a kilometer away. I killed my headlights and slowed down. The oncoming lights were too low to the ground to be a truck or bus, so it had to be something smaller, like a four-wheel drive, probably a military patrol.

Susan said, "Paul, pull off the road."

"I know." I put the Nissan in four-wheel drive and drove down the raised road embankment. There was no drainage ditch because the rice paddy was right at the bottom of the embankment. I drove parallel to the road with my right wheels in the rice paddy muck, and my left wheels on the side of the embankment. We were at a forty-five degree angle, maybe more, and I was concerned that the Nissan might flip. My rear wheels were starting to slip and sink into the muck. I stopped.

I looked up at the road and saw that I wasn't really out of sight. But it was dark enough to hope for the best, while preparing for the worst. I said to Susan, "Give me the tote bag."

I could hear the vehicle approaching now and saw the head beams coming closer.

She passed the bag to me, and I put my hand inside and found the pistol grip. I didn't want Mr. Cam to see the gun because that could be the thing that sent him to the police.

I could feel the end of the magazine seated in the pistol grip. I clicked off the safety. I asked Susan, "Magazine fully loaded?"

"Yes."

"Is there a round chambered?"

"No."

"Extra magazines?"

"Two." She added, "I'm frightened."

I looked at Mr. Cam, who seemed apprehensive. I had the impression he was rehearsing his story for the authorities, and was glad he was tied up.

Within a few seconds, I could see the top of the vehicle as it approached. It was a big enclosed jeep-like vehicle, painted dark, not yellow, and I recognized it as military. I saw the driver, who was concentrating on the road, and a man in the rear.

The Nissan's roof was about level with the raised highway, it was painted dark blue, it was a dark night, and the gods were with us. The military vehicle kept going.

We sat there for what seemed like a long time, then I put the Nissan into reverse, the rear wheels caught, and the Nissan backed up the embankment.

I sat on the road for a few seconds with the headlights still off and looked around. It was so dark I could barely see ten yards in any direction.

I began moving forward again without lights toward Quang Ngai. The glow from the town silhouetted some buildings on both sides of the road, and I saw something that looked promising. I pointed the Nissan toward the silhouette, stopped, and snapped on the headlights.

There on the right, at the end of a dirt trail, was a ruined structure without a roof. I hoped it wasn't a Buddhist temple or we'd have another problem with Mr. Cam.

I drove slowly onto the dirt path that cut through the rice paddies, and I pulled up to the front of the white stucco structure. On the front peak, I could see the remains of what had been a church belfry. I said to Susan, "Catholic church. I hope this guy isn't also Catholic."

She said something to Mr. Cam, and he nodded.

I drove through the wide doorway and into the church, then cut the wheels and backed the

Nissan into the front corner of the church so it couldn't be seen from the road.

The headlights illuminated what was basically just a shell of a building with vegetation growing through the rubble-strewn concrete floor.

I killed the lights and the engine, and said, "Well, this is it for the night."

We all got out and stretched, except that Mr. Cam couldn't stretch his arms very well, so I untied him.

Susan got the water and the snacks out of the car, and we had a terrible dinner. I asked her, "Didn't they have Ring Dings or cheese crackers in that gas station? What is this stuff?"

"I don't know. Candy. Stop complaining. In fact, you should say grace."

Mr. Cam ate more than his share of the stuff in the cellophane bags, and he drank a whole liter of water by himself.

I had no choice but to tie him up again, so I bound his thumbs behind his back, took his sandals, and put him in the rear of the Nissan, where he lay down on the seat.

Susan and I sat cross-legged in the corner opposite the Nissan. The only illumination came from the starlight into the roofless building. She observed, "It must have been a nice country church once."

"These were all over when I was here—ruined

churches and pagodas. They were the only substantial buildings around, and civilians and military used to take cover in them. You'd be safe
from small arms fire, but not rockets or mortars."

She said, "It's hard to imagine a war raging
around you every day. I'm glad you were able to
talk about it back there in Bong Son."

I didn't reply.

She took out her cigarettes and very expertly
cupped the lighter and lit up quickly, just like an
old combat soldier. She shielded the cigarette in
her hands as she smoked. She said, "I'm cold.
Can I borrow something from your suitcase?"

"Sure. I'll get it."

"Bring my backpack, too." I stood and went
to the Nissan. I opened the hatch door and got
my blue blazer out of my suitcase, and took her
backpack. I put my blazer over her shoulders.

She said, "Thank you. Aren't you cold?"

"It's about seventy degrees."

Susan had a travel alarm clock in her backpack, and she set it to go off at midnight. She
said, "We'll set it every hour, so if we both drift
off, this should wake us up."

"Okay. I'll take the first watch. Try to get
some sleep."

She lay down on the concrete floor with her
backpack for a pillow.

We talked awhile, then I realized she'd drifted
off.

I took the Colt .45 out of her tote and chambered a round. I put the pistol in my lap.

The alarm rang at midnight, and I shut it off before it woke her. I set it again for one A.M., in case I drifted. But, oddly, I had no trouble staying awake, and I let her sleep until 4 A.M.

We switched places, and I gave her the pistol.

I lay my head on her backpack and remembered when my own backpack had been my pillow for a year, and my rifle had been my sleeping partner. We always slept fully clothed, with our boots on, swatting mosquitoes all night, worrying about snakes and about Charlie. We were dirty, miserable, sometimes wet, sometimes cold, sometimes hot, and always frightened.

This wasn't the worst night I'd ever spent in Vietnam; far from it. But I couldn't blame this one on anyone but myself.

The sky lightened, bringing a false dawn, which was common to the tropics, then an hour later, the real dawn broke, and a rooster crowed. A stream of sunlight came in through a small arched window to the right of where the altar had once been. A shard of blue glass, still stuck in the window frame, cast a streak of blue light across the floor and up the opposite wall.

I sat up, and Susan and I watched the dawn unfold.

The interior of the small church was clearly visible now, and I could see the whitewashed walls and the crumbling stucco, and the places where the bullets had hit, and where exploding shrapnel had scarred a faded fresco of the Virgin Mary.

There wasn't a single scrap of wood left in the structure, except the charred remains of a fire that someone had lit on the floor where the altar once sat.

The rice paddies don't attract many birds, but I heard a lone bird singing somewhere. Then I heard the first vehicle on the road.

Susan said, "Today is Lunar New Year's Eve." She took my hand. "I don't think I've ever been so happy to see a sunrise in my life."

I could hear a truck on the road and a motor scooter. I glanced out through the open doorway and saw a farm cart and two girls on bicycles.

I remembered when the first vehicles on the road were minesweepers, tanks that could safely set off explosive devices buried in the potholes during the night. Then would come the Jeeps and trucks filled with American and Vietnamese soldiers, rifles and machine guns ready to take on any ambush that had been set in place during the night.

Then came the civilians, on foot, in ox carts, on bicycles, off to the fields, or to school, or wherever.

Within an hour of sunrise, Highway One would be open, piece by piece, from the Mekong Delta to the DMZ, and life would go on until the sun set.

I said to Susan, "Highway One is open to Hue."

CHAPTER TWENTY-FOUR

——————★——————

In the daylight, I could see that the driver's side of the Nissan had picked up some yellow paint from my contact with the police jeep. Susan and I each had Swiss army knives, and we scraped the paint off, while Mr. Cam, who I'd untied, used a shard of glass to help.

I cut our plastic water bottles in half and collected some rice paddy muck outside, which we smeared along the scrapes.

In the muck, we found a few bloodsucking leeches. Susan was repulsed by the leeches, Mr. Cam didn't seem to care, and I had some unpleasant memories.

She looked at a big, fat leech in the muck of the plastic water bottle. "Do they bite?"

"They attach themselves to your skin somewhere. They have a natural anesthetic in their saliva, so you don't know you've gotten bitten. Also in the saliva is a blood thinner, so your blood just keeps flowing into these things while they suck. You can have them on you all day and not know it, unless you do periodic checks. I had one under my armpit once that got so fat and bloated with my blood that I accidentally squashed it when I lay down on my side to take a break."

Susan made a face.

After I'd returned from Vietnam, I'd probably told more leech stories than combat stories. These stories never failed to gross out people, and I got really good at it.

We used one of my polo shirts to wipe our hands.

I let Mr. Cam drive, and this made him happier than having his thumbs tied together. I sat in the front and Susan in the rear. We pulled out of the church and onto Highway One. A few people on bicycles and motor scooters looked at us, but by all appearances, we were two Western tourists with a Vietnamese driver, who had pulled over to check out a war ruin or make a pit stop.

Within a few minutes, we were in the provincial capital of Quang Ngai. I kept a close eye on Mr. Cam, and Susan was engaging him in conversation. He seemed okay, but Susan said, "He wants something to eat, and he wants to telephone his family."

"He can do whatever he wants after he drops us off at Hue–Phu Bai Airport."

Susan relayed this to him, and he seemed quietly unhappy.

Quang Ngai was nothing to write home about. It was, in fact, an ugly town, but I spotted a beautiful gas station.

We pulled over, and I said to Susan, "You pump. I'll keep Mr. Cam company."

Susan got out and pumped gasoline. A few people hanging around the gas station watched her pumping while Mr. Cam and I sat in the front. They probably concluded that Western men had their women better trained than the Vietnamese men did. They should only know.

Susan paid the guy, who had been standing near her, and the guy seemed very curious about us and the Nissan. He even drew Susan's attention to the scrape marks and the dent. Susan pretended she spoke no Vietnamese.

I looked at Mr. Cam. If he was going to make a break for it, this was his best shot.

The pump attendant said something to Mr. Cam, who replied, and they exchanged another few words.

Susan got in the car and said to Mr. Cam, "Cu di."

Mr. Cam started the engine and threw the car into gear.

I asked Susan, "What did he and the guy say?"

Susan replied, "The guy noticed the Nha Trang license plates and asked if we'd driven through the night. Mr. Cam said no, then the guy asked him where we'd stayed last night, and Mr. Cam didn't have an answer. It was just polite conversation, but it didn't go well."

I said, "Well, no one calls the police about anything here. Right?"

Susan didn't reply.

We passed through the rest of the ugly town and crossed the Tra Khuc River via a bridge that looked like it had been the prize in a game between Viet Cong sappers and the U.S. Army Corps of Engineers. In the end, it looked as though the engineers had narrowly won.

We were in the open country again, and Highway One was now crowded with motor vehicles, ox carts, bicycles, scooters, and pedestrians. We were barely making fifty KPH, and I could see how the drive from Nha Trang to Hue could take eleven or twelve hours during the day.

I looked at the map and saw an asterisk north of Quang Ngai, which meant a point of interest. The point of interest, which was only a few kilometers from here, was described in Vietnamese and in English. It said: *My Lai Massacre.* It went on to say: *War crime occurred here, March 16, 1968, when three U.S. infantry companies killed several hundred unarmed villagers. A memorial commemorates the dead and reminds one of the insanity and tragedy of war.*

I said to myself, "Amen."

We approached a small road that had a hand-painted sign with an arrow that read in English *My Lai Massacre.*

As I said, I hadn't seen any helpful road signs so far, so I had to wonder who put up that one and why. I wondered, too, if any of the surviving three hundred American soldiers who had been there had ever come back.

I looked at the terrain. There were long stretches of rice paddies and small villages clustered on pieces of high ground, shaded with palm trees, and surrounded by growths of towering bamboo. This was typical of what I recalled when I thought of Vietnam, though I'd also operated in much more rugged terrain, away from the coastal populations, which I preferred.

When the war was in the jungles and the highlands, it had a better feel to it, a sort of boys' adventure, the ultimate rite of passage. In the hills and the jungles, you didn't kill civilians by mistake or on purpose, as at My Lai, and there were no villages to burn, or water buffalo to shoot. The boys seemed more focused and intent in the quiet presence of the primeval jungle and the highland forests; it was just us and them in the greatest game of survival ever conceived or carried out. The war had clarity, and the kills were clean, and there were no women or children dying around you, and no My Lais.

We passed into the province of Quang Nam, and approached the once huge American air force base at Chu Lai. This, I recalled, was where some of my air force friends from Apocalypse Now had been stationed.

I saw strands of rusted barbed wire from the old base, then abandoned concrete buildings. I saw a few hangars and dozens of concrete aircraft revetments built in the white sands that stretched to the east down to the sea. I could also make out a runway, covered with white objects that I couldn't identify.

Susan saw me looking and said, "The farmers use the old runways to dry manioc root."

"Really? You mean that millions of U.S. tax dollars were spent to build jet fighter runways that are now used to dry manioc roots?"

"Looks that way. Swords into ploughshares. Runways into—"

"What the hell is manioc?"

"You know. Like cassava. You make tapioca pudding out of it."

"I hate tapioca. My mother force-fed it to me. Call an air strike on that runway."

Susan laughed, and Mr. Cam smiled. He liked happy passengers.

I said, "I'd love to be here when those jet jockeys from Apocalypse Now get up to Chu Lai. They'll have a fit."

The Chu Lai base was big and sprawling, and we kept passing pieces of it. I saw kids pulling wagons through the area, and I asked Susan, "What are they doing?"

"They're scrap metal scavengers. It used to be a huge business in Vietnam, but most of the easy stuff has been found." She added, "A lot of the stuff blew up in their faces. There were hundreds of scavengers killed and maimed every year, according to what I've heard. Now, the pickings are slimmer, but safer."

I watched the kids digging in the sand. After thirty years of war, and nearly thirty years of peace and recovery, this nation still had scars and unhealed wounds that continued to bleed. Maybe that's what we had in common with them.

Susan said, "When or if you go into the interior, be advised that a lot of the unexploded stuff is still lying around."

"Thank you." In truth, even during the war, there was so much unexploded stuff around that you had just as much chance of being blown up by your own duds as by their booby traps.

I looked at Mr. Cam, who had obviously not had a good night's sleep. He was starting to nod a bit, and I shook his shoulder. I asked him, "Do you know that twenty-five percent of U.S. auto fatalities are caused by fatigued drivers?"

"Eh?"

Susan translated something, but not quite what I said. She said to me, "He wants some coffee."

"Next Burger King, we'll stop."

She said something to Mr. Cam, and I didn't hear the words Burger King.

The coast curved inland now, and the highway passed over several small bridges that spanned creeks and streams, which ran down

from the hills into the sea. It really was a beautiful country, and I appreciated it more now than
I did when I had to walk it seven days a week.

Susan said, "This area was the center of the
Champa civilization. Did you see Cham Towers
when you were here?"

"Actually, I did, though I didn't know what
they were. We used them as watchtowers or artillery spotting towers. I saw everything through
the eyes of a soldier. I'm glad I came back. I'm
glad you're with me."

"That's very sweet. Don't forget you said that."

We drove awhile, and I looked at the map. I
said, "According to the map, Highway One runs
far to the west of Da Nang, so we don't have to
go through the city."

"Didn't you say you left Vietnam from Da
Nang?"

"Yes. November 3, 1968. Caught a helicopter
from Quang Tri to my base camp at An Khe and
collected the stuff in my trunk, which I hadn't
seen since my R&R, got all my paperwork in order, saw the pecker checker about VD, said
good-bye to a few people, and di di mau'ed the
hell out of there. Caught a big Chinook chopper
to Da Nang. We drew fire someplace over the
highlands. I mean, I had less than seventy-two
hours left in-country, and these bastards are trying to kill me on the way to Da Nang. But aside
from a few holes in the chopper, we made it.
Then, while I'm in the transit barracks waiting

for my flight home, the next day, at about three in the morning, Charles lobs in a few mortar rounds on the going-home barracks." I added, "He did it on purpose."

"Was anyone hurt?"

"The empty mess hall next door got blown up, and some shrapnel flew through the barracks. I got knocked out of my upper bunk bed and sustained yet another head injury. But no one noticed, and I caught my flight to San Francisco."

"I'll bet you were happy to be going home."

I didn't reply for a while, then said, "I was . . . but . . . I thought about staying with my company . . . everyone who left had mixed feelings about leaving their friends . . . it was weird, and it stayed with me for months . . . it wasn't a death wish, it was a mixture of emotions, including the thought that I wasn't going to fit in among normal people. It's hard to explain, but nearly everyone who's been to war will tell you the same thing."

She didn't reply.

We continued in silence awhile, then we crossed a bridge that spanned the Cam Le River, and I said to Susan, "Ask Mr. Cam if the Cam Le River is named after him."

She said to me, "There aren't that many words in Vietnamese, Paul, and fewer proper names, so you'll see a lot of names and words appearing with great frequency. Try not to be confused, and no, the river was not named after Mr. Cam."

Mr. Cam knew we were talking about him, and kept looking over his shoulder at Susan. Susan put her hand on his shoulder and said something. He laughed.

I guess he got over being kidnapped, almost killed in a high-speed chase, being tied up, sleeping out in the cold, and being threatened with death. Or, maybe he was smiling because he was thinking about his tip. Or maybe his revenge. The unhappy truth is, if Susan hadn't been with me, I'd have had no choice but to kill Mr. Cam. Well, of course I had a choice, but the right choice was to get rid of him. And yet, deep inside of me, I knew I'd killed too many Vietnamese, including the two cops, and the thought of killing yet another made my stomach knot up. But if I believed that what I was doing here was important and right, then just like in 1968, when I believed the same bullshit, I'd do what I had to do for God, for country, and for Paul Brenner.

The Da Nang airport was off in the distance to our right, and beyond the airport, I could see the low skyline of the big city.

The airport, I recalled, was bigger and better than Tan Son Nhat because the Americans had built it from scratch. Now, according to my map, it was designated as an international airport. I said to Susan, "You could dry a lot of manioc on those runways."

"It's a major civilian and military field. In a

few years, you'll be able to fly to the States from there."

"How about right now?"

"There are already American cargo planes making the run once in a while."

Actually, I knew this. This was escape Plan C, according to Mr. Conway. Paul Brenner in an air shipment container labeled bananas or something. Might work. Might not.

She got her camera out and took a picture of the airport in the distance. She said, "A souvenir for you. And no one is trying to kill you this . . . well . . . you know what I mean."

"Right."

"I fly up here once in a while on business. Did you say you never got to China Beach?"

"Nope."

"Monkey Mountain?"

"Hate monkeys."

"I guess you weren't here too long."

"I was here for exactly seventy-one hours and ten minutes. And I never stepped foot out of the airbase."

"Right. You wanted to go home."

"In a passenger seat, not the cargo hold."

I recalled another television show from the last days of South Vietnam and said to Susan, "In about late March of 1975, as the end drew near, World Airways sent two 727s on a mercy mission to rescue civilian refugees at Da Nang Airbase. When the first plane landed, about a thousand hysterical men, women, and children mobbed the aircraft. But the South Vietnamese military decided that they deserved to be saved instead of the civilians, and they began firing at the refugees, and two hundred soldiers from the South Vietnamese Black Panther regiment threw everyone off the aircraft but themselves."

"That's awful."

"The pilot of the second 727 had the good sense not to land, but television cameras in that aircraft captured the sight of refugees hanging in the wheel wells of the first aircraft as it flew over the South China Sea. One by one, the people in the wheel wells fell off."

"My God . . ."

I tried to imagine the panic and desperation of those last days before the final surrender. Millions of refugees, entire military units falling apart instead of fighting, paralysis in Saigon and in Washington, and the mesmerizing images of chaos and disintegration flashing across television screens around the world. A total humiliation for us, a complete disaster for them.

As it turned out, the bad guys weren't that bad, and the good guys weren't that good. It's all perception, public relations, and propaganda anyway. Both sides had been dehumanizing each other for so long, they'd forgotten they were all Vietnamese, and all human.

Susan said, "I never knew any of this . . . no one talks about it."

"Probably just as well."

Highway One came to a T-intersection, and I looked at my map and pointed to the left. Mr. Cam made the turn, and we continued on. The highway around Da Nang was heavy with trucks, cars, and buses, and Mr. Cam played chicken with oncoming traffic every minute or so.

Susan told him to cool it, and he stayed behind a truck, which made him unhappy. It was Tet Eve, and he wanted to be back with his family in Nha Trang. He'd come very close to being there in spirit only.

The land started to rise, and I could see huge mountains up ahead, with spurs running right down into the South China Sea. The map showed that the highway went through these mountains, but I didn't see how. As we continued to climb, I said to Susan, "Have you taken this road?"

"Yes. I told you, I took the torture bus, Saigon to Hue. It was a nightmare. Almost as bad as this trip."

"Right. Is this mountain road dangerous?"

"It's breathtaking. There's a single pass through the mountains called Hai Van Pass. In French it's called Col des Nuages."

"Cloudy Pass."

"Oui." She continued, "These mountains used to separate what was then all of Vietnam to the north from the kingdom of Champa that we just drove through. There's a distinct weather difference on either side of the pass, especially now in the winter."

"Is it snowing in Hue?"

"No, Paul. But it will be much colder on the other side of Cloudy Pass, and possibly raining. This is the northern boundary of the tropics." She added, "I hope you brought something warm to wear."

In fact, I did not. But I shouldn't blame Karl or anyone for that. I'd been on the other side of the pass in January and February of '68, and I recalled the rainy days and the cold nights. I said to Susan, "Do you have something to wear in that bottomless backpack?"

"No. I'll shop."

"Of course."

We kept climbing up the mountain. To the left of the road was a steep wall of rock and to the right, not far from the wheels of the car, was a sheer dropoff into the South China Sea.

Susan said, "This is spectacular."

Mr. Cam was not sightseeing, thank goodness, and I saw that his knuckles were white. I said to Susan, "Tell him to pull over. I'll drive."

"No. There are police at the top of the pass."

We climbed to about five hundred meters elevation, judging by the water below. The mountain towering over us to the left was at least another thousand meters. If I had driven this last night in the dark, it would not have been fun.

After what seemed like a long time, we approached the top of Cloudy Pass. The terrain flattened out, and I could see old concrete bunkers and stone fortifications on both sides of the road.

We reached the summit of the pass, and there were more fortifications scattered around. There was also a tour bus, a few cars with Vietnamese drivers and Western tourists, dozens of kids selling souvenirs, and a police outpost with two yellow jeeps parked out front.

Mr. Cam said something, and Susan said to me, "He wants to know if you want to stop and take pictures."

"Next time."

"Everyone stops. We should stop. It will look less suspicious."

"Tell him to pull over."

He pulled over close to the precipice, which dropped down to a small peninsula that was the end of the mountain spur. I said to Susan, "Take a picture, and let's get out of here." I kept my eyes on the cops hanging around near their jeeps on the other side of the road. They were glancing at all the cars and the tourists, but seemed too lazy to cross the road. Then again, you never know.

About twenty kids descended on the Nissan, pushing useless and stupid souvenirs at the windows.

A few of the kids had these aluminum can

origamis of Huey helicopters, and I was amazed that these things had been faithfully reproduced for almost thirty years since the Americans had left.

One kid was banging the window with this tin Huey, and I saw that on the side of the helicopter was a perfectly painted black and yellow First Cavalry insignia. I said, "I have to have that."

I lowered the window a crack, and the kid and I argued price. We each held on to the helicopter until I released a buck, just like a drug deal going down.

I cranked up the window and said to Mr. Cam, "Cu di."

He threw the Nissan into gear, and we continued across the pass, then down the other side.

Susan asked, "Do you like your toy?"

"You don't see these all over." I hand-flew the tin helicopter around, then made a whooshing noise like rockets firing, followed by the chatter of a Gatling gun.

Mr. Cam laughed, but it was a nervous laugh.

Susan asked, "Are you all right?"

"Coming in for a landing." I hovered the chopper and landed it on the dashboard.

Mr. Cam and Ms. Susan were quiet. I love acting nuts.

By now, we were on the downslope side of Cloudy Pass, and sure enough, there were clouds obscuring the road and a wind came up, then rain started to splatter against the wind-

shield. Mr. Cam turned on his wipers and headlights.

We continued down, and the rain got heavier,
and the wind rocked the Nissan. I glanced at Mr.
Cam, and he looked a little concerned. When a
Vietnamese driver is concerned, his round-eye
passengers should be terrified.

Traffic was light both ways, but there was
enough of it to make the descent more treacherous.

Within fifteen minutes, we'd gotten to a
lower elevation where the clouds thinned out,
and the wind and rain eased off a little.

Susan said, "Those winds come from the
northeast and are called the Chinese winds. It's
winter here, and not a good time to travel cross-
country."

We got down to near sea level, and within a
few minutes, I could see a large expanse of flat
land spreading from the sea to the mountains
farther west.

Susan said, "We have left the ancient kingdom of Champa, and are now in the province of
Hue. The people here are a little more reserved,
and not nearly as easygoing as where we just
came from."

"So, Cloudy Pass is sort of like the Mason-
Dixon line."

"I guess."

I looked at the sky, which was heavy with a
solid, low, gray cloud, as far as the eye could

see. The terrain, too, looked gray and wet, and the vegetation seemed colorless and stunted.

I remembered this winter landscape very clearly, and in fact I remembered the sodden smell that I smelled now, and the burning charcoal in every hut, a little heat against the cold, damp wind.

We were down in the flatlands now, and off to the right was a squalid bamboo hut, and out front, a peasant stood in his doorway, smoking a cigarette and staring out at the rain. In the brief moment that I saw his emotionless face as we passed by him, I understood just a little the lives of these rice farmers; work from sunup to sundown, home to a meal cooked over an open fire, then to bed.

And then there were the leeches, and the foot rot, and the vermin inside the huts and the lice in their hair.

And when the wars came, as they always did in this country, the peasants were the first to be recruited and the first to die—millions of them, wearing their first decent clothes, and carrying a weapon that would cost them two years of earnings made in the rice paddies.

I'd seen all of these things long ago, although I only now understood it. I understood, too, why so many of them joined the Viet Cong in hopes of a better life after the victory. But, as my French friend at Tan Son Nhat said, the more things change, the more they stay the same.

The sky was gray, the rain fell in the fallow black paddies, the countryside seemed dead and deserted.

It was Tet Eve, and I recalled the Tet Eve of many years ago, huddled in a hastily constructed bunker in the foothills west of Quang Tri, not far from here. It was raining, and I was smoking a cigarette, looking out at the rain and the dripping vegetation, not unlike that peasant back there. The gray dampness seeped into the muddy bunkers, and into our souls.

We didn't know it then, but within a few hours, a battle would begin that would last a long, bloody month. And at the end of that month, Hue and Quang Tri would lie in ruins, the body bags would run out before the ammunition, and nothing would be the same again here, or at home.

Susan said, "Hue, fifty kilometers ahead."

I thought of my close calls getting out of here in '68, and my more recent close calls here. This place had colored my life, and changed the course of my personal history, not once, or twice, but three times now. I should ask myself what kept drawing me back.

—BOOK V—

Hue

CHAPTER TWENTY-FIVE

——— ★ ———

It was a little after noon, and the rain had stopped but the sky remained gray. I could see a small propeller aircraft landing at Hue–Phu Bai Airport to the right of Highway One. This, too, had once been an American airbase, though not a major installation.

Susan spoke to Mr. Cam, and he pulled into the airport gate, where a police jeep sat. The rain had washed the mud from the car damage, and I pictured specks of yellow paint on the front fender. The two cops gave us the eye as we passed. I recalled Mr. Conway's advice to avoid airports, but as it turned out, I needed to drag the red herring through an airport.

As we drove through the airport, I could see a few remnants of the American army and air force—concrete bunkers, revetments, and a concrete control tower that I remembered.

It wasn't a busy place, so Mr. Cam was able to park in a space near the small terminal.

We got out of the Nissan, I opened the rear hatch, and put our luggage on the ground.

Mr. Cam stood by anxiously, waiting for what would happen next. He wasn't dead, so he was way ahead of the game already.

I got out my wallet and counted out two hundred dollars, which I gave to Mr. Cam and said, "For Mr. Thuc."

He smiled and bowed.

Then I pointed to the damage on the Nissan and asked him, "How much?"

He understood and said something, which Susan translated as three hundred dollars. I gave it to him without argument, looking forward to putting in this expense when I got back: *Damage to hired car incurred while running police vehicle off road and killing two cops— $300. No receipt.*

I looked closely at the damage and pointed out to Mr. Cam a few streaks of yellow paint. I pantomimed scraping them off, and he nodded quickly. Then I counted out another hundred and gave it to Mr. Cam, indicating that this was for him.

He smiled very wide and bowed lower.

I asked Susan, "You think that's enough for almost getting him killed?"

"Sure. How much do I get?"

"You volunteered. He was kidnapped." I reached in the car and took the toy helicopter off the dashboard and handed it to Mr. Cam. I said to him, "A gift for you so you can remember this trip forever." As if he needed a reminder.

Susan translated something, and Mr. Cam bowed and said in English, "Thank you. Good-bye."

I looked at my watch and said to Mr. Cam, "We fly to Hanoi now. You buying that?"

He smiled and said, "Hanoi."

"Right." I said to Susan, "Give him a final pitch about not going to the cops."

She put her hand on Mr. Cam's shoulder, and spoke to him in a low, soothing tone. He kept nodding. I kept looking at his eyes.

We all wished each other Chuc Mung Nam Moi, and Mr. Cam got into the Nissan and drove away.

I asked Susan, "Police station or Nha Trang?"

"Nha Trang."

We gathered our luggage and walked into the terminal past two uniformed and armed men. The terminal, which had a Sixties air to it, was crowded, but not packed. The arrival and departure board showed flights only to 6 P.M.

Susan said, "Most of the Tet traveling has ended, and everyone is home by now."

"I'm not. You're not." I looked around and said, "I was here once to catch a military flight to An Khe. The flight was full, and I couldn't get on. The aircraft took off and hit a helicopter rising at the end of the runway. Killed everyone. Makes you wonder."

Susan didn't respond.

I looked around and saw armed uniformed guys walking in pairs, and they wore the same kind of uniform that Pushy had worn at Tan Son Nhat. Must be border patrol types. Two of them stopped a Westerner and asked for tickets and identification.

I said to Susan, "Okay, we've been here long enough. You and I will take separate taxis to the Century Riverside Hotel. I'll go first and check in. You follow and try to get a room. If you can't, just wait in the lobby, and I'll meet you there."

"Make it the lounge. I need a drink."

"Me, too. Where's the pistol?"

"On my person."

"Why don't you go to the ladies' room, transfer it to your tote, and I'll take the tote?"

"Why don't you go catch a taxi?"

"Susan—"

"It's my gun. If I get stopped and searched, I'll tell them it's a cigarette lighter. See you later."

We stood there a moment, and I said, "Keep low when you pass that police jeep at the gate."

"I know."

I didn't kiss her, I just turned and left the terminal. Outside, there were a few taxis, and I got into one, carrying my luggage, and said to the driver, "Hue. Century Riverside Hotel. Biet?"

He nodded and off we went. As we approached the police jeep, I bent down and tied my shoelace.

It was about ten kilometers to Hue, and we passed through the town of Phu Bai on the way, which I vaguely remembered. In the distance, I could see pagodas and the tombs of the emperors scattered through the low, rolling landscape.

We crossed a stream, and Highway One became Hung Vuong Street. I didn't know Hue, but I knew of Hue, and I knew that we were in the New City on the east bank of the Perfume River. The old Imperial City was on the opposite bank.

The New City was a pleasant and prosperous-looking place, small in size, but bigger than the last time I'd seen it, which was from a helicopter in 1968, when it was basically a mound of rubble.

Within a few minutes, the taxi pulled into a circular driveway in front of the Century Riverside, which was set back from the street in its own gardens, and was indeed on the river. It was a fairly large, modern structure, five stories high, beautifully landscaped out front with a pond and a fountain. A big gold sign hung over the front doors that read *Chuc Mung Nam Moi—Happy New Year*.

I deserved this place.

I paid the taxi driver, and a bellboy appeared, who took my suitcase and gave me a receipt. I kept my overnight bag.

A doorman opened the front door and said, "Welcome to the hotel, sir."

I walked into the big, expansive lobby, which was done in a tasteful modern style. Kumquat trees sat in urns on the floors, and branches of Tet blossoms were in vases.

The long check-in counter was to the left, and I picked the prettiest girl behind the counter and went over to her.

I said, "Checking in. Bond. James Bond."

I gave her my voucher, and she looked at it, then at me. "You are . . . ?"

"Brenner. Paul Brenner. It's on the voucher."

"Oh . . . sorry."

She played with her keyboard and looked at her computer screen. I imagined a message in big red letters that said WANTED: DEAD OR ALIVE—CALL THE POLICE.

But the pretty lady, whose nametag said Dep, which means pretty, was smiling as she read her screen. She said, "Ah, yes. Mr. Paul Brenner. Welcome to the Century Riverside, Mr. Brenner."

"Thank you."

I had the feeling I was a little underdressed, and probably I smelled, and I needed a shave and some toothpaste, but Dep didn't seem to notice. She asked me, "Did you have a pleasant journey?"

"I had an interesting journey."

"Yes? Where are you arriving from?"

"Nha Trang."

"Ah. How is the weather there?"

"Very nice."

"It's very cloudy here, I'm afraid. But you might enjoy the cooler weather."

"I'm sure I will."

She got all the computer stuff in order and said to me, "We have a very nice suite for you,

Mr. Brenner, with a terrace overlooking the river and the Old City."

"Thank you."

"Have you been to Hue before?"

"Close. Quang Tri. '68."

She looked up at me and said, "Ah."

"Precisely."

She asked, "May I see your passport and your visa?"

"You may, but I need them back."

"Yes, of course. But I need to make a photocopy. Meanwhile, please fill in this registration card."

I filled in the registration card while Dep turned around and made copies of my visa and passport. She came back to the desk and gave me my documents, and I gave her the registration card.

She said, "You will be staying with us three nights, correct?"

"Correct." *Do I get a refund if I'm arrested before then?* I asked her, "By the way, do you have any rooms available?"

She played with her computer and said, "A few. We're very busy for the holiday." She found my key and said to me, "If there is anything we can help you with, the concierge is at your service."

"Thank you. Are there any messages for me?"

"Let me see."

She turned around and went through a file box. She extracted a big envelope and said, "I believe this is for you."

I took the envelope and signed for it.

"Your luggage will be up shortly. Suite Six is on the fifth floor. The elevators are right behind you. Have a pleasant stay."

"Thank you. You're very pretty. Chuc Mung Nam Moi."

She smiled, bowed her head and said, "Thank you. And Happy New Year."

I went to the elevators and pushed UP. I've noticed that hotel people, in good hotels, all speak the same language, all over the world. They must be trained in someplace like Switzerland, perfect little androids with clockworks in their heads. And then they're wound up and released on the world.

The elevator came, and I went up to the fifth floor and found my suite.

It had a large sitting room, and an equally large bedroom, a big bathroom, and sure enough, a terrace that looked out over the river to the Old City on the opposite bank.

The modern furniture looked comfortable, but my standards had dropped so low that I had lost any judgment.

There was a large alcove with a desk, and I sat behind the desk and opened the envelope.

It was a fax, addressed to me. It was from Karl, and it didn't say Happy New Year.

I glanced at the message and noticed that the words weren't couched in business jargon, where double entendres are easier to write and to understand. Karl had to use a friendly format because I wasn't supposed to be here on business; I was a returning vet, a tourist, and Karl knew this fax would be in the hands of the police long before I saw it. Karl had also changed his sex, and was now Kay.

I read: Dear Paul, I hope this finds you well, and that your trip is everything you hoped it would be. Regarding that lady we discussed, I've heard that she may be married to another American, so you should be careful of pillow talk, and a jealous husband. As your friend, I advise you to end this relationship. No good will come of it. On a happier note, your Hue itinerary looks good. Hope you are having fun. Let me hear from you. It was signed: Love, Kay.

So, all I had to do was figure this out, which wasn't that hard. *Married to another American*. Obviously, he meant that Susan might be working for another American intelligence service. But I already suspected that. So what? I wasn't even sure who *I* was working for.

Your Hue itinerary looks good. Tomorrow's rendezvous was on.

I opened the pencil drawer and found a fax transmittal form and wrote: Dearest Kay, Have arrived in Hue and received your fax. You're so sweet to worry about my love life. But if you sleep with the enemy, you know where they are at night. The trip is going well—very moving, very enlightening. I love the Vietnamese people, and the government is doing a wonderful job here. I can't thank you enough for suggesting this trip.

I looked up from my note, thought a moment, then added: The long shadows of the past do indeed still stretch from here to there, but the shadows in my mind and in my heart are fading, so if you don't hear from me for a long time, know that I have found what I was looking for, and that I have no personal regrets about this journey. My love to C.

I looked at what I'd written, decided it was fine for Karl, for Colonel Mang, for Cynthia, for me, and for posterity.

I recalled my letters home in 1968, and remembered them as a mixture of news, some GI complaining, and a little homesickness. But like most of the guys in combat, who realized that each letter could well be the last, I always ended on a note that suggested I was at peace with myself; that I accepted the possibility of death, was not frightened by it, but, of course, hoped for a happier outcome. Implicit in the message was always the idea that the experience was doing me some good, so that I'd be a better person when I returned. I hoped God was reading the letter, too.

It was all pretty heavy stuff for an eighteen-year-old, but you grow up fast when you're measuring your allotted time on earth in minutes.

And now, nearly three decades later, here I was again, my life still in danger, and my letter home still saying pretty much the same thing: I've prepared myself for whatever happens, and so should everyone there.

I left Karl's fax to me on the desk because to destroy it might look suspicious to the people who'd already read it.

I stood and carried my overnight bag into the bathroom. I brushed my teeth, washed up, and combed my hair.

The doorbell rang, and I went into the living room and answered the door. It was my suitcase, and I gave the guy a buck. I opened the suitcase and threw on a wrinkled blue blazer. I was anxious to see Susan, so I didn't unpack, and took my fax from the desk and went down to the lobby.

I gave the fax to a desk clerk along with a dollar, and asked the clerk if he'd fax this now and give me the fax back.

He replied, "Sorry, sir, fax machines are all day busy. It take one, two, hour. I fax for you and return original to room."

I knew this routine, and what we'd gotten away with at the Grand Hotel in Nha Trang, I wasn't going to get away with here. I could have gone to the General Post Office, but for all I knew, they photocopied your fax for the cops right in front of you. In any case, my fax to Karl was clean, and I was in a hurry. I left it with the clerk. I then went to the cashier and cashed five hundred dollars in traveler's checks, for which I was given two trillion dong or something like that.

I looked around the lobby to see if Susan was there, but she wasn't. I didn't want to ask the desk clerk if she'd checked in, so I stood there awhile and waited. The lobby was bustling on this Saturday afternoon, the eve of Tet. Virtually all the guests were Western, and most of them looked European by their dress.

I did see three middle-aged guys who were obviously Americans, and just as obviously veterans. They were fairly well dressed for Americans—long pants, collared shirts, and blazers—and they carried themselves well. One of them had a Hemingway-type beard, and he looked familiar, like I'd seen him on TV or something.

I'm good at making educated guesses about people—I do it for a living. As I watched them standing in the lobby, talking, I guessed that they had all been officers, probably army or marines, because they didn't have the sloppy and goofy mannerisms of air force officers, and they didn't strike me as navy. They may have been combat veterans, rather than rear echelon types, and for sure they'd become financially successful over the years. They had gotten together and decided it was time to go back. They may have had women with them, but they were alone now. The guy with the beard made a command decision, and they all headed for the cocktail lounge. I followed.

The lounge had no bar, so I sat at a cocktail table facing the door. I was supposed to be at the Immigration police station now, but I'd decided that they could wait. Actually, they could go fuck themselves.

A waitress came by, and I ordered a San Miguel, then made it two. The waitress asked, "Person join you?"

"Yes."

She put down two napkins and a bowl of peanuts.

I looked at my watch and looked at the door. Susan wasn't the kind of woman you had to worry about to accomplish a simple task like taking a taxi from the airport. It was the gun thing that had me totally bummed out. All it would take was a random ID check at the airport, a minor auto accident, or a routine police stop on the road, and we'd be talking about a shoot-out or an arrest for a capital offense. Despite my job, I'm not crazy about guns, but I could see why so many Americans were enthusiastic about their rights to bear arms.

This made me wonder what happened to the millions of M-16s we'd given the South Vietnamese army. I hadn't seen one American M-16 carried by a cop or a military man since I'd been here; they all had their Russian AK-47s, which they loved during the war.

Maybe, I thought, there were millions of M-16s hidden by the former ARVN, buried in plastic out in the vegetable patch or something. But probably not. This was a country of unarmed civilians and armed cops and soldiers. The defeat was complete, and the chances of an insurgency starting was nil. I recalled the photographs in the Museum of American War Crimes, the mass executions of insurgent tribespeople and former ARVN. Hanoi didn't mess around.

Where was Susan?

The beers came and the waitress put them on the table with two glasses. I signed a chit and gave her a buck.

I drank some beer and ate some peanuts, staring at the door and glancing at my watch.

I could hear the three guys at a table nearby, and I listened, to take my mind off worrying about Susan.

I could only catch pieces of the conversation, but I heard some military talk and acronyms, so I'd gotten that right. One guy said something about a dustoff, meaning a medical evacuation by helicopter, and another guy said, "incoming," meaning unfriendly rocket, artillery, or mortar fire. The third guy said something about the "pucker factor going up," which meant everyone's sphincter was tightening with fear. They all laughed.

Definitely combat vets. I glanced at them, and I could see they were having a good time, old vets like myself, back to kick the beast in the balls.

I wondered if they felt as strange and disconnected as I'd felt on the roof of the Rex, and was starting to feel here in the nice cocktail lounge of the luxury hotel built on the bank of the Perfume River where the marines had been dug in, exchanging fire across the river with the enemy, who held the opposite bank. I think if you keep the patter and chatter going, you block out the sounds of the machine guns and rockets. But if you sat silently, as I was doing now, you could still hear the distant thunder as it receded in time.

Susan should have arrived by now, and I needed to check with the desk clerk. I stood and started toward the door.

Just as I reached the door, she appeared suddenly, and I almost bumped into her. I said, by way of greeting, "Where the hell have you been?"

"It's good to see you, too."

"I was worried about you."

"Sorry. I had to freshen up."

In fact, she was wearing one of the silk blouses she'd bought in Nha Trang, black pants, and sandals. She'd obviously showered and put on makeup.

"I *rushed* down here to meet you, and you're up in your room taking a bubble bath or something."

"Can I buy you a drink?"

I turned and walked to the cocktail table. I sat and drank my beer.

Susan sat opposite me and said, "Is this my beer?"

"Obviously."

She poured herself some beer, took a few peanuts, and threw one at me. Hit me in the forehead.

She sat back, sipped her beer, and lit up.

She wasn't saying anything, and she wouldn't until I calmed down. I know women.

I said, "I could have gotten a massage if I'd known you were going to take your sweet time."

She threw another peanut at me.

"We were supposed to meet here, right after—forget it. Where's the heat?"

"Safe."

"Safe *where?*"

"Under my bed."

"Are you crazy?"

"No. And I'm not stupid either. I went out to the flower garden and buried it in a plastic bag."

I calmed down a bit and asked, sarcastically, "Do you remember where you buried it?"

"Orange birds-of-paradise. I buried it while I sniffed the flowers."

"Okay. And no one saw you?"

"I hope not."

"And you wiped the prints clean?"

"Only mine. I left yours on the gun."

I ordered another beer. I saw the three Americans glancing at Susan—leering, actually, and making comments. Men are pigs.

She asked me, "Any messages?"

"Yes. From K. He wants me to dump you."

"Well, what difference does it make now?"

"None. Subject closed. Did you get a message?"

"No one knows what hotel I'm at."

"I'll bet they could figure it out real quick."

She smiled. "Uh . . . duh . . . ? Hey, did you know this is the Year of the Ox?"

"I thought it was the Year of the Toronto Blue Jays."

"I mean the astrological year. Stop jerking me around."

"Sorry. Year of the Ox."

"Right. It's forecast to be a propitious year."

"What does that mean?"

"Lucky. Good fortune."

"You mean for everybody?"

"I don't know. Sorry I mentioned it. You're a pain in the ass."

She got sulky, which gave me a minute to reflect on a few things. *Married to another American.* Karl was teamed up with the FBI for this case, so he must mean that Susan was with the CIA or State Department Intelligence. SDI people fainted at the sight of a gun, so that kind of narrowed it down to CIA. Of course, there could be another player out there, like Military Intelligence. In any case, this wasn't quite like sleeping with the enemy, but more like sleeping with a business competitor. Either that, or Karl was messing with my head, and that wouldn't be the first time. Karl could also be wrong, and that, too, wouldn't be the first time.

Susan interrupted my thoughts and said, "I've made a reservation here for an early dinner. They have this huge Tet meal laid on. Then we'll walk around the Old City and see the celebration—dragon dances, puppet shows, music, and all that. Then we'll go to the cathedral for midnight mass."

She had to be CIA—who else would be so arrogant as to plan my evening for me?

She said, "Are you listening to me?"

"Yeah . . . Look, let's have the early dinner and turn in—"

"Paul, it's New Year's Eve."

"No, it's not. That was a month ago."

"It's New Year's Eve *here*."

"I don't believe it. You only lose or gain a day when you cross the International Dateline. Not a month."

"I think we should go to your room, and you shower, since you obviously have not, then we'll get very comfortable in bed, then dress for dinner."

I couldn't find anything wrong with that, so I stood and said, "Okay. Let's go."

"Can I finish my beer?"

"I have a mini-bar in the room. Let's go."

"Are you hot?"

"Yes, let's go."

She stood, we walked out to the lobby, took the elevator up to the fifth floor, and I led her to my suite.

She said, "Oh, this is very nice. They gave me a small room on the first floor overlooking the street." She added, "Room 106."

She walked to the glass doors and went out to the long terrace. I followed.

The Perfume River was spanned by two bridges that connected the Old and New City, and alongside the closest bridge were the ruined remains of another bridge that had been destroyed, probably in '68.

Across the river sat the walled city of Hue, known as the Citadel, the capital of the emperors. From this height, we could see over the Citadel walls and into the city, and what struck me was that about half the central part of the city seemed to be missing, replaced by open fields in which lay the outlines of what had once been buildings.

Susan said, "You see those walls within the

Citadel walls? That's the Imperial Enclosure, and within those walls are the walls of the Forbidden Purple City, where only the Emperor, his concubines, and the eunuchs were allowed."

"So I'm not allowed in there, but you are."

"Very funny." She went on, "Most of the ancient buildings were destroyed in 1968."

"I see that." Somewhere down there, at noon tomorrow or later, I was to meet my contact. I hoped it wasn't a woman.

Susan said, "My guide told us that the Americans bombed the city mercilessly for thirty days and destroyed most of the antiquities."

I didn't feel like defending the American use of overwhelming firepower, but I said, "The North Vietnamese army captured the city by surprise on Tet Eve, during the Tet truce. It took thirty days of bombing, shelling, and ground action to get them out. It's called war."

She nodded and said, "But . . . it's such a shame."

"The Communists went around with names and addresses of people they wanted liquidated. They shot over three thousand soldiers and civilians who were on their lists. Did your guide tell you that?"

"No."

I looked off to the northwest and said, "My infantry company was dug into those foothills way out there on the horizon. We could see the bat-

tles raging in Quang Tri and Hue. We moved
down from the hills and tried to block the escape of the Communist troops after they'd given
up Quang Tri. Then we moved farther south toward Hue, and set up a blocking force to intercept the stragglers coming out of Hue so they
couldn't disappear into the hills."

She looked out at the countryside to the north
and west, and said, "So you were right out there?"

"Yes."

"And the battle was going on right here in
the city?"

"Yes. On this side of the river, right where we
are now, the marines were dug in and controlled this riverbank and the New City." I said,
"Quang Tri is about sixty kilometers due north
of here, right up Highway One, which you can
see over there."

"You should go to Quang Tri."

"I think I will. I've come this far."

"I'd like to go with you, if you want the
company."

I nodded. "This stretch of Highway One from
Hue to Quang Tri was called by the French soldiers the Street Without Joy. The name stuck,
and that's what we called it, although some guys
called it Ambush Alley, or Fucked Up Road One."

She asked me, "Where is the A Shau Valley?"

I pointed due west. "Right over that mountain range, maybe seventy kilometers, near the

Laotian border. It's a very isolated place, more of a box canyon than a valley, surrounded by mountains, and socked in by clouds most of the year. It may be hard to get there."

"I'm game."

I looked at her and smiled. "Were you really boring once?"

"Boring *and* coddled. I used to throw a fit if room service was slow."

I took a final look at the city of Hue, turned and walked off the terrace.

I went into the bathroom, shaved and showered.

Susan and I made love in the comfortable bed, then fell asleep.

We got up at six, dressed, and went down to the hotel dining room where New Year's Eve dinner was being served, buffet style.

Every seat seemed to be filled, and we sat at a small table for two near the riverside garden, which, according to Susan, was not far from her buried pistol.

Everyone there was a European or American, and I spotted the three guys I'd seen before. They were sitting at a table with a group of women, and I could tell by the body language that the ladies were not their wives or girlfriends. The guys were on their game, and the women were either entranced or faking it.

A band played elevator music, and the dining room was a sea of smiling faces, sparkling crystal, and hustling waiters. In 1968, I wouldn't have thought this was possible.

One buffet table was laden with real Vietnamese holiday food, which had signs in several languages, so that everyone could avoid most of it. The other tables had make-believe Vietnamese food, Chinese food, and Western dishes. Susan and I ate like pigs, using chopsticks, knives, forks, and our fingers.

We left the hotel at nine and walked across the Perfume River via the Trang Tien Bridge.

The night was cool, and the sky had become clear. The moon was now a thin sliver that would disappear shortly, and the stars were brilliant. Thousands of people strolled along the tree-shaded embankment, between the river and the towering walls of the Citadel. The city was festooned with red flags, and many of the buildings were outlined in lights and Chinese lanterns.

The focus of activity seemed to be around the historic flag tower opposite the main gates of the wall. Entire families sat or walked, greeting one another and wishing each other a Happy New Year.

Susan said, "Fireworks are banned for individuals, but the city will probably fire off a few rockets like they do in Saigon. When I arrived in Saigon three years ago, fireworks were still legal, and on Tet Eve, the whole city sounded like a war zone."

"I know that sound."

Opposite the flag tower, the massive Citadel gates were open, and beyond the gates was an ornamental bridge, which led to the Emperor's Palace. The palace was big, made of stone and red lacquered wood, and had a traditional tiled roof. It was all lit up with floodlights, and decorated for the holiday. I wondered how this place had escaped the bombing.

But then Susan said, "People and organizations from all over the world donated money to rebuild the palace in its original style."

"Good. Let's go in. I'll donate a fiver."

"You can't go in tonight. See those soldiers? They're turning people away. Must be a government ceremony or something."

"I'll give them a ten."

"Forget it. You're in enough trouble."

So we continued our stroll along the embankment, then passed through a smaller gate into the city.

There were lots of people around, and we saw a dragon dance, and a few silly puppet shows set up in makeshift theaters. There were groups of musicians playing traditional music on stringed instruments, which was very whiny and irritating.

Most of the cafés and restaurants had closed,

but we found a café owned by a Catholic couple who stayed open to get the Buddhist business.

The café was crowded with Viets and Westerners, but we found a table and had coffee.

I said to Susan, "This is nice. I'm glad I'm here."

"Me, too."

"You're missing the Vincent party in Saigon."

"There's no place in the world that I'd rather be than here, with you."

I said, "I feel the same way."

We finished our coffee. There were no taxis or cyclos around, so we walked back across the Perfume River by the Phu Xuan Bridge into the New City where Susan said the cathedral was located.

From the bridge, I could see a big sports complex along the riverbank, with tennis courts, a swimming pool, and playing fields. Susan said, "That's the Cercle Sportif. The old French sporting club. There's one in Saigon, and in a lot of major cities. Used to be whites only. Now, it's mostly Party members only."

"Commies play tennis?"

"I don't know. I guess so. Why not?"

"I'm trying to picture Colonel Mang in tennis whites."

She laughed, then said, "When no one is looking, the pigs walk on their hind legs."

"So I've heard."

We continued across the bridge, and suddenly there were flashes of orange light in the sky, followed by a series of explosions; I flinched, then realized it was sky rockets. My heart was actually racing, and I took a deep breath.

Susan looked at me.

I felt a little foolish and joked, "I thought Charles was back."

She said, "That's why I mentioned the fireworks before."

As we came off the bridge, I started to cross the street, but Susan stopped me. "See that little booth on the opposite corner? That's the police checkpoint. Avoid that corner. They sometimes harass Westerners, as I found out when I was here."

"I haven't been harassed by the police since Thursday night. I'm feeling neglected. Let's go have an argument with them."

"Please."

We avoided the police booth and crossed in mid-block. As we walked, I said to her, "Maybe we can skip mass."

She replied, "You should get down on your knees and thank God that you're even here in one piece."

It was a hike to the cathedral, and the city streets were starting to become deserted. Susan said, "Everyone is home now for the traditional meal."

"Why don't the Buddhists go to the pagodas for midnight mass?"

"I don't think it's called mass, and they pray when they feel like it."

We arrived at the Cathedral of Notre Dame at about quarter to midnight, and there were still people arriving, mostly on foot. The majority were Viets, but there were a number of round-eyes as well.

The cathedral was impressive, but not old. It was, in fact, fairly modern, with some Gothic and Vietnamese touches. I assumed that whatever old churches had existed had been destroyed.

We went inside and found space in a pew toward the rear. I said to Susan, "If this is a Buddhist holiday, why is there a Catholic mass?"

"I don't know. You're Catholic. E-mail the Pope."

The mass began. The entire mass and the hymns were in Vietnamese, which was funny, like it was being dubbed. I skipped communion as I'd done in Notre Dame, Saigon, but most of the congregation, including Susan, went up to the altar. There wasn't any of this sign of peace stuff that they do now in Catholic churches in the States, which was good because this crowd would probably bow instead of shaking hands, and everyone would bump heads.

I noticed that the citizens of Hue were better

dressed than the Viets south of the Hai Van Pass, and I supposed that had to do with the cooler weather, and maybe the sophistication of this city.

My multicultural experience came to an end, and we followed the recessional out into the open plaza in front of the cathedral.

People stood around and chatted, and somehow, don't ask how, Susan got into a conversation with a Viet family. They were very impressed with her fluent Vietnamese, and her rudimentary French, which they also spoke.

Long story short, we were on our way to dinner with the Pham family.

On the way there, walking with this entire clan, I said to Susan, "Didn't you tell them I wasn't of good character?"

"Fortunately, they didn't ask about either of us."

On the way, Susan gave me a quick course in Vietnamese table manners. She said, "Don't leave your chopsticks sticking up in the rice bowl. That's a sign of death, like the joss sticks in the bowls in cemeteries and family altars. Also, everything is passed on platters. You have to try everything that's passed to you. If you empty a glass of wine or beer, they automatically refill it. Leave half a glass if you don't want any more."

"Sounds like South Boston."

"Listen up. The Vietnamese don't belch like the Chinese do to show they enjoyed the meal. They consider that crude, as we do."

"I don't consider belching crude. But then, I don't belong to the Junior League."

She made a sound of exasperation, then said, "Okay, when you've had enough to eat, you stick your chopsticks in your nostrils."

"Are you sure?"

"Trust me."

The Phams lived in a nice private house, not too far from the cathedral, and they obviously had a few dong.

I still had rice coming out of my ears from the meal at the hotel, but that was no excuse not to eat.

I found myself wedged in at a long table between a hundred-year-old grandma and some snotty kid. Across from me, however, was a number one co-dep, and she spoke a little English, but not enough for me to show her how charming I was. She may have belonged to someone, but she kept smiling and giggling, and passing me platters.

Everyone spoke ten words of English, and they weren't the same ten words, so the conversation moved okay. Plus, most of them knew some French, and my limited French was coming back to me. The Vietnamese phrases that I knew well, as I said, were not appropriate for a family dinner. I did, however, consider asking co-dep to show me her ID card.

Susan was down at the other end of the table, and she was having a good time.

The Vietnamese seemed very pleasant in a family setting, but the public and commercial life of this whole country was a disaster.

A guy of about thirty sitting next to Susan said in passable English, "Mr. Paul, Miss Susan tell me you here in 1968."

"Quang Tri."

"Yes? You fight Communists."

"That's why I was here."

"You kill?"

"Uh . . . I guess."

"Good." He stood and said something to the crowd, raised his glass to me, and said in English, "To this brave soldier who kill the . . ." He asked Susan something, then finished his sentence with, "kill the Antichrists."

Everyone toasted, and I felt compelled to stand. I had the distinct feeling this was an anti-Communist crowd, and I wouldn't have been surprised if the door burst open and the Ministry of Public Security goons came in and arrested everyone. Karl would not approve of me being here. I raised my glass and said, "To the brave Catholics of Vietnam. The only good Red is a dead Red."

My host seemed momentarily confused, but Susan translated, and everyone applauded.

I looked at Susan and saw she was rolling her eyes. I sat and waited for the door to burst open.

At about 2 A.M., I considered sticking my chopsticks up my nostrils, but we didn't get out of there until about 3 A.M., and the streets were deserted. Also, I was a little inebriated.

Susan said, "Wasn't that an experience?"

I burped. "It was."

"I'm having such a good time with you."

I burped again. "Good."

"They were such nice people."

"Right. A little bloodthirsty, but nice."

"Mr. Uyen, the man sitting next to me, who toasted you, told me that many of his family were murdered by the Communists in 1968. That's why they're so . . . hateful of the regime."

"You know, everyone here is full of suppressed hate and rage over what happened. Colonel Mang, Mr. Uyen, all of them. They'd love to get their hands around each other's throats again."

Susan didn't reply.

I said, "Anyway, the Phams should be careful. The Ministry of Public Security does not play games."

"I'm sure they're careful."

"They didn't even know us."

"We're Americans, and Catholics. One of us is Catholic."

"Right." It was interesting that the Viets assumed all Americans were anti-Communist. I guess they hadn't met any Ivy League professors. I said, "I don't think we were followed from the cathedral, and no one is following us now. But you didn't do the Pham family any favors by inviting yourself to dinner. Conversely, they're probably on a few watch lists, so we didn't do ourselves any favors by going there."

She stayed silent awhile, then said, "Point made." She added, "But I think even the cops are celebrating tonight."

"I hope so."

We walked through the quiet streets, then Susan said, "You seemed to be enjoying the company of that young lady across from you."

"What young lady?"

"The one you were speaking to all night."

"Oh, that one. She's a nun."

"I don't think so."

"Susan, I'm tired, I have a headache, and we're lost."

"We're not lost. The hotel's that way."

We kept walking, and sure enough, we turned a corner and saw the hotel.

Susan suddenly stopped. "Paul."

"What?"

"Weren't you supposed to report to the Immigration Police today?"

"I was busy today. I'll do it tomorrow." We continued walking.

"You should have gone today. They know

you're here because the hotel reported your check-in."

"Well, then, they know I'm here. Fuck 'em." I added, "Colonel Mang has me on a long leash. He wants to see what I'm up to."

"How do you know that?"

"I know."

"So what happens tomorrow when you have to make a rendezvous? What if you're being watched?"

"You always plan a secret rendezvous as if you're being watched. That's why they're called secret." I added, "I have to ask you to stay out of the Citadel tomorrow."

"Oh . . . okay."

"Unless you're my contact."

"That would be interesting."

We got to the hotel, and I said, "Let's go around back, and you can show me where it's buried."

"Tomorrow."

"Now."

"Okay . . ."

We walked on a path to the gardens at the rear of the hotel. The land sloped down to the river, and the gardens were terraced and lit with small ground lights.

We walked down a path toward the river, and Susan nodded to her right. "See them? Orange birds-of-paradise."

"Is that the flower that eats flies?"

"No, Paul. Do you see them or not?"

"I do. Someplace in there?"

"Yes. A foot to the right of the middle garden light. The soil is very loamy. I can dig it up with my hand."

"Okay. I'll get it before we leave."

"*I'll* get it."

I didn't reply. We stood in the garden and looked out at the river. At this hour, we were the only ones there; we turned and walked back to the front of the hotel.

We went into the lobby, and I checked for messages. There were two for me, and I signed for them.

Susan and I took the elevator up to my suite, where I collapsed in an armchair. "God, I'm getting old."

"You're in great shape. Open the envelopes."

I opened the small one first and read aloud, " 'You to report to Immigration Police tomorrow in morning.' "

Susan said, "That leash is not that long."

"Long enough. If they were really pissed, they'd be sitting here now."

"It's New Year's Eve. What's the other message?"

I opened the big envelope and took out a fax. It was from Karl, and I read it to myself: Dear Paul, Perhaps my last message was not clear—You really need to end that relationship. Please tell me you have. It was signed: Love, Kay.

The nice thing about not being in the army was that you don't have to obey a direct order from someone who was.

I noticed a P.S. It said: C sends her love. Will see you in Honolulu.

That could be pure bullshit to keep me in line. In any case, the situation vis-à-vis Susan had become complicated, and I didn't know how I felt about meeting Cynthia in Honolulu.

Susan was looking at me. She asked, "Who is the message from?"

"Kay."

"Is everything all right?"

"Yes."

"You don't look all right. Can I see the message?"

"No."

She looked hurt, offended, and pissed.

I stood, went toward the terrace with the message, then turned around, and handed her the fax. I said, "It's Ms. Kay now. Same guy."

She took it and read it, then handed it back. She stood and said, "I think I'll sleep in my room tonight."

"Probably you should."

She turned, walked to the door, and without hesitation opened it and left.

I went out on the terrace and looked at the

city across the river. The holiday lights were still on, mostly red, as you'd expect in a Red country.

I thought of the Pham family. There was, I thought, a gray cloud over this country, formed from the smoke and fire of war, and it rained down hate, sorrow, and mistrust.

If that wasn't bad enough, this cloud, or, as Karl called it, this shadow still covered my own country.

Truly, Vietnam was the worst thing that ever happened to America in this century, and perhaps the reverse was also true.

The phone rang, and I went back inside and answered it. "Hello."

"I just wanted to say good luck tomorrow."

"Thank you."

"If something happened to you, and we parted—"

"Susan, the phones aren't secure. I know what you're saying, and I was about to call you."

"Do you want me to come to your room?"

"No. We're both tired, and we'll have a fight."

"Okay. Where and when can we meet tomorrow?"

"At six here in the lounge. I'll buy you a drink."

"Okay . . . and if you're very late?"

"Fax Ms. Kay directly. Do you have the number?"

"I remember it."

"Give her all the details, and be sure you stand at the fax machine, or try the GPO."

"I know."

"I know you do. You're a pro."

"Paul . . . ?"

"Yes?

"I had no right to get upset about that P.S. I apologize."

"Forget it."

"This is what it is. This is here and now. I said that, and I meant it."

I didn't reply to that, and I said, "Hey, I had a good day. Happy New Year."

"Me, too, and you, too."

We both hung up.

So, I'm having lady problems in a hostile country halfway around the world, people are trying to arrest me or kill me, and it's 4 A.M., and I need to see the cops in the morning, then make a possibly dangerous rendezvous at noon. And yet, for some reason, none of this bothered me. In fact, the entire Highway One ordeal, including killing the two cops, and the flashbacks, and all of the rest of it, didn't bother me.

I recognized this feeling for what it was: survival mode. Life was no longer complicated. It all came down to getting home one last time.

★

CHAPTER TWENTY-SIX

———— ★ ————

It wasn't the worst New Year's Day hangover I've ever had, but it may have been the earliest I'd ever been awake to fully appreciate it.

I showered and dressed for success—blue blazer, white button-down shirt, khaki slacks, and docksiders with socks.

I took an orange juice from the mini-bar and swallowed two aspirin with my malaria pill. I was glad they hadn't given me a suicide pill because I felt lousy enough to take it.

I went downstairs, skipped breakfast, and walked the few blocks to Ben Nghe Street, where the Immigration Police were located.

It was a cool, damp morning, high cloud cover, and the streets were nearly deserted, and strewn with trash from the night before.

I thought maybe I should have called Susan, but sometimes a little separation is good. I'd been separated from Cynthia more than we'd been together, and we got along great. Maybe not great, but okay.

I got to the police building, a structure of prefab concrete, and went inside.

In a small foyer sat a uniformed guy at a desk, and he said to me in English, "What you want?"

Rather than reply and confuse the idiot, I gave him a photocopy of Colonel Mang's note, which he read. He stood and disappeared into a hallway behind him.

A minute later, he reappeared and said to me, "Room." He held up two fingers.

I returned the peace sign and went to Room 2, a small office whose door was open. Behind a desk sat a man about my age in uniform, who looked more hungover than I did.

He didn't invite me to sit, but just looked at me awhile. I looked at him. Something not pleasant passed between us.

On his desk lay his gun belt and holster, which held a Chicom 9mm. There wasn't a police station in America where you'd get this close to a cop's gun. Here, the cops were sloppy and arrogant. This offended me, and having to stand also pissed me off.

The cop looked at the note in his hand and said to me, "When you arrive Hue?"

I'd had enough of this crap, and I replied, "The Century Riverside Hotel told you when I arrived. You know that's where I'm staying for three nights. Any other questions?"

He didn't like my reply or my tone of voice. He raised his voice, which became sort of high pitched, and he almost shouted, "Why you not report here yesterday?"

"Because I didn't want to."

He did not like that. I mean, he's working on

New Year's Day, he's got little rice wine demons smashing gongs in his head, and he's getting attitude from a round-eye.

So, we stared at each other, and as I said, something unhealthy was passing between us, and it wasn't just irritation brought on by mutual hangovers. He said to me, "You soldier here?"

"That's right. How about you?"

"Me, too."

We kept staring at each other, and I now noticed a jagged scar running down from half an ear, zigzagging over the side of his neck and disappearing beneath his open collar. Half his teeth were missing or broken, and the rest were brown.

He asked me, "When you here?"

"I was here in 1968, I was with the First Cavalry Division, I saw combat at Bong Son, An Khe, Quang Tri, Khe Sanh, the A Shau Valley, and all over Quang Tri Province. I fought the North Vietnamese army and the Viet Cong, you killed a lot of my friends, and we killed a lot of your friends. We all killed too many civilians, including the three thousand men and women you murdered here in Hue. Any other questions?"

He stood and stared at me, and I could see his eyes go nuts before his face even twitched.

Before he could say anything, I said, "Any more questions? If not, I'm leaving."

He shouted at the top of his lungs, "You *stay!* You stay here!"

I pulled up a chair, sat, crossed my legs, and looked at my watch.

He seemed confused, but then realized he should sit, which he did.

He cleared his throat and pulled a piece of paper toward him. He clicked a ballpoint pen, got himself nearly under control, and asked me, "How you get to Hue?"

"Bus."

He wrote that down and asked, "When you leave Nha Trang?"

"Friday afternoon."

"Get to Hue what time?"

I took a guess and replied, "Ten or eleven o'clock Friday night."

"Where you stay Friday night?"

"Mini-motel."

"What is name of mini-motel?"

"I don't know."

"Why you not know?"

When you need to explain missing time periods to the police, always come up with a sexual liaison, but do not use this excuse at home. I replied, "Meet lady on bus. She take me to mini-motel. Biet?"

He thought about that and asked again, "What is name of mini-motel?"

"The Ram-It Inn. Fucky-fucky Mini-Motel.

How the hell do I know the name of the place?"

He stared at me a long time, then said, "Where you go from Hue?"

"I don't know."

"How you leave Hue?"

"I don't know."

He tapped his fingers on his desk near his holster, then said, "Passport and visa."

I threw the photocopies on his desk.

He shook his head. "Need passport and visa."

"In hotel."

"You bring here."

"No."

His eyes narrowed and he shouted, "You bring here!"

"Go to hell." I stood and walked out of the room.

He ran after me and grabbed my shoulder. I pushed his arm away, and we faced off out in the corridor.

We looked into each other's eyes and both of us, I think, saw the same thing: a bottomless pit of pure hate.

I had been this close to only three enemy soldiers, and with two of them, what I'd seen and smelled was fear. On the other one, however, I'd seen this look that was not combat hostility, but a pure hatred that was ingrained in every atom of that man's being, and which ate at his heart and soul.

And for a second, which seemed like an eternity, I was back in the A Shau Valley, and that man was staring at me again, and I was staring back at him, both of us looking forward to killing the other.

I came back to the present and tried to regain some sense of sanity, but I really wanted to kill this man with my bare hands, to bash his face to a pulp, pull his arms out of their sockets, smash his testicles, crush his windpipe, and watch him suffocate.

He sensed all of this, of course, and was having murderous fantasies of his own, probably having more to do with a sharp filet knife.

But unlike on a battlefield, we both had other orders, and we each reluctantly pulled back from that darkest place in our hearts.

I felt drained, as though I'd actually been in battle, and the cop, too, looked spent.

Almost simultaneously, we each nodded in recognition, and we turned and parted.

Outside, on the street, I stopped and took a deep breath. I tried to clear the bad thoughts from my head, but I had this almost uncontrollable urge to run back in there and smash that son of a bitch into a bloody pulp. I could actually feel his flesh splitting under my knuckles.

I put one foot in front of the other until I was well away from the police station.

I walked aimlessly awhile, trying to burn off the adrenaline. I found myself kicking bottles in the street and punching signposts. This was not good, but it was inevitable, and maybe it *was* good. Unfortunately, it wasn't cathartic; quite the opposite.

It was about 9 A.M. now, and the New City was starting to stir. I walked toward the Perfume River via Hung Vuong Street, which took me to the Trang Tien Bridge. In the river near the bridge was a floating restaurant that I'd noticed the night before. There were a few people sitting at café tables on the deck, so I walked to the restaurant, crossed the gangplank, and was greeted by a young man who looked like he hadn't yet gotten to sleep.

He showed me to an outdoor table, and I ordered a coffee with a double cognac, which pleased him and would please me more.

The deck was strewn with decorations, paper party hats, champagne bottles, and even a lady's shoe. Clearly, not everyone had spent midnight gathered around the family dinner table and the home altar.

The coffee and cognac came, and I poured half of it down my throat. My stomach was already churning with bile and acid, and the coffee and cognac just added to the unhealthy brew.

I sat there on the gently swaying deck of the floating restaurant, and stared across the misty river at the gray, brooding walls of the Citadel.

I really didn't want to dwell on what happened at the police station—I knew what happened, why it happened, and I knew it could happen again, any time, any place.

I finished the coffee and cognac and ordered another. The young man put the cognac bottle on the table, recognizing, I guess, a guy who needed a few drinks.

After my second C&C, I felt a little better and thought about my job. My problem at the moment was to shake any tail I might have, and meet someone on the other side of the river at noon, or two, or at four. And if those rendezvous didn't work out, I was to await a message at the hotel, and be prepared to leave at a moment's notice.

If, however, I made a successful rendezvous, I'd know where I was supposed to go next.

Every man or woman on a dangerous assignment has a small, secret wish that the whole thing would just fizzle out. You want to know in your guts that you'll go, but you're not going to be disappointed if they say "Mission canceled."

I remembered this feeling when we'd moved out of the foothills toward Quang Tri City with orders to retake the city from the Communists. By the time we got there, the South Viets had done the dirty work, and we were all secretly relieved, but outwardly we expressed great disappointment that we hadn't gotten a piece of the action. No one, including ourselves, believed a word of it. But that's what macho posturing is all about.

Then, in late March, we got our wish to get a piece of the action; we were told we were going to Khe Sanh to face twenty thousand well-armed, well-entrenched North Vietnamese troops who had surrounded the marines at the Khe Sanh firebase since January. This is not the kind of news that brightens your day.

I don't think I'll ever forget the sights and sounds of hundreds of helicopters picking up thousands of infantrymen and air-assaulting into the hills around Khe Sanh. If ever there was an apocalyptic vision on this earth, short of a nuclear explosion, this air assault was it; fighter-bombers dropping hundreds of thousand-pound bombs that made heaven and earth shake, jet fighters releasing tumbling canisters of napalm, the earth aflame, rivers, streams, and lakes burning, forests engulfed in fire, and great fields of elephant grass and bamboo ablaze and, all the while, the helicopters are firing rockets and machine guns into the inferno below, and artillery shells are raining down high explosives and burning white phosphorus, making the dark earth erupt like mini-volcanoes. The sky is black with smoke, the earth is red with fire, and the thin layer of air in between is a killing zone of streaking red and green tracer rounds, hot,

jagged shrapnel, and plummeting helicopters.
Apocalypse *now*.

I remember the helicopter I was on swooping
in for a touch-and-go landing, and I was standing
on the landing skid, ready to jump, and the guy
standing on the skid beside me put his lips to my
ear and shouted over the din of explosions,
"Hey, Brenner, you think this is a go?"

We both laughed in recognition of what we
and everyone had been thinking before the assault began, and in that moment, we formed a
communal bond with every soldier in history
who ever waited for the sound of the bugle, the
war pipes, the whistle, the red flare, or whatever
it was that meant Go.

Go. You are no longer human, you have no
mothers, no wives, no one you care about, except the man beside you. *Go.* This is the moment you have been dreading for as long as you
can remember, this is the fear that comes to you
in the night before you sleep, and the nightmare
that wakes you out of your sleep. This is it—it's
here, it's now, it's real. *Go.* Meet it.

I wiped the clammy sweat off my face and
dried my hands on my trousers.

And then there was the A Shau Valley.

When you think you've plumbed the depths
of fear, when you've gotten to a place at the end
of the tunnel, where it can't get any more narrow or any more black, a place where you no
longer have the capacity for fear, in a little corner

of the tunnel where you laugh at death, you discover a secret room with the greatest fear of all: inside that room is yourself.

I stood, left five dollars on the table, and walked over the bridge to the Citadel.

CHAPTER TWENTY-SEVEN

———————— ★ ————————

I spent the next few hours sightseeing with my guidebook in hand, snapping photos, taking cyclos and taxis, doubling back on streets, and generally making life miserable for anyone who was trying to follow me.

The crowds around the sights were thin because of the late celebration the night before, and I had the feeling that my contact might wait until 2 P.M., when there were more people around.

Almost everyone who was meandering about were Caucasians, so I didn't stick out. Most of the morning sufferers, I noticed, were with organized tour groups but as the morning got later, I saw a few Viet families out for a stroll. The walls of the Citadel were over two kilometers on each side, and I stayed within the walls where most of the people were.

At 11:30 A.M., I left the walled city through a gate that put me back on the river walk. I headed south along the embankment where there were a good number of people strolling, and dozens of cyclos, which followed me wherever I went, the drivers yelling, "Hello! Cyclo? Hello! Cyclo?"

The cyclomen, as in Saigon and Nha Trang,

looked like what was left of the losing side in the war. The winning side looked like the cop in the Immigration police station. It had been one of those wars where the vanquished looked slightly more well adjusted than the victors. The only hope I saw in this country was in the eyes of the children, and even those eyes didn't always look hopeful.

I continued along the river and came to the main gates opposite the flag tower where Susan and I had been the night before. The gates were open to the public today, and I re-entered the walled city and crossed the ornamental bridge where dozens of tourists were snapping pictures. I was now in the Imperial Enclosure, formerly reserved for the Emperor and his court. The Emperor's Palace was also open, and I entered the huge, dark structure. The entrance hall was red and black lacquered wood, with lots of gilded dragons, and green demons with glassy eyes, the sort of stuff that doesn't help a hangover.

I exited the rear of the palace and directly in front of me was the Halls of the Mandarins, Number 32 in my guidebook.

This was another ornate building, which, according to my book, had been resurrected from the ashes of 1968, and it had that old/new look, like a Disneyland pavilion. I snapped a photo.

It was 11:45, and I had no idea where, exactly, I was supposed to meet this person. The Halls of the Mandarins was big, and like all buildings, it had an outside and an inside, but Mr. Conway had not been specific, though common sense would dictate inside if it was raining, which it wasn't.

I walked around the perimeter of the building, and by now I was certain I wasn't being watched or followed. TV shows to the contrary, it's almost impossible to tail someone for three hours unless you're on a treadmill, and then it's easy to spot your tail.

At this point, if I did spot someone who was watching me, it could very well be my contact, and I looked out for that, too.

The danger, I knew, wasn't in me being followed; I'm better at shaking a tail than a married man with a jealous wife.

The real danger was that my contact might be well known to the Ministry of Public Security, Sections A, B, C, D, and E. It's almost always the local amateur, hired by some half-wit in Washington, who shows up at a secret rendezvous with fifteen cops on his tail, half of them with video cameras.

Thank God this guy didn't have to pass anything to me that would be incriminating, like a box full of documents marked "Top Secret."

No one approached me, but I still had about five minutes, so I walked through yet another gate, this one leading into the Forbidden Purple City, which was the inner sanctum within the outer sanctum of the Imperial Enclosure. These emperors liked their privacy, and according to Susan, only the Emperor, his concubines, and his eunuchs were allowed in the Purple City. In other words, this whole compound was reserved for two balls. I need a place like this.

Actually, there wasn't much left in the Forbidden Purple City—no emperors, no eunuchs, and unfortunately, no concubines—only wide expanses of fields and low foundation walls where buildings once stood. The only intact structure was the rebuilt Royal Library, Number 23 on my guidebook map, and my second rendezvous point at 2 P.M., if the first one didn't come off.

There were a number of Westerners in the Purple City, and I overheard a middle-aged couple speaking in American English. She was saying how awful it was that the American military bombed these architectural treasures into rubble. He agreed and added, "We cause death and destruction wherever we go."

I didn't think he meant him and his wife, who only caused stupidity wherever they went. As part of my cover, I offered to take their picture together in front of a grassy expanse of waste and rubble. They seemed pleased and gave me their idiotically complex camera that had more stops than the Washington Metro.

As I focused, I said to them, "Did you know that the Communists attacked this beautiful city during the Tet truce, the holiest night of the

Buddhist year? Smile. Did you know that the Communist political cadres executed over three thousand citizens of Hue, men and women, by shooting, bashing their heads in, or burying them alive? Smile."

They weren't smiling for some reason, but it was a photo that they'd remember, so I fired off two shots, the second with the guy coming toward me, holding out his hand for the camera.

The guy took his camera without a word of thanks, and he and his wife walked away, a little less ignorant than a minute ago, but obviously not happy with this new information. Hey, you're supposed to learn things when you travel; I had.

I walked out of the Purple City, back to the Halls of the Mandarins, and wandered around inside. The place was big, and I had no idea how this person was going to spot me. If we both had tails, maybe the tails could sort of help us get together for a photo and a bust.

Despite my flippancy, I was getting a little concerned. Again, I knew I was alone, but I had not one iota of confidence that the other guy was similarly alone.

At 12:20 P.M., I was still wandering the building, and the fire-breathing dragons started to look like I felt.

I went outside. The sun was peeking through small cracks in the cloud cover, and it was a little warmer.

I circled the Halls of the Mandarins, but no one seemed to want to make my acquaintance.

The rendezvous had not come off. I had about an hour and a half until the next one, during which time I could go and have my head examined.

I exited the walled city onto the river embankment where I'd noticed a few snack bars. I bought a liter of water and a rice ball wrapped in banana leaves.

I ate on a bench beside a young Viet couple and stared at the Perfume River, eating my ice cream with a plastic spoon and sipping tepid water out of a plastic bottle.

I bit into the sticky rice ball. This really sucked. James Bond never sat on a park bench with a hangover, sipping warm water and eating a sticky rice ball with his fingers.

The Perfume River was flowing fast because of the winter rains, and downriver I could see the three stone pylons where the old bridge once spanned the river. I'd spoken to a marine years ago, who'd been here during the battle, and he said that you could cross the river by walking on the dead bodies floating downstream. This, of course, was a typical marine exaggeration, but all war stories have a seed of truth before they grow into gigantic bullshit trees. I've never actually known a war story to get smaller with a retelling.

Two co-deps in pink ao dais walked along the

river, and their long, straight hair, parted in the middle, reminded me of Susan. I stood, called out to them, and indicated my camera.

They stopped, giggled, and posed. I took a picture and said, "Chuc Mung Nam Moi."

They returned the greeting and walked past me, still giggling and glancing over their shoulders.

This gave me a little lift.

Most people, I think, lead normal lives; I have not. In this whole world, at this moment, there couldn't be more than a few dozen men and women, if even that, doing what I was doing now. Most secret rendezvous were of the sexual kind, and there were millions of them happening right now, and there would be millions more tomorrow, and the next day. And a few of those lovers would wind up dead, but most would wind up in each other's arms.

Paul Brenner, on the other hand, was going to wind up either arrested, or in possession of a piece of information that could get him arrested, or killed, or, best scenario, might get him a few more bucks in retirement pay, and the lady of his dreams back in the States.

This had all seemed like a good idea back in Washington—well, not a good idea, but at least an idea that might do me some good, and it had.

I stared at the river, and the New City on the opposite shore. I watched a thousand people stroll by. Having missed the first rendezvous was sort of a reprieve, and I had a lot of legitimate reasons to abort the mission, Colonel Mang being not the least of those reasons. Time to go back to the hotel and clear out of this country.

I sat there.

At 1:30 P.M., I stood, re-entered the Citadel through the outer wall and into the Imperial Enclosure, then through the final wall into the Forbidden Purple City. It hit me then that the symbolism of the name had not been lost on the dramatically inclined dolts in Washington, and I knew that this was where I'd meet my contact and possibly my fate.

CHAPTER TWENTY-EIGHT

──────★──────

I entered the walled enclosure of the Forbidden Purple City, and walked through the vegetable plots and flower gardens toward the Royal Library, which, as I noticed before, was the only surviving structure within the inner walls.

A few tourists stood around the building, but most people were wandering through the gardens.

About twenty meters from the library, a Vietnamese man was squatting beside a garden, examining the flowers. He stood up and stepped on the path in front of me. He said in near perfect English, "Excuse me, sir. Are you in need of a guide?"

Before I could answer, he went on, "I am an instructor at Hue University, and I can show you the most important sites of the old walled city." He added, "I am a very good guide."

The man who was standing before me was in his mid-thirties, dressed in the standard black slacks, white shirt, and sandals. He wore a cheap plastic watch, like everyone here, and his face was unremarkable. I could have passed him a dozen times and not picked him out of a crowd. I said to him, "How much do you charge?"

He replied with the countersign, "Whatever you wish to pay."

I didn't respond.

He said, "I see you have a guidebook. May I look at it?"

I handed him the book, and he opened it. He said, "Yes, you are right here, within the Forbidden Purple City. You see?"

Without looking at the book, I replied, "I know where I am."

"Good. This is an excellent place to begin our journey. My name is Truong Qui Anh. Please call me Mr. Anh. And how shall I address you?"

"Paul would be fine."

"Mr. Paul. We Vietnamese are obsessed with forms of address." He squatted again and said, "Look at this mimosa plant. You see, when I touch the leaves, they are touch-sensitive and they curl."

My luck, I get a talker. While Mr. Anh was annoying the mimosa, I glanced around to see if anyone was watching.

Mr. Anh straightened up and flipped a few pages of my guidebook. "Is there anything specific you'd like to see?"

"No."

"Then I will pick a few places. Are you interested in the emperors? The French colonial period? Perhaps the last war. Were you a soldier here?"

"I was."

"Ah. Then you may be interested in the battle of Hue."

I was starting to think this guy was really a guide, then, as he looked in my guidebook, he asked, "Mr. Paul, are you quite sure you weren't followed here?"

"I'm quite sure. How about you, Mr. Anh?"

"I'm sure I'm alone."

I said to him, "Why did you miss the first rendezvous?"

He replied, "Just to be on the safe side."

I didn't like that reply and asked him, "Did you think you were under surveillance?"

He hesitated, then replied, "No . . . to be honest with you, I lost my nerve."

I nodded. "You got it back?"

He smiled in embarrassment. "Yes." He added, "I'm here."

I wasn't going to tell him that I almost wasn't here for Rendezvous Two myself.

I asked him, "Are you really a university instructor?"

"I am. I would be lying to you if I said I haven't come to the attention of the authorities. I am a Viet-Kieu. Do you know what that means?"

"I do."

"Good. But other than that, the authorities have no reason to watch me."

"You've never done anything like this before?"

"Well, once, about a year ago. I like to help

when I can. I've been back four years, and now and then I'm asked to do a small favor. Come, let's take a walk."

We walked together on the paths, and Mr. Anh said, "The Communists take all the credit for the rebuilding here, but the fact is, they let this entire imperial compound fall from ruin to decay because it was associated with the emperors. The Communists are suspicious of history, and whatever came before them. But Western organizations have put pressure on them to restore much of what was lost in the war. The West provides the money, of course, and the Communists reap the rewards of tourism."

We were in the outer sanctum now, near the Emperor's Palace, and Mr. Anh led me to a flower garden formed by the ruined foundation of a building. He said, "My father was a soldier with the army of South Vietnam. A captain. He was killed right here, where this garden is, and where an imperial building once stood. He was found after the battle in the rubble here along with fifteen other officers and men, their hands tied behind their backs, and bullet holes in their heads. Apparently, they were all executed by the Communists."

I understood that Mr. Anh was establishing his anti-Communist credentials, but this story could be totally false and how would I know?

He said, "I was very young when he died, but I remember him. He was stationed here, where my family lives. We were home that evening, the evening of Tet 1968, across the river in the New City, when suddenly my father jumped out of his chair and shouted, 'Gunfire!' Well, my mother laughed and said, 'Dear husband, those are fireworks.'"

I watched Mr. Anh as he stared down at the garden and relived this memory. He continued, "Father grabbed his rifle and started for the door, still wearing his sandals—his boots were in the corner. He was shouting for us to go into the bunker behind the house. We were all very frightened now because we could hear screaming in the street, and the fireworks had become gunshots."

Mr. Anh stayed silent, staring at the ground, and he almost looked like a little boy staring at his shoes while he tried to get something out. He continued, "My father hesitated at the front door, then came back and embraced my mother and his mother, then the five children, my brothers and sisters. We were all crying, and he pushed us out the back door where the bunker was dug into the garden."

Mr. Anh picked a flower, twirled it in his fingers, and threw it in the garden. He said, "We stayed in the bunker with two other families for a week until the American marines came. When we re-entered our house, we saw that all the Tet food had been taken, and we were very hungry. We saw, also, that our front door had been broken in, and many things were taken, but the house had survived. We never knew if Father had been taken prisoner in the house, or on his way to rejoin his soldiers. The attack was a complete surprise, and the Communists were within the city before the first shot was fired. Father would have liked to die with his soldiers, and at first we thought he had. But then in March, as the people and the soldiers were clearing rubble, they found the decomposed bodies of many massacres. My father wore dog tags, which the Americans had made for him, and that was how he was identified, right here, where a building once stood. The Communists must have shot them all in this building. I'm glad he was still wearing his dog tags so we had a body to bury. Most families did not."

Mr. Anh stood there a moment, then walked away. I followed.

We left the walled Citadel and walked along the riverbank. Mr. Anh asked me, "So you were a soldier here?"

"First Cavalry Division, 1968, mostly up at Quang Tri."

"Ah, so you know this area?"

"I remember some of it."

"How does it seem to you? Vietnam."

"Peaceful."

"This is a country whose people have had their spirit crushed."

"By whom?"

"The regime."

"Why did you come back?"

"This is my country." He asked me, "If America were a dictatorship, would you live there?"

Interesting question. I replied, "If an American dictatorship was as inefficient as this one, I might."

Mr. Anh laughed, then said, "Well, they may appear to you as inefficient, but they did a thorough job of destroying all opposition to the regime."

"They didn't get you. Or a lot of other people I've met who seem to hate the regime."

"Perhaps I should have said, organized opposition." He added, "They have not won many hearts or minds."

We passed the Phu Xuan Bridge, and Mr. Anh insisted he take my camera and shoot pictures of me with the river in the background, then from the opposite angle with the walls of the Citadel behind me. He didn't look particularly nervous about this meeting, which could get him shot, but I could see a little anxiety in his eyes now and then.

I said, as he was shooting, "I'm assuming if they were going to arrest us, they would wait to see if we met anyone else."

He handed me the camera and replied, "Yes, they would wait."

"Are you frightened right now?"

"I am beyond frightened." He smiled and added, "You know that we are inscrutable."

We continued our walk along the river. All I wanted from Mr. Anh was the correct name of the village I needed to get to, some directions, and anything else he might have been told to pass on to me. But the man was in no hurry, and maybe it was a good idea to look like a tourist and guide.

Mr. Anh informed me, "I attended the University of California at Berkeley."

"I thought you wanted to get away from the Communists."

He sort of giggled and continued, "I lived mostly in northern California, but I took a year and traveled all over America. It's an amazing country."

I inquired, "Where did you get the money?"

"Your government."

"That was nice of them. And now you're paying them back."

He stayed silent a moment, then replied, "Your government has a program to . . . how can I say this . . . to cultivate agents of influence, Vietnamese refugees, who, like myself, promise to go back to Vietnam for a period of at least five years."

"I've never heard of that."

"And you never will. But there are thousands of us who have come back to live, Viet-Kieus, whose sympathies lie more with Washington than Hanoi."

"I see. And what are you supposed to do? Start a revolution?"

"I hope not." He laughed again and said, "All we have to do is be here, and in subtle ways, influence the thinking of the people, and of the government, if possible." He added, "Most Viet-Kieus are entrepreneurs, some like myself are academics, and a few have even entered the civil service, the police, and the army. Individually, we have no power, but as a whole, there are enough of us so that the Hanoi government hesitates before they take a step backward, toward socialism and isolation. Private enterprise, trade, and tourism are here to stay. You understand?"

"I think so. And do you put subversive thoughts into your students' heads?"

"Certainly not in the classroom. But they know where to come when they want to hear the truth. Do you know that it is forbidden to mention that the Communists executed three thousand citizens of this city? Everyone knows that, everyone has lost a family member, but none of the textbooks mention this."

"Well, Mr. Anh, if it makes you feel any better, American history books rarely mention the Hue massacre either. You want to read about massacres, go to the index under My Lai."

"Yes, I know this."

We were at the far corner of the wall, and on

the riverbank was a huge marketplace, where Mr. Anh led me.

He found a small snack bar with tables and chairs near the river, and he said to me, "May I get you something to drink?"

"A Coke would be fine."

He went to the snack stand.

I sat and looked around. It was hard in this country to determine if you were seeing the same people twice or three times, especially the men, who all favored black slacks and sandals with socks. Some of the shirts were different, but most were white. The hair came in one color and one style, and it was all on the guys' heads; no beards or mustaches, except on very old men, and no one wore hats. A few of the men wore windbreakers, but all the windbreakers were the same style and color, which was tan. Some of the Viets, I'd noticed, wore reading glasses, but barely anyone wore glasses for distance, though all of the drivers should consider this.

A Viet crowd was a sea of sameness here in Hue, more so than in Saigon or Nha Trang.

Mr. Anh sat and gave me a can of Coke. He had hot tea in a bowl, and a paper bag of un-shelled peanuts, which he seemed to enjoy crushing.

He finally got down to business and said, "You wish to visit a certain village, correct?"

I nodded.

He pushed a handful of unshelled nuts toward me and said, "The village is in the far north. North Vietnam."

Bad luck. I was hoping it was in the former South Vietnam, and I was hoping it was nearby, but Tran Van Vinh was a North Vietnamese soldier, so what did I expect?

Mr. Anh pretended to be looking through my guidebook as he said, "This village is small, and does not appear on most maps. However, I have done some extensive but discreet research, and I believe this is the place you seek."

"What if it's not?"

He chewed on some peanuts and replied, "I've been in direct fax contact with someone in America, and your analysts there are in agreement that this village that I've found is the one you are seeking." He added, "I am ninety percent certain this is the place you are looking for."

"Close enough for government work."

He smiled, then informed me, "Very few Westerners go to this area, and you would need a reason to be there."

"Do I have to supply my own reason?"

Mr. Anh replied, "By luck, there is a place close to this hamlet that does draw some tourists. This place is called Dien Bien Phu. You have heard of this place?"

"The final battle of the French-Indochina War."

"Yes. Military men of all nationalities go there to study this historic battlefield. So you should go there. When you have seen the museum and taken some photos, ask a local person where is this hamlet you are looking for. It is less than thirty kilometers north of Dien Bien Phu. But be careful who you ask. Up north, they report everything to the authorities."

He sipped his tea, then continued, "I have been to Dien Bien Phu, and so I can tell you that there are many hill tribespeople who gather near the museum and in the market to sell their crafts to the tourists. The tribesmen are mostly H'mong and Tai. You will recall from your time here that the tribespeople have little loyalty to the Vietnamese government." He added, "They are not anti-Communist, they are anti-Vietnamese. Therefore, you should direct your inquiries to a tribesman, not an ethnic Vietnamese. You may find a few tribesmen who speak some English, but mostly they speak French for the tourists who are mostly French. Do you speak French?"

"Un peu."

"Bon. You should try to pass as French." He added, "I think you can trust these people."

"Tell me why I should trust *you*."

Mr. Anh replied, "That would take some time, and whatever I say would not convince you. As I see it, Mr. Brenner, you have no choice."

"How do you know my name?"

"If I needed to contact you at your hotel in an emergency."

I informed Mr. Anh, "It's very unusual in these situations for you to know who I am. I don't mean to sound racist, but you're not a native-born American, and you don't qualify as a person who should know either my name or my destination."

He looked at me a long time, then smiled and replied, "I still have relatives in the new country. Your government trusts me, but to be sure, they have arranged a family reunion for me in Los Angeles. I am to leave for the States on the same day you leave Hue. If I don't show up in Los Angeles, they will assume I have betrayed them and you."

"That's a little late for me, partner."

"I have no intention of betraying you, Mr. Brenner. In fact, I wish you a successful trip because if something happens to you, it will not go well for me or my family in Los Angeles."

"I see. Well, we don't shoot people."

"That's not what they told me."

I didn't reply to that. Bottom line here, the stakes were very high, whatever the game was, and Mr. Anh was either loyal to Uncle Sam, or scared shitless about his family, or both. They weren't fucking around in Washington. I said, "Okay. Sorry if I insulted you."

"Not at all. It was a legitimate and necessary question. Your life is at stake."

"Thanks."

"For you, it doesn't matter if I'm loyal or under duress. I'm on your side."

"Great."

Mr. Anh stayed silent, chewing on his peanuts, then said, "Whatever your mission is, Mr. Brenner, I assume it is important enough for you to risk your life. If not, you should take the next plane to Hanoi or Saigon, and get out of this country. This can be a pleasant place for the average Western tourist—but if you are deviating from tourism, the government can be very unforgiving." He added, "I have been asked to help, and I agreed, thereby putting my own safety in jeopardy. I don't know what this is about, but I am one of those Vietnamese who still trust the Americans."

"Well, I don't."

We both smiled.

I said to Mr. Anh, "Okay, if you are who you say you are, then thank you. If you're not, then I suppose I'll see you at my trial."

"You would be lucky to get a trial. I'll tell you something you may not know—the Hanoi government is obsessed with the FULRO. You have heard of this group—Front Unitié de Lutte des Races Opprimées—the United Front for the Struggle of the Oppressed Races?"

I recalled again the photos I saw in the American War Crimes Museum in Saigon. I said, "Yes. I've heard of the FULRO."

Mr. Anh had more good news for me. He said, "You will be passing through FULRO territory. The Hanoi government is merciless in hunting down these guerrillas, and merciless in their treatment of Americans who have made contact with them. If this is your mission, and you are caught, you can expect to be tortured, then shot. I know this for a fact."

Well, this was not my mission, but it occurred to me that I'd have a hard time explaining that if I were arrested. I always assumed that the worst that would happen if I were caught would be a few weeks or months of unpleasantness, followed by a diplomatic solution to the problem, and repatriation back to the States. But if I put the FULRO into the equation, I might very well wind up being the last American MIA in Vietnam.

Mr. Anh was a bottomless well of interesting facts, and he said, "There have been CIA men, Special Forces men, and American freelance mercenaries who have gone into the remote areas of the country to aid the FULRO—most of them have never been heard of again."

"Thanks for the encouragement."

Mr. Anh looked at me and said, "This is an unhappy country, a country whose history has turned brother against brother, father against son. Here, in the south, you never know who to trust. But when you get to the north, it is much easier—trust no one."

"Except the hill people."

Mr. Anh did not respond. He sipped his tea and asked me, "Has your visit brought back memories?"

"Of course."

"In this country, most of the war generation are dead, or have fled. Those who remember do not speak of it. The government celebrates every Communist victory, and they have changed each of their defeats into victories. If they had thirty years of victories, what took them so long to win the war?"

It seemed like a rhetorical question, but the answer was, "The winners write the history."

Mr. Anh continued, "I had to go to America to learn the history of my own country. If you listen to Hanoi long enough, you start to doubt your own memory and your own sanity."

"Same in Washington, Mr. Anh."

"Well, but you make that a joke. Here, it is not a joke."

"How many more years do you have here?"

"One."

"Then what?"

"I don't know. I may stay . . . things are changing for the better here . . ."

"I have an American friend who's been here three years, and she can't seem to leave."

"Everyone has his or her own reasons for staying or for leaving. This is an interesting country, Mr. Brenner, a dynamic country in many ways, coming out of a long nightmare, filled with social and economic change. For many people, especially Americans, the transition is exciting, and offers many opportunities. An American expatriate once described Vietnam to me as being like the Wild West, a place where you leave your history behind, and where anything goes in pursuit of your fortune."

"God help Vietnam."

Mr. Anh smiled and added, "You could die of boredom in Japan, or Singapore, or Korea. Here, you won't die of boredom."

"That's for sure." I finished my Coke and looked at my watch.

Mr. Anh noticed and said to me, "The name of the village you seek is not Tam Ki, it is Ban Hin, in the province of Lai Chau." He spelled it out for me and added, "It's a difficult journey. The only air service is twice weekly from Hanoi, and you are not to go via Hanoi, according to what I have been told. In any case, the seats on the aircraft are usually booked weeks in advance. So you need to go by land. Unfortunately, there is no bus service from here, only from Hanoi. The roads, especially now with the rains, are treacherous, and you know by now that you are not allowed to rent a car yourself. You need a car and driver."

"Maybe I'll stay home."

"That is your decision. But if it were me going, I would take a four-wheel drive and a good driver. The road distance from Hue to Dien Bien Phu is between nine hundred and a thousand kilometers, depending on your route." He added, "Fortunately, the first five hundred kilometers will be on Highway One toward Hanoi. At some point south of Hanoi, you must choose a road to take you to Route 6, which will then take you northwest through the mountains to Dien Bien Phu."

He found a map of northern Vietnam in the guidebook and pushed the book toward me. "Do you see Dien Bien Phu?"

I looked at the map and found it in the far northwestern part of the country, near Laos. I could also see Route 6, coming out of Hanoi and winding through the mountains to Dien Bien Phu. I asked, "How's Route 6?"

"Not a good road at this time of year, or any time for that matter. The roads that lead you to Route 6 are worse."

"Worse than New Jersey?"

He smiled and continued, "You will see on the map two or three roads leading from Highway One to Route 6 before you get to Hanoi. You must pick one, depending on weather conditions, the condition of the road, and perhaps other factors that only you can decide upon when the time comes for you to leave Highway One." He looked at me.

I said, "I understand. Tell me what I should tell my driver about why I don't want to go through Hanoi to get to Highway 6 to Dien Bien Phu?"

"Tell him you enjoy treacherous mountain roads in the rain."

Not funny.

Mr. Anh said, "With luck, you can be in Dien Bien Phu in two days."

I thought about this, and wondered what those idiots in Washington were thinking. I said, "Is it possible to hire a small plane from Hue–Phu Bai?"

"Not in this country, Mr. Brenner. Private flights are strictly forbidden."

"How did the French get to Dien Bien Phu?"

He smiled. "They parachuted in." He said, "There is an alternative route. You could fly from here to Vientiane, the capital of Laos, then fly to Luang Prabang in Laos, and you will be only about a hundred fifty kilometers from Dien Bien Phu. But you'll first need a visa for Laos, and then you would have to cross the border back into Vietnam by road, and that could present a difficulty."

"Well, thank you for the geography lesson, Professor. I'm sure I can get to Dien Bien Phu before my visa expires."

He reiterated, "Hire a very good private driver with a good four-wheel drive. You should make it." He added, "Do not go through Vido-tour."

"I know that."

Mr. Anh played with his pile of broken peanut shells and said to me, "I have been told to pass on some instructions."

I didn't reply.

Mr. Anh said, "If you find this person you are looking for, you are to offer to buy all his war souvenirs. If he is dead, document his death, and make the same offer to his family. If he is alive, you are to photograph him, and establish his residence with maps and photographs. This person may be contacted at a later date for whatever purpose your government needs him for."

Again, I didn't reply.

Mr. Anh seemed a bit uncomfortable about something, and he was avoiding my eyes when he said, "Or you may wish to finalize the matter yourself, thereby saving the trouble of a further visit to this individual."

I said to Mr. Anh, "I'm sorry, could you repeat that?"

He did, and I said to him, "I'm not quite sure I understand what that means. Do you?"

"No, I don't, Mr. Brenner. They said you would understand."

"Did they? What if I misunderstood and thought they meant I should kill him, when they meant something else?"

Mr. Anh did not reply to that directly but said, "After a long, bitter war, there are many grudges left to be settled."

I didn't think this had anything to do with an old grudge, or a payback for something that happened in the secret world of espionage or the Phoenix assassination program, or anything like that. Tran Van Vinh was a simple soldier who'd seen something he wasn't supposed to see. But Mr. Anh assumed that it had to do with the dirty, back-alley war, which was a logical assumption; or that's what he'd been told.

Mr. Anh concluded with, "In any case, your mission is then complete, and you are to go directly to your next destination with the items you have acquired. This message is verbatim, and I know nothing further."

I didn't reply.

Mr. Anh said, "You are to stay here tonight and tomorrow night, as you know, then make your way to Dien Bien Phu, and the village in question. I am to contact you at your hotel if there is a change in plans, or if I have any further information for you. I have a secure means of informing someone in Saigon that this meeting was successful, and you have the opportunity now to give me a message that I will pass on."

I replied, "Just tell them that I understand my mission, and my duty, and that justice will be done."

"Very well. Should I leave, or do you wish to go first?"

"I'll go." I took some peanuts and put them in my pocket. I said to Mr. Anh, "I'm leaving this guidebook with you. What I want you to do is to return it to my hotel on the morning I'm to depart for Dien Bien Phu, which is the same morning you are departing for Los Angeles. In that way, I'll know you haven't been arrested, and that my mission is not compromised. If I don't receive the book, I reserve the right to leave the country. You can pass that on."

He said, "I understand."

I stood and took ten dollars out of my pocket and put it on the table. "Thank you for an interesting tour."

He stood, and we shook hands. He said to me, "Have a safe journey, sir. Happy New Year."

"Same to you."

I left and made my way through the market, out onto the river walk, and I headed toward the bridge to the new city.

It was not yet four o'clock on New Year's Day, the first day of the Year of the Ox. It might also be the last day of the year for the jackass, meaning me. How do I get myself involved in things like this? For a take-charge kind of guy, I keep falling into vats of shit: career-limiting homicide cases, dangerous assignments to hostile countries, and complicated love affairs.

I got onto the pedestrian walk of the Trang Tien Bridge, and I stopped halfway. I cracked open some peanuts and dropped the shells into the river. I popped a few peanuts in my mouth and chewed.

The sky was a layer of clouds and a few raindrops fell. The air was damp and cool, and the Perfume River ran swiftly to the sea.

Well, I thought, I hadn't misunderstood Mr. Conway at Dulles, or Mr. Anh in Hue. Washington wanted Tran Van Vinh dead, and they'd be happy if I killed him. And they didn't even bother to give me a reason, beyond national security, which could mean anything and usually did.

The reason the geniuses didn't tell me ahead of time why this guy needed to be whacked was because if he was already dead, then I would have information I didn't need.

But for some reason, they seemed to think that if and when I met Mr. Tran Van Vinh, I'd know the reason, and I'd do what I had to do.

Whatever this poor bastard saw in the ruins of Quang Tri during Tet of 1968 was going to come back to haunt him, and to kill him. And that really wasn't fair, if he had indeed survived the whole war and had grown old . . . well, about my age, which is not old, but mature.

I tried to bring all my considerable powers of deductive reasoning to this puzzle, and I was getting close to something, but it kept slipping away.

The thing that was easy to deduce was this: If what Mr. Vinh saw was going to get him killed, then what Mr. Vinh told me could also get me killed.

★

CHAPTER TWENTY-NINE

— ★ —

I sat in the cocktail lounge of the Century Riverside Hotel sipping a Scotch and soda while the little guy at the piano was playing "Strangers in the Night."

It was ten after six, and the place was filled with Westerners chatting away while pretty cocktail waitresses in short skirts hurried around getting drink orders wrong.

I started wondering if Susan had gotten herself re-pissed and was going to stand me up. Women don't care where they are when they're pissed off at the guy they're with. I've had women make scenes in Soviet Moscow, East Berlin, and other places where it's not a good idea to attract attention, with no regard to their surroundings or the situation; when they're pissed, they're pissed.

Another possibility was that Susan had been picked up for questioning. After that little scene this morning at the police station, I wouldn't be surprised if they decided to harass me through her. Despite our charade, they knew we were together.

A bigger anxiety, however, was the gun, and the possibility that someone had seen her burying it. But even if the cops had been alerted, they wouldn't make a move until someone came to dig it up, which was why I intended to leave it there.

I ordered another Scotch. The three veterans were a few tables away, and they'd acquired some company in the form of three women in their mid-twenties, young enough to be their daughters. These guys may have once been officers, but they were not gentlemen; they were pigs.

The women looked and acted like Americans, but beyond that, I couldn't tell much about them, except that they were tourists, not expats, and they liked middle-aged guys with bucks.

Anyway, it was 6:30, and I was getting a little concerned. This is why it's better to travel alone, especially when you're on an assignment that could get dicey. I have enough trouble watching my own ass without worrying about a civilian.

But maybe she wasn't a civilian. This got me thinking about Mr. Anh, who, like Susan, was doing a little favor for Uncle Sam. This place was becoming the East Berlin of the post–Cold War world: shadowy people running around doing deals, doing favors, keeping their eyes and ears open. The CIA must feel re-energized now that they had a place where they could stir up the shit again.

The Americans, of course, don't like losing, and they'd learned a good postwar lesson from the Germans and the Japanese; if you lose the war, buy the winner's country.

Susan appeared at the door and looked around. She spotted me as I stood, and she smiled. You can always tell when someone is sincerely happy to see you by how they smile when they spot you in a crowd.

She walked over to the cocktail table, and I saw she was wearing black jeans, which I hadn't seen before, and a white silk V-neck sweater, which I also hadn't seen.

She gave me a big hug and kiss and said, "I knew you'd returned safely because I checked with the desk."

"Safe and sound."

She sat, and I sat across from her. She asked, almost excitedly, "So, how did it go? You had the rendezvous?"

"Yes. It went fine. What did you do today?"

"Shopping and sightseeing. So, who met you?"

"A Eurasian woman named Dep Throat."

"Come on, Paul. This is exciting. Was it a guy? An American? A Viet?"

"A guy. And that is *all* I'm saying."

"Do you know where you have to go next?"

I didn't seem to be getting through to her. I said, "Yes, and that's the end of the conversation."

"Is it far from here?"

"What are you drinking?"

"San Miguel."

I signaled the waitress and ordered a San Miguel beer.

Susan asked, "Where did you meet this guy? Where is Number 32? I'll bet that refers to the map in the guidebook."

"Did you sleep well?"

"I slept like a baby until noon. Did you go to the Immigration Police?"

"Yes."

"Did it go all right?"

"Yes." I added, "Actually, we had some words."

"Good. When you're nice to them, they think you're up to something. When you mouth off, they figure you're clean."

"I know that. I was a cop."

"I stayed away from the Citadel, as you asked, and now you have to tell me where you met this guy."

"Obviously, I met him in the Citadel."

"Do you think you were followed?"

"I wasn't. I don't know about him. Did you buy that outfit today?"

"Yes. You like it?"

"Very nice."

"Thank you."

Her beer came, and she poured it into a glass. We touched glasses, and she said, "Sorry about last night. You don't need the hassle."

"That's okay. I did the same thing to you about Bill."

"You did. I got rid of him."

I didn't reply.

I noticed the three vets again, and they were looking at Susan even though they already had three babes. What swine.

"What are you looking at?"

"Three Americans over there. Former army or marines. I saw them here yesterday and also at dinner. They're eyeing you."

"They're cute."

"They're pigs."

"The women seem to be having a good time."

"They're pigs, too."

"I think you're jealous."

"No, I'm not. You're the most beautiful woman in the room."

"You're so sweet." She changed the subject back to business and asked, "So, do you know how to get to this place you're supposed to go to?"

"I think so."

There was a good deal of background noise in the lounge, so no one could overhear us, and the piano player was playing Tony Bennett's "Once Upon a Time." I decided that the time had come to get at the bottom of some things that could affect my health. I said to her, "Now, let me ask you a few questions. Look at me and keep eye contact."

She put down her beer and sat up in her chair. She looked at me.

"Who are you working for?"

She replied, "I work for American-Asian Investment Corporation. Sometimes I do favors for the American consulate in Saigon, and the embassy in Hanoi."

"Have you ever done favors for the resident CIA guy in Saigon or Hanoi?"

"Saigon. Just once."

"You mean now."

"Yes."

"Do you get paid?"

"Expenses."

"Did you have formal training?"

"Yes. A month at Langley."

Which explained the trip to Washington. I asked, "Is American-Asian Investment a CIA front?"

"No. It's a real investment company. But it is a vetted facility."

"Anyone else at AAIC doing favors?"

"I can't answer that."

"What were your instructions regarding me?"

"Just meet and greet."

"They didn't tell you to pump me?"

"No. Why bother? Are you going to tell me anything about why you're here?"

"No. Did they tell you to travel with me?"

"No. That was my idea."

"Right now, Susan, are you on the job or off the job?"

"Off the job."

"I'm believing everything you say. You understand that? If you say it, it's the truth."

"It *is* the truth."

"Are you in love with me?"

"You know I am." She smiled for the first time and said, "I did fake one orgasm."

I tried not to smile and asked, "Do you know anything about my assignment that I don't know?"

She didn't reply.

"Tell me."

"I can't. I can't lie to you, so I can't say anything."

"Let's try again. What do you know about this?"

She took a sip of beer, cleared her throat, and said, "I don't know what your purpose here is, but I think the CIA does. They certainly weren't going to tell me. I think everyone has little pieces of this, and no one is telling anyone else what they know."

That was probably true. I wondered if even Karl had the whole picture. I said to Susan, "Meet and greet doesn't quite cut it."

"Well, obviously there was more to it. I was asked to brief you about the country without it sounding like I was briefing you. More like acclimating you and making sure you were good to go." She added, "You figured that out."

"Okay, aside from the resident CIA guy in Saigon, did you speak to anyone from the American embassy in Hanoi?"

"Yes, I did. The American military attaché. Colonel Marc Goodman. He flew to Saigon and spoke to me."

"About what?"

"He just wanted to be sure I had the right stuff."

"To do what?"

"To . . . win your confidence."

"I'm not getting a clear picture."

"You're putting me on the spot."

"My life is on the spot, lady. Talk to me."

"I wasn't supposed to travel with you. But I was supposed to offer to meet you here in Hue, to tell you I had to go there anyway on business or whatever. Then I was to say I would meet you again in Hanoi."

"What if I didn't like you?"

"Most men like me."

"I'm sure. And what was the point of you meeting me here in Hue?"

"To see if I could help you, to report on your health, your attitude, any problems with the police, the outcome of your rendezvous, and so forth. You know that."

"Okay. Did this military attaché guy, Colonel

Goodman, and the CIA guy talk to each other in Saigon?"

"They did. But I wasn't there for that meeting."

"You understand that a military attaché is actually Military Intelligence?"

She nodded.

"Who's the CIA guy in Saigon?"

"I can't tell you."

Apparently everyone was in on this, but me. Army Intelligence and the CIA were talking to each other about a CID/FBI case that they weren't supposed to know anything about; but obviously they did. What was the connection? Actually, the more I thought about Mr. Conway at Dulles, the more he seemed less FBI and more military; but they wanted to give the appearance of FBI involvement so that it seemed more like a homicide case and less like an international problem. Not only was Colonel Mang running around passing himself off as one thing when he was another, but so was Mr. Conway. And so was Susan. By this time, I wouldn't have been surprised to discover that I was working for Colonel Mang.

"Paul?"

"What?"

"Are you angry with me?"

"Not yet. Okay, so when they motivated you to use your many charms to win my confidence, what did they tell you to motivate *you?*"

"National security. My patriotic duty. Stuff like that."

"What else?"

"Do you still love me?"

"More than ever. What else?"

"I've already told you a few times. It has to do with the emerging relationship between America and Vietnam. Business. Oil. Trade. Cheap labor. They don't want it screwed up. Neither do I."

"Who's trying to screw it up?"

"I told you that, too. The hard-liners in Hanoi, and maybe in Washington."

"And did they tell you that my mission was going to help or hurt that cause?"

"They indicated that you could help."

"I guess they did, or you'd have already pushed me off the roof of the Rex."

"Don't be silly. I was told to help you."

"If I told you what I was doing here, do you think that my little piece of the puzzle and the little piece of the puzzle that you have might fit together?"

"I don't know."

"Do you want to swap pieces of the puzzle? You go first."

"I have no need to know why you're here, and no desire to know."

"Or, you already know."

"I don't. Are you pissed off at me?"

"Not yet."

"Still love me?"

"More than ever."

"Good. Can I have a cigarette?"

"Sure. Fire away."

She pulled a pack out of her purse and lit up. She took a long drag and exhaled, then sat back and crossed her legs. She said to me, "It has to do with Cam Ranh Bay."

"Okay."

"We built it, we want it back."

"I know that."

"The Philippines has kicked us out, and the Japanese are moving to reduce our presence. The Russian lease on Cam Ranh Bay expires in a few years, and they're paying rent under the old 1975 lease price in new rubles, which are almost worthless. Hanoi wants them out."

"Real money talks English."

"Right. We're talking about *billions* of greenback dollars to Hanoi for a long-term lease."

"Go on."

"The Viets hate and fear the Chinese. Always have. The Americans fear the Chinese. Strategic Pentagon projections show us at war with Red China within twenty years. We're short on military bases in this area. Plus, there's a *lot* of offshore oil here."

"So, this isn't about coffee, rubber, or betel nuts?"

"No. Oil and military bases."

"Got it. Continue."

"The Pentagon and others in Washington

are very excited about this. The present admin-
istration is not. They don't want to piss off the
Chinese, who would go totally ballistic if we
set up a military base at Cam Ranh Bay."

I nodded. I now had a little piece of the puzzle, but it didn't fit my piece. I mean, it must,
but there was another piece in between.

Susan continued, "Hanoi is willing to sign
Cam Ranh Bay over to us, despite some hard-
line opposition from the old Reds who still hate
us. But it's the present American government
who doesn't have the balls to go for it, despite
nearly everyone in the Pentagon and the intelligence community saying go for it. It's crucial in
case of a future war. It's good for us, and good
for the Vietnamese."

I didn't reply, but the thought of American
soldiers, sailors, and airmen back on Vietnamese soil was mind-boggling.

She sipped her beer and lit another cigarette.
She said to me, "You surprised me when you
asked Captain Vu about American warships in
the area."

"This is not rocket science. It's Political Science 101. Some of it's been in the news."

"Give yourself more credit, Paul."

"Okay. Let me guess how you know all this.
You're the CIA station chief."

She smiled. "No. I'm just a kid, a spoiled, up-
per-class MBA expat, looking for adventure."
She put her cigarette in the ashtray and without

looking at me said, "The CIA station chief in Saigon is Bill Stanley. Please don't tell anyone I told you."

We made eye contact, and I asked her, "Does Bank of America know about that?"

"He doesn't work for Bank of America. You arrived in Saigon on a weekend so you couldn't check things out, but I did take you to my office."

"Yes, you did. And are you and Bill . . . involved?"

"That part is true. Was true."

"Are you having fun?"

"Not if you're angry at me."

"Me? Why should I be angry at you?"

"You know. Because I lied to you about some things."

"Really? Are you still?"

"I've told you everything I know. They're going to fire me."

"You should be so lucky. Tell me why I'm here."

"I really don't know."

"Does Bill know?"

"He must know something."

"But he didn't share that with you?"

"He did not."

"Why were you supposed to meet me in Hanoi?"

"I'm not sure. They said you might need someone to talk to in Hanoi that you could trust.

Not an embassy person. They said if you returned from your mission, you might be . . . upset by what you discovered." She added, "I'm
supposed to tell the embassy your state of mind,
what you're thinking."

"And you just let that statement slide by?"

"I understand that the less I know, the better."

"Where did you get the gun?"

"From my company safe. That was the truth."

"Do you realize that about half of what
you've said to me over the last week has been
lies, half lies, and bullshit?"

She nodded.

"So? Why should I believe anything you say
now?"

"I won't lie to you anymore."

"I really don't care."

"Don't say that. I was just doing a job. Then I
fell in love. Happens all the time."

"Does it?"

"Not to me. But to people. I really hated myself for not being honest with you. But I thought
you figured it all out anyway. You're very
bright."

"Don't try to butter me up."

"You *are* pissed at me."

"You bet."

"Do you still love me?"

"No."

"Paul? Look at me."

I looked at her.

She gave me a sort of sad smile and said, "It's not fair, you know, if the gods in Washington come between us. If we part, we'll both turn to stone."

She had a point there about Washington, and I suppose you could say we were both being manipulated and lied to. I said to her, "Of course I love you."

She smiled.

I asked her, "What orgasm did you fake?"

She smiled wider. "You tell me." She added, "I won't do it again."

So, we sat there, had another round, and retreated into our own thoughts, trying to figure it all out.

Finally, she asked me, "Did you get any messages today?"

"No."

"Why do they want you to drop me?"

"Don't know. Do you know?"

"Probably because they don't like what happened between us. They really don't want us pooling information." She added, "I'm supposed to be working for them, but they don't trust me anymore. And neither do you."

I didn't reply to that last statement and said, "I think on a personal level, your friend Bill was pushing Washington to push me to dump you."

"I'm sure of it. He's really pissed at you." She laughed.

"He should thank me for getting his headache."

"That's not nice."

I didn't reply. I asked her, "Did *you* get a message?"

"Yes. They know I'm here, of course. Message from Bill *ordering* me to return to Saigon. Business jargon. Said I'd be fired and disciplined and so forth if I didn't report to work Monday. There's a ticket waiting for me at Hue–Phu Bai Airport."

"You should go straighten that out."

"I should, but I'm not. I want to go with you to Quang Tri."

"Fine. I booked a four-wheel drive and driver, 8 A.M., to take us to the A Shau Valley, Khe Sanh, and Quang Tri. I requested Mr. Cam."

She laughed and said, "Mr. Cam is home now in front of the family altar, asking the gods to erase us from his memory."

"I hope so."

"Paul?"

"Yes?"

"Can I give you some advice?"

"Is it free?"

"Yes. And from the heart. Don't go where they're sending you. Come back to Saigon with me."

"Why?"

"It's dangerous. You know that. That's not

what I'm supposed to tell you. That's from me personally."

I nodded. "Thank you. But as they may have told you, I'm counter-suggestible."

"I don't know about that. But I know that you think this is a personal test of your courage, and maybe you have a lot of other personal reasons for pushing on. This is no longer about duty, honor, and country, if it ever was. Well, you've proven your courage to me, and I'll write a full report about Highway One and everything else that's happened. You have to make the decision to abort. We'll go to Quang Tri and the A Shau Valley tomorrow and Khe Sanh, and you'll put that to rest. Then we'll go back to Saigon together, take a bunch of crap from everyone, then . . . you go home."

"And you?"

She shrugged.

I thought about that tempting offer for about half a second, then replied, "I'm finishing the job. End of conversation."

"Can I go with you?"

I looked at her and said, "If you thought Highway One was bad, wait until you see this trip."

"I really don't care. I hope by now you know I can handle it."

I didn't reply.

She informed me, "You'll increase your chances of success by about five hundred percent if I'm along."

"But can I double my money?"

"Sure. Look, Paul, there's no downside to having me along."

"That's a joke—right? Look, I appreciate your willingness to risk jail and maybe even your life to be with me, but—"

"I don't want to spend the next week worrying about you. I want to be with you."

"Susan . . . this may sound very chauvinistic, but there are times when a man—"

"Cut the crap."

"Okay. How's this? I keep thinking of those photos in your office, and sometimes I see you as Mr. and Mrs. Weber's little girl again, and I see the rest of your family back in Massachusetts, and even though I don't know them, I could never face them or face myself if something happened to you because of me."

"That's a very nice thought. Actually sensitive. But you know, Paul, if something happened between here and Hanoi, it would most probably happen to both of us. We'd have adjoining cells, adjoining hospital beds, or matching air shipment coffins. You won't have to explain anything to my parents, or to anyone."

I looked at my watch. "I'm hungry."

"You can't have dinner until you say yes."

I stood. "Let's go."

She stood. "Okay, you can have dinner. I knew I should have asked you when we were in bed. I can get anything I want out of you in bed."

"Probably."

We went outside, and it was raining, so we took a taxi across the river into the Citadel where Susan said she'd made a dinner reservation.

The restaurant was called Huong Sen and was a sixteen-sided pavilion built on stilts in the middle of a lotus pond.

We got a table by the rail, ordered drinks, watched the rain fall on the water, and listened to bullfrogs croaking. It was a very nice, atmospheric place, lit with colored lanterns and candles on the tables. Romantic.

Neither of us mentioned a word of business or anything that had been said in the cocktail lounge.

We had dinner and talked about home and about friends and family, but not about us or about any future plans.

Somewhere back there in the cocktail lounge, I think I used the "L" word, and I was trying to remember what I'd said. Maybe I didn't actually use it, but I remembered agreeing to it.

Susan was staring out at the rain on the pond, and I looked at her profile.

I should have been incredibly angry at her; but I wasn't. I shouldn't trust another word she said; but I did. Physically, she was flawless, and intellectually she gave me a run for my money. If I were writing an officer's evaluation report on her, I'd say: brave, intelligent, resourceful, decisive, and loyal. Divided loyalty, to be sure, but loyal.

But was I in love?

I think so. But what happened here could probably not happen elsewhere, and maybe could not be transplanted. And then there was Cynthia.

Susan turned and saw me staring at her. She smiled. "What are you thinking about?"

"You."

"And I'm thinking about you. I'm trying to think of a happy ending."

I didn't reply.

"Can you think of a happy ending?"

"We'll work on it."

We looked at each other, and we both probably had the same thought that the chances of a happy ending were not good.

★

CHAPTER THIRTY

―――――★―――――

The following morning, Monday, Susan and I waited in the hotel lobby for our car and driver. We both wore jeans, long-sleeve shirts, and walking shoes. Susan had her tote bag filled with things for the road.

The lobby was full of tourists waiting for their buses, cars, and guides. Hue was a tourist mecca, I realized, a destination between Saigon and Hanoi, and as it turned out, a good place for my rendezvous.

She asked me, "How are you getting to where you need to go tomorrow?"

"I don't know yet. We'll talk about it later."

"Does that mean you'd like my help?"

"Maybe."

"I'll give you some advice now—do not hire a car with a Vidotour driver. You might as well have Colonel Mang along."

"Thank you. I already figured that out."

We walked outside, and it was another gray, overcast day, cool and damp, but no rain.

Susan said to me, "You really pumped me last night."

"I was very horny."

"I wasn't talking about *that*. I meant in the lounge."

"Oh. That was overdue, darling."

An open white RAV4 pulled into the circular driveway and stopped. A guy got out and spoke to the doorman, who pointed to us.

The driver came over to us, and Susan spoke to him in Vietnamese. They chatted for a minute, probably about price, which is Susan's favorite subject with the Viets.

He was a man of about forty, and I'd gotten into the habit of matching the age of a Viet with his or her age in relation to the war. This guy had been in his mid-teens when the war ended, and he may have carried a rifle, either for the South Vietnamese local defense forces, made up mostly of kids and old men, or for the Viet Cong, who had lots of boys and girls in their ranks.

Susan introduced me to our driver, whose name was Mr. Loc. He didn't seem particularly friendly and didn't offer to shake my hand. Most Viets, I noticed, in their dealings with Westerners, were either very slick, or very good-natured. Westerners equaled money, but beyond that, the average Nguyen was polite until you pissed him off. Mr. Loc did not look or act like a hired driver; Mr. Loc reminded me of the close-faced guys I'd seen in the Ministry of Public Security in Saigon. In my job as an army criminal investigator, I assume many roles, and I'm good at it;

Mr. Loc wasn't very good at getting into his role as a driver, any more than Colonel Mang was at trying to pretend he was an immigration cop.

Susan said to me, "Mr. Loc needs to know where we're going now so he can telephone his company."

I spoke directly to Mr. Loc and said, "A Shau, Khe Sanh, Quang Tri."

He barely acknowledged this and went into the hotel.

I said to Susan, "I booked this through the hotel, who, as you know, are required to use Vidotour. Ask that clown for his business card."

She nodded in understanding, and when Mr. Loc came out of the hotel, she asked for his card. He shook his head as he said something to her.

She walked over to me and said, "He says he forgot his cards. The Viets who have business cards are proud of them, and they'd forget their cigarettes before they forgot their cards."

"Okay, so we're under the eye. Ask him if he has a map."

She asked him, and without a word of reply, he took a map from the front seat and gave it to me. I opened it and spread it on the hood.

As Mr. Loc stood nearby, I said to Susan, "Here's the A Shau Valley, due west of Hue. The road ends in the middle of the valley at this place called A Luoi, near the Laotian border, where I air-assaulted in by helicopter in late

April '68. From A Luoi is this dotted line that may or may not be passable. It was part of the Ho Chi Minh Trail. Ask Mr. Loc if we can take that to Khe Sanh."

She asked him, though he probably understood what I was saying. He said something to Susan, and she said to me, "Mr. Loc says the road is mostly dirt, but as long as it doesn't rain, we can make it to Khe Sanh."

"Good. Ask him if we can all speak English and stop pretending."

"I think the answer is no."

"Right. Okay, after A Shau, we travel what looks like seventy klicks north to Khe Sanh, where I also air-assaulted in by helicopter, in early April '68. Then we head east, back toward the coast on Highway 9 along the DMZ, and arrive at Quang Tri City, where my old base camp was located, and where I was stationed during most of the Tet Offensive in January and February 1968. So, we're traveling back in time in reverse chronological order." I added, "We'll do it in that order because I wouldn't want to be in the A Shau Valley when it gets dark."

She nodded.

I said, "It's a total of about two hundred kilometers, then due south again for about eighty kilometers, and we're back in Hue." I folded the map and threw it on the front seat.

Susan lit a cigarette, looked at me, and asked, "Did you ever think you'd be back this way?"

I moved away from the vehicle and from Mr. Loc, and thought about that. I replied, "Not at first. I mean, when I left here for the last time in '72, the war was still going on. Then, for a decade after, the Communists had a tight grip on this country, and Americans weren't exactly welcome. But . . . by the late '80s, when things here loosened up, and as I got older, I started to think about going back. Veterans were starting to return, and almost no one I knew regretted the trip."

"And here you are."

"Right. But this wasn't my idea."

"Neither were the other two times."

I replied, "Actually, I volunteered for my second tour."

"Why?"

"A combination of things . . . good career move—I was a military policeman by then, and not a front-line infantryman. Also, things were getting a little rocky at home, and my wife wrote a letter to the Pentagon on my stationery saying I wanted to go back to 'Nam."

Susan laughed. "That's silly." She looked at me and said, "So, basically, you went to Vietnam to get away from your marriage."

"Right. I took the coward's way out." I thought a moment and said, "Also . . . I had a brother, Benny, who . . . they had an unwritten policy of one male family member at a time in a combat zone . . . and Benny was very accident-prone, so I bought him some time. Fortunately, the American involvement in the war ended before he got his orders to go. He wound up in Germany. I don't like to tell that story because it makes me sound more noble than I am."

She put her hand on my shoulder and said, "That was a very brave and noble thing."

I ignored that and said, "The little bastard kept sending me pictures of himself in beer halls with fräuleins on his lap. And my mother, who is totally clueless, kept telling everyone that Benny got sent to Germany because he took a year of German in high school. And Paul took French, so they sent him to Vietnam, where she'd heard they spoke French. She thought Vietnam was near Paris."

Susan was laughing.

"Ready to roll?"

"Yes."

She put out her cigarette, and we got into the back seat of the RAV. Susan asked me, "Are your parents alive?"

"Yes."

"I'd like to meet them."

"I'll give you their address."

"And Benny?"

"Still leading a charmed life. I also have another brother, Davey, who still lives in South Boston."

"I'd like to meet all of them."

I tried to picture the Webers of Lenox getting

together for a few beers with the Brenners of South Boston, and I wasn't getting a good image of that gathering.

Mr. Loc got behind the wheel and off we went.

We drove along the tree-shaded river road past a few hotels and restaurants, past the Cercle Sportif, and the Ho Chi Minh Museum, and within a few minutes, we were out of the small city and into the low rolling hills, heading south.

I could see the tombs of the emperors scattered around, walled compounds surrounded by huge trees in park-like settings. Susan took a picture from the moving vehicle.

Most tourists, I suspected, came out of the city to see the tombs and pagodas, but I was going elsewhere. I said to Susan, "You didn't have to come with me. There are better things to see here than battlefields."

She took my hand and said, "I saw most of the sights when I was here last time. This time I want to see what you saw."

I wasn't sure *I* wanted to see what I saw.

The road continued south, through the necropolis, then swung west. Since it was the Tet holiday week, there was not much traffic on the road. Within the villages, I could see kids playing, and whole families gathered outside, talking and eating under trees.

I took the map from the passenger seat and looked at it. This was basically a road map, and not a very good one. The maps I'd used were detailed army terrain maps, partly taken from the French military maps. The army maps were covered with plasticine to survive the climate, and we used grease pencils to show the American firebases, airfields, base camps, and other installations. Army Intelligence would give us updates on the suspected locations of Viet Cong and North Vietnamese army units, which we'd note on the map. I don't know where they got this information, but most of our firefights were in places where the enemy wasn't supposed to be.

I looked up ahead and saw we were approaching the Perfume River. There was no bridge, according to the map, and no bridge in reality, in case I was expecting a pleasant surprise.

Mr. Loc drove onto a barge that could accommodate two vehicles. We were the only car waiting, and the ferryman said something to us. Susan said to me, "We can pay for two vehicles, or we could be here all day. Two bucks."

I gave the ferryman two bucks, and we got out of the RAV. Susan and I stood on the deck as the ferry made its way across the Perfume River. She took a picture from the boat.

I said to Susan, "Ask Mr. Loc if you can take his picture."

She asked him, and he shook his head and replied in a sharp tone.

Susan said to me, "He does not want his picture taken."

I looked across the river to the opposite shore and said to Susan, "The Army Corps of Engineers used to bridge these rivers with pontoon bridges. Chuck, however, didn't like to see standing bridges, and he'd load up a bamboo raft with high explosives and wait for a convoy to cross. Then he'd float along with the other craft, trying to look like Tom Sawyer or Huckleberry Finn, and at the last minute, he'd set a timer, abandon ship, and swim underwater with a breathing reed. Usually, though, we could see this coming, and we'd blow Chuck and his raft out of the water before he got to the bridge."

Susan had no comment.

I added, "This was why we all liked bridge duty. It was one of the more interesting games we played." I looked at Susan, who was processing this, and said, "I guess you had to be there."

She asked, "Paul, now that you're grown up and mature, when you look back on this, do you see it as . . . well, not within the normal range of behavior?"

"It seemed normal at the time. I mean, most of what we did, said, and thought was appropriate for the situation. Any other kind of behavior that you'd call normal would be considered abnormal here. Getting excited about sitting on a bridge all day, waiting to blow Charlie out of the water—instead of patrolling the jungle all day— is, I think, quite normal. Don't you agree?"

"I guess. I can see that."

"Good." I admitted, however, "It does seem a little weird, now that I think about it."

We reached the opposite bank, and we got back into the vehicle.

Mr. Loc drove off the barge onto the road, and we continued on, west toward the hills and mountains looming in the distance.

We were making only about fifty KPH, and it would take us over an hour to get to the A Shau Valley, if the road stayed this good.

The countryside was hilly, but the Viets had managed to extend their rice paddy cultivation through a series of dikes and waterwheels. The countryside looked prosperous and more inhabited than I remembered it.

We came to a small town called Binh Bien, which was the last town on this road. Beyond this was what we used to call Indian Territory.

The road rose, and before long, we were in the hills, which were covered with scrub brush and red shale.

I said to Susan, "We had to dig in every night, and we'd find a hill like that one over there with the steepest sides possible, and the best fields of fire. This is mostly shale, and it would take us hours with these little entrenching tools just to scratch out a shallow sleeping hole that would also become our firing hole, if we got hit during the night. The hole looked like a shallow grave, which it sometimes became. We'd set out trip flares and claymore mines around our perimeter. The claymore had a hand-squeeze generator attached to an electrical wire that put out enough juice to blow the detonator. The claymore mine fired hundreds of ball bearings downrange, like a giant shotgun blast, and anyone within about a hundred feet to the front of it would be mowed down. It was a very effective defense weapon, and if it weren't for the trip flares and the claymores, most of us would not have slept for the entire year we were here."

She nodded.

The road started to twist through a very narrow pass with steep slopes rising on either side, and the vegetation became thicker. A mountain stream ran along the road, and I could imagine that it flooded during the monsoon, making the road impassable.

I said to Susan, "This is the only way into the valley from Vietnam, but the Americans never went in overland because this pass was an ambush waiting to happen. We flew in by helicopter and brought everything we needed by air."

The blacktop had mostly disappeared, and as we got higher, the clouds drifted across the slopes, a mist rose off the ground, and it was getting cold. Mr. Loc was not too bad a driver and took it easy. We hadn't seen a vehicle or a human being in about twenty kilometers.

Susan said, "I've never been this far into the interior. It's spooky."

"It's like another country. Totally different from the coastal plains. Lots of Montagnards up here."

"Who are they?"

"Hill tribespeople. There are lots of tribes with different names, but collectively we called them Montagnards, after the French name for them."

"Oh. Now we call them ethnic minorities, or indigenous peoples. That's politically correct."

"Right. They're Montagnards. Just means mountain people. Anyway, they used to like Americans and hated the ethnic Vietnamese, north and south. We armed them to the teeth, but the trick was to get them to kill only North Viets and Viet Cong, and not kill our ARVN allies. I think their motto was 'The only good Vietnamese is a dead Vietnamese.'" I asked her, "Have you ever heard of the FULRO?"

Mr. Loc's head turned, and we made eye contact. Now this idiot would go back and report that I was here to lead a Montagnard insurrection.

Susan said, "I saw some photos once in the war museum of—"

"Right. Me, too."

Susan thought a moment, then said, "In all the years I've been here, I've never seen a hill tribesman."

"Not even in the Q-Bar?"

She ignored that and asked me, "Are they . . . you know . . . friendly?"

"They used to be. They're actually quite pleasant, if you're not Vietnamese. Maybe you should re-comb your hair."

I looked up and saw Mr. Loc staring at us in the rearview mirror. The man obviously understood what we were saying, and he didn't like this talk about FULRO and the Montagnards' hatred of the Vietnamese.

We crested a rise in the road and started down. The pass was still very narrow and twisting, and partly obscured with fog and mist, so we couldn't see down into the A Shau Valley.

"Look, Paul." Susan pointed to a ridge on which stood a long structure of logs and thatch, built on stilts. She asked me, "Is that a hill tribe house?"

"Looks like it."

As we got within about a hundred meters of the longhouse, three men with very long hair, dressed in what looked like multicolored blankets, appeared on the ridge above us. Two of them were carrying AK-47 rifles, and the other had an American M-16. My heart skipped a beat, and I guess Mr. Loc's did, too, because he slammed on his brakes.

Mr. Loc stared at the three armed men, less than fifty meters from us now, and said something to Susan.

Susan said to me, "Mr. Loc says they are Ba Co or Ba Hy tribesmen. They aren't allowed to carry rifles, but they hunt with them, and the government doesn't seem to be able to do anything about it."

This was a piece of good news. I liked the idea of armed civilians that the government couldn't control. I just hoped they remembered that they liked Americans.

The three tribesmen were looking down at us, but not making a move. I decided to make sure they knew only the driver was a Viet. I stood on the seat and waved. I shouted, "Hello! I'm back!"

They looked at one another, then back at me.

I called up to them, "I'm from Washington and I'm here to help you."

Susan said, "You want to get us shot?"

"They love us."

The three tribesmen waved their rifles, and I said to Mr. Loc, in English, "Okay, they say we can go. Move it." I sat.

He threw the vehicle into gear.

We continued down the pass into the valley. Susan said, "That was incredible. Damn, I should have taken a picture."

"If you take their picture, they cut off your head and try to stuff it into the camera."

"You're being an idiot."

"I'll tell you what they used to do to North Vietnamese soldiers and Viet Cong—they'd skin them alive, then filet them with razor knives, and feed the pieces to their dogs and make the prisoner watch as the dogs ate him, piece by piece. Every time they captured an enemy soldier, the dogs would go crazy with anticipation. Most enemy soldiers killed themselves rather than get captured by the Montagnards."

"My God . . ."

"I never saw this . . . but I saw the aftermath once . . . I think it made us feel good that we weren't quite that psychotic yet."

She didn't reply.

Mr. Loc turned and looked at me. It was not a very nice look. I said to him, "Drive."

The pass widened and became less steep. The ground fog lifted, and we could see the A Shau Valley, dotted with patches of white mist, which looked like snow from here.

I stared at the valley, and it was very familiar. Not only did I never think I'd see this place again, but when I was here, I thought this was the last place I'd see on this earth.

Susan was looking at me and asked, "Remember it?"

I nodded.

"You flew in. Then what?"

I didn't say anything for a while, then I said, "We flew in from Camp Evans, the First Cavalry Division's forward headquarters. A huge flight of helicopters carrying infantry for an air assault. It was April 25, and there was a window of good weather. We came in from the north-east, over these hills that we just drove through. In the north end of the valley is this place called A Luoi, which was once a Viet village, but by that time, there was no trace of it. That's where this road ends. At A Luoi, there was once a French Foreign Legion post that was overrun by the Communist Viet Minh, back in the '50s. The Communists then controlled this valley, which was called a dagger pointed at the heart of Hue. So, in the early '60s, the Special Forces arrived and set up a camp, right in the middle of Indian Country at A Luoi. They rebuilt the French airstrip, and recruited and trained the Montagnards to fight the Viet Cong and the North Viets."

We were almost at the floor of the valley now, and I could see the small river that ran through it.

I continued, "The valley opens out into Laos over there, beyond those mountains, and a branch of the Ho Chi Minh Trail runs right into the valley. So one day in 1966, the enemy massed his forces in Laos, thousands of them, and overran the American Special Forces camp, and the Communists controlled the valley again."

We were now entering the flat valley, and Mr. Loc sped up a little.

"After the Special Forces camp was overrun and the surviving hill people fled, this whole valley and the hills and mountains became a free-fire zone, a dumping ground for the air force. If they had to abort a precision bombing mission because of weather, they'd unload their bombs in this valley. When I got here, this place looked like Swiss cheese. These huge, house-sized craters became firing holes for us and them, and we'd fight, crater by crater . . . in the valley, in the hills, in the jungle up there." I looked to the southwest and said, "Somewhere over there near Laos is the place called Hamburger Hill, where, in May 1969, the army had about two hundred men killed and hundreds more wounded, trying to take this useless hill. This whole fucking valley was drenched in blood for years . . . now . . . it still looks gloomy and forbidding . . . but I see that the Viets and the Montagnards are back . . . and I'm back."

Susan stayed silent awhile, looked around, then said, "I can understand why you wouldn't want to come back here."

"Yeah . . . but . . . it's better than reliving it in bad dreams . . . like the guy at the Cu Chi tunnels . . . you go back, look it in the eye, and see that it's not what it used to be. Then, the new memory replaces the old one . . . that's the theory. But meanwhile . . . the place bums me out."

"Do you want to leave?"

"No."

The road headed toward the resurrected village of A Luoi, which I could see in the distance.

Around us, where there had once been elephant grass, bamboo, and brush, fields had been cleared for vegetable farming.

I said, "So, now it's April 1968, and the American army wants the valley back. So we air-assault into here, and I'm sitting in a Huey with six other infantry guys, not happy about any of this, when all of a sudden flak starts to burst around the chopper. We'd never been shot at with Triple A—anti-aircraft artillery—and this was absolutely terrifying . . . these big black air bursts, like in a World War II flick, are filling the sky, and huge chunks of shrapnel are whizzing through the air around us. The chopper in front of me got hit in the tail rotor and the whole aircraft spun around, throwing infantry guys out the door, then the chopper fell like a rock and exploded on the ground. Then another chopper gets hit, and by now our pilot is in a rapid vertical descent, trying to get below the flak. So there're two choppers down that I could see, each carrying seven infantry and four crew, so that's twenty-two killed before we even hit the ground. We lost ten more choppers on the initial air assault. Meanwhile, we're drawing machine gun fire from all these hills around the valley as we're descending, and our chopper takes a round right through the plexiglass windshield, but we're okay, and the pilot gets us about ten feet off the ground, we jump, and he gets the hell out of there."

"Good lord. You must have been—"

"Scared shitless. So, now we're on the ground, and it's what's called a hot landing zone, meaning, we're drawing fire. The bad guys are in the hills all around us, and they're lobbing in mortar rounds, rockets, and machine gun fire. We're landing thousands of men by helicopter into this killing zone, and we start to spread out to engage the enemy in the hills. Meanwhile, the air force is dropping napalm and cluster bombs on the hills, and the army Cobra gunships are firing rockets and Gatling guns to try to suppress the enemy fire. It was a total fucking mess, sort of like the Normandy Beach landings, but by air instead of boat. By the end of the day, the situation was under control, we'd secured the A Luoi airstrip, and we were fanning out into the hills, searching for Chuck."

I looked in the rearview mirror and said to Mr. Loc, "We beat the pants off the People's Liberation Army that day, Mr. Loc."

He didn't reply.

"Paul. Don't."

"Fuck him. His mommie was a Commie."

"Paul."

I got myself calmed down a bit and saw that we were entering A Luoi, a muddy village of wooden structures. There was one stucco building with a flag that was obviously the government building. The only vehicles I could see were scooters, a farm truck, and two yellow police jeeps. There were electric wires overhead, so the place had electricity, which was an improvement over the last time I'd been here.

Mr. Loc stopped in the village square. There were no parking meters.

Susan and I got out, and I looked around, trying to orient myself. The hills hadn't changed, but the valley floor had.

I said, "So, this is the shithole we fought for in three weeks of bloody combat."

I said to Mr. Loc, in English, "We're going to take a walk. You can report to your bosses." I jerked my thumb toward the government building.

Susan and I walked through the small square and down a narrow path that ended in a field west of the village. Running through the farm fields was the old airstrip, a mile-long stretch of PSP—perforated steel planking—overgrown now with weeds, but still usable.

I said to Susan, "Here's the airstrip, and at the far north end of it over there was the ruins of the Special Forces camp that the First Cav used as the command post when we landed. The engineers threw up sandbag bunkers all around the strip, and within two days, we had barbed wire and claymore mines encircling the whole runway. My company spent three days in the hills pushing the bad guys farther back, away from the airstrip. Then, we got a two-day break by manning the bunkers. My bunker was about over there, at the foot of that hill."

I looked out over the farmland to where the hills rose, about five hundred meters away. I said to Susan, "One day, we're sitting on top of the bunker, six guys playing poker, and Charlie starts dropping mortar rounds in from those hills farther back. And here's what's totally nuts—we barely looked up at the impacting rounds because we're old pros by now, and we knew Chuck was trying to hit the command bunkers over there or the ammo dumps or the airstrip itself. So we kept on playing cards. And then—here's the funny thing—some Commie son of a bitch up there in the hills—obviously the mortar spotter with field glasses—must have noticed us and got pissed off that we weren't paying any attention to his mortar fire. So, he gets personal and starts directing the mortar fire toward our miserable little bunker. The rounds started walking in on us, and we realized they were getting too close when dirt and stones started falling on us. Well, I'm sitting there with three aces and about thirty bucks in the pot, and everyone drops their cards, grabs a handful of money, and jumps off the roof of the bunker and dives inside. I jumped in just as a mortar round exploded outside and shook the bunker. I'd kept my cards, and I'm showing these idiots my three aces as the bunker is starting to come apart, and we're arguing if I won, or if it should be called a misdeal. We laughed about that for weeks afterward."

Susan said, "I guess you had to be there."

"I was."

I walked on a path between two cultivated fields, and Susan followed. The path ended in a treeline, and we went through the trees to where the small river flowed. It was a shallow, rocky river, and I recalled crossing it at a rock ford somewhere upstream. I went down to the river's edge and stood on a flat rock. Susan stood beside me.

"One day, we crossed this river a little upstream, over there. We had only about a hundred men in the company that used to number about a hundred and sixty. We'd lost a lot of people during the Tet Offensive in January and February, then at Khe Sanh in early April. So, now it's around April 30, and we've already lost a few guys here in the A Shau, and the meat grinder needs fresh meat, but no replacements are arriving, and we're also getting low on C rations and purified water . . ."

I looked at the water and said, "This is a clean mountain river, so we took a chance and filled our canteens here and drank directly out of the river."

I walked along the rocky bank until I reached the natural rock ford I remembered. Susan followed, and we stepped into the river on the first rock. The water came up to our ankles, and it was as cold as I remembered it. We crossed the river and scrambled up the opposite bank.

I said, "So we crossed here, and what do we see? About ten dead enemy soldiers lying on the riverbank here, some of them half in the water. They were decomposing into the river, all green and bloated, and one guy's jaw was just hanging by a piece of muscle and it was resting on his shoulder, with a full set of teeth . . . it was very weird." I added, "Everyone emptied their canteens. One guy vomited." I knelt down and scooped some water in my hands and stared at it, but didn't drink.

Susan was quiet.

I stood and turned away from the river. I could see where the trail began through the thick vegetation, and I climbed the bank onto the trail.

Susan followed, but said, "Paul, this is the kind of place where there could still be land mines."

"I don't think so. This is probably a well-used ford, and this trail is also well traveled. But we'll be careful." I started up the trail and Susan followed. "We'll do a leech check later."

She didn't reply.

"So, we're moving up this trail, and something moves in the bush. But it's not Chuck, it's a deer. I'm near the front of the lead platoon, and like idiots, we all fire at the deer. We miss, and we start chasing it through this bush while the rest of the platoon is jogging up the trail to keep up with us."

I kept moving up the trail that rose into the thick woods and up into the foothills.

"The company commander, Captain Ross, was back by the river with the other two platoons, and he thought we were in contact, but my platoon leader radioed that we were chasing a deer. This got us a chewing out from the captain, who was now leading the rest of the company to our rescue." I laughed. "I mean, totally nuts."

I kept moving up the rising trail. The rain forest was very thick here, and I kept thinking I felt land leeches falling on my neck.

Susan said, "Where are we going?"

"There's something up here I want to see. I can't believe I found this place."

We passed by a few bomb craters that were now choked with trees and bush, but which had been fresh earth back then.

Finally, we got to a clearing that I remembered, and which was still pocked with bomb craters. Across the open clearing was a wall of rain forest, and about a hundred meters beyond the forest rose a tier of steep hills. This was the place. I walked toward the forest.

I stood at the wall of vegetation and said to Susan, "So, about twenty of us are chasing this deer and blasting away, and the deer runs right into this treeline, which then had an opening that we thought was another trail. We follow, and all of a sudden, we break into the open, but it's not a natural jungle clearing because we see a lot of cut tree stumps, and we realize it's an enemy base camp, hidden in the jungle, and also hidden from the air with the high triple-canopy vegetation overhead to form this huge sort of sky dome. Sunlight is filtering into these acres of open space, and it's totally surreal. Huts, trucks, hammocks, open air kitchens, a field hospital, a damaged tank, and lots of anti-aircraft weapons, just sitting there."

I tried to find a break in the vegetation, but couldn't. I said to Susan, "It's in there." I pushed through the thick growth and got tangled in a wait-a-minute vine, which I cut with my Swiss army knife.

"Paul, *this* is not a well-traveled path. You're going to get yourself killed."

"You go back."

"No, *you* come back. That's enough."

"Just stay there, and I'll call for you." I pushed farther into the bush, knowing that this place could be littered with cluster bombs that had a habit of exploding when disturbed. But I needed to see this old base camp.

Finally, the bush thinned out, and I stood at the edge of what had once been a huge enemy base camp under the triple-canopy jungle. There was so little sunlight in here that the vegetation wasn't very thick or tall, and I could see all the way to the rising hills about a hundred meters away.

Susan came up behind me and asked, "Is this it?"

"Yes. This was the North Vietnamese base camp. Look over there. You see those bamboo huts? This whole place was filled with huts, ammunition, trucks, weapons . . ."

I stepped farther into the old camp and looked up at the jungle canopy. "They'd actually hoisted camouflage nets up there. Very clever people."

Susan didn't reply.

"So, we charge in here after this deer, about twenty of us, and we stop dead in our tracks. The funny thing is that we're chasing dinner, but the North Viets must have thought we were attacking with hundreds of troops because they'd all di di mau'ed. Gone. Someone noticed that a cooking fire was still smoking."

I moved a few more meters into the camp and said, "We're moving very cautiously now, tree by tree, stump by stump. We'd just scored a big hit by finding this camp, and my platoon leader, Lieutenant Merrit, radios the company commander with the good news, not mentioning the deer this time. But as it turned out, Charlie hadn't really left, and they were hiding around the perimeter of this camp, mostly on those steep hills over there. But we're not totally stupid either, so we get down behind the tree trunks and the stumps, and do what's called recon by fire, which is basically shooting the place up to see if we can draw any fire in return before we get too deep into this compound. Sure enough, one of the bad guys loses his nerve or got overanxious, and fires back before the whole platoon is in the killing zone. All of a sudden, we're in this huge firefight, and we're firing grenades and rockets into these drums of gasoline, which are blowing up, and ammo dumps are blowing up, and by now, the rest of the company is right behind us."

I walked farther into this overgrown camp and looked around. It was obvious that metal scavengers had been here because there wasn't a shard of steel left anywhere—no blown-up gas drums, no wrecked trucks, and not even a scrap of shrapnel on the ground.

Susan came up beside me and stared at these open acres beneath the jungle canopy. "This is incredible . . . I mean, there must be places like this all over Vietnam."

"There are. They managed to hide a half million men and women at any given time in jungle camps like this, in the Cu Chi tunnels and other tunnels, in villages along the coast, in the swamps of the Mekong Delta . . . they'd come out to fight when and where they wanted, on their terms . . . but this time, we trapped them in this valley, and they had to stand and fight on our terms . . ."

I moved farther into the deserted, spooky camp. "Unfortunately, it turned out that we'd tangled with a much bigger force than ours, so we broke contact and got the hell out of there. We moved back toward the river, but they kept trying to get around us to cut us off, and we kept blasting our way out. We called in helicopter gunships and artillery, which is the only thing that saved us from being surrounded and annihilated that day. It was a real mess, but the worst was yet to come. Our battalion commander, a lieutenant colonel, had been wounded in the air assault, and his replacement, a major, really wanted to be a lieutenant colonel, so for two days, he ordered us to counterattack, supported by artillery and gunships. But we were still outnumbered, and by Day Three, we'd lost a third of the company, killed and wounded, but we retook the camp, or so we thought. All of a sudden, we hear something strange over there at the far end of the camp, and out of that jungle comes two tanks, and they weren't ours because we had no tanks in the valley. None of us had ever run into an enemy tank, and we're . . . frozen. The tanks had twin 57 millimeter rapid-fire cannon mounted on turrets, and they open up. One guy gets hit square in the chest with a cannon shell, and he disintegrates. Two guys get hit by flying shrapnel, and everyone is diving for cover or running, but you can't outrun a tank. Then, one guy takes his M-72 anti-tank rocket—this little thing in a cardboard tube—stands, adjusts his aiming device very coolly as these tanks are coming at us, and he fires. The rocket hits the turret of the lead tank, and the gunner is blown out of the turret. Another guy fires a rocket and knocks out the other tank's tread. The enemy tankers get out and start running, and we mow them down. Now we have two tank kills, and the captain radios this to battalion headquarters, and we're heroes. So, do we get relieved and go back to A Luoi? No, the new battalion commander is trying to get a reputation or something, and he orders us to push on. That's not what we had in mind, but the guy is slick, and he tells us on the radio that according to intelligence reports, there may be American POWs kept in bamboo cages farther into the hills. So this motivates us, and off we go."

I walked toward where I thought we'd hit the tanks, and Susan followed. "We climbed this steep hill over here and pursued what was left of the enemy, and kept a lookout for those POW cages." I took a breath and continued. "By Day Six, we'd had about a dozen fights with the North Viets as they withdrew. We actually did find some bamboo cages, but they were empty. By now, we were completely exhausted, overcome with the worst kind of combat fatigue where you can't sleep at night, you can't eat, and you have to remind yourself to drink water.

We're barely speaking to one another because there's nothing to say. Every day more people are getting killed or wounded, and the group becomes smaller, until platoons and squads no longer exist, and we're just a horde of armed men without any real leadership or command structure . . . all the officers are dead or wounded, except the company commander, Captain Ross, a twenty-five-year-old who's the old man of the company by now, and all the sergeants are dead or wounded . . . the medics are all wounded, and so are the radio operators and the machine gunners, so we're trying to remember what we learned in basic training about radios, the M-60 machine gun, and first aid . . . and we keep pushing on . . ."

I stared at the hills in the distance.

Susan said in a soft voice, "Paul, we can go back now."

"Yeah . . . well, we should have asked to be relieved or reinforced, and maybe the company commander did, though I don't remember . . . but this running battle had taken on a life of its own, and I think it had a lot to do with killing more of the people who'd killed and wounded so many of us . . . it was like a fight to the finish, and as frightened and fatigued as we were, all we wanted to do was kill more of them. In fact, something very strange had happened to us."

I stood. "It went on for a total of seven days, and by the seventh day, you couldn't guess that we were nice American kids from a nice, clean country. I mean, we literally had blood on our hands, on our ripped fatigues, we had seven-day beards, and hollow bloodshot eyes, and filth on our bodies, and we weren't thinking about shaves and showers, or food or bandages . . . we were thinking about killing another gook."

We both stood there and finally Susan said, "I understand why you wouldn't want to talk about this."

I looked at her and said, "I've told this story a few times. This is not the story I don't like to talk about."

I walked fifty meters farther into the camp, and Susan followed. "We moved deeper into these hills, and on the seventh day, we were patrolling down a ridgeline, looking for another fight. The company commander put out flank security—two guys in the ravines on either side of this ridge. I was one of the guys. Me and this other guy scramble down into this ravine, and we're walking parallel to the company, who we could still see on the ridgeline above us. But then the ravine got deeper, the ridgeline turned, and the other guy was way out in front of me, and now I've lost visual contact with him and the rest of the company. So, I'm walking by myself, which is not a good thing to do, and I'm trying to catch up to the guy in front of me, but as it turned out, he'd scrambled back up the side of the ridge to try to find the company."

I moved to the base of the steep hill where there were still some huts, collapsed and over-grown with vines. I looked up at the hill. "It was over there, on the other side of this hill . . . I'm walking by myself, and I decided it was time to climb back up the ridge and find everyone. Just as I was about to do that, I caught a movement out of the corner of my eye, and standing on the other side of the ravine, not twenty meters away, is a North Vietnamese soldier with an AK-47 ri-fle, and he's looking at me."

I took a deep breath and continued, "So . . . we're staring at each other, and this guy is dressed in tiger fatigue pants, but he's bare-chested, and he has bloody bandages wrapped around his chest. My rifle is not at the ready, and neither is his. So, now it's a matter of who gets off the first shot, but to be honest, I was frozen with fear, and I thought he was, too. But then . . . the guy throws his rifle down, and I started to breathe again. He was surrendering, I thought. But no. He starts walking toward me and I raise my rifle and yell, 'Dung lai!' Stop. Halt. But he keeps coming at me, and I yell again, 'Dung lai!' He then pulls a long machete out of his belt. He's saying something, but I can't figure out what the hell he's trying to tell me. By this time, I'd had enough of this, and I was going to blow him away. But then I see he's pointing to the entrenching tool—the shovel hanging from my web belt, and all of a sudden, I realize that he wants to go hand-to-hand."

I felt a cold sweat forming on my face, and I listened to the birds and the insects in the trees, and I was back in that ravine again.

I said to Susan, or to myself, "He wants to go hand-to-hand, and he's spitting out these words. I didn't understand a thing he was saying, but I knew exactly what he was saying. He was saying, 'Let's see how brave you are without your artillery, your gunships, your jet fighters.' He was saying, 'You fucking coward. Let's see if you have any real balls, you overfed, overindulged, fucking American pig.' That's what he was saying. Meanwhile, he's coming closer, and he's not even ten feet from me now, and I looked into his eyes, and I've never seen hate like that before or since. I mean, this guy is totally around the bend, he's been wounded, and he's alone like maybe he's the last survivor of his unit . . . and he's motioning for me to come closer, you know, like in a schoolyard fight. Come on, punk. Let's see if you have any balls. Take the first swing . . . then . . . I have no idea why . . . but I threw my rifle down . . . and he stops and smiles. He points again to my shovel, and I nod to him."

I stopped talking and stood on a rock at the base of the hill. I took a few breaths and wiped my face.

Susan said, "Paul, let's go."

I shook my head and went on, "So, who's crazier, me or him? I reached around, unsnapped my entrenching shovel, and set the blade at a ninety degree angle to the handle and locked it in place. I took my helmet off and threw it on the ground. He's not smiling anymore, and his face is intent and focused. He's looking in my eyes, and he wants me to look at him, but I'm from South Boston and I know you keep your eyes on the other guy's weapon. So, now we're circling around each other, stalking, and neither of us is saying a word. He swings the machete, and it cuts the air in front of my face, but I don't step back because he's not close enough . . . but his machete is longer than my shovel, and this is going to be a problem if he comes closer. So, round and round we go, until finally he makes his move and aims a diagonal blow at the side of my neck."

I stopped speaking and thought about what happened next. Strangely, though I'd rarely relived it in detail, it all came back to me. I said, "I jump back and it misses, then he comes in again with the point of the machete aimed at my throat. I step to the side, stumble, and fall. He's on me in half a second and goes for my legs with the machete, but I swivel my legs away, and he cuts the ground. I jump to my feet as he delivers another blow toward my neck, but I deflect it with my shovel, then bring the shovel up, like an uppercut, and catch the side of his jaw. The shovel blade, which I keep sharp, shaves off a piece of his jaw, and this big piece of bloody flesh is hanging there, and he's in temporary shock, which is all I need. I swing the shovel around like I'm swinging a bat at a fastball and the blade nearly severs his right forearm and the machete flies out of his hand."

I thought I should let this story end there, but I continued. "So . . . he's standing there and the game is over. I have a prisoner, if I want one, or I could let him walk away. Or . . . I could kill him with my entrenching tool . . . he's staring at me, this big bloody piece of his jaw hanging, and his forearm running blood . . . so, what do I do? I throw my entrenching tool down and pull my K-bar knife. His eyes show fear for the first time, then he shoots a quick look at his machete on the ground, and he goes for it. I kick him in the head, but he's still scrambling for the machete. I come around him and grab his hair with my left hand, jerk him upright and pull his head back. Then I cut his throat with my knife. I can still feel the blade slicing through the cartilage of his windpipe, and I hear a hiss of air as the windpipe is severed . . . I cut the artery, too, and blood is gushing out all over my hand . . . I let him go, but he's still standing, and he turns to me and we're face-to-face, and blood is gushing out of his throat, and I could see the life dying in his eyes, but he won't stop staring at me, so we look at each other until his legs collapse, and he falls face forward."

I avoided looking at Susan and said, "I wiped the blood off my knife on his pants, clipped the shovel on my belt, sheathed my knife, gathered my helmet and rifle, and started walking away. I looked up and saw two guys from my company, who'd come to find me, and they'd seen some of this. One guy took my rifle out of my hand and fired three signal shots in the air. He said to me, 'The rifle works, Brenner.' These guys looked at me . . . I mean, we were all a little nuts by then, but . . . this was above and beyond nuts, and they knew it."

I thought a moment, trying to recall what happened next, then I said, "The other guy retrieved the AK-47, and he says to us, 'The gook has a full magazine.' He looked at me and says, 'How the fuck did you get into hand-to-hand with this guy?' I didn't say anything, and the other guy says, 'Brenner, you're supposed to shoot these fuckers, not get into knife fights with them.' They both laughed. Then the guy picks up the machete and hands it to me, and he says, 'Take the head back. No one's going to believe this shit.' So . . . I hacked off the dead man's head . . . and the other guy fixed his bayonet to my rifle, and he picks up the head and sticks it on the bayonet and hands me my rifle . . ."

I glanced at Susan and continued, "So we go to rejoin the company, me holding up the head on the end of my rifle, and as we approach the company positions, one of the guys with me yells out, 'Don't shoot—Brenner's got a prisoner,' and everybody laughs . . . everybody wants to know what happened . . . a guy cuts a bamboo pole and sticks the head on the pole . . . I talk to the captain along with these two guys who found me . . . and I'm kind of out of it . . . I'm looking at this head, which is being paraded around on the pole . . ." I drew a deep breath. "That night, I was on a helicopter back to base camp . . . along with the head . . . where the company clerk handed me a three-day pass to Nha Trang."

I looked at Susan and said, "So, that's how I wound up in Nha Trang on R&R."

CHAPTER THIRTY-ONE

───────★───────

Susan and I walked silently down to the river where we did a leech check. She was clean, but I had a land leech on my back starting to bloat with blood.

I said to her, "Light up."

She lit a cigarette, and I instructed her to heat the leech's rear end without burning it or me. She put the cigarette close to the leech, and it backed off. She plucked it off my back and threw it away with a sound of disgust. She said, "You're bleeding."

She put a tissue on the leech bite and held it there until it stuck. We put our clothes on, and we sat on a rock by the riverbank.

She smoked, and I said, "I'll take a drag."

She handed me the cigarette, and I took a long pull, coughed, and gave her the cigarette. I said, "These aren't good for you."

"Who said they were?"

We sat there quietly and listened to the flowing water.

She finished her cigarette and asked, "How are you doing?"

"Okay." I thought a moment and said, "Men who've been here have worse stories than that to tell . . . and I've seen worse . . . but there's something about hand-to-hand. I can still smell that guy and see his face, and I can still feel his hair in my hand and the knife cutting into his throat . . ."

"Finish it."

"Yeah . . . well, afterward, I was sorry I killed him. He should have lived. You know, like a defeated warrior who's shown bravery."

"Do you think he would have let you live?"

"No, but I shouldn't have taken his head. An ear or a finger would have been enough."

She lit another cigarette and said to me, "That's not what's really bothering you."

I looked at her, and our eyes met.

We sat there, watching the river. Finally, I said, "I frightened myself."

She nodded.

"I mean . . . where did that come from?"

She threw her cigarette in the river. She said, "It came from a place you never need to go to again."

"I'd be lying if I said I didn't feel good about it . . . about taking the challenge and killing him."

She didn't reply.

I said, "But like a lot of traumatic events, I buried it very quickly, and by Day One in Nha Trang, it was the furthest thing from my mind. Except, now and then, it would pop back in my head."

She nodded and lit another cigarette.

I said, "Then after I got home, I started to think about it more . . . like, Why did I do that? No one was egging me on, except him, and there was no rational reason for me to throw down my rifle and try to kill this guy with my shovel while he's trying to hack me up with his machete. What the hell was I thinking?"

"Sometimes, Paul, it's better to leave these things alone."

"I suppose . . . I mean, I've seen war psychosis, and I've seen guys in combat who lose all fear for some reason, and I've seen the most inhuman and brutal behavior you can possibly imagine from normal guys. I've seen skulls used as paperweights or candle holders on the desks of officers and sergeants, I've seen American soldiers with necklaces made out of teeth or dried ears or finger bones, and I can't tell you all the day-to-day atrocities I've seen on both sides . . . and it makes you wonder about who we are, and about yourself when you barely pay attention to it, and you really start wondering about yourself when you start participating. It was like a cult of death . . . and you wanted to belong . . ."

Susan stared at the flowing river, the smoke rising from her cigarette.

"Most guys arrived here normal, and they were shocked and sickened by the behavior of the guys who'd been here awhile. Then within a few weeks, they'd stop being shocked, and within a few months, a lot of them joined the club of the crazies. And most of them, I think, went home and became normal again, though some didn't. But I never once saw anyone here who had gone around the bend ever return to normal while they were still here. It only got worse because in this environment they'd lost any sense of . . . humanity. Or, you could be nice and say they'd become desensitized. It was actually more frightening than sickening. A guy who'd sliced off the ear of a VC he'd killed that morning would be joking with the village kids and the old Mama-sans that afternoon, and handing out candy. I mean, they weren't evil or psychotic, we were normal, which is what really scared the hell out of me."

I realized I'd gone from "they" to "we," which was the whole point; "they" became "we," and "we" became me. Fuck Father Bennett, fuck St. Brigid's church, fuck Peggy Walsh, fuck the Act of Contrition, fuck the confessional booth, and fuck everything I'd ever learned in school and at home. Just like that. It took about three months. It would've taken less time, but November and December in the Bong Son were kind of quiet. After Tet, Khe Sanh, and the A Shau, I would have killed my own brother if he was wearing the wrong uniform; in fact, a lot of the Vietnamese did.

Susan was still staring at the river, motionless, as though she didn't want to make any abrupt movements while I was carrying my sharpened shovel.

I took a deep breath and said, "I don't mean to pretend that I was the chaplain's assistant. Far from it. We'd all gone crazy, but we all figured it was temporary and conditional. And if you're lucky, someday you go home. But unfortunately, you take it home with you, and it changes you forever because you went to that dark place in your soul, the place most people know exists but have never been to, but you've been there for a long time and didn't find it so terrible, nor do you feel an ounce of guilt, and that itself becomes the fear . . . and you go on with your life in the U.S.A., mingling again with normal people, laughing and joking, but carrying this thing inside you . . . this secret that Mom doesn't know, and your girlfriend can't guess at, except sometimes she knows something's wrong . . . and now and then, you run into one of your own, someone who was there, and you swap stupid stories about getting drunk and getting laid, and hot landing zones, and dumb officers who couldn't read a map, and the worst case of black clap you've ever had, and poor Billy or Bob who got greased, and this and that, but you never touch on things like those villagers who you blew away by accident, or not by accident, or about how many ears and heads you collected, or the time you cut someone's throat with a knife . . ."

Susan asked, "Was anyone . . . normal?"

I thought about that and said, "I'd like to say that there were men among us who . . . who held on to some degree of morality or humanity . . . but I really can't remember . . . I think maybe. A combat unit is self-selecting . . . you know, guys who couldn't handle it either never made it to the front, or were sent back. I remember guys who cracked very quickly and were sent to the rear to do menial jobs, and that was sort of a disgrace, but we got rid of them . . . and yes, there were men among us who held on to their religious or moral beliefs, but I think that in war, as in life, the good ones die young and die first . . ." I said to her, "That's the best answer I can give you."

She nodded.

I looked at the river, which I'd crossed so many years before with my own tribe, chasing the deer who led us into the dark rain forest to a darker place than we'd ever been before.

We re-crossed the river at the rock ford and started back to A Luoi. As we walked on the straight path through the ground mist and the farm fields, Susan said to me, "I feel that anything I say would be trivial or patronizing or stupidly sensitive. But let me say this, Paul—what happened here, to you and the others, was history, in both senses of the word. There was a war, you were in it, it's over."

"I know. I believe that."

"And if you're wondering, I don't feel any differently toward you."

I didn't reply, but I wanted to say, "You say that now. Think about it."

Susan took my hand and squeezed it. She said, "And there I am, having dinner on the roof of the Rex Hotel, bugging this total stranger about not wanting to talk about the war. Can I apologize for that?"

"No need. This whole trip has done me good. And if you weren't along, I might not have been as honest with myself as I'm being with you."

"I appreciate that."

I changed the subject and said, "Somewhere in this valley, in May of 1968, a North Vietnamese soldier named Tran Quan Lee was killed in battle. Found on his body was a letter from his brother, Tran Van Vinh, also a soldier in the North Vietnamese army."

I didn't elaborate and waited for her to respond. Finally, she asked, "And you found this body and letter?"

"No. Someone else did."

"And you saw this letter?"

"Yes, about a week ago. Do you know anything about this letter?"

She looked at me as we walked and said, "Paul, I'm not sure what you're getting at."

I stopped and she stopped. I looked at her. "Susan, do you know anything about this letter?"

She shook her head, thought a moment, then said, "This has something to do with why you're here."

"That's right."

"You mean . . . someone found a letter on the body of an enemy soldier . . . who found the letter?"

"An American soldier in the First Cavalry Division found the letter."

"You knew this man?"

"No. It was a big division. Twenty thousand men. This guy who found the letter kept it as a war souvenir, and recently the letter was translated, and what was in the letter is the reason I'm here."

She mulled that over, and I looked at her. I knew this woman by now, and I could tell she knew something and was trying to fit it in with what I'd said.

I asked her, *"What* did they tell you?"

She looked at me and replied, "Only that some new information had come to light and that you had to find someone here and question that person about it."

"I told you that."

"I know. And that's all they told me in Saigon. Is this letter the new information?"

"It is."

"What does the letter say?"

"Well, what it says is one thing, what it means is something else. That's why I need to find and question the person who wrote the letter."

She nodded.

We continued on toward the village of A Luoi, about a hundred meters away across the flat terrain. It was irrelevant where and how Tran Quan Lee died, but it would be interesting to know. If I'd had time back in Washington, I'd have found and questioned Victor Ort, and maybe swap some A Shau Valley stories.

I was certain that Victor Ort had made a photocopy of the letter for himself, or had kept the original and sent the VVA the photocopy. In either case, Victor Ort had an original text that I could have had translated rather than relying on the altered translation I'd seen. But probably Karl sent someone to Ort's house and got the letter. Bottom line, Karl wasn't going to let me do any standard detective work on this case; he'd made certain I went off half in the dark to Saigon on a weekend, where Susan Weber did some smoke and mirrors until I was on the train to Nha Trang.

Also, I didn't see how that letter and Susan's statement about Cam Ranh Bay fit together, if indeed they did. That could be smoke and mirrors, too.

Susan asked me, "Do you have a copy of the letter?"

I replied, "You must have skipped a few classes at Langley."

"Don't be sarcastic. I'm not a trained intelligence officer."

"Then what did they teach you there?"

"How to be useful. I assume your contact in Hue told you how to find . . . what's his name?"

"Tran Van Vinh. And yes, he did." I asked her, "Does that name mean anything to you?"

"No. Should it?"

"I suppose not." But I'd had another thought that Tran Van Vinh had become a high-ranking member of the Hanoi government, and somehow the true translation of this letter could be used to blackmail him into cooperating with the Americans on something, like maybe Cam Ranh Bay.

Mr. Vinh could actually live in Hanoi and be in Ban Hin only for the Tet holiday, which would make sense. But if he was going to be blackmailed, why did they want him dead? It was possible that Washington didn't want him dead, and just told me that as more bullshit so I couldn't figure this out. But if that were the case, why did Mr. Anh in Hue give me that message, which as far as I knew, were my final instructions from Washington?

It's very difficult to solve a case when all the evidence you have is written or verbal, and the written evidence is bogus, and the verbal stuff is lies.

The truth of the matter lay in the village of

Ban Hin—formerly known as Tam Ki—in the person of Tran Van Vinh, a simple peasant and former soldier, who might well be neither of those things. In fact, he might be long dead, or about to be dead, or about to be bribed or blackmailed.

War, as I've said, has a stark simplicity and honesty to it, like trying to kill someone with a shovel. Intelligence work was, by its nature, a game of liar's poker, played with a marked deck and counterfeit money.

Susan said, "I'm sorry I can't help you with that letter. But I can help you find the guy who wrote it, and if he doesn't speak English I can give you an accurate translation of what he says to you, and you to him." She added, "I'm pretty good at winning the confidence of the Vietnamese."

"Not to mention horny American males."

"That's easy." She added, "Trust me, or don't trust me. You're not going to find anyone better than me to help you."

I didn't reply.

We reached the outskirts of A Luoi, where an old woman was throwing rice to a flock of chickens in a bamboo enclosure behind her house. She looked at us in surprise, and our eyes met, and we both knew why I was here. This valley certainly wasn't an attraction for the average tourist.

We walked through a cluster of houses and

back into the square. The RAV sat where we'd left it, and Mr. Loc was sitting under a thatched canopy in what looked like a primitive café or canteen filled with locals. He was drinking something by himself and smoking. Most Viets, I'd noticed, never sat alone and would strike up a conversation with anyone. But Mr. Loc gave off bad vibes, which the Viets in the canteen recognized, and they kept their distance from him.

Susan asked me, "Do you want to get something to eat or drink?"

"No. Let's head out."

She went to the canteen and spoke to Mr. Loc, then came back to where I was standing near the vehicle. "He'll be ready in a few minutes."

"Who's paying for this trip—him or me?"

"I don't think he likes you."

"He's a fucking cop. I can smell them a mile away."

"Then maybe he has the same thought about you." Susan asked me, "Do you want a picture here?"

"No."

"You'll never be back this way again."

"I hope not."

"Do you have pictures of when you were here last time?"

"I never once took my camera out of my backpack." I added, "I don't think anyone took a picture here, and if they did, the odds were that their family developed them when the deceased's personal effects were sent home."

She dropped the subject.

Mr. Loc finished whatever he was drinking and approached the vehicle.

I took the map off the seat and opened it. I said to Susan, "This dotted line to Khe Sanh says something about the Ho Chi Minh Trail, right?"

She looked at the map and read, " 'He Thong Duong Mon Ho Chi Minh.' Means sort of network of the trail, or part of the trail network of Ho Chi Minh."

"Right. It wasn't actually a single trail—it was an entire network of jungle trails, shallow streambeds, underwater bridges, log roads through swamps, and who knows what else. Most of it, as you can see, goes through Laos and Cambodia, where we weren't supposed to operate. This trail to Khe Sanh skirts the Laotian border, and I hope this clown doesn't get lost, and we wind up in Laos without a visa."

Mr. Loc was standing nearby, and I motioned him toward me. He moved slowly and stood too close. I wanted to deck him, tie his thumbs together, and drive myself. But that might cause a problem. I pointed at the map and said to him, "Ho Chi Minh Trail. Biet? Khe Sanh."

He nodded and got in the driver's seat. Susan and I got in the rear, and off we went.

There were a number of narrow farm paths

in the valley, which we drove on, and at some point, we headed north on a dirt road through the foothills. The trees came up to the road, and the branches blocked out most of the sunlight. This was, indeed, the Ho Chi Minh Trail.

The terrain got rougher and more mountainous, and now and then part of the road was paved with rotting logs, what we used to call corduroy roads. There were spectacular waterfalls and cascades in the distance, and shallow brooks ran right across the road. Susan took photos as we bounced along. Mr. Loc seemed to enjoy running through the mud as fast as possible to maximize the splashes, and Susan and I got splattered a few times. In the rearview mirror, I could see Mr. Loc smiling.

We were barely making thirty kilometers per hour, and the RAV was bouncing badly. Now and then, the road wound around what looked like small ponds, but which were actually gigantic bomb craters made by thousand-pound blockbusters dropped by B-52 bombers from thirty thousand feet. I pointed this out to Susan and said, "We spent a fortune blowing the hell out of these dirt trails. We may have killed between fifty and a hundred thousand North Vietnamese soldiers, men and women, along these infiltration routes. But they kept coming, filling in the holes or changing the route now and then, like a line of army ants that you're trying to stomp on before they reach your house." I added, "I didn't appreciate this until I saw those Russian-made tanks in that base camp. I mean, those vehicles were made near Moscow, wound up somehow in North Vietnam, and traveled thousands of kilometers over roads like this, under constant attacks, carrying their own fuel and spare parts, and one day, one of them makes it all the way to the gates of the presidential palace in Saigon. I give those bastards credit. They never understood that we were beating the hell out of them and that they couldn't possibly win." I slapped Mr. Loc on the shoulder and said, "Hey, you little guys are tough. Next war against the Chinese, I want you on my side."

Our eyes met in the rearview mirror, and I could swear that Mr. Loc nodded.

The rain forest thinned out, and we could see that the hills and mountains were dotted with longhouses on stilts, and we saw the smoke of cooking fires curling into the misty air.

Susan said, "This is absolutely beautiful. It's so pristine. Can we stop and meet some tribespeople?"

"They don't like unannounced visitors."

"Are you making that up?"

"No. You have to call ahead. They only receive visitors between four and six."

"You're making that up."

"You make stuff up," I said.

"No, I don't. Let's stop."

"Later. There are lots of tribespeople around Khe Sanh."

"Are you sure?"

"Ask James Bong."

She smiled. "Is that what you call him?"

"Yeah. James Bong, secret agent. Ask him."

She asked him, he replied, and she said to me, "He says there are Bru tribesmen around Khe Sanh." She added, "He wants to know what business we have with the Moi—Moi means savages."

"Well, first of all, it's none of his business, and second, we don't like racial epithets, unless it's gook, slant, or zipper head."

"Paul. That's awful."

"I know. I'm regressing. I apologize. Tell him to go fuck himself."

Mr. Loc, I think, understood this. I said to Susan and to Mr. Loc, "If we were trying to make contact with insurgent tribesmen, would we have a secret policeman driving us?"

No one answered.

Susan took a few more photos and carried on a chat with Mr. Loc. After a while, she said to me, "Mr. Loc says there are about eight million tribesmen in Vietnam, and over fifty distinct tribes with different languages and dialects. He says the government is trying to bring education and agriculture to the tribespeople, but they resist civilization."

"Maybe it's the government they're resisting."

Susan said, "Maybe they should be left alone."

"Correct. Look, I happen to like the Montagnards I've met, and I'm happy to see that they still carry rifles. My fantasy is to come back, like Colonel Gordon, Marlon Brando, or Mr. Kurtz, and go native. I'd organize those eight million people into a hell of a fighting force, and we'd own these mountains. We'd hunt and fish all day, and perform weird and spooky ceremonies at night, gathered around blazing fires with the heads of our enemies impaled on poles. Maybe I'd organize tour groups of Americans. Paul Brenner's Montagnard World. Ten bucks for a day trip, fifty for overnight. I saw Montagnards once stake out a bull and skin it alive, then cut its throat and drink its blood. That would be the climax of the evening. What do you think?"

She didn't reply.

We rode in silence through the fog-shrouded mountains under a sunless sky, the smell of wood fires hanging in the heavy air, and the damp chill seeping into my bones and my heart. I think I hated this place.

Susan said something to Mr. Loc and he stopped.

I asked, "What's up?"

She replied, "There's a trail there that leads up this hill to some longhouses." She took her camera and got out of the RAV. She said, "I want to see a Montagnard village."

She started up a steep trail off the side of

the road. I said to Mr. Loc, "Be right back, Charlie. Don't go away."

I got out and followed Susan up the trail.

About two hundred meters up the side of the hill, the land flattened, revealing a large clearing in which were six longhouses built on stilts.

In the clearing were about two dozen women and twice as many kids, all going about their daily activities, which seemed to consist mostly of food preparation. The whole area looked very clean and free of vegetation, except for short grass on which grazed small goats and two tethered hill ponies.

The women were wearing long, dark blue dresses with white embroidery, gathered at the waist with scarves.

The dogs started barking as soon as they smelled us, but the Montagnards kept at their tasks, and barely gave us a glance, though a few of the kids stopped what they were doing.

The dogs ran toward us, but they were small dogs, as all the dogs were in Vietnam, and I didn't remember them as being particularly vicious. Still, I wished I had little doggie treats. I said to Susan, "They won't bite."

"Famous last words."

"Don't kneel to pet them—they don't get petted and they might think you're looking for lunch."

Susan waved to the Montagnards and said something in Vietnamese.

I said to her, "This is the Tribingo tribe. They're cannibals."

A short, stocky old man, who had been sitting on the stairs of a longhouse, rose and walked toward us. He wore an embroidered long-sleeve shirt, black pants, and leather sandals.

I looked around again, but didn't see any young or middle-aged men. They were all hunting, or maybe drying heads in the smokehouse.

The old man came right up to us, and Susan said something to him, which included the word My, and they both bowed.

Susan introduced me to the old man, whose name sounded like John, and we shook hands. This guy was old enough to have been a Montagnard fighter, and he was eyeing me like I might be here to give him new orders.

Susan and the old man, who was obviously the village chief—the honcho, as we called them, even though that was a Japanese word— chatted, and I could tell they were having a little trouble communicating in Vietnamese.

John looked at me and surprised me by saying, "You GI? You fight here?"

I replied, "A Shau."

"Ah." He motioned us to follow him.

I said to Susan, "I think they're going to have us for lunch."

"Paul, stop being an idiot. This is fascinating."

The old man informed us that he and his people were of the Taoi tribe, which I hoped weren't into human sacrifices, and he showed us around the small village, which had no name; according to Susan, it was called the Place of the Clan of dai-uy John, or Chief John. Dai-uy is also captain, and John was not his name, but that's what it sounded like. I didn't think I'd find this place in the *Hammond World Atlas,* especially if it changed names every time they got a new chief.

Susan asked for and got permission to take photographs of everything and everybody. The dogs followed us wherever we went.

John pointed out all sorts of things that he thought would interest us, and which did interest one of us.

He introduced us to everyone, even the kids, and Susan kept up a conversation with him as she translated for me. Susan said to me, "He wants to know if we'll have food with him and his people."

"Next time. We need to get moving."

"I'm hungry."

"You won't be when you see what's on the menu. Also, they take forever to eat a meal. They must have learned about four-hour lunches from the French. Tell him we need to be somewhere."

"We're in the middle of nowhere."

I looked at the old man and tapped my watch, which maybe he understood, and I said, "Khe Sanh."

"Ah." He nodded.

We finished the village tour, and I noticed

that the kids were not following us, or begging for money or candy, like the Viet kids usually do in Saigon. Only the dogs dogged us each step of the way.

The old man led us to the wooden stairs where we'd first seen him sitting and invited us to come into the longhouse. There were leather sandals and homemade shoes all over the steps, so Susan and I took off our shoes and so did John.

We climbed the stairs, and the dogs did not follow. Americans should learn to keep their dogs outside, like the primitive Montagnards did.

We entered this wooden structure about fifty feet long and twenty feet wide. The floor was wood planking, with multicolored throw rugs scattered around. Tree trunk poles ran down the center of the longhouse and held up the peaked roof.

There were small windows covered with thin fabric that let in some daylight and a few hanging oil lamps, which were lit. Obviously, there was no electricity. Toward the center of the longhouse was a big clay oven, but no chimney, and I recalled that the smoke rose to the roof and filled the room, which kept the mosquitoes away at night.

There weren't any people in the longhouse, and the hammocks were folded and hung along the walls. I counted about twenty of them, and I tried to picture twenty people of all ages and both sexes sleeping together in this communal house filled with smoke. No wonder there weren't as many Montagnards as there were Vietnamese. I asked Susan, "You ever do it in a hammock?"

"Can we change the subject to something cultural?"

John led us to the center of the longhouse where his space was. He was the honcho, so he had a big area, filled with bamboo chests and boxes. There were machetes and knives hung on the wall, along with some scarves and strips of leather.

I noticed a big square table in the center of the longhouse about a foot off the ground, stacked with porcelain and pottery.

In an odd way, this communal society was the Communist ideal, yet the Montagnards hated the rigidity and control of the Communist government, and were basically free-spirited and independent. Plus, they didn't like the Vietnamese anyway.

John sat cross-legged beside a big wooden chest and so did Susan, so I did the same, which is easier than squatting like the Viets do.

John opened the chest, pulled out a green beret, and handed it to me.

I took it and looked at it. Inside was the label of an American manufacturer.

John said something to Susan, who translated, "He says this was given to him by his American dai-uy during the war."

I nodded.

He took out another green beret, said something, and Susan said to me, "This was given to him only three years ago by another American—a former soldier who had come to visit."

I said to Susan, "I don't have any green berets to give him."

"Give him your watch."

"Give him *your* watch." I asked, "What the hell is he going to do with a watch?"

John showed us a few other treasures from his chest: a GI web belt, a plastic canteen, a compass, a K-bar knife, and a few ammo pouches. I was reminded of my own steamer trunk in the basement of my house, like a million other trunks all over America, filled with bits and pieces of a former military life.

John then took a small blue box from his chest, which I recognized as a military medal box, like a jewelry box, and he opened it, very reverentially. Lying on the satin lining was a round bronze medal with a red and white ribbon. Stamped on the medal was an eagle perched on a book and sword. Around the eagle were the words "Efficiency, Honor, Fidelity."

I stared at the medal and recognized it as the Good Conduct Medal. I recalled that the Special Forces guys used to buy them in the base camp

PXs and award them to their Montagnard troops for bravery, though the medal had nothing to do with bravery, but the Montagnards didn't know that, and the army wasn't bummed out about the Special Forces guys handing out these nothing medals to their Montagnard fighters.

I took the box as if it held the Congressional Medal of Honor and looked at the Good Conduct Medal and showed it to Susan. I said, "John got this for extraordinary bravery, above and beyond the call of duty."

Susan nodded and said something to John in a respectful tone.

John smiled, took the box from me, and snapped it closed. He put it gently back in the big chest.

I thought about my Vietnamese Cross of Gallantry, given to me by the Viet colonel who kissed both my cheeks, and I wondered if I'd actually gotten a medal for having a clean uniform or something.

Anyway, last but not least, John lifted a long object out of the chest wrapped in an oilcloth, and I knew what it was before he unwrapped it; Dai-uy John still had his M-16 automatic assault rifle, the plastic stock and hand grip glistening with oil, and the cast aluminum parts and blued steel barrel gleaming like they'd just passed a company inspection.

He held it toward me with both hands, like it was a sacred object, and our eyes met. I put my hands on the rifle, and we both clasped it for a few seconds. His smile had faded into a sort of stern and faraway look, and I think my own face had the same expression. We both nodded in re-membrance of things past—the war, the missing comrades, and the defeat.

Without a word, he re-wrapped the rifle and put it back in the chest. He closed the chest and stood.

Susan and I stood, also, and we walked out of the longhouse into the overcast daylight.

John led us back to the path, and we waved to everyone on our way. At the head of the path, he said something to Susan, and she replied. She said to me, "John wishes us a safe journey, and welcomes you back to the hill country."

I replied, "Tell John I thank him for showing me his medal, and for introducing me to his people." I didn't know if the Montagnards cel-ebrated Tet, so I said, "I wish the Taoi tribe good fortune, good hunting, and happiness."

Susan translated, John smiled, then said something. Susan turned to me and said, "He wants to know when the American soldiers are coming back."

"How about never? Is that soon enough?" I said, "Tell him the Americans are returning only in peace, and there will be no more war."

Susan told him, and he seemed, I thought, a little disappointed. He'd have to postpone killing Vietnamese for longer than he'd hoped.

I reached into my pocket and took out my Swiss army knife. I handed it to John, who smiled. He seemed to recognize the knife, and in fact, began pulling out the blades and the other gadgets.

I said, "That's a Phillips head screwdriver, John. Just in case you run into any screws. This weird thing is a corkscrew for your Château Lafite Rothschild, or you can screw it into a commissar's head, if you want."

Susan was rolling her eyes while I showed John all the handy gadgets on the knife.

John took the dark blue scarf from his neck and put it around Susan's neck. They exchanged some words, and we bid each other farewell.

Susan and I started down the trail.

She said, "That was fascinating . . . and moving. He still . . . well, he seems to idolize the Americans."

"They also liked the French, which shows bad judgment on both accounts." I added, "They just don't like the Vietnamese, and the feeling is mutual."

"I understand that." She thought a moment and said, "I can't believe I've been here three years, and I didn't know anything about any of this."

"It's not in the Wall Street Journal or the Economic Times."

"No, it's not." She asked me, "Glad you stopped?"

"*You* stopped. I went along to see that you didn't wind up on a cooking spit."

We got to the end of the path, and I said, "I'll bet Mr. Loc is hanging by his heels from a tree with his throat slit and the dogs are lapping his blood."

"Paul, that's gross."

"Sorry. I wanted to drive."

We found the RAV, and Mr. Loc was alive and well, but looking a little annoyed, and maybe nervous.

We got back into the vehicle, and I said to Mr. Loc, "Cu di."

Susan asked, "Is your Vietnamese coming back?"

"Yeah. Scary." Most of my Vietnamese had to do with getting laid, but I did remember some common expressions. I said to Susan, "Sat Cong," which means, "Kill the Communists."

Mr. Loc did not like that, and he glanced back at me. I said, "Keep your eyes on the road."

The bad road continued north, and we came to a small place on the map called Ta Ay, a cluster of primitive bamboo huts in a flat mountain meadow whose inhabitants looked Vietnamese. The Viets lived in the villages and cultivated the land; the tribespeople lived in the hills and mountains and lived off the land. It *was* fascinating, as Susan said, and under other circumstances and without a personal history of these hills, I might have been in a better mood.

We passed through another hamlet, which, according to the map, was called Thon Ke, and the road turned west toward the Laotian border and dropped into a narrow valley, then turned north again and followed this meandering mountain valley until, an hour later, we came to a low-lying area of rice paddies, and a village called Li Ton. The road here was actually the tops of wide rice paddy dikes. *The Ho Chi Minh Trail*. Amazing if you thought about it; more amazing now that I'd seen a piece of it.

A little more than two hours after we'd left A Luoi, we crossed a new concrete bridge at a place called Dakrong, and a few kilometers further, the Ho Chi Minh Trail intersected with Highway 9, which was two lanes of semi-paved blacktop, partly compliments of the U.S. Army Corps of Engineers. Mr. Loc turned left onto the highway, and we traveled west, toward Khe Sanh.

I said to Susan, "This road was blocked by the North Vietnamese army during the siege of Khe Sanh, from early January to April 1968. Even an armored convoy couldn't get through. But in early April, we air-assaulted into these hills all around the besieged camp, and about a week later, an armored column with a few regiments of marines and ARVN soldiers forced the road open again and relieved the siege."

"And you were here?"

"Yeah. The First Air Cavalry got around a lot. It's nice to have hundreds of helicopters to take you around, but usually you don't want to go where they're taking you."

We continued a short distance on Highway 9. Traffic was moderate and consisted mostly of scooters, bicycles, and produce trucks.

To the right was the plateau of Khe Sanh combat base, beyond which rose tree-covered hills, which were obscured by mist and fog. Geographically, this place resembled the A Shau Valley, though it wasn't as remote or narrowly hemmed in by the hills.

Historically, Khe Sanh was a place where, like the A Shau and Dien Bien Phu, a great Western army had gathered in a remote, godforsaken valley, to do battle with the Vietnamese. Dien Bien Phu had been a decisive military defeat, while Khe Sanh and the A Shau had been at best a military stalemate, and in the end, a psychological setback for the Americans, who believed that a tie score was no substitute for victory.

We passed by the plateau of the old combat base and came to the town of Khe Sanh, which, like A Luoi, had disappeared during the war, but Brigadoon-like, had reappeared years later.

The sky was still gloomy and overcast, and this was the way I remembered it in April of 1968, a sky as gray and heavy as my mood had been, a place where the stench of thousands of dead bodies hinted at your own fate.

CHAPTER THIRTY-TWO

——★——

We drove into the town of Khe Sanh, where substantial buildings of stucco and red tile roofs were springing up everywhere on well-laid-out streets.

We pulled into a big square where a large market building was under construction. Obviously, this was a showplace town, a place with an evocative name that the government wanted to look good for the tourists and newspeople. And, in fact, there were five tour buses parked in the square and dozens of Western tourists were wandering around the market stalls, probably trying to figure out why they were here in this remote corner of the country.

Mr. Loc pulled into a gas station, and Susan and I got out of the vehicle and stretched. I said, "I need a cold beer."

She said something to Mr. Loc as he pumped gas, and we headed across the square toward an outdoor café.

As we walked, Susan asked me, "This wasn't the base, was it?"

"No. We passed it on the way in—that high plateau. Khe Sanh combat base took its name from this town that no longer existed at the time. We'll go up to the base later."

There were a number of outdoor stalls on the way toward my beer, and Susan, true to form, had to stop at most of them. A lot of the stalls sold two-kilo bags of coffee, which must be the local produce, and some stalls had pineapples and vegetables. There were a cluster of stalls that sold war souvenirs, mostly junk, like jewelry made from scraps of brass shell casings. I spotted some 105 millimeter brass shell casings with flowers growing in them, a mixed metaphor if ever there was one. There were bud vases, which had once been .50 caliber machine gun shell casings, plus the short, squat shell casings of grenade launchers that were being sold as drinking cups with handles welded on them.

Susan said, "Where did all this stuff come from?"

I said, "The United States of America."

"My God, there's so much of it."

"It was a hundred-day siege. This is probably a minute's worth of ordnance expenditure."

She wandered over to a stall that had bits and pieces of armaments—plastic stocks from M-16 rifles, the release levers and pins of hand grenades, the cardboard telescopic tubes of M-72 light anti-tank rockets, and so forth. Plus, there were plastic canteens, GI web gear, ammo pouches, bayonet scabbards, belt buckles, and all sorts of odds and ends, the archaeological evidence of an army that once fought here, for sale now as souvenirs to the survivors, who might want to take home a piece of hell.

Susan questioned me about the bits and pieces, what they were and what they had been used for. I answered, then said, "Cold beer."

"Just a minute. What's this?"

I looked at what she was holding and said, "That happens to be the canvas carrying case of an entrenching tool. You clip it on your web belt, and the shovel blade fits right inside."

She put it down and walked to another stall where a family of Montagnards was selling crafts. She whispered to me, "Paul, do you know what tribe this is?"

They were dressed in bright blue and red clothing with elaborate embroidery, and the women had their hair in huge piles on top of their heads, bundled in brightly colored scarves. The ladies wore huge hoop earrings and were smoking long pipes. I said to Susan, "I think they're from California."

"You're a wiseass. What tribe are they from?"

"How the hell do I know? They're all Montagnards. Ask them."

She spoke to an old lady in Vietnamese, and both of them were surprised that they each knew Vietnamese. Susan chatted with the old woman, then said to me, "Her Vietnamese is hard to understand."

"So is yours."

The whole family was gathered around now, talking away, the ladies puffing on pipes, the men smoking cigarettes. They discussed Susan's Taoi tribe scarf and showed her their more brightly colored scarves. At some point they started looking at me, and I could tell that Susan was informing them that I was once here.

A very short old man with bow legs approached me, dressed in an orange sort of tunic with a yellow sash around his waist. He took my hands and looked into my eyes, and we stared at each other. His hands were like leather, and so was his face. He said something, and Susan said to me, "He says he was an American soldier."

"Really? I don't think he meets the minimum height requirement."

He kept talking, and Susan translated as he spoke. "He says he fought for the Americans with . . . the green berets . . . he spent seven years with them . . . they paid him well . . . gave him a fine rifle and knife . . . he killed . . . many, many . . . he said beaucoup, beaucoup . . . you hear that?"

The old man said, "Beaucoup, beaucoup, vee-cee—" He made a cutting motion across his throat, which I understood very well, having done it myself. I said to Susan, "Ask him if he still has his rifle."

She asked him and he looked at me and nodded almost imperceptibly.

So, I'm standing there, looking at this incredibly wrinkled old face with narrow slit eyes, and we're holding hands in the Khe Sanh town square, and we don't have much in common, except the bond of war, which can never be broken.

Susan said, "He wants to know if you know Captain Bob, his commanding officer."

I replied, "Tell him I once met Captain Bob in America, and that he's doing well, and he speaks often of the bravery of his Montagnard soldiers."

Susan translated this, and the old man totally bought it. He squeezed my hands, then went into the stall and came out with a bronze Montagnard bracelet, which you can't buy, but which they'll give you if they like you or if you're brave. He opened the thin bracelet, put it on my left wrist, and squeezed it closed. He stepped back and saluted me. I returned the salute.

By now, we had a few Americans around us, plus a few Viets who didn't look happy with this.

I said to Susan, "Tell him thank you, and tell him that Captain Bob and I will be back to organize another Montagnard army."

She said something to the old man, he smiled, and we shook hands.

Susan absolutely had to have six scarves and sashes of multi hues, and for the first time since she'd been in Vietnam, she didn't argue price, but gave the old lady a ten.

Susan wanted to take pictures, of course, so she asked the Montagnards if that was all right, and they said it was. I said to Susan, "They'll cut your head off." But she took pictures anyway, and they didn't cut her head off. We all posed for shots, wearing scarves around our necks, then bid one another farewell, and I made directly for the café.

Susan said, "They're from the Bru tribe. Let me see your bracelet."

I held my arm out, like a sleepwalker.

She examined the simple bracelet and asked me, "Is there any significance to this?"

I replied, "It's a token of friendship. I actually have one at home. Now I have two."

"Really? Who gave you the first one?"

"A Montagnard, obviously."

"Why did he—or she—give it to you?"

"He. You didn't mess around with their women, or you'd wind up with your dick on a stick."

"Good. So, why did they give you a bracelet?"

"Just a token of friendship. They handed them out pretty easily if they liked you. Unfortunately, they expected you to eat with them, and they ate things that were worse than C rations."

"Such as?"

"Well, nothing as bad as the Viets. They're into meat—deer, boar, birds, weasels, and other horrible wildlife. They burned their meat to a cinder. But it was the cup of warm blood that was a little hard to get down."

"You drank the blood?"

"It went well with the red meat."

We got to the outdoor café. It was nearly one P.M., and the place was filled with Euros and Americans, including backpackers. There were a few guys who could have been veterans, but mostly there were a lot of tour groups sitting together, who I didn't think had any association with this place; Khe Sanh was obviously on the tour route, and I supposed most of these people had signed up for this at their hotels in Hue. The brochure probably said something like: *Khe Sanh! See the actual site where the famous bloody three-month siege of the U.S. Marine Combat Base took place—Relive the horrors of 30,000 men locked in mortal combat from the comfort of your air-conditioned bus. Side trip to a Montagnard village—Lunch included.*

Anyway, the tables were full, but I spotted a table for four where only an American guy and a Viet guy sat, having a beer. I went over to the table and said, "Mind if we sit here?"

The American, a big guy of about my age, said, "No. Go ahead."

Susan and I sat.

The guy said, "My name's Ted Buckley." He put out his hand.

I took it and said, "Paul Brenner. This is Susan Weber."

He took Susan's hand. "Pleased to meet you. This is Mr. . . . what's your name?"

The Viet guy, who looked about sixty, said, "I am Mr. Tram. It is a pleasure to make your acquaintance."

Ted Buckley said to us, "Mr. Tram was a North Vietnamese army officer, a captain—right? He saw combat here. Can you believe that?"

Mr. Tram sort of smiled and bowed his head.

Ted added, "And I was here with the Twenty-sixth Marine Regiment, January to June '68." He smiled and said, "So Mr. Tram and I were here at the same time, but on different sides of the wire."

I looked at Mr. Tram, and our eyes met. He was trying to figure out if I had been here, too, and if I was carrying a grudge, or if, like Ted Buckley, I just found this a hell of a coincidence.

Ted said, "Mr. Tram said he would be my guide at the base. Are you guys going to the base, or were you there?"

I replied, "We're on our way."

The waitress came over, and Susan and I ordered whatever beer was cold.

Ted looked at me and asked, "Marines?"

I replied with the standard, "Hell, no. Do I look that stupid?"

He laughed. "Army?"

"First Cav."

"No shit?" He looked at Susan. "Sorry." Then he asked me, "Were you here?"

"I was." In the spirit of good-natured interservice rivalry, I added, "Don't you remember that the cavalry flew in and bailed your butts out?"

"Bullshit. We had Charlie right where we wanted him."

"He had you surrounded for three months, Ted."

"That's where we wanted him."

We both laughed. This was fun. I think.

Mr. Tram and Susan were both smoking now, sitting quietly and listening.

Ted said to Mr. Tram, "This guy was here, too. First Cavalry Division. You understand that?"

Mr. Tram nodded and said to me, "You arrived on the first day of April."

"That's right."

He informed me, "I remember it well."

"Good. Me, too."

The beers came, and we all raised our bottles. Ted said, "To peace."

We all touched bottles and drank.

I looked at Ted Buckley. He was, as I said, a big guy, but had acquired some pounds since those lean, mean months of the siege of Khe Sanh. His face was weathered, and his hands were rough, so he did outdoor manual labor.

Susan asked him, "Are you here alone?"

"My wife's with me. She stayed in Hue. Said I'd get more out of this if I came alone." He explained, "We're with a tour group. Came up from Saigon by mini-bus. Just met Mr. Tram. He said he'd give me a private tour. Hey, you're welcome to join us."

I said, "Thanks. We will."

Ted looked at Susan and asked, "How'd you get dragged along?"

She smiled and replied, "I volunteered."

"Never volunteer for anything. Right, Paul?" He added, "You guys staying in Hue?"

Susan replied, "We are."

He said, "We saw the Citadel there yesterday. Jesus, most of it's still leveled." He asked me, "You see any action there?"

"No. I was mostly up in Quang Tri."

"Right. LZ Sharon. I remember that. What did you do with the Cav?"

"Regular grunt."

"Me, too. I spent six months of my tour in this shithole." He said to Susan, "Sorry. I can't think of a better word for it."

Susan replied, "I'm used to it by now." She turned to Mr. Tram and asked him, "How long were you here?"

He replied, "Four months. I arrive in December of 1967, and I leave here in April." He looked at me and said, "When Mr. Paul arrive, I leave." He thought that was a little funny and sort of giggled.

Ted regarded Mr. Tram a moment and asked him, "How was it on the other side of the wire?"

Mr. Tram understood the question, thought a moment and replied, "Very bad. The American bombers come day and night, and the cannons fire day and night . . . it was very bad for us . . . and for you, too, I am sure . . . but the bombers were very bad."

Ted replied, "Well, buddy, I was on the receiving end of your cannons for three fucking months."

"Yes, war is terrible for everyone."

It got quiet for a while, then Ted said to me, "Hey, can you believe this? I mean, can you *believe* you're back?"

"I'm working on it."

Ted said to Susan, "You look too young to remember any of this."

She replied, "I was, but Paul has been kind enough to share his memories with me."

Ted obviously wanted to ask about our relationship, so before it bugged him too much, I said to him, "Susan and I met in Hue, and I invited her to come with me today."

"Okay. So, you just met." He asked Susan, "Where you from?"

"Lenox, Mass."

"Yeah? I'm from Chatham, New York, just across the state line. I have a small construction company." He smiled and said, "I dug so many trenches here and built so many bunkers, when I got home, I wanted to sandbag my house and dig firing trenches around it. My old man got me a job with a bricklayer instead."

Susan smiled.

Ted asked me, "Where you from, Paul?"

"Boston originally. I live in Virginia now."

Susan asked Mr. Tram, "And where are you from?"

He smiled and replied, "I am from a small city on the coast called Dong Hoi." He added, "It is in the former North Vietnam, but there is no border since the reunification, and so I move here to Khe Sanh with my family six years ago."

Ted asked, "Why?"

He replied, "It is an economic development zone."

"Yeah? But why *here?*"

He thought a moment and replied, "I remember the beautiful green hills and valley when I arrive here, before the battle . . . many Vietnamese are moving away from the coast where there are many people. This is, as you would say, the new frontier."

Ted replied, "It's a frontier, all right. Complete with Indians."

Susan asked Mr. Tram, "And you are a tour guide here?"

Mr. Tram replied, "I instruct English at the high school. It is the Tet holiday now, so I come here to see if I can be of any service to the tourists." He added, "For veterans only."

I looked at Mr. Tram. He seemed pleasant enough, and if he was with the Ministry of Public Security, it was probably only part-time. In any case, I'd found him, he hadn't found me, so he had nothing to do with me. Maybe he and Mr. Loc knew each other.

Mr. Tram asked me, "May I inquire about your profession?"

I replied, "I'm retired."

"Ah. You retire so young in America."

Susan said, "He's older than he looks."

Mr. Tram and Ted chuckled, and Ted glanced at both of us and decided we were sleeping together.

We all chatted awhile, had another round of beers, and everyone hit the backhouse.

Mr. Tram was not the first North Vietnamese soldier I'd met here, but he was the first I'd had a few beers with, and my curiosity was aroused. I asked him, "What do you think of all these Americans coming back here?"

He replied without hesitation, "I think it is a good thing."

I don't like to get into politics, but I asked him, "Do you think what you were fighting for was worth all the death and suffering?"

Again, without hesitation, he replied, "I was fighting for the reunification of my country."

"Okay. The country is reunified. Why does Hanoi treat the south so badly? Especially the veterans of the South Vietnamese army."

Someone kicked me under the table, and it wasn't Mr. Tram or Ted.

Mr. Tram thought about that, then replied, "There were many mistakes made after the victory. The government has admitted this. It is time now to think of the future."

I asked him, "Do you have any friends who were former South Vietnamese soldiers?"

"No, I do not. With my generation, it is hard to forget." He added, "When we see each other in the street or on a bus or in a café, we are reminded of the suffering and the death we brought to each other. We look with hatred, and turn away. This is terrible, but I think the next generation will be better."

We all went back to our beers. Oddly enough, ex-Captain Tram would have a beer with two Americans who'd tried to kill him, not far from here, but he wouldn't even say hello to a former South Viet soldier. This animosity between the North and South Viets, the victors and the vanquished, went on, and it was a very complex thing, having less to do with the war, I thought, than what came after. War is simple; peace is complex.

Ted said to Susan and me, "The bus leaves in about half an hour. I don't think they'd mind if you came along."

I replied, "We have a car and driver. You can come with us now."

"Yeah? Okay." He looked at his guide. "Okay?"

"Of course."

Ted insisted on paying for the beers, and we left the crowded café.

We found Mr. Loc where we'd left him, and he said something to Susan, who replied in Vietnamese. This blew Ted away, and he said, "Hey, you speak gook? I mean, Vietnamese?"

Susan replied, "A little."

"Jesus, who the hell speaks Vietnamese?"

Susan and I and Mr. Tram squeezed into the rear of the RAV, big Ted got in the front, and off we went.

We headed east on Highway 9, and Mr. Tram, wanting to start earning his pay, said, "If you will look to your right, you will see the remains of the old French Foreign Legion fort."

We all looked, and Susan snapped a picture and so did Ted.

Mr. Tram continued, "The People's Army occupied the fort until the arrival of the . . ." He looked at me, sort of smiled, and said, "Until Mr. Paul arrived with hundreds of helicopters."

This was really a little strange. I mean, here I was sitting ass to ass with this guy who I'd have painted bright red in a heartbeat if I'd seen him here way back when. Or he'd have killed me. Now he was my guide, telling me when I'd air-assaulted in here.

Mr. Tram went on with his tour and said, "This road to your right that intersects here was part of the Ho Chi Minh Trail, and it travels south to A Luoi in the A Shau Valley, the scene of

many terrible battles. On this trail, one kilometer south is the Dakrong Bridge, which was a gift
to the Vietnamese people from our socialist
Cuban brothers. We can visit the bridge later, if
you wish."

Susan said something to Mr. Tram in Vietnamese, and he nodded as she spoke.

Ted heard this and turned around again.
"What's happening?"

Susan explained. "We just came from the A
Shau Valley. Paul was there once."

Ted said, "Oh, right. You guys went from
here to the A Shau. How was it?"

I replied, "It sucked."

"Couldn't be worse than Khe Sanh, buddy."

There are descending circles of hell, even in
war, and every soldier is convinced he's in the
worst circle, and there's no use trying to convince him otherwise. Your hell is your hell, his
hell is his hell.

Mr. Tram said, "I had a brother who was in
the A Shau Valley."

No one asked him how his brother was doing
now.

Mr. Tram returned to the packaged tour and
said, "As you see, the fields on both sides of the
road are under cultivation. Coffee and vegetables and pineapples are the main produce. During the war, the valley was uninhabited, except
for some hill people who had allied themselves
with the Americans. Very few of the original in-

habitants have returned, and there are mostly new settlers from the coast. They name their villages after their old villages, so when family or friends from the coast come to visit, they need only ask for such and such a village, and the local people can direct them to the new village, which has the same name as the village from which the settlers have come."

Ted informed Mr. Tram, "We have the same thing in the States. New York, New Jersey, New London, New whatever. Same thing."

"Yes? Very interesting," said Mr. Tram, who hadn't gotten paid yet. Mr. Tram continued, "You see those many ponds in the area? These are not ponds, but bomb craters. There were once thousands of them, but most have been filled in with earth. The remaining ones are used to raise ducks or to water the animals."

I remembered this landscape when I flew in, and from the air all you could see was the dead brown defoliation, the gray ash, mile after mile of North Vietnamese trenches, and crater after crater, like the surface of the moon.

I imagined Captain Tram and his comrades sitting in their bunkers or slit trenches at night, smoking and talking, hoping for a quiet evening. Meanwhile, six miles overhead, too high to be seen or heard, a flight of huge, eight-engine B-52 bombers all released their thousand-pound bombs simultaneously. The bombs did not whistle or shriek on the way down—the shrieking came from the people on the ground as the hundreds of bombs hit without warning.

Arc Light Strikes, they were called, and they transformed the earth below into a here-and-now hell, as though the nether regions had surfaced to engulf the world. And there wasn't a bunker built or a tunnel deep enough to withstand a delay-timed fuse, which let the thousand-pound bomb burrow into the earth before exploding. And if the bomb didn't actually hit you and vaporize you, the concussion turned your brain to Jell-O, or ruptured your internal organs, burst your eardrums, and threw you into the air like another clod of dirt. Or sometimes you got buried alive when your tunnel, trench, or bunker collapsed.

We'd found hundreds of North Vietnamese here, lying down, staring up at the sky, blood running from their ears, nose, mouth, or wandering around like zombies. They weren't worth taking as prisoners, they were beyond medical help, and we didn't know if we should shoot them or not waste the time.

I glanced at Mr. Tram, and knew he'd seen this, from his perspective, and I wondered if he thought about it much, or if it was always there.

We traveled about two kilometers on Highway 9, then Mr. Loc turned left at a sign that said, in English, *Khe Sanh Combat Base*.

We drove up a dirt road that climbed to the plateau. A bus was coming down, and a line of backpackers was climbing up. Within a few minutes, we were in a parking field where about six buses sat, along with a few private cars and motor scooters. Mr. Loc stopped, and we all got out.

The plateau on which the combat base once sat was nothing more than an expanse of windswept grassy field. The misty green hills towered over the plateau, and I could imagine the North Vietnamese artillery, rockets, and mortars up there, firing down onto the open plateau. What military genius picked this place to defend? Probably the same idiot who set up the base at A Luoi, and since both places had once been French strongholds, I thought also of Dien Bien Phu, which was geographically similar. I said to Ted, "They taught us to take the high ground and hold it. I think they forgot Lesson Number One."

Ted agreed and said, "Jesus, we were sitting ducks here." He looked around at the hills. "The fucking gooks would fire, then quick-move the artillery into a cave. We'd return counter–artillery fire from here, and the air force would hit the hills with high explosives and napalm. This game went on for a hundred fucking days, and this camp was hell on earth, buddy. You went out to take a piss, and you got your weenie blown off. We lived like fucking animals in the trenches and bunkers, and the fucking rats were everywhere, and I swear to God it rained every day, and the fucking red mud was so thick it pulled your boots off. In fact, we had a guy stuck up to his knees in the mud, and a Jeep tried to pull him out, and got sucked in up to the windshield, then a deuce-and-a-half truck tried to pull the guy and the Jeep out, and got buried up to the roof, and then two bulldozers came and they both got buried, then we called in a sky crane chopper with cables, and the chopper got sucked right in and disappeared. You know how we got everybody out?"

I smiled and asked, "No, how?"

"The mess sergeant yelled 'Hot chow!'"

We both laughed. Truly, the marines were full of shit.

Mr. Tram and Ms. Susan smiled politely. Mr. Loc, who ostensibly didn't speak English and had no sense of humor anyway, stood stone-faced.

Mr. Tram said, "Here we are on the combat base. As you can see, there is nothing left here, except the outline of the runway over there, where nothing seems to grow."

We all looked at the runway in the distance. Susan and Ted snapped a few pictures of the barren landscape and of us.

Ted said, "I was here in June when the bulldozers buried the whole fucking base. We didn't leave shit for Charlie."

Mr. Tram, who had once been Charlie, agreed and said, "When the Americans abandoned the base in June, they did not want to leave anything which could be used in a propaganda film, and so now we see nothing. But you see the holes in the earth where the metal scavengers have mined everything that was buried. They have found even trucks that had been destroyed by artillery and buried." He added, "There is talk of reconstructing some parts of this combat base because when the tourists come, they see nothing."

I said to Ted, "Hey, I got a job for you."

He laughed. "Yeah. No fucking way I'm filling one more fucking sandbag on this fucking hill."

Mr. Tram smiled and said, "Many American marines have been helpful in providing information to the local authorities about this base, and now we have maps and drawings of how it may have looked."

Ted said, "It looked like a shithole. Red mud and sandbags. No grass when I was here."

Mr. Tram went on a bit about reconstructing hell for the tourists. I looked around and saw that there were maybe fifty people wandering around, trying to figure out what all the fuss was about. I guess you had to have been here.

We walked around awhile, and Mr. Loc stayed with the vehicle. Mr. Tram pointed to the west and said, "You can see the hills there of Laos, twenty-five kilometers. Near that border is the American Special Forces camp of Lang Vei, which my regiment captured in the early days of the siege." He paused, then said, "They were very brave men, but there were too few of them."

I said, "Their Montagnard fighters were also very brave."

Mr. Tram did not reply.

We continued walking across the plateau, and I spotted two middle-aged American men together, who were having a very emotional moment while their wives stood off to the side and looked away.

Ted noticed them, too, and stared at them awhile, then went over and spoke to them. Big Ted didn't look like the huggy, kissy type, but within a minute, the two guys and Ted were embracing.

A few minutes later, Ted returned, cleared his throat, and said, "They were artillery guys. Both got hurt when the ammo dump exploded in January, and they got medevaced out." He added, "They missed most of the fun."

No one commented on this, though Mr. Tram must have remembered when the main ammo dump got hit by a North Vietnamese artillery round. Guys I knew who had been patrolling in the hills near Quang Tri City said they could see and hear it thirty kilometers away. It must have been a big morale booster for the North Viets, and a bad omen for the besieged marines.

We continued our walk.

Ted stopped near the edge of the plateau and said, "I remember that my bunker was on this side, the south side, about the middle of the perimeter here, and we could see down to Highway 9."

Mr. Tram said, "Yes? My regiment was also to the south, on the other side of the highway, so perhaps we exchanged some bullets."

"Hey, I'm sure we did, pal." Ted asked me, "Where were you, Paul?"

I looked out over the valley to the hills in the far distance and said, "Also here on the south side. We air-assaulted into those hills, near where we drove in from A Shau. They told us we were going in behind the enemy—behind Mr. Tram here—but there were plenty of North Vietnamese troops where we landed."

Mr. Tram nodded thoughtfully and said, "Yes, I recall quite clearly the afternoon when the helicopter cavalry arrived." He added, "They bombed us for days before the helicopter assault began and dropped much napalm, and when the helicopters arrived with the air soldiers, we were very frightened."

I said, "*You* were frightened? I was scared shitless. Biet?"

Mr. Tram nodded and kept nodding, and I saw he was far away, thinking of the day the helicopters came.

Ted said, "I remember when the Cav arrived, and we said, 'Shit, now they're going to run Charlie off, and the fun is over.'"

There seemed to be two different versions of this battle: The First Cavalry looked at this as saving the besieged marines; the marines looked at it as the cavalry spoiling their fun. I said to Ted, "I wouldn't have minded staying home."

He laughed.

Mr. Tram came back from wherever he'd gone and asked Ted, "Did you have rats?"

"Did we have rats? Christ, we had trench rats so big we thought they were deer. And those were *hungry* rats. You had to sleep with your boots on or you'd get your toe bit off. I kid you not. These fuckers were mean and ballsy. We had special buckshot rounds for the .45 automatics, and we'd do rat hunts once a day. One time, two rats picked up a case of C rations and carried it into a hole, then one comes back out and tries to swap a pack of C ration cigarettes for a can opener." He laughed. "That's balls."

Susan seemed mildly amused. Mr. Tram was still thinking about rats. He said, "Our trenches were filled with rats. They ate . . ." He looked at Susan and didn't finish the sentence, but I knew that it wasn't C rations that the rats ate.

Mr. Tram said, "These rats carried disease . . . you understand, the . . . in French it is les puces."

Susan said, "Fleas."

"Yes, and these fleas carried the plague . . . the dark plague, when the skin becomes black . . . bubonic . . . many men died that way."

We stood there under the gray, gloomy sky,

with this constant wind sweeping down from the hills, and three of us retreated into our own thoughts. We could have stood there for a week playing Can You Top This, but what was the point?

Finally, Ted said, "Yeah, I remember now, a cargo plane came in one day carrying this stuff . . . gamma something."

I said, "Gamma globulin."

"Yeah. You remember that? They stuck this horse needle in your ass and squirted this shit into your butt. This stuff was on ice, and I swear it was thick as putty. I had a lump in my ass for a week, and we asked the medics what it was for, and they said, 'measles.' But afterward, we found out it was because of the plague. Jesus H. Christ, as if the incoming rounds wasn't enough to worry about."

Susan asked, "Did anyone get sick?"

Ted replied, "You think they'd tell us? You went to the field hospital with a fever, and sometimes you got sent back to duty with penicillin, and sometimes they took you out of here on the next thing flying out. Nobody used the word plague."

I nodded, recalling the fear of bubonic plague, the evidence of which we'd seen among the dead and wounded North Vietnamese. We had gotten gamma globulin before the air assault, and our medics had been mostly up-front about this and told us to avoid flea bites from the rats, and, of course, direct rat bites. And while we were at it, quit smoking and try not to get hit by a bullet. Thanks, Doc.

The First Cavalry had named this operation Pegasus, after the mythological flying horse, but it could more aptly have been named the Four Horsemen of the Apocalypse—War, Famine, Pestilence, and Death.

Mr. Tram continued, "So, this terrible siege went on for all of January, February, March, until April. We had perhaps twenty or twenty-five thousand men around this camp, and the American marines had . . . how many, Mr. Ted?"

"About five or six thousand."

"Yes. And when we left here, they told us we had left ten thousand of our comrades behind, sick, wounded, and dead . . . and we had many more thousands with us who were sick and wounded . . . and many of them died afterward. I lost many friends here and some cousins and an uncle who was a colonel. And I know many Americans died also, so when I left here, I thought to myself, 'What was the purpose of this?'"

Ted said, "Beats the hell out of me."

Mr. Tram walked silently for a while, then stopped and pointed. "Do you see that trench out there? It is one of the surviving trenches that we dug. We began digging trenches toward this camp—just as my father and uncles had done at Dien Bien Phu. Each night we dug, and the trenches came closer and closer to your barbed wire. And when we were very close, we would come out of the trenches at night and attack a place where we thought the defenses were weak, and where we could penetrate into your camp . . . but we could not . . . and many men died out there, where the barbed wire once was."

Ted picked up the story and said, "If we thought we saw movement out there, or if a flare tripped, our mortars would fire parachute flares above the area, and everything got lit up like day . . ." He looked down from the plateau where the wire had once been and said, "We'd see them coming at us, like hundreds of them, real quiet, not shooting, just coming at the wire, and they wouldn't even take cover, they just kept running toward us, and we'd open up and they'd start dropping like tenpins. Christ, one night one of them blows a fucking bugle, and they all start running and screaming, and my asshole gets tight, and I'm shaking so fucking bad I can't steady my rifle, and they start throwing those bangalore torpedoes into the outer wire, and the wire blows, and it's breached, and they come in toward the second wire, and mortar rounds are falling all around my bunker, and I'm afraid to put my face to the firing slit because mortar and grenade shrapnel and tracer rounds are coming in through the slit, so I hold my M-16 up to the slit by its pistol grip, and I'm crouched below the slit, so I can't see shit, but I'm emptying magazine after magazine downrange . . . and then I get hit in the hand by hot shrapnel, and I drop the rifle and see that it's damaged, so what the hell am I thinking when I run out of the bunker and start chucking grenades down at the wire. Five frags and two white phosphorus, and everything down there is burning, including people, and these little . . . these guys are still fucking coming, and they've breached the second wire, and there's nothing between me and them except the last wire because we've blown all our claymores now, and the machine gun got knocked out, and I'm looking around for a fucking rifle . . . then, all of a sudden, the bugle blows again, and they're gone."

Ted stared down the slope of the plateau and said, in a barely audible voice, "And they're gone . . . except for a few dozen of them tangled in the wire, or moaning on the ground. So, we go down there and . . . well . . ." He looked at Mr. Tram, who looked away from Ted.

We walked around the perimeter of the big camp, and there wasn't a scrap of anything left, except the ghostly trace of the long airstrip, where, as Mr. Tram said, nothing seemed to grow.

Mr. Tram said to me, "If you do not mind, could you tell me what was your experience here?"

We continued our walk, and I thought a min-

ute and said, "Well, after we air-assaulted in, we
made contact with the enemy . . . with the North
Vietnamese army, but it was obvious they were
retreating into Laos. We had light contact for the
next week or so. I really can't remember how
long we stayed. We saw many hundreds of dead
soldiers, many wounded, many graves . . . and
the rats . . . and there was a terrible stench of
death, and the land was devastated . . . and I had
never seen anything like this . . . the aftermath
of a great slaughter, and in some ways, it was
more terrible than battle itself. I kept saying to
myself, 'I am walking through the Valley of
Death, and God has abandoned this place.'"

We were back in the town square of Khe Sanh
again. I gave Mr. Tram a ten and said to him,
"Thank you. I'm sure this is difficult for you to
relive this."

He bowed and replied, "I can only do this
with Americans who have been here. To the others, it is meaningless."

Susan said, "Well, I wasn't here, but you
three guys made me feel like I was."

Ted asked Susan, "Hey, do you think my wife
should have come?"

Susan replied, "Yes. Come back with her tomorrow."

Ted bit his lip and nodded. "She wanted to
come . . . it was me who didn't want her to."

Susan said, "I understand."

Susan said something in Vietnamese to Mr. Tram. He bowed and replied, we all shook hands, and Ted was off to his bus, and Mr. Tram to wherever.

We got back in the RAV, and I said to Mr. Loc, "Quang Tri."

He pulled onto Highway 9, and we headed east, back toward the coast, to the place where I'd spent most of my time here, when they weren't air-assaulting me into the middle of another nightmare.

Susan said, "That was incredible. What an experience."

I didn't reply.

She asked me, "How are you holding up?"

"Fine."

"Paul . . . why do you think you survived this place?"

"Beats me."

"I mean, half the men who were with Mr. Tram died, and he survived. Ted Buckley survived, you survived. Do you think it was fate? Or skill? Or luck? What?"

"I really don't know. The dead, if they could speak, would tell you why they died, but the living have no answers."

She took my hand, and we rode in silence down Highway 9 through the peaceful valley of Khe Sanh, which means the Green Valley, and which must have seemed like a cruel joke to the twenty thousand North Vietnamese who came here and watched the valley turn red with their blood and the bomb-blasted earth, gray with ash, and black with rotting corpses.

And the South Vietnamese, who were fighting for their land, must have wondered if inviting the Americans to help them was a blessing or a curse because no one can level the terrain like Americans, and the destruction must have been beyond anything the South Vietnamese could comprehend.

And for the six thousand American marines surrounded and besieged at Khe Sanh combat base, so far from home, they must have wondered how they wound up in the epicenter of hell on earth.

And Khe Sanh, the Green Valley, had passed into military legend for the marines, right up there with the Halls of Montezuma, the Shores of Tripoli, Okinawa and Iwo Jima, and all the other blood-soaked battlefields around the world.

And for the First Air Cavalry Division, casualties were mercifully light, victory was claimed, we put another battle streamer on our regimental flags, received a commendation from the president, and flew into the A Shau Valley, where fate awaited us in yet another dark and misty place.

I looked at the countryside as we passed through the valley, and I saw it was green again, and life had returned, coffee and vegetables grew over the bones, and the human race marched on toward something hopefully better.

Yet, standing there on that plateau, I knew that I, and Ted, and Mr. Tram could hear the whispers of ghosts on the wind, and the distant sound of that bugle that split the quiet night and roused the beast in each man's heart.

CHAPTER THIRTY-THREE

——★——

We continued east on Highway 9. In the hills, I could see acres of fire and smoke, like the war had returned, but then I remembered that some of the Montagnards practiced slash-and-burn agriculture.

The mouth of the valley widened and the hills on both sides retreated into the distance. The landscape became less verdant the farther east we traveled.

Around us were flat, open stretches of scrub brush and some hardscrabble farms. I recalled seeing this from the air as the armada of helicopters, in nice neat formations, carried us to the hilltop landing zones of Khe Sanh.

I said to Susan, "The DMZ is about five kilometers north of here. This entire strip of land south of the DMZ, from the coast to the Laotian border, was the marine area of operations. The marines set up a series of firebases from Cua Viet on the coast to Khe Sanh in the east. This whole stretch of land was fought over for a decade, and the marines said that DMZ meant Dead Marine Zone."

Susan asked, "Did it always look this bleak?"

I replied, "I don't know. This might be the result of defoliation, napalm, and high explosives." I added, "The motto of the defoliation people was, 'Only We Can Prevent Forests.'" I had thought that was funny once, but it didn't seem funny anymore.

We came to the former marine base called the Rockpile, a towering, seven-hundred-foot-high rock formation, which we could see to our left as the road swung east again.

We continued on, and I saw a sign near a dirt road to the right that said *Camp Carroll*. A minibus was coming toward Highway 9 from the dirt road, and on the side of the bus it said *DMZ Tours*.

I remarked, "DMZ World." I said to Susan, "When I was back here for Part Two in 1972, Camp Carroll had been turned over to the South Vietnamese army as we were trying to turn the whole war over to the South Viets. During the Easter Offensive of '72, the South Viet commander of Camp Carroll surrendered to the North Viets without a shot fired. We heard about this down in Saigon, and we couldn't believe it at first. The whole garrison just laid down their arms."

It was then, I recalled, that I knew that as soon as the last American soldier left, the South Vietnamese would lose the war, and all the American blood that had been spilled here was wasted.

We continued on and passed through the town of Cam Lo, which would never be a picture on a postcard. There were a number of DMZ Tour buses parked on the street near a café, and I said to Susan, "Just north of here is Con Thien firebase, which as you know means the Hill of Angels, and where a high school buddy of mine was killed."

We left Cam Lo, passed the turnoff for Con Thien, and continued east.

The landscape hadn't improved much, and the sky was even grayer as we came toward the coast.

There were a few buildings on both sides of the road now, and there was even a decent-looking four-story stucco hotel with a big banner sign that said *DMZ Visitor Welcome Here—Rooftop Restaurant Sees DMZ*. I said to Mr. Loc, "Dung lai."

He glanced back at me and pulled over.

Susan and I got out and walked back to the hotel, named the Dong Truong Son. The lobby was small but new, and we took the one elevator up to the rooftop restaurant.

It was well past lunchtime, and not yet the cocktail hour, so no one was there, except a young man who had to be the waiter because he was sleeping in a chair.

Susan and I took a table by the low wall of the covered restaurant where we had a panoramic view to the north.

I knew this place; I'd seen it from the ground and from the air, I'd seen it on maps, and I still saw it in my mind. I said to Susan, "That's the Cua Viet River, which runs out to the South China Sea over there. To the east is Con Thien on the Cam Lo River, and all along the Cam Lo were smaller fire support bases, starting with Alpha One to the east, Alpha Two, Three, and Four." I pointed and said, "Beyond the Cam Lo River, you can see the Ben Hai River, which runs right through the center of the old DMZ at the 17th Parallel, which was the border that partitioned North and South Vietnam. I'll be going that way tomorrow."

She didn't reply.

Susan and I looked out over the still devastated landscape, and from up here, I could see the telltale ponds, some of them running in a straight line, evenly spaced, so there was no mistaking that they were created by a bomb pattern.

She said, "It's bleak. So much different than around Saigon and Nha Trang."

"I had the same feeling when I came from Bong Son in January '68. We came into the winter monsoon, then the Tet Offensive, then Khe Sanh, and the A Shau. Rain, fog, mist, mud, gray skies, scorched earth, and too many corpses. I remember thinking that my father may have had it easier fighting the Germans in France in the summer of '44, although I never said that to him."

"Your father was in World War II?"

"He was an infantryman, just like me. The Brenners pride themselves on never having had an officer in the family, or anyone with a safe military job. We're just South Boston cannon fodder for the wars. I lost an uncle in Korea."

Susan said, "My father was an air force officer in Korea. A flight surgeon." She added, "As I said in Saigon, I think you'd like each other."

"Fathers have a tough time liking guys who are having sex with their daughters."

"I've never had sex. I'm still a virgin. Ask my father."

I smiled. "Well, then there's the age difference."

"Paul, I'm past thirty—my parents wouldn't mind if you were a Civil War veteran. They're desperate." She added, "So am I, or I wouldn't bother with you."

The waiter had woken up. He saw us and ambled over. We ordered two coffees.

Susan said to me, "How does it feel sitting in a rooftop restaurant overlooking the DMZ?"

"I'm not sure. I feel sort of . . . disconnected, like I know I'm here, though it's hard to think of this as a tourist attraction." I paused. "But I'm glad it is. None of this should be trivialized, but maybe it's inevitable that it will be. On the plus side, maybe the tourists can learn something, and maybe the vets can come to terms with a lot of things, and the Vietnamese can meet a lot of Americans and make a few bucks while they're at it."

She nodded. "I'm glad I came here."

The coffee came, Susan lit up, and we looked out over the silent battlefields below.

I said to Susan, "Okay, here's the brochure copy—DMZ Tours: A pleasant morning in the minefields where you can gather shrapnel and participate in a sandbag-filling contest, followed by a picnic lunch in the ruins of Con Thien firebase, after which we look for unmarked graves along Highway One, and we end our day at the Dong Ha Soccer Stadium, where we'll see a re-creation of the surrender of Camp Carroll, performed by the original cast. Picnic lunch included."

She looked at me awhile and decided not to respond.

Somewhere around her second coffee and third cigarette, she said to me, "As if this isn't stressful enough for you—this return to your old battlefields—you're probably worried about the trip up country and what you have to do there, and the people in Washington are giving you a hard time, and this Colonel Mang is shadowing you—"

"Don't forget you."

"I was getting to that. So, on top of all this, along comes this pushy bitch—"

"Who's that?"

"This very forward, very brazen broad, who decides to pursue you—"

"Seduce."

"Whatever. And you've got a million things on your mind, and your heart is back in the States, and your soul is on temporary loan to the dead."

I didn't reply.

She said, "And yet, Paul, I think it worked. Between us."

I nodded.

She said, "But I'm thinking maybe I shouldn't go up country with you."

"I never asked you to."

"Maybe I'd be more of a burden than a help."

"I think you should go on to Hanoi, and I'll meet you there."

"No, I think I should go back to Saigon."

This sort of surprised me, and I said, "Why?"

"I think you have to finish your job here, then go to Honolulu . . . see how that works out, then . . . give me a call."

"From Honolulu?"

"No, Paul, from Virginia."

"Okay. Then what?"

"Then we can both see how we feel."

"You mean, we have to be in different hemispheres to see how we feel?"

Susan seemed a little impatient with me for some reason and said, "I'm giving you an out. Are you dense?"

"Oh. Where's the out? I missed the exit ramp."

"You're a complete idiot. I'm trying to be sensitive to your situation, and I'm willing to give up the man I love—"

"You already did that. You sent him a fax."

She stood, "Let's go."

I gave the waiter a few bucks, and we rode down the elevator. I said, "I'm sorry. It's been a stressful day. I make jokes when I'm stressed, and when I sense danger—old combat habit. Don't mean shit, as we used to say about things that meant a great deal. Xin loi. Sorry about that." And so forth. By the time we got to the lobby, Susan was holding my hand and telling me she understood, which was more than I could say for myself. I mean, sometimes I'm full of shit, but Susan's self-sacrificing performance was a whole barnyardful of it. I know an out when I see one, and that wasn't it. For better or worse, we were going to complete this tour of duty together.

★

CHAPTER THIRTY-FOUR

—————— ★ ——————

B ack on the road, we drove into the town called Dong Ha Junction, which looked a lot like a truck stop in New Jersey. There was a railroad station, a bus station, two gasoline stations, and a few guest houses. We came to the T-intersection of Highway One and turned south. On the other side of the two-lane highway I saw a building whose sign said, in English, *Quang Tri Tourism Office*, in front of which were a few tour buses.

Susan asked me, "Do you know this town?"

"I was never here, but I know it was a marine and army logistics base."

Susan spoke to Mr. Loc, who responded, and Susan said to me, "Dong Ha is the provincial capital of Quang Tri Province."

"Quang Tri City is the provincial capital. Send Mr. Loc back to school."

Susan spoke to Mr. Loc again, and then said to me, "Quang Tri City was completely destroyed by the American bombers in April 1972 and has never been rebuilt. This is now the provincial capital."

"Shit happens."

We drove south on Highway One, which was

nearly deserted, and I said to Susan, "From here to Hue, this was called the Street Without Joy."

She looked around at the sparse vegetation, and the ramshackle houses, and the occasional rice paddy and said, "Were you guys fighting to hold on to this, or make the enemy take it?"

I laughed. "I have to remember that line the next time I run into someone who was here." I said, "Somewhere around here is where the marine area of operations ended, and the army AO began."

We came to a newly constructed bridge that crossed a branch of the Cua Viet River, and I said to Mr. Loc, "Stop."

He stopped on the bridge, and I got out. Susan followed.

I looked downstream and saw the pylons of the old bridge, and I said to Susan, "My platoon guarded this bridge a few times. Well, not this bridge, but the one that was over there." I could see the remains of a French pillbox where the old bridge had crossed the river and said to her, "I slept in that concrete pillbox a few times. I scratched my name in the wall, along with a few hundred other names, including guys named Jacques and Pierre."

She took my hand and said, "Let's go see."

"Ask James Bong if he has a flashlight."

She asked him, and he produced one from the glove box. Susan and I walked about ten meters along the riverbank to where the destroyed bridge had been. The French pillbox or bunker was a round structure, about ten meters across, made of reinforced concrete with a domed roof to deflect rockets and mortar rounds. There must have been a time when boxes of pills looked like this, thus the name, but to me, it looked like an igloo. I could see embedded in the ground at the base of the concrete structure scraps of green plastic, which had been American sandbags. I said to Susan, "We used to sandbag the old French concrete fortifications because the newer munitions were able to penetrate six or eight inches of steel-reinforced concrete, and the sandbags would absorb that direct hit. Still, if you were inside one of these things when it took a direct, it would scramble your brains for a few hours. We used to call it 'becoming a marine.' Old joke."

I took the flashlight from Susan and shined the light inside the bunker. I said, "Looks nasty in there. I can't even see the concrete floor, just mud."

She asked, "Any leeches?"

"Not in there. I'll go in first and throw the snakes out." I stepped through the narrow slit opening.

The center of the dome was about five meters high, allowing a man to stand at any of the firing slits with plenty of overhead room.

I shined the flashlight around the concrete walls and floor and saw creepy crawlers, like centipedes, and lots of webs with big walnut-sized spiders on them, plus lots of slugs, but no snakes. The walls were all mildewed, but I could see names scratched in the concrete.

Susan called in, "Throw some snakes out."

"No snakes. But be careful and don't touch the walls."

She squeezed into the pillbox and stood beside me. She said, "Yuck. It smells."

"We kept these things very clean, but no one's been here since 1975."

Gray light came in through the firing slits, and I kept the flashlight moving to pick out anything I didn't want to come in contact with.

Susan said, "Where's your name?"

I moved the flashlight slowly across the round walls, and I stopped the beam at a grouping of names. I moved closer, avoiding the spiderwebs, and focused the beam on the names scratched into the concrete. They were all French names, and there was a date of Avril 1954. I seemed to remember these names and the date, which in 1968, was only fourteen years before, but to me, an eighteen-year-old kid who had been four years old when the French Indochina War ended, this seemed like the writings of an ancient army. Now, I realized the proximity of the two wars and the passage of time since.

Susan said, "Someone wrote something under the four names. See that?"

I placed the beam on the French words. "It says, 'This place sucks.'"

"No, it doesn't." She moved closer and read the French, "Les quatre amis, les âmes perdues—four friends, lost souls."

I moved the beam around and stopped at the name of Sal Longo. I said, "This man was in my platoon. He was killed in the A Shau Valley . . . incredible . . ."

I found my name, etched into the concrete with the tip of my beer can opener. The letters were barely legible, covered with black mildew. I stared at Paul Brenner's name, followed by the date of 11 Jan 68.

Susan looked at where the beam had come to rest and said, "That's amazing."

"Better here than on the Wall in Washington."

I looked at my name awhile, then moved the light around and saw a few other names I recognized, and some I didn't. Someone had scratched a heart and arrow in the wall that said *Andy and Barbara, forever*. If that was Andy Hall, then forever arrived in May 1968, also in the A Shau. Basically, Delta Company, my company, had ceased to be an effective fighting unit after that three weeks, and the survivors almost all got another stripe on their sleeves, what the army called rapid battlefield promotions, but which we called blood stripes.

I took Susan's arm and led her to the entrance.

We stood outside under the overcast sky and Susan said, "I can't believe that. There was your name written almost thirty years ago . . . and those French soldiers . . . it's sort of . . . sad . . . almost creepy . . . I mean, I know some of those men didn't make it back."

I nodded.

We walked back to the RAV and continued south on the Street Without Joy.

We passed an airstrip on our left that I recalled was the Quang Tri airport, which was where the army kept their small observation and reconnaissance aircraft. The airstrip was abandoned now and grass grew through the concrete. The control tower had disappeared and so had a huge French watchtower that had been right near the airstrip. I recalled that the concrete watchtowers had once dotted the landscape, but I hadn't seen a single one so far. In fact, every substantial landmark that I remembered—schools, churches, pagodas, French and American fortifications—had disappeared.

I said to Susan, "Most of this area was damaged during the Tet Offensive, but they were rebuilding when I left. It looks like nothing survived the Easter Offensive of '72, or the final offensive of 1975."

She said, "That pillbox survived."

"Hey, I should have spent the whole fucking war in there."

Up ahead, on the left side of the road, I saw a

big, ruined concrete building that I could tell had not been hit by bombs or artillery because most of the roof was intact. The damage had been caused by what appeared to be a vicious firefight. The walls were pockmarked with bullet holes, and there were distinctive small round holes in the thick walls where concrete-piercing rockets had entered the building and exploded inside, leaving scorch marks on the interior walls. It took me a minute to recognize this as the Buddhist high school, the place where Tran Van Vinh wrote the letter to his brother.

Susan said, "Oh, my God. Look at that building."

I said, "A Buddhist high school."

Susan seemed fascinated by the war ruin and took a photo. She said, "You don't see any war-damaged buildings like this around Saigon—hey, look. A tank."

Beyond the high school on the side of the road was a huge M-48 Patton tank, the olive drab paint still looking good after thirty years. I should get some of that paint for my exterior house trim.

Susan told Mr. Loc to stop, and he did. She said to me, "Go sit on the tank."

"You go sit on the tank. I've sat on enough tanks." I took the camera from her.

She jumped out of the vehicle and scrambled up the sloping rear of the tank. She was athletic and agile, I noticed, and climbed like a tomboy.

She got up on the turret and sat cross-legged. I took a picture and said, "I wish all the tank crews looked like you."

She hammed it up for the camera, and I took a few more shots as she posed, lying and standing on the derelict tank.

She jumped down and walked back to the RAV.

I pointed to the east, where a wall of low hills rose out of the flatlands, about five kilometers away. I said, "I was in those hills on the night the Tet Offensive began at the end of January. We were constructing yet another firebase, and about ten that night we could see what we thought were fireworks, but then we realized it was something else. The radios came alive and reported an enemy attack on Quang Tri City. We were put on full alert and as the night went on, we got reports that Quang Tri City and Hue had been taken from the South Vietnamese troops and that our brigade headquarters, called Landing Zone Betty, which was on the edge of Quang Tri City, was under siege."

I looked around. "Our main base camp was called Landing Zone Sharon, and it was around here somewhere, but I don't see any sign of it." I stared out toward the hills. "So that's where I celebrated Tet 1968, the Year of the Monkey." I added, "It was not a lucky year for anyone."

She said, "This year will be much better."

We jumped in the RAV, and off we went.

Another hundred meters up Highway One, Mr. Loc turned left where the railroad station used to be, onto a two-lane road that I remembered led to Quang Tri City, about a mile off Highway One. The road was flanked by small wood and thatch houses surrounded by vegetable plots. There were trees here, but probably none that predated the 1972 battle. I said to Susan, "This road used to be lined with vendors selling things to GIs."

"Like what?"

"Mostly stuff they'd stolen from us. You could buy it back here."

Mr. Loc stopped the car, then looked around. He said something to Susan, and she said to me, "This is Quang Tri, and the citadel of the city used to be somewhere there to the left."

I looked to the left, but there was nothing there except more small houses, bamboo fences, gardens, and chickens.

Susan and Mr. Loc spoke, and she said to me, "He thinks the moat of the Citadel is still there, and a villager can direct us."

"Okay. We'll be about an hour."

Susan took the camera out of the bag, spoke to Mr. Loc, and we jumped out. Mr. Loc reached back into the rear, handed Susan the tote, and said something.

We started down a dirt path between vegetable gardens and small houses that were made of bits and pieces of the vanished city and the fortifications that had once been here. I saw chunks of concrete and bullet-riddled wooden planks, and the corrugated metal that the Americans used for barracks roofs, and the green plastic sandbags from disassembled bunkers, and garden paths made of red roof tile. The ruined city and the fortifications had been recycled by the peasants.

I said to Susan, "This was once a small city, now it's a big village. Back to basics through air-power."

"Incredible," she said.

I asked Susan, "What did he say to you?"

"About what? Oh, he's going to park and leave the vehicle, so he wanted me to take my stuff."

I nodded.

A few kids saw us, and soon there was a mob of them following us. A few adults watched us curiously from their gardens.

We continued on the village paths, and Susan was looking around. She said, "I've never really been in a rural village."

I replied, "I've been in hundreds of them. They all look the same. Except some held Viet Cong and some didn't." I looked around. "See that haystack? Once we found a whole room hidden in a big haystack. Chuck was gone, but he'd left some equipment. So we Zippo'ed the haystack, then got carried away and burned some nearby hootches—that's what we called the peasant houses." It was all coming back to

me, and I continued, "Then there'd be these little holes hidden in the gardens, big enough for
one tiny VC to stand in—we called them spider
holes, and they were hard to find, unless Chuck
decided to pop out and open up with his AK-47.
Plus, every hootch had an earth bunker in the
garden, where the family would go if the shit hit
the fan. But each bunker could also hold some
VC, and you didn't want to go in there and
check it out because if you did, you'd never
come out again, so you shouted for everyone to
come out with their hands up, and usually
you'd get a few co-deps who Mama-san wanted
to hide from the GIs in case we had things on
our minds beside finding Mr. Charles. So, after
everyone was supposed to be out, you chucked
a tear gas grenade in, and now and then Mr.
Charles would come running out with his AK-47
blazing, and you'd waste him, then move on."

I was amazed that this was all coming back to
me so vividly, and I went on, "Buried in the
thatch roofs you'd find rifles, ammunition, plastic explosives, and all that good stuff, and you'd
arrest the family and turn them over to the National Police and burn their house, though nine
times out of ten the poor bastards who were hiding VC or weapons were doing it under threat.
One time—and I guess this was funny—we
pulled on a water well rope and sure enough,
whatever was down there was too heavy to be a
water bucket, and so about three guys pull

Charles up, his black pajamas dripping wet, his feet in this wooden bucket, and before he got to ground level, he threw his AK-47 rifle up so we wouldn't blow him away. So, up he comes, looking almost sheepish—like, you found me—and we laughed our asses off, then someone punched him in the face, and he fell down into the well, and we let him tread water for fifteen minutes before we lowered the bucket down and fished him up. Then the same guy who punched him in the face gave him a cigarette and lit it for him, then burned the house where the well was, and we tied Chuck up and put him on a chopper back to a POW camp, and the beat goes on. Day by day by day, village by village by village, until we were sick to death of searching these miserable villages and searching the people and trashing their hootches looking for weapons and wondering when Charlie was going to pop up out of nowhere and blow your head off. And other days, we'd help deliver a baby, medevac some sick kid back to an aid station, put first aid ointment on some old guy's festering sore, and hand out candy. Acts of human kindness, alternating with acts of extreme cruelty, usually on the same day, and often in the same village. You just never knew how a hundred armed boys were going to act at any given moment. I guess a lot of it depended on how many casualties we'd taken the day before, or if we found anything in the village, or maybe how hot and thirsty we were, or if the

officers and sergeants were minding the boys
closely, or if they didn't give a shit that day because they'd gotten a bad letter from home, or
they'd gotten chewed out on the radio by a superior officer, or if they themselves were starting
to go around the bend. As the war went on, the
young lieutenants got younger, and the sergeants
had been PFCs just a month before . . . and the
normal constraints of more mature people . . .
you know, like Lord of the Flies . . . kids can get
crazy . . . and if somebody kills one of the gang,
they want blood in return . . . and so the village
sweeps got . . . they got out of hand, and it wasn't
war anymore, it was kids on the prowl with short
fuses, who were just as likely to throw a fragmentation grenade into a family bunker as a tear
gas grenade, or just as likely to give Papa-san a
box of cookies from home as to crush a lit cigarette in his face if they found a spider hole in his
garden."

Susan walked silently beside me, and I wondered if I should be telling her any of this. I
also wondered if I should be telling me any of
this. Back in the States, you could forget it, or
sanitize it in your mind, or put it all down to
false memory syndrome, the result of watching
too many 'Nam flicks. But here . . . here is
where it happened, and there was no way to
spin it.

We kept walking through the village, the kids
following, but not begging or being annoying,

like they were in Saigon. These were rural kids, who didn't see many Lien Xo, and so maybe they were shy; but maybe they had an ancestral memory of big Americans who had walked through their fathers' and grandfathers' villages, and they kept their distance.

I said to Susan, "Imagine being a villager— you don't sleep at night, and you don't smile during the day. You and everyone around you are on the brink of madness and despair, and you're totally at the mercy of two armed enemies who say they want to win your hearts and minds, but who may one day rape you and slit your throat. And that was life in the villages of this tortured country. By the time it was all over, the peasants didn't care who won. The devil himself with his legions from hell could have won, and that would be wonderful because the war had stopped."

Susan stayed quiet for a while, then said, "I would have joined the guerrillas and gone into the hills to fight. I'd rather die fighting."

I forced a smile and said, "You're a fighter." I added, "In fact, most of the young men and women chose one side or the other and did just that. But some stayed in the villages to plant and harvest, and to take care of aging parents and younger siblings and hope for the best. In any case, if you ever get to a rural village again, when you see people of that age, you'll understand what they went through."

She nodded.

As if on cue, an old man stood on the side of the path, and he bowed to us. Susan spoke to him, and he smiled at her Vietnamese. They talked for a few minutes, and Susan said to me, "The Citadel is just up this path. He says he's a longtime resident of Quang Tri, and if you are a returning soldier, you must be surprised at what you see."

"I am. Tell him I was with the First Cavalry, and my brigade headquarters was in the old French fort."

She told him, and he replied at some length. She said to me, "In 1972, the Communists and the Army of the Republic . . . the ARVN . . . fought back and forth for the city, and it changed hands many times, and lay in ruins, then the ARVN withdrew toward Hue, and the American bombers came and destroyed all that was left of the city, and killed many Communist soldiers who were in the Citadel and the French fort, and the American base camp outside the city. There is nothing left."

I nodded.

He said something else, and Susan said to me, "He says other Americans from the cavalry have returned, and they are always sad and surprised that nothing is left of their presence here. He also met a Frenchman once who came to see the fort where he was stationed, and the Frenchman was convinced he was in the wrong place and spent all day looking for his fort, and the . . . watchtowers, I think he means."

The old man thought that was funny, laughed, and said something else, which Susan translated as, "The Frenchman expected to find the café where he once drank, and maybe his former . . . ladies."

"Hey, that's why I'm here. Tell him."

Susan told him, and he laughed harder. Why he got a kick out of this, I don't know, but maybe he'd done all the crying he had in him, and there was nothing left to do except laugh at the death and destruction.

We thanked the old man and moved on.

At the end of the path, we came to a huge open space, about a half a kilometer on each side, surrounded by peasant huts and gardens in the distance. The space was covered with high grass and small trees, and at first it looked like a village commons. But all around the space was a weed-choked moat, which had once surrounded the walls of the Citadel. Here and there around the open areas, I could see pieces of wall, none of them over three feet high, and a bomb-blasted stone arch stood where a destroyed bridge once spanned the moat.

I said to Susan, "This was the Citadel, sort of like the one in Hue, but obviously it's in much worse shape. This was the center of the city, and it held government buildings, a hospital, bank, a few cafés, the barracks and headquarters of the

South Vietnamese army, and the MACV compound—that's the Military Assistance Command, Vietnam—American military advisors to
the ARVN." I told her, "Most of the MACV guys
were killed when the Communists took the city
during the Tet Offensive. Same in Hue. It's a
risky job when you have to depend on unreliable allies for your safety."

Susan looked around at the open space in
the center of the sprawling village. "It looks
like a park or a sports field, but it's completely
barren."

"I guess it's been left as a monument to a destroyed city and to the people who died here,
but I don't even see a marker."

"Neither do I . . . but look, Paul, there's a
bridge across the moat."

I looked to where Susan was pointing and
saw an intact, but shell-blasted concrete bridge
that had once led to a gate in the vanished walls.

We walked to the bridge and crossed the dry
moat into what was once the Citadel. The kids
who were following us didn't cross, and one of
them yelled something to us. Susan said to me,
"He says it is government property, and we are
not allowed to be here." She added, "He also
said, 'Thanh Than.' Ghosts."

I replied, "That's what they tell the kids to
keep them away from any unexploded ordnance."

"You're probably right. Meanwhile, don't step

on an unexploded shell, or we'll both be ghosts."

"Stay on the paths."

"There are no paths, Paul."

"Well, step lightly."

We walked into the center of the grassy field that had once been a city, and I said, "The parade ground was about here, and the military side of the Citadel was across the field, over there . . . I think."

"You remember this?"

"Sort of. I was here only once, when I had to participate in some idiotic awards ceremony that the ARVN liked to schedule too often."

"You mean you got an award here?"

"Yeah. And it wasn't the Good Conduct Medal."

"What was it?"

"Something called the Cross of Gallantry, after the French medal of the same name. It was the equivalent to our Bronze Star, I think."

"What did you get the medal for?"

"I'm not real sure. The whole ceremony was in Vietnamese."

"Come on, Paul. You know why they gave you a medal."

"Yeah. For propaganda. They filmed the whole thing, and showed it before the feature film—in the six movie theaters that probably existed in the whole country. Our brave American allies, and so forth. The ARVN just took the list of GIs who got American medals for whatever and gave the equivalent Viet medal. I got the Bronze Star for the A Shau Valley without a ceremony, and the Viets gave me the Cross of Gallantry here, with a lot of pomp and ceremony."

She asked, "Did they give you a copy of the tape?"

I smiled and replied, "It was a *film*, Susan. I don't think they had videotape then, but if they did, they'd have sold me a copy, which they didn't."

"Maybe we can find the original film in the archives in Saigon."

"I hope the fucking thing got blown up."

"You're so sentimental."

"Right. Anyway, I stood about right here with maybe a hundred other Americans from the First Cav, and I got kissed on both cheeks by a colonel . . . it was June or July by this time, and the temperature was ninety degrees on this parade ground, but my reconstituted company, filled with cherries now—that means new guys from the States—were out patrolling somewhere, so this wasn't that bad. I thought I could hit a few bars in town after the dog-and-pony show, but the U.S. Army was nice enough to collect us all in trucks and take us back to Landing Zone Sharon, which, I guess, no longer exists." I looked at Susan and asked her, "Am I a great date or what?"

She smiled and put her arm through mine.

She said, "This is really an incredible experience for me."

"Well . . . this is the last duty station for you. I've sort of taken you through my first tour—the Bong Son in November and December '67, Quang Tri for the Tet Offensive in January and February, then Khe Sanh in April, and the A Shau in May, then back here to Quang Tri Province, where I stayed until I went to An Khe base camp in November, collected my stuff, flew to Da Nang, and on to San Francisco."

"That must have been a hell of a weekend in San Francisco."

I said, "I was ready to party hard with a few other guys I knew who I'd come home with . . . but we weren't overly welcome in San Francisco . . ."

She didn't reply.

"In truth, I wasn't really in a partying mood anyway, and I stayed a few days in a hotel, getting my head on right . . . showering and flushing the toilet every half hour." I smiled. "I slept in the soft bed, watched a lot of TV, finished two bottles of gin, and kept pinching myself to make sure I wasn't dreaming . . . then I flew home to Boston. But I wasn't completely right yet."

"And there was no counseling available?"

I almost laughed. "We're talking 1968 here at the height of a huge war. You saw a shrink *before* you got inducted, and they always said you were mentally healthy enough to go off and kill people, but they never examined your head when you came back. And you know what? I don't blame them."

"Counseling might have helped."

"Sigmund Freud in consultation with Jesus Christ wouldn't have helped. Most of us found our own way back."

We walked across the moated acres that had once been Quang Tri City, and I stooped down and picked up a piece of jagged shrapnel that the metal scavengers had missed and looked at it. I said, "It could be from a bomb, a rocket, a mortar round, an artillery round, or a fragmentation grenade, and it could be ours or theirs. And it doesn't make a difference when it hits you." I gave it to Susan. "Souvenir of the lost city of Quang Tri."

She put it in her pocket.

We continued walking under the gray sky, and I could see a few Viets across the moat looking at us, probably wondering if we were scouting this place as part of the DMZ tour. Two bucks to cross the surviving moat bridge and wander around the Citadel. The tour operators would throw scrap metal around each morning before the tour buses arrived, and everyone could take a piece home.

I said to Susan, "Okay, here's another piece of the puzzle. The letter to Tran Quan Lee that was found on his body in the A Shau Valley was written by his brother, Tran Van Vinh, who was wounded here during the battle for Quang Tri City during the Tet Offensive of 1968. Vinh lay wounded in one of the buildings that were here, and he saw something that had to do with two Americans. Do you know this?"

"No."

"Okay. So, a day later, he writes this letter from the cellar of the Buddhist high school that we saw on the way in, and that letter made its way to his brother in the A Shau Valley."

"What did he see?"

"What he saw was why I'm here. The question is, Did Tran Van Vinh survive this battle, or the battles of the next seven years, and if so, is he still alive today, and can I find him, and if I do, what can he tell me?" I left out the part about me killing Tran Van Vinh, and then maybe me being terminated.

We continued walking, and Susan finally said to me, "And that's it?"

"That's it."

"What he saw is important?"

"Apparently, or I wouldn't be here spending government money."

"What did he say in the letter?"

"He said he saw an American army captain murder an American army lieutenant in cold blood, right here in a damaged building of the Citadel, as he, Tran Van Vinh, lay wounded on the floor above."

She thought a moment and said, "So . . . this is a murder investigation."

"Apparently."

She stayed quiet awhile, then said, "But . . ."

"But."

She stopped walking and looked out over the empty field. "Right here?"

"Somewhere. I couldn't tell you where any of the buildings were, but it's always good to return to the scene of the crime, even if it's nearly three decades later, and the scene has been pulverized by bombs and artillery. Cops are as superstitious and mystical as combat soldiers, and there's this feeling that the dead—the ghost—will speak to you, or at least inspire you to find their killer. I don't actually believe that, but I don't dismiss it either." I smiled and asked, "Should we try a séance?"

She smiled in return and said, "I can see how you could be inspired by being where the murder took place." She looked at me. "But you think there's more to this than a murder?"

"What do you think?"

"I have no idea."

I asked her, "Why did they tell you it had to do with Cam Ranh Bay?"

"I don't know."

"What could that have to do with a murder during the war?"

"I don't know."

"Why is the intelligence community involved with an army Criminal Investigation Division murder case?"

"I have no idea. Do you?"

"I have too many ideas. Some of them fit some of the facts, but none of them fit all the facts. What I need is more facts. You got any?"

"No . . . except . . . by the way Bill and Colonel Goodman were getting hyperventilated, it sounds like more than an old murder case."

I nodded. "You're very bright. So take a guess."

She thought a moment, then said, "The murderer, this captain, or the witness, Tran Van Vinh, was then, or is now, a very important man."

"That's a very astute answer."

She forced a smile and said, "I'm getting messages from the beyond."

We stood there awhile in this place that had witnessed at least two great battles, but was now deathly quiet. Beneath this earth were bones at rest, and perhaps bombs that I hoped remained at rest and had not been waiting for my return.

Susan asked me, "Do you think this man Tran Van Vinh is alive?"

I replied, "Here's another irony, or coincidence . . . we were ordered to come down from the hills two days after the North Vietnamese captured the city, and we were ordered to set up a blocking force to interdict the North Vietnamese soldiers fleeing the city . . . and we did kill a number of them . . . so, in effect, I or my company may have killed my star witness."

"That would be ironic, not to mention eerie . . ."

I nodded and said, "Yet, I feel that Tran Van Vinh is alive."

Susan asked, "And he lives in the village of Tam Ki?"

"Well, no. That was sort of a cover name. My guy in Hue gave me the actual name of the village."

"What *is* the name of the village?"

"I can't tell you right now. Maybe later."

"Where is it?

"Way up north." I added, "Near Dien Bien Phu. You know where that is?"

"Sort of. It's a hike. And that's where you're going tomorrow?"

"That's the plan."

"Good. Dien Bien Phu is on my list of places to see. How are we getting there?"

"Don't know how *I'm* getting there. I thought I'd take a train up the coast as far north as I can get, then travel cross-country by four-wheel drive."

"Good idea. The trains start running again Friday. Does that present a problem?"

"I guess it does. How would you get there?"

"Well, if you buy me dinner tonight, I'll tell you."

I looked at her and asked, "Do you really have an idea?"

"I didn't spend all day yesterday shopping."

"Tell me."

"No." She said, "You have no need to know, until you need to know."

She took my arm, and we turned toward the bridge.

The first thing I noticed was that all the kids on the other side of the moat were gone.

The second thing I noticed was somebody standing in the middle of the Citadel field, watching us. It was Colonel Mang.

★

CHAPTER THIRTY-FIVE

— ★ —

Colonel Mang and I stared at each other across a hundred meters of open field.

Susan asked me, "Who is that?"

"Take a guess."

"Oh . . . what's he doing here?"

"Well, for starters, he wants me to walk to him, which I'm not going to do."

Susan said, "Paul, I know these people. If you make him lose face, he'll go nuts."

"You know, Susan, I'm really fucking tired of Westerners worrying about East Asians losing face. Fuck him."

"I'll go talk to him."

"You stay right here."

She didn't reply or move.

I noticed two other men a hundred meters behind Colonel Mang, standing on the moat bridge. They were in uniform and were carrying rifles. In fact, even from this distance, I could pick out my chubby friend Pushy from Tan Son Nhat.

Colonel Mang, I noticed, was dressed in a dark green dress jacket, shirt, and tie, which was more appropriate for this cooler climate. He also wore a peaked hat and a holster and pistol.

A wind had picked up, and the sun was dropping below the trees. Long gray shadows stretched across the acres of the former Citadel, and soon it would be dark. I was prepared to stand there until dawn.

Susan said, "Paul, let's walk about a third of the way. He'll do the same."

"Fuck him. I didn't invite him here."

"He doesn't need an invitation. Trust me on this. Come on." She took a step.

I hesitated, then started walking. Susan walked beside me. I stopped after about thirty paces.

Colonel Mang got the idea and took exactly thirty paces toward us. This was all very silly, of course, but men will be boys when balls are involved.

I took a tentative step toward Colonel Mang, he did the same, and we began walking toward each other. We closed the distance to about ten meters, and the little shit stopped. I stopped.

We looked at each other. He didn't seem happy, so that made at least two of us.

Susan said, "Come on, Paul. Point made. Let's go see what he wants."

"Fuck him."

Colonel Mang must have not heard me correctly because he said, "Good evening, Mr. Brenner."

I didn't reply.

Susan had had enough of the pissing contest

and walked up to Colonel Mang. She spoke to him a minute, and I couldn't hear her, so I didn't know what language she was using. She turned to me and said, "Paul, why don't you join us?" She motioned me to come forward.

Well, this had been a hell of a day—the A Shau, Khe Sanh, the DMZ, and now Quang Tri. My brain was filled with war memories, and my body was pumped with nasty male hormones. I had the bad attitude of a combat infantryman, and I was no longer a tourist in Saigon, listening to Mang's crap; it wasn't going to take much to set me off. If I'd had my M-16, I could have wasted the two clowns with the rifles before Mang could even go for the pistol on his hip.

"Paul. Come and join us. Please."

I took a deep breath and walked the ten paces to where Susan and Colonel Mang were standing.

We didn't exchange greetings, but I spoke without being spoken to. I asked him, "What are you doing here?"

He stared at me a long time, then replied, "That is my question to you."

"I told you I was coming to Quang Tri to see where I was stationed. So don't ask me why I'm here."

He regarded me for a moment, and I could tell that he understood that I'd dropped my firm but polite manner of speaking to him. He said to me, "Well, what did you see? Nothing. I told you, there is nothing here. Your bombers laid waste to an entire province. Is this what you want to see?" He motioned around the empty acres. "Do you enjoy this?"

I took a deep breath and replied, "Colonel, you know very well why the bombers destroyed this province. Why don't you try to deal with reality as I've tried to do since I've returned?"

He replied without hesitation, "Reality is whatever we say it is."

"No, reality is what happened. The massacre at Hue happened, and the massacre here at Quang Tri happened in 1968. I saw it with my own eyes. And, yes, the massacre at My Lai also happened. We all have blood on our hands. Deal with it, and stop pushing the fucking war in my face. I didn't start it, and neither did you. Get over it."

He didn't appreciate the lecture or my tone of voice, but he kept his cool and replied, "There was no massacre at Hue or Quang Tri. There was a liquidation of the enemies of the people. The massacre was at My Lai."

"What do you want?"

"You can tell me why you and your companion here are trying to contact the hill people."

"You mean the Moi? The savages?"

"The hill people, Mr. Brenner. What is your business with them?"

"I have no business with them."

"Mr. Loc says otherwise."

"Mr. Loc is an idiot."

Susan chimed in and said, "Colonel, tourists come from all over the world to see the indigenous people of Vietnam. We did the same."

Colonel Mang regarded Susan a moment, wondering, I'm sure, why a woman was answering for a man. This country was so sexist, I might like it here. Colonel Mang said, not to Susan, but to me, "You were out of sight of Mr. Loc several times. You climbed into the hills in the A Shau Valley. You stopped at a hill tribe settlement. You spoke to hill people in the square at Khe Sanh."

I said, "So what? I'm a tourist."

"Yes? And do the hill people give all tourists that bracelet you are wearing on your wrist? Or the Taoi scarf that Miss Weber now wears? And do tourists exchange military salutes with former American mercenary troops?"

I thought about that, and he had some good points there. I replied, "Colonel, I think you're being overly suspicious, and overly sensitive to the issue of the Montagnards."

"Do you think so? You do not live here, Mr. Brenner." He asked, "Would you care to explain your actions?"

Actually, no. I said to Colonel Mang, "Where is Mr. Loc? Bring him here and we'll discuss this." I added, to lighten the moment, "I have the constitutional right to face my accuser."

Colonel Mang smiled and said, "Mr. Loc, unfortunately, had to leave for a while." He asked me, "Why did you go to A Shau Valley and Khe Sanh?"

I didn't reply.

Colonel Mang said to me, "Mr. Loc said you told many war stories, Mr. Brenner, and none of those stories involved your duties as a cook."

I replied, "Mr. Loc doesn't speak English, Colonel."

"Ah, but he does. And you know that. You remarked on it to him several times."

"Correct. So why would I incriminate myself in front of him if I knew he understood English?"

"Because you did not know he was an agent of the Ministry of Public Security."

"Of course I knew that. I told him I knew that."

"He did not mention that to me."

Susan spoke up and said to Colonel Mang, "Then he hasn't spoken the truth to you. We knew from the minute we met him that he was a policeman. I've been in this country for three years, Colonel, and I know a secret policeman when I see one."

Colonel Mang stared at Susan awhile, then said to her, "I am speaking to Mr. Brenner." He turned back to me and said, "I do not believe that you knew—"

Susan said sharply, "I am speaking to *you*, Colonel. And you will answer me."

Colonel Mang turned back to Susan. "Excuse me? I do not believe I heard you correctly."

"No? Then understand this—" She switched to Vietnamese and laid a whole lot of shit on Colonel Mang, who I was certain was about to slap her. Then, I'd have to clock him, and then the goons with the rifles would charge across the field, and before you knew it, I'd have Colonel Mang's pistol to his head, and we'd be in a standoff for the rest of the night, or a shootout, or whatever. This was not good. But I let Susan vent.

Before Susan finished yelling at Colonel Mang, he began yelling back at her, and they were really going at it. I wondered what happened to her concern about Colonel Mang saving face. I love it when peacemakers go nuts and try to start World War Three. I noticed, too, that the goons with the rifles were alert and watching. They couldn't hear much from that distance, but they knew a pissed-off lady when they saw one, especially if they were married. On the plus side, at least Susan and Colonel Mang were still talking—or yelling. If Mang got quiet, we'd have a problem.

I needed to cool this down, so I said to Susan, "Okay. Im lang. Fermez la bouche. Shut up. That's enough."

She shut up.

Colonel Mang was really worked up, and even if he hadn't come here to arrest us, he was thinking about it now, especially with the two goons watching him taking lip from the American bitch.

Colonel Mang got himself cooled down and turned back toward me. He said, as though nothing had happened, "I do not believe you knew that Mr. Loc was an agent of the Ministry of Public Security."

"Do I look stupid?"

Colonel Mang resisted saying, Yes, you look stupid. Why else would you be here? Instead, he said, "If you are so clever, why did you speak so freely of your battles in the presence of Mr. Loc when you told me you were a cook?"

I replied, "Obviously, I was not a cook. I was an infantryman."

"Why did you lie to me?"

Because the half-wits in Washington told me to. I replied, politely, "I saw no reason to upset you, Colonel, with the fact that I fought your compatriots here."

"Yes? But you lied."

Cops love to pick on a lie. I said, "I lied. I killed North Vietnamese and Viet Cong soldiers, here, in and around Quang Tri City, in Khe Sanh, in the A Shau Valley, and down in the Bong Son. So what? You, too, were a combat soldier, and you killed my compatriots. It was wartime. That's what we got paid for. Subject closed. You didn't come here to tell me you discovered I was a combat soldier. What do you want?"

He replied, "I told you. I want to know what business you have with the hill people."

"None."

"Then why did you go into the hills?"

This guy was dense, or paranoid. Probably both. I said, "I went to the A Shau Valley and to Khe Sanh to see where I fought. I thought we understood that."

He thought about that and replied, "Perhaps the lie is that you were never stationed in those places, but now you go there to make contact with the hill people on behalf of your government, and you use the excuse of visiting your battlefields when, in fact, these were not your battlefields. It is the hill tribes you are interested in."

I needed a second to follow this logic. Apparently, Colonel Mang already had it in his mind that I was up to no good, so he had to make what he knew fit with what he suspected. In fact, I *was* up to no good, but he wasn't even close to the truth. Actually, he didn't have to be; any criminal charge would do in this country.

I applied some logic of my own and said, "If I needed an excuse to go into the hills, why wouldn't I tell you at Tan Son Nhat that I had an interest in, perhaps, trees and wildlife? Follow?"

He thought about my counterlogic and replied, "In fact, you told me you were not even sure you were going to your base camp at An Khe, which is in the highlands, and where there are many tribespeople. Why were you hiding that?"

"Hiding *what?* I never went to An Khe."

"But you went to other hill areas."

This guy was giving me a headache, and I saw that Susan, too, was getting impatient with Mang's paranoia and silliness regarding the hill people.

He said to me, "You have, of course, heard of the FULRO?"

I knew that was coming. I replied, "I learned about them at the American War Crimes Museum. I saw the photographs of the mass executions of tribespeople. That upsets the tourists, by the way."

"Yes? It is intended as a lesson."

"Why couldn't you just put the hill people in re-education camps and teach them to be happy citizens? Why did you have to shoot them?"

He looked at me and informed me, "Enemies of the state, who lay down their arms, are given the opportunity to reform themselves in special schools. Enemies who are captured with weapons are shot." He added, "Anyone, armed or not, who makes contact with armed insurgents is also shot." He looked at me, then at Susan, and asked, "Do you understand?"

Of course I understood. We did the same thing in 1968, so I couldn't give Colonel Mang a lecture on due process, guilt by association, or the right to bear arms. It was time, however, to bring this to a head. I looked Mang in the eye and said to him, "Colonel, are you accusing me of being a spy?"

He stared at me, and choosing his words carefully, replied, "I am attempting to discover the true purpose of your visit to my country."

Well, so was I. But Colonel Mang couldn't help me on that. I said to him, "Surely you have better things to do during the Tet holiday. Perhaps your family would like to see you."

He didn't like that remark at all and said, "It is none of your business, Mr. Brenner, what I do. But for your information, I have been home, and now I have come to speak to you."

"I'm sorry that you've come a long way for nothing, Colonel."

"I would not come a long way for nothing, Mr. Brenner."

That sounded like there was more unpleasantness coming. I said, "Colonel, I don't respond well to subtle threats. You may find this unbelievable, but in my country, as I told you, a citizen can refuse to answer the questions of a policeman, and the citizen has the right to remain silent. The policeman then has his choice of arresting the suspect or releasing him. So, if you've come here to arrest me, then do it now. Otherwise, I'm leaving."

Colonel Mang had probably not been lectured on the limits of police power before, so he chose his own option, which was none of the above. He said to me, "If you answer my questions truthfully, you and your companion can be on your way."

I looked at Susan, who nodded to me. Having her along, as I've said, had its pluses and minuses, and right now was a minus. If I wound up in the slammer under interrogation, I could handle it. But if Mang decided to throw Susan in the clink, too, I'd have a problem.

Colonel Mang said, "Mr. Brenner? I have a few more questions for you. May I?"

I nodded.

He smiled and said to me, "Please describe for me the relationship between you and this lady."

I saw that one coming, too, and replied, "We met for the first time in Saigon—Ho Chi Minh City—and are now traveling together."

"Yes? To where?"

"To Hanoi."

"Oh, yes. To Hanoi, and where are you going between Hue and Hanoi?"

"I think I told you, Colonel. Up the coast."

"Ah, yes. You wanted to see how the people of the former North Vietnam, as you call it, live and work."

"That is what I said."

"And how do you propose to get to Hanoi?"

"I don't know. Any suggestions?"

He smiled and said, "You could come with me. I have a car and driver."

"That's very good of you to offer, but I don't want you to go out of your way."

"I am going that way. My family home is near Hanoi."

"I see. So, I suppose I'll be seeing you again in Hanoi."

"You can be sure of that, Mr. Brenner."

"I'm looking forward to it. Perhaps we can meet at my embassy."

"Perhaps not." He took out a cigarette and lit it.

Susan took out her cigarettes and said to Colonel Mang, with a bit of sarcasm, "Would you like a cigarette?"

He ignored her, which was a big improvement over a screaming match. He learned fast.

He drew on his cigarette and said to me, "So, you are traveling along the coast to Hanoi?"

"How else can I get to Hanoi?"

"Well, one could take the long route through the hills, toward Laos, then come back to Hanoi via the Red River. It is very scenic."

"Are there any hill people there?"

He smiled and didn't reply.

This was too much fun for one day. It was cold and almost dark, I needed a Scotch, and I'm playing cat and mouse with Sherlock Holmes's evil East Asian twin, standing in a place where a murder had been committed while soldiers and civilians died by the thousands all around the murder scene. *That* was why I was here, and this guy is trying to pin a capital offense on me. I couldn't wait to see Karl and have a good laugh over this.

Colonel Mang returned to the subject of my

love life and said to me, "So, you and Miss Weber are traveling as friends. Correct?"

I replied, "As you already know, we share the same bed."

He put on an expression of mock surprise. This guy needed an acting coach. He said, "But you had separate rooms in Nha Trang and now Hue. And you share the same bed. What an extravagance."

I replied, "Americans are extravagant in their attempts at propriety and good taste."

"In fact, you indulge yourselves in whatever you like or want, then attempt to pretend you are simple, virtuous people. I believe the word in English is hypocrisy. Correct?"

"That's a very good observation, Colonel. Now can I tell you about the Vietnamese? They are the only people I've ever met who worship the American dollar more than the Americans."

"You are insulting me and my country, Mr. Brenner."

"You have insulted me and my country, Colonel Mang."

He drew on his cigarette and said, "Perhaps we should get back to our business." He looked at Susan and said something to her in Vietnamese. She didn't look happy with the question and replied curtly.

I said, "This conversation will be conducted in English."

Susan said to me, "He asked me if American women make a habit of sleeping with men they've just met. I told him it was an insulting question."

I said to Colonel Mang, "Do Vietnamese officers make a habit of insulting women?"

He said to me, but not to Susan, "I am trying to determine the true nature of your relationship."

"Why? It's not your business."

"I think it is. You are aware, of course, that your friend here has been sleeping with the CIA station chief in Ho Chi Minh City."

I took a deep breath and replied, "I am aware she had a boyfriend."

"Yes? And you know this boyfriend. You told me so yourself. Mr. Bill Stanley. The CIA station chief for all of the south of Vietnam."

Of all the names for me to pick when I was telling Mang who booked my train reservations to Nha Trang, I pick the fucking CIA guy. But that's what happens when the bozos in Washington decide you have no need to know something you need to know.

"Mr. Brenner? Why are you sleeping with your friend's girlfriend?"

I said, "I only know Bill Stanley as an employee of the Bank of America."

"Yes? So, you did not know your friend was the CIA station chief?"

"You say he is, and he's not my friend."

"But you said you went to university to-gether. Princeton."

I glanced at Susan, who looked confused. Someday, my flip remarks were going to get me into trouble; in fact, the day had arrived. I said to Colonel Mang, "How could we have been classmates when he's at least ten years younger than me?"

"That's what I wondered, Mr. Brenner."

"Well, I was making a joke."

"What is the joke?"

"It's hard to explain. Colonel, I don't know Bill Stanley, and he's not my friend."

"But he *is* a CIA agent. It is perfectly all right. The CIA knows who our intelligence man is in our embassy in Washington. One cannot hide these things. In fact, Mr. Stanley has nothing to do with the Bank of America and is a consulate officer in the Economic Development section. That is not his real job, of course, but it provides him with the diplomatic immunity he needs to carry out his other work. And yet you, Mr. Bren-ner, his friend, did not know this. Amazing."

Truly amazing. And Colonel Mang was a little sharper, and more sarcastic and ironic than I'd thought.

"What am I to believe, Mr. Brenner?"

I glanced at Susan, who looked a little anx-ious. She could have been pissed off at me for using Bill Stanley's name, but she was probably more pissed off about how this whole thing had been handled.

"Mr. Brenner? What am I to believe?"

I replied, "I don't know Bill Stanley."

"But you told me you did know him."

"I lied."

"Why?"

"Well, I'll tell you why. It was Ms. Weber who arranged the train tickets to Nha Trang, but I didn't want to use her name, so I used her boyfriend's name. Biet?"

"No, I do not understand. Why would you do that?"

"Look, Colonel, if I knew that Bill Stanley was a CIA agent, why would I use his name in a conversation with you?"

"That is what I am trying to determine, Mr. Brenner."

"Right. Well, the answer is, I don't know Bill Stanley, or who he works for, and I don't know anyone in Saigon, but I remembered his name and place of employment from something Ms. Weber said, so I gave you his name instead of hers."

He asked, "But *why?* You have not answered that question."

"You answer it for me."

"How can I answer it for you? You should answer it."

"Okay . . . I didn't want Ms. Weber's name to come to the attention of the police in any way, no matter how innocent the context. She lives here, and I didn't want to compromise her business activities. You understand that."

"Perhaps. But I do not understand your connection to Mr. Stanley."

"There *is* no connection." *Asshole.*

"Ah, but there is. You are sleeping with his girlfriend." He smiled.

I hated to admit it, but this guy was almost as good and as sarcastic as I was on the job. I said to him, "Answer *my* question. If I knew or believed that Bill Stanley was a CIA agent, why would I use his name? I'll answer for you, Colonel. I didn't know, and I still don't know. And why should I believe you that he is a CIA agent?"

He nodded. "Why, indeed?" He looked at Susan and asked her, "Do you know that the man you were sleeping with was a CIA agent?"

She replied, "Why would he tell me?"

"This is a very annoying habit of the Americans to answer a question with a question."

Susan asked, "Why is it annoying?"

Colonel Mang was losing his patience with Susan, who truly could be irritating. He took a step toward her, and I took a step toward him. We all stopped taking steps and stood motionless, but ready.

Finally, Colonel Mang turned back toward me, lit another cigarette without offering one to the lady, and said to me, "So, you do not know Mr. Stanley."

"I do not."

"But you spoke to him in front of the Catholic cathedral in Ho Chi Minh City."

"Was that Bill Stanley?"

"You know it was, Mr. Brenner. Do not play games with me."

"I was introduced to Bill Stanley for the first time in front of the cathedral, we spoke for about three minutes, as you know, and we have not seen each other or spoken since."

"So you say. Why should I believe you? You lied to me about your duties during the war, you met a CIA agent on your second day in Ho Chi Minh City, you show too much interest in the hill people, you are vague about your itinerary, and you told me you were going alone to Nha Trang, but in fact you were not. You went with the girlfriend of a CIA agent. So how many other lies have you told me?"

"Two or three."

"Yes? What lies have you told me?"

"I think I told you how well run and prosperous Vietnam looks. In fact, it is neither. The people are miserable, and everyone I've met in the south hates Hanoi. There are more prostitutes and pimps in Saigon than when I was here, and you've treated the former soldiers of the Republic of Vietnam very badly, and I know you've desecrated their graves and reduced the survivors to near slavery, and as a former soldier, I find this dishonorable and offensive, and so should you. The Hanoi government has no legitimacy, and is not supported by the will of the people. Now, Colonel, you have the real truth, not what you say or believe is the truth."

Colonel Mang did not look at me. He looked off into the distance while he hyperventilated. He really had a strange look on his face, and his shoulders were heaving. I didn't know if he was going to faint, cry, pull his gun, ask me for asylum in America, or what. I was going to suggest the lotus position, but he seemed to be getting himself under control without it.

He took a deep breath and snapped out of his trance, or whatever. He cleared his throat and continued, as though he hadn't been on the verge of a psychotic episode. He asked me, in a matter-of-fact tone, "Mr. Brenner, the Immigration Police in Hue inform me that you took a bus from Nha Trang to Hue. Is that correct?"

Another question I didn't want to hear. I replied, "That's correct."

He mulled that over a moment, then said, "And you left Nha Trang in the early afternoon and arrived in Hue that evening, before midnight. Correct?"

"That's about right."

"I see." He pretended to be digesting this information, and a look of perplexity, almost worry, passed across his face, as if something was bothering him. I knew that look because most interrogators use it. Colonel Mang said, "The officer at the Hue Immigration police station said you told him you traveled alone. Is that correct?"

I realized that if these questions had been asked of Susan and me separately, we might have different answers. I replied, "I never said I traveled alone. In fact, he didn't ask me. But probably you asked him, and so like subordinates everywhere, he fabricated an answer for you."

He thought about that, then said, "I suppose, then, I must ask him again." He said to me, "So you and Miss Weber traveled together."

"Correct."

"By bus."

"Correct."

"And where did you stay when you arrived in Hue?"

"A mini-motel."

"Ah, yes. That was what I was told." He smiled and said to me, "The police officer was under the impression you spent the night with a prostitute." He looked at Susan, then back at me and said, "But he must have mistaken your description of your traveling companion."

I said, "The policeman in Hue, like Mr. Loc, needs to understand English better if they're going to question or eavesdrop on English-speaking people. Don't you agree?"

He probably did, but he said to me, "My English, I hope, is to your satisfaction. I understand English quite well, but I do not understand your answers."

"I understand them."

Colonel Mang smiled and said, "Let me ask you a simple question—what was the name of the mini-motel where you and Miss Weber spent the night?"

"I don't know. Do they have names?"

"They are usually named by their street address. Does that help you?"

"No."

He looked at Susan. "Can you recall the name of this motel?"

"No."

He kept looking at her and said, "I am rather surprised, Miss Weber, that you, who have been in Vietnam for three years, would go to such a place."

She replied, "Colonel, when you're tired, you sleep anywhere."

"Is that so?" He turned back to me and asked, "And did you go to the Century Riverside when you arrived in Hue to see if there was a room available for you?"

"No."

"And why not? You would have discovered, as I did, that there were rooms available."

I replied, "I'm on a budget. The mini-motel was very cheap."

He wasn't buying that at all, and I don't blame him. He said, "Mr. Brenner, you say you arrived in Hue Friday evening, and you never bothered to see if your hotel, or any other Western hotel, or even a guest house, had a room available for you and your traveling companion. Instead, you say you went from Hue bus station to a mini-motel frequented almost exclusively by prostitutes and their men, and you took a room there, but you do not remember the hotel. Then at 12:35 P.M. the next day, you register at the Century Riverside Hotel, alone, then approximately twenty minutes later, Miss Weber arrives and requests a room. Then, at some point, you meet in the lounge, and after a while, you retire to your rooms—or Mr. Brenner's room. Am I understanding this correctly?"

I replied, "You are."

"And yet, none of it makes any sense to me. Perhaps you can explain to me your actions."

This was clearly not going well, and it wasn't going to get any better. I said to Colonel Mang, "Colonel, Ms. Weber and I are having a clandestine affair. Do you understand?"

He kept staring at me.

I continued, "We're trying to avoid any possible confrontation with Mr. Stanley, which explains all of our actions."

Colonel Mang didn't think so. He said, "I am no less confused, Mr. Brenner, but let me continue." He looked at Susan and me again, then said, "You are a handsome couple. The sort of people who would not be easily forgotten. And so, I had the police in Nha Trang question the two bus drivers who drove the noon and one P.M.

buses. And neither of these drivers remembers a middle-aged Western couple of any description on their bus. In fact, aside from a few Western backpackers, both buses were filled only with Vietnamese." He paused. "It seemed odd to me that you would travel by bus."

I replied, "There was no other transportation available, and you know that. I was on the one P.M. bus from Nha Trang to Hue, and again, Colonel, someone has given you incorrect information."

"Yes? So much incorrect information. From different people." He looked at Susan and asked her, "And you, too, were on that bus?"

"That's right."

He thought awhile, or pretended to, then said, "Unfortunately, I believed this incorrect information from the bus drivers, that you were not on these buses, so I made further inquiries. I first inquired of Vidotour if either of you hired a car and driver, and they informed me that you had not. They keep very careful records, and so, of course, that is correct information. Then I began making inquiries of private tour operators." He looked at me and asked, "And do you know what I discovered?"

I didn't reply to the rhetorical question. In fact, I doubted if Mang had been able to contact any of those people during this holiday period.

Colonel Mang kept staring at me, and neither of us played a card. Finally, he said, "Nothing.

But we are still making inquiries in Nha Trang."

I said nothing.

He added, "I think, Mr. Brenner, that you and Miss Weber came to Hue via a private mini-bus, or more likely a private car and driver. I believe my instructions to you, Mr. Brenner, were clear. You were not to travel by private transportation."

I needed to respond to this and said, "Colonel, I think I've had enough of your questions, your suspicions, and your sarcasm. I don't know what the purpose of this is, but I'm going from Hue directly to Hanoi, and I'm making a formal complaint to my embassy, then I'm leaving the country. And when I return to Washington, I'm making a complaint directly to the State Department. Your behavior is unacceptable and unwarranted."

He didn't seem concerned about any of this; by now, he was certain he had something on me, and he seemed more confident. He said to me, "I think I will discover that you hired a car and driver to take you to Hue, and that you stopped some place for the night, and perhaps deviated from your direct route to Hue. And when I find that driver, I will question him about what you did, and who you saw or met with on your journey. Unless, of course, you would like to tell me now."

I didn't want to tell him I killed two policemen on the way, so I replied, "I have nothing further to say to you."

"Well, I have more things to say to you." He lit another cigarette and said, "The policeman you spoke to in Hue informed me that you were very uncooperative."

I didn't reply.

"He said you attempted to leave his office without permission."

I couldn't resist replying, "Not only did I attempt to leave his office, I did, and he didn't stop me."

Colonel Mang seemed a bit surprised. Clearly, his subordinates told the boss what they wanted to tell him. Oddly, I think he believed me and not them, which maybe wasn't so odd; in a police state, everyone is terrified of the truth.

He said to me, "I believe if you put yourself in my situation, you would see that my questions and suspicions are indeed warranted. There is a great deal of what you call circumstantial evidence to suggest that your purpose here is not tourism. And then we have the lies you told me, and which you now attempt to correct."

I replied, "I think, Colonel, other people have lied to you, or misled you, or made false assumptions. If I were a policeman, I'd go back and question everyone again, and I'd see if I was barking up the wrong tree. Biet?"

He turned to Susan, who said something to him in Vietnamese. He nodded and looked back at me. "Interesting expression. But I am not a dog."

I resisted a reply.

He said, "I had the impression from Mr. Stanley's faxes to Miss Weber at the Grand Hotel that your affair was not so clandestine."

I replied, "Which is why we're trying to avoid Mr. Stanley."

"Yes? Is the CIA station chief so stupid that you think you can avoid him by staying in a mini-motel for one night, then checking into a hotel that almost all Westerners use?" He added, "I may have believed you were trying to avoid Mr. Stanley if you had stayed for your entire time in Hue at the mini-motel where they do not ask for passports or visas."

"Right. We should have done that. Anything else?"

"Yes. How does your lady friend, Kay, know of your involvement with Miss Weber? And why is this lady friend warning you against this involvement?"

"Why don't you stop reading my mail?"

"It is my job to read your mail, Mr. Brenner. Answer my question."

This was an easy one, and despite my anger at Colonel Mang's snooping, I replied, "I faxed her from Nha Trang about my new romance, and I believe she's jealous. I assume you know something about women, Colonel, so you understand. Also, your question is another example of your barking up the wrong tree."

"Is it? Then let me ask you a question about

your fax response to Kay. You said, 'If you sleep with the enemy, you know where they are at night.'" He looked at Susan, then me, and asked, "So, is this lady here the enemy you referred to?"

I glanced at Susan, then looked back at Mang and replied, "It's an idiomatic expression. You should not take all the English you hear or read literally."

"Yes? Well, I thank you, Mr. Brenner, for that lesson."

"You're quite welcome. And stop reading my mail."

"I find it interesting. You also said in your response to Kay . . . let me try to recall . . ." He recited the last paragraph verbatim, "'The long shadows of the past do indeed still stretch from here to there, but the shadows in my mind and in my heart are fading, so if you don't hear from me for a long time, know that I have found what I was looking for, and that I have no personal regrets about this journey. My love to C.'"

I didn't look at Susan, but kept staring at Colonel Mang. I didn't mind too much that he was trying to stick me with a capital offense, but he was making my love life more difficult than it already was.

Colonel Mang asked, "Why would Kay not hear from you for a long time? And what is it that you found here that you were looking for?"

I took a deep breath and replied, "I have found inner peace and happiness."

"Yes? Where? At Khe Sanh? The A Shau Valley? Hue? Here?"

"You're upsetting my karma, Colonel. Change the subject."

"You do not like any of my subjects."

"Try again."

"Perhaps I should try at police headquarters in Hanoi."

"Fine. Let's go."

He didn't understand bluffing very well, and he seemed surprised. He cleared his throat and said, "In due time, Mr. Brenner."

I looked at my watch.

He said, "Am I keeping you from an appointment?"

"You're keeping me from my dinner."

He ignored that and asked Susan, "Are you married to another American?"

She replied, "Why don't you check my work visa application?"

"I did. You stated you were unmarried."

"Then there's your answer."

He added, "And there seems to be no evidence of a husband in your apartment." He smiled.

Susan stared at him. I mean, this is the lady who had a little fit when she realized someone had been in her hotel room in Nha Trang. Now she finds out that Colonel Mang has been through her apartment. She took a deep breath and said something to him in Vietnamese. It was a short sentence, in a soft voice, but whatever she said, Colonel Mang's face tightened like someone was sticking something up his ass. I had requested that the conversation be in English, but sometimes you need to use the native language to say, "Fuck you, asshole."

I looked at Colonel Mang, who was undoubtedly thinking ahead to a time when he could speak to us separately with the help of electric shocks to the genitals and breasts.

I was waiting for him to ask me about New Year's Eve at the Phams', or Sunday, New Year's Day, with Mr. Anh, but he wasn't asking, which worried me more than if he had. It occurred to me that if Colonel Mang were *very* clever, he'd be purposely giving me the impression he was barking up the wrong tree regarding the FULRO. In fact, he may know something about my real purpose here, though there was no way he could know—except if he'd arrested Mr. Anh.

I actually wanted him to ask me about Saturday and Sunday, but instead, he brought up a much worse subject. He looked directly at me and played his trump card. He said, "Eventually we will discover how you traveled from Nha Trang to Hue. We will also discover if you have any knowledge of an automobile accident that occurred on Highway One outside Nha Trang, in which two police officers were killed."

I looked him right in the eye and said, "Colonel, I don't know what the hell you're talking about. But you've accused me of everything from itinerary violations to sexual misdeeds, spying, being in contact with the FULRO, and now something about an automobile accident. This is outrageous. I won't stand here one more second and listen to this."

I took Susan's arm and walked away.

Colonel Mang shouted, "Stop! Do not take one more step."

I let go of Susan's arm and walked directly up to Colonel Mang, very close.

We looked into each other's eyes, and he said to me in a quiet voice, "I could shoot both of you right here and now, and throw your bodies into that moat for the dogs to eat."

"You could try. But you'd better be very fast with your gun if you're going to stand this close to me."

Colonel Mang took a step back, and I took a step toward him. He reached for his gun, and Susan shouted, "No!" She yelled something in Vietnamese, rushed toward us, and grabbed my arm, trying to pull me away from Mang.

I looked over Colonel Mang's shoulder and saw the two goons running across the field.

Colonel Mang took another step back, heard the sounds of running footsteps behind him, and motioned for the two men to stop, which they did.

He took another step back and said to both of us, "You have threatened an officer of the

Socialist Republic, and for that I could arrest you and have you imprisoned for ten years." He looked at Susan, "Correct?"

Susan replied, "You don't need an excuse or a charge, and you know it."

He looked at her and said, "You have been in this country for far too long, Miss Weber. It may be time for you to leave."

My sentiments exactly.

But Susan replied, "I'll leave when I'm ready to leave."

"You will leave when I have you expelled."

"Go ahead and try it."

He glared at her and said, "In fact, Miss Weber, it may be time for your whole company to leave."

She sort of smirked and said, "My company, Colonel, has more influence in Hanoi than you do."

Colonel Mang did not like this. I could almost see him pining for the days when a pistol shot in the head resolved annoying problems. But there was a new reality out there, and neither Colonel Mang nor I completely understood it.

Colonel Mang took a deep breath and said to Susan, "Hanoi is a long distance from Ho Chi Minh City. If you stay, Miss Weber, your pleasant life in your expensive apartment with your servants, and your illegal motorcycle, and your evenings at the Q-Bar will no longer be as pleas-

ant or peaceful." He smiled and added, "In fact,
I think you should stay in Vietnam."

"That's exactly what I'm going to do."

We had really pissed this guy off, and I knew
he had some parting words for me, which I
hoped were, "Mr. Brenner, your visa is canceled. Go home." Okay.

He turned to me, smiled wickedly, and said,
"Have a pleasant and safe journey to Hanoi. I
may see you there. But perhaps not."

"I plan to be there."

He looked again at Susan and said to her,
"Remove the film from your camera and give it
to me."

"I will not."

He motioned to the two men behind him,
and they came forward. Pushy and I made eye
contact, and he smiled.

I said to Susan, "Give him the film."

She hesitated, took the camera from her tote
bag, and instead of taking out the film, she
snapped a picture of Colonel Mang. This was
not a Kodak moment.

He shouted, "The film! Now!"

She opened the camera, ripped the partially
exposed film out, and threw it on the ground.

Pushy retrieved it, and he looked up at Susan
with an expression of surprise, bordering on
awe, as if to say, "You don't fuck with a colonel
in the MPS, lady. You nuts?"

Colonel Mang decided to break off the confrontation while he was ahead on points. He looked at me and said, "You and I, Mr. Brenner, survived many brutal battles here. It would be very ironic if you did not survive your vacation."

My thoughts exactly.

He turned and walked away across the desolate field with his two henchmen. Pushy turned his head toward us as he walked and made a cutting motion across his throat.

CHAPTER THIRTY-SIX

———★———

The sky was dark now, and we stood there in the cold wind

Finally, Susan spoke. "I'm shaking."

"It got cold."

"I'm shaking with fear, Paul."

I knew what she meant. "You did fine. Terrific, actually."

She lit a cigarette and her hand trembled, which it hadn't in the presence of Colonel Mang.

I said, "Let's roll."

We started walking toward the bridge.

Susan asked me, "Did you two get along a little better in Saigon?"

"A little, but not much."

She thought a moment, then said, "Weird, but I think he . . . he has some positive feelings toward you. Don't laugh."

I replied, "The cat has positive feelings toward the mouse. Lunch."

"No, it's more than that. There's something between you . . . like a game, a challenge, a respect—"

"We're bonding. But you know what? If I had a shovel and he had a machete, someone's head would wind up on a pole."

She didn't reply, and we kept walking across the dark acres of the former Citadel. Susan said, "We lost all those good shots of Chief John's village, Khe Sanh . . . everything. That *really* pisses me off."

"You should have asked for a confiscated property receipt."

"Now we have to come back and take more photos."

"Not in this lifetime, sweetheart."

"We'll be back here someday."

I didn't reply.

She said, "He was going for his gun, Paul."

"Don't piss off people who have guns."

"*You* pissed him off," she reminded me.

"I was trying to bond with him. It came out wrong."

She ignored that and said, "This makes the rest of the trip more difficult."

"It makes it more challenging."

We crossed the small bridge over the moat and headed back through the paths of the village toward the road.

There were electric lights in the houses that we passed, and I could smell the distinctive odor of charcoal in the cool, humid air. This was the smell I most remembered at twilight in the winter of 1968.

Susan said to me, "Sorry I didn't tell you about Bill sooner."

I replied, "It wasn't your place to tell me." I
smiled and said, "So I need a name, and I use
the name of the CIA station chief. Nice going,
Brenner."

She held her cigarette between her middle
fingers, Viet style, and said in a Vietnamese accent, "So, Mr. Brenner, you have made contact
with the hill people. Yes? And Miss Weber in-
forms me you are going to organize them into
an army. Yes? And you will own the hills. Yes?"

"Not funny. Hey, do you think Mr. Loc is waiting for us?"

"I very much doubt that."

We kept walking through the dark village,
and at night it was difficult to find the main path
from the road where Mr. Loc had left us. I could
smell fish cooking and rice steaming in the humid air.

We came to the road, and I said, "Mr. Loc did
not wait for us. Too bad. I wanted to break his
neck. How do we get back to Hue?"

"I don't know. You want to stay in Quang Tri
City?"

"There is no Quang Tri City," I said.

"Maybe there's a guest house. Or I'll bet we
could stay in any one of these houses for a few
dollars."

"They'd have to pay *me*. Let's get on the
highway."

We walked toward Highway One over a kilometer away. I said, "That bastard left us here in the middle of nowhere."

We got to the highway, but there weren't any vehicles in sight, and it was two days into the new moon, so it was pitch dark.

Susan looked around, then said, "The buses go up and down Highway One until maybe midnight. I'll go check with a local. You stay here and flag down a bus, if one comes along. They stop if you flag them down."

Susan went into the closest hootch, about thirty meters down the road, and I waited.

I thought about the day and realized I'd done a five-month tour of combat duty in an afternoon. I may have wanted to linger awhile in the A Shau or Khe Sanh, but maybe enough was enough. I knew I'd never be back.

I thought also about all the stuff I'd filled Susan's head with and decided that that, too, was enough.

Susan came back up the road and said, "We're invited for dinner and to stay overnight." She added, "We missed cocktails."

"What's for dinner?"

"Rice."

"Long grain or sticky?"

"Sticky. There will be a bus along within half an hour. It's a local."

"When does it get to Hue?"

"When it gets there."

"Did you have fun today?"

"Paul, I had an incredible day, and I truly thank you. The question is, How are you?"

"I'm fine. When I'm not fine, I'll let you know."

She lit a cigarette. "This war . . . that war was unimaginable. I can't even begin to comprehend how you and the others lived like that for a whole year."

Not everyone lived the whole year, but I didn't say that.

We stood silently on the blacktop of Highway One and waited for headlights going south.

Susan asked, "What if an army patrol comes by? Do we duck out, or just stand here?"

"Depends on the mood I'm in."

"Well, we're waiting to flag down the Hue bus. Ten-dollar fine."

"This place sucks."

Susan replied, "The people are mostly nice. That family I just spoke to practically begged me to stay for dinner."

"Peasants are nice. Cops, politicians, and soldiers suck."

"You're a cop *and* a soldier. You're nice."

"Sometimes." I said, "Colonel Mang wants to kick you out. Why don't you go?"

"Where am I going to?"

"Lenox, Massachusetts."

"Why?"

"Why not?"

She asked me, "Why don't you go back to Boston instead of living in Virginia?"

"There's nothing for me in Boston."

"What's in Virginia?"

"Nothing."

She stared at the glow of her cigarette awhile, then asked, "Why don't we go some-place together?"

"You have to quit smoking."

"Can I have one after sex?"

"That's still half a pack a day."

She laughed. "Deal."

The headlights of a big vehicle approached from the north, and I could see the lit windows of a bus. I stood out on the deserted highway and waved.

The bus stopped, the door opened, and we got on. I said to the driver, "Hue."

He looked at Susan and me with curiosity and said, "One dollar."

Best deal in town, so I gave him two, and he smiled.

The bus was half empty, and we found two seats together. The seats were wood, and the bus was old, maybe French. The passengers were looking at us. I guess we didn't look like bus people.

The bus continued south down the dark highway and stopped in every little village, and whenever someone flagged it down. People got on and people got off. Susan was happy to be on a smoking bus, which was one hundred percent of the bus fleet. She held my hand and looked out the window at the black, desolate terrain.

There was not one major town between the dead city of Quang Tri and the resurrected city of Hue. But at some point, the countryside started to look better, from the little we could see—houses, lights, rice paddies—and I had the feeling we'd passed out of Quang Tri Province and into the province of Hue.

I thought about Quang Tri. I would've liked to have seen my old base camp, Landing Zone Sharon, or the old French fort named Landing Zone Betty. But those places where I'd spent most of a year existed now only in my mind, and in a few faded photographs. It was strange to feel any nostalgia for a war zone, but those places—the base camps, the vendor stalls, the whorehouses and massage parlors, the hospital where we'd donated food and medicine, the Buddhist and Catholic schools where we'd given paper and pens from our monthly allotment, the church where we'd befriended the old Viet priest and the nun—were all gone now, obliterated from the earth and from the memories of everyone except the oldest of us.

Maybe I'd waited too long to return. Maybe I should have come back before so many of the visible and psychological scars had healed, before most of that wartime generation had died or grown too old. I may have seen something different here ten or fifteen years ago; more rubble, and more amputees, and more poverty, to be sure. But also some of the old Vietnam, before the DMZ tour buses and Cong World, and backpackers, and Japanese and American businesspeople.

But life goes on, things get better—Quang Tri Province notwithstanding—and one generation passes away, and another is born.

I said, "Sorry if I upset your pleasant life here."

"It wasn't that pleasant. I asked for a little excitement, and I got it. I asked about the war, and you told me."

"I'm done with that."

The bus continued on, and we didn't speak for some time, then I asked her, "How are we getting up country tomorrow?"

"Elephant."

"How many elephants?"

"Three. One for you, one for me, and one for my clothes."

I smiled.

She asked me, "Do you think Colonel Mang will be following us?"

"I'll see that he isn't." I added, "You're leaving the gun here."

She didn't reply.

We retreated into our separate thoughts as

the old bus chugged on over the bad road. Finally, Susan said, "I'm not upset about that fax."

"Good. Which fax?"

"The one where you said, 'Sleeping with the enemy,' and 'Love to C.'"

I didn't reply.

She changed the subject and said, "When Colonel Mang mentioned the police car accident, my heart stopped."

Again, I didn't reply.

She said, "What if he finds Mr. Cam or Mr. Thuc?"

I replied, honestly, "Then we've got a big problem."

"Paul, I'm frightened."

I didn't reply.

"Maybe we should get out of the country before we get charged with murder."

"That's a good idea. You should fly to Saigon tomorrow and get out."

"And you?"

"I need to push on. I'm not available to Colonel Mang after I head up country tomorrow. Then when I get to Hanoi, I'll call a guy in the embassy and have him get me inside. After that, it's up to Washington and Hanoi to cut a deal to get me home." I added, "I hope it costs Washington at least a billion in foreign aid."

"This isn't funny."

"Susan, go home. Fly to Saigon and catch the first plane out."

"I will if you will."

"I can't."

She said, "Your Vietnam luck has run out, Paul."

I didn't reply.

I thought about our encounter with Colonel Mang in the desolate ruins of the Quang Tri Citadel, and I recalled the South Vietnamese colonel, probably dead now or re-educated, who had pinned the medal on me. Two very different occasions, but the same place. Actually, it wasn't the same place; time and war had changed that place from a field of honor to a wasteland so crowded with ghosts that I swear I could feel their cold breaths on my face.

The bus continued on toward Hue.

Susan, coming out of her thoughts, said, "Plus, he was insulting. He practically accused me of being a slut."

"You should have slapped him. Hey, what did you say to him about searching your apartment?"

She hesitated, then replied, "Well, I asked him if he masturbated while he was searching my underwear drawer."

"Are you crazy?"

"I felt violated. I was angry."

"Anger, Ms. Weber, is a luxury you can't afford here."

"Maybe I shouldn't have said that. Notice, however, he didn't deny it."

I laughed. But it wasn't funny. Colonel Mang hadn't thought so, either. He was probably in the Hue police station by now testing his electrodes.

An hour after we left Quang Tri City, the bus came into the northern end of Hue, and stopped at the An Hoa bus station, just outside the walls of the Citadel. This seemed to be the last stop, so we got off. A taxi took us to the Century Riverside Hotel.

There were no faxes or other messages for us at the front desk, making me believe that everyone in Saigon and Washington had the utmost confidence in my ability to carry out the mission; or maybe they were all just fed up with Susan and me. In either case, no news is good news.

We hit the bar before the bathrooms, showing where our priorities lay.

We hadn't had anything to eat since breakfast, but strangely I had no appetite for anything but Scotch whiskey. Susan, too, drank dinner.

At about 10 P.M., we retired to my suite and sat on the terrace with beers from the mini-bar and watched the city and the river through the mist.

She said to me, "In Saigon, I told you that for people of my generation, Vietnam was a country, not a war. Do you remember that?"

"I do. Pissed me off."

"I can see now why it would. Well, I hope I've shown you the country as well as you've shown me the war."

"You have. I learned some things."

"Me, too. And did you work through some things?"

"Maybe. I won't really know until I'm home for a while."

Dark storm clouds had rolled in from the north, and it began to rain. A flash of lightning lit up the city and the river, and the bolt crackled to the earth, followed by the distant sound of rolling thunder, like an artillery barrage.

The rain blew in on the terrace but we sat there drinking, and within a few minutes, we were soaking wet and cold.

It was easy to imagine it was the winter of 1968 again; the Tet Offensive was raging, and to the north of here, the city of Quang Tri lay burning across the flooded rice paddies, and we were dug into night positions, into the mud, and we waited for the retreating enemy army trying to reach the hills behind us, pursued by the American and South Vietnamese troops. Hammer and anvil, it was called. We were the anvil, the pursuing troops were the hammer, and the poor bastards in between were hamburger meat.

I may have seen Tran Van Vinh that night

and may have fired a burst of rounds at him. I would have to ask him, when I saw him, how he'd escaped from the cauldron of the embattled city.

Susan asked me, "Wet enough?"

"Not yet."

"Where are you now?"

"In a foxhole, outside Quang Tri City. It's raining, and the artillery is firing."

"How long do you need to be there?"

"Until I'm ordered to leave."

She stood. "Well, when you get ready to make love, not war, I'll be waiting." She tousled my wet hair and went inside.

I sat in the rain for another few minutes, did my penance, and went inside.

Susan was in the shower, and I got undressed and joined her.

We made love in the shower, then went to bed.

Outside, the thunder clapped and the lightning lit up the dark room.

I slept fitfully, and the lightning and thunder provided the background for my bad dreams of battle, and I was aware of a cold sweat on my face, and a trembling in my body. I kept reaching for my rifle, but I couldn't find it. I knew none of this was real, but my body reacted as if it were, and I dreamed that I'd been knocked unconscious by an explosion, and when I awoke, I was being flown to a hospital ship, the USS *Sanctuary*, in a very quiet helicopter.

I opened my eyes.

I sat up in bed with the feeling that something black and heavy had been lifted off my heart.

CHAPTER THIRTY-SEVEN

───★───

I looked at the digital clock on the nightstand. It said 4:32, or, as we say in the army, Oh-dark-thirty. I could hear rain, but not thunder. I turned toward Susan, but she wasn't in bed.

I got out of bed and checked the bathroom, but she wasn't there. My thrashing around might have woken her, so I went into the sitting room of the suite and checked the couch, but she wasn't there either.

I picked up the telephone and dialed her room. As the phone rang, I pulled it toward the terrace, but she wasn't on the terrace, and she wasn't answering the telephone.

I went back to the bedroom to get dressed so I could go to her room, or to the garden out back.

As I was dressing, I heard the door open in the sitting room. I went into the room as she turned on a lamp. She was dressed in jeans and a black sweater, and she was wearing a black quilted jacket, which I hadn't seen before. She was also carrying her backpack and some other items in a large plastic bag, which she threw on the couch.

I said, "Going somewhere?"

"Going up country."

"Are the elephants watered and fed?"

"They are."

"And you left the gun in the garden?"

"I did."

"Swear?"

"Swear." She said, "We need to check out by five-thirty and meet someone."

"Who and where?"

"Are you showered?"

"No." I yawned. "Why should I be?"

"Go ahead and shower. Look, I bought you a backpack when I went shopping Sunday, and this leather jacket, and two rubber rain ponchos, plus some other stuff for the road. You need to pack light and ditch your luggage and dress clothes."

I moved toward the couch and said, "How will anyone know I'm an American without my blue blazer?"

"That's the point. Look." She buttoned her quilted jacket, put on a pair of biker goggles, tied a Montagnard scarf around her neck and face, and put on a black fur-trimmed leather hat with earflaps. "Voilà."

"What are you supposed to be?"

"A Montagnard."

"What tribe?"

"I've seen pictures of them in newspapers and magazines and on TV. This is how they dress in the highlands and the hill country when they're riding their motorcycles in the winter."

"Is that a fact?"

"Yes. And as you know, they're a little heavier and stockier than the Viets, so we should be able to pass as Montagnards from a distance."

"What distance? Ten miles?"

She added, "Also, there are a number of Amerasians left over from your visit here, and many of them live in the hills . . . they're sort of outcasts."

I said, "There won't be any Amerasians on the other side of the DMZ; I never got that far."

She said, "Well, then north of the DMZ we're Montagnards. Point is, you want to blend in. From a distance."

I didn't reply.

She took a dark brown leather jacket from the plastic bag and handed it to me. She said, "I bought you the biggest one I could find. Try it on."

I tried it on, and I was able to get into it, but it was tight, and barely reached my waist.

Susan said, "You look sexy in leather."

"Thank you. I assume we're going by motorcycle."

She looked at me and said, "I can't think of another way. Can you?"

"Yes. Four-wheel drive and a driver. I'm going to check out the private tour companies today—Slicky Boy Tours, Hue office. I've got some days to get to where I'm going, so I'm not pressed."

She shook her head and said, "You don't want a third party involved. Colonel Mang will be all over this town interrogating private tour operators, if he hasn't already."

"Well . . . let's go to another town to hire a car and driver. Or we can just ask any guy in a four-wheel drive. Any Nguyen will drive us to Dien Bien Phu for three hundred bucks."

Susan replied, "That may be true, but my idea is better and doesn't involve a third party, and gives us complete control of the agenda."

She was right, up to a point. Transportation in this country was a matter of making the least bad choice. I asked her, "Where did you get a motorcycle?"

"Go shower. I'll start packing for you."

I turned, went back into the bedroom, peeled off my clothes, and went into the bathroom. I tried to remember when I'd given Susan control over this mission.

Through the bathroom door, I could hear her rummaging around in the bedroom. I called out, "Can I have one blazer for Hanoi?"

"It's a small backpack."

I shaved, showered, and took my malaria pill.

I came out of the bathroom wearing a towel, and Susan had my suitcase and overnight bag on the bed, plus a dark green backpack. My clothes were strewn on the sheets. I said, "I'll do that."

I spent the next ten minutes putting the bare necessities in the backpack; everything that I was going to ditch, I put into the suitcase and overnight bag.

She saw me packing my docksiders and Ho Chi Minh sandals and said, "Just wear your running shoes. You have too many pairs of underwear. Why don't men wash underwear when they travel?"

Now I remembered why I wasn't married. I said, "It's easier to throw them out. Okay, how's that?"

She rolled up a rain poncho, pushed it in my backpack, and strapped it shut. "Good. That's it. You want to get dressed?"

I took off the towel and put on the outfit I'd kept aside—athletic socks, one pair of underwear, jeans, a polo shirt, and my black running shoes. I slipped my passport and visa into my wallet and put that into a little waterproof pouch that Susan had bought. I said, "Where'd you go for this stuff? L. L. Bean?"

"I went to the central market. They have everything."

We gathered her quilted jacket and my leather jacket, plus the two hats, two pairs of leather gloves, and a bunch of Montagnard scarves, and stuffed them in the plastic bag so no one downstairs could see and remember them. I put my camera in a plastic laundry bag along with my exposed and unexposed film and shoved it in a side pouch of my backpack. This reminded me too much of 1968.

Susan said to me, "I've got my camera, so we can ditch one to save space."

I knew I'd have to photograph Tran Van Vinh's souvenirs if he wouldn't sell them to me, and I'd definitely have to photograph Mr. Vinh himself, or his grave. Also, I needed to photograph his house and locale, so if he wasn't dead, someone could come by later, find him, and kill him. I said to Susan, "I need a camera for this job, so we'll take two to play it safe."

"Okay."

I asked her, "Is all your exposed film accounted for, including the roll Colonel Mang confiscated?"

She nodded. "I never had the film out of my sight."

"Good." I asked her, "You have that snow globe?"

She didn't reply for a second, then said, "No. It's missing again."

"Why didn't you tell me?"

"What difference does it make?" She forced a smile and said, "I can pick it up at the Metropole in Hanoi."

I replied, "You can be sure that we're not going to the Metropole when we get to Hanoi."

She informed me, "It's impossible to find a no-questions-asked place to stay in Hanoi. They report every guest to the police. It's not South Vietnam."

"We'll deal with that when we get there. Ready?"

"Ready."

We carried everything down to the lobby and walked to the front desk. We checked out, and I noticed on my bill a hundred-dollar charge for the Vidotour car and driver, which wouldn't have been unreasonable, except that the driver was a secret policeman, who'd left us stranded in the next province. But I didn't want to quibble over this with the clerk.

Susan asked the clerk, a young man named Mr. Tin, "Can you check to see if we have any messages?"

I said to him, "I'm also expecting a small parcel, a book, which someone was to deliver this morning."

"Let me look." He went to the key box and took out a few notes, then went into the back room.

Susan asked, "What book?"

"My Lonely Planet Guide." I explained it to her and she didn't comment.

Mr. Tin returned with a fax message, and a manila envelope that was not thick enough to be a book. He said to me, "Here is a fax for you, Mr. Brenner, and this envelope is for the lady."

I asked, "And no book?"

"Sorry, sir."

I moved away from the desk and looked at my watch. It was only 5:35 and still dark outside the lobby doors. I asked Susan, "What's the latest we can leave here?"

"Now."

I thought a moment. I had no way of knowing if Mr. Anh had been picked up by the police after our rendezvous. Therefore, I had no idea if Colonel Mang had already applied electric shocks to Mr. Anh and learned of my destination.

Susan said, "Sorry about the early departure, but I had no choice. Let's be optimistic that the book would have been here in a few hours."

"Yeah . . . okay. We'll try to call here later." I opened my fax envelope and read the short message: Dear Paul, Just a quick note to say have a good journey to Hanoi. Heard from friends in Saigon that all went well in Hue. C is looking forward to seeing you in Honolulu. God bless. Love, Kay. P.S. Please reply.

I handed the fax to Susan, who read it and handed it back without comment. I said, "It would seem that my contact here in Hue did contact Saigon, and said the rendezvous came off okay. But I still don't know if this man got picked up later."

I went to the desk, got a fax form, and wrote: Karl, replying to your fax—meeting in Hue was successful, as you know. Went to A Shau, Khe Sanh, and Quang Tri City Monday. Very moving. You need to come back,

Colonel. Leaving now by private transportation to find T-V-V. Ms. W will accompany me. She has been an invaluable asset, translator, guide, and companion. Remember that, whatever happens. Ran into Colonel M in Quang Tri. He seems to suspect I'm here to start a Montagnard insurrection. Look up FULRO, if you don't know about it. Mang to meet me in Hanoi, or sooner, so Metropole is out. I'll try to contact Mr. E in USEmb in Hanoi on my arrival. I'm still visualizing success. My love to C. I hesitated, then wrote: For a variety of reasons, not the least of which is my possible extended stay here, do not have C make journey to Hawaii. I'll see her in the States. See you wherever and whenever. I added: I gave this my best shot, Karl, but I feel somewhat used. Biet? I signed it Paul Brenner, Chief Warrant Officer, retired.

I gave Mr. Tin two dollars and said, "Let's fax this now."

"Sorry, sir, the fax machine—"

"It's six o'clock in the morning, pal. The fax machine is not busy." I came around the counter and helped Mr. Tin into the back room where the fax machine was. I also helped him dial and within a few seconds, the fax was sent. I borrowed matches from Mr. Tin, emptied a trash can on the floor, and burned the fax in the can. I looked at Mr. Tin, who didn't seem happy with me in his space. I said to him, "Mr. Tin, I'm going to call you later. I want to know if that book arrived for me. Biet?"

He nodded.

I patted him hard on the shoulder, and he stumbled sideways. "Don't disappear."

I left the back room, came around the counter, and walked over to where Susan was sitting on a couch. She had her envelope open, and I could see photographs on the coffee table and on her lap.

I sat next to her and said, "Okay, I got the fax off, and I told Mr. Tin I'd call later about . . ." I looked at the photographs lying on the coffee table. I picked one up. It was a color photograph of a beach, taken from a high elevation on the land side of the beach. It took me a second to recognize the beach at Pyramide Island, and the photo had been taken from the pyramid rocks where the bird's nest collectors had been climbing.

I picked up the photograph that had first caught my eye and saw it was a grainy image of Susan walking out of the water, obviously taken with a telephoto lens. It was a full frontal nude and there I was in the background, still in the water.

I looked at a few other photos—Susan and me embracing in the water, Susan talking to the Swedish couple, and me lying facedown in the sand while Susan sat on my butt. I put the pictures down and looked at her. She had a faraway look on her face, staring out at nothing.

I said, "I'm going to kill that son of a bitch."

She didn't reply or move.

"Susan? Look at me."

She took a deep breath, then another, and said, "It's okay. I'm okay."

"All right . . ." I gathered up the photos and put them in the envelope. I stood. "Ready to go?"

She nodded, but didn't stand. She said softly, "That bastard."

"He's an asshole," I agreed. "A sneaky, perverted, sadistic, sick little shit."

She didn't reply.

"Okay, let's go." I took her arm and lifted her up. She stood motionless for a second then said, "That bastard . . . why did he do that?"

"It doesn't matter."

She looked at me and said, "He could mail those pictures to Bill."

Actually, the pictures were already on the way, and not just to Bill.

Susan said, "And my office . . ."

"Let's go." I took her arm, but she wasn't moving.

She said, "And . . . my friends here . . . my family . . . the police have my home address in Lenox . . . my office in New York . . ."

"We'll deal with that later."

She looked at me and said, "They only have your home address . . . they've got a police file on me . . . every letter I've ever sent from here has the address recorded before it goes out . . ."

"But you used the company pouch to New York for mail. Correct?"

"I sent Christmas cards directly from the GPO . . ." She tried to smile. "I wanted a Vietnamese stamp on them . . . I *knew* I shouldn't have done that . . ." She looked at me and asked, "Do you think he'd send those photos to people in the States?"

"Look, Susan, not to make light of it, but you were on a nude beach. Not a big deal. Okay? You weren't photographed in a sexual act."

She gave me an angry look. "Paul, I don't want my family, friends, and co-workers to see pictures of me naked."

"We'll deal with it later. We need to get out of here. Out of Vietnam. Alive. *Then* you can worry about the pictures."

She nodded. "Okay. Let's go."

We gathered our luggage and headed for the door. I said to the doorman, "We need a taxi for Hue–Phu Bai Airport."

He motioned out at the darkness and said, "Airplane not go. No light Hue–Phu Bai. Sun. Airplane go." He smiled. "You go have breakfast."

"I don't want breakfast, sport. I want a taxi. Bay gio. Maintenant. Now."

Susan said something to him, and he smiled, nodded, and went outside.

She said to me, "I told him you were a compulsive, anal-retentive, worrywart." She smiled.

I smiled in return. She was looking better. I said, "What's the word for anal-retentive?"

"Asshole."

The doorman came back and helped us with our bags. A taxi pulled up the circular driveway, we got in, and off we went.

The rain had turned into a light drizzle, and the road glistened. The taxi headed toward Hung Vuong Street, toward Highway One and the airport. She looked out the rear window and said, "I don't see anyone behind us."

"Good. Where are we going?"

"I don't know. I thought you knew."

I put my arm around her and kissed her on the cheek. I said, "I love you."

She smiled and replied, "So will about a hundred more men in a few days."

"The mail here is slow."

She took my hand and said, "Don't you feel violated?"

"That's what Mang wants us to feel. I'm not playing into that."

"But you're a guy. It's not the same."

I didn't want to return to that subject, so I asked again, "Where are we going?"

"Close."

We kept heading south on Hung Vuong Street, through the New City and toward Highway One. Susan said something to the driver, and he slowed down and made a U-turn on the nearly deserted street. As we headed back the way we'd come, I didn't see any other vehicles doing the same thing.

We continued north, and Hung Vuong crossed the Perfume River at the Trang Tien Bridge, near the floating restaurant. I could see the Dong Ba market on the opposite bank, where Mr. Anh and I ate peanuts and talked.

The taxi stopped at a bus terminal that also said Dong Ba, and Susan and I got out, got our luggage, and I paid the driver.

I said, "Are we going by bus?"

"No. But the terminal is open now, and that's what the driver will remember. We have to walk to Dong Ba market, which is also open at this hour."

We put our backpacks on, and I wheeled my suitcase down the road. Susan carried my overnight bag. I said, "I'm going along with this because you had some training in these things at Langley, and you know this country. So of course you know what you're doing."

"I know what I'm doing."

We were in the Dong Ba market within five minutes, and it was already open in the predawn darkness; people who were probably restauranteurs were haggling over the price of strange-looking fish and slabs of meat.

A man stood under a naked light bulb hanging from a wire and said in English, "You come see number one fruit."

I ignored him, but Susan followed him around to the back of a big produce stall. I followed.

The man opened a rickety door in the back of the stall, and Susan entered. The man stood at the door and said to me, "Come. Quickly."

I went through the door and he closed it. We were in a long narrow room, lit by a few light bulbs. The room smelled of fruit and damp earth.

Susan and the man spoke in Vietnamese, then Susan said to me, "Paul, you remember Mr. Uyen from dinner at the Pham house."

Indeed I did. To show him I really remembered him, I said in Vietnamese, "Sat Cong."

He smiled and nodded enthusiastically. "Yes. Sat Cong. Sat Cong."

I said to Susan, "The kiwis look good."

She replied, "Mr. Uyen has offered to help us."

I looked at Mr. Uyen and said, "Do you understand that we are under surveillance by the Ministry of Public Security, and they may have seen us talking to you and your family after mass, and that they may have followed us to your home? Do you understand all that?"

His English wasn't so good, but he understood every last word. He nodded slowly and said to me, "I do not care if I die."

"Well, Mr. Uyen, I care if *I* die."

"I no care."

I didn't think he understood that *I* cared if *I* died. In any case, I said to him, "If police arrest me with motorcycle, they find you. License plate. Biet?"

He replied to Susan, who said to me, "The plate was taken from a motorcycle that was destroyed in an accident."

I said to Susan, "Okay, but if they trace the motorcycle to him, tell him we'll tell the police we stole it from him. Okay? And tell him we'll drop it in a lake or something when we're done with it."

She told him, and he replied in Vietnamese to Susan, who said to me, "He says he hates the Communists, and he is willing to become one who suffers . . . a martyr . . . for his faith."

I looked at Mr. Uyen and asked, "And your family?"

He replied, "All same."

It's hard arguing with people who are looking for martyrdom, but at least I tried.

It occurred to me, too, that Mr. Uyen was probably motivated not only by his faith, but also by his hatred for what happened in 1968 and since then. Mr. Anh, too, was not completely motivated by ideals, such as freedom and democracy; he was motivated by the same hate as Mr. Uyen—they'd both had family members murdered. You can forgive battlefield deaths, but you don't forget cold-blooded murder.

I said, "Okay, as long as everybody here knows the consequences."

In the dim light, I saw a large tarp draped over what must be the motorcycle.

Mr. Uyen saw me looking at it and walked to it, and tore off the tarp.

Sitting there on the earth floor of the narrow room was a huge black motorcycle of a make that I couldn't identify.

I went over to it and put my hand on the big leather saddle. On the molded fiberglass fairing it said BMW and under that Paris-Dakar. I wasn't going to either of those places, though Paris sounded good. I said to Mr. Uyen, "I've never seen this model."

He said, "Good motorcycle. You go to mountain, to big . . . road . . ." He looked at Susan and tried it in Vietnamese.

She listened, then said to me, "It's a BMW Paris-Dakar model, probably named after the race of the same name—"

"Dakar is in West Africa. Does this thing float?"

"I don't know, Paul. Listen. It's got a 980cc engine, and it holds forty-five liters of fuel, and it has a two-liter reserve, and the range is about five hundred to five hundred and fifty kilometers. Mr. Uyen says it's excellent for mud, cross-country, and the open road. That's what it's made for."

I replied, "I guess so if you can go from Paris to West Africa with it." I looked at the big tank, which rode high on the frame so it couldn't be punctured from the ground. With a range of over five hundred kilometers, we might only have to refuel once during the 900 kilometer trip to Dien Bien Phu. I knelt and checked out the tires, which were big, about eighteen inches, and they had good tread.

Susan was talking to Mr. Uyen, then said to me, "He says it's very fast and . . . I think he means maneuverable . . . and it has not bumps. I guess that means it's an easy ride. My biker vocabulary is a little thin."

I turned to Mr. Uyen and asked, "How much?"

He shook his head. "Free."

I hadn't heard that word in any context since I'd stepped off the plane at Tan Son Nhat, and I almost fainted. I said to Mr. Uyen, "We cannot give motorcycle back to you. One way. Bye-bye. Di di."

He was nodding, but I didn't know if I'd made myself clear.

Susan said, "I already told him that. He understands."

"Really? Where and when did you speak to him?"

"During dinner I mentioned I had a problem, and I was invited to breakfast Sunday morning. You were, too, but you had appointments."

I seemed to recall she'd said she slept until noon. I said, "So this is a done deal?"

"Only if you want it."

I thought about that and said to Susan in cryptic English, "Aside from my concerns that other people might be on to us, and on to these people, it's a thousand klicks to you-know-where. That's a lot of saddle sores and mud. You up for that?"

She said something to Mr. Uyen, and he laughed hard.

"What's so funny?"

She said to me, "I told Mr. Uyen you wanted to know if he has an elephant instead."

I wasn't amused.

Mr. Uyen was patting the saddle and said, "Good motorcycle. Buy from French man. He . . ." He spoke to Susan.

She said to me, "There was a cross-country race here last year. Hanoi to Hue."

"Did the Frenchman win?"

Susan smiled and asked Mr. Uyen. He replied, and she said to me, "He came in second."

"Let's find the bike that came in first."

She was getting impatient with me. "Paul. Yes or no?"

Well, the price was right, so I jumped on the bike and said, "Take me through this."

Mr. Uyen gave Susan and me a quick and confusing lesson on how to drive a BMW Paris-Dakar motorcycle. I had the impression Mr. Uyen didn't really know how to drive this machine, or he drove it like all Vietnamese drive everything—by trial and error, with a lot of horn honking.

I got off the bike. "Full tank?" I patted the tank.

Mr. Uyen nodded.

"Okay . . ." I looked at Susan. "Okay?"

She nodded.

We opened the plastic bag and put on our Montagnard biker costumes: leather jacket for me, quilted jacket for Susan, fur-trimmed leather hats, and Montagnard scarves. Mr. Uyen was amused.

We emptied our backpacks into the big saddlebags and stuffed the collapsed packs on top.

I said to Mr. Uyen, "You keep suitcase and overnight bag. Okay? Take care of my blue blazers."

He nodded, then took a map from a zippered leather pouch mounted on the fiberglass fairing and gave it to me. He said, "Vietnam."

"You got one of Paris?"

"Where you go?"

"To kill Commies."

"Good. Where you go?"

"Dalat."

"Okay. Good. Go safe."

"Thank you." I took out my wallet and handed him the last two hundred dollars I had, which was not a bad price for an expensive Beemer.

He shook his head.

Susan said, "He really wants to give us the motorcycle."

"Okay." I said to Mr. Uyen, "Thank you."

He bowed, then looked around at his stack of fruit, chose a bunch of bananas and stuffed them into the Beemer's saddlebags, then he took two liters of bottled water and lay them on top of the bananas. He motioned me to wheel the bike to the door, which I did.

Mr. Uyen went to the door, opened it a crack, and peeked out. He looked at us and nodded.

I zippered my leather jacket, wrapped the dark scarf around my neck, and put on the tinted goggles, then pulled on the leather gloves, which were tight.

Susan was doing the same, and we looked at each other. It was funny, but it wasn't funny. She asked me, "Are you driving that thing, or flying it?"

"This was *not* my idea."

Susan and Mr. Uyen exchanged Happy New Year greetings and bows. I shook hands with Mr. Uyen and said, "Thank you, again. You are a good man."

He looked at me and in perfect English said, "God bless you and God bless Miss Susan and God bless your journey."

I said, "And you be careful."

He nodded and opened the door.

I wheeled the heavy bike out into the dark marketplace with Susan right behind me. I glanced back at Mr. Uyen, but the door was closed.

Susan said, "Keep wheeling the bike to the road over there."

I wheeled the bike through the dimly lit marketplace. The drizzle had stopped, replaced by a cold river mist. A few people glanced at us, but my own mother wouldn't have recognized me, so it didn't matter.

Susan said, "Okay, I think the best way out of here is along the river road to the left. Ready?"

I jumped on the bike and started the engine. The roar sounded terrific and I could feel the power pulsating through the frame. I revved the engine and glanced at the gauges, which all seemed to be working. I flipped on the lights as Susan climbed on behind me. I kicked the bike into first gear, and off we went up a grassy slope to the river road.

I drove along the embankment with the Perfume River to our left and the towering walls of the Hue Citadel to our right. The bike had lots of power, even with two people on it. This could be fun. Then again, maybe not.

There wasn't much traffic, so I was able to learn how to drive this big machine without killing us or anyone else.

We passed the two river bridges, then passed by the flag tower, then a few minutes later, the south wall of the Citadel ended, and Susan called out, "Turn right."

I turned onto a road that paralleled the west wall of the Citadel and which ran north along the railroad track. The two-kilometer-long wall of the Citadel ended, and we crossed over the wide moat that surrounded the walls. The road got wider, and I realized I was on Highway One.

Susan tapped me, and I glanced over my shoulder at her. She had her arm out, and I looked to where she was pointing. Receding in the distance were the Citadel walls within which lay the imperial city of Hue, the capital of the emperors, the flower of Vietnamese cities, that had died in 1968, and was born again on the bones of its people.

I thought of Mr. Anh, and his father, the army captain, and of Mr. Uyen and the Pham family, and the sixteen-sided restaurant where Susan and I had dinner in the rain, and Tet Eve and the Perfume River, and the cathedral, and the holiday lights and the sky rockets. The Year of the Ox.

Susan wrapped her arms around me, put her mouth to my ear and said, "I always feel sad when I leave a place where I had a good experience."

I nodded.

The sky was brightening in the east, and Highway One, the Street Without Joy, on which we'd traveled to Quang Tri and back, and hell and back, was filled with morning traffic.

I looked at the foothills in the distance as they caught the first light of the sun rising over the South China Sea. I remembered those hills and the cold rain of February 1968. Most importantly, I remembered the men, who were really boys, grown too old before they'd finished their boyhoods, and who had died too young, before any of their dreams could come true.

I always felt I had been living on borrowed time since 1968, and each day was a day that the others never had; so to the best of my ability, whenever I thought about it, I'd tried to live the days well and to appreciate the extra time.

I reached back and squeezed Susan's leg.

She held me tighter and closer, and rested her head on my shoulder.

It had been a long, strange journey from Boston, Massachusetts; the destination was unknown, but the journey was a gift from God.

—BOOK VI—

Up Country

CHAPTER THIRTY-EIGHT

———————★———————

W e continued north on Highway One, and the traffic became heavier as the sky lightened. Now and then I got the motorcycle up to one hundred KPH, and I got good at doing the Vietnamese horn-honking weave.

Susan said into my ear, "Before Cu Chi, when was the last time you drove a bike?"

"About twenty years ago." I added, "You never forget. Why do you ask?"

"Just wondering."

We passed the turnoff for Quang Tri City, and we saw the abandoned tank and the destroyed Buddhist high school where this all began. A while later, we crossed the bridge where the pillbox sat with my name inscribed inside.

Fifteen minutes later, we slowed down for Dong Ha Junction and passed slowly through the ugly truck stop town. As we came to the intersection of Highway 9, we saw two policemen in a yellow jeep parked on the opposite side of the road. They barely gave us a glance.

Susan said, "Those cops thought we were Montagnards."

"I don't know what they thought we were, but this limited edition bike stands out."

"Only to you. There are so many new imported goods in this country that the Viets barely notice anymore."

I wasn't totally buying that. I had another thought and said, "I don't see any other Montagnards on motorcycles."

She replied, "I saw two."

"Point them out to me next time."

I continued on toward the DMZ. We were north of Highway 9 now, in the old marine area of operations, and I'd been on this stretch of road only once, when I caught a convoy to go see the Boston friend of mine who was stationed at Con Thien. He was in the field on an operation, so I missed him, but I left a note on his cot that he never saw.

There was a string of market stalls along the highway north of Dong Ha, but once I cleared them, I got the bike back up to one hundred KPH. I could see now from this perspective that it wasn't as dangerous as Susan had made it look on the road to Cu Chi.

Within fifteen minutes, the landscape changed from bleak to dead, and I said to Susan, "I think we just crossed into the DMZ."

"God . . . it's devastated."

I looked at this no-man's-land, still uninhabited, pocked with bomb and shell craters, the white soil covered with straggly, stunted vegetation. If the moon had a few inches of rainfall, it would probably look like this.

I saw some barbed wire in the distance, and the wreck of a rusting Jeep, sitting in a posted minefield where even the metal scavengers wouldn't go.

Up ahead in the mist, I could see the hazy outline of a bridge which I knew must cross the Ben Hai River. I slowed down and said to Susan, "When I was here, the bridge wasn't."

I drove onto the middle of the bridge and stopped. I looked at the river that had divided North and South Vietnam for twenty years and said, "This is it. I'm in North Vietnam."

She said, "I'm still in South Vietnam. Pull up."

"Walk."

She got off the motorcycle, opened a saddlebag, and removed the manila envelope that held the photographs from Pyramide Island. With her cigarette lighter, she lit the corner of the envelope. The envelope blazed in her hand, and she held it until the last second, then dropped the flaming photos off the bridge and into the river.

We mounted up and continued on across the bridge.

On this side of the bridge was a statue of a North Vietnamese soldier, complete with pith helmet and an AK-47 rifle. He had the same lifeless eyes of the American statues at the Wall.

We continued on into former enemy territory. The farther we went away from the DMZ, the better the land looked, though there were still a large number of bomb craters and destroyed buildings dotting the landscape.

The road was no better here, and it was slick from the mist and drizzle. I kept wiping my goggles and face with my Montagnard scarf, and my leather jacket was shiny with moisture.

We passed a motorcycle going south, and the riders were dressed like we were. They waved as they passed, and we waved in return.

Susan said, "See? Even Montagnards think we're Montagnards."

Within an hour, we approached a good-sized town that had a sign that read *Dong Hoi*.

We entered the town, and I slowed down and looked around. What struck me was that the place looked more gloomy and run-down than anything I'd seen in the former South Vietnam. The cars and trucks were older, and there were not as many motor scooters or cyclos. Nearly everyone was riding a bicycle or walking, and their clothes looked dirty and worn. Also, there was not nearly as much commercial activity here as south of the DMZ; no bars, no shops, and only a few cafés. It reminded me of the first time I'd crossed from West Germany to East Germany.

Susan said, "This is Mr. Tram's hometown— our guide at Khe Sanh."

"I see why he moved."

Again, we passed a parked yellow police

jeep, and again the cop behind the wheel barely looked up from his cigarette. This might actually work.

Up ahead, I could see a convoy of military vehicles: open trucks and jeeps filled with soldiers and a few staff cars. I accelerated and began passing them.

I glanced to my right and saw that the drivers and passengers were all looking at us—actually, they were looking at Susan. Susan's face was tightly wrapped in scarves, leather cap, and goggles, and for all they knew, she could have looked like their grandmothers, but they recognized a nice ass when they saw one, and they were waving and calling out to her. Susan had her face turned away modestly, which was what a Montagnard woman would do.

I looked at the driver of the open jeep next to me, and we made eye contact. I could see by his expression that he was trying to figure out what tribe I came from. In fact, I didn't think I was passing for a Montagnard. I gassed the bike, and we accelerated up toward the front of the convoy and passed the lead vehicle.

Highway One was flat and ran near the coast on this stretch of the road, and we made good time, but the road was shared by so many different types of vehicles of varying size and power, along with bicycles, carts and pedestrians, that there was no such thing as cruising; it was an obstacle course, and you needed to keep alert and terrified at all times.

We were about two hundred kilometers from Hue, and it was almost 9 A.M., so we'd covered about 120 miles in two and a half hours. And Highway One was the easy part.

Up ahead, a mountain range to the west ran down to the South China Sea, as they have a habit of doing in this country, creating a high pass right beside the sea. As the road rose, bicyclists were walking their bikes, and the ox carts were getting slower. I moved to the left and accelerated. Within twenty minutes, we approached the crest of the twisting mountain pass. It was cold and windy up here, and I had trouble controlling the bike.

Before we got to the crest, I started noticing people on the road. They were wrapped in layers of filthy rags, their faces barely visible, and they were coming out of the rock formations, walking toward us with their hands out. Susan called into my ear, "Beggars."

Beggars? They looked like extras in *Revenge of the Mummy*.

Susan yelled at them as we drove past, but some of them actually got their hands on us as we accelerated up the pass, and I had to weave around a bunch of them in the middle of the road.

I reached the crest of the pass, and we

started down to the coastal plains. The bike skidded a few times on the slippery blacktop, and I kept downshifting.

Below, I could see that the flat rice paddies were flooded up to the dikes, and small clusters of peasants' huts sat on little islands of dry ground. There were more pine trees here than palms and more burial mounds than I'd seen in the south. I recalled that North Vietnam had lost about two million people in the war, nearly ten percent of the population, and thus the countless burial mounds. War sucks.

An hour and a half from the mountain pass, we approached a large town. I turned onto a dirt road and drove until I got the bike out of sight of the highway.

Susan and I dismounted and stretched. We also used the facilities, which consisted of a bush.

I took the map out of the zippered leather pouch and looked at it. I said to her, "That town just ahead is Vinh."

She informed me, "That's a tourist town. We can stop there if you want to make that phone call to the Century Riverside."

"Why is it a tourist town?"

"Just outside Vinh is the birthplace of Ho Chi Minh."

"And there are Westerners there?"

She replied, "I don't think many Westerners

care about Uncle Ho's birthplace, but you can be sure Vidotour does, so the place is a must-see. Also, it's about halfway between Hue and Hanoi, so it's the overnight stop for the tour buses."

"Okay. We'll stop there and get Uncle Ho T-shirts."

She opened a saddlebag and took out two bananas. "You want a banana, or a banana?"

We ate the bananas standing up and drank some bottled water as I studied the map. I said, "About two hundred klicks from here is a town called Thanh Hoa. When we get there, we need to look for a road that heads west. Take a look. We need to get to Route 6, which takes us to . . . well, it's supposed to take us to Dien Bien Phu, but I see that it ends before it gets there . . . then there's a smaller road to Dien Bien Phu."

Susan looked at the map and said, "I don't think that last stretch qualifies as a road."

I said, "Okay, let's take off the Montagnard stuff and try to look like Lien Xo on a pilgrimage to Uncle Ho's birthplace."

We took off the tribal scarves and the leather hats and stuffed them in a saddlebag.

We mounted up and drove back to Highway One.

Within a few minutes, we were on the outskirts of the town of Vinh. On the right was a painted billboard, and I slowed down so Susan could read it.

She said, "It says . . . 'The town of Vinh was totally destroyed by American bombers and naval artillery . . . between 1965 and 1972 . . . and has been rebuilt by the people of Vinh . . . with the help of our socialist brothers of the German Democratic Republic . . .'"

"That's a real tourist draw."

As we entered the town, it did indeed look like East Berlin on a bad day; block after block of drab, gray concrete housing, and other concrete buildings of indeterminate function.

A few people on the street glanced at us, and I was having second thoughts about stopping. "Are you sure there are Westerners in this town?"

"Maybe it's off-season."

We came to a Y-intersection at a park, and Susan said, "Go left."

I took the left fork and, as it turned out, this was the street that took us to the center of town, another Le Loi Street, on which we made a right turn. I wondered how she knew that.

There were a number of hotels on the left side of the street, and none of them would be mistaken for the Rex. In fact, I've never seen such grim-looking places, not even in East Germany, and I wondered if the East Germans were playing a joke on the Viets. In any case, I saw tour buses and Westerners on the street, which made me feel better.

I said to Susan, "Maybe you can try the call from one of these hotels."

She replied, "I have a better chance of getting through from the post office. Also, if I can't get through by phone, the GPO will have a fax and telex." She added, "You can't choose your long-distance carrier here."

We drove around awhile and spotted the post office. Susan got off and walked directly into the building.

A few passersby gave me a glance, but thanks to Uncle Ho, I didn't attract too much attention. After about ten minutes, a yellow jeep pulled up beside me with two cops in it. The cop in the passenger seat was staring at me.

I ignored him, but he yelled something at me, and I had no choice but to look at him.

He was saying something, and I thought he was motioning for me to dismount, then I realized he was asking me about the motorcycle. Recalling that foreigners were not supposed to drive anything this big, and knowing that the BMW had Hue license plates, I said in French, "Le tour de Hanoi à Hue."

The cop didn't seem to understand, and quite frankly I don't understand my own French half the time. I repeated, "Le tour de Hanoi à Hue," which didn't fully explain why I was sitting in front of the post office, but the cop in the passenger seat was now speaking to the cop behind the wheel, and I could tell that the driver understood something.

The cop in the passenger seat gave me a hard, cop look, said something in Vietnamese, and the yellow jeep pulled away.

I took a deep breath, and for the first time in my life, I thanked God that I passed for a Frenchman.

I was going to dismount and go find Susan, but I saw her coming out of the post office. She jumped on, and I drove onto Le Loi Street, which I'd figured out was Highway One, and within five minutes, we were out of Vinh. A sign on the side of the road said in about a dozen languages, *Birthplace of Ho Chi Minh; 15 Kilometers*. I said to Susan, "Want to see the log cabin where Uncle Ho was born?"

"Drive."

We continued north on Highway One.

Susan said to me, "I couldn't get through by phone, so I telexed and faxed. I had to wait for a reply."

"Bottom line."

"The book hasn't arrived, or so Mr. Tin said in his telex."

I didn't reply.

She said, "But the book is worth about fifteen bucks to a backpacker or a tourist who doesn't have a guidebook . . . and we're not there . . . so, it's possible that Mr. Tin did get it, and it's now for sale. That's a lot of bucks here."

Again, I didn't reply.

Susan said, "There was a message, however, from Colonel Mang. For me."

I didn't ask what it said, but Susan told me. "Colonel Mang wishes me a safe trip and hopes I enjoyed the photographs."

I didn't reply.

She added, "He also said he noticed bathing suits in my apartment, and he's sorry I forgot them."

We approached the turnoff for Ho Chi Minh's birthplace, where two mini-buses of Western tourists were turning in. I pulled over and took Susan's camera out of the backpack and snapped a photo of the sign, in case this film wound up in the hands of the local police. I said to Susan, "I got the once-over from a couple of cops in a jeep. I convinced them I was a Frenchman on a cross-country motorcycle race. My Parisian accent impressed them."

"The North Viets have some positive feelings for the French."

"Why?"

"I'm not sure. But in Hanoi, you'll see middle-aged men wearing berets, and it's still très chic to speak a little French among that age group and to affect French manners and read French literature. In Hanoi, they consider the French to be cultured, and the Americans to be uncouth, materialistic, war-mongering capitalists."

"That doesn't make us bad people."

She tried to smile, then got pensive. She said, "I'm upset about those photographs."

I replied, "I'm upset about the book not showing up."

She looked at me and nodded. "Sorry." She asked, "What do we do about the book not showing up?"

I thought about that. Mr. Anh could have spent some time strapped to a table as Colonel Mang clipped electrodes to his testicles and cranked up the juice. If that was the case, Mr. Anh would have said, "Dien Bien Phu! Ban Hin!" and anything else that Colonel Mang wanted to hear.

Susan asked again, "What do you want to do?"

"Well . . . we could go to Hanoi and try to get out of here on the first flight to anywhere. Or we can go to Dien Bien Phu. For sure, we can't sit here all day."

She thought a moment, then said, "Dien Bien Phu."

I reminded her, "You said my Vietnam luck has run out."

"It has; you were mistaken for a Frenchman. My luck is still good, notwithstanding my Playboy centerfold. Let's roll."

I kicked the BMW into gear and accelerated onto the highway.

Susan leaned forward and looked at the gas

gauge. She said, "We need gas. We just passed a station. Turn around."

"There should be another one up ahead. Some of them give away rice bowls with a fill-up."

"Paul, turn around."

I made a sharp U-turn, and we pulled into the gas station and up to a hand crank pump. I shut off the engine, and we dismounted.

The attendant sat in a small open concrete structure and watched us, but didn't move. Clearly, this was a state-owned facility, and unlike anything I'd seen south of the DMZ. It was still very socialist here, and the good news about capitalist greed and consumer marketing had not reached into Uncle Ho territory yet.

I turned the hand crank, and Susan held the nozzle in the gas fill.

Susan said, "Crank faster."

"I'm cranking as fast as a European socialist would crank."

She said to me, "When we pay this guy, we're French."

"Bon."

I squeezed thirty-five liters into the big tank, and I looked at the total. I said, "Twenty-one thousand dong. That's not bad. About two bucks."

She said, "It's in hundreds, Paul. Two hundred and ten thousand dong. Still cheap."

"Good. You pay."

The gas station attendant had wandered over, and Susan said to him, "Bonjour, monsieur."

I added, "Comment ça va?"

He didn't reply in any language, but looked at the bike as Susan counted out 210,000 dong with Uncle Ho's picture on the notes. I pointed to Uncle Ho and said, "Numero uno hombre," which may have been the wrong language. Susan kicked my ankle.

The attendant looked us over, then looked again at the bike. We mounted up, and Susan said to the guy, "Le tour de Hue–Hanoi."

I accelerated out of there before the guy got wise to us.

We continued north on Highway One, then we pulled over and got into our Montagnard scarves and the fur-trimmed leather hats.

Susan said to me, "Why the hell did you say 'numero uno hombre'?"

"You know—Uncle Ho is a number one guy."

"That was Spanish."

"What difference does it make? You're French, I'm Spanish."

"Sometimes your joking around is inappropriate for the situation."

I thought about that and replied, "It's an old habit. Infantry guys do that when it gets tense. Cops, too. Maybe it's a guy thing."

She informed me, "Sometimes you make the situation worse with your smart-ass remarks—

like with Colonel Mang, and you and Bill going to Princeton together."

Susan was in a bitchy mood, and I hoped it was PMS and not morning sickness.

Highway One was the only major north–south artery in this congested country, and even though traffic was supposed to be light because of the holiday, it seemed like half the population was using the two pathetic lanes of bad blacktop. We never got above sixty KPH, and every inch of the road was a challenge.

It took us nearly two hours to travel the hundred kilometers to the next major town of Thanh Hoa. It was pushing 3 P.M., and it was getting cold. The sky was heavy with gray clouds, and now and then we passed through an area of light rain; crachin, rain dust. My stomach was growling.

I called back to Susan, "This should be Thanh Hoa. This is the first place we can head west and north toward Route 6."

"Your call."

I looked at the odometer. We'd come almost 560 kilometers from Hue, and it had taken us over eight hours. It was now 3:16 P.M., and we had less than four hours of daylight left.

I played around with a few options and decided that since it wasn't raining, I should get on the bad road now, and get as close as I could to Route 6 before the sun set; tomorrow could be raining and the next secondary road

to Route 6 could be impassable, which was
what Mr. Anh had been trying to tell me in his
little briefing. I said to Susan, "We'll take the
road out of Thanh Hoa. If we don't like it, we
can go back and try the next one."

We entered the town of Thanh Hoa, still
wearing our Montagnard scarves and leather
hats. The town apparently hadn't been obliterated in the war, and it had a little charm. In fact,
I saw an old gent wearing a beret, and there
were a few hotels and cafés that hadn't been
built by the East Germans.

A few people glanced at us, and a few cops in
front of the police station gave us the eye.

Susan said, "They don't see that many Montagnards on the coast, so they're curious, but
not suspicious. It's like American Indians coming into a Western town."

"Are you making this up?"

"Yes."

We got through the town, and I saw a small,
blacktopped road to the left. A sign said *Dong
Son* and something in Vietnamese. I slowed
down and pointed.

Susan said, "It's an archaeological site . . . the
Dong Son culture, whatever that is . . . one
thousand years before the common era. Maybe
the road is newer."

I turned into the narrow road and drove
about a hundred meters, then stopped.

I pulled the map out of the pouch and looked

at it. I said, "This is the road. We take this about fifty klicks to some little village called Bai-whatever, then head north on Route 15 to Route 6."

"Let me see that."

I handed her the map, and she studied it in silence. She put the map in her jacket and said, "Okay. Let's go."

I kicked the BMW into gear and off we went. The road passed the archaeological digs, then the blacktop disappeared. The dirt road was rutted from carts and vehicles, and I kept the motorcycle between the ruts, which was a little better.

We were barely bouncing along at forty KPH, a little over twenty miles an hour, less sometimes.

The terrain was still flat, but rising. There were some rice paddies, but these disappeared and vegetable plots took over.

The BMW Paris-Dakar was indeed a good dirt bike, but the dirt wasn't so good. I had trouble holding on to the grips, and my ass was more off the saddle than on. Susan was holding on to me tight. I said, "We're going to feel this in the morning."

"I feel it now."

It took us nearly two hours to cover the forty kilometers to the end of the road. We entered the little village called Bai-something, and the road ended in a T-junction. I took the road to the right, which was Route 15, and the dirt was in better condition. In fact, there was gravel on the road, and the road was crowned and had drainage ditches on both sides.

According to the map, it was over a hundred kilometers to Route 6, and at this speed, it would take at least four hours to get there. It was now 5:40 P.M., and the sun was going down behind the mountains to my left.

The road rose into the hills ahead, and I could see higher hills with mountains behind them. We didn't speak much because it was hard to get the words out with all the bouncing.

It was almost dark, and I was looking for a place to stop for the night. We were definitely in the hills now, and the Viets didn't live much away from the towns, villages, and agricultural areas. Pine trees came up to the sides of the road, and it was getting spooky. I stopped the bike and took a rest. I said to Susan, "Maybe there's a ski lodge up ahead."

She took the map out of her jacket and looked at it. "There's a village up ahead called Lang Chanh, about twenty klicks."

I thought a moment, then said, "I don't think I want to go into a North Viet village after dark."

"Neither do I."

"Well . . . I guess this is it." I looked around. "Let's find a place to hide us and the bike."

"Paul, nothing is moving on this road now. You could sleep in the middle of it."

"Good point." I wheeled the bike up a few meters and rested it against the trunks of some pine trees.

Susan opened a saddlebag and took out the last two bananas, the last bottle of water, and the two rain ponchos.

We sat near the bike with our backs against two pine trees, and I peeled my banana. I said, "Here's some good news. No land leeches in the pine forest."

"Chiggers and ticks."

We ate the bananas and drank the water and watched the light fade. There was a thick cloud cover, and it was pitch dark around us. We could hear sounds in the pine forest, like small animals scurrying around.

She lit a cigarette and looked at the map by the flame of her cigarette lighter. She said, "Another four hundred kilometers to Dien Bien Phu."

We sat in silence and listened to the night. I asked her, "Did you camp out as a kid?"

"Not when I could avoid it. Did you?"

"Well, not when I lived in South Boston. But in the army, I camped out a lot. I once figured that I spent over six hundred nights under the stars. Sometimes it's nice."

A loud clap of thunder rolled through the hills and a breeze came up. It was either cold here, or I'd been in 'Nam too long. I said, "Sometimes it's not."

Susan lit another cigarette and asked me, "Want one? It curbs your appetite."

"I just had a banana."

It started to rain, and we put our ponchos over our heads. We moved closer together to conserve body heat and wrapped the ponchos tighter around us. I said, "Crachin. Rain dust."

"No, this is real fucking rain."

The rain got heavier, and the wind got stronger.

Susan asked me, "How much are they paying you for this?"

"Just expenses."

She laughed.

We were both soaked, and we started to shiver. I remembered these cold, wet evenings in the winter of 1968, dug into the mud with nothing more than a rubber poncho, and the sky was filled with pyrotechnics that had a terrible beauty in the black rain.

Susan must have been thinking the same thing, and she asked me, "Is this how it was?"

"Sort of . . . actually, it was worse because you knew it was going to be the same every night until the winter rains ended in March . . . and you had the extra problem of people on the prowl who were trying to kill you." I paused and said, "That's it for the war, Susan. It's over. Really."

"Okay. That's it for the war. The war is over."

We wrapped the ponchos around us, and lay down together in the rain under the pine trees.

It rained through the night, and we shivered in the rubber ponchos and got as close as we could to each other.

Tomorrow was Dien Bien Phu, if we made it, then the hamlet of Ban Hin, and the person or grave of Tran Van Vinh.

CHAPTER THIRTY-NINE

———★———

A gray dawn filtered through the dripping pine trees.

We unwrapped ourselves from the wet ponchos, yawned and stretched. We were both soaking wet and cold, and a chill had seeped into my bones. Susan didn't look well.

We shook out our ponchos and rolled them up. We opened the saddlebags and took out dry socks, underwear, and clothes from our backpacks, changed, and threw our wet jeans and shirts into the trees; we didn't need many more days of clothes. Maybe fewer than we thought.

Susan had more Montagnard scarves in the saddlebags, and we used one to wipe down the bike, then put on the others and changed tribes.

We did a quick map check and got on the BMW. The engine started easily, and off we went, north on Route 15 to Route 6.

The road was mostly red clay and bits of shale that provided some traction if I didn't gas the engine too quickly.

A kilometer up the road, I spotted a small waterfall cascading from a rock formation into a stream by the side of the road.

I pulled over, and Susan and I washed up

with a piece of orange soap she'd brought along, and we drank some cold and hopefully clean water.

We mounted up and continued on. There wasn't anything moving on the road except us, but I couldn't get the speed past sixty KPH without losing control. Every bone and muscle in my body ached, and the last real meal I'd eaten had been in the sixteen-sided pavilion restaurant, and that was Sunday, New Year's Day. Today was Wednesday.

We approached the small village of Lang Chanh, and beyond the village was the beginning of the higher hills, and beyond that, the mountains whose peaks I couldn't see because of the low clouds and mountain mist.

I slowed down as we entered the squalid village of bamboo huts and ramshackle pine log structures. It was just a little after 7 A.M., and I could smell rice and fish cooking.

There were a few people around and lots of chickens. Susan said, "I need to get something to eat."

"I thought you had a banana yesterday."

She put her hands around my throat and playfully squeezed. Then she wrapped her arms around me and laid her head on my shoulder. I noticed her arms weren't very tight around my chest, and I knew we needed to get some food.

We passed through Lang Chanh and continued on. The road rose more steeply here, but the BMW was an incredible machine, and it ate up the mud as we climbed into the high hills.

Susan said in my ear, "This is actually nice. Almost fun. I like this."

It *was* actually fun, in the middle of nowhere, on the way to the end of nowhere.

I had no way of telling how high we were, but the map had shown benchmark elevations of 1,500 to 2,000 meters, over a mile high on the mountain peaks, so we were about half that elevation on this road. It was cold, but there was no wind, and the drizzle had stopped, though the cloud layer had not one break in it.

Now and then I saw huge stands of mountain bamboo surrounded by taller pine trees, and I was reminded of corn fields in Virginia, surrounded by towering forests of white pines. I recalled from last time I was here that when things that don't look anything like home start to look like things from home, then it's time to go home.

I glanced at my odometer and saw we'd come forty kilometers from Lang Chanh, so right ahead should be the village of Thuoc. The last forty klicks on Route 15 had taken an hour, but I felt confident I could make up some time when I reached Route 6, which was designated on the map as an improved road, though that's a relative term.

The road swung sharply to the left and a few

minutes later, I slowed down for Thuoc, which looked like Lang Chanh, except there were fewer chickens here.

As we passed through the village, a few people followed us with their eyes. I was fairly sure that they saw dirt bikes now and then, and I was also sure they couldn't tell what or who we were. I could tell what *they* were, however, ethnic Vietnamese, so we weren't yet in hill tribe territory and, in fact, I hadn't seen any longhouses.

We continued on for another twenty or thirty kilometers, and the hills got higher. The road followed a mountain stream, and up ahead I could see towering peaks. I have a good sense of direction, and though the sun wasn't visible, I knew we were going the wrong way.

I pulled over, stopped, and looked at the map. I studied it awhile, then scanned the terrain, trying to figure out which way I was heading. I'm a good terrain map reader, but the map wasn't that good, and there was not one single road marker. "Moss grows on what side of the tree?"

"Are we lost?"

"No, we are, as they say in the army, temporarily disoriented."

"We're lost."

"Whatever."

We both got off the bike, put our heads together, and looked at the map. I said, "I think we were supposed to turn someplace near Thuoc in order to stay on Route 15, but I didn't see a sign or a road."

Susan put her finger on the map and said, "When 15 swung west on that curve before Thuoc, the road continued on as Route 214, which is where we are. We needed to turn hard right to stay north on 15."

I said, "The Laotian border is just ahead."

"And that means border guards and soldiers."

"Right. Let's get out of here."

I started to wheel the bike around and noticed on a ridgeline ahead, smoke curling into the air, and the silhouettes of longhouses against the gray sky. I said, "We're in Montagnard territory."

She looked around at the hills and asked, "Are there FULRO here?"

"I don't know. I'm new at this FULRO stuff, despite what Mang thinks." As I was swinging the bike around, I heard something and looked down the road in the direction we'd come from. Coming toward us was an open dark green army jeep with two men in the front. "Jump on."

We both jumped on, and I started the engine. The bike was pointed perpendicular to the narrow road, and I had my choice of going toward the jeep and passing them, or heading west toward the Laotian border, where they were going; neither of these were my first choice.

The jeep was less than a hundred meters from me now, and the driver spotted us. He purposely put the jeep in the center of the narrow road so I couldn't squeeze past him, thereby limiting my choices to one.

I cut the wheel to the right, kicked it into gear, and accelerated toward the Laotian border.

Susan called out, "Paul, we could stop and try to talk our way out of this. We haven't done anything wrong."

"We're dressed as Montagnards, and we're not Montagnards. We're Americans, as our passports say, and I don't want to have to explain what we're doing here."

I looked in my rearview mirror, and I saw that the jeep was keeping up with me. I was doing seventy KPH and the bike was handling well, but I had trouble staying in the saddle, and Susan was holding on for dear life.

To make matters worse, I was heading toward the border post where I'd be stopped, or where I could charge right through, ducking AK-47 automatic rifle fire from the Viets, and probably from the Laotian border guards on the other side, who were also Commies and sort of friendly to the Viets now and then. So, this was like hammer and anvil; the guys in the jeep were the hammer, the border post was the anvil, and we were hamburger meat.

I glanced in my rearview mirror again and saw that the jeep was a little farther back; he was just going to follow me until I got to the border, which must be very close now, then we'd have a chat. I looked for a place to try to put the bike in the hills to my left or right, but it didn't seem possible, and the soldiers behind me knew that.

Susan said, "Paul, if you don't stop or slow down, they're going to assume we're running from them. Please, stop. I can't hold on. I'm going to fall. Slow down and pull over and see if they just want to pass us. Paul, I'm going to fall off. Please."

I slowed down and moved the motorcycle to the right and the jeep started to gain on us. I said to Susan, "Okay . . . we'll just take it easy here and see what they want." We pulled off our scarves and leather hats.

I had the strong feeling this was the end of the road.

The jeep was right behind us now, and the soldier in the passenger seat was standing, holding an AK-47 rifle. The jeep drew abreast of us, and the guy with the rifle looked us over. He shouted, "Dung lai! Dung lai!" which used to be my line back in '68. He motioned with his rifle for me to pull over and stop.

As I started to slow down, I saw a strange expression on the guy's face, then a loud explosion right beside my head, and the soldier with the rifle did sort of a backflip. The rifle went flying, and he fell in the rear of the open seat. Another gunshot rang out, and the driver's head exploded. The jeep bucked to a halt and stalled, then rolled slowly backward down the slope until its rear wheels went into the ditch.

I stopped the motorcycle.

I sat there staring straight ahead. I could smell the gunpowder. Without turning, I said to Susan, "You swore you left the gun in Hue."

She didn't reply, but dismounted and walked over to the jeep, the Colt .45 still smoking from the barrel.

She paid no attention to the driver, who had half his skull missing, but very expertly she examined the other soldier, who was sprawled half in the back of the jeep. She said, "They're both dead." She stuck the .45 under her quilted jacket. "Thank you for slowing down."

I didn't reply.

We looked at each other for a few seconds. Finally, she said, "I couldn't let them stop us."

I didn't reply.

She took out a cigarette and lit it. Her hand was steady as a rock. I knew I was in the presence of someone who was no stranger to guns.

She took a few drags, then threw the cigarette in the water and watched it flow downstream. She asked, "What do you think we should do with this mess?"

I said, "Leave it. They'll think it was the FULRO. But we have to take the rifles to make it look like it was them."

She nodded and went over to the jeep and

collected two AK-47s and a Chicom pistol from the holster of the driver.

I went to the jeep and took the extra magazines and threw them into the woods, then took their wallets, cigarettes, and watches and stuffed everything in my pockets.

I looked at the two dead men covered with blood and gore, but I didn't get any flashbacks; that was then, this was here and now, and one had nothing to do with the other. Well, maybe a little.

Susan rummaged around the open jeep for a few seconds and found a cellophane bag of dried fruit. She opened the bag and offered it to me.

I shook my head.

She grabbed a handful of the dried fruit, put it in her mouth, chewed and swallowed, then put another handful in her mouth and stuck the bag in her side pocket.

We walked back to the motorcycle, each carrying an AK-47 slung over our shoulders.

I turned the bike around, we mounted up, and started downhill on the muddy road, back toward Thuoc, where I'd missed my turn.

Before we got to Thuoc, I stopped, and we tossed the rifles, the pistol, and the personal effects of the dead men into a thicket of bamboo.

We continued on and reached Thuoc. I saw the turn now, and got back on Route 15.

We rode in silence. We crossed a wooden bridge over a mountain stream, and drove through the village of Quan Hoa. After another twenty kilometers, we intersected with Route 6, and I turned left, west toward Dien Bien Phu.

It was a decent road, two narrow lanes, but wide enough for two trucks to pass in opposite directions if they squeezed hard to their right. The road surface was a sort of oiled gravel, which now and then turned to thin asphalt. I got the BMW up to eighty KPH.

Most of the sparse traffic consisted of logging trucks, a few four-wheel drives, and now and then a motorcycle. I saw no motor scooters or ox carts, and no bicycles or pedestrians; this was, indeed, the road to and from nowhere.

To the left rose the hills and mountains that ran along the Laotian border, and to the right were more hills, and beyond them were the towering peaks of what was called the Tonkinese Alps.

All in all, it was a spectacular road, though now and then the surface deteriorated without warning, and I had to slow down.

The general direction of the road was northwest and uphill. As we got farther west, the few signs of habitation disappeared, except for the smoke from hill tribe settlements, rising out of the forest and into the misty air, the smoke sometimes indistinguishable from the mountain fog.

I drove for two hours, and neither Susan nor

I spoke a word. Finally, she said, "Are you going to speak to me?"

I didn't reply.

"I need to make a pit stop."

Up ahead, I could see a flat area off to the side where pine trees had been cleared. There was a small culvert in the stream, and I drove over it and stopped among the pine stumps. I shut off the engine.

I sat there for a minute, then dismounted. Susan, too, dismounted, but did not use the facilities. She stretched, lit a cigarette, and put her foot up on a tree stump. She turned to me and said, "Say something, Paul."

"I have nothing to say."

"Tell me I did a good job."

"You did a good job."

"Thank you." She said, "I couldn't let them stop us."

"So you said."

"Well . . . if you hadn't taken a wrong turn, none of that would have happened."

"Sorry. Shit happens."

She watched the smoke curl from her cigarette. After a while, she said, "The part that's true is that I'm madly in love with you."

"Is that the good news or the bad news?"

She ignored that and said, "And that's the part they don't like . . . if they believe it."

I said, "I think that's the part I wouldn't like either, if I believed it."

"Please don't say that."

"Do you need to go behind a bush?"

"No. We need to talk."

"No, we don't."

"We do." She glanced at me and said, "Okay, I *do* work for the CIA, but I'm also a real civilian employee of American-Asian, so neither of us has any direct government involvement, and they could let us hang if they wanted to. And, no, they really didn't want you to dump me, they wanted you to trust me, so they told you to dump me. And, yes, I'm supposed to keep an eye on you . . ." She smiled and said, "I'm your guardian angel." She continued, "And yes, I was involved with Bill, and yes, he really is the CIA station chief, and they'll go ballistic if they find out I told you, and no, they didn't tell me to sleep with you—that was my idea. Made the job easier, but yes, I did fall in love with you . . . and yes, they really are suspicious of me now because they know or suspect that we're sexually and romantically involved, and I don't care."

She looked at me, then continued, "And no, I don't know what Tran Van Vinh knows or saw, but yes, I know all about this mission, except for the name of the village, which they didn't want me carrying around in my head, and at 4 P.M. on Sunday, after you met Mr. Anh, I met with him, and he briefed me about everything I didn't know except the name of the village, which he could give only to you." She added, "He says he likes you and trusts you to do the job." She looked at me and asked, "Did I miss anything?"

"The Pham family."

She nodded. "Right. That was an arranged meeting in front of the cathedral. This motorcycle was already bought, and you passed your motorcycle driving test on the way to Cu Chi." She added, "I met Pham Quan Uyen last time I was in Hue. He can be trusted."

"That's more than I can say about you."

She looked upset. "Okay . . . don't trust me. But ask me anything you'd like, and I swear I'll tell you the truth."

"You swore you were telling me the whole truth back in Saigon, Nha Trang, and Hue. You also swore you didn't have the gun."

"I *needed* the gun. *We* needed the gun in case something like what happened, happened."

I said to her, "And you need the gun to blow Tran Van Vinh's brains out. Correct?"

She didn't reply.

I asked her, "Why does he need to be killed?"

She replied, "I swear I don't know. We're about to find out, though." She added, "I believe he's alive."

"So, you've agreed to kill a man without knowing why."

"You killed people without knowing why."

"They were trying to kill *me*."

She looked at me and said, "How many of them were actually trying to kill you?"

"All of them. Don't try to turn this back on me, Susan. I may have been a combat soldier, but I was never an assassin."

"Never?"

I wanted to tell her to go to hell, but then she'd bring up the A Shau Valley, and whatever else I'd been stupid enough to tell her, and I really didn't want to go there.

She said, "Look, Paul . . . I know you're angry, and you have every right to be angry. But this isn't as cold-blooded and devious as it seems—"

"Fooled me."

"Let me finish. They told me they picked you because you were good, but also because your boss thinks a lot of you personally. He wanted to resurrect your career, or at least have it end well—"

"Like me being killed? How good is that?"

She continued, "He also thought that if you came back here, it would be good for you, and good for . . . your relationship with . . . your girlfriend. So, don't be so cynical. People care about you."

"Please. If I'd had lunch, I'd blow it now."

She moved closer to me and said, "I'd like to think there's a human element in what we do . . . I mean, as Americans. We're not bad people, though we sometimes do bad things. And I think we do them with the hope that we're doing the bad things for a good reason. In another country, they'd just have sent two assassins to kill this guy, and end of story. But we don't work that way. We want to be certain that if something has to be done with this man, that's he's the guy we're actually looking for, and that what he knows, if anything, cannot be dealt with in any other way." She looked at me and said, "I'm not going to walk up to a guy named Tran Van Vinh and blow his brains out." She added, "We may take him with us to Hanoi."

"Are you finished?"

"Yes."

"Can we go now?"

"Not until you tell me that you really believe that I love you. I don't care about anything else. If you want, we can turn around right here and drive to Hanoi. Tell me what you want to do, or what you want me to do."

I thought about that and said, "Well, what I really want to do is to push on, find this guy, and find out what the fuck this is all about." I looked at her and said, "And what I want you to do is to go back to Saigon or to Hanoi or Washington or wherever the hell you came from."

She stared at me a long time. Then she reached into her jacket and pulled out the Colt .45.

NELSON DEMILLE

I looked at the gun—you always keep your eye on the weapon—and it looked bigger than a Colt .45 in her small hand.

She turned the butt toward me and handed me the gun. I took it. She pulled two extra magazines out of her pocket and put them in my other hand. She pulled her backpack out of a saddlebag and put it on.

I looked at her face and saw tears streaming from her eyes. She didn't say anything, but took my head in both her hands, kissed me hard on the lips, turned and walked quickly across the road.

She stood there, not looking at me, but looking at the Hanoi-bound traffic. A four-wheel drive vehicle approached driven by a Viet with two male passengers, and Susan held up her hand. The vehicle slowed down and pulled onto the shoulder.

Well . . . I could let her go, then I'd regret it down the road and wind up chasing the four-wheel drive halfway to Hanoi. Or I could call out to her and tell her I changed my mind. Or I could let her go for real.

Susan was crouched down and speaking to the two Viets in the front seat. The rear door opened, and she got in without looking at me. The driver pulled back on the road.

I crossed the road and stood in front of the vehicle. The driver turned his head toward Susan, then he stopped. I went around to the rear door and opened it. I said to her, "Let's go."

She said something to the three Viet guys, who all smiled.

She got out, and I slammed the door. The vehicle continued on.

Susan and I crossed the road, and she put her backpack in a saddlebag. We mounted the motorcycle. I turned to her, and our eyes met. She was crying again, but silently, which I don't mind too much. I said to her, "If you're lying about being in love with me, I swear to God, I'll blow your brains out. Understand?"

She nodded.

I started the engine, kicked the bike into gear, and we got on the road.

We continued farther into the mountains toward Dien Bien Phu, where an army had met its fate, and where my fate had been waiting patiently.

★

CHAPTER FORTY

---- ★ ----

We continued northwest on Route 6. It was just before noon, and the fuel gauge showed less than half a tank. We weren't going to make it all the way to Dien Bien Phu without refueling. If Susan wasn't on the motorcycle, I might have been able to reach Dien Bien Phu on this tank of gas. Then again, if Susan wasn't on the motorcycle, I might be in a military prison answering difficult questions.

But to take it a step further back, to the rooftop restaurant of the Rex Hotel, my life had taken a wrong turn sometime between my second lucky beer and dessert, and so had this mission. I had the perceptive glimpse into the obvious that everyone involved with this mission knew a lot more than I did, and a lot sooner than I did.

Mud slides, caused by overlogging, covered sections of the bad blacktop, but had the advantage of filling in the potholes. I was averaging only about sixty KPH, which was better than most four-wheeled vehicles were doing. In fact, I spotted two four-wheel vehicles at the bottoms of ravines.

Back to Ms. Weber, who was not riding with

her arms around me any longer, but who was holding on to the C-strap. The tears had been real, and so had the tears in Apocalypse Now. This was a woman who was as conflicted as I was about life, Vietnam, and about us. But so what? I don't like being manipulated or lied to any more than anyone else, and when my life is at stake, I like it even less. With a guardian angel like Susan Weber, I didn't need to worry about meeting the Angel of Death, which led me to the thought that if Susan had been instructed to take care of Tran Van Vinh, then maybe she'd also been instructed to take care of Paul Brenner, if necessary. But I couldn't come to terms with that, so I put it out of my mind. But not completely.

The road dropped into a highland plain, and I could see Montagnard longhouses in the hills. A wind swept over the open area from the northeast, so I had to keep compensating by leaning into the crosswind. Plus, it was starting to rain, and I slowed down to see what was in front of me.

Another thought on the subject of this very strange mission was, Why me? Surely there were more gung ho individuals in the CID who couldn't wait to risk their lives and go to Vietnam, and who knew how to follow orders.

But maybe Karl had calculated correctly that Paul Brenner was the guy they needed. My most obvious asset was my status as a non-government employee, thereby giving everyone lots of plausible deniability if things went bad. Susan, too, I was certain, appeared on no government payroll, and she had all the Vietnam stuff necessary to the mission: knowledge of the land, the language, and the culture; Viet knowledge that American intelligence had forgotten over the last quarter century. Plus, she was a female, which was less suspicious to the Viets, who didn't think much of women.

It all looked good on paper, I guess, but there's always the problem of agents of the opposite sex getting the hots for each other. It happened to me and Cynthia. Karl, however, had convinced his colleagues that Paul Brenner was in love with Cynthia Sunhill, and Paul was a monogamous guy, who had a good, if not perfect, record of keeping his dick in his pants on the job. Plus, Susan Weber was very involved with Bill Stanley, CIA station chief, Saigon office.

Last thought was that Karl really did care about me and wanted this for me, for career purposes and personal reasons, partly having to do with my strained relationship with Cynthia. And as for Cynthia, I had no idea what she knew, or what she'd been told, but I'd bet half my retirement pay they hadn't mentioned Ms. Weber to Ms. Sunhill.

We passed through a small agricultural town that was actually signposted and whose name was Yen Chau. There was a big produce market on both sides of the road, and the people seemed to be mostly Montagnards in traditional garb. A lot of vehicles were parked under the roofs of the produce stalls, their drivers talking and watching the rain as they smoked. A dark green military jeep sat on the side of the road facing me, but the canvas top was up, and the two men inside were smoking, not looking at anyone.

I pushed on.

The road made a few thrilling twists and turns, and I had to keep the speed down so we wouldn't skid out. The ravines were so deep, I'd still be falling past my visa expiration date.

We passed through a small Montagnard village where a steel and wood bridge crossed a rain-swollen gorge.

About an hour later, the rain eased off, and I could see signs of civilization ahead. Susan said to me, "Son La, right ahead. Provincial capital."

We entered the small town of Son La, which looked like a Wild West town strung along Main Street. There were a few guest houses and cafés on either side of Route 6, which was very narrow here. A faded wooden sign in French pointed to a side road and read *Pénitentiaire*. The French really knew how to pick some lousy prison locations. I mean, this place made Devil's Island look like Tahiti.

Many of the inhabitants of Son La appeared to be Montagnards in modern dress, and many of them wore berets. There was an old French concrete kilometer marker on the side of the road which said *Dien Bien Phu, 150 KM*. I looked at my gas gauge and estimated that I had about another one hundred kilometers of fuel, maybe less.

Susan asked me, "Want to stop for gas?"

"No."

We pushed on through the outskirts of Son La. The Department of Public Works ran out of dong, and the road became a thin mixture of mud and bitumen. I was skidding and spinning a lot, and the road was all upgrade.

We were going into the high hills again, and the road became steeper and narrower. In front of me was a wall of fog which I entered. It was surreal riding through the mountain fog, and if I let my imagination run away, it was like flying the motorcycle through turbulent air.

Susan said, "This is Pha Din Pass. I need to stop."

I stopped on the road, and we dismounted. I wheeled the motorcycle to the edge of a shallow creek and kicked down the stand.

Susan and I used the facilities. We were splattered with mud, and we washed up in some frigid water running down the side of the rocks, then drank some of the water.

Susan offered me the cellophane bag of dried fruit, and I shook my head. She ate some of the fruit, then lit a cigarette.

She said to me, "If you're not going to speak to me, or if you hate me, you should have let me go."

True enough, but I didn't reply.

She said, "I gave you the pistol. What more can I do to make you trust me?"

"You have any other guns on you?"

"No."

I wanted to ask her if she was supposed to whack me if I became a problem, but I couldn't bring myself to ask, and for sure I wasn't going to get a straight answer.

She said, "Do you want to talk?"

"We did that."

"Okay." She threw her cigarette in the stream, then pushed the cellophane bag at me. She said, "I'm not going any farther until you eat something."

I don't like fruit, even dried fruit, but I was getting a little light-headed, maybe because of the altitude. I took the bag and ate some of the fruit. I said, "Let me see the map."

She handed me the map, and I studied it.

She asked, "How are we doing for gas?"

I replied, "It's mostly downhill from here."

She came up beside me and looked at the map. She said, "There should be gas available in Tuan Giao, where Route 6 turns north and this other road heads south to Dien Bien Phu."

"I figured that out. Ready to go?"

"I need another cigarette." She lit up again.

I waited.

She said, "If you don't love me or trust me, I'm going to jump off this cliff."

I replied, "There is no cliff, and I'm not in the mood for your bewitching charms."

"Do you hate me?"

"No, but I'm fed up with you."

"Will you get over it?"

"Let's go." I got on the motorcycle.

"Do you love me?"

"Probably." I started the bike.

"Do you trust me?"

"Not at all."

She threw her cigarette down and said, "Okay. Let's go."

She mounted up, I pushed off, and kicked the motorcycle into gear.

We continued on over the pass, and the visibility in the fog was less than ten feet. At some point, we were on a straight downgrade, and I kicked the bike into neutral to save fuel. Even without being in gear, we were moving too fast, and I had to keep tapping the rear brake.

I saw a pair of oncoming yellow lights, and within a few seconds, an army jeep appeared out of the fog. The only thing that anyone could see of our faces were our round eyes, but even that feature was covered with goggles. The driver, however, was staring at us, and I had the thought that the word was out on the apparent FULRO attack on the army jeep near the Laotian border. Things like that didn't make the news, but I guessed that it happened more often than the Viets admitted, and the army guys were very alert and wary.

The jeep was slowing down, and the guy in the passenger seat had his AK-47 at the ready. I thought he was going to block the road, so I kept one hand on the brake, and the other ready to go for the pistol tucked in my belt.

The jeep came to almost a complete stop and watched us pass by. I counted to five, then threw the motorcycle into gear and accelerated. I also killed the lights, which actually made the fog easier to see through. I got up to eighty KPH, which was much too fast for the road or the bad visibility. I was basically flying blind, trusting in my nonexistent luck, and my sense of how this road was turning. To her credit, Susan said nothing, showing how much she trusted me, or maybe she had her eyes closed.

I kept looking in the rearview mirror, but I didn't see any yellow fog lights behind us.

Within half an hour, we drove out of the fog, and I could see a stretch of curving road running through forested hills.

I'd never been in such a godforsaken place, even during the war, and I could see that there wasn't any room here for misjudgment; one misstep was all it would take to end this trip.

I got into third gear, and we continued on through the forest. I looked at the gas gauge and saw that we were near empty. I had counted on being able to buy some overpriced fuel from a passing car or truck if I ran out, knowing that all vehicles carried gas cans and probably siphons. But I seemed to be the only idiot on the road, except for the army jeep, and I didn't think he'd sell me gas.

I heard the engine cough, and I switched over to the reserve tank.

Susan heard it, too, and asked, "Are you on reserve?"

I nodded.

She didn't offer any advice or criticism of my fuel management.

At about the point where the reserve tank should have been empty, I saw some cleared land and a few huts up ahead.

Within a few minutes, we were in the small junction town of Tuan Giao, where Route 6 turned north toward China, and another road headed south toward Dien Bien Phu.

I saw a sign that said *Et-xang*, and I said to Susan, "We're French."

We both took off our Montagnard scarves and leather hats and stuffed them into our jackets as I headed toward the sign.

We ran out of gas before we got to the so-called service station, and Susan and I pushed the motorcycle the last hundred meters.

The et-xang place consisted of a muddy lot and a crumbling stucco building inside of which were bottles and cans of gasoline of all sizes, shapes, and volume.

The proprietor was an old Viet wrapped up like it was snowing, and he smiled when he saw two Westerners pushing the BMW through the mud. This could be Slicky Boy's father.

Susan said to the old guy, "Bonjour, monsieur."

He replied, "Bonjour, mademoiselle," being very kind about her age.

There wasn't much else to say; the guy had no trouble figuring we were out of gas, and he began funneling fuel into the BMW tank from various containers. He'd hold up a finger or two or three and say in French, "Litres," as he poured. He reached forty liters by his count, more than the tank held, and I cut him off.

The price was the equivalent of about a buck and a half a liter, which was expensive for Vietnam, but I wasn't sure where the hell we were anyway, so I paid him in dollars.

It was 6:15 P.M., and the sun was starting to set behind the mountains to the west. The distances in this part of the world weren't long, but the traveling times were deceptive. We'd come close to a thousand kilometers, which should have taken maybe eight hours on a real road, but had taken us two twelve-hour days, and we weren't even there yet.

The next day, Thursday, was the official end of the Tet holiday, though in reality it would run through the weekend. But I had this thought that we'd find the village of Ban Hin, and the house of Tran Van Vinh, only to be told, "Oh, sorry, you just missed him. He's on his way back to Saigon where he lives now. He manages the Rex Hotel," or something like that.

Susan said to me, "It's nice to see you smiling again. What are you thinking about?"

"You don't want to know."

"Whatever makes you happy, makes me happy."

"If I had anything in my stomach, I'd puke."

"Don't be mean to me."

"Get on."

We mounted up and headed south. I saw a concrete kilometer post that said *Dien Bien Phu, 81 KM*.

We were Western tourists now, on our way to see the French equivalent of Khe Sanh and the A Shau Valley, the Viet version of Yorktown, Thermopylae, Armageddon, and dozens of other Last and Final Battlefields that were in reality only a prelude to the opening shots of the next war.

And as for my pistol-packing, cigarette-smoking friend behind me, I needed to figure out if I had a guardian angel back there, or something more dangerous. Guns are like bugs; if you see one, there are more. Or, to be more trusting, maybe Ms. Weber's last round of true confessions was the whole truth and nothing but the truth.

The road was bad, so she put her arms around

me. I was still pretty pissed off, but there's nothing like hunger and fatigue to take the piss and vinegar out of you. This lady could ride, and she could shoot, and she talked the talk, and I had enough enemies in these parts to worry about, so I patted her hand.

She rubbed my stomach and asked, "Are we friends?"

I replied, "No, but I love you."

She kissed my neck. I was reminded of a very big cat with very long fangs licking a captured antelope before snapping its neck.

CHAPTER FORTY-ONE

——————★——————

A bout forty kilometers from Dien Bien Phu, the road deteriorated instead of getting better as it approached the town. What is wrong with this place? There was not one reflective arrow or reflective anything, the ground mist was getting heavier, and it was diffusing the head-beam, and I was starting to get disoriented.

Susan said, "Paul, let's stop and sleep here."

"Where?"

"*Here*. On the side of the road."

"I can't see the side of the road."

We pushed on, averaging about fifteen KPH, and the bike was wobbling at the lower speeds. About two hours later, pushing 10 P.M., a valley suddenly opened up on both sides of the road. The grade began a downhill descent, and within fifteen minutes, the road came into a wide, open plain. I couldn't actually see much of the plain, but I could sense it, and I could see lights scattered around. There was a break in the clouds now and the weak moonlight and starlight reflected off what I thought was a lake, but then I recognized it as a series of rice paddies. Back in '68, there were a lot of valleys in 'Nam nicknamed Happy Valley, meaning that GIs on patrol in the hills were happy to see the valley. This was Happy Valley.

The road curved sharply to the right, and there were huts on both sides. It took me a while to realize I was in the town of Dien Bien Phu. I saw a lighted sign to my left that said *Nga Luan Restaurant*, and to my right was a place called the Dien Bien Phu Motel. This was all like an apparition, and I thought I'd gone over a cliff and was now in Viet heaven. I said, "The Dien Bien Phu Motel looks like a winner." We drove up to the motel office in the middle of a long stucco building and dismounted. I stretched and discovered that none of my muscles were connected or working. I actually had trouble walking to the reception office, and I thought I was going to fall on my face. I couldn't even peel off my leather gloves.

Before we went inside, Susan said to me, "They'll want our passports and visas, and they don't take no for an answer in the north, nor will they take ten bucks instead."

"So, we're Americans. Doesn't make us bad guys."

She said, "Eventually, our names will be sent to the Ministry of Public Security in Hanoi, and there'll be a record that we were here."

"I understand. But I think we'll be in Hanoi before our names are. We're on the last leg of this journey, but if you want, we can sleep under the stars."

She thought a moment, and I could see the trained professional now, weighing the risks. She said, "Let's get a room."

"Take it for four nights so they think we're hanging around awhile."

She replied, "They'll take our passports until we check out, so when we check out tomorrow, they'll know we're gone. This is a police state."

"Right. But make it four nights anyway, and that's what will be reported to Hanoi. You go in. They don't have to see me."

"They do. Did I mention this was a police state?"

We went inside the small reception area. A middle-aged woman behind the counter was reading a newspaper.

Susan asked for a room in French, and the woman seemed surprised that we were checking in so late. She and Susan exchanged bad French, a little English, and a few words of Vietnamese. We had to produce our passports and visas, which the woman insisted she had to keep.

For ten American bucks a night, we got the key to Unit 7. My lucky number.

We left the reception room, and I wheeled the motorcycle to Unit 7 at the left end of the motel. Susan opened the door and said, "The lady said put the bike in the room, or we'll never see it again."

I pushed the motorcycle into a small room and left it near the foot of the twin bed.

The place had a small bathroom and one night stand, one lamp, and a clothes pole hanging on chains from the ceiling that looked like a trapeze for sexually adventurous couples.

We took our backpacks out of the saddlebags and put them on the bed, then Susan went into the bathroom, turned on the electric water heater, and washed her hands and face in cold water. She then went to the door and said, "The lady said she'd get something for us to eat. Be right back."

She left.

I sat on the bed and took off my running shoes, then peeled off my wet socks. I got my leather jacket and gloves off and put the Colt .45 under the pillow. I looked around. I knew, somewhere deep down inside, that this place was awful, but at this moment, it looked to me like the Ritz-Carlton in Washington.

Susan returned with a bamboo tray on which were bamboo containers that when uncovered revealed soggy meat dumplings. She put the tray on the bed. Also on the tray were bowls of cold rice, chopsticks, and a bottle of water.

We knelt at the side of the bed and ate the meat dumplings and rice with our fingers. It took about thirty seconds to get the stuff down, and we killed the water in less time than that.

Susan commented, "I guess you were hungrier than you thought." She added, "The meat was porcupine. No joke."

"I wouldn't care if it was dog."

She smiled and put the tray on the floor, then stood and took off her wet, muddy clothes. As she was undressing, she said, "The reception lady was very surprised that we'd come in over the mountains at night on a motorcycle."

"So was I."

"She said this is the latest she'd ever checked anyone in, and she was about to turn out the lights and leave. We may have aroused a little suspicion."

"Whatever we do here seems to arouse suspicion."

Susan replied, "I think we're okay now. She said there are some Westerners in town, though most of them come later in the season."

"This place has a season?"

She put her hands on the clasp of her bra, then looked at me as if to say, "Is it all right if I get naked in front of you? Or are we no longer lovers?"

I stood and unbuttoned my shirt. Susan unclasped her bra and threw it on the motorcycle, then slipped off her panties.

Susan asked me, "You want to kill some time while the water is heating?"

Well, as pissed off as I was, Dickie Johnson was not at all angry. In fact, he was happy, and he and I were about to have an argument. But my big brain was nearly dead with fatigue, and little Dickie's brain had slept for the whole ride, so I was no match for his insistent demands. I peeled off my shirt, pants, and undershorts as Dickie stretched.

We stood there in the lamplight, and our faces were dirty, except for where the goggles and scarves had been, and our bodies were covered with a damp sweat and who knew what else after two days without a shower.

She turned down the sheets, which had a reddish cast from what must have been heavily iron-oxidized water.

Susan crawled into the bed, rolled on her back, and motioned for me to come to her. I got into bed, Dickie pointing the way.

I got on top of her and slid right in. I mean, I couldn't even walk or control the movement of my limbs, and my backbone felt as if I'd made a parachute jump with seventy pounds of field gear and tangled shrouds into a concrete pit; but I wanted to get laid. Amazing.

So, Dickie was home where he wanted to be, but I couldn't get the old in and out going. Susan sensed this and moved her hips up and down.

I think we had simultaneous orgasms, or maybe simultaneous muscle spasms, followed by a brief period of unconsciousness. When I woke up, I was still on top of her. I got out of bed and shook her awake.

I practically carried her into the bathroom and turned on the shower. There was a sliver of soap on the sink, and we got in the small fiberglass stall together. We let the tepid water run over our bodies, then dried off with small hand towels.

We staggered back to the bed and flopped down side by side. Susan yawned and asked me, "Did we have sex?"

"I think so."

"Good." She yawned again and said, "Are we friends?"

"Of course."

She stayed quiet for a while, and I thought she was sleeping. I turned off the lamp.

In the dark, she asked me, "Where's the gun?"

"Under my pillow. Leave it there."

She stayed silent for a while, then said, "Everything I told you about my personal life is true."

"Good night."

"The other stuff . . . well, what choice did I have?"

"I don't know. Sweet dreams."

She stayed quiet, then said, "I have a photo pack with me, Paul."

This woke me up. I asked, "A photo pack of the victim?"

"Yes. And of the possible murderer."

I sat up and turned on the light. "And?"

"And that's it. They're both young men, in uniform, and the photos are not captioned."

"Where are the photos?"

"In my backpack."

I got out of bed and opened her backpack at the foot of the bed. I completely emptied it out on the bed, finding no second pistol, which made me feel better.

I found the photo pack, a vinyl-bound and plastic-wrapped album that held single shots on each page. I took the album to the lamp and held it under the light. I started flipping through the pages, and the first ten photos, in color and black and white, were all of the same man in various uniforms—khakis, stateside fatigues, green dress uniform, and even one in a blue formal uniform. In some photos, the guy was bareheaded, and in some he wore a helmet or the appropriate head-gear for the uniform. I could see from the rank insignia that the guy was a lieutenant, and he wore the crossed rifle insignia of an infantryman. In one photo, he was in jungle fatigues, and I could make out the shoulder patch of the First Cavalry, and the patch of the Military Assistance Command, Vietnam. He was about twenty-five, maybe a little younger. He had sandy hair, cut short, big innocent eyes, and a nice smile.

I knew, even without the rank, that this guy

was not the killer; he was the victim. He looked like a lot of guys I'd known in 'Nam who had something in their smiles and their eyes that told you they wouldn't be around long. Truly, the good died young, and everyone else had a fifty-fifty chance. I imagined that these photos came from the man's family.

The second group of about ten photos showed a guy with captain's bars. He, like the other guy, wore the crossed rifle insignia of the infantry, and in a few photos, he wore jungle fatigues with the same two shoulder patches as the lieutenant.

I studied this man's face, but my eyes were blurry, and my mind was half asleep. Yet, there was something familiar about his face, though I couldn't place the face in the proper context, and nothing was jelling—except that I knew the face.

In one photo, the captain was in a green dress uniform, and with the tie on, the face looked more familiar. He was a rugged-looking man, with dark hair, cut military short, dark, piercing eyes, and a smile that was put on, but could pass for sincere.

On his green dress uniform, I could make out two rows of ribbons, and I recognized most of them, including the Vietnamese Cross of Gallantry, like my own, but also the Silver Star, which showed bravery above and beyond the call and so forth, plus the Vietnamese Service

Medal, indicating, like the medals for bravery, that this photo was taken post-Vietnam. This guy also had the Purple Heart, but since he was in uniform, post-'Nam, it was not a disabling wound. Whoever this guy was, he'd come home in honor and glory, and might still be alive, if he hadn't gone back to 'Nam and run out of luck. Of course he was alive; that's why I was here.

I stared at the photograph of the captain in his green uniform, and I looked into his eyes, which seemed to be far away, like the eyes of a man whose mind was elsewhere. Whoever this man was, someone in the CID and/or the FBI thought he was a murderer.

I flipped through the photos again, and this time I concentrated on the uniform nametags that were visible in some of the photos. Not one of the nametags was readable, and I had the distinct impression the photos had been retouched to blur the names. Interesting.

Susan asked, "Do either of them look familiar?"

I made eye contact with her and replied, "No. Why should they?"

"Well . . . I thought we discussed that one of them might now be famous."

I didn't respond to that, but said, "Maybe our witness can identify one or both of them, though it's a long shot."

I put the photo pack on the night table. I needed to sleep on those photos, and maybe it would come to me. I had the feeling that Susan could put name captions on both those men.

I turned off the light and fell into bed.

Susan was saying something, and I could hear a sentence that began with, "Tomorrow," and ended with "conclusion," which was a good place for me to pass out.

CHAPTER FORTY-TWO

——————★——————

I dreamt of my farmhouse in Virginia; a light snow was falling outside my window. I awoke at dawn to a different reality.

Susan was awake and said to me, "If we went back to the States together, I think we could put all this behind us."

I said, "Let's get back to the States."

She took my hand and said, "And when people ask us how we met, we can say we met on vacation in Vietnam."

"I hope this is not your idea of a vacation."

"Or we can say we were secret agents on a dangerous mission, and we're not allowed to talk about it."

I sat up. "We have to get moving."

She squeezed my hand and said, "If something happens to me, and you get out of here, will you visit my family and tell them about this? About . . . the last few weeks . . . ?"

I didn't reply. I'd made that promise to three Boston area guys in '68, and one of them didn't make it back, so when I'd gotten home, I kept my promise and visited the parents in Roxbury, and it was the longest two hours of my life. I truly would rather have been back in combat than there. Mom, Pop, two younger brothers, and one sister, about four years old, who kept asking me where her brother was.

"Paul?"

I said, "I will. Do the same for me."

She sat up and kissed me, then got out of bed and went into the bathroom.

I got dressed, then squared away all our gear, and stuck the pistol in the small of my back.

Susan came out of the bathroom. As she got dressed, she asked, "What's the plan?"

"We'll be Canadian tourists and take a look around."

We left the motorcycle in the room and walked out of the motel onto the street, which was the road we'd come in on.

It was cool and partly overcast, and in the daylight, I could see that most of the buildings were French colonial, set among lush vegetation. There were dozens of people walking and bicycling on the dirt road. The men wore pith helmets, like the North Viet soldiers had in '68, and those helmets still sent a shiver down my spine. The Viet women wore conical straw hats, and the Montagnards, who seemed to make up the majority of the population, wore the traditional garments of at least two distinct tribes.

Judging from the distance of the surrounding mountains, this valley was bigger than Khe Sanh or A Shau.

We walked down the road and passed a small hill on the left, atop which was an old French tank. We continued on and passed an army museum and a big military cemetery, then turned right at a sign that showed crossed swords, the international symbol for battlefield.

As we walked, I saw a bunker with a wooden sign in French, Vietnamese, and good English. The sign read *Here is the bunker of Colonel Charles Piruth, commander of the French artillery. On the second evening of the battle, Colonel Piruth, realizing he was surrounded by overwhelming Viet Minh artillery, apologized in person to all of his artillery men, then went into this bunker and killed himself with a hand grenade.*

I stared at the bunker, which was open, and I assumed they'd cleaned up the mess.

Susan said to me, "I don't think I get it."

I replied, "I guess you had to be here."

I looked at the hills that ringed this valley, and thought maybe I got it. The French were looking for a set-piece battle, like the Americans at Khe Sanh, and they came here, in the middle of nowhere, to lure the Communists into a fight. They got more than they bargained for. Shit happens.

Susan took a photo, and we continued on. We crossed a bridge over the small river that flowed through the valley. On the other side of the bridge was a monument to the Viet Minh casualties, built on the French stronghold named Eliane.

Small groups of Western tourists were walking around, all of them with guides.

We followed a group, who made a left turn on a rural road. A few rusting tanks and artillery pieces sat in vegetable fields, and there were a few markers in French and Vietnamese.

We came to a big bunker around which a group was standing. The sign near the bunker said *Here is the bunker of General Christian de Castries, commander of the French forces, and the site of the French surrender.*

A Viet guide was giving a talk in French to ten middle-aged men and a few women. I wondered if any of them had been survivors of this place. One older guy, I noticed, had tears in his eyes, so I guess that answered my question.

A young Vietnamese man came up to us and said something in French. I said, "Je ne parle pas français."

He seemed surprised, then looked us over and asked, "American?"

I replied, "Canadian," which I'd been taught is good cover for Americans in certain parts of the world where Americans aren't fully appreciated. Thank God for Canada.

The guy spoke English and asked, "You come to see battlefield?"

Remembering my many covers, I replied, "Yes.

I'm a military historian, a botanist, and a naturalist. I collect butterflies."

Susan was smiling rather than rolling her eyes. I think she had missed the old Paul Brenner and was happy he was back.

The guide said, "You please give me one dollar, I tell you about battle."

Susan gave the guy a buck, and it was like putting quarters in a jukebox. He began a rap that was barely comprehensible, and when he was stumped on an English word, he used French, and when French became a problem, he used Vietnamese.

The long and the short of it was that in early 1954, ten thousand soldiers of a French army including Foreign Legionnaires and about three thousand Montagnard and Vietnamese colonial troops set up a string of strongpoints in this valley, all named after women who had been mistresses of General de Castries. There were seven strongpoints, and I was immediately impressed with the French general.

The Viet guide made what was probably a standard joke and said, "Maybe more mistresses, but he no have enough soldiers."

"Good point."

The guide went on awhile, and the whole sorry episode sounded like a replay of Khe Sanh, except the French didn't have the airpower to neutralize the overwhelming force of fifty thousand Viet Minh soldiers led by General Vo

Nguyen Giap, the same guy who'd planned the Siege of Khe Sanh, and the '68 Tet Offensive, and who I was starting to dislike, or maybe admire.

The guide said, "General Giap men carry many hundred cannon through hills and surround Dien Bien Phu. Shoot many thousand cannon shell at French. French colonel kill self when thousand cannon shell fall. He very surprised."

I looked at the hills I'd driven through the night before. I'd be surprised, too. I'd barely gotten the motorcycle through here; hundreds of artillery pieces would be a real challenge.

There was something about the Vietnamese that made them incredibly patient, plodding, and persevering. I thought of the Ho Chi Minh Trail, the Cu Chi tunnels, dragging hundreds of huge artillery pieces over terrain that was barely passable on foot. I asked our guide, "Did they dig tunnels and trenches here?"

"Yes, yes, many, many kilometer—les tranchées. See there? Les trenchées. Viet Minh soldier dig close, attack Eliane, Ann-Marie, Françoise, Dominique, Gabrielle, Beatrice, Claudine."

I said to Susan, "I'd name a fortress for you. Strongpoint Susan."

The guide understood and smiled politely. "Yes? You name fort for this lady?"

Susan was back to rolling her eyes and didn't reply.

The guide informed us that the French dropped another three thousand paratroopers into Dien Bien Phu to try to save the besieged army. In the end, however, after two months, all thirteen thousand French and colonial troops had been killed, wounded, or captured, and the Viet Minh, according to our guide, had lost half their fifty thousand men, but won the war. He said, "French people have enough war. French soldiers go home."

This story had a familiar ring to it, like it was 1968 instead of 1954, and since no one in Washington had learned anything from Dien Bien Phu, I suppose you could say that the American war in Vietnam started right here.

The guide said, "Two thousand French solider lay here—" He made a sweeping motion with his arm to encompass the vegetable fields where water buffalo walked and women worked with hoes. "French people make monument there. See there? Many French come to see here. Some American come, too. I never meet Canada people. You like?"

I thought I'd seen enough battlefields in the last two weeks to last me the rest of my life. Notwithstanding that, I felt a bond with the men who'd fought and died here. I said, "Interesting."

Today was Thursday, and by Sunday, I should be in Bangkok. I was feeling like most short-timers feel with four days left and counting: paranoid. I recalled what my platoon sergeant was nice enough to say to me a few days before I left the field to go home: "Don't get your hopes up, Brenner. Charlie still has seventy-two hours to fuck you up."

Susan gave the guide her camera, and he took a photo of us near General de Castries's command bunker. The photo album should be titled *My Worst Winter Vacation Ever.*

The guide asked us, "You want see all battlefield? I take you. One dollar."

I replied, "Maybe tomorrow. Hey, what do you do for fun in this town?"

"Fun? What is fun?"

I was wondering about how to get Tran Van Vinh to Hanoi on a motorcycle built for two, assuming he was alive and was going to stay alive—and also assuming I actually needed to take him to Hanoi, which I didn't know, though Susan knew. It occurred to me that maybe Susan would be riding alone, and I didn't need to worry about this. Nevertheless I asked, "What's the best way to get to Hanoi?"

"Hanoi? You want go Hanoi?"

"Yeah. Is there a train? Bus? Airplane?"

"Airplane. Bus very dangerous. No train. French people go plane. Plane no go tomorrow, go samedi. But maybe no place for you. Biet?"

"How about car and driver?"

"No. Tet now. No driver go Hanoi. Lundi driver go Hanoi. You want driver?"

"Maybe. Okay, thanks for the history lesson. Viet people very brave."

He almost smiled, then pointed to himself and said, "Ong die here. You understand? Grand-père."

"I understand."

We left the guide and walked up the dirt road, back toward the town. We passed a gutted tank and a few French bunkers overgrown with weeds. I observed, "This is somehow quieter and more dignified than Cong World or DMZ World."

Susan replied, "The north is more somber and less commercial. Plus, they're dealing with the French here, who are a little more dignified and solemn than some of our compatriots at Cong World or Apocalypse Now."

I said, "I'm Canadian."

She informed me, "I barely understood that guide's Vietnamese. They speak a different dialect up here."

I had the suspicious thought that Ms. Weber was setting me up for some juke and jive if we got to speak with my star witness. I said, "The written language is the same. Correct?"

She hesitated, then replied, "Mostly."

"Good. Bring a pen."

We kept walking, and she asked me, "What's the plan now?"

"Our mutual rendezvous person in Hue, Mr.

Anh, suggested I go to the market and chat with a few Montagnards. Didn't he tell you that?"

"Yes, he did."

"That's the plan."

She inquired, "Are you concerned about what may have happened to Mr. Anh?"

"I am."

"Do you think he'd crack under interrogation?"

"Everyone does."

She didn't reply.

We turned onto a street at the edge of the town. There were enough Westerners around so that we didn't stand out, and they were mostly middle-aged or older people, and no backpackers, which was a treat. I saw the bus station to our left; an old stucco building with two incredibly dilapidated buses in front of it.

She saw me looking at the buses and asked, "Why did you ask the guide about transportation to Hanoi?"

"I might want to take my witness to Hanoi. I can't take the motorcycle unless you're willing to stay behind."

She changed the subject and said, "You need to tell me now the name of the village we're looking for."

If I believed her, this was the one thing she didn't know, and if I told her, then she didn't need me any longer. But the time had come, and I said to her, "It's called Ban Hin. It's about thirty kilometers north of here." I added, "If something happens to me, you push on."

She didn't reply.

We got to the market, which was a partially paved area covered by roofs in long rows.

As we walked through the market, I noticed that no one was badgering us to buy anything. I remarked on this to Susan, and she said, "The merchants in the north are not aggressive or pushy. As a businesswoman, I find the North Viets hopeless."

I said, "You can drop your cover, Ms. Weber."

"I have to stay in practice for the next guy I do this with."

I looked around the market and noticed lots of porcupines hanging, along with weasels, red squirrels, and other tasty wildlife. I asked Susan, "So, what's our story? We have relatives in Ban Hin? A pen pal? Looking for a retirement spot?"

She said, "I'll take care of it."

There was a whole section of the market taken up by Montagnards and their wares, and we walked through this area. Susan said to me, "Meet me in Aisle 8, paper products and light bulbs."

I looked around to see if the aisles were actually numbered, and she laughed at me. "Go find the tea section. I'll find you there."

I kept walking, then glanced back and saw Susan sitting cross-legged on a blanket, talking to some Montagnard women and handling some ladies wear while she smoked a cigarette; the salesladies smoked whatever was in their pipes. Maybe they were less pushy because they were stoned out of their minds.

I found the covered stall where tea leaves lay on the ground in wicker baskets. The vendors were mostly Montagnards of the same tribe, and they were brewing tea, so I got a bowl of hot tea for two hundred dong, about two cents, and sipped it. It was awful, but it was hot and I was cold.

This was a weird place, and I was sure that nearly all the Westerners were with organized groups. Only an idiot would come here alone.

Four soldiers with AK-47s came into the tea area, and they gave me the eye, then ordered bowls of tea.

They stood not ten feet from me, drinking tea, smoking, and talking softly. One of them kept glancing at me. Do I need this shit?

If it weren't for the Colt .45 stuck in my belt, I wouldn't be too concerned. Yet, when you're carrying, and you're not supposed to be carrying, the fucking gun seems to get bigger and bigger under your clothes, so that in your mind, it's the size of an artillery piece.

The four soldiers finished before I did and walked away.

I stood there listening to my heart beat.

Susan appeared and put down a large plastic bag filled with brightly colored clothes. She ordered tea, sipped from the bowl, and said, "That feels good."

"How'd you make out?"

"Pretty good. Ban Hin is about thirty kilometers north of here."

"I know that. How do we get there?"

She said, "These Montagnards are all Tai and H'mong, and they live in the north hills and walk into Dien Bien Phu with their wares, or sometimes they take a pony, or the once-a-day bus, and the rich ones have scooters or motorcycles."

"Is that a fact? How do we get to Ban Hin?"

"I'm getting to that. I found a lady who lives near Ban Hin."

"Good. She draw you a map?"

"No. But I got directions. Problem is, she and her people use a lot of trails and shortcuts, so she wasn't clear on the road route. Plus, I couldn't understand half her Vietnamese. The Montagnards have a worse accent than the North Viets."

"Go back and get the directions written out."

"They're illiterate, Paul."

"Then get her to draw a map."

"They don't understand the concept of maps. Maps are abstract."

"To you and her maybe. Not to me."

"Take a break. I think I can follow her directions."

I thought about all of this. Mr. Anh had been

very clear about not asking an ethnic Vietnamese anything because they'd run off to the cops if they thought you were up to something. Montagnards were all right because they kept to themselves. But Mr. Anh failed to mention that they spoke differently, took trails instead of roads, were illiterate, and had never seen a map in their lives. Minor problems, but Susan thought she knew the way to Ban Hin.

I asked her, "What did you tell her about why you wanted to go to Ban Hin?"

"I said I'd heard there was beautiful jewelry made there." Susan added, "It's a girl thing."

I rolled my eyes, but I don't do that well, and Susan missed it.

She said, "She mentioned that Ban Hin was a Vietnamese village, not Montagnard, as we probably knew, and that the Vietnamese made bad jewelry, plus she never heard of jewelry being made in Ban Hin."

She finished her tea, then went around to other stalls and bought some bottled water, rice cakes, and bananas. I looked for a taco stand.

We left the market carrying plastic bags and walked toward the motel, a hundred meters up the dirt road. We went into Unit 7, packed our stuff in the BMW's saddlebags, and I wheeled the bike out of the room and down to the reception office.

Inside, we checked out early, and got our passports and visas back. I hoped they hadn't yet faxed copies to the Ministry of Public Security, but I wasn't going to ask.

There was a guy behind the desk, and he asked me, "Where you go now?"

I replied, "Paris."

Susan said to him, "We drive Hanoi."

"Ah. Big water, Road 6. You go only Son La. You wait Son La. Two day, three day."

I said, "Thanks for the traffic and weather, sport. See you next season."

We left the office, and I said to Susan, "Am I to understand that Route 6 is blocked by floods or mud slides?"

"Sounds that way. Mr. Anh said this was common, but they usually get bulldozers and open it up in a day or so."

"What the hell is wrong with this place?"

"Don't take it personally."

"Okay, how do we get to Hanoi from here if Route 6 is closed?"

"There is another route along the Red River. Goes right to Hanoi."

"What if we have three people?"

She replied, "There's a train along the Red River at a place called Lao Cai on the Chinese border, about two hundred kilometers north of here."

"Okay, how do we get to Lao Cai with Tran Van Vinh?"

"Maybe by bus. Let's worry about that after we get to Ban Hin and see how many people we need to get to Lao Cai. Also, the trains start running again tomorrow morning. It's about 450 kilometers from Lao Cai to Hanoi, so we should make it in ten to twelve hours." She looked at me and said, "In case I'm not with you, you know the way."

I nodded.

She said, "If all else fails, find a Hanoi-bound logging truck. The only questions they ask is if you have ten bucks and if you'd like to buy some opium."

"Did Mr. Anh tell you all this?"

"Yes, but we could have read it in the guide-book, if you hadn't given it to Mr. Anh. When you give someone a signal object, you don't use something you need. Use a bag of peanuts or something. Were you sleeping during that class?"

"I'm retired." I asked her, "Why didn't you get the book back when you saw him?"

"I didn't know he had it." She added, "Another amateur."

"And you?"

"Investment banker."

"Right." We mounted up, and I pulled onto the road. I headed south, in case anyone was looking, and I was out of Dien Bien Phu in a few minutes. I pulled over near the hill where the tank sat. A sign informed me that this was Dominique. I wondered what happened to all the general's ladies, and I wondered if any of them had ever come here to see their namesakes.

Susan got off the bike and opened a saddle-bag. We put on the fur-lined leather caps and the goggles, and Susan took out two dark blue scarves she'd bought and said, "H'mong tribe."

"I know that."

She laughed. "You're so full of shit."

We wrapped the scarves around our necks and chins, and she said, "Unfortunately, the tribespeople here don't know how to set dyes, and you'll have blue dye on your face." She showed me her hands, which indeed had blue dye on them. No one in Washington was going to believe this shit.

I studied the map for a few minutes, and I said to her, "Where's Ban Hin?"

She pointed to a place on the map and said, "Someplace up here in the Na River Valley. It's not marked, but I can find it."

We looked at each other, and I said, "This is going to be okay."

She got on the motorcycle, I twisted the throttle, and we sped off.

I found a dirt trail that ran through the rice paddies and, within a few minutes, we were on the road that ran past General de Castries's command bunker. I also wondered what happened to him, and if he ever saw his seven mistresses again. If I had seven mistresses, I might decide to stay in a POW camp.

We drove through the vegetable fields, passed the rusting tanks and artillery pieces, and traveled north toward the hills and mountains we'd come out of last night, though by a different road, this one west of the one I'd taken to Dien Bien Phu.

I looked at my watch and saw it was not yet noon. This one-lane road was dirt, but dry, hard-packed, and smooth between the wheel ruts, so I was doing thirty KPH without too much trouble. In about an hour, unless we got lost, I'd be asking someone in Ban Hin if they knew a guy named Tran Van Vinh. I couldn't even guess at the outcome of this day.

This road that was marked Route 12 on the map ran through the Na Valley, which was not even five hundred meters wide in most places. The river was small, but swift-flowing, and the road was actually a levee that ran along the side of the river.

The hills got higher and towered over the narrow valley, which was no more than a gorge in some places. Wherever the valley widened, there were flooded rice paddies and peasant huts on both sides of the dirt road. The few people we saw looked to be ethnic Vietnamese in traditional black silk pajamas and conical straw hats, working in the rice fields much as they did on the coastal plains, but very far from their ancestors.

The hills were over two thousand meters high now, and a constant headwind blew down from the north, through the tunnel-like valley, and Susan and I had to lean forward or get blown off the bike.

No one was working in the fields, and there was no traffic on the one-lane road. I remembered it was the last day of Tet, and people stayed home, including, I hoped, Tran Van Vinh. The Viets who had traveled to get to their ancestral homes wouldn't be on the road again until tomorrow or the next day. It occurred to me, of course, that Tran Van Vinh might have an earlier ancestral village on the coast, and he may have gone there for Tet. But if that was the case, I'd catch him on his way back to Ban Hin, though that would be pushing my time frame. I really wanted to be in Bangkok Sunday, or anywhere other than Vietnam. But I knew I'd stay until Mr. Vinh and I had a talk.

In the hills, I could see Montagnard long-houses clinging precariously to cleared ridge-lines, and it struck me that two very different civilizations existed in the same space, but vertically to one another.

About an hour after we'd started, I saw on the odometer that we'd come thirty kilometers. "What do your directions say?"

"Ban Hin is right on this road."

"It is? You made it sound complicated."

"Sometimes you want to leave me behind, so I need to sound invaluable."

I didn't reply to that interesting statement, but said to her, "See that hut there? Go ask about Ban Hin."

"We speak only to Montagnards. We haven't come this far to blow it at the last minute."

We continued on slowly, north on Route 12. About ten minutes later, coming toward us, were three young men, Montagnards, on their ponies.

I stopped the motorcycle and shut it off.

As the Montagnards approached, I could see that the ponies were saddleless, which they always were, and there were sacks of something tied over their backs.

Susan and I took off our scarves, hats, and goggles, and Susan dismounted and walked toward the riders. She greeted them with a wave, and they reined up, looking at her.

She spoke to them and they were nodding. They looked at me, who had been a Montagnard myself just two minutes ago, then looked back at Susan. Almost simultaneously, the three of them pointed back over their shoulders. So far, so good.

Susan seemed to be thanking them and was about to walk away when one of them reached into his sack and pulled out something, which he gave to her. She waved and walked back toward me.

The three riders overtook her and chatted again. They obviously liked what they saw. They came abreast of me and the motorcycle, and sort of saluted as they continued south.

Susan walked up to me and said, "They were nice. They gave me this skin." She held up a two-foot-long animal skin with black fur on it. She said, "I think it's a wolverine. Unfortunately, it isn't tanned and it smells."

"It's the thought that counts." I said, "Get rid of it."

"I'll hold it awhile."

"Where's Ban Hin?"

"Up the road a piece."

"How far?"

"Well . . . they apparently don't measure in time or distance. They travel by landmarks, so it's the big village after two small villages."

"Good. Mount up." I added, "You have blue dye on your face."

She mounted up, and I started the engine and kicked the bike into gear. We continued on without our Montagnard accessories.

Within five minutes, we passed a small cluster of huts. Village One.

Five minutes later, we passed small Village Two.

Five or six minutes later, we approached a bigger village situated along the right side of the road. In front of the village were four stucco structures set back from the road, and I could tell that one was a modest pagoda, the other a clinic, and the third was a school. The fourth flew a red flag with a yellow star, and had a dark green military jeep parked in front of it. I knew this had been too easy. I stopped the bike.

Susan said, "This is Ban Hin."

"And that's a military jeep."

"I know. What do you want to do?"

I said, "I haven't come this far to turn around."

"Me neither."

I went quickly past the military post, then cut into the landscaped yard in front of the pagoda, and pulled the bike around to the rear, out of sight of the road and hopefully of the military building.

I shut off the engine, and we dismounted.

Susan said, "Okay, how do you want to ask if Tran Van Vinh is alive and at home?"

I replied, "We're Canadian military historians, who speak some French. We'll ask about some veterans of the Tet Offensive, then get down to the battle of Quang Tri. Wing it. You're good at bullshitting people."

We got our backpacks and cameras out of the saddlebags, and Susan went around to the entrance of the pagoda.

I followed her through the open doors, and there was no one inside. Tet blossoms were stuck in ceramic urns, and there was a small shrine at the far end of the small, windowless structure, and joss sticks burned on the altar.

Susan went up to the altar, took a joss stick,

and lit it, then threw a few dong in a bowl. Hey, whatever it takes.

She turned and joined me near the front door. She said, "Today is the last day of the Tet holiday, the fourth day of the Year of the Ox. We have arrived in Ban Hin. Let's go find Tran Van Vinh, then let's go home."

We left the pagoda and walked into the village of Ban Hin.

CHAPTER FORTY-THREE

———————— ★ ————————

The village of Ban Hin was not like the tropical and subtropical villages of the coastal plains; there were no palm trees, for one thing, but lots of pine and huge leafy trees, plus thick clumps of wild rhododendron that were starting to bloom on this cool February afternoon.

The village was hemmed in by the steeply rising mountain to the east, the rice paddies to the north and south, and the one-lane dirt road we'd arrived on.

The peasants' huts were mostly rough-hewn pine with roofs of thatched bamboo leaves. Each house was surrounded by a vegetable garden, and in some of the gardens I could see the entrances to earthen bomb shelters, remnants of the American bombing.

I wouldn't have imagined that a valley this remote had been bombed, but I recalled in Tran Van Vinh's letter to his brother, Lee, that Vinh had mentioned that their cousin, Liem, had written and described trucks filled with wounded soldiers, and columns of fresh troops heading south. I could picture this now, this remote valley road that began at the Chinese border, where much of the war matériel originated, then wound its way to the Laotian border where the Ho Chi Minh Trail network began. I had the feeling that anyone here over thirty years old remembered the United States Air Force.

The village was filled with kids and adults of all ages, and it seemed that most of the residents of Ban Hin were home on this last day of Tet.

In fact, everyone was staring at us, the way people in a small rural American village might stare at two East Asians who were wandering around in black silk pajamas and conical straw hats.

We reached the center of the village, which consisted of a red dirt square, no bigger than a tennis court, surrounded by more houses and an open pavilion that housed a small produce market. I could see some picnic-like tables where people sat, talked, drank, and ate. They stopped what they were doing and looked at us.

I always knew that if we got this far, the biggest problem would be here in this village. The military facility on the road added to the problem.

In the center of the square was a simple concrete slab about ten feet long and six feet high set on another concrete slab on the ground. The vertical slab was painted white, and on the white paint was what appeared to be red lettering. At the base of the slab were Tet blossoms and joss sticks burning in ceramic bowls. We walked over to the monument and stood before it.

The red lettering was, in fact, names, running in rows top to bottom. Across the top were larger letters, and Susan read, " 'In honor of the men and women who fought for the Reunification of the Fatherland in the American War of 1954 to 1975.' " She said, "These are the names of the missing, and there are a lot of them, including Tran Quan Lee." She pointed.

I saw Tran Quan Lee, and saw, too, that there were many people of the family of Tran listed as missing.

We both read the names, but did not see Tran Van Vinh. So far, so good. I said, "The dead must be on the other side."

We walked around the monument, whose entire surface was painted with red-lettered names that looked as though they'd been recently touched up.

A crowd of about a hundred had gathered, and they were inching a little closer to us. I noticed that a number of middle-aged men and women had missing arms or legs.

I looked at the names of the dead, which were listed chronologically, like the names on the Wall in Washington. If Tran Van Vinh had been killed in action, we'd have no idea when, but it wasn't before February 1968, so I started there, while Susan began at the end with April 1975.

I held my breath as I read the names.

Susan said, "I don't see him yet . . ."

"Neither do I." But I didn't want to see his name, and I may have unconsciously blocked it out, though every time I saw a "Tran," my heart skipped a beat.

The crowd was right behind us now. It felt a little odd staring at the monument to the dozens of dead and missing of this village, all of whom had been killed by my compatriots, and maybe even by me. On the other hand, I had my own wall to deal with. Also, I was Canadian.

Susan and I kept reading the names, and she said softly to me, "A lot of these names are women and children, and the names are noted as having been killed on the homefront, which I guess means by bombs."

I didn't reply.

Susan and I met in the middle of the list and read the last of the names to ourselves. I said, "He's not here."

"Not here, either. But is he still alive?"

"I'll bet everyone behind us can answer that question."

As I stared at the simple slab of concrete with hand-painted names, I couldn't help but think of the polished granite wall in Washington. In the end, there was no difference in these two memorials.

I said to Susan, "Canadian. Ready?"

"Oui."

We turned around and looked at the crowd. In rural South Vietnam, we had aroused passing curiosity; here, we aroused intense interest, and if they discovered we were Americans, they might get hostile. I couldn't read anything in the faces of the crowd, but they didn't look like a welcoming committee. I said, "Bonjour."

There was some murmuring, but no smiles. It occurred to me that with Dien Bien Phu so close, there might be some residual animosity toward the French. *Ong die here . . . grand-père.* I said, "Nous sommes Canadiens."

I thought I saw the crowd relax a bit, or maybe that's what I wanted to see.

Susan, too, said, "Bonjour." She then said something about us coming from Dien Bien Phu, and was it okay if we made une photographie of Le Monument?

No one seemed to object, so Susan stood back and made une photographie of the names of the dead.

Finally, someone came forward, a middle-aged gent in black wool pants and an orange sweater. He said something to me in French, but I totally didn't get it, and I didn't think he cared if the pen of my aunt was on the desk of my uncle.

Susan said something to him in halting French, and he replied.

The guy's French was a little better than Susan's, so she mixed in some halting Vietnamese, which had the effect of startling the crowd and bringing everyone closer.

It couldn't be long before a few soldiers showed up and asked for our passports and discovered we weren't actually Canadians.

I was starting to feel less like James Bond and more like Indiana Jones in a movie titled *Village of Doom*.

Susan was giving this guy the line of crap about l'histoire de la guerre américaine, which he seemed to be half buying.

Finally, she said something to him in more fluent Vietnamese, and I could hear the name Tran Van Vinh.

Asking for someone by name in a small town in Vietnam, or Kansas, or anywhere sort of stops the show.

There was a long silence, then the man looked at both of us, and I held my breath until finally he nodded and said, "Oui. Il suvivre."

I knew I had not come this far to visit a grave, and here I was in the village of Ban Hin, and the answer to the question of whether or not Tran Van Vinh was alive was, "Yes, he's alive."

Susan glanced at me, nodded and smiled. She turned back to the guy and continued in broken Vietnamese, with a little French thrown in, and he replied to her in slow Vietnamese, with lots of French. We were actually getting away with this.

Finally, he spoke the magic word, "Allons."

And off we went, following him through the crowd, which parted for us.

We passed through the covered market, and the man stopped at a community bulletin board covered with clear plastic. He pointed to two faded black and white photographs of Americans in flight suits with their hands in the air, surrounded by pajama-clad peasants carrying old bolt action rifles. There was some room left for another picture of me and Susan in a similar pose.

The man said, "Les pilotes Americains." I glanced at Susan, and we made eye contact.

We continued on a narrow tree-shaded path between small houses toward the towering mountain at the end of the village where a group of low hillocks lay at the base of the mountain, which I recognized as burial mounds. Beyond the burial mounds were small wooden houses.

We followed the guy up a winding path toward a house built of hand-hewn pine and thatched with bamboo leaves.

We got to the door of the house, and the guy motioned us to wait. He entered through an open door.

A few seconds later, he came out and motioned us inside. As we entered, he said something to us in French about chez Tran.

We found ourselves in this one-room house whose floor was packed red clay. Glass windows let in some gray light, and I smelled charcoal burning somewhere in the damp air.

As my eyes adjusted to the dim light, I could see hammocks folded along the walls with blankets in them, and on the floor were a number of woven bamboo baskets and chests. A low table without chairs sat in the center of the floor on a black rug.

In the far corner was a clay cooking stove, which glowed red from the firebox with burning charcoal. To the right of the clay stove was a simple altar against the wall, and on the altar were burning joss sticks and framed photographs. Hanging on the wall to the right of the altar was a big poster of Ho Chi Minh. Beside that hung a Vietnamese flag and some framed certificates or awards.

I looked around again to confirm that no one was home.

We stood there a moment, then Susan said, "He says this is the house of Tran Van Vinh, and we should wait here."

I don't like being boxed in by walls, but it was too late to worry about that now. We had arrived, one way or the other, at the end of our journey. I asked, "Did he say where the liquor cabinet was?"

"No. But he said I could smoke." She walked to the charcoal stove, took off her backpack, sat on a hearth rug, and lit a cigarette.

I slipped off my backpack and put it next to hers. I saw that the roof was only about six feet high at the far wall, and I went over to it and pulled out the pistol from under my leather jacket. Having learned a thing or two from the Viet Cong, I slipped the .45 and the two extra magazines between two rows of tied thatch.

Susan said, "Good idea. I think if the soldiers arrive, we could talk ourselves out of just about anything but that gun."

I didn't reply to that overly optimistic statement, but I asked her, "What did you tell that guy?"

She replied, "His name is Mr. Khiem, and he's the village schoolteacher. As you suggested, I told him we were Canadian military historians who had been to Dien Bien Phu, and that we were also studying the American War. I also said that we were told in Dien Bien Phu to see the war memorial in the square of Ban Hin. I made that up."

"You're good at that."

"I said I'd heard that many veterans of the American War lived in the Na Valley, and we were especially interested in veterans of the '68 Tet Offensive, and more specifically the battle of Quang Tri City." She drew on her cigarette and continued, "But Mr. Khiem wasn't offering any names, except his own. He was at the battle of Hue. Finally, in frustration, I just said I'd heard the name of Tran Van Vinh come up in Dien Bien Phu. We'd heard that he was a brave soldier who'd been wounded at Quang Tri." She looked at me and said, "I didn't want to hang around that square any longer so I went for broke."

"Did Mr. Khiem buy it?"

"Maybe. He was somewhere between incredulous and proud that they spoke well of Ban Hin in Dien Bien Phu." Susan added, "Mr. Khiem is also a Tran and is related to Vinh in some way or another."

I said, "There were lots of dead and missing Trans on that memorial. I'm glad we're Canadians."

She tried to smile and said, "I hope he believed that."

"He didn't get hostile, so I guess he did. On our next mission to Vietnam, we'll be Swiss."

She lit another cigarette. "Send me a postcard."

I said to her, "You did fine. I'm really proud of you, and if Mr. Khiem went to get the soldiers, it wasn't your fault."

"Thank you."

I asked her, "Does Tran Van Vinh live here, or is he visiting for Tet?"

"Mr. Khiem said Tran Van Vinh lives here in Ban Hin and has lived here all his life."

"Where is he now?"

"Mr. Khiem said something about seeing his relatives off."

"That should put him in a good mood. When is he expected back?"

"Whenever the daily bus arrives from Dien Bien Phu."

I looked at the picture of Uncle Ho and asked, "Do you think this is a setup?"

"What do you think?"

"I think you Canadians have an annoying habit of answering a question with a question."

She forced a smile and smoked.

I walked over to the family altar and looked at the framed photographs in the dim light. I noticed that all the men and women were young, in their early to mid twenties. I said to Susan, "No one gets too old around here."

She glanced at the photographs. "They use photos of the deceased when they were in their prime, no matter how old they were when they died."

"Really? So if I died today and I was Buddhist, they could use one of the photos you just took of me."

She smiled. "I think they'd call your mother for a slightly less recent photograph." She added, "The family altar is more ancestor worship than Buddhist. It's sort of confusing. The Vietnamese who are not Catholic call themselves Buddhist, but they also practice a primitive ancestor worship. Plus, they practice Confucianism and Taoism. They call it Tam Giao—the Triple Religion."

"I count four."

"I told you, it's confusing. You're Catholic. Don't worry about it."

I looked at the small photographs and noticed that many of the young men were in uniform. One of them, I was certain, was Tran Quan Lee, who though not officially dead, could be presumed so after nearly thirty years of not showing up for the holidays.

We still had the option of coming to our senses, and I said to Susan, "If we hustle, we can be on the BMW in about five minutes."

She didn't even hesitate before replying, "I don't know who's going to come through that door, but we both know we're not going anywhere until someone does."

I nodded.

Susan asked me, "How do you want to handle our conversation with Tran Van Vinh?"

"First of all, it's *my* conversation, not our conversation, and I'm going to be straight. This is how I'd do it with a witness in the States. You bullshit suspects, but you're straight with witnesses."

"Including the fact that we're Americans sent by our government?"

"Well, not *that* straight. We're Americans, but we've been sent by the family of the murdered man to seek justice."

"We don't know the murdered man's name."

"Tran Van Vinh does. He took the dead man's

wallet. Let me do the talking, Susan, and the thinking. You do the translating. Biet?"

We made eye contact, and she nodded.

We waited.

I looked at Susan. We had come a long way, but beyond that, this moment of truth, which had been abstract up to now, was suddenly real and immediate. Tran Van Vinh was alive, and what, if anything, he told us would present a whole new set of problems.

Susan stood and put her arms around me. "I have deceived you, and I may still have to do some things that you don't like, but no matter what happens, I love you."

Before I could reply, I heard a noise behind me, and we both turned toward the door. Standing in the open doorway was the dark outline of a man who I hoped was Tran Van Vinh.

★

CHAPTER FORTY-FOUR

—————— ★ ——————

Susan walked directly to the man at the door, bowed, and said something to him in Vietnamese.

He bowed in return, said something, then looked at me. We made eye contact, and I had no doubt this was Tran Van Vinh.

He looked to be about sixty, but was probably younger. He was thin, and taller than the average Viet. He had all his hair, which was still jet black and cut short. He wore baggy trousers and a black quilted jacket, and on his feet were socks and sandals.

Susan said to me, "Paul, this is Mr. Vinh."

I walked directly to him and put out my hand.

He hesitated, then took my hand. I said, "I am Paul Brenner, an American, and I have come a long way to see you."

He stared at me as Susan translated.

I said to him, "We told your compatriots that we were Canadians because we felt that there may be some unpleasant feelings toward Americans in your village."

Again, Susan translated, and again Mr. Vinh kept staring at me.

I looked into his eyes, and he looked into

mine. The last American he'd seen had probably wanted to kill him, and vice versa, but I saw no hostility in his expression; in fact, I couldn't see anything.

I took my passport out of my pocket and handed it to him with the front page open.

He took it and looked at it, then closed it and handed it back to me. He said something, which Susan translated as, "What do you want?"

I replied, "First, it is my unpleasant duty to inform you that your brother, Lee, was killed in action in the A Shau Valley in May of 1968. His body was found by an American soldier, who removed personal items that identified him as Tran Quan Lee."

Mr. Vinh understood A Shau and coupled with his brother's name, he must have known this wasn't good news.

Susan translated, and Mr. Vinh listened without emotion. He kept staring at me, then walked over to the family altar, picked up a photograph and looked at it a long time. He put it back, turned, and said something to me.

Susan replied to him directly, then said to me, "He wants to know if you killed his brother. I told him you did not."

I said, "Tell him I was a soldier with the First Cavalry Division, and that I saw combat in the A Shau Valley in May of 1968, and that it could have been me who killed his brother, but it was not I who found the body."

Susan hesitated and asked me, "Are you sure you want—"

"Tell him."

She told him, and he looked at me, then nodded.

I said, "Tell him I was also outside Quang Tri City at the time he was recovering from his wounds in the Buddhist high school, and it was my duty to kill the North Vietnamese soldiers who were trying to escape from the city."

Susan translated, and Mr. Vinh looked surprised that I knew a little of his war experiences. We made eye contact again, and again I saw no hostility, and I knew I would not. In fact, as we looked at each other, I had no doubt that he was saying to himself, "This poor bastard was there, too."

I said to Mr. Vinh, "I'm glad I didn't kill you, and glad you didn't kill me."

Susan translated, and I saw a faint smile pass over his lips, but he didn't reply.

I was getting somewhere with him, but I didn't know where. I said to him, "Quite frankly, Mr. Vinh, I'm very surprised that you survived seven more years of war."

Susan translated, and Mr. Vinh stared off into space, nodding to himself as though he, too, were surprised. I thought I saw a slight tremble in his upper lip, but that might have been my imagination. The man was very stoic, which was partly for our benefit, and also an old wartime habit.

I said to Susan, "How we doing with your translating?"

She replied, "He spent a lot of time in the south during the war, and he's aware of my southern accent. I'm catching most of what he's saying."

"Good. We like true and accurate translations."

She didn't reply.

I didn't say anything further to Mr. Vinh, and I let him think if he wanted to say anything to me. Finally, he spoke and Susan listened, then said to me, "Mr. Vinh says he was in the 304th Infantry Division of the People's Army of Vietnam."

Mr. Vinh continued and Susan translated. "He was sent into the south in August 1965 and fought in Quang Tri Province. He says you should know where his division was during the Tet Offensive in the winter of 1968."

Indeed I did. The 304th was our main adversary when I got to Quang Tri in January 1968. This guy had already been there two and a half years, with no end in sight and no R&R.

Mr. Vinh was speaking, and Susan said, "In June of 1968, the division returned to the north . . . there were few men left in the division . . . the division was rebuilt with new soldiers, and returned to Quang Tri in March 1971, then participated in the Spring Offensive of 1972 . . . the Easter Offensive . . . and his division captured the province and the city of Quang Tri . . . and suffered heavy losses from the American bombing and withdrew north again to rebuild the division." Susan added, "He wants to know if you were there for the Spring Offensive."

I replied, "I, too, had returned home in 1968, in November, then came back to Vietnam in January 1972, and was stationed at Bien Hoa during the Spring Offensive."

Susan told him this, and he nodded, then looked at me. I doubted if he'd ever spoken to an American veteran before, and he was obviously curious, but arriving as I had, out of nowhere, he was trying to collect his thoughts; he hadn't been thinking about this meeting for the last two weeks as I had.

Mr. Vinh spoke, and Susan translated. "He says he returned to the front in 1973, then participated in the final Spring Offensive of 1975, and the 304th Division captured Hue, then drove down the coast on Highway One on captured tanks. He entered Saigon on April 29 and was present at the surrender of the presidential palace the next day."

And I thought I had a few war stories. This guy had seen it all, from the alpha to the omega, ten years of slaughter. If my year had seemed like ten, then his ten must have seemed like a hundred. And here he was, home in his native village, getting on with life after having had a decade of his youth taken from him.

I said to him, "You must have received many medals and decorations."

Susan translated, and without hesitation, he walked to a wicker chest, as I hoped he would, and opened it. I needed to get him into the habit of opening trunks of war memorabilia.

He removed a black silk cloth, which he unfolded on the low table. He knelt and spread out twelve medals of different shapes and sizes, which were all painted with various colors of enamel, and each had multicolored ribbons attached; and there lay the pretty evidence of ten years in hell.

Mr. Vinh named each medal, and Susan translated.

I didn't want to patronize Mr. Vinh by saying how impressed I was; he seemed to me capable of detecting bullshit, so I just nodded and said, "Thank you for showing me."

Susan translated, and she and I made eye contact. She nodded, as if to say, "You're doing pretty good for an insensitive idiot."

Mr. Vinh replaced his medals, closed the trunk, and stood.

So we all stood there for a few seconds, and I'm sure that Mr. Vinh knew I hadn't come twelve thousand miles to see his medals.

The moment had arrived, and I said to him, "I'm here to speak to you about what you saw while you lay wounded in the Citadel at Quang Tri City."

He recognized Quang Tri, and perhaps even

Citadel, and his eyes went to Susan, who translated.

He looked back at me, but didn't respond.

I said to him, "The American soldier who found the body of your brother in the A Shau Valley removed from his body a letter written by you to your brother, as you lay recovering from your wounds at the Buddhist high school. Do you recall that letter?"

As soon as Susan translated, he nodded in understanding of how I knew what I knew.

I lied to him for the first time and said, "I am here on behalf of the family of the lieutenant who was killed by the captain," which maybe wasn't a complete lie. I continued, "I have been asked to inquire about this matter and to bring understanding and justice to the family." I looked at Susan, as if to say, "Get that right."

She glanced at me and translated.

Mr. Vinh did not reply.

I tried to put myself in his position. He'd seen his generation wiped out and was not impressed or moved by the desire of an American family trying to find justice in that mass slaughter, or to bring closure to the death of one soldier. The Hanoi government, in fact, was always a little incredulous regarding the American government spending millions of dollars to find the remains of a few MIAs. I don't know if this was a cultural difference, or a matter of practicality;

Vietnam didn't have the time or money to look for a third of a million missing soldiers. We, on the other hand, had become obsessed with the search for our two thousand missing men.

Mr. Vinh remained silent, and so did I. You can't rush these people, and they don't get nervous during long periods of silence the way Americans do.

Finally, Mr. Vinh spoke, and Susan translated. "He said he does not want to participate in any inquiry unless ordered to do so by his government."

I took a deep breath. I wasn't going to insult this old soldier by offering him money, but I reminded him, "This family has learned of the fate of your brother, Lee, which I have passed on to you freely. Would you be kind enough to tell me the fate of their son, so I may pass that on to them?" I paused, then added, "This is a private family matter, and has no government involvement."

Susan translated, and there was again a silence in the room, broken by the crackling of the charcoal on the hearth, and the sound of a songbird outside.

Mr. Vinh turned and walked to the door.

Susan and I looked at each other.

Mr. Vinh left, and we could hear him talking to someone outside, then he returned and said something to Susan.

She bowed to him, and I thought we were

being asked to leave, or to stick around until the soldiers came, but Susan said to me, "Mr. Vinh has asked his grandson to find a female relative to make tea."

Why do I doubt myself? I'm good at this. Witnesses love me. Suspects fear me. Also, I'm very lucky.

Mr. Vinh motioned us toward the low table, and we joined him there. He sat cross-legged with the warm stove at his back and indicated a place on the floor for Susan at his left and me across from him.

Susan took out her cigarettes and offered one to Mr. Vinh, who accepted. She offered one to me with a nod, and I took the cigarette. Susan lit all three cigarettes and put her plastic lighter on the table. The ashtray was a scrap of twisted steel that looked like a bomb fragment.

I took a puff on the cigarette and left it in the ashtray. Mr. Vinh seemed to like his Marlboro Light.

I said to him, "May I tell you the story of how I came to read your letter to your brother?"

Susan translated, and he nodded.

I related the story of Victor Ort, and the Vietnam Veterans of America, emphasizing the VVA's humanitarian program of helping the Hanoi government discover the fate of their missing soldiers. The story changed somewhat, however, and Mr. Ort and I both became members of the Vietnam Veterans of America, and by chance I knew a family whose son, a First Cavalry lieutenant, had been killed in Quang Tri City. Sounded good to me.

I further explained that the family was convinced that this lieutenant who was mentioned in Mr. Vinh's letter could be their son. I spun a little more stuff, and being Boston Irish, this is my specialty. I did not mention the army Criminal Investigation Division, nor did I mention the name of the deceased lieutenant, because I didn't know it; but Mr. Vinh did.

Mr. Vinh listened as Susan translated.

A middle-aged woman entered and without a word went to the hearth where a water kettle hung permanently over the charcoal. She put three bowls on the rug and took a pinch of tea leaves from a ceramic canister and sprinkled the leaves in each bowl. Then, with a ladle, she filled each bowl with hot water, put the bowls on a wicker tray, and on her knees walked to the table, where she bowed.

I really liked this country. I looked at Susan and winked. She stuck her tongue out at me.

Anyway, the tea ceremony complete, the lady disappeared.

We sipped our tea. I smiled and said, "This is awful."

Susan said something else to Mr. Vinh, and he smiled.

Susan and Mr. Vinh smoked, sipped tea, and chatted. Susan said to me, "Mr. Vinh asks if we are lovers. I told him we began as friends when you hired me in Saigon to translate, then we became lovers."

I looked at Mr. Vinh, who had a faint smile on his face, probably thinking, "Way to go, old man."

Susan said, "Mr. Vinh is amazed at the number of American veterans who have returned to visit in the south. He sees this in the newspapers and in the schoolhouse where there is a television."

I nodded and had the thought that Ban Hin was not completely cut off from the world, and this fact might be relevant if my suspicions about the murderer were true.

Susan and Mr. Vinh continued their tea chat and lit up again. This was necessary, I knew, before you got down to business, but I was becoming a little impatient, not to mention concerned about who might show up next.

I said, directly to Mr. Vinh, "May I ask you if that woman was your wife?"

Susan translated, and he nodded.

I asked, "Was that Mai, who you mentioned in your letter?"

Susan hesitated, but then translated.

Mr. Vinh put down his bowl of tea and looked straight ahead. He said something to no one in particular.

Susan said to me, "Mai was killed in a bombing of Hanoi in 1972. They had been married when he returned from the front in 1971, and they had no children."

"I'm sorry."

He understood and nodded.

Susan and he exchanged a few more words, and she said to me, "He has remarried and has seven children, and many grandchildren. He wants to know if you have children."

"Not that I know of."

Susan gave him a one-word answer that was probably "No." The pleasantries over, Mr. Vinh asked me something, and Susan translated, "He would like to know if you have the letter which he wrote to his brother."

I replied, "I had a photocopy of it, but lost it in my travels. I will send him the original, if he tells us how to do that."

Susan passed this on to him, and he replied. She said, "He has a cousin in Dien Bien Phu, and you can send it there."

I nodded.

I wished I had the letter, of course, to see if what he'd written was what had been translated and what I'd read. But, hopefully, I'd find that out soon.

There were no refills on the tea, thank God, and Mr. Vinh and Susan were keeping the mosquitoes away with cigarette smoke.

I asked Mr. Vinh, "Do your wounds bother you?"

Susan translated, and his reply was, "Sometimes. I have more wounds after Quang Tri, but none so serious as to keep me from my duties for more than a month."

He pointed to me.

I replied, "I had no wounds."

Susan translated, and he nodded.

I asked him, "How did you escape from Quang Tri City?"

He replied and Susan translated, "I was able to walk, and all the walking wounded were told to try to escape at night. I left in the early morning, and I walked alone, through a rainstorm in the moonless night. I passed within ten meters of an American position and escaped into the hills to the west."

I hoped he took the dead lieutenant's stuff with him.

He said something else, and Susan said to me, "Mr. Vinh says he may have walked right past you."

"He did."

That got a smile from everyone, but no belly laughs.

Okay, down to business. I said to Mr. Vinh, "May I show you some photographs so that we may discover if the lieutenant whose family has sent me here is the same lieutenant you saw in the bombed building in Quang Tri City?"

Susan translated, and he nodded.

Susan stood, went to her backpack, and returned with the photographs. She placed the small album on the table and opened it to the first page.

Mr. Vinh stared at the photo, then stood and went to a wicker trunk. He returned with something wrapped in cloth, and produced a canvas wallet. He opened the wallet and removed the plastic photo holder, which he laid next to the photo on the table.

Susan looked at both photos, withdrew the one from the album, and passed both photographs to me.

I looked at the photo from the wallet, which was of a young couple. The woman was good-looking, and the man was the same one in the photo pack.

We now had the victim, and what we needed next was the victim's name, though of course the CID already knew that; but I didn't.

I said to Mr. Vinh, "May I see the wallet?"

Susan asked, and Mr. Vinh pushed the wallet across the table.

I opened it and went through it. There were some military payment certificates—what we used for money instead of dollars—and a few more family photos—Mom and Pop, two teenage girls who looked like his sisters, and an infant who could be the child of the deceased.

There were a few other plasticized odds and ends in the wallet: the Geneva Convention card, the card that listed the Rules of Land Warfare, and another card with the Rules of Engagement.

Lots of rules in war. Most of them didn't mean shit except Rule One, which was, "Kill him before he kills you."

This young officer, however, had the required cards, and I got a sense of a young man who did the right thing. This was reinforced somewhat by his PX liquor ration card, which only officers had access to. The card had only two punch holes in it, indicating two liquor purchases. If I'd had this card in 'Nam, it would have looked like Swiss cheese hit by shrapnel.

The final card was the man's military identification.

I looked at the ID and saw that the name of the dead man was William Hines, and he was a first lieutenant in the infantry.

I looked at Mr. Vinh and said to him, "May I return this wallet to Lieutenant Hines's family?"

Mr. Vinh understood without translation and without hesitation he nodded.

I pushed the wallet aside. If nothing else came out of this, the Hines family was going to get this wallet returned after nearly thirty years, assuming that Paul Brenner returned from Vietnam.

I said to Mr. Vinh, "In your letter, you said to your brother that an American captain killed this man."

Susan translated, and Mr. Vinh nodded.

I continued, "We have some photographs of a

man who we believe to be this captain. Perhaps you can recognize this man."

Susan spoke to him and opened the photo pack to the last ten photos and showed them, one by one, to Mr. Vinh. I watched his face as he looked intently at the photographs.

When Susan came to the last one, Mr. Vinh stared at it and said something, then went back and looked through the photos again, and again he spoke. I had the feeling he was unsure, or unwilling to commit to an identification, and I didn't blame him.

Susan said to me, "He says the light was not good. The captain's face was covered with dirt, and he wore a helmet, and from where Mr. Vinh lay on the second floor, he could not see the face clearly, and in any case, he could not remember after all these years."

I nodded. I was close, but approaching a dead end. I asked Mr. Vinh, "Can you tell me what you saw that day?"

Susan asked him, he replied, and she translated directly. "What was in the letter is what I saw."

I didn't want to tell him that his letter and my letter might not be the same. So, putting my detective hat on, I said to him, "In your letter, you said to your brother that you could attach no meaning to the murder of the lieutenant by this captain. But you said they argued. Is it possible that the lieutenant threatened the captain? Or was the lieutenant showing insubordination or cowardice? It seems unusual that an officer would draw his pistol and shoot another officer over an argument. Could you think about what you saw, and perhaps another thought will come to you."

Susan translated, and Mr. Vinh stared at me, though I couldn't tell why. Finally, he said something, and Susan said to me, "He says he can still attach no meaning to it."

I wasn't going to give up that easily, especially after we'd risked our lives to get here and killed four men in the process. I said to Mr. Vinh, "Perhaps my memory of the letter is not good, and perhaps the translation of the letter was not accurate. Could you please re-tell the story as you remember it?"

Susan translated.

Mr. Vinh took a deep breath, as though he didn't want to tell a war story, and didn't reply.

I said, "Mr. Vinh, no one likes to re-live that time, but since I've been here, I've visited the sites of my old battles, including Quang Tri, and also the A Shau Valley. I have re-lived those times in my mind, and I've told these stories of war to this lady, and I believe this has been good for me. I ask you now to re-live this time, only so that some good may come of it."

Susan translated, and Mr. Vinh said something, which she translated as, "He does not want to speak of it."

Something was wrong here, and I said to Susan, "Are you translating accurately?"

She didn't reply.

"Susan, what the fuck is going on here?"

She looked at me and said, "You really don't want to know, Paul."

I felt a shiver run down my spine. I said, "Yeah, I really fucking want to know."

"Paul, we've come a long way, and we've found Mr. Vinh alive. Now we need to see if he has more souvenirs, then go back to Hanoi and make a report."

I glanced at Mr. Vinh and saw that he understood that his guests were having an argument.

I took the wallet and held it up. I said to Mr. Vinh, "Souvenir?," a word that most Viets understood. "Souvenir de guerre? Dai-uy souvenir? Captain's souvenir? Trung-uy souvenir? Lieutenant's souvenir?" I pointed to the wicker chest. "Beaucoup souvenir? Biet?"

He nodded, stood, and went to his war chest.

I looked at Susan and asked, "Do you know what this is about?"

"I do."

"You saw the true translation of the letter?"

"I did."

"You're a lying bitch."

"I am."

Mr. Vinh returned with a few items in his hands, which he put on the table.

I looked at them. There was an American military watch, whose second hand had stopped long ago, a plastic army canteen that would still be in use by Mr. Vinh, except it had shrapnel tears in it from some other battle, a gold wedding ring, a set of dog tags, and some papers in a canvas pouch.

I picked up the dog tags and they said *Hines, William H.*, followed by his serial number, then his blood type, and his religion, which was Methodist.

I looked at the ring and inside was inscribed *Bill & Fran, 1/15/67*, about a year before he was killed.

I opened the canvas pouch and found a bundle of letters from Fran, from Mom and Pop, and other people. I put the letters aside and found an unfinished letter that he'd been writing, dated February 3, 1968. It said:

Dear Fran,
   I don't know when or if I'll be able to finish this letter. As you know by now, the VC and NVA have attacked all over the country, and have even attacked the Citadel here at Quang Tri. MACV Headquarters has been hit by mortars, and we've got lots of wounded guys who can't get medical attention. The ARVN soldiers have cut and run, and the MACV guys are fighting for their lives. So much for this soft job as an advisor. I know this letter sounds very pessimistic, and I don't even know if you'll get it, but maybe you will, and I want you to know

And there it stopped. I put the letter down.

Also in the canvas pouch was a small note-book, and I opened it. It was a typical officer's log, showing radio frequencies and call signs, codes, names of South Vietnamese army contacts, and so forth. Plus Lieutenant Hines had used the pages as a diary, and I flipped through it and read a few dated entries. It was mostly stuff about the weather, staff meetings, thoughts on the war, and other random notes.

One entry, dated 15 January, caught my eye. It read, "Capt. B. much beloved by sr. officers, but not by me or others. Spends too much time wheeling & dealing on black market & every nite in whorehouse."

I closed the diary. It sounded like Capt. B. was enjoying his war, until Tet.

I looked at Mr. Vinh and pointed to the stuff on the table, then to myself.

He nodded.

I looked at Susan and said, "The Hines family will want this. They'll also want to know how Lieutenant William Hines died."

Susan said to me, "You know how he died. In battle."

"Sorry. He was murdered."

"They don't need to know that."

"Well, I can't speak for the Hines family, but I was sent here to find out who killed Lieutenant Hines."

"No, that's not why you were sent here. You

were sent here to see if the witness to this murder is still alive. He is. And does he have any souvenirs? He does. And can we get those souvenirs? We have. The people in Washington already figured out the name of the murderer—the other guy in these photos, obviously—and neither you nor I need to know that name. You don't *want* to know."

"Wrong." I looked at a folded sheet of yellowed paper on the table, the last souvenir from Mr. Vinh's trunk. I'd recognized it as a unit roster, and I pulled it toward me. It had been typed on an old ditto stencil, and the names were hard to read, but not illegible. The paper was headed *U.S. Army, MACV, Quang Tri City, RVN.* It was dated 3 January 1968.

I scanned the names and saw that there were sixteen Americans in the advisory group, all officers and senior sergeants. It wasn't a particularly dangerous job, until something went wrong, as it had during the Tet Offensive.

The commander of the group was a lieutenant colonel named Walter Jenkins, and his executive officer was a Major Stuart Billings. The third in command was a captain, the only captain listed above a string of lieutenants, which included William H. Hines. The captain's name was Edward F. Blake.

I stared at the name awhile, then pulled the photo pack toward me, and looked at one of the pictures, the one where the captain was wearing a tie. I looked at Susan and said, "Vice President of the United States Edward Blake."

She lit a cigarette and said nothing.

I took a deep breath. If I'd had a Scotch and soda, I would have downed it. *Edward F. Blake. Capt. B.*

Vice President Edward Blake, one heartbeat and one election away from becoming the next president of the United States. Except he had a problem: He murdered someone.

I glanced at Tran Van Vinh, who sat patiently, though perhaps he was getting bad vibes now. I tried to look cool and calm so as not to upset Mr. Vinh. In a normal tone of voice, I asked Susan, "What are the chances of our host here recognizing Vice President Edward Blake?"

She drew on her cigarette and replied, "That's the question, isn't it?"

"Yeah. I mean, TV reception is not real good out here."

She said, "We discussed all of that in Washington. They asked me my opinion."

"What's your opinion?"

"Well, my opinion is that almost every Viet in the country can recognize the president and maybe even the vice president of the United States from pictures in the newspapers. Newspapers here, as in most Communist countries, are universal, cheap, and available to the masses, who are almost all literate. That's what I told them in Washington."

She added, "Also, the news is heavily political and focuses on Washington. The Viets are not badly informed, even in Ban Hin. Plus, we have the television set down at the schoolhouse. And as you might know, Vice President Blake, when he was a senator, was on the Foreign Relations Committee and the MIA Committee, and he has made numerous trips to Vietnam. You may recall that he's a close personal friend of our ambassador to Hanoi, Patrick Quinn." Susan glanced at Mr. Vinh and said, "There could be a potential problem, especially if Edward Blake becomes president." She looked at me and asked, "What do *you* think?"

I pictured Tran Van Vinh sitting in the marketplace downtown, smoking and reading the local *Pravda*, and he's staring at a photo of Edward Blake, and a little bell goes off in his head, and he says to himself, "No . . . can't be. Well, maybe. Hey, Nguyen, this guy who's president of the Imperialist States of America is the guy I told you about—the guy who blew away that lieutenant in Quang Tri."

But then what? Would he report this interesting coincidence to the local authorities? And if he did, what would come of it? *That* was the question.

Susan asked again, "What do you think, Paul?"

I looked at her and said, "I can see why some people in Washington could be nervous, and why Edward Blake may be losing some sleep, assuming he knows about all of this, including Paul Brenner's mission to Vietnam. In any case, the chance of our host here making the ID and reporting it is very slim."

"Better safe than sorry." She added, "I feel a little better now that we've got all these war souvenirs."

"And if you kill this guy, you'll feel even better."

She didn't reply to that, but said, "He sort of recognized the photo. I mean, he's not going to put a name to it right away, but someday he may. Like when he reads about a visit from Edward Blake in one of the national newspapers. In fact, Vice President Blake is right now in Hanoi on an official visit."

I replied, "What a coincidence." I asked, "Does Blake know that he's got a problem? Is that why he's here?"

"I really don't know . . . I think if he doesn't know now, he's going to find out from his aides, if and when we get to Hanoi. That's my guess."

"So, we don't know if the people who sent us on this mission are trying to cover for Blake, or blackmail him?"

She didn't respond to that and continued, "The rural newspapers are weekly, so the next one will have something about Blake's visit, with accompanying photos. The Viets often show wartime photos with a current photo, and they always mention wartime duty, so they'll say that Edward Blake fought at the battle of Quang Tri in 1968, but has since become a friend of Vietnam. They love that." She looked at me. "What do you think? Would our friend here put it together if he saw side-by-side photos of Captain Blake and Vice President Blake?"

"Am I defending this guy's life?"

She didn't reply.

I said, "This man did not go through ten years of hell to be whacked by you in his own home because he may remember something someday."

Mr. Vinh continued to smoke as his guests spoke in English. He probably thought we were very rude, but he was polite enough not to mention it. I wondered, too, if he could recognize the name Edward Blake whenever Susan and I said it. I asked Susan, "Can he understand the name?"

Susan replied, "No. It would be read and pronounced differently. Not so Anglo-Saxon as we pronounce it. Without accent marks, it reads differently to him. But we need to take that roster so he can't match the name in a newspaper . . . plus, our presence here will be recalled by him, and so will that photo pack."

I stared at Susan and thought about all of this. Time to take a Susan reading: Did I still love her? Yes, but I'd get over it. Did I trust her? Never did. Was I pissed? Yes, but impressed. She was very good. And, finally, Was she about to do something rash and violent? She was thinking about it.

She puffed thoughtfully on her cigarette, then said to me, "I really wish you hadn't been so damned nosy."

"Hey, that's what I get paid for. That's why they call me a detective."

She smiled, then realizing we'd been ignoring our host, she chatted with him awhile about God knows what. Maybe she was asking him where he'd gotten his dirt floor. She gave him another cigarette, then she found the bill from the Dien Bien Phu Motel in her pocket, and wrote something on the back as she spoke to Mr. Vinh. Maybe they were exchanging pho recipes, but then she said to me, "I'm getting Mr. Vinh's cousin's address in Dien Bien Phu so we can mail Mr. Vinh's letter back to him."

"Why? You or someone else is going to kill Mr. Vinh."

Susan didn't reply.

Mr. Vinh smiled at me.

I said to Susan, "Let's get out of here before the fuzz shows up."

Susan said to me, "We're okay. You're not going to believe this, but Mr. Vinh is the district Party chief." She nodded toward the poster of Uncle Ho on the wall. "The soldiers won't come unless Mr. Vinh summons them."

I looked at Mr. Vinh. My luck, I'm in the house of the top Commie in the county. That aside, he

seemed cooperative, and if Susan had translated
my questions about what transpired on that day
he'd seen Captain Blake shoot Lieutenant Hines,
Mr. Vinh would have answered. I asked Mr. Vinh,
"Parlez-vous français?"

He shook his head.

"Not even a little? Un peu?"

He didn't respond.

Susan said, "Okay, maybe we should go, Paul,
before Mr. Vinh starts to smell a rat."

"I'm not finished."

"Leave it alone."

"Tell me, Susan, why it's important that Edward Blake be covered."

"You should read the papers more, and I told
you, Edward Blake is well connected here. He's
made lots of friends in the Hanoi government—
the new people who want to be our friends. Edward Blake is close to a deal on Cam Ranh Bay,
as well as a trade deal and an oil deal. Plus, he'll
stand up to China."

"Who cares? It looks to me like he committed
a murder."

"Who cares about *that?* He's going to be the
next president. The people like him, the military likes him, the intelligence community likes
him, and the business community likes him. I'll
bet even you liked him ten minutes ago."

In fact, I did. War hero and all that. Even my
mother liked him. He was handsome. I said,
"Okay, let's give Edward Blake the benefit of the

doubt and assume that he killed Lieutenant Hines for a good military reason. Now you ask Mr. Vinh, without any bullshit, what he saw that day. Now."

Susan replied, "We'll never know the reason, and it's irrelevant, and Mr. Vinh doesn't know." She stood. "Let's go."

I said to her, "*You* know. Tell me."

She moved toward the back wall near the roofline, and she was much closer to the gun than I was. She said to me, "I don't want you to know. You know too much already."

Mr. Vinh was trying to figure this all out and looked from me to Susan.

I stood and kept my eyes on Susan.

She knew that I knew where she was heading, and she said to me, "Paul . . . I love you. I do. That's why I don't want you to know any more than you already know. In fact, I'm not going to even mention that you discovered the name of Edward Blake."

I said, "*I'll* mention it. Now you ask him what I want to know, or you tell me what you know."

"Neither." She hesitated, then said, "Give me the keys."

I took the keys out of my pocket and threw them to her.

She caught them, looked at me, and said something to Mr. Vinh. Whatever she said caused Mr. Vinh to look back at me and start talking.

I saw Susan reach into the thatch and take

the pistol. She held it behind her back. I wondered if a shot could be heard in the village. Or two shots.

I said to her, "I killed people for my country and did all kinds of nasty things for my country. You ever hear that old saying, 'I'd rather betray my country than my friend?' There was a time when I didn't believe that. Now I'm not so sure. When you get to be my age, Susan, and you look back on this, you might understand."

We looked at each other, and I could see she was near tears, which was not a good sign in regard to my health or Mr. Vinh's health.

Mr. Vinh was standing now and looking back and forth at us.

Susan said something to Mr. Vinh, and he began gathering up the stuff on the table.

I wanted to stop him, but I didn't think that was a good idea for several reasons, not the least of which was the gun.

Mr. Vinh gave the photo pack to Susan, which she put in the side pocket of her quilted jacket, then the canvas pack with the letters and the MACV roster, the dog tags, the wallet, the wedding ring, and the watch, which she also stuffed in her pockets.

Mr. Vinh by now realized that Susan and I were not agreeing on something, but polite chap that he was, he didn't want to get in the middle of a tiff between two Westerners of the opposite sex.

Meanwhile, Ms. Weber was contemplating her next move, which might be a clean exit or a messy one. She'd have to muffle the sound of the gun, and she might be thinking about that. I had trouble picturing Susan Weber killing Tran Van Vinh, or her new lover, but then I remembered her blowing away those two soldiers without blinking an eye. She moved toward her backpack and removed the pelt that the Montagnards had given her. That's how I would muffle the gunshot. I looked at her, but she wouldn't make eye contact with me, which was not a good sign.

She hesitated a long time, then made her decision and stuck the gun in the small of her back without Mr. Vinh being aware of what just transpired.

She presented the pelt to Mr. Vinh with a bow, which he returned. She looked at me and asked, "Are you coming with me?"

"If I come with you, I'm taking your gun and the evidence. You know that."

She took a deep breath and said, "I'm sorry," and left.

So, there I was in the middle of nowhere in the house of the local Commie chief who didn't even speak French, let alone English, and my new girlfriend takes a powder with the bike keys and the gun. Well, it could have been worse.

I put my finger to the side of my head and said to Mr. Vinh, "Co-dep dien cai dau. Crazy."

He smiled and nodded.

"So, any more buses out of here today?"

"Eh?"

I looked at my watch. It was almost 3 P.M. Dien Bien Phu was thirty kilometers. On a forced march, I could make six or seven kilometers an hour over flat terrain. That should get me into town at about 8 P.M.; or maybe I could hitch a ride.

I said to Mr. Vinh, "Cam un . . . whatever. Thanks. Merci beaucoup. Great tea." I put out my hand and we shook. I looked into his eyes. This old veteran had survived hell times ten, and he was now basically a poor peasant, an agrarian Communist of the old school, totally uncorrupted and totally irrelevant. If Washington didn't whack him, maybe the new people in Hanoi would. Mr. Vinh and I had a few things in common.

I took off my watch, a nice Swiss army brand, and handed it to him. He took it reluctantly and bowed.

I picked up my backpack and left the house of Tran. I walked down through the foothills, through the burial mounds, and back into the village of Ban Hin.

I didn't attract as much attention as last time, or if I did, I didn't notice.

Bottom line, despite my bravado and my sarcasm, I was still in love with Ms. Bitch. In fact, I felt my stomach turning and my heart ached. I thought back to Saigon, to the roof of the Rex, the train to Nha Trang, the Grand Hotel, Pyramide Island, Highway One to Hue, Tet Eve, and A Shau and Khe Sanh and Quang Tri, and if I had it all to do over again, I'd do it with her.

Then there was the Edward Blake thing. I still couldn't get it all straight, and I wasn't ready to analyze it. What I knew for certain was that some power circle or the other had gotten wind of this letter and intruded themselves into it, or maybe it was the other way around; the letter had come to the attention of the CIA first, or the FBI, and the army CID was only the front. And Paul Brenner was Don Quixote, running around the countryside on knightly errands with Ms. Sancho Panza, who was the real power and the real brains. Of course, I'd figured some of this out a while ago, but I hadn't done much about it.

In any case, some people in Washington had talked themselves into a deep paranoia, which they're good at. And Edward Blake was a winner, according to the polls; handsome war hero, beautiful wife and kids, money, friends in high places, so anyone or anything who threatened his coming presidency was dead meat.

That aside, I didn't think the guy was in trouble, especially if someone whacked Mr. Vinh, and whacked me. Susan, in the final analysis, couldn't pull the trigger, so maybe I should send her a thank-you note.

I passed through the village square and

glanced at the monument to the dead. This war, this Vietnam War, this American War, just went on killing.

I came to Route 12 and looked around for a lift, but it was the last day of the holiday, and I supposed everyone was stretching it out to the weekend, and no one was going anywhere for a while.

I began walking south toward Dien Bien Phu. I passed the military post and noticed that the jeep was gone.

About a half-kilometer down the road, I heard a big motorcycle behind me, but I kept walking.

She pulled up beside me, and we looked at each other.

She asked, "Why are you going to Dien Bien Phu? I told you how to get to Hanoi. You don't listen to me. You should be hitching a ride to Lao Cai. I'm going that way. Jump on."

"Thanks, but I'd rather crawl, and I'd rather go where I want to go." I kept walking.

I heard her call out to me, "I'm not going to follow you, or beg you. This is it. Come with me, or you'll never see me again."

We'd already done this routine on Highway 6, but this time I was hanging tough. I acknowledged that I'd heard her with a wave of my hand and continued on.

I heard the motorcycle rev, then listened to the engine growing fainter as she drove off.

About ten minutes later, the motorcycle engine was behind me again. She pulled up to me and said, "Last chance, Paul."

"Promise?"

"I was afraid you'd gotten a ride, then I'd lose you."

I kept walking, and she kept up with me by accelerating and downshifting the bike. She said, "You can drive."

I didn't reply.

She said, "You have to get to Hanoi, then fly out of here Sunday. I need to get you to Hanoi or I'm in trouble."

"I thought you were supposed to kill me."

"That's ridiculous. Come on. Time to go home."

"I'll find my own way home, thank you. Did it twice."

"Please."

"Susan, go to hell."

"Don't say that. Please come with me."

We both stood there on the dirt road and looked at each other. I said, "I really don't want you with me."

"Yes, you do."

"It's over."

"Is this the thanks I get for not killing you and Mr. Vinh?"

"You're all heart."

"Mind if I smoke?"

"I don't care if you burn."

She lit up and said, "Okay, here's what happened. In Tran Van Vinh's letter, he said that he was in the Treasury Building in the Citadel of Quang Tri City, wounded, on the second floor, looking down. He saw two men and a woman enter, and they opened a wall safe and began taking out bags. They were civilians, and Mr. Vinh, then Sergeant Vinh, speculated that they were either looting the treasury, or they were on official business and were taking the loot to a safe place. Mr. Vinh said in his letter that these people opened some of the bags, and he could see gold coins, American currency, and some jewelry." She drew on her cigarette. "You see where this is going. Do you want to go there?"

"This is why I'm here. You don't listen to me."

She smiled and continued, "This story comports with the fact that the treasury at Quang Tri was looted during the battle. It's in the history books. I looked it up."

"Finish the story."

She continued, "Sergeant Vinh in his letter says that he had run out of ammunition several hours before, so he just watched. A few minutes later, the lieutenant—Hines—came into the building, and he spoke to the three civilians, as though he might be on a mission with them to save the contents of the safe. But all of a sudden, Lieutenant Hines raises his rifle and kills the two men. The woman was pleading for her life, but he killed her with a rifle shot to the head. Captain

Blake enters, sees what happened, and he and Lieutenant Hines have an argument, and Lieutenant Hines starts to raise his rifle, but Captain Blake fires his pistol and kills Lieutenant Hines. Then, Captain Blake secures the cash and gold by putting it back in the safe and locking it shut. Then he leaves." She added, "The loot disappeared afterward."

She threw away her cigarette and said, "So that's what happened, and that's what Tran Van Vinh saw and wrote to his brother in the letter."

I looked at her for a while, then said, "I think you got the two Americans reversed."

She sort of smiled. "You may be right. But I think it sounds better that way."

I said, "So Edward Blake actually killed four people in cold blood and is also a thief. And this is the guy you want to be president?"

"We all make mistakes, Paul. Especially in war. Actually, I wouldn't vote for Edward Blake myself, but he'd be good for the country."

"Not for my country. See you around." I turned and walked away.

She stayed abreast of me and said, "I like a man who stands up for what's right."

I didn't reply.

She said, "So now you know the secret. Can you keep it?"

"No."

"You can't prove it."

"I'll try."

"That's not a good idea."

I stopped and looked around. There wasn't a soul in sight. I said to her, "Hey, this would be a good place for you to kill me."

"It would be." She drew the .45 automatic out of her belt and very expertly twirled it by the trigger guard and handed it to me, butt first. "Or, you can get rid of me." I took the gun and flung it as far as I could into a flooded rice paddy.

She said, "I have another gun. Two more, in fact."

"Susan, you're not well."

"I told you, my family is crazy."

"*You're* crazy."

"So what? It makes me interesting. Do you think you're completely well?"

"Look, I don't want to argue with you out here—"

"Do you love me?"

"Sure."

"You want my help in blowing Edward Blake out of office?"

"He's good for the country," I reminded her.

"Not my country. Come on. I'm running out of gas, and you're too old to walk."

"I was an infantryman."

"Which war? Civil or Spanish-American? Get on. You can deal with me in Hanoi. I need a spanking."

I smiled.

She made a U-turn around me and reached for my hand. I took it, and she pulled me toward the bike.

I got on.

We headed north, past Ban Hin, toward Lao Cai and on to Hanoi.

This would have been a pleasant outcome if I truly believed even half of what she told me.

CHAPTER FORTY-FIVE

——————— ★ ———————

We continued north on Route 12, which remained a single-lane dirt road that ran along the Na River to our left.

The sky was heavy with low, dark clouds, which looked like they were going to hang around until spring. I hadn't seen a sunny day since we'd gone over the Hai Van Pass on the road to Hue.

To the extent that weather affects the culture, there really were two distinct Vietnams: sunny, noisy, and smiley in the south; gray, quiet, and somber up here. Guess who won the war?

Susan and I hardly said a word to each other, which was fine with me. I hate these lovers' quarrels where one person wants to kill someone and the other doesn't.

I tried to figure this all out, and I guess I understood most of it, at least the political, economic, and global strategy part of it. And as usual, it made about as much sense as how we got involved here in the first place. In the final analysis, it only had to make sense to the people in Washington, who thought differently than normal people.

Regarding Washington's motivations, this

was a mixture of legitimate concern about China, an unhealthy obsession with Vietnam in general, and the deeply held belief that power was like a big dick that God gave you to use and have fun with.

Aside from these profound thoughts were the human elements. For starters, Edward Blake needed to go to jail for murder. Someone else could be president.

Then there was Karl. Colonel Hellmann needed a general's star or he'd be forced to retire, and a senior colonel trying to get a star was like a high school girl trying to get a date the night before the prom; blow jobs were not out of the question. I didn't blame him, really, but he didn't need to drag me into it.

And then there were the bit players, like Bill Stanley, Doug Conway, and who knew who else, who were reading from a script titled, "God Bless America," which the producers and directors were actually going to present as, "Mr. Blake Goes to Washington," in which President Blake fucks the Russians out of Cam Ranh Bay, makes Vietnam into an American oil company, thereby redeeming the past, and in the last act, the Seventh Fleet sails out of Cam Ranh Bay toward Red China and scares the shit out of everyone.

Maybe these people should take up tennis.

And there was Cynthia, who was manipulated by Karl Hellmann to suggest to Paul Brenner that Paul needed a mission; that this was the best way to save the relationship. Cynthia's motives may have been pure, but if she really understood me, she would have been totally honest instead of pretending that she and Karl were not in cahoots. God save me from women who have only my best interests at heart.

And then there was Susan, my furry little kitten with the big fangs. The really scary thing was that she was truly in love with me. I seem to attract intelligent women with mental health problems. Or, to look at it another way, the problem might be me. I can usually blame Dickie Johnson for most of my lady problems, but I think, this time, it was my heart.

There was a big town ahead, according to the map, Lai Chau, which unfortunately was not Lao Cai, and not even close.

We had the Montagnard wrappings on so that out on the road, the military wouldn't spot us for Westerners and pull us over for fun. But as we approached Lai Chau, we took off the scarves, the fur-trimmed leather hats, and goggles, and pulled into a gas station in the middle of the town, which looked like a less prosperous Dien Bien Phu.

Susan used the facility while I pumped gas with a hand crank. Is it slower if you're pumping liters instead of gallons? Or faster?

Susan returned, sans blue dye on her face and hands, and said, "I'll pump. You can go use the bucket."

"I like pumping."

She smiled and said, "Can I hold your nozzle?"

Totally nuts. But a great lay.

"Are you angry at me?"

"Of course not."

"Do you trust me?"

"I think we did this."

"Okay, do you believe that I'm on your side? That I believe as you do that Edward Blake needs to give a public accounting of how William Hines died?"

"Absolutely." I finished pumping and asked her, "You got any dong?"

She paid the attendant, who was standing near us, looking us over, and checking out the BMW. Why don't these guys pump the gas? Things will be different here when all the gas stations are American-owned and -operated. That'll show these bastards who really won the war.

I wanted to drive, so I mounted up. Susan came up beside me and said, "Look at me, Paul."

I looked at her.

She said, "I could not have killed that man. You have to believe that."

I looked into her eyes and said, "I do believe that."

She smiled and said, "You, however, piss me off."

I smiled, but said, "It's not a joke."

"I know. Sorry. I make bad jokes when I'm tense."

"Jump on."

She got on the back and put her arms around me.

I started the engine and off we went, up Route 12, which was mostly uphill as the Na Valley rose higher.

Susan was hungry, as usual, and we pulled over and had a picnic lunch beside a foul-smelling rice paddy. Bananas and rice cakes, and a liter of water. The last good protein I'd had was the porcupine last night.

Susan lit a post-prandial cigarette and said, "If you're wondering why they picked you, one reason was because they wanted a combat veteran. There's this sort of bond between old soldiers, even if they fought on different sides, and I could see that immediately between you and Mr. Vinh."

I thought about that and replied, "There's no bond between me and Colonel Mang."

"Actually, there is."

I ignored that and said, "So, I was picked by a computer? Handsome, bilingual in French and Vietnamese, extensive knowledge of the country, loves native food, motorcycle license, and people skills."

She smiled. "Don't forget good lay."

"Right. Tell you what—they miscalculated."

"Maybe. Maybe not."

I let that one go, and we mounted up.

About sixty kilometers and two hours out of

Lai Chau, the road forked and there was actually a sign: to the left was the Laotian border, ten kilometers, and to the right was Lao Cai, sixty-seven kilometers. I took the right fork, not wanting to go to Laos on this trip, and definitely not wanting to run into any more border guards or military.

In my rearview mirror, however, I saw a military jeep kicking up dust behind me. I said to Susan, "Soldiers."

She didn't look back, but bent over and found the jeep in the mirror. "You can easily outrun them on a rutted dirt road."

What she meant was that the tire ruts were very bumpy, whereas the crown in the middle was smoother. I twisted the throttle and got the bike up to sixty KPH, and I saw that the cloud of dust behind me was getting farther away.

We kept up that speed for half an hour, and I figured if the jeep was going half our speed, then he was fifteen kilometers behind us.

She said to me, "I told you a motorcycle was better."

A lot of this trip had been thought out ahead of time, and what seemed to me random or serendipitous had been calculated. I'd made the mistake of underestimating my friends in Washington, who I knew couldn't be as stupid as they seemed.

This was a totally desolate stretch of road, called, according to the map, 4D, which obviously meant desolate. It was getting cold and dark. I took Susan's hand and looked at her watch. It was about 7 P.M. The sun sinks fast in these latitudes, as I found out in '68, and you can get caught in the dark by surprise.

Route 4D was starting to climb into high mountains, and I could see towering peaks to our front. To make matters worse, a ground fog was developing. We were not going to make it to Lao Cai.

Once again, I started looking around for a place to pull over where we could spend the night. I could actually see my breath, and I guessed the temperature was close to freezing.

Just as I was about to pull over on a small patch of ground near a mountain stream, I saw a sign that said *Sa Pa*, and in English, *Scenic Beauty. Good Hotels*. I stopped and stared at the sign. Maybe it was a backpacker joke. I said, "Is that for real?"

Susan informed me, "There's a hill station town up here called Sa Pa. Old French summer resort. Someone in my Hanoi office went there. Let's see the map."

I took out the map, and we both looked at it in the fading light. Sure enough, there was a little dot called Sa Pa, but no indication on the map that this was anything other than another two-chicken town. The map elevation showed 1,800 meters, which explained why I could see my breath and not feel my nose. I said, "It's another thirty kilometers or so from Sa Pa to Lao Cai. We'll stop in Sa Pa."

I accelerated up the sharply rising road. The fog was thick now, but I left my headlight off and stayed in the middle of the dirt road.

Within fifteen minutes, we could see the glow of lights, and a few minutes later, we were in Sa Pa.

It was a pleasant little place, and in the dark, I could imagine I was in a French alpine village.

We drove around awhile, and the town was dead in the winter. There were lots of small hotels and guest houses in Sa Pa, and every one of them would report our check-in to the Immigration Police.

I saw few people on the streets, and most of them were Montagnards. I spotted a Viet on a motor scooter ahead of me, and I said to Susan, "Ask that guy what's the best hotel in town." I accelerated and came up beside him. Susan spoke to him, and he gave her directions. She said to me, "Make a U-turn."

I made a U-turn on the quiet street, and Susan directed me to a road that climbed above the town.

At the very end of the road, like a mirage, was a huge, modern hotel called the Victoria Sa Pa.

We gave the bike to a doorman, took our backpacks, and entered the big, luxurious lobby.

She said to me, "Nothing but the best for my

hero. Use your American Express. I think I'm not being reimbursed anymore."

"Let's have a drink first."

There was a lounge off the lobby, and I took Susan's arm and led her into this modern lounge with a panoramic view of the misty mountains. We put our backpacks down and sat at a cocktail table. A waitress took our orders for two beers. I looked around and saw about a dozen Westerners in the big place, so we didn't stand out, which was why I wanted the best place in town.

Susan said to me, "I have the feeling we're not checking in here."

"No, we're not." I added, "By now, Colonel Mang may know we stayed at the Dien Bien Phu Motel, so he knows we're in northwest Vietnam. He'd like to know exactly where, but I'm not sure what he'd do with that information. In any case, I don't want him or the local goons joining us for cocktails. So we'll push on."

She replied, "I agree we shouldn't check into a hotel or guest house, but maybe we should find a place to sleep in town, like a church, or that park we saw. Lao Cai is about two hours of dangerous driving through the mountain fog. If a military jeep came up behind us, we wouldn't hear him over the motorcycle, and we might not be able to outrun him. If he came toward us on a narrow mountain road, we'd have to turn around, and we might not be able to outrun him." She looked at me and said, "And you threw away my gun."

"I thought you had two more."

She smiled.

I said, "Well, I have an infantryman's solution to escape and evasion at night. We walk."

She didn't reply.

The beers came, and Susan raised her glass to me. "To the worst three days I've ever spent in Vietnam, with the best man I've ever spent them with."

We touched glasses. I said, "You wanted a little adventure."

"I also wanted a hot shower and a soft bed tonight. Not to mention a good dinner."

"You wouldn't get any of that in jail." I looked at her and said, "We've come too far to make a mistake now."

"I know. You're the expert on getting out of here with only hours left before the flight leaves."

"Did it twice."

Susan called the cocktail waitress over and in French made her understand we wanted something to eat.

Susan smiled at me and said, "Maybe we'll come back here in the summer."

"Send me a postcard."

She sipped her beer thoughtfully, then said, "They'll have a fax machine here." She looked around at the dozen or so people in the lounge.

"We can ask one of these Westerners to send a fax for us. Just to say we've made it this far."

I replied, "If we don't make it all the way to Hanoi with a mission report, they won't care how far we got."

"Well . . . we should at least tell them that we met TVV, and he's given us some souvenirs."

"Susan, the less they know in Saigon, Washington, and the American embassy in Hanoi, the better. I don't owe them anything after the bullshit they—and you—have been feeding me for two weeks."

The waitress brought a bowl of peanuts and two plates of satay on skewers, covered with what smelled like peanut butter sauce.

"What is this meat?" I asked.

"Don't obsess on the meat. You have a long walk ahead of you." Susan stood. "I saw some tourist brochures in the lobby. I'll be right back."

I sat there with my beer and mystery meat. Jealous men don't like their women out of their sight. I'm not a jealous man, but I've learned that I shouldn't let Susan out of my sight.

She returned a few minutes later with a few brochures in her hand, sat, and scanned one of them. She said, "Okay, here's a little map of Sa Pa, and I see the road to Lao Cai. You want to hear about the road?"

"Sure."

"All right . . . surrounding us are the Hoang Lien Mountains, which the French called the

Tonkinese Alps . . . the area is home to an abundance of wildlife, including mountain goats and monkeys—"

"I hate monkeys."

"It's very cold in the winter. If we're hiking, and I guess we are, there are no mountain huts or shelters, and we'll need rain gear and a heating stove—"

"Susan, it's only thirty-five kilometers. I can do that in my underwear. Do we have to go through any villages?"

"I don't think so . . . doesn't say . . . but there are Red Zao tribesmen in the mountains, and it says here they're very shy and don't like visitors."

"Good."

"Okay . . . twelve kilometers from Sa Pa is the Dinh Deo Pass, the highest mountain pass in Vietnam at 2,500 meters. On this side of the pass, the weather is cold, wet and foggy. After we cross the pass, it will often be sunny."

"Even at night?"

"Paul, shut up. Okay . . . there are strong winds over the pass, but only a few hundred meters down, the weather starts to get warmer. Sa Pa is the coldest place in Vietnam, and Lao Cai is the warmest. That's good . . . the Dinh Deo Pass is the dividing line between two large weather systems."

"Can I speak?"

"No. About ten kilometers out of Sa Pa is the

Silver Waterfall where we can ditch the motor-cycle."

"It says that in the brochure?"

She looked up from the brochure and said to me, "They told me in Saigon that this guy Paul Brenner had a reputation of being a diffi-cult-to-work-with wiseass. They didn't know the half of it."

I informed her, "They told me in Washing-ton you were a businessperson who was doing a favor for Uncle. They didn't tell me one per-cent of it."

"You lucked out."

I said, "Let's get out of here before we have company."

We paid the bill, walked outside, tipped the doorman, and got the motorcycle.

Susan said, "It's cold out here."

"It's sunny on the other side of the pass."

We put on our gloves, leather hats, and Mon-tagnard scarves, mounted up and drove off. We went back into the town, and Susan directed me to the road leading north to Lao Cai.

The dark, foggy road climbed higher into the mountains. The road was paved, but the visibil-ity was so bad I had to keep the speed down to between ten and fifteen KPH.

About forty-five minutes out of Sa Pa, I could hear the crashing of a waterfall ahead, and a minute later we saw the falls cascading from a high mountain off to our left front. There was a drop-off on the side of the road, and I dismounted. I couldn't see down through the fog, so I picked up a big rock and threw it. A few seconds later, I heard it strike another rock, then another, until the echoes died away. I said to Susan, "Well, as the brochure said, this is where we ditch the bike."

We left the engine running, and we both pushed the BMW Paris-Dakar off the edge of the road. About two seconds later, we heard it hit, then hit again and again, until we couldn't hear it any longer. I said, "Good motorcycle. I think I'll buy one."

We continued on foot, up the steeply rising road. It was bitter cold, and the north wind was blowing in our faces.

It took us almost an hour to cover the two or three kilometers to the Dinh Deo Pass. As we approached the crest of the pass, the wind began to howl, and we leaned into it and trudged on in silence.

At the top of the pass, the wind was so strong we had to stop and take a break on the leeward side of a boulder. We sat there and caught our breath.

Susan spent a few minutes getting her cigarette lit in the wind. She said, "I need to stop smoking. I'm winded."

"It should be better on the downslope. Are you okay?"

"Yeah . . . just need a break."

"You want my jacket?"

"No. This is a tropical country."

I looked at her in the dim light, and our eyes met. I said, "I like you."

She smiled. "I like you, too. We could have a hell of a life together."

"We could."

She put out her cigarette, and we both started to stand, then she froze and said, "Get down!"

We both dropped to the ground and lay flat.

I heard the engine of a vehicle over the noise of the wind, and I could see yellow lights refracted in the fog. We lay there, and the lights got brighter as the vehicle approached from the direction we'd come from. I caught a glimpse of a big military truck as it passed.

We lay there for a full minute, then Susan said, "Do you think he's looking for us?"

"I have no idea, but if he is, he's looking for two people on a motorcycle."

I let another minute pass. Then we stood, came around the boulder, and walked on into the wind. I pushed the scarf down to my neck and raised the flaps on my leather hat so I could hear better. Now and then, I looked over my shoulder for lights. The chance of anyone in a vehicle spotting us on foot before we heard or saw them was slim. But we needed to keep alert.

We crossed the crest of the pass, and the wind

picked up, but it was downhill now, and we made good time.

About five hundred meters from the top of the pass, the wind became a breeze, and I could actually feel the air get warmer.

Five minutes later, I saw yellow fog lights coming at us and heard the sound of the engine, carried toward us on the wind.

There was a drop-off to our left, and to our right was a narrow stream between the road and the wall of the mountain. We hesitated half a second, then fell into the ice cold stream.

The vehicle approached slowly, and the engine got louder and the yellow lights got brighter.

We lay there, motionless.

Finally, the vehicle passed, but I didn't get a glimpse of it.

I gave it thirty seconds, then got up on one knee and looked south. I could see the lights climbing up toward the pass. I stood. "Okay. Let's move."

Susan stood, we got back on the road and continued on. We were soaked and cold, but as long as we were moving, we wouldn't freeze to death.

There was not a single sign of habitation along the route, not even a Montagnard house. If the Viets and hill people thought Dien Bien Phu was cold, they definitely wouldn't live up here.

Two hours after we crossed the pass, the fog

lifted, and the air was warmer. We were almost dried off, and I removed my gloves, scarves, and leather hat and put them in my backpack. Susan kept hers on.

Within half an hour, we could see the lights of a town down in what appeared to be a deep valley that I guessed was the Red River Valley, though I couldn't actually see the river.

We stopped and sat on a rock. Susan took out one of the tourist brochures, which was soggy, and read the brochure by the flame of her lighter. She said, "That must be Lao Cai, and on the northwest side of the river is China. It says Lao Cai was destroyed during the Chinese invasion of Vietnam in 1979, but the border is open again, if we want to visit the People's Republic of China."

"Next time. What's it say about transportation to Hanoi?"

She flicked on the lighter again and said, "Two trains run daily. First one is at 7:40 A.M., arrives in Hanoi at 6:30 P.M."

I looked at my watch, but it wasn't there. I asked Susan, "What time is it?"

She looked at her watch and said, "Almost one A.M. Where's your watch?"

"I gave it to Mr. Vinh."

"That was nice of you."

"I'll send him a new battery next year."

She asked me, "What do you want to do for the next six hours?"

"Have my head examined."

"I can do that. You want to hear it?"

"No. Let's get down to a warmer elevation, closer to Lao Cai, then find a place to hide out until dawn." I stood. "Ready?"

She stood and off we went, down the road.

The mountains became foothills, and we saw huts and small villages now, but no lights on. The road dropped steeply toward the valley, and I could now make out the Red River and the scattered lights of two towns on both sides of the river; this side was Lao Cai, and the town on the other side, up river about a kilometer, must be in China.

I only vaguely remembered the 1979 border war between China and Vietnam, but I clearly recalled that the Viets kicked some Red Chinese ass. These people were tough, and as I said to Mr. Loc on the way to the A Shau Valley, I wanted them on our side in the next war. And I guess, in a way, that was partly what this mission was about.

I mean, I didn't want to be accused of upsetting the global balance of power; the military and political geniuses in Washington were obviously working hard to forge a new Viet-American alliance against Red China. Somehow, Vice President Blake was important to this alliance, and he needed to become president. All I had to do was forget what I'd seen and heard in Ban Hin, and with luck, we'd have Cam Ranh Bay again, and the sailors of the Seventh Fleet could get laid a lot in Vietnam, plus we'd have some new oil resources, and we'd have a big Vietnamese Army poised on that border right ahead of me, and we could all kick some Chinese butt—or at least threaten to if they didn't stop acting like assholes. Sounded good.

Even better, I could blackmail President Blake into making me Secretary of the Army so I could fire Colonel Karl Hellmann, or bust him to PFC and put him on permanent latrine duty.

Obviously, lots of good things could happen if I just shut my mouth—or maybe I'd get it shut for me.

I didn't know, nor would I ever know, if Susan Weber was supposed to terminate my career and turn my pension into a death benefit for Mom and Pop. The stakes were high enough for her to be motivated into such a course of action—I mean, if Washington had threatened to kill Mr. Anh's whole family if he turned rat, then certainly the stakes were high enough to add Chief Warrant Officer Paul Brenner to the hit list.

During the war, the Phoenix Program had assassinated over 25,000 Vietnamese who were suspected of collaborating with the Viet Cong. Add to that number a few Americans in Vietnam who had VC sympathies, and some local Frenchmen who were outright VC collaborators, and other Europeans who lived in Vietnam and leaned too far left. It was an amazing number—25,000 men and women—the largest assassination and liquidation program ever carried out by the United States of America. And I could assume that some of those Americans, who had been involved with the program and who were my contemporaries, were ready, willing, and able to whack a few malcontents and troublemakers like me at the drop of a hat.

On a happier note, I had found the girl of my dreams. Right here in Vietnam. A guy shouldn't be so lucky.

As we walked toward Lao Cai, I said to Susan, "You understand that I'm going to blow the whistle on Edward Blake."

She didn't reply for a while, then said, "Think about it." She added, "Sometimes, Paul, truth and justice are not what anyone wants or needs."

"Well, when that day comes—if it hasn't already arrived—then I'll move to someplace like Saigon or Hanoi, where at least no one pretends that truth and justice are important."

She lit a cigarette and said, "Underneath it all, you're a Boy Scout."

I didn't reply.

She said, "Whatever you decide to do, I'm with you."

Again, I didn't reply.

We found a thicket of bamboo and made our way into it, then unrolled our ponchos and lay on the ground. I'm not a big fan of bamboo vipers, and I hoped it was cold enough to keep them snoozing until the sun warmed them. That's what it said in the escape and evasion manual.

Susan slept, but I couldn't. The sky was clearing, and I could see stars through the broken cloud cover. Some hours later, the sky began to lighten, and I could hear birds that sounded like parrots or macaws squawking. I also heard the stupid chattering of monkeys somewhere in the distance.

We needed to get moving before the bamboo vipers did, and I shook Susan awake. She sat up, yawned and stood.

We got back on the road and continued on.

To our right was a wide stream, flowing swiftly out of the mountains to the Red River. There were clusters of huts near the road, but it was too early for people or vehicles to be out and moving.

The road flattened, and we were on the valley floor now. Within thirty minutes, we entered the incredibly ugly town of Lao Cai.

I could tell that all of these buildings were relatively new and that the entire town must have been destroyed in the 1979 war. At least this was one destroyed Vietnamese city that no one could blame on the United States Army, Marines, Navy, or Air Force.

There were a few people around, but no one took any note of us. I saw a group of about fifteen young backpackers sitting and lying in a group in the marketplace, as though they'd spent the night there.

I said to Susan, "With our backpacks, we can pass for college kids."

"Me maybe."

Susan stopped a Vietnamese lady and asked, "Ga xe lua?"

The woman pointed, pantomimed something, and spoke.

Susan thanked the woman in French and I thanked her in Spanish, and off we went.

Susan said, "We have to cross the river."

We crossed the Red River on a new bridge, and I could see pylons of two destroyed bridges further upstream. Also up the river, where it split into two branches, I could see buildings with Chinese characters painted on them.

Susan saw them, too, and said, "China."

I looked around as we came off the bridge and saw a few ruined buildings on the Vietnamese side that hadn't been rebuilt. It had been an odd war, and I couldn't even remember what it was that got the Chinese and Vietnamese at each other's throats so soon after the Chinese had given aid to the Viets during the American War. Basically, they didn't like each other, and hadn't for about a thousand years. It probably wouldn't take much to get them at each other's throats again.

We followed a road that paralleled the train

tracks, which I noticed were narrow-gauge. I could see the station ahead, and it, too, was a new concrete slab structure, the original station being probably the first casualty of the war.

We entered the station house and saw hundreds of people at two ticket windows, and hundreds more camped on the Hanoi-bound platform. There were a few people on the westbound platform for the train to China, which was only about 1,500 meters up the line.

The station clock said 6:40, and it looked like we'd be waiting in line for an hour and might not get a seat. The next train, according to the posted schedule, left at 6:30 P.M. and got to Hanoi at 5:30 Saturday morning.

I didn't need to be in Hanoi until Saturday, but I didn't want to hang around Lao Cai for twelve hours. Plus, it's sometimes nice to show up early and surprise people.

I said to Susan, "Why don't you use your charm and your American bucks and jump the line?"

"I was about to do that." She went to the front of one of the lines and spoke to a young man. Money changed hands and within ten minutes, she returned with two tickets to Hanoi. She said, "I got us each a soft seat for ten bucks, plus I bought the kid a sleeper bunk for seventeen bucks, and gave him another five. Are you keeping track of our expenses?"

"I'll just put in for combat pay. Actually, since

you're with me, I can also put in for hazardous duty pay."

"You're funny."

Not a joke.

We moved out to the platform where hundreds of people stood, sat, and lay on the cold concrete. The narrow-gauge train was on a siding, and it looked like the Toonerville Trolley.

The sky was light, but overcast, and the temperature was in the mid-fifties. There were a number of young backpackers and middle-aged Western tourists, and many of them wore recently purchased articles of Montagnard clothing from different tribes, probably mixing tribes as well as genders. The real Montagnards on the platform thought this was funny and were pointing and snickering.

Susan lit a cigarette and asked me, "How much money was combat pay?"

"Fifty-five bucks a month. Six hundred and sixty dollars a year. Not that good a deal. Meanwhile, guys like Edward Blake, who weren't out in the jungle getting their asses shot off, did things like black market, currency dealing, and outright looting. Some people here got rich off the war, most got killed, wounded, or fucked up, plus, of course, fifty-five bucks a month for their troubles."

Susan thought a moment and then said, "I can see why you'd take this personally."

I didn't reply.

She asked me, "I wonder if Blake got that loot home."

"We may never know, but it wasn't that difficult. Before you went home, you got checked out here to make sure you weren't bringing home drugs or military ordnance. Other than that, they didn't care what you brought home in your duffel bag. At the U.S. end, Customs just waved you through because they knew you'd been checked for drugs and explosives at this end. Also, officers, like Captain Blake, were on the honor system."

She nodded and said, "Behind every great fortune, there is a crime."

Because this was a border town, there were too many uniformed guys around, mostly border patrol types, but also a lot of heavily armed soldiers, as though they were expecting another war momentarily. This place was a little creepy, but there were enough adventure travelers from Europe, Australia, and America to provide us some cover.

Border cops began patrolling the platform, asking people for ID and soliciting contributions for the widows and orphans fund. I noticed that they gave the ethnic Chinese a really hard time, and also they were picking on Westerners who were alone or in small groups without a guide.

Susan, too, noticed this and said to me, "See that group over there? I think they're Americans. Let's mingle."

I knew they were Americans because two of the guys were wearing shorts in fifty-degree weather, and the women had bought and put on enough Montagnard jewelry to look like radar antennas.

We walked over to the tour group of about twenty Americans who had a male Viet guide with them.

Susan, who's more sociable than I am, struck up a conversation with a few of the ladies. They talked jewelry and fabrics.

The cops kept their distance from us.

At about 7 A.M., the Toonerville Trolley started to move off the siding and ran onto the main single-line track and stopped at the platform. Susan said good-bye to her new friends, and we went to our car in the short eight-car train. We boarded car Number 2 and found our seats.

The coach was narrow, with only two seats on the left, and the aisle running along the windows to the right.

We put our backpacks overhead, and Susan said, "You take the aisle so you can stretch a little. This is really cramped." We sat.

Neither of us spoke, and I think we both realized that we'd had more than our share of good luck, and we shouldn't comment on it. Of course, skill, brains, and experience had a lot to do with it, too. As it turned out, Susan Weber was a good traveling companion. I wondered if I'd have made it on my own, and I knew that I'd be wondering about that for the rest of my life.

At 7:40, the train pulled out of the station, and we were on our way to Hanoi.

The tracks ran along the north bank of the Red River, and on both sides of the river, the Tonkinese Alps stretched along the valley. With a little imagination, I could picture myself in Europe going someplace nice.

The coach was filled with Viets and Westerners, and there were people standing in the vestibule, but no squatters in the narrow aisle beside us.

We sat in silence awhile, watching the scenery, which was actually quite spectacular. The train made a lot of noise over the tracks, and I realized the coach wasn't heated. I also assumed there was no bar car.

Susan turned away from the window and looked at me. She said, "So far, so good."

"So far, so good."

She asked, "So, was I a good buddy?"

"Am I home in one piece yet?"

She lit a cigarette and looked out the window for a few minutes, then asked me, "What are your instructions regarding Hanoi?"

"What are *yours?*"

She didn't reply for a while, then said, "I was told to go to the embassy for a debriefing."

I asked her, "Are there Viet police guards around the embassy?"

She replied, "Well, I've only been there once
. . . but yes, there's a Vietnamese police post.
Plus I was told there were undercover embassy
watchers, checking out everyone who goes in or
out, and even taking photos, and sometimes
they stop people."

"What were you doing in the embassy?"

"Just visiting."

"Right."

She asked me again, "What are your instructions?"

I replied, "I was told to go to the Metropole
and await further instructions. I may or may not
be contacted. I may or may not be wanted in the
embassy. I'm to leave for another city tomorrow—"

"Bangkok. I saw your tickets, and so did
Colonel Mang."

"Right. The Metropole is out, Hanoi airport is
out, and the embassy is watched."

"So? What are we going to do?"

"Is the Hanoi Hilton still open?"

"This is not a joke."

"I make jokes when I'm tense. Anyway, am I
to understand from you that Vice President
Blake is visiting Hanoi?"

"He's here to see his old friend, Ambassador
Patrick Quinn, and to participate in a conference
on MIAs, and I'm sure a few other less publicized
meetings with the Vietnamese government."

I nodded. "He should also have an unscheduled meeting. With us."

Susan didn't reply for a while, then said, "That might be a good idea, or a very bad idea."

"If he knows about this problem, he wants to be in Hanoi where he can have some hands-on control of the situation where and when the mission ends. We can help him with that."

Susan replied, "I honestly don't know if he's aware that he has a problem. But other people do, and I think Mr. Blake will be made aware of it in Hanoi. The bad news, Mr. Vice President, is that we know you murdered three Viets and an American officer in Vietnam. The good news, sir, is that we have the situation under control."

"It's not under control," I pointed out.

"It was supposed to be."

The train continued east toward Hanoi. Susan and I discussed a few ideas and options and tried to come up with a game plan. I made believe I trusted her completely. She made believe, too.

I kept getting the feeling that I wasn't supposed to have gotten this far, and that Susan was making adjustments for my living presence. But that might be too paranoid. Maybe I was supposed to make it as far as Bangkok, then be evaluated as to how much I found out, and, as Mr. Conway said, how I would be dealt with. Maybe Susan was supposed to be a witness for or against me. And maybe my friend, Karl, who cared about me, was to be my judge. I asked Susan, "Are you supposed to go to Bangkok?"

She didn't reply.

"Hello? Susan?"

"Yes."

"Good." I pointed out to her, "If there exists a possibility that I might need to be . . . let's say, given a full military funeral before I was ready for one, has it occurred to you that you, too, might be in a similar predicament?"

"It has occurred to me."

"Good." I left it at that.

We moved into the rising sun, toward Hanoi, toward the end of the mission, and toward the end of my third, and definitely last, tour of duty in Vietnam.

The train from Lao Cai moved slowly through the northern outskirts of Hanoi, and at 6:34 P.M., we pulled into Long Bien Station.

The journey from sultry, sinful Saigon had taken me to the battlefields of South Vietnam and into the heart of my own darkness, and up country on a journey of discovery and hopefully self-awareness.

I had finally come to terms with this place, as had a lot of men who'd been here, and as had a lot of my generation, men and women, who hadn't been to Vietnam, but who had lived through Vietnam so many years ago.

And yet, at unexpected moments, the war still had the power to haunt our dreams and intrude into our waking hours. And for Edward Blake, this was one of those times.

—BOOK VII—

Hanoi

CHAPTER FORTY-SIX

──────★──────

*H*anoi. An evocative name to people of my generation, as Berlin and Tokyo were to my father's generation. Hardly a week went by during the war that didn't have a news report of a Hanoi bombing raid. *American bombers struck two miles from the center of Hanoi today, targeting a railway bridge over the Red River, a power plant, and suspected enemy surface-to-air missile sites.* After about five or six years of these news stories, they ceased to be news, except for the pilots and the people on the ground.

The passengers around us were gathering their luggage and began filing off the train.

Susan and I remained seated and watched the platform.

There were a large number of uniformed Border Police on the platform scanning the departing passengers, plus some plainclothes guys, who were easy to spot. I said to Susan, "Some of those guys have what could be photos in their hands."

She kept staring out the window and said, "This is not an uncommon sight at transportation terminals . . . we shouldn't automatically assume they're looking for us . . . but they *are* looking at Westerners."

"Right." I also assumed they had the photographs from Pyramide Island, so maybe they wouldn't recognize us with our clothes on. In fact, a few of the cops seemed more interested in the photos than the departing passengers.

I said, "Let's hook up with that American group you were talking to."

We stood, got our backpacks, and made our way to Car 6 where the American group was filing out with their Vietnamese tour guide.

There was a Viet lady standing in front of Susan as we shuffled out, and Susan spoke to the woman in Vietnamese, then spoke to me. Susan discovered that Long Bien Station was located in a remote district on the east side of the Red River, and the passengers from our train needed to board a standard-gauge train to the central station if they were going to downtown Hanoi. There were also buses and taxis available. And police cars.

One of Susan's most striking features is her straight shoulder-length hair, and she asked me to tuck it under her quilted jacket.

I have many striking features, but I couldn't wrap them all in scarves without attracting attention or running out of scarves, so I just wrapped a dark blue Montagnard scarf around my neck and chin. Susan did the same.

"Separate when we get out."

We got out on the platform, separated, and placed ourselves in the center of the group of about twenty Americans with their guide.

Susan was chatting with the people around her, and I struck up a conversation with two guys while my eyes followed the cops. A few of them were looking at our group, but not showing any signs of recognition.

The tour group was assembled, and we began moving off the platform. We might just make it, but I held my breath anyway.

The railway station was a combination of old and new, and I could see where bomb damage had been repaired with newer concrete. A country that has seen war never looks quite the same again, at least not to the people who remembered how it used to look.

The weather was overcast, and a lot warmer than it had been in the mountains. This country needed a sunny day. I needed a sunny day.

I noticed a taxi stand to my left, where two Border Police and a plainclothes guy stood, looking at Westerners who were getting in the cabs.

Our American tour group was moving toward a waiting bus whose sign said *Love Planet Tours*. I wasn't feeling any particular love at the moment, but fugitives can't be choosy.

Our group began boarding the Love Planet bus. Susan was ahead of me, and she spoke to the Viet tour guide for a moment, handed him some money, which made him smile, and she boarded. I reached the guide and handed him five bucks. He smiled and nodded.

I boarded the bus. The driver, who had never met this group, didn't pay any attention to me, but if he had, he'd have gotten a few bucks, too.

The bus could hold about forty people, and there were lots of empty seats, but Susan had placed herself in an aisle seat beside a middle-aged woman wearing Montagnard hoop earrings. I took the seat across the aisle from Susan and threw my backpack on the empty window seat. I could hear the luggage being thrown into the compartment below my feet.

It took forever for the poky Americans to board, and I watched the Border Police outside moving around, still staring at pictures and still looking for someone.

The bus was finally loaded, and the Viet guide came aboard. He said, "Okay, every person here?"

The tour group replied in unison, "Yes."

I hate tour groups, but the alternative in this case—a police car—might actually be worse, but not by much.

I saw a border cop walking toward the bus, and he got on.

I needed to tie my shoelaces, which I did, and so did Susan. Meanwhile, the woman next to her was keeping up a non-stop rap and to the cop it must have looked like she was talking to herself.

I could hear the tour guide and the cop

exchanging words, and I figured it was only a matter of seconds before the cop would be tapping me on the shoulder. I glanced at Susan, who was looking at me, and we kept eye contact.

After what seemed like eternity plus a few minutes, I heard the hydraulic sound of the door closing. A second later, the bus was in gear and moving. Nevertheless, Susan and I kept tying our shoes until the bus was out of the station area and on the road.

I sat up, and so did Susan. I said to her, "Hi, I'm Paul. Is this your first time in Vietnam?"

She closed her eyes, put her head back on the headrest, and took a long, deep breath. The lady next to her never missed a beat and kept jabbering.

The bus headed south, and the setting sun came in through the right-side windows. We both took off our blue Montagnard scarves and put them in our backpacks. I said to Susan, "Where you from?"

She replied, "Please shut up."

The woman beside her took offense, shut up, and turned toward the window.

Susan said to her, "Sorry. I was talking to this pest."

The woman turned toward me and gave me a hard look.

I glanced at the tour guide, who was standing near the driver, facing the rear. I saw that he was looking at me, and our eyes met for half a second, then he looked away.

I had no idea what motivated him to keep his mouth shut, but it probably had a lot to do with fear; not of Susan and me, but of the cop. Taking a few bucks from unauthorized passengers was a small offense; harboring fugitives, even unintentionally, could get him fined, fired, and arrested. This was a country that was running scared, and I've been in countries like that, and that could work for or against the authorities. This time, it worked against them. Next time, we might not be so lucky.

The bus continued on a wide street, and the guide said, "So, we now come to Chuong Duong Bridge, who go over Song Hong—Red River. Beautiful river. You take picture."

Everyone dutifully took photos of the bridge and the Red River. The guide said, "We go now Hanoi. Hoan Kiem District—Old Quarter. Very beautiful. You take picture."

We crossed the bridge into the Old Quarter of Hanoi, and the streets and sidewalks were crowded, but not nearly as bad as Saigon. In fact, instead of the frenzied, horn-honking suicidal motorists and pedestrians of Saigon, there was a quiet determination on everyone's faces here, a slower and more purposeful movement of people and vehicles. I was reminded of army ants in a terrarium.

The buildings were mostly French colonial, very quaint, very run-down, but still charming. There were lots of leafy trees on the streets, and if it weren't for the signs in Vietnamese, I could imagine I was in a French provincial town, which is where I'd rather be.

On the horizon, I could see the lights of towering new skyscrapers. I said to Susan, "It's not as grim as I imagined."

Susan excused herself from the one-way conversation with the woman and said to me, "Looks are deceiving."

"Don't be negative. Visualize success."

She was in no mood for me and turned her attention back to Blabbermouth.

I looked out the window again. I recalled that we'd never actually bombed the center of Hanoi; just the military targets on the outskirts of the city, which is why it still looked French and not East German. I didn't recall, however, the U.S. getting any favorable press for sparing the central city. It's hard to put a good spin on bombing attacks, even sensitively planned ones.

The bus made its way through the narrow, winding streets. The guide was giving a running commentary, and he, too, didn't congratulate the Americans for leaving the Old Quarter intact. People don't appreciate Americans.

The guide said, "Tomorrow, we see Ho Chi Minh tomb, Ho Chi Minh house, Lenin monument, Army Museum, Air Defense Museum, and lake in city where American B-52 bomber crash and still in lake."

I said to Susan, "We're going to miss all of that."

She didn't reply.

I glanced out the window, then asked Susan, "Do you know where we are?"

She replied, "I have a general idea where we are. Do you have any idea where we're going?"

I hadn't actually thought much beyond the immediate problems as they had evolved. In truth, I never thought we'd get this far, but we had, so now I needed to figure out where we were going to spend the night. I said to her, "Well, we can't go to the embassy or the Metropole if they're looking for us. How about your Hanoi office?"

She replied, "My office is closed, I don't have a key, and it may be watched."

"Can you call one of your employees at home?"

She said, "I don't want to get them involved."

"You mean none of them are working for the CIA?"

She didn't reply.

I said, "Well, I have a contact in the embassy. His name is John Eagan, FBI guy here on assignment. I'll call him tomorrow from a pay phone and arrange a rendezvous somewhere."

She said, "You know the embassy phones

are tapped. Don't you have a pre-arranged rendezvous?"

"No. But I can work it out." I asked her, "Do you know what a big ugly fucker is?"

"I'm sitting across from one."

I smiled. "It's a B-52 bomber. Military slang. Someone in the embassy should know that. The military attaché, Colonel Marc Goodman, will know."

The lady next to Susan was eavesdropping on our conversation, and her hoop earrings were sticking straight up.

I asked Susan, "Do you know the lake where the big ugly fucker is?"

The lady's eyes widened. Susan smiled and nodded.

"Good. That's our rendezvous. Eagan is the guy. Just in case we're separated. Okay?"

Again, she nodded.

I asked her, "Who's *your* contact in the embassy?"

She didn't reply for a second, then said, "Also Eagan."

I didn't pursue that.

I said, "As for tonight, we should try to find an American who will let us share his or her hotel room. But not this group."

She replied, "I'll have no problem finding someone who will share his hotel room with me. Where are *you* sleeping?"

"Brothel."

"Not in this city."

Susan seemed to be thinking, then said to me, "Actually, there is a place we can go tonight . . ."

By the expression on her face, I thought she meant an old lover, which would not have been my first choice of overnight accommodations. But then she said, "I was invited to a reception tonight . . . at the American ambassador's residence."

"Really? Am I invited?"

"That depended."

"On what?"

"On whether or not we got to Hanoi tonight."

I think it mostly depended on whether I was alive or dead. I said, "I thought you told me everything."

She didn't make eye contact and replied, "My presence at this reception was tentative, and not important."

"I see. So, let me guess who's at this reception. Well, since the Vice President is in town, I'll take a wild guess that Edward Blake is the guest of honor." I looked at her.

She nodded.

"And you are supposed to brief him about some subjects that he may have some interest in."

"Not him directly."

The lady beside Susan was leaning so far left, I thought the bus might flip over.

I said to Susan, "Am I dressed for a diplomatic reception?"

She smiled and replied, "You're so sexy, Paul, you could show up in dirty jeans, running shoes, and a muddy leather jacket."

"Good. What time is this soiree?"

"Starts at eight."

I looked at my watch, which was still on Mr. Vinh's wrist. I said, "What time is it?"

She looked at her watch. "It's 7:15."

"Can I buy a watch in this town?"

"I'll buy you one."

The bus pulled over on a narrow street and stopped. The guide said, "We here at hotel. Good hotel."

I looked out the window and saw an old stucco hotel that the *Michelin Guide* may have overlooked.

Our tour guide said, "We register in hotel, then meet in lobby, and go to good dinner at Italian restaurant."

This got a round of applause from the group, which had probably been eating rice and weasel up country for the last week. I applauded, too.

Everyone began filing out of the bus, and I found myself behind Susan's chatty friend. She turned her head toward me and gave me a look like I was an unshaven, mud-splattered, smelly pervert. She asked, "Are you with our group?"

"No, ma'am. I'm Canadian."

We stepped off the bus and encountered our

guide. He looked away from Susan and me, but I took a twenty and pressed it in his hand as we passed by him.

So, there we were, in Hanoi, on a narrow street crowded with pedestrians, cyclos, and a few motor vehicles. It was dark now, and the streetlights were on, but the trees blocked most of the light, so the street was in shadow.

We walked away from the hotel, and I asked Susan, "Do you know where we are?"

She said, "Not far from the ambassador's residence." She suggested, "Let's find a place to have a drink, use the facilities, and wash up. Also, I want to make a call to the embassy duty officer."

"Good idea." I looked across the street for a café or bar, then something made me turn back toward the hotel about fifty meters away. Parked in front of the bus was an olive drab car, a sedan, which you don't see many of in this country. I had the impression it was some sort of official vehicle. There was a uniformed man standing on the sidewalk with his back to us, and in the light from the hotel marquee, I could see he was speaking to our guide and to the bus driver. I didn't like the looks of this; I liked it even less when the bus driver pointed toward Susan and me. The uniformed guy turned around and looked toward us. It was, in fact, Colonel Mang.

★

CHAPTER FORTY-SEVEN

──── ★ ────

Colonel Mang walked toward us and called out, "Mr. Brenner! Miss Weber!"

I said to Susan, "Did he say something?"

"Oh, shit . . . Paul . . . should we make a run for it?"

Before I could decide, the sedan moved up and stopped beside us. The uniformed guy in the passenger seat pulled a pistol and pointed it at me.

Colonel Mang came strolling down the sidewalk, wearing his green dress uniform, but no gun holster. He motioned for his goon in the car to put away his gun, then stopped a few feet from us and said, "I was afraid I had missed you at Long Bien Station."

I replied, "In fact, you did."

"Yes. But now I have found you. May I offer you both a ride?"

He may have been feeling bad about leaving us stranded in Quang Tri, and now he wanted to make it up to us. I said, however, "That's okay. I need the exercise."

"Where are you going?"

"To the Metropole."

"Yes? The Metropole is the other way. Why did you ride on that tour bus?"

I replied, "I thought it was a city bus."

"You know it is not that. In fact, you are acting as if you are running from something."

"No, we're going to the Metropole. That way, correct?"

He looked at Susan and inquired, "Did you get my message at the Century Hotel?"

She didn't reply.

Colonel Mang said, "Mr. Tin told me he delivered it to you via telex to the post office of the city of Vinh. What were you doing in Vinh?"

Susan replied, "Visiting Ho Chi Minh's birthplace."

"Ah, yes. You are both Canadian historians, as I recently discovered."

Neither of us replied. And neither of us were happy with that statement.

Colonel Mang lit a cigarette. Maybe he'd drop dead of a heart attack.

I noticed over Mang's shoulder some Americans from the tour bus looking at us as two uniformed men in front of the hotel motioned them inside. Also, I saw that the bus driver and the guide had disappeared; they were probably on their way to where we were going, and it wasn't the Metropole Hotel.

I noticed, too, that pedestrians were crossing to the other side of the street to avoid whatever police state activity was happening on this side.

Colonel Mang said to me, "You both left very early from the Century Hotel in Hue."

"So what?"

He ignored my snotty reply, but he had to get even with me so he said to Susan, "Unfortunately, there are no naked beaches for you here on the Red River."

Susan snapped, "Go to hell."

He smiled unexpectedly and said to her, "You have become very popular with the men of my department who have closely studied the photographs of you on Pyramide Island."

"Go to hell."

Colonel Mang remained composed, and I figured he didn't want to start a screaming match in front of his men, who probably didn't understand that Susan was telling him to go to hell.

Mang looked us over and said, "You appear to have spent some time in the countryside."

Neither of us replied.

He asked me, "Where is your luggage?"

"Stolen."

"Yes? And where did you both get those coats which were not in your luggage?"

"Bought them."

"Why?"

"Why not?"

"And I see blue dye on your face and hands from Montagnard scarves. It appears to me that you are both trying to disguise yourselves."

"As what?"

"I do not like your replies, Mr. Brenner."

"I don't like your questions."

"You never do." He switched subjects and said, "Your reservation at the Metropole, Mr. Brenner, is for tomorrow. Why did you arrive a day early?"

Susan replied, "Colonel, we have an invitation—"

"Later," I interrupted. The reception at the ambassador's residence was an ace, which could only be played once, and this might not be the right time.

Susan understood and said to Mang, "I have an early appointment tomorrow at the embassy."

"With whom?"

"To speak to the commercial attaché."

"About what?"

"About commerce, obviously."

He gave Susan a hard stare, then said to her, "I made some inquiries and discovered that you are also booked at the Metropole, but for today."

Colonel Mang had more information than I did about Ms. Weber's travel itinerary. But to be fair, she had mentioned to me in Nha Trang something about business in Hanoi, although by now I didn't think it had anything to do with the commercial attaché.

Colonel Mang, who enjoyed his own sarcasm, said to Susan, "Since Mr. Brenner has no room tonight, I could suggest that you share your room with him, but that would give the appearance of impropriety."

Susan suggested, "Go to hell."

It was time to see if this guy was fishing, hunting, or setting traps. I said to him, "Colonel, I appreciate your going out of your way to welcome us to Hanoi, and if there's nothing further, we'll be on our way."

He didn't reply.

I added, "You're frightening the tourists."

"Yes? But I do not seem to frighten you."

"Not even close."

"The night is young. Have you ever been to Hanoi, Mr. Brenner?"

"No, but friends of mine flew over during the war, though they didn't stop." Good one.

He smiled and said, "In fact, some did stop and were lodged in the Hanoi Hilton."

Not bad. I love pissing contests. It was my turn, and I said, "I wanted to see the Air Defense Museum, but I was told there was nothing to see."

He asked me, "Would you like to see the inside of the Ministry of Public Security?"

"Thank you, but I've already seen the one in Saigon."

"Ho Chi Minh City."

"Whatever." He seemed reluctant to act on his threat, or maybe he was having too much fun here on the street. In any case, I said to him, "Ms. Weber and I have called the duty officer at the embassy to register our presence in Hanoi. Perhaps you and I can speak tomorrow. Let's say cocktails at six, Metropole bar. I'll buy. Date?"

He stared at me in the dim light and said, "You did not call your embassy." He continued, "I understand that you think I am influenced by diplomatic considerations. But I tell you this, Mr. Brenner, if I have fifteen minutes alone with you and Miss Weber, I will prove that both of you are in this country on behalf of your government and that you are acting against my country."

"Can you be more specific?"

"I will be very specific when I have you in an interrogation room."

We seemed to be at an impasse here. I wanted to go to a five-star hotel, and Colonel Mang wanted me in jail. But he wanted to be sure he wasn't making a bad career decision, so we were chatting on the street, and he wanted me or Susan to do or say something to justify an arrest. I've been there myself, but I wasn't too sympathetic to his dilemma.

Colonel Mang had a solution and said to me, "I would like both of you to accompany me, voluntarily, to the Ministry of Public Security for a discussion."

I've said this thousands of times to suspects, and most of them never went home that day. I replied, "This is a joke. Right?"

"No. It is not a joke."

"Sounds like a joke."

He seemed either confused or annoyed that I'd turned down his invitation. He said, "If you come voluntarily, I promise you, you will be free to leave within an hour."

Susan reminded him, "You said you needed only fifteen minutes with us."

I'd gotten to the point where I could read Colonel Mang, and I saw that he was really pissed. I noticed, too, that Susan pissed him off more than I did. I don't think Mang and I had actually bonded, but I was certain he hated Susan. For this reason, among many others, I didn't want her in his clutches. I said to him, "Colonel, I have a suggestion. Take us to the embassy and let Ms. Weber go inside. Then, I'll go with you voluntarily to the ministry."

He didn't think too long about that and said, "No."

Susan, too, said, "No, wherever we go, we go together."

No one was cooperating with me, so I said to Mang, "Okay, let us make a call to the duty officer at the embassy and inform him or her that we've arrived in Hanoi, and that Colonel Nguyen Qui Mang would like to ask us a few questions and that we are accompanying him to the Ministry of Public Security. Voluntarily, of course. You can listen to the call."

He shook his head.

Colonel Mang didn't know how to do a deal. Or, he didn't think he had to make one.

I said to him, "Well, Colonel, I'm out of ideas." I took Susan's arm and said to Mang, "Good evening."

Mang lost it and shouted, "Dung lai!" forgetting his English.

I looked at him.

He was hyperventilating again, and now that we'd called him out, he needed to do something. He spoke to the guy in the passenger seat, who got out and opened the rear door. I hoped Colonel Mang was leaving, but no such luck. He looked over his shoulder to be certain the American tourists were all gone, then said to us, "Get in the car."

Neither Susan nor I moved.

He smiled and said, "Are you frightened?"

"No. Are you?"

"Why should I be frightened? Get in the car."

I replied, "Someone has to pull a gun on us for us to get in the car."

He understood and nodded in appreciation. He said something to the guy standing near the car, who was happy to be of assistance, and he pulled his gun on us.

I took Susan's arm, and we got in the rear of the sedan. Mang got in the passenger seat, and the guy with the gun stayed behind.

We drove in silence through the streets of the Old Quarter, and within a few minutes, we slowed down in front of the Metropole Hotel, a huge stately building that looked as if it belonged in Paris.

I thought Colonel Mang had changed his mind, and I said to him, "Thanks for the ride."

He turned in his seat and said, "I wanted you to see where you will *not* be spending the night."

Asshole.

The sedan headed west through the Old Quarter. Just to satisfy myself that these people weren't complete idiots, I tried the door handle, but it was locked.

This situation had gone from bad to worse, and it showed no signs of getting better. I explored my options, but there weren't any except going violent, which I was prepared to do. Mang had no weapon that I could see, but the driver did, so the driver had to be taken out first. I glanced out the rear window and saw a backup car following. I had to decide, as they'd taught me in my army POW escape and evasion course, if physical resistance was possible, and if it was, what the consequences were of a failed attempt. Sometimes you compound a small or medium problem by snapping someone's neck; other times, you solve the problem. It depended, I guess, on what was at the end of this ride.

I mulled this over, taking into account the backup car, and the fact that Susan and I were not pre-rehearsed for a coordinated escape attempt.

The car made a turn, and I leaned toward her and whispered. "Gun?"

She shook her head and said, "That was a joke."

Mang said, "No talking."

We turned down a narrow, badly lit street whose sign said *Yet Kieu*, and we stopped in front of a large colonial-era five-story building. The backup car stopped behind us.

Colonel Mang took an attaché case from the seat and got out without a word.

Susan poked me and said softly, "Ambassador's reception, Paul."

"Is that tonight?"

"Paul."

"Only play the ace when you need it."

She looked at me. "I think we need it."

Two guys from the backup car came toward the sedan and opened the rear doors. Susan and I got out, and we were escorted, not gently, to the front door of the Ministry of Public Security, where Colonel Mang stood.

A guard opened the door, and Colonel Mang entered, followed by Susan and me with the two goons.

The big lobby was very run-down, and it reminded me of its counterpart in Saigon. There were a few uniformed and civilian-dressed men walking around, and they looked at us as though they didn't see that many Westerners inside this ministry, though they'd probably like to see more.

Colonel Mang led us to an old, cage-type elevator and said something to the operator as the five of us entered.

We rode up in silence and got out on the fourth floor, which was dimly lit and decrepit. There were a number of closely spaced doors on one side of the corridor, and from behind one of them I could hear a man cry out in pain, followed by the sound of a slap, and another cry of pain. One door was slightly ajar, and I heard a woman weeping.

Colonel Mang didn't seem to notice any of this, and neither did the two goons. I guess they were used to it, like it was just background noise on the fourth floor.

Colonel Mang opened a door, and as he started to enter, I caught sight of a man lying naked on the floor, covered with blood and moaning softly. Behind a desk sat a uniformed man, smoking and reading a newspaper.

Colonel Mang exchanged a few words with the man behind the desk, and closed the door. He said, "That room is being used."

I exchanged glances with Susan, and I knew she'd seen what I'd seen. Most people have no point of reference for scenes like this, and I recalled my first combat experience, the dead and the dying lying everywhere, and it does not register as reality, which is how you cope with it.

Colonel Mang found an empty room, and we all entered.

The room was windowless and warm, lit by a single hanging light bulb. There was a desk and chair in the middle of the room and two wooden stools.

Mang placed his hat and attaché case on the desk, sat, and lit a cigarette. He motioned us toward the stools and said, "Sit."

We remained standing.

The floor was old parquet wood, and it was stained with something brownish red. Through the wall behind me, I could hear shouting, followed by a thud against the wall.

Colonel Mang looked pretty blasé, as though beatings in the police station were no more remarkable than fingerprinting and mug shots.

He commented, "People who do not cooperate in the interrogation rooms are brought to the basement where we always get full cooperation, and where you are not invited to sit." He motioned with his hand and said, "Sit."

The two goons behind us kicked the stools into the back of our legs and pushed us down.

Colonel Mang regarded Susan and me for a long time, then informed us, "You have caused me a great deal of trouble." He added, "You have spoiled my holiday."

I replied, "You're not making my vacation much fun either."

"Shut up."

Susan, without asking, took out her cigarettes and lit up. Mang didn't care or notice, as if smoking was the one inalienable right of a prisoner in a Viet jail.

We all sat there while two of us smoked, and the goons behind me breathed heavily. My instincts told me that Susan and I were in some difficulty. Our biggest problems, of course, were the two dead cops on Highway One, and the two dead soldiers on Route 214. The fact that Susan and I were in both areas at the time of those deaths could be pure coincidence, but I didn't think Mang would buy that. And then there was Mr. Cam, our driver, who I should have killed. The truth was, Susan and I were possibly facing a firing squad for murder, and the U.S. government couldn't help us with that.

Mang looked at us, and we looked at him in the light of the hanging bulb. He said, "Let's begin at the beginning." He drew on his cigarette, then informed us, "I did finally discover how you traveled from Nha Trang to Hue. Mr. Thuc was very cooperative when I paid him a visit at his travel agency."

For the first time, I felt a little fear alarm go off.

Colonel Mang said, "So, Mr. Brenner, you

hired a private car, which you were told not to do—"

I interrupted and said, "Ms. Weber was free to travel any way she wished. I was a passenger."

"Shut up." He continued, "And the car was driven by Duong Xuan Cam, who has told me of your journey in great detail." Colonel Mang stared at me and said, "So perhaps you would like to tell me in your own words of your journey so there will be no misunderstanding."

I concluded from this bullshit that Mr. Cam either died under interrogation before he admitted to being an accessory to murder, or Mr. Cam was hiding or running for his life. I said, "I'm sure I can't tell you anything more than the driver told you. Ms. Weber and I slept for the entire trip."

"That is not what your driver said."

"What did he say?"

Colonel Mang replied, "If you ask me one more question, Mr. Brenner, or you, Miss Weber, then this session will move immediately to the basement. Do I make myself clear?"

I replied, "Colonel, I need to remind you that neither Ms. Weber nor I are POWs in the Hanoi Hilton, where your compatriots tortured hundreds of Americans during the war. The war, Colonel, is over, and you will be held accountable for your actions."

He stared at me a long time, then replied, "If in some small way, I can cause your country to again become the enemy of my country, that

would make me, and others here, very happy."
He smiled unpleasantly and added, "I think I
have found a way to do that. I am speaking, of
course, of the trial and execution of an American so-called tourist and an American so-called
businesswoman for either murder, or anti-
government activities, or both."

I think he meant us, so again I reminded
him, "You will be held accountable, not only by
my government, but by yours as well."

"That is not your concern, Mr. Brenner. You
have other problems."

He sat there a moment, thinking perhaps
about my problems, and hopefully his potential
problems. He said to me, "When we last met in
Quang Tri City, we discussed your visit to Hue,
your missing time period on your journey from
Nha Trang to Hue, your insolence to the police
officer in Hue, and other matters relating to
Miss Weber's choice of male companionship.
We also discussed your visit to the A Shau Valley,
to Khe Sanh, and your contact with the hill
tribes. I believe I have enough evidence right
now to keep you in custody."

I said, "I think you're harassing an American
army veteran and a prominent American businesswoman for your own political and personal purposes."

"Yes? Then we need to continue our talk until you and I think otherwise." He asked me,
"How did you leave Hue?"

I said to him, "We left Hue on a motorcycle and arrived, as you know, in Dien Bien Phu the same way."

"Yes, and became Canadians along the way."

I didn't reply.

"Where did you get this motorcycle?"

"I bought it."

"From whom?"

"A man in the street."

"What was his name?"

"Nguyen."

"I'm running out of patience with you."

"You can't run out of what you don't have."

He liked that and smiled. "I think I know where you obtained this motorcycle."

"Then you don't need to keep asking me."

He stared at me and said, "In fact, I don't know. But I know this—before you and Miss Weber leave here, you will be happy to tell me."

So far, Mr. Uyen was safe, Slicky Boy's greed had gotten him in trouble, and Mr. Cam was dead or missing. That left Mr. Anh, who I hoped was having a pleasant family reunion in Los Angeles.

Mang asked me, "Where did you stop during your two-day motorcycle trip to Dien Bien Phu?"

"We slept in the woods."

"Is it possible that you slept in a Montagnard village?"

We were back to Montagnards again. I said, "I think I would have remembered."

He looked at me closely and said, "Two soldiers were murdered near the Laotian border on Route 214. One had a .45 caliber bullet lodged in his chest, the ammunition used in a United States Army Colt automatic pistol." He stared at me, as if he thought I might know something about that. "You would have been in that vicinity at about that time."

I kept eye contact with him and replied, "I don't know where Route 214 is, but I took Highway One to Route 6 to Dien Bien Phu. Now you tell me I was on Route 214 and you accuse me of murdering two soldiers. I can't even respond to such an absurd accusation."

He kept staring at me.

I reminded him, "As it stands now, we accompanied you voluntarily to answer some questions. A very short time from now, we will consider that we've been detained against our will, and you, Colonel, whose name is known to my embassy, will need to account for our absence." Sounded good to me, but not, I think, to Colonel Mang.

He smiled and said, "You were not listening to me, Mr. Brenner. I do not care about your embassy or your government. In fact, I welcome a confrontation."

"Well, Colonel, you're about to have one."

"You are wasting my time." He looked at Susan and said, "I realize I have been ignoring you."

"Actually, I'm ignoring *you.*"

He laughed. "I think you do not like me."

"No, I don't."

"Why? Because of those photographs? Or because you have a racially superior attitude toward the Vietnamese, like so many of your countrymen?"

I said, "Hold on. This line of questioning is—"

"I am not speaking to you, Mr. Brenner." He added, "But if I were, I would ask you how many times you used the racial expressions gook, slope, zipperhead, and slant-eyes. How many times?"

"Probably too many times. But not in the last twenty-five years. Get off this subject."

"This subject interests me." He looked at Susan. "Why are you in my country?"

"I like it here."

"I do not believe that."

She said to him, "I don't care if you believe it or not, but I love the people of this country, and the culture, and the traditions."

He said, "You forgot to mention the money."

"But I don't like your government, and, no, the government and the people are not the same." She added, "If you were an American, I'd still find you disgusting and detestable."

I figured we'd be on the elevator to the basement in about three seconds, but Colonel Mang just stared off into space. Finally he said, "The problem is still the foreigners." He added, "There

are too many tourists here and too many businesspeople. Soon, there will be two less."

Again, I was fairly sure he was referring to us.

Susan advised him, "Look closer to home for
the cause of your problems. Start here in this
building."

Colonel Mang said to her, "We do not need
you or any foreigners to tell us how to run our
own country. Those days are over, Miss Weber.
My generation and my father's generation paid
in blood to liberate this country from the West.
And if we need another war to get rid of the capitalists and the Westerners, then we are prepared to make the sacrifice once again."

Susan said, "You know that's not true. Those
days are also over."

Colonel Mang changed the subject back to
getting Susan and me in front of a firing squad
where he felt more confident. He turned his attention to me and said, "You left Hue by motorcycle early Tuesday morning and arrived in Dien
Bien Phu very late on Wednesday evening where
you registered at the Dien Bien Phu Motel."

"Correct."

"And on Thursday morning you visited the
battlefields, and told the guide you were Canadian historians, and I believe botanists."

"I said Connecticut historians."

"What is that?"

"Connecticut. Part of the United States."

He seemed a little confused, so I added, "Nutmeg State."

He let that go and continued, "Later that day, you both arrived by motorcycle in the village of Ban Hin, again posing as . . . historians."

I didn't reply.

"Miss Weber very specifically told a man in the village market square that you were Canadians. Why did you pose as Canadians?"

"Some people don't like Americans. Everyone likes Canadians."

"I do not like Canadians."

"How many Canadians do you know?"

He saw I was getting him off the subject, and he also saw I was stalling for time. In truth, if we had any chance of getting out of here, it had to do with whether or not he intended to keep us beyond the time we might be missed. But I wondered if anyone in Washington, Saigon, or the embassy here would really be concerned at this point. Tomorrow, yes, tonight, maybe not. The Ambassador's reception sounded like an optional attendance, and we might not be missed. Certainly I wouldn't be missed if I was supposed to be floating in the Na River next to Mr. Vinh. I considered playing my little ace, but my instincts said Colonel Mang wasn't ready for it.

He asked me, "Why did you go to Ban Hin?"

"You know why."

"I do. But to be quite honest, I cannot make

much sense of your visit to Tran Van Vinh. So, you can explain it to me."

There were five names I didn't want to hear from Colonel Mang tonight, or ever: Mr. Thuc, Mr. Cam, Mr. Anh, Mr. Uyen, and Tran Van Vinh. He'd already used three of them. As for Tran Van Vinh, loyal comrade that he was, he'd been fully cooperative with Colonel Mang, but not totally enlightening. I was more concerned about Mr. Anh and Mr. Uyen, who'd made the mistake of sticking out their necks for the Americans, just as twenty million other South Viets had done during the war. You'd think these people would learn. In any case, those two names hadn't yet come up, but I understood Colonel Mang's interrogation techniques by now, and I knew that he skipped around, and saved the best for last.

He was getting impatient with my silence and asked again, "Perhaps you can explain to me the purpose of your visit to Mr. Vinh."

I replied, "I'm sure Mr. Vinh told you the purpose of my visit."

"He told me of your visit by telephone, but I have not had a chance to speak to him in person." Colonel Mang looked at his watch and said, "He should be arriving shortly by plane, then I will discuss this with him further. In the meantime, you should tell me why you paid him a visit."

"All right, I will." Sticking close to the truth, I gave Colonel Mang the same story I gave to Tran

Van Vinh about the letter, the Vietnam Veterans of America, the family of Lieutenant William Hines, the apparent murder of the lieutenant by an unknown captain—no use mentioning the vice president of the United States—and that while I was in Vietnam on a nostalgia trip, I had promised I'd look into this matter for the Hines family.

I finished my story, and I could see that Colonel Mang was deep in thought. He'd already heard this from Tran Van Vinh, and this story was sort of a curveball and didn't fit into anything he suspected or knew. Of course, this turn of events raised more questions than it answered for Colonel Mang, and I could see he was perplexed. Next, he'd want to see the war souvenirs in Susan's backpack. I had the feeling we'd be here a long time. Like maybe forever.

Colonel Mang looked at Susan and asked her, "Do you agree with this story?"

She replied, "I'm just the slut along for the ride."

He looked at her and inquired, "What is a slut?"

She replied in Vietnamese and he nodded, like this was the first thing he'd believed from either of us so far. He did say, however, "But you have this connection to Mr. Stanley that makes me suspicious."

She replied, "I've slept with half the Western men in Saigon, Colonel. You shouldn't attach any meaning to my relationship with Bill Stanley."

Sometimes, as they say in my profession, naked is the best disguise. Colonel Mang seemed genuinely pleased to have his opinion of Susan confirmed by the slut herself, even though that made the Bill Stanley liaison not so incriminating.

Also, of course, Colonel Mang was now wondering about my attachment to Susan Weber, and if he could get to me through her. In truth, I've been very loyal to sluts in the past, but Colonel Mang didn't know that, so I gave Susan a glance of annoyance, and turned my body away from her.

Colonel Mang seemed to notice, and he said to Susan, "You are no better than the prostitutes on the streets of Saigon."

She replied, "I don't charge."

"You would be more honest if you did."

So, having put Susan in her place, he turned his attention back to me and said, "Tran Van Vinh describes an argument between you and Miss Weber. He said she left his house without you, then you left some minutes later. Correct?"

"That's correct."

"Why?"

"We disagreed on many things during the journey, and finally disagreed on how best to get to Hanoi."

He thought about that, then said, "And you both decided to take the train from Lao Cai."

"I guess so, if we arrived together at Long Bien Station."

"I knew where you were, and I knew you were going to Hanoi. You were not listed as an airline passenger, so I had the Long Bien Station watched as well as the bus terminal, and of course the Metropole Hotel and the American embassy in the event you took a car or your motorcycle to Hanoi."

"How did you know we were on the tour bus?"

"Ah. The policeman who boarded the bus observed that the tour guide seemed nervous, but he did not want to cause a problem in front of your compatriots, so we waited." Colonel Mang informed us, "You may meet the tour guide later in another part of this building." He smiled and said, "I told you we would meet again in Hanoi."

"What if we had gone to Ho Chi Minh City instead?"

He seemed happy to answer questions about how good he was at his job, and he replied, "If we were not sitting here, we would be in the same ministry in Ho Chi Minh City. Very little escapes our attention, Mr. Brenner."

I should have left that alone, but I said, "You have no idea what escapes your attention."

He smiled again. "You and Miss Weber did not escape my attention. Here you are."

"You make a point." I said to him, "The Immigration Police in this country are very relentless, Colonel. We could use such Immigration Police in America."

He smiled again and replied, "Itinerary viola-

tions, illegal means of travel, and visa irregulari-
ties are serious matters, Mr. Brenner."

"They must be to mount a nationwide man-
hunt for me and Ms. Weber."

"Are we finished playing games?"

"I hope so. Are you Section A or B?"

He replied, "Section A. The equivalent of
your Central Intelligence Agency."

"Well, next time I come to Vietnam, I'll apply
for my visa earlier."

He smiled yet again and said, "There will not
be a next time."

"Are we finished?"

"No. And do not ask again."

I would have looked at my watch, but I remembered where it was.

So, we all sat while Susan, Mang, and the two
goons smoked, and I inhaled secondhand
smoke, and there wasn't even a window to
open. As if this place wasn't unhealthy enough,
there were old bloodstains on the floor, and the
interrogator in the room behind me seemed to
enjoy bouncing his guest off the wall, which
made the light bulb sway.

Colonel Mang let us listen to the Vietnamese
squash game next door for a while, then turned
to Susan and asked her, "Why did you send a
telex to Mr. Tin at the Century Hotel in Hue?"

Susan replied, "Mr. Brenner loaned his
guidebook to a tour guide and asked that it be
returned by Tuesday morning. It wasn't, and I

sent a telex asking if it had arrived. I'm sure you read the telex."

He didn't indicate that he had and asked Susan, "And what would you have done if the book was returned to the hotel? Drive back to Hue?"

"Of course not. I would have asked Mr. Tin to send it to us at the Metropole."

He looked at me and asked, "And who was this guide you gave the book to?"

I think I'd run out of Nguyens, so I said, "I think his name was Mr. Han. A student."

"Why would you give him your guidebook?"

"He asked to borrow it. Did I break another law?"

Even Colonel Mang saw the humor in that and smiled. Usually, though, when he smiled, it wasn't a good sign. He said to me, "I have a confession to make."

"Good, because I don't."

He continued, "I had you followed in Hue."

I didn't reply, and we all sat there awhile listening to someone being dragged screaming down the hallway. It could have been the tour guide.

Finally Colonel Mang said, "My colleagues lost sight of you, but they did report that your movements were those of a man who thought he was being followed."

"What did you expect them to say? That I was sitting on a park bench, and they lost sight of me?"

He didn't like that and turned to Susan. "And the same for you, Miss Weber. You moved in a suspicious manner."

"I was shopping."

"Ah, yes. For your disguises."

"For suitable attire to travel to Dien Bien Phu." She added, "I can tell you about my shopping in great detail if you'd like to hear about it."

Neither Colonel Mang nor I warmed to that subject. Also, Mang may have thought he was barking up too many trees. In fact, he wasn't, but I felt fairly sure that Mr. Anh was safe. But with Colonel Mang, you never knew what surprises he had in store.

He turned to me and asked, "Where is the motorcycle that you bought in Hue?"

"I sold it to an Australian in Lao Cai."

"What was the name of this man?"

"Woman. Sheila something. Blond, blue-eyed, nice smile."

Colonel Mang suspected I was jerking him around, but he played the game. He asked, "How much did you pay for it in Hue, and how much did you sell it for?"

"I paid three thousand American, but I could only get five hundred from the Aussie lady in Lao Cai." I added, "She knew we had to catch a train, and she drove a hard bargain."

"I see. And did you exchange any paperwork with this lady, or the person in Hue?"

"Colonel, I haven't seen a sales receipt in this country since I've been here."

He let that go and looked at Susan. "I have found your motorcycle keys in your apartment, but we can't find your motorcycle. Can you help us?"

"It was stolen."

"I think it is hidden."

Susan asked him, "Doesn't Section A have anything better to do than look for motorcycles?"

"In fact, Miss Weber, we do, which is why you are here."

"I have no idea why I'm here."

"You do."

Susan told him, "I don't think *you* know, Colonel."

He informed her, "What I do not know, I always discover from the suspect." He reminded both of us, "This is only a preliminary interrogation. The next interrogation is what you see and hear in these rooms. The final interrogation is in the basement. At that time, we will return to the subjects of the two policemen who were killed, and the soldiers who were killed, and other subjects, such as motorcycles, which need further explanation."

I informed Colonel Mang, "Torture is the last resort of a stupid and lazy interrogator. And the confessions are useless."

He looked at me as if he'd never heard this

before, which he probably hadn't. He asked me, "What do you know about interrogation?"

"I watch a lot of police shows on television."

"Actually, I have been trying to find out more about you through my embassy in Washington."

"I don't know anyone there."

"I do not like your sarcasm."

"No one does."

He returned to the subject of my past life and said, "We discovered that you retired from the American army last September, and that you held the rank of chief warrant officer."

"I told you that at Tan Son Nhat."

"But you were not clear about your job."

"No one in the army is clear about their job."

"Apparently not, considering your past performance here."

"We did fine here, Colonel, and you know it. Ask any of your high school classmates."

Colonel Mang totally lost it and started screaming in Vietnamese, pounded the desk and stood. I actually saw spittle at the corners of his mouth. I had the feeling I shouldn't have mentioned the war.

He ran around the desk and came at me. I stood, but before I could react, both goons had me in an armlock. Colonel Mang slapped me across the face, and I spun out of the grasp of the two goons, who weren't very strong, and one of them went down. The other came at me again, and Susan stood and kicked my stool in front of his legs. He fell face down on the floor, and Mang and I squared off.

Before I could take him apart, the two goons scampered across the floor toward a wall, pulled their pistols, and began shouting.

Colonel Mang said something to them, then unexpectedly left the room. I guess he had to take a piss or something.

Susan said to me, "Paul, the fucking reception."

One of the goons spoke sharply to Susan in Vietnamese, and she said to me, "He says sit and shut up. If we move, or talk, he'll shoot us."

So, we sat with the two goons behind us, holding their pistols pointed at us. If they were closer, I'd have both pistols in five seconds, but they kept their distance.

The banging around in this room hadn't attracted any particular attention because of the banging around in the other rooms. Colonel Mang hadn't closed the door when he left, and I heard a lot of slapping going on down the hall.

We sat for about five minutes before Colonel Mang returned. He had two more armed goons with him, who also stood behind us. As Mang passed by, I smelled alcohol.

He sat behind the desk and lit a cigarette. He tried to appear as though nothing had happened and said to us, "Let me return to the subject of the murders of two policemen and two soldiers. Whether you confess to these murders or do not confess, there are witnesses to these murders, who will identify both of you as the murderers. So, you should consider yourselves charged with murder."

I thought about playing my ace, but that ace was starting to look like the deuce of clubs.

Colonel Mang let us think about the murder charge, then said, "I am willing to dismiss these murder charges in exchange for a written statement from both of you admitting that you are agents of the American government, and explaining in detail what is your mission here."

"Then we all go to the Metropole for a drink?"

"No. You stay in prison until you are expelled."

"And my government apologizes and writes a check."

"I hope they do not apologize. And you can keep your money."

"What would you like me to confess to?"

"I want you both to confess what you have done—making contact with armed insurgents, aiding the FULRO, espionage, and being in contact with enemies of the state."

"I've only been here two weeks."

He wasn't catching all of my sarcasm, and he nodded. He looked at me and tried to be reasonable. He said, "Surely you see the advantage of confessing to political crimes rather than being charged with common murder. Political crimes can be negotiated between our governments.

Murder is murder." He reminded me, "I have witnesses to four murders. I also have witnesses to
the political crimes. The choice is yours."

The justice system worked a little differently
here than at home. I think I mentioned that to
Karl.

Colonel Mang said, "I need a decision from
you, Mr. Brenner."

Susan said, "You're ignoring me again."

He looked at her. "I do not need anything
from you, except for you to shut your mouth."

Before Susan could tell him to go to hell
again, I said, "I'll let you make the decision,
Colonel. My voluntary cooperation has come to
an end, as you may have noticed."

Colonel Mang said something to the goons,
and I thought we were headed for the nether regions, but one of the goons took our backpacks
and put them on the desk.

Another goon motioned for us to remove
our coats. We took them off, and he threw them
on the desk.

Colonel Mang emptied my backpack on the
desktop. He didn't remark specifically about my
lack of underwear, but did say, "Where are all
your clothes?"

"In the luggage that was stolen, obviously."

He ignored that, looked at my camera, film,
Montagnard bracelet, and my last clean shirt. He
took apart my toilet kit and squeezed my toothpaste and squirted shaving cream on the desk.

As he played with my personal items, he spoke to me and asked, "So, what was your profession in the army?"

"I told you."

"You told me you were a cook. Then you admitted to being a combat soldier."

"I was. Then I became a cook."

"I think, actually, you are an army intelligence officer."

Close, but no cigar.

He tired of my paltry possessions and emptied Susan's backpack on the desk. He went out of his way to ignore her bra and panties, and rummaged through her stuff, including the Montagnard scarf given to her by Chief John, some brass Montagnard jewelry, and other odds and ends.

He set her camera next to mine along with all our exposed film.

Eventually, he focused on the items given to us by Tran Van Vinh. He examined the watch, the dog tags, the wedding ring, the logbook, the wallet, and the items in the wallet, and finally the canvas pouch with the letters and the MACV roster. The roster held his interest for only a few seconds, then he riffled through the letters. Finally, he looked at Susan and asked, "These are all the items given to you by Tran Van Vinh?"

She nodded.

"Why do you have them and not Mr. Brenner?"

"What difference does it make?"

"What do you have on your person?"

"Nothing."

"We will see about that shortly."

She said to him, "If you touch me, I'll kill you. If not today, then someday."

He replied, "Why would a slut care if a man touched her?"

"Fuck you."

I said to Susan, "Take it easy." I said to Mang, "If you touch her, Colonel, and she doesn't kill you, I will. If not today, then someday." I added, "You know I can do that."

He looked up from his poking around and said to me, "Ah, so you like this lady. And you would kill for her."

"I'd kill you just for fun."

"And I would kill *you* just for fun. In fact, you no longer have the choice of confessing to political crimes. I certainly do not want anyone as dangerous as you and Miss Weber being set free someday. You might kill me."

I said to him, "If not me, then someone else."

He glanced at me, and I could see that he understood that I was revealing that I wasn't alone. This is what he suspected and was happy to have it confirmed, but not too happy about being put on a hit list.

He chose to ignore my statement and turned his attention to the coats, which held nothing of interest for him. He asked Susan, "Where are the photographs I sent you?"

She said something to him in Vietnamese, which is not usually something he wants to hear.

He replied sharply in Vietnamese, and I reminded everyone, "Speak English."

Colonel Mang said to me in good colloquial English, "Shut your fucking mouth."

The situation called for diplomacy, so in French, the international language of diplomacy, I said to him, "Mangez merde."

It took him a second to realize I'd told him to eat shit. He said to me, "You may as well have your fun now, Mr. Brenner, and take this opportunity to act bravely in front of your lady. Later, neither of you will be so brave."

I didn't reply.

He opened his attaché case and took out a stack of photographs. He studied a few of them, then threw about six toward us and a few landed on the floor face up. They were, of course, the photographs from Pyramide Island. Colonel Mang said to Susan, "Perhaps I am confused about the issue of Western modesty. You put me in a difficult situation in regard to searching you."

Susan said, "Don't touch me."

Mang looked at me. "Mr. Brenner? Can you help me?"

I said, "You should get a female to do the search in another room."

"Why can we not all pretend we are on the beach?"

I said, "Why don't you stop being an asshole?" I stood and felt something cold on my neck.

Colonel Mang said, "Sit."

The gun at the back of my neck was mine if I wanted it, but I wasn't sure if the other three guns were drawn and aimed. I sat.

It was time to play the ace. I said to Mang, "Colonel, the American Ambassador, Patrick Quinn, has invited me and Ms. Weber to a reception at his residence at 8 P.M. The reception is in honor of the Vice President of the United States, Edward Blake, who, as you know, is in Hanoi. We need to be at that reception, which has already started."

Colonel Mang looked at me, then at Susan. He said, "And what will you wear to the Ambassador's reception? I see no suitable attire on your person or in these bags."

Susan said, "Mrs. Quinn has appropriate attire for me. You shouldn't worry about that."

Colonel Mang looked at me. "And you, Mr. Brenner?"

"I'm just playing the guitar. And I'm late."

He ignored that and asked, "Why would either of you be invited to such an affair?"

Susan replied, "I'm a friend of Mrs. Quinn."

"Are you?" He looked at me. "And you, Mr. Brenner?"

"Pat Quinn and I went to school together."

"Ah. So many famous people from that class.

So, then I am keeping you both from dinner with your compatriots."

Susan informed him, "Your Foreign Minister, Mr. Thuang, will also be there, and so will the Interior Minister, Mr. Huong, who I believe is your superior. I may or may not mention this matter to them."

I'm not usually impressed with name dropping, but I made an exception in this case. Of course, Colonel Mang may now have a good reason not to let us out of here alive. I looked at Colonel Mang, but he was being inscrutable, and I couldn't tell which way he was going to tip.

I said to him, "I sent a telex from Lao Cai to the embassy informing them we'd be arriving by train, checking into the Metropole, and would be at the reception at eight."

"The post office is not open at the time the Lao Cai train leaves for Hanoi."

Whoops. I said, "I gave the message to the Australian lady who promised to send it. The lady who bought my motorcycle." I'm really glad I was born Irish.

Colonel Mang lit another cigarette and thought this over. Finally, he asked me, "Will this man Blake be your next president?"

"Probably." I added, "We have elections."

He thought a moment, then said, "I do not like this man."

Well, finally, we had something in common.

Mang said, "He was a soldier here during the war."

"Yes, I know."

"He makes too many visits here."

I replied, "He's a friend of Vietnam."

"So he says." He added, "I have heard rumors that he wishes to place American military on Vietnamese soil again."

Neither Susan nor I responded. Colonel Mang had a lot to consider here, and I didn't want to interrupt his thoughts with threats, or with promises to put in a good word for him at the reception.

He looked at us and said, "I am still not satisfied with any of your answers. It is my duty to protect my country."

He didn't sound real sure of himself, and he knew it. He glanced at his watch, which was a good sign. Yet, he still couldn't make a decision.

He looked at me and said, "I am going to ask you some questions, Mr. Brenner, and if you answer me truthfully, I may consider releasing you and Miss Weber."

I didn't reply.

He asked me, "Are you here to investigate the murder of this Lieutenant Hines by an American captain in Quang Tri City in February 1968?"

"I told you I was."

"But you indicated you were conducting this investigation on behalf of the family."

"That's right."

"Are you also conducting this investigation on behalf of your government?"

"I am."

He seemed surprised at the truthful answer. So was I, and so was Susan. I saw a way out of this building, and the way out had to do with Edward Blake, who in a way got me here in the first place.

Colonel Mang asked me, "And Miss Weber is your professional colleague?"

I wasn't sure about that, and I replied, "She has volunteered to assist me with the language and the travel."

He looked at Susan, "What connection do you have to your government?"

"I slept with Bill Stanley."

"And what else?"

"I'm a citizen and a taxpayer."

He wasn't bonding with Susan at all, so he turned his attention back to me and asked, "And what is your connection to your government?"

I'd once slept with a female FBI agent on a case, but I didn't think he wanted to know about that now. I said, "I'm a retired criminal investigator for the United States Army." I was also allowed to give him my service number, but I can't always remember it.

He thought awhile, probably wondering what an army CID guy did. He asked me, "What is your present connection to your government?"

"A civilian employee."

"Do you work for the Central Intelligence Agency?"

Probably, but I replied, "No, I do not. This is a criminal matter. I'm investigating a murder, not committing one."

He missed the Beltway humor and continued, "When you spoke to Tran Van Vinh, did you discover the identity of this murderer?"

"Perhaps."

"Why is this important after so many years?"

"Justice is important."

"To whom? The family? The authorities?"

"To everyone."

He drew thoughtfully on his cigarette. The man was not stupid, and neither am I, so I kept quiet. He needed to arrive at the end of this by himself.

He said to me, "So, you have returned to Vietnam after nearly thirty years to find the truth about this murder."

"That's right."

"For justice."

"For justice."

"This murdered Lieutenant Hines must come from a wealthy and powerful family for your government to go through all this trouble."

"It wouldn't matter if he was rich or poor. Murder is murder. Justice is justice."

He looked at Susan and asked her, "Where are the photographs you showed to Mr. Vinh?"

"I got rid of them."

"Why?"

"I didn't need them anymore."

He said to her, "Mr. Vinh said you had two sets of photographs. One of Lieutenant Hines, the other of a captain that you suspected was the murderer."

Susan nodded.

"Mr. Vinh was able to provide you with this photograph of Lieutenant Hines from his wallet, and these items confirm he was the man who was murdered."

"That's right."

"But Mr. Vinh was not able to identify the photographs of the captain as the man he saw murder this lieutenant in Quang Tri City. Correct?"

"That's correct."

He asked Susan, "What is the name of this captain?"

"I don't know."

"How could that be? You had his photographs."

I interrupted and said, "Those were my photographs, Colonel. Ms. Weber was just translating."

"Ah, yes. So, I ask you, what was the name of that captain?"

"I have no idea."

"You were not told who you were looking for?"

"No, I was not. What difference does it make to you? Do you think you would know him?"

He looked at me and said, "In fact, Mr. Vinh thought about your visit after you left, and . . ."

I could see that Colonel Mang was burning the neurons, and like me a few days ago, he had something almost in his grasp, but it kept slipping away.

I reminded him, "I've answered you truthfully. Now you know the purpose of my visit here. We've broken no laws. We need to leave."

He was really in deep thought, and he knew instinctively that he was finally on to something. He asked me, "If you are investigating the murder of an American by an American, why did your government not request the help of my government?" He reminded me, "You pay millions for information about your missing soldiers."

This was a really good question, and I recalled that I'd asked Karl the same thing, though within the question was the answer. It had taken me about two minutes at the Wall to answer it myself. It was taking Colonel Mang longer, so he repeated the question, as if to himself.

I replied, "As you learned from Mr. Vinh, this captain also murdered three Vietnamese civilians and stole valuables from the treasury at Quang Tri. My government thought it was best to avoid a situation where your government insisted on putting this captain on trial."

Colonel Mang didn't actually say, "Bullshit," but he gave me that look that said, "Bullshit." He said, "That answer is not satisfactory."

"Then answer the question yourself."

He nodded and rose to the challenge. He lit another cigarette, and I thought I heard a game show clock ticking.

Finally, he began studying the personal effects of Lieutenant William Hines. He picked up the MACV roster and looked at it. He said, "Mr. Vinh observed that a document with American names caused both of you to show some emotion." He read the roster, then looked at me, then at Susan. He said something to her in Vietnamese, and I thought I heard the word dai-uy, captain, and definitely heard a Vietnamese-accented Blake.

Susan nodded.

Colonel Mang had the look of a man who had arrived at the truth. He was pleased with himself, but also a bit agitated, and maybe a little frightened. Like Karl, he could be looking at a general's star, but if he used this knowledge the wrong way and took it to the wrong people in his government, he could wind up stamping visas on the Laotian border for the rest of his life. Or worse.

He looked at me and asked an astute question. "Are you going to protect this man, or expose him?"

I replied, "I was sent here to find and report the truth. I have no control over what happens to this man."

He said to me, "You should have said you were

sent here to expose him. I told you I did not like him."

"I know what I should have said. You asked for the truth, and I gave you the truth. Do you want me to start lying again?"

He ignored that and said to us, "Give me your visas."

This was the best news I'd heard in a while, and I gave him my visa. Susan, too, handed over her visa. He didn't bother to ask for our passports because all three of us knew that the American embassy could issue two new passports in ten minutes, but without the Vietnamese-issued visas, we were not getting out of this country. But we *were* getting out of this building.

Colonel Mang said something to one of the goons, who left the room. He said to me, "I am going to let you and Miss Weber go to your reception."

I wanted to congratulate him on a wise decision, but I said instead, "When may we expect to get our visas returned?"

"You do not need a visa to be re-arrested, Mr. Brenner."

"I suppose not."

The door opened and the goon returned with a female in uniform. She spoke to Susan in Vietnamese, and Susan let herself be subjected to a pat-down, which seemed to satisfy the requirements of a search without giving Susan too much to talk about at the Ambassador's reception.

It was my turn, and the male goon patted me down.

All we really had on us were our wallets, and Mang examined the contents of both, then threw them on his desk. He said, "Take your wallets and leave."

We both took our wallets and began packing our backpacks.

Mang said, "You know you are not taking any of that."

I said, "We need the personal effects of Lieutenant Hines."

"So do I. Leave."

"I need my airline ticket."

"You have no use for it."

"We need our jackets."

"Leave. Now."

Susan said, "I want my film and camera."

He looked at her, then at me and said, "Your arrogance is absolutely astounding. I give you your life, and you argue with me about what I have taken in exchange for your life."

He had a point, and I took Susan's arm.

He said, "Wait. There is something you can take with you to your party. Take the photographs from the floor."

I could almost hear Susan telling him to go fuck himself, so I said quickly, "Ms. Weber already sent her set to the commercial attaché at the embassy. Thank you."

He smiled, "And I will send this set to Ambassador and Mrs. Quinn. They should know they are hosting a whore in their house."

Susan smiled sweetly and said, "I'll pass on your regards to the Interior Minister."

"Thank you. Be sure to tell him that his friend Edward Blake is a murderer and a thief."

I shouldn't have replied, but I said, "You should tell him yourself, Colonel. You have the evidence and you have Tran Van Vinh. But be careful. You have a tiger by the tail."

We made eye contact, and in that brief moment, I think we saw ourselves in each other's faces; we, he and I, America and Vietnam, kept bumping into each other, at all the wrong times, in all the wrong places, and for all the wrong reasons.

★

CHAPTER FORTY-EIGHT

——— ★ ———

The goons escorted us down to the lobby and out the front doors. Susan said something they didn't like, and they said good-bye with a push.

We stood in the dark street a second, then Susan took my hand, and we moved toward a lighted avenue a few blocks away. Susan said, "Why didn't you tell him about the Ambassador's reception sooner?"

"I kept forgetting."

She squeezed my fingers together in a powerful grip and it hurt. She said, "Not funny."

I said, "I don't think the Ambassador's party is what got us out of there. Edward Blake got us out of there."

She didn't reply.

We put some distance between us and the Ministry of Fear, and reached a broad avenue named Pho Tran Hung Pao, which should be renamed.

Susan got her bearings, and we turned right. We passed a big, ugly modern building that Susan said was the Cultural Palace, and where a lot of cabs and cyclos were parked. I said, "We should get a taxi."

"I need to walk. It's not far."

We continued down the busy avenue. She took her cigarettes out of her jeans and lit up with a match. She said, "At least he didn't take my smokes."

"He's not that sadistic."

We continued along the busy avenue, and because the weather was cool many of the men wore sweaters or heavy sports jackets, and most wore berets or pith helmets. No one was wearing a smile, including me. This place somehow wiped the smile off your face, especially if you'd just come from Yet Kieu Street.

Susan said, "He's got all our evidence. What do you think he's going to do with it?"

"That's the question."

"We go through hell to get that stuff, and now he's got it, and he figured it out . . ." She said to me, "Washington is going to have a fit."

I didn't reply.

She asked me, "So, what's the plan now?"

"I need a drink."

"I'll get you one at the reception."

"Do you really know the Ambassador's wife?"

"I do. I met her twice here in Hanoi, and I went shopping with her and her friends in Saigon, and we went to dinner. Do you play the guitar?"

"I lied. Do you know the Ambassador?"

"I met him in Hanoi at the embassy once, and at his residence another time."

"Would he remember you?"

"Probably. He hit on me."

"How'd he do?"

"He was doing fine until Bill butted in." She laughed and put her arm through mine. "I can be a handful. But you can handle me."

We came to another wide avenue that Susan recognized, and we turned left and continued walking. We approached a big lake surrounded by parkland and vendors, and people playing chess. On the lighted lake were an assortment of small boats, and I could see an island in the lake where a pagoda stood, topped with a red star. I asked, "Is this the lake where the B-52 bomber is?"

"No. There are lots of lakes in Hanoi. This is the Lake of the Returned Sword."

"Is there a Lake of the Returned Evidence?"

"I don't think so."

We walked along the lake, and Susan asked again, "Paul, what is the plan?"

"Whatever it is, it's my plan."

She didn't respond for a while, then said, "You still don't trust me."

I didn't reply.

"After all we've been through together . . ."

"That's the point."

She stopped walking, and I stopped and turned to her. We looked at each other, and I could see she was upset. She said to me, "I would and did risk my life for you."

"You did risk your life."

She didn't pursue that and asked me, "Do you really love me?"

"I do, but I don't have to trust you."

"You can't have love without trust."

"That's female bullshit. Of course you can. Let's go." I took her arm, and we continued on.

She pulled away from me and said, "I'm going to the hotel. You go to the reception."

This sounded like something from my last three or four relationships. It must be me. I said to her, "I need you there."

"Try again."

"You have the invitation, and you know the way. You know the host and hostess."

"Try again."

"I want you there."

"Why?"

"I don't know. But *you* know. Tell me what was supposed to happen tonight."

She didn't answer for a few seconds, then said, "If I made it this far, I was supposed to go to the reception and tell someone whether or not I was successful, and turn over whatever I have."

"Was I supposed to make it this far?"

She thought a moment and replied, "Situation A was we didn't find Tran Van Vinh or we didn't get any evidence. Then you go to Bangkok, and I go back to Saigon. Situation B, we found what we were looking for, but you don't know what it means. You go to Bangkok, I go to Saigon. Situation C, you understand what we discovered, and you're okay with it. You talk it over in Bangkok, I go to Saigon. Situation D is where you want to be a hero and a Boy Scout, and you and I go to Bangkok together. That's the situation now."

I watched the boats racing, or maybe engaging in mock naval battles; it was hard to tell with the Vietnamese.

"Paul?"

I looked at her.

She said, "Of course, it got complicated because I fell in love with you."

"Everyone does. That's Situation E."

"All right. Situation E."

I said to her, "Let's go back to D. What are you supposed to do when I tell you that I'm going to report everything I've found out to my boss, then to the FBI, and to the Justice Department, and to the press, if I have to?"

She didn't reply.

"And this will result in an official investigation, and possibly an indictment of Edward Blake, and his trial for murder, which might upset his plans to become president. Okay, if I told you this, which I did, then what were you supposed to do?"

"Reason with you."

"I'm unreasonable. Then what?"

"You're putting me in a difficult position."

"Welcome to a difficult position. Talk to me."

"What do you want me to say? That I was

supposed to kill you? I told you, I was just supposed to keep an eye on you until I got you to Bangkok." She paused, then said, "After that, I had no idea what they intended to do with you."

"That's pretty cold and heartless."

"I know. But it sounded all right in the briefing. Haven't you ever been to a briefing where tough decisions are discussed very logically and matter-of-fact, and they sound right, but then you go out and see the people you're supposed to get tough with." She looked at me.

In fact, most of my professional life, from battle briefings to JAG meetings, have been like that. I said, "I understand, but what you're talking about is illegal, not to mention immoral and dishonest."

"I know."

"What was your motivation?"

She shrugged. "Stupid things. Excitement, adventure, the feeling that important men trusted and relied on me." She looked at me. "I see you're not buying that."

"No, I'm not."

"Good. You're not as stupid as you look."

"I hope not. Where'd you learn to use a gun?"

"Lots of places."

"Who do you work for?"

"I really can't tell you, and it doesn't matter." She added, "Don't bother to ask again."

I didn't reply.

She said, "Look, Paul, you were ordered to

lie to me from day one, and I was ordered to lie to you from day one. You have no right being pissed off at *my* lies while thinking your own lies are justified."

I nodded. "Okay. But that's why I'm out of this business."

"You should consider staying in. You did a brilliant job with Tran Van Vinh, and with Colonel Mang, and with putting two and two together."

"It's good to quit when you're ahead and alive."

She looked at me and said, "I told you when we stood there in the Na Valley, when I gave you the gun, that I'd help you expose Edward Blake, though that is not what I'm supposed to do. I meant that, and I'll do it, because it's the right thing to do, and because . . . I'll do anything you ask me to do. Even if you and I never see each other again, I want you to think well of me . . ."

I could see tears running down her face, and she wiped them with her hands.

I said, "Let's go."

We continued past the lake, and Susan knew the way. We turned up a street called Pho Ngo Quyen, and came to the Metropole Hotel on a corner. Susan said to me, "I can check in, and we can shower, and if you'd like, we can make love."

"Why spoil such a perfect day?"

"Are you being cruel or funny?"

"Funny. Let's get to the Ambassador's digs and get this over with."

"We're dirty and we smell."

"So does this job. How far is this place?"

"Another block."

We passed the Metropole, made a turn, and continued down a small tree-shaded street. Up ahead, I could see a well-lighted area that I knew must be the ambassador's house.

Susan stopped and looked at me. She said, "I'm upset, and I can't go in there looking upset."

"You look fine."

"I have no makeup on, I've been crying, I'm not dressed, and you're making me miserable."

"You can borrow some lipstick."

"Look at me."

"No."

"Paul, look at me."

I looked at her.

She said, "Three things—I'm on your side, you can trust me, and I love you."

"Okay."

"Kiss me."

I kissed her, and we put our arms around each other and held the kiss. How far back was that hotel?

We separated, and she looked at me. She said, "Three more things—we have no evidence, Tran Van Vinh is under Colonel Mang's control, and when you do get out of Hanoi, you need to be as careful in Bangkok as you were here."

I said, "Which is why I want you to just keep quiet and make yourself scarce. You don't need to get involved with my Boy Scout merit badge."

She didn't reply.

We walked the short distance along a high stucco wall toward a set of wrought iron gates at the entrance to a driveway.

There was a Viet police booth along the wall, and a guy in plainclothes approached us and said in English, "Passports."

We gave him our passports, which he examined with a flashlight. He looked at us as though he knew who we were, as though Colonel Mang had called ahead.

If Colonel Mang had changed his mind, we'd be on a return trip to the Ministry of Public Security. I could see the gates of the ambassador's residence not twenty feet away, and I saw two United States Marine guards standing there.

The plainclothes cop wasn't saying anything, and I couldn't determine if I needed to kick him in the balls and make a dash for the gates. There were two uniformed cops outside the police booth, both armed, and they were watching us.

The plainclothes cop said to me, "Where are you going?"

"To the American Ambassador's reception."

He looked at our clothing, but said nothing.

I put out my hand and said, "Passports."

He slapped both passports in my hand, turned, and walked away.

We continued toward the gates, and I said to Susan, "Getting out might not be so easy."

"I had the same thought."

The gates were open and the two marine guards in dress blues were a welcome sight, though I'd never tell that to a marine.

The marines were at parade rest with their hands clasped behind their backs, and they looked us over. They didn't come to attention and salute, but our round eyes got us through.

A few yards past the gate on the right was a guardhouse where another marine stood in an olive drab uniform, armed with an M-16 rifle. A marine sergeant approached us and said, "Sorry, folks, this is private property."

Susan said, "We're here for the Ambassador's reception."

"Uh . . ." He looked us over. "Uh . . ."

Susan said, "Weber. Susan Weber. And this is my guest. Mr. Paul Brenner." She added, "Chief Warrant Officer Paul Brenner."

"Okay . . . uh . . ." He looked at the clipboard in his hand with a penlight and said, "Yes, ma'am. Here you are." He looked at her, then at me and asked, "Can I see some form of identification?"

I gave him my passport, which he studied with the penlight, then handed the passport back and said, "Thank you, sir."

Susan handed him her passport and he checked it out and handed it back to her. He

said, "Uh . . . the event tonight is business attire."

Susan said, "We've just come in from the
country, and there are clothes waiting for us
here. Thank you, Sergeant."

"Yes, ma'am." He asked me, "Have you been
here before, sir?"

"Not here, no."

He pointed to the house and said, "You follow this circular driveway to the front door. The
reception is in the garden tonight. Have a good
evening."

I looked at this young marine sergeant and
thought of Ted Buckley at Khe Sanh. The world
had come a long way since the winter of 1968,
but if you were never there, you wouldn't
know that.

I was about to turn away when the marine
asked me, "Did you serve here?"

"I did. A long time ago."

He came to attention and saluted former PFC
Brenner.

I took Susan's arm, and we walked up the
stone-paved driveway.

The house was a three-story French villa with
a slate mansard roof. The cream-colored stucco
was molded to look like stone blocks, and there
were French ornamental details on the facade,
including wrought iron balconies and louvered
shutters. An illuminated American flag flew
from a pole near the front entrance. A breeze

snapped the flag, and I felt a little tingle run down my spine.

A Vietnamese man dressed in a dark suit stood at the entrance. He smiled and said, "Good evening."

Susan replied in English, "Good evening."

I like people who don't show off their second language whenever they get a chance. Nevertheless, I said to him, "Bon soir," so he could tell his friends about a Frenchman who came to the American Ambassador's reception dressed like a pig.

He replied, "Bon soir, monsieur." He opened the door and we entered.

We went up a short flight of marble stairs, at the top of which was yet another Viet, this one a woman in a blue silk ao dai, who also greeted us in English and bowed. She said, "Please follow me. The reception is in the garden."

Susan said to her, "I'd like to use the ladies' room."

The Viet lady probably thought that was a good idea.

She bowed us toward a sitting room to the right, off of which was a staircase that went up to the next floor, but Susan passed it and kept going.

As we crossed the well-appointed sitting room, Susan motioned to a set of closed double doors on the left-hand wall and said, "The Ambassador's office."

She opened another door that led to a big bathroom and said, "Come on in. I'm not shy."

We both entered the bathroom and I locked the door.

Susan made right for the toilet.

There were two marble washbasins along the wall, with soap and towels, and I washed the grime and blue dye off my face and hands. I looked in the mirror and a very tired unshaven man looked back at me. This wasn't the worst two weeks of my life—the A Shau Valley still held first place—but it might have been the most emotionally draining. And it wasn't over. Nor would it ever be.

Susan stood at the basin beside me and looked at herself in the mirror. "I look good without makeup . . . don't I?"

"See if the Ambassador hits on you again."

I didn't see any mouthwash, so good soldier that I am, I bit off a piece of soap, put a handful of hot water in my mouth, and gargled. The soap foamed around my lips.

Susan laughed and said, "What are you doing?"

I spit into the sink. "Gargling."

She washed up and tried the soap in the mouth. "Ugh."

I went to a window that overlooked the front garden where we'd come in. I could see the marine guards at the entrance, the two marines at the guardhouse, and the American flag flapping outside the window. Over the wall was Hanoi, Mang territory.

I said to her, "We need to stay here tonight. Or in the embassy."

Susan came up beside me with a hot, wet towel and put it on the back of my neck. "How's that feel?"

"Great."

She looked out the window and said, "You know, Paul, you don't have to have a confrontation here. Why make yourself persona non grata in the embassy?"

"Why not? I'm persona non grata in the rest of this country. Am I persona non grata in this bathroom?"

She smiled. "Your safety zone is definitely shrinking. You know, Colonel Mang might do the job for you."

"I need a drink."

We left the bathroom and went back to the Viet lady, who led us down a hallway past a large living room or salon, beyond which I could see a larger dining room. The furnishings here were top-notch, a mixture of French and East Asian, though a lot of bad modern paintings hung on the walls.

We came to a long gallery that ran along the rear of the house, and the lady motioned us toward a set of French doors. I could hear music and talking out in the garden.

As Susan and I walked toward the doors, she said to me, "Bill is supposed to be here."

"I kind of figured that out."

"Does that bother you?"

"No. We were classmates at Princeton."

We went through the doors onto a set of marble stairs flanked by pink granite banisters. I said, "You could buy a B-52 bomber for what this place costs."

Susan took my hand, which was a very nice gesture, and we moved halfway down the stairs. There was a big pavilion pitched in the yard, which was all lit up with Chinese lanterns. The yard was surrounded by walls and gardens, which were also lit. To the left, I saw a big lighted swimming pool. I could be the next ambassador to Vietnam if I played my cards right.

Susan looked out over the crowd of about two hundred people, none of whom wore jeans or polo shirts. She said to me, "There's the Ambassador . . . and there's Anne Quinn . . . I don't see the Vice President . . . but wherever you see a crowd and hear the kissing of ass, he should be in the center."

"I think I see him."

Susan said, "We're a bit late for the receiving line, so we should first go and announce our presence to Mrs. Quinn."

"You learn this in the Junior League? Can't we hit the bar first?"

"No. Protocol before alcohol."

We descended the last steps, and a few people noticed us, then a few more. There seemed to be a little lull in the noise level.

Susan went right up to the Ambassador's wife, who was speaking to a group of men and women under the pavilion. Susan put out her hand and said, "Anne. How are you? You look fabulous."

Anne Quinn was a handsome woman of about fifty with an expressive face. In fact, her face expressed something close to shock, but she recovered nicely and said, "Susan! How wonderful to see you!"

Barf.

They did a little air kiss, and Mrs. Quinn's nose twitched, like she'd just smelled Vietnam.

The rest of the group seemed to be backing away.

Susan said to our hostess, "You'll never guess what a week I've had."

No, she never would.

Susan said, "Oh, Anne, please let me introduce you to my friend, Paul Brenner. Paul, Anne Quinn."

I tried to stand downwind from her as I took her hand and said, "Very pleased to meet you. Chuc Mung Nam Moi."

She smiled weakly and returned my New Year's greeting.

I still had the taste of soap in my mouth, and I tried to blow a bubble, but it wasn't working.

Susan said to Mrs. Quinn, "Please forgive us for arriving late. Paul and I spent a week traveling up country, and the train from Lao Cai was late, and to top it off, we had our luggage stolen."

"Oh, how awful."

I guess that explained our attire without mentioning it directly. Susan, I noticed, seemed to fit in here, and even her voice had changed from sexy to sort of chirpy. I needed a drink.

Mrs. Quinn glanced at me and started processing something. She said to Susan, "You . . . you traveled to where . . . ?"

"To Dien Bien Phu and Sa Pa. You absolutely must go there."

"Well . . . yes . . ."

"Paul and I spent three wonderful days in Nha Trang. Have you been there?"

"No . . ."

"You must go. And don't miss Pyramide Island. Then we went to Hue and stayed at the Century. Where you stayed last year."

"Oh, yes . . ." She glanced at me again, then said to Susan, "Bill Stanley is here . . ."

The lady never finished a sentence. Probably never finished a thought.

Susan sort of looked around. "Oh, is he? I'll have to say hello."

"Yes . . . he was actually asking . . ."

Susan said to her and to the other people who were still moving backward, "Paul served in Vietnam during the war, and we visited some of his old battlefields."

Mrs. Quinn looked at me. "How interesting . . . did you . . . find it difficult . . . ?"

"Not this time."

Susan said to her, "Paul has been looking for a drink since Lao Cai. And I can use a few myself. Terrible train ride. If you'll excuse us."

"Of course."

She took my arm, and we moved toward one of the bars. Susan said, "Lovely woman."

"Don't look for another invitation in the mail."

We made our way through the crowd, and everyone was glancing at us. The thing about a beautiful underdressed woman is that she's still beautiful.

We got to the open air bar where two Viet guys in white coats stood smiling. Susan ordered a gin and tonic, and I ordered a double Scotch on the rocks, which they understood.

I looked around. The crowd of about two hundred was mostly round-eyes, but there were also a good number of Vietnamese, a few in military uniforms, which reminded me of Colonel Mang. Maybe I should have invited him here. He would have enjoyed himself. Also, I could take him in the bushes and beat the shit out of him.

Most of the Westerners and even the Asians looked like business types, but I saw a number of people who could be from other embassies, East and West.

Bottom line here, Vice President Edward Blake was a big draw.

I made a mental note to find my FBI contact, John Eagan, though I was sure he'd find me first.

A four-piece Viet combo was playing "Moonlight in Vermont" out on the lawn, and I noticed a few guys around with earplugs and bulges under their coats, who were obviously Secret Service detailed to the VP. By now, some spotter somewhere was talking into their earplugs saying something like, "Two vagrants at the south bar. Keep an eye on them."

Our drinks were made, and I turned around and bumped into one of the Secret Service guys, who had removed his earplug so he could talk to me. He looked about fifteen, and he was smiling. He put out his hand and said, "Hi, I'm Scott Romney."

I ignored his hand and said, "I'm an American citizen."

He kept his smile plastered on his face and said, "Sir, do you think we could have a word inside?"

"No, I don't think so, sonny."

Susan interrupted my fun and said to him,

"Go speak to Mrs. Quinn. She knows us personally."

He looked at Susan and still smiling said, "Yes, ma'am. I'll do that." And off he went.

I took a sip of my Scotch, gargled, and swallowed.

Susan made me hold her glass while she lit a cigarette. She said, "I'm almost out of smokes." She took her glass and said, "I told you, you look suspicious. That's never happened to me before."

I smiled.

She puffed away and said, "You want to meet the Ambassador now?"

"I want to finish my drink."

"He's coming this way."

I looked to my right toward the pool, and saw a man who must be Patrick Quinn coming toward us alone, but followed at a distance by a few other men. He was about my age and my height, well built, and not bad looking. He was wearing a dark blue suit, like almost every other guy here, and he was beaming a smile at Susan. He came right up to her and shouted, "Susan!" and gave her a big hug and kiss. He said, "You look lovely! How are you?"

He was able to finish short sentences by raising his voice at the end.

Susan replied, "I'm wonderful. You look very fit and tan for February."

Barf.

He replied, "Well, my secret is a tanning lamp and a new gym in the basement. You look very tan yourself. Where have you been?"

"To Nha Trang. With this gentleman. Mr. Ambassador, may I introduce you to my friend, Paul Brenner."

He never missed a beat or batted an eye as he turned to me and stuck out his hand. "Paul! Great meeting you!"

He had a good grip, and he liked to pump, so my Scotch splashed around. He said, "Welcome to our little gathering. Glad you could make it, Paul."

"Thank you, Mr. Ambassador."

"Call me Pat. So, you and Susan were in Nha Trang?"

"For a few days."

"I have to get there. God, I'd love to travel more around this country."

"It's an adventure," I told him.

"I'm sure it is. I'm sure it is."

You can say that again. "It is." I couldn't tell if he knew who I was, or why I was in Vietnam, or if my appearance here was a surprise, a shock, or meaningless. The ambassador is almost always kept in the dark about what the spooks are doing, so he can deny it all later and sound sincere. But it struck me as odd that with two hundred other people here, he'd gone out of his way to charge across the lawn toward Susan. Of course, he probably wanted to fuck her, which could also explain his enthusiasm.

Susan was telling him about the Lao Cai train and the luggage, and he was hanging on every word and nodding sympathetically. He definitely wanted to fuck her, but that was the least of my problems, and in fact, maybe not my problem at all.

He said to Susan, "I'm sure Anne has something for you to wear."

Susan replied, "I actually like my old jeans."

He laughed. Ha ha. He turned to me, "Paul, can I get you a sport jacket?"

"Not if the lady is in jeans. I'm not that brave."

Ha ha.

Susan told him, "Paul served with the army in Vietnam. We visited his battlefields."

"Ah. Is this your first time back?"

"It is."

"I was here with the navy. Off the coast. Never saw any real action."

"You didn't miss anything."

He laughed and slapped my shoulder. He said, "As you know, Vice President Blake saw combat, too. Remind me later to introduce you. Well, I'm glad you both came despite your misadventures. Get yourselves something to eat. The Metropole is catering."

He turned to Susan and said in a softer voice,

"Bill Stanley was asking about you." He looked at her. "You should let him know you're here."

"I will."

Patrick Quinn moved back to his group on the lawn.

I finished my Scotch and said to Susan, "Is that guy for real?"

"He's very charming."

"Your taste in men worries me."

She smiled and looked around. "There's a buffet table. Do you want something to eat?"

"No. I get silly when I eat." I handed my empty glass back to the bartender and he re-filled it.

Susan asked, "Do you mind if I go find Bill?"

"Bill will find you, darling."

"Am I under arrest?"

"No, I just feel so much safer when you're at my side."

She shrugged.

We moved around a little, and Susan knew a few people, mostly American businessmen and women who lived in Hanoi. There was a guy there from her Hanoi office, and they chatted awhile.

Meanwhile, I kept catching glimpses of Edward Blake getting his butt smooched.

Power.

Edward Blake was soon to become the most powerful man in the most powerful country that the world has ever known. And I had his balls in my hand. But if you're going to squeeze the king's balls, you better be ready for all the king's men.

I glanced at Susan talking to her colleague. She was the wild card in this game.

A man approached me and put out his hand. "Hi, I'm John Eagan. You must be Paul Brenner."

I took his hand and replied, "How many other people here are dressed like this?"

He smiled, then glanced at Susan and said to me, "Could I have a word with you?"

Susan noticed him, and I said to her, "I'll be right back."

John Eagan and I moved off to the far side of the lawn, behind the combo band, who were playing "Carry Me Back to Old Virginia." I was getting homesick.

Eagan had a drink in his hand, and he touched my glass with his. "Welcome to Hanoi."

I said to him, "I'll bet you didn't think you'd be saying that tonight."

He didn't reply, and we stood there.

He was about forty, too young for the war, but he may have been military before becoming FBI. I had another thought that, if Susan was telling the truth that Eagan was her embassy contact, then he could be CIA. I'd learned not to believe anything I'd been told about this mission.

He said to me, apropos of nothing, "This place sucks."

"What was your first clue?"

He smiled. "Training Viet narcs. They're all on the take, and they grow opium in their back-yards."

I said to him, "Okay, you've established that you're an FBI guy training the Vietnamese police. I believe every word of it. What can I do for you?"

He didn't seem to appreciate my cynicism, and his demeanor changed. He asked me, "How did you wind up here tonight?"

"Where was I supposed to wind up?"

"At the Metropole, tomorrow."

"What difference does it make?"

"Probably none." He asked me, "So, how did it go?"

"How did *what* go?"

"Your trip."

"Fine."

"Can you be more specific?"

I said to him, "Look, I don't know what you know, or what you're supposed to know, or even who the hell you are. I'm supposed to contact you only if I'm in deep shit. I'm in deep shit. The police have my visa, and I want you to get me the fuck out of here tomorrow. I need to be debriefed in another country, and I need a visa or a diplomatic passport, and a plane ticket, and an embassy escort to the airport. Okay?"

He thought about that and asked me, "How did the police get your visa?"

"You're not helping me with these questions, John."

"Okay . . . here's a piece of news for you. You're going to be debriefed tonight. Here."

"This is a CID homicide investigation. I only talk to my boss. Those were my last and only instructions."

"You were told by Doug Conway and your boss that this is a joint investigation with the FBI. You can talk to me. What we'd like, Paul, is for us to meet in the Ambassador's office at midnight."

"You're not listening to me, John."

"Just be there, okay? We can resolve your exit at that time."

"Who wants to see me?"

"Me, for one. Plus Colonel Goodman, the military attaché, and a gentleman from Saigon, who you met briefly at the cathedral, and maybe one or two others. We just need a little of your time before we send you on your way."

I said to him, "I assume the VP is staying here tonight."

"I can't say for security reasons, but that would be a good assumption. Why do you ask?"

"I wanted to meet him."

"I'll try to arrange that."

"I'll also need a room here."

"Why?"

"Because if I step outside these gates, I could be arrested."

"Why?"

"I like scrambled eggs for breakfast."

He looked at me. "Are we having a problem, Paul?"

"We are. And my traveling companion, Susan Weber, needs a room here, too. She's in the same situation as I am."

"This should be an interesting story."

I said to him, "Just get me out of here. Fish and house guests smell after three days." I turned and walked back toward the pavilion.

I really didn't know who John Eagan was, but Bill Stanley used to work for Bank of America, and Susan Weber worked for American-Asian Investment Corporation, and Marc Goodman, the military attaché, was actually Military Intelligence, and Colonel Mang was an Immigration cop, and Paul Brenner was a tourist. I should write all this down.

In any case, I got my message across, and at midnight, I'd see what their problem was.

I got another Scotch and looked around for my date. A tall, slim, good-looking woman in an evening dress came up to me and asked, "Are you looking for someone?"

I replied, "I've been looking for you all my life."

She smiled and put out her hand. "Let me introduce myself. I'm Jane Blake."

I suddenly recognized her face. I cleared my throat and said, "Oh, I'm terribly sorry—"

She smiled again. "That's all right. I'm totally ignored when Ed is in the room. Or in the garden. Or anywhere."

"I can't imagine why."

She smiled and said, "Let me be very bold. Everyone wants to know who you are."

Finally, a James Bond moment. I said, "You mean, why am I dressed in dirty jeans and haven't shaved recently?"

She laughed. "Yes, that's right."

"Well, Mrs. Blake, I could be the Count of Monte Cristo returning from prison. But my name is Paul Brenner, and I've just come from a remote village called Ban Hin, where I needed to find a man named Tran Van Vinh." I looked at her, but she showed absolutely no sign that this meant anything to her.

She asked me, "Why did you have to find this man?"

"It goes back to the war, and I'm afraid I'm not at liberty to discuss it."

"Oh, that sounds intriguing."

"It was."

"And who is that woman with you?"

"Susan Weber. My guide and interpreter. She speaks fluent Vietnamese. Lives in Saigon."

"Oh, this *is* mysterious." She smiled. "And romantic."

"We're just friends."

"Well, I think you're looking for your friend. She's over there, near the pool." She informed me, "No one even came close to guessing who you were. Ed thought you were a famous actor. They dress so badly. Most of us thought you'd lost a bet, or came dressed like that on a dare."

"Actually, I did come on a dare. Good luck to your husband with the nomination."

She smiled, nodded, and moved off to spread the news. I hope she wasn't measuring for drapes in the White House.

I walked toward the pool where I spotted the woman I'd *really* been looking for all my life. She was talking to her old lover, Bill Stanley, who could possibly be pissed at me for stealing his girlfriend, though he should thank me.

They both saw me coming and stopped their conversation and stood there with their drinks as I approached. I love this shit.

I got within speaking distance and said, "Am I interrupting?"

Susan replied, "No. Paul, you remember Bill Stanley."

I put out my hand and he took it. I asked him, "How are things at the bank?"

He didn't reply, and he wasn't smiling at me.

Dapper Bill was dressed in a dark blue tropical wool suit, which had undoubtedly been tailor-made for him in Saigon, with an extra short trouser rise to fit snugly against his undersized genitalia.

Susan said to me, "I was just telling Bill about our run-ins with Colonel Mang."

Bill spoke for the first time and said, "I've researched this man, and you're lucky to be alive."

I told him, "If you'd researched me, you'd know that it's Colonel Mang who's lucky to be alive."

Bill didn't seem impressed with my macho moment.

I informed him, "Mang thinks he knows you, too. He told me you were the CIA station chief in Saigon. Can you imagine that?"

Again, Bill had nothing to say, but at least Susan was covered regarding how I knew Bill was CIA.

So, we all stood there awhile in a moment of awkward silence. I wondered if Susan felt uncomfortable standing between two men who she'd recently slept with. She looked composed, so maybe this had been addressed in a Junior League meeting. She said, "Paul, Bill tells me you're invited to a meeting here tonight. He asked me to join you. I think this would be a good idea."

I said to Bill, "As I just told John Eagan and as he will tell you, I'm not at liberty to discuss anything with you, the CIA, Military Intelligence, the FBI, or anyone here. This is still a CID homicide investigation, so you can't change the rules or the players."

He replied, "You can and you will discuss this if ordered to by your boss, or by a proper higher authority."

I didn't like his tone of voice, but to be nice,

I said, "If and when my orders change, I'll follow them. However, I'm a civilian, and I reserve the right to pick the time and place of my debriefing. And it's sure not here."

Bill Stanley looked at me and said, "It would be a good idea for you to come to this meeting since we'll be discussing your exit from the country. You don't have to say any more than you want to say."

"Goes without saying." This was a diplomatic reception, and I was trying to be diplomatic, but this is not my strong point, and I asked Bill, "What were you thinking?"

"Excuse me?"

"What were you thinking when you teamed up your girlfriend with me to go on a dangerous mission?"

He seemed to be thinking about what he was thinking. He cleared his throat and said, "Sometimes, Mr. Brenner, matters of national security take precedence over personal considerations."

"Sometimes. And if this is one of those times, then you shouldn't have any gripes about what happened."

He didn't like that and replied, "To be honest with you, this was not my idea."

I didn't bother to ask him whose idea it was, though I said, "You could have said no."

He was seething, but said nothing.

I continued, "Though that wouldn't be a good career move."

Bill may have thought I was implying that he was an ambitious company man who would pimp his girlfriend to advance his career. He remained politely silent, however, the way people do when they're speaking to someone with a terminal condition.

Susan thought it was time to change the subject and said, "Paul, I told Bill that we did discover the identity of the murdered lieutenant, but that we still can't determine the identity of the murderer."

"Did Bill believe that?"

Bill answered, "No, Bill did not believe that."

I said to Susan, "Bill doesn't believe that."

Susan said, "Well, it's the truth." She continued, "I told Bill we'd found Tran Van Vinh, but that we'd decided not to chance carrying those things with us, so we hid everything."

Our eyes met for a half a second, and I looked at Bill to see his reaction, but Bill was as inscrutable as Colonel Mang.

I really didn't know if Susan had said this, because Susan says lots of things. She knew the identity of the murder suspect all along, and Bill knew that, so she was trying to protect me, which was nice, but it wasn't going to play. I said to Bill, "Actually, it would be a good idea if the Vice President attended this midnight meeting."

Bill looked at me a long time before informing me, "The Vice President has no interest in a murder investigation."

"He may be interested in this one. Tell his staff that it's in his best interest to be there."

Bill reminded me, "You have signed various statements relating to national security and official secrets. Regardless of your present status, they are all still binding."

"I also swore to defend the Constitution."

He gave me a long, hard stare and said, "I'm sure you were told in Washington that if you took this assignment, your life could be in danger."

That was usually the type of statement made before a mission, not after, so in this context, it could actually be a threat.

I said to Bill, "Could I have a word with you alone?"

Before Bill could reply, Susan said, "No."

I said to her, "Personal only. No business."

She informed me, "I won't be discussed like that."

Bill picked up the theme and said to me, "We're all mature enough to discuss this together."

I informed everyone, "I'm not that mature." I moved off and motioned for Bill to join me. "Guy talk."

Susan looked pissed, but stood where she was and lit a cigarette.

Bill and I moved out of earshot, and I said to him, "We need to talk about Susan, and . . . oh, one piece of business. If I find out, or even suspect, which I do, that I was the expendable party in this operation, and that you knew of, approved of, or planned that, then I'll kill you. Now, let's talk about Susan."

He stood staring at me and said nothing.

I can do soap opera for about five minutes before I revert to my true self, and I felt I needed to do this, so I said, "On a personal level, I'm truly sorry about what happened. I admit to knowing about your involvement with Susan, and it's not my habit to chase other men's wives or girlfriends." Most of the time. "And as I'm sure you've been told, I'm in a committed relationship with someone at home. So I make no excuses for what happened, and you should know that Susan resisted my attentions. The mission is over, and I'm going home. I apologize again for any trouble I've caused between you and her, and I hope you both can put this behind you."

I studied his face as he processed this gentlemanly, man-to-man bullshit. I actually believed some of it myself, and I really was conflicted about Susan. I was fairly sure, however, that Susan had no further interest in Bill, and maybe Bill had no further interest in Susan. But I needed to clear the air, as they say, and give Bill a chance to say his piece.

But Bill had nothing to say, so I continued to take the blame for whatever vague involvement I was admitting to. I told him, "Susan, in fact, kept the relationship platonic and businesslike until we were forced by circumstances to share a room in Dien Bien Phu." Bill would like to believe that, and I felt I'd done my chivalrous duty toward the lady, and I was ready to get back to the subject of me killing him, and vice versa.

Bill said to me, "I'm staying at the Metropole."

"Good choice."

"When I checked in yesterday, there was a sealed envelope waiting for me, sender unknown."

"Really? You shouldn't open packages without a return address."

"Yes, I know that. But I did. Inside the envelope were twenty photographs of you and Susan at a beach, labeled Nha Trang, Pyramide Island." He added, "All you were wearing were your smiles."

Whoops. I said, "Well, I remember being at the beach, and we were wearing bathing suits. Those pictures must have been digitally altered."

"I don't think so. What the hell possessed you two to cavort publicly in the nude when you knew you were being followed? Did they teach you anything at whatever school you went to?"

The man had a point, so I said, "I admit to a lapse of judgment."

"And then you tell me you and she had a platonic relationship until a few days ago."

"Well, we just went skinny-dipping. It was my idea."

"I'm sure. Haven't you ever heard of telescopic lenses?"

"I really don't want a lecture from you."

"These photographs could be used for blackmail."

"Actually, I think the police are sending them to everyone, yourself included, to embarrass Susan. So that rules out blackmail."

"My God . . ." He asked me, "Have you seen these photographs?"

"Actually, I have. Colonel Mang was kind enough to give us a sneak preview."

He shook his head and seemed lost in thought. He said to me, "You may not care, but Susan comes from a good family with some social standing, and—"

"Bill, cut the Ivy League, Junior League shit, before I lose my temper. We both care about Susan. End of discussion."

"All right . . ." He looked at me. "Susan told me she loves you. Certainly she told you that."

"Yes, she did, but this was such an artificial situation. She should think about it."

"How do you feel about her?"

"Conflicted."

"Meaning?"

"Meaning that I keep discovering new facets of her personality." I think it's called bipolar disorder, but Bill already knew that. To be honest, I'm not always sane myself, and that's when Susan really appealed to me. But to be more loyal to Susan, I said to Bill, "She's a remarkable woman, and I could easily fall in love with her."

He mulled this over. My five minutes of "Days of Our Lives" was drawing to a close, so I said to him, "I think this may be Susan's decision and not ours."

Bill didn't really know me at all, and he probably took everything I said at face value, despite what was in his briefing memo about me. He said to me, "I had the impression from Susan that you . . . that you felt the same way about her."

Before I could reply, Susan joined us and said, "I think that's enough."

Time for a commercial break. I said, "I have to insist that nothing further is discussed about this case that I'm not privy to."

Bill replied, "That's absurd and outrageous."

"Nevertheless, I insist."

Bill snapped, "For your information, you have no say over who speaks to whom. Susan does not work for you, and neither do I."

I asked him, "Who does Susan work for?"

"Not for *you*."

Susan said, "Please, both of you—"

I interrupted, "Look, Bill, it's time for you to take a reality check. Fate, luck, and hard work have put Edward Blake's balls in my hand. I didn't ask for this, and I didn't want it. But there it is." I held out my hand palm up and curled my fingers. "Now, I fully understand this is dangerous information, so I really need to be careful about who, what, where, when, and how it's disseminated. Everyone will thank me later for my diligence and foresight. Including you, Bill. So, we have our choice of all three of us hanging out together until midnight, which is not my first choice, or all of us going our separate ways with no cheating, or Susan and I keeping each other company. Someone make a decision."

Susan said to Bill, "Paul and I are going to have a drink. We'll see you later."

We left Bill Stanley smoking, and he didn't even have a cigarette.

As Susan and I moved to a bar, she asked, "So, who won me?"

"We're going to flip a coin later." I said to her, "Regarding this meeting, I do *not* want you to back me up. Just stay neutral or pretend you're voting for Edward Blake in the next election."

"If that's what you want."

We got a drink, and Susan said, "I think my days as a contract employee are over."

"Is that what you are?"

"I told you, I'm a civilian. No direct government involvement." She thought a moment and said, "They'll also get me fired from my day job."

I said to her, "Look, sweetheart, there are maybe ten people in this world who know what this is about, and we're two of them. The other eight think we have the evidence and they want it. If we had it, we could cut a deal. Also, if we'd told them there was no evidence, they might have believed us. But you told Bill we found the evidence and hid it. Now, we're in the worst possible situation in regard to our health. Bottom line, all we have is too much knowledge and nothing to trade."

"Well . . . that's one way to look at it."

"Tell me the other way so I know if I should bother to make my next car payment."

"Well . . . tell them the truth. Colonel Mang has the evidence and the witness, and he's put two and two together. They'll go nuts, but that takes the pressure off us. They'll have to deal with Mang. Best scenario, Mang blows the whistle, Blake is ruined, the CIA kills Mang, and we live happily ever after."

"I don't think life works like that. Look, there were two reasons to use civilians—one was plausible deniability if things went bad, the other was that they rarely whack one of their own. But if they think they have to, they'd whack us in a heartbeat."

"They're not that ruthless."

"The CIA and Military Intelligence assassinated over 25,000 people here during the war."

"No they didn't."

"You want to dance?"

"Sure."

We put our drinks down and went out to the

small dance floor in front of the band. They were playing another American name place song, Ray Charles's "Georgia on My Mind," and I pictured Edward Blake tallying electoral votes in his mind.

A lot of people were looking at us dancing, and the public affairs photographer took a picture of us, which I could see in the *Washington Post* captioned: *"Paul Brenner and Susan Weber, Hours Before Their Disappearance."*

I caught a glimpse of Edward Blake looking at us, but he didn't seem particularly disturbed. I was starting to think that he was clueless about his problem.

The band swung into "Moon Over Miami," where there were lots of votes. I saw Bill talking to John Eagan, and they kept glancing at Susan and me as though they were trying to decide what size air shipment coffins we needed.

Susan said, "I wish we were back in Saigon dancing on the Rex roof, and that I'd told you then all I knew."

"That would have been a long dance."

"You know what I mean."

I didn't reply.

"Did you tell Bill you loved me?"

"I don't share my feelings with other guys."

"Okay, share them with me."

For some reason, I remembered an old army expression: The enemy diversion you are ignoring is the main attack.

But that was being cynical and paranoid again. I said to Susan, "I do love you. And you know what? Even if you're still deceiving me, and even if you betray me, I'll still love you."

She held me tighter as we danced, and I could tell she was crying. Hopefully, these were tears of joy, and not premature remorse.

CHAPTER FORTY-NINE

──────★──────

A t about ten minutes to midnight, the last of the guests were leaving, the band was packing, and the bartenders were corking the Chardonnay.

Susan and I went into the ambassador's residence and made our way through the quiet house toward the sitting room.

There were a few Secret Service guys standing around in the salon. I saw my young friend, Scott Romney, near the staircase, and he tensed up when he saw me. I said to him, "There are milk and cookies in the kitchen."

We entered the sitting room, and Bill Stanley and John Eagan were already there. Also there was a man in an army green dress uniform whose rank was colonel, and whose nametag said *Goodman*. This was the Military Intelligence guy, Marc Goodman, and he would not normally have any interest in a homicide investigation. I guess it was Cam Ranh Bay that he was interested in.

He was a tall, lanky man, a few years older than me. I remembered seeing him out on the lawn. He recognized Susan from their meeting in Saigon, and they shook hands, and she introduced me.

The door to the Ambassador's office was closed, and John Eagan said, "The Ambassador is with someone and will be finished shortly."

Colonel Goodman said to me, "I understand you and Ms. Weber had a bit of trouble."

I replied, military style, "Nothing we couldn't handle, sir."

Goodman wore the insignia of an infantry officer and had enough ribbons to make a bed quilt. I saw, too, the Combat Infantryman's Badge, which I also owned, and the Silver Star, Bronze Star, and two Purple Hearts. My instinct said this guy was okay, but my instincts had also said that about Edward Blake.

Neither Bill nor John Eagan felt like making small talk, but Goodman said to me, "So, you were with the First Cav in '68."

"Yes, sir." I called him sir because I was ex-army on an army assignment, and he outranked me. In about two days, if I saw him again, he'd be Marc.

He asked, "Saw action where?"

I told him, and he nodded. We exchanged a few details about our military careers, and he asked me, "Do you miss the CID?"

"Not recently."

"Are you pursuing a career in civilian law enforcement?"

"I've thought about it."

"I'm sure you'll have no trouble landing a job in federal law enforcement after this assignment."

That sounded like a joke, but he wasn't smiling. So, maybe it was an incentive to be cooperative. I didn't reply.

He said to Susan, "Have you been properly thanked for volunteering to be a translator and guide?"

Susan replied, "I was happy to help."

"I'm sure it wasn't easy for you to leave your work."

This conversation had a surreal quality to it, the way all government meetings do, especially if the subject is sensitive; the art of innuendo, double-talk, evasive phrasing, and arcane code words. You could think you were being asked to go out for coffee, when they really meant you should assassinate the President of Colombia. You had to pay attention.

Bill struck me as a quiet sort of guy, which might be the only thing I liked about him. Nevertheless, he decided to speak. He said to Susan, "I've indicated to Colonel Goodman, and to the Ambassador, that you may be leaving the country involuntarily."

She said to all assembled, "I'd like to stay. But as you know, my resident work visa has been taken by the police, and my status here is uncertain."

I clarified this by saying, "We were arrested and may be arrested again."

John Eagan said, "I've spoken to the Ambassador about both of you staying here tonight."

"Good. It's either here or Yet Kieu Street."

Everyone knew that address, and it needed no further explanation. I said to Bill, "Where is your boss?" meaning the resident Hanoi CIA bureau chief—top spook in Vietnam.

He replied, "He's out of town."

Why he would be out of town at the culmination of a very important mission was a little mysterious. It could be that he wasn't on the Blake team and was unreliably honest and couldn't be trusted. But I had another thought, and I looked at John Eagan. I asked him, "How long have you been with the FBI?"

"Not long."

"About two weeks?"

He didn't reply directly, but said to me, "Paul, I know you have some issues with the world of intelligence, and it all probably seems like silly cloak-and-dagger stuff to a cop. But there are lots of good reasons why nothing is as it seems. It works for everyone, yourself included."

"It's not working for me, John."

"It really is, Paul."

There was a coffee bar in the sitting room, and I poured myself a cup. Susan went to the bathroom to smoke.

Bill took the opportunity to ask me to step

out into the hallway, which we did. He said, "We can get you out of here in a day or two. Susan will be staying a few days longer."

"Says who?"

"She'll need some time to wrap up her personal and business affairs in Saigon. From here, of course. Then, we'll arrange her safe exit from the country."

"In other words, she's a hostage."

"I'm not following you."

"We're leaving together."

"Not possible."

"Make it possible."

He told me something I already knew. "You're on thin ice. Don't stomp your feet."

I asked Bill, "How worried are you right now?"

He turned and walked back into the sitting room.

I finished my coffee in the hallway and returned just as Susan came out of the bathroom. She'd found a tube of lipstick somewhere and had repainted herself.

One of the double doors to the Ambassador's private office opened, and Patrick Quinn exited without his usual smile. He looked around, found his smile, and said, "Bill, Marc, John, Paul, Susan!"

He was into first names, like he'd aced the Dale Carnegie course. He said, "I know you have some business to attend to, so please make yourselves comfortable in my office."

Everyone mumbled their thanks. I said to Patrick Quinn, "I was to remind you to introduce me to your friend, the Vice President."

He looked at his watch and said, "I'll see if he's available." He said to Colonel Goodman, "Marc, if you need anything, ring the guardhouse or the kitchen." He said to everyone, "Thank you all for joining us tonight." He left.

Whoever he was with in his office was still there, or had exited from the window.

We all moved toward the open door, Susan first, followed by Bill, Marc, and John.

I entered the dimly lit office last, and the first thing I noticed was a man sitting in a leather wing chair in the corner. He bore a striking resemblance to Karl Hellmann.

He stood and moved toward me with a smile. He put out his hand and said, "Hello, Paul."

He even *sounded* like Karl, right down to the accent. I took his hand and said, "Hello, Karl."

We were so thrilled to see each other, we could barely speak. I finally found my voice and said to him softly, "You're a lying, double-dealing, devious son of a bitch."

He replied, "I'm glad to see you're well. I was worried about you. Please introduce me to Ms. Weber."

"Introduce yourself."

He turned to Susan and said, "I am K. Karl Hellmann. We've communicated by fax and e-mail."

Susan said, "It's a pleasure to meet you. Paul speaks so highly of you."

"We hold each other in mutually high regard." Karl said to the others, "Thank you for inviting me."

Karl shook hands with Bill, Marc, and John, and from the snatches of conversation, I was able to determine that they'd never met, or pretended they'd never met or communicated, and that they were happy to make one another's acquaintance. Karl said, "My flight arrived only an hour ago, and I haven't checked into my hotel. So please bear with me if I seem somewhat forgetful."

Everyone understood that bullshit.

I said to Karl, "Could I have a word with you?"

"Of course."

We moved out into the sitting room, and I closed the door. I said to Karl, "You almost got me killed."

"How could that be? I was in Falls Church. You look tired."

"I've spent two fucking weeks in this hell-hole, the last few days on a motorcycle on the run from the cops."

"How was Nha Trang, by the way? Did I tell you I had a three-day R&R there?"

"Why are you here?"

"They asked me to come."

"Why?"

"So you could be fully debriefed here, rather than Bangkok."

"Why?"

"They're very anxious about this."

I pointed out, "They could debrief Susan here. She's probably working for the CIA."

"Well . . . it appears that you and she have developed a friendship, and they felt they needed to do this here and now."

"What you mean is that they want to see whose side I'm on."

"Whatever."

"Can I assume you know what this is about?"

He saw the coffee setup and poured himself a cup. He asked me, "Do you think I could smoke here?" Without waiting for my answer, he lit a cigarette.

"Karl, do you know what this is about?"

He exhaled a stream of smoke and replied, "Actually, I was the first person to know. When the Tran Van Vinh letter landed on my desk, I thought about who to assign the case to. But the more I read the letter, the more intrigued I became with it. So, I assigned it to myself. I was able to determine the identity of the murdered man from my investigation of army files, combat records, and official unit histories. As you suggested in Washington, it was a fairly simple case of narrowing the list of men who served in Quang Tri City in February 1968. Lieutenant Hines, a MACV advisor, was killed in action at the Citadel on or about 7 February 1968. And his name is on the Wall. And then I came across the name of Captain Edward Blake, and I realized, of course, that I'd possibly found something of immense importance. Captain Blake was William Hines's commanding officer, and most probably the only American First Cavalry captain he'd be in close contact with. Of course, I couldn't be sure of that, and in fact, we're still not sure."

"I'm sure."

"Don't be so sure." He reminded me, "You don't convict a man of murder on flimsy circumstantial evidence."

"No. You blackmail him and let him become president of the United States."

He looked around for an ashtray as he changed the subject and said, "She's quite beautiful."

"You haven't seen her at 7 A.M. with a hangover."

"She would still be beautiful. Is Mr. Stanley upset with you?"

"He may be actually relieved."

"Ah." Karl smiled, just a little, and flipped his ash in a potted plant. He said, "She strikes me as the type who may be too much to handle for any man. Even you."

"Is that a compliment?"

"It was meant to be. So, I have just arrived and know almost nothing, except what the Ambassador has just told me."

"What did he tell you?"

"Only what he knows and what Bill Stanley

told him, which is that you were investigating a wartime murder, and that your investigation was fruitful. True?"

"Depends on your definition of fruitful."

"Have you found Tran Van Vinh?"

"I have. In Ban Hin."

"And he had some war souvenirs."

"He did."

"And you have these?"

"How is Cynthia?"

The shift in the subject didn't bother Karl. He replied, "She's well and sends her love. She was disappointed that you changed your Hawaii plans. But I see why you did that."

"Don't make assumptions based on flimsy evidence."

"I never do." He drank his coffee and flipped his ash in the cup. He continued, "Mr. Stanley told the Ambassador that you had committed some sort of travel violation, and that the police had questioned you."

"That's correct."

"Was this a serious violation?"

"I killed two policemen, and two soldiers."

Karl didn't seem shocked or upset. "I assume the police are not sure about this."

"It really doesn't matter here."

"This is true. The Ambassador seems upset about having you as his houseguest, but he seems to look forward to Ms. Weber's company."

"I can't imagine why."

"We need to get you out of this country before the government discovers that you are in residence here and asks for you to be turned over to the police."

"Which government?"

"The Hanoi government, of course. Are you having paranoid delusions?"

"No, I'm quite certain some people in Washington want to kill me."

"If anyone did want you dead, they're probably all here. Starting with Mr. Stanley, but not for the reasons you think."

"Karl, your warped sense of humor is not appreciated at this time. Plus, I'm pissed off at you."

"You'll thank me for this someday. I see you've lost some weight. Did you not eat well?"

"Look, Colonel, I want to be out of here by tomorrow night, latest. I got the short-timer shakes, and the single-digit fidget. Biet?"

"Oh, I remember that feeling too well. Do you think I should go down to Cu Chi and Xuan Loc?"

"Why not? You're here. Also, I want Susan out with me."

"That's not my problem."

"It is now."

"I'll see what I can do." He asked me, "Is this Colonel Mang the cause of your problems?"

"Well, there are many causes to my problems, but he's the most obvious, and the most honest about it."

Karl ignored the innuendo, and asked me, "Where is this man now?"

"About a ten-minute drive from here. Susan and I spent an unpleasant hour with him at Gestapo Headquarters earlier this evening."

"But if he released you, Paul, then you shouldn't be too concerned."

"It's a very long story, and we shouldn't leave those people in there alone too long."

"Why not?"

"Karl. Look at me. Look closely. How stupid do I look?"

He played the game and studied my face. He said, "You look fairly intelligent. Perhaps too intelligent."

"Why did you send me on this assignment?"

"Because you are the best man I have."

"This is true. But not the best man for the job."

"Probably not. But they tried to take this case away from me, and I needed to impress them with my best agent."

"Who are *they?*"

"It doesn't matter."

"What's in this for you?"

He anticipated the question and replied, "Only the satisfaction of having done a difficult job well."

"Am I invited to your promotion party?"

"Of course."

I looked at him a long time and said, "Colonel, do you understand that the next president of the United States may be a thief and a murderer?"

"An alleged thief and murderer."

"While you and I were getting our asses shot off, this guy is sitting in his office at MACV Headquarters in the Citadel at Quang Tri, wheeling and dealing on the black market, and getting stoned. Then when the shit hits the fan and American soldiers and marines are dying all around him, he finds the fucking time to commit murder and robbery. You've read the original of that letter. Doesn't this bother you?"

He thought a moment and said to me, "I assume Ms. Weber translated this story from Tran Van Vinh."

"Answer my question."

He answered, "What's past is past. We can't change what happened to us there . . . here. We did our duty, some did not. We should not hold on to the anger, as you seem to do—"

"You're damned right I'm angry." I thought about my advice to Colonel Mang to let go of the anger, but I often don't take my own good advice. I said to Karl, "You asked me at the Wall if I was angry at the men who didn't serve, and I told you I was not. I told you I was angry at those who served dishonorably. Do you remember that?"

"I do. That was my first indication that I might

be making a mistake by sending you on this assignment."

"You should have known ten years before that."

He nodded. "Perhaps I did. I have some ambivalence myself about this."

"You shouldn't have any ambivalence, Karl."

He didn't reply to that and said, "Your anger shouldn't affect your judgment. We don't know, nor will we ever prove, that Edward Blake is guilty of anything."

"That's for a jury to decide."

"No, it's not. Look at this problem as an opportunity. An opportunity for me, and for you, to belatedly profit from the war."

"I can't believe I'm hearing that from you. Colonel Karl Law and Order Hellmann. You'd indict your own mother if you caught her shoplifting in the PX."

"My mother is not going to be the next president of the United States, and she's not surrounded by powerful and ruthless people."

I stared at him.

He said, "You can't judge a man's life by a moment in time. If you or I were judged that way, we'd have a lot to answer for. The fact is, Paul, Edward Blake has led what appears to be an exemplary life since the war, and he is what the country needs and wants at *this* moment in time. What possible difference could it make to you if he became the next president?"

I turned toward the office door, but Karl grabbed my arm. He said, "Don't make my life difficult, and don't make your own life more difficult than it already is. We have both escaped many bullets, Paul, and are about to earn well-deserved promotions and comfortable retirements. Our military funerals with full honors will come soon enough. There's no reason to accelerate that date."

I pulled my arm away from him and went into the office.

Susan was sitting in a club chair, John Eagan and Bill were on a leather couch, and Marc Goodman had moved the desk chair around to the group. I stood with my butt on the Ambassador's desk. Karl entered and took the big leather chair he'd claimed earlier.

The room was half lit with two green-shaded lamps, and outside the windows I could hear the sounds of chairs being folded on the lawn.

Colonel Goodman said to me, "It's been decided that I lead the discussion."

I didn't say anything.

Goodman said to me, "While you were outside, Susan gave us a briefing of your travels from Saigon to Nha Trang, to Hue, and then to Dien Bien Phu, and your problems with the police and the soldiers, and your run-ins with this Colonel Mang. We're up to Ban Hin." He looked at me and Susan and said, "I commend you both on an outstanding job."

I didn't respond.

He said to me, "If it's all right with Colonel Hellmann, Paul, perhaps you'd like to tell us what happened in Ban Hin."

Colonel Hellmann said, "Paul is free to speak. But I should tell you at this time that Mr. Brenner has some serious questions about the purpose of this mission and this meeting."

Everyone looked at me, and I made brief eye contact with Susan. This is what is called a defining moment. My personal life has always been a shambles, and my professional life has been marked by brilliant triumphs that I've always managed to eclipse later through some stupid stubbornness, or a run-in with authority. I didn't see why this case should be any different from any other, so I said, "As Bill probably told you, I'm on thin ice, and all I have to hold on to is the Vice President's nuts."

There was some throat-clearing and a little squirming around in the seats. Susan had her hand over her face, and I couldn't tell if she was upset or smiling.

I said, "Let me make it clear that Susan Weber did her job in regard to the mission, Tran Van Vinh, and me. I was totally in the dark about the subject of my investigation until the very end when I discovered among Mr. Vinh's war souvenirs a MACV company roster that listed Lieutenant William Hines and Captain Edward Blake. At that time, I indicated to Susan that I understood what this was about, and that I also understood the necessity of keeping the information secret and limited. She made an evaluation, based on my representation, that I was going to be a team player, though that's not what I—"

Susan interrupted, "Paul, your memory is not good. You went totally bonkers when you discovered that Edward Blake was a suspect in a murder case. You wanted to blow the whistle, and I told you you'd be nuts to do that. We argued, and you won. I agree with you. We need to uphold the law. It's really that simple."

There was a long silence in the room, and I could see that no one was happy, least of all Bill, who'd undoubtedly vouched for Susan. Karl, too, was having disturbing thoughts about his best agent, and both he and Colonel Goodman were waving good-bye to their general's star. Only John Eagan seemed cool, and by now I was certain he wasn't the FBI guy sent here to train Viet narcs.

I looked at Susan, who had just put herself in a very bad situation. She winked at me.

I said, "I'm a cop, so I'm going to pretend this is a CID staff meeting, and I'm going to pretend that all of you want me to present my evidence regarding a murder case. There are no personal or political considerations in this case, and no bullshit about national security or anything but the law."

John Eagan said, "You can present your case

any way you wish, Paul. That doesn't change the reality."

"In fact, it will change *your* reality. And you can deal with it. It's not my problem."

No one offered any new realities, so I continued, "I was contacted two weeks ago by Colonel Hellman, who asked me to conduct an investigation of a possible wartime murder. During the course of this briefing, I concluded that there was more to this than a thirty-year-old murder. But I took the case anyway, which may have been my first mistake."

I continued with my little tale, using the language of the criminal investigator. I skipped over our journey up country from Saigon, but I did mention Mang, the Highway One incident, and the Route 214 incident. I left out the sex because I'm a gentleman, it was irrelevant, and Bill was in the room. Marc Goodman and John Eagan, however, had probably figured out that Susan and I were more than partners, and they were factoring this in.

I jumped ahead and described in a little detail our last interrogation by Colonel Mang and gave the impression that Mang still thought this had to do with the FULRO.

I moved back to Dien Bien Phu and Ban Hin and the house of Tran. I went into enough detail so that they understood that if I was in front of a congressional committee or people from the Justice Department, I'd sound believable.

I concluded with, "Tran Van Vinh, in my opinion, is a reliable and believable witness. The translation of the letter that was given to me by Colonel Hellmann, though edited for my benefit and not an original document, is an important document. So much so, that I faxed it from Dulles Airport to a friend with a note asking him to hold it for me."

This bullshit got a few heads turning toward one another.

I went on, "As for the physical evidence, it consisted of the personal effects of Lieutenant William Hines. A wallet, a wedding ring, a canvas pouch containing letters, unread by me or Susan, a logbook in which Lieutenant Hines described Captain Blake in unflattering terms—called him a black marketeer and a good customer of the local hookers."

I saw a little squirming from John and Bill. Colonel Goodman, too, seemed uncomfortable. I said, "I'm not being judgmental, though Lieutenant Hines was. I admit to some whoring myself when I was here, and a little cannabis to take the edge off. But no black marketeering."

John said, "This is not relevant."

I informed him, "Nearly everything in a homicide investigation is relevant if you want to find out why one man killed another."

Karl, my good buddy, agreed. "Everything is relevant, and the most inconsequential things, when put together, give a picture and establish the motives and the personalities of the victim and the suspect."

I said, "Very good, Karl. In fact, from what I could glean from the effects of the deceased, William Hines was a Boy Scout, and Edward Blake was a bad boy. No, that doesn't make him a murderer. But we have some facts that point to him as a suspect. We have the MACV roster, which shows that both men were in the same small advisory group at the same time, and there was only one captain in the group. Army records will back this up—if they haven't been destroyed in that famous and convenient storage fire. We have the testimony of the witness, who saw and identified an American army captain of the First Cavalry Division shoot and kill a lieutenant, now identified as William Hines, who wore the same shoulder patch as the captain, and whose personal effects this witness took."

I milked this thin evidence for all it was worth, but if this group was a jury, and I was a prosecutor, I'd be worried. So, when you're losing your case, you make shit up. I said, "As Susan may have told you, Tran Van Vinh identified the photos of Edward Blake as the killer."

I glanced at Susan, who said, "Positive identification."

Bill, John, and Marc seemed upset; Karl seemed skeptical, as he should be.

I finished my presentation with, "And then there's the loot from the treasury. Someone will need to investigate Edward Blake's financial past, specifically after he returned from Vietnam. There was jewelry in the treasury vault, and that may be traceable, or still in the possession of Mr. Blake or his former lady friends or his present wife."

There was silence in the room, then Bill spoke. "It sounds to me that this evidence is not only circumstantial, but also weak and inconclusive, not to mention three decades old. I certainly wouldn't make an accusation based on what I've heard."

John Eagan agreed and said, "An accusation this serious against Edward Blake wouldn't stand up in court, but it would result in a field day for his political enemies and the media."

Marc Goodman seemed deep in unhappy thoughts, then asked me, "And in your opinion, this witness is reliable?"

"I think he is. But I understand that an American jury may not."

John asked me casually, "Where is this witness?"

I said, "Probably sleeping. He's a peasant."

Bill, who had observed my wit earlier, asked in an annoyed tone, "Sleeping *where?* In his village?"

"I guess so. It wasn't practical for us to bring him here." I looked at Bill and John and said, "And it wasn't practical for Susan to blow his head off."

No one, including Karl, feigned any shock or surprise, which was a treat. But neither did anyone comment.

Colonel Goodman looked at Susan and asked, "And you and Paul have hidden this physical evidence?"

"Yes."

"Where?"

Susan replied, "If I told you, it wouldn't be hidden."

Colonel Goodman smiled good-naturedly and said, "It doesn't need to be hidden any longer."

Susan didn't reply.

Colonel Goodman asked, "Is it nearby?"

Susan replied, "No. We anticipated having a police problem when we got off the Lao Cai train."

"So, you hid these items back in Lao Cai or near Ban Hin?"

"Around there."

Bill was embarrassed by his ex-girlfriend's lack of cooperation, and if Eagan was his boss, which he probably was, then Bill's next assignment would be watching Russian ships off the coast of Iceland. Bill said sharply, "Susan, tell us where you hid the evidence."

She fixed Bill with a look that Bill had probably seen before. "I don't like your tone."

He changed his tone. "Susan, can you describe for us the hiding place of Lieutenant Hines's personal effects?"

"Later."

"Susan—"

John Eagan butted in and addressed a question to me. "Are you withholding evidence in a criminal case?"

"No. I just hid it."

"Why?"

"We're in a hostile country, John. I secured the evidence in a safe location."

"Which you will now reveal to us."

"Why? You don't think much of it. Don't worry about it."

He ignored that and repeated, "You will tell us now where you hid it."

"Why? Who are you?"

Eagan looked at Karl, who said to me, "I'm making that a direct order, Paul."

"All right. I'll tell you later. In private."

Karl was happy to be the only one who could control me, and happier to be the sole recipient of some important information. He said, "Fine. We'll speak later."

Everyone had to be satisfied with that, and Colonel Goodman moved on and said to Karl, "You, Colonel, are an experienced and professional investigator. What is your opinion of this evidence? Would you recommend further investigation? The bringing of charges? Or a dismissal of the case?"

Karl played with his lower lip for a moment,

then answered, "You must factor in the passage of time, and the nature of the witness. He may seem reliable and believable, but I wouldn't want him as my witness unless I had some other evidence to back up his testimony . . . and the single piece of relevant physical evidence described, an army roster, is simply not enough. If this was my case at this point, I'd drop it."

I said, "Karl, that's not true and you know it. It is at this point that you do the only thing you *can* do. Question the suspect."

John Eagan jumped right in and said, "That will not happen, here or anywhere." He looked at everyone and reminded us, "We're losing sight of the most important issue. This . . . this matter could ruin the life and political career of an honorable man, a decorated veteran, a husband, father, and dedicated public servant. The American people do not need any more scandal or witch hunts. And there *are* international considerations. I dismiss this whole thing as unworthy of further discussion."

Colonel Goodman thought a moment, then said, "I'd like to know how each of us who have this information would proceed. John?"

"Drop it and this meeting never took place."

"Bill?"

"Drop it. And forget it."

"Colonel Hellmann? This is an actual case for you, is it not?"

Karl Hellmann replied, "It never was official, and it never will be. Consider the file destroyed."

I thought I heard a sigh of relief.

Colonel Goodman looked at me. "Paul?"

"I want time with the suspect."

Goodman started to say something, then thought better of it and turned to Susan. "Ms. Weber?"

"I have absolutely no experience with the law or criminal matters, and I wouldn't know what constitutes good evidence or circumstantial evidence, or a reliable or unreliable witness. But I know that four murders and a robbery were committed by an army captain, and the only captain we have who might have done it is in the guest room upstairs. Common sense says to talk to him. He may be able to tell you where he was that day. I mean, he could have been on leave, or in a hospital, or with ten other guys. You need to dig a little deeper, and maybe you'll be happy with what you find, or maybe you'll find you need to dig even deeper."

Again, a long silence, then I said, "Look, I'm not convinced myself that Edward Blake is a murderer. I might even want to be convinced otherwise. Susan is right. There's nothing lost by talking to the man."

Eagan said to me, "So, you want me to go upstairs and roust the Vice President of the United States out of bed so he can come down here and answer questions about his possible involvement in a murder?"

"Why not?"

"Because, if I was him, I'd tell you to go fuck yourself."

"I've been told that many times, John. That's when I get a subpoena."

"Are you crazy?"

"Karl can answer that."

Eagan didn't bother to ask Karl. Eagan said to me, "Look, if you want to get legal, you have no power and no authority to question anyone here, and certainly not the Vice President."

"Voluntary questionings are done all the time, John. You first ask the person if he wants to voluntarily answer some questions. If he doesn't, then you get a little suspicious, then you get a little subpoena."

"Bullshit."

Army officers rarely swear, and Goodman said, "Language, please."

Eagan said, "Jesus Christ . . . I can't believe this."

John Eagan was obviously the hatchet man here, and probably had the most to lose, except for Edward Blake. Eagan, if he was the CIA bureau chief, had planned most of this mission along with Bill, and if it came off okay, John and Bill would be at Edward Blake's inauguration ball, and in private they'd call him Eddie.

Washington has a different system of rewards and punishments, and it goes like this: If I know you did something wrong and I don't punish you, then I want a reward. That, however, is not how I or the law works.

I said to Karl, "You and I, Karl, are sworn officers of the law. We are on United States property. The alleged crime was committed while the suspect was in the military. Do we have the right to ask Edward Blake to voluntarily answer some questions?"

Karl wanted to shake his head, but his training called for a nod. The result looked like a neck spasm. Finally, he said, "There may be a jurisdictional question."

I said to Eagan, "Are you FBI?"

"No."

"Who's the FBI guy in the embassy?"

Eagan replied, "Who gives a shit? You're pissing me off, Paul."

Bill asked me, "Are you showing off for Susan?"

Before I could say "Fuck you," Susan said, "No, he's been a pain in the ass about this since he discovered the truth. He really means it."

I slid off the desk and said, "I'm going upstairs to find Edward Blake."

Eagan stood. "You take one step up those stairs, and you're history, pal."

"John, don't make me hurt you."

Everyone was standing now, and Colonel

Goodman, our discussion leader, said, "That's quite enough from both of you." He looked at me and asked, "Paul, if I can arrange for the Vice President to join us, do I have your word that you'll be satisfied that this investigation is concluded?"

I can see why Military Intelligence has a bad reputation. But *I'm* not stupid and I answered, "Of course."

"And I have your word that you understand that anything that has been said tonight is for all time classified information?"

"Absolutely."

"And your two weeks in Vietnam were tourism and nothing else."

"Correct." I noticed Bill and John looking at each other. They weren't protesting, so that meant I'd won. Actually, it meant I was dead.

Colonel Goodman walked to the door and said, "I'll get a Secret Service man to speak to the Vice President." He left.

Karl said to me, "Paul, you may want to reconsider."

I replied, "I just want to meet the VP. And get an autograph for my nephew."

Susan stood and came over to me. She said, softly, "If you had one day left in Vietnam before you went home, would you volunteer for a dangerous mission?"

"No. But I'd follow orders. My last orders were to find a murderer."

"I think Karl would like you to stop looking."

"Fuck Karl. How about you?"

"I'm on your side. Do what you need to do."

Goodman returned and said, "The Vice President will be joining us shortly." He said to me, "You have ten minutes. You *will* be polite and respectful."

"Yes, sir."

"You will *not* make any accusations. You will present the facts, and if the Vice President wants to make a statement, he will. If not, it's his right to remain silent."

"Yes, sir. I do this all the time."

"Good."

The door opened, and everyone stood, but it was only my little friend Scott Romney. He looked around, gave me what was supposed to be a tough look, then left.

A few seconds later, Vice President Edward Blake walked in the Ambassador's office. He was about my height and build, but not as good-looking as I am. He wore suit pants, a white dress shirt without the tie, and a silly silk kimono.

Edward Blake did not look annoyed, impatient, or puzzled, and certainly not personally worried, only officially concerned, like some crisis might be developing. He said, "Good evening. Problem?"

Colonel Goodman cleared his throat and said, "No, sir . . . nothing like that. May I introduce everyone?"

Goodman had given some thought to the

intros, and introduced Susan Weber first as a
Saigon resident and a friend of the Quinns'.
Goodman then introduced Bill Stanley and
Karl Hellmann, explaining, "Bill is here from
Saigon and is a friend of Susan's and also a col-
league of John's, whom you know. Colonel
Hellmann is army, just in from D.C." He saved
the best for last and said, "This is Paul Brenner,
also a friend of Ms. Weber's, and a colleague of
Colonel Hellmann's."

I shook the future president's hand, and he
said to me, "Ah, I know who you are. My wife
spoke to you."

"Yes, sir."

"You cost me a ten-dollar bet."

More than that, Ed. "Yes, sir. She told me."

The Veep explained this in a good-humored
way, and everyone laughed politely. Edward
Blake said to Susan, "And you're his traveling
companion."

"Yes, sir."

"Any friend of Pat and Anne's is a friend of
mine."

The guy was slick, but also charismatic, a
man's man, a lady's dream, and maybe a nation's nightmare.

Edward Blake looked around and said, "Well,
it was a pleasure meeting you all."

Not so fast, Ed.

Colonel Goodman said to the Veep, "Sir, this
is not purely social . . . could we impose on you

to give us a few minutes of your time? A serious matter has come up that should be brought to your attention."

I studied Edward Blake's face. The question that had been on my mind since Washington was, Did he know about this? In a way, it didn't matter, except as it related to his participation, if any, in the cover-up of a crime. My hunch was that he hadn't yet been told that the past had returned. You do the investigation first, then you tell the boss that you've got good news and bad news. The bad news is that we know what you did; the good news is that we can help.

Goodman motioned the Veep to Karl's vacated chair, and he sat back, crossed his legs, and motioned for us to sit. We all sat, except me, who parked my ass on the edge of the desk.

Colonel Goodman said to Edward Blake, "Sir, this has to do with the reason that Mr. Brenner is in Vietnam, and why Colonel Hellmann is here . . ."

Blake looked at both of us, but said nothing.

Goodman continued, "I can assure you, sir, that everything that has been discussed in this room, and whatever will be discussed is limited to a handful of people, most of whom are here . . . and that anything that is discussed now will be considered confidential and privileged . . ."

Blake said, "Okay, you've assured me and you've aroused my curiosity. Can we get to the point?"

"Yes, sir. Perhaps Mr. Brenner would like to speak. It was his idea that we ask you to join us."

Blake said to me, "You're on, Paul."

"Yes, sir. It's my duty to inform you that Colonel Hellmann and I are with the army Criminal Investigation Division."

This didn't seem to get any reaction out of him, and maybe it didn't sink in.

There are two opening questions you always ask in a homicide investigation, and I asked the first one. "Do you know a man named William Hines?"

This caught him completely off guard, and his expression went through a remarkable change, and I swear the color drained from his face. Everyone there saw it, and everyone had to come to the same conclusion.

"Sir?"

"Uh . . . don't . . . what was that name?"

"William Hines. Lieutenant William Hines."

"Oh . . . yes . . . I served with him. In Vietnam."

"Yes, sir." I asked the second question. "When was the last time you saw him alive?"

"Uh . . . alive? Oh, yes, he was killed in action. That's right."

"When was the last time you saw him alive, sir?"

"Uh . . . let me see . . . the Tet Offensive had started in late January . . . I guess I saw him a few days after . . . he went missing . . . our Headquarters was overrun . . . so . . . I'm not really sure, but about February 4 or 5 . . . 1968." He did what they all do and asked me, "Why do you ask?"

I usually say, "I'll ask the questions, you give the answers." But even I'm not that ballsy. I said, "Sir, it's come to the attention of the army Criminal Investigation Division that Lieutenant William Hines was murdered in the Treasury Building within the Citadel at Quang Tri City, on or about 7 February 1968. We have good reason to believe that his assailant was a United States Army captain. We have some evidence and an eyewitness, and what we're trying to do now is learn the identity of that assailant."

He was starting to compose himself, and he looked shocked. "My God . . . are you sure?"

"Yes, sir. We're sure he was murdered by an army captain."

"Good Lord . . ." He wasn't looking at anyone in the room and wasn't really looking at me. He said, "That was a terrible time . . . I was with the MACV group then, and we were surrounded in the Citadel and fighting for our lives. I think there were only about twenty American officers and NCOs—"

"Eight officers and nine NCOs, according to the unit roster."

He looked at me. "Is that right? Anyway, I think only seven of us survived . . ." He thought it might be a good idea to change the subject and said to me, "Pat Quinn tells me you saw combat in 'Nam."

"Yes, sir. First Cav, like you, 1968, like you. I was a rifleman with Delta Company, First Battalion, Eighth Cavalry, First Air Cav, outside Quang Tri City about that time."

"Really?" He forced a smile and said, "What were you guys doing *outside* the city? We needed you inside."

I smiled in return. "Looked too dangerous in there."

He laughed and said, "Well, if I can think of anything that might help you, Paul . . . and Karl . . . in this matter, I'll contact you." He stood, and everyone stood.

I said to him, "Sir, would you like to speak to me in private?"

He replied, "About what?"

"About the incident in question."

"I know nothing about it. But I'll think about it." He moved toward the door.

At this point, I sometimes inform the witness that he's a suspect, but then I have to read him his rights, and I usually can't find the little card in my wallet. I said to Edward Blake, "As I mentioned, sir, there was a witness to this murder, and I've questioned him." I didn't bother to mention that the witness was an enemy soldier, and I let Blake conclude that it was an American GI. I said, "He was lying wounded on the second floor of the Treasury Building, and through a hole in the floor, he saw this army captain murder not only Lieutenant Hines, but three Vietnamese nationals. The murderer then proceeded to loot a vault in the treasury."

I could see the color drain out of his face again. Not in a million years did he ever think he'd hear an eyewitness account of this story; he thought he'd killed all the witnesses. I could actually see his knees wobbling and he put his hand on the doorknob, which shook audibly. He said to me, "There have been many instances of witnesses coming forward years after the fact, who are suffering from one psychological disorder or another, or who are just plain liars. I'm sure you're familiar with that."

"Yes, sir. That's why we need your help."

"I'm sorry, I can't help you. But I wish you good luck with your investigation." He started to leave, then remembered his manners and said to Susan, "Ms. Weber, a pleasure. Gentlemen, good night." He started to leave again, then he did something strange and came over to me and shook my hand. He turned and left the room.

Karl and Susan reached for their smokes at the same time and lit up.

I went to a sideboard and helped myself to a Scotch on the rocks.

There was an almost embarrassed silence in the room. I looked at the face of each person there, and I knew that they all believed that Edward Blake had murdered three men and one woman in the commission of a robbery, and one of the men was a comrade in arms, which didn't sit well with Colonels Goodman and Hellman, nor with me.

But we all knew this from the beginning, and no one was shocked. They were worried. Worried about their careers, about their lives, and maybe even worried about their country. For sure, they were worried about me. In fact, I was worried about me, too.

It was Colonel Goodman who spoke first, and he said to me, "Could you find it in your heart to give Captain Edward Blake a pass on this one?"

I didn't reply.

He said to me, "I was a young infantry lieutenant during the war . . . I wouldn't expect everyone to understand that time and that place, Paul, but you and I do, and Colonel Hellmann understands. None of us would want to be called to account for that madness."

Again, I didn't reply.

Karl said to me, "The issue here, Paul, is not guilt or innocence, or even justice or morality. The issue here is the past. I told you, the shadows stretch from here to home. We, as soldiers, were collectively reviled and spit on at that time, and we don't owe anyone any explanation for our actions, or any new revelations about that war. If we have any guilt, it is a shared guilt, if we have any honor, it's amongst ourselves only. We are bound together for all time by blood and common nightmares. I tell you this, my friend, this has little or nothing to do with Edward Blake; to a greater or lesser degree, we are all Edward Blake."

I took a deep breath and didn't reply.

Bill said, "Paul, Edward Blake will be the first Vietnam veteran to become president of the United States. Don't you want that?"

"Bill, shut the fuck up."

The quiet room got quieter. I said, "Even if I bought that . . . and maybe I do . . . the other issue is all of you and your ambitions, your lying, your deception, and your bullshit. Edward Blake may have had a bad moment; you've had bad careers."

I put my drink down and moved to the door. I said to Karl, "I told you to find someone else." To Susan I said, "Come with me."

★

CHAPTER FIFTY

---★---

At noon the following day, an embassy staff car took me and Susan to Noi Bai Airport, north of Hanoi. We didn't speak much during the twenty-minute ride.

Two embassy security guys accompanied us into the terminal, and we bypassed airport security and check-in and went straight to the diplomatic lounge.

Mr. Uyen and Colonel Mang had my luggage, so I was traveling pretty light: the clothes on my back, my wallet, my passport, an airline ticket, and a diplomatic laissez-passer.

Susan wore a nice jade green dress, loaned to her by Anne Quinn, and I wore my dirty jeans, but clean boxer shorts and a horrible pink golf shirt given to me by Mrs. Quinn, who indicated that it was okay if she never saw me or the shirt and shorts again. A souvenir from Vietnam.

The diplomatic lounge was a little squalid despite its name, but there weren't many diplomats or their families traveling that Saturday, so we had the place pretty much to ourselves. The two embassy security guys stayed with us, which wasn't a bad idea.

The night before, Susan and I had slept on the pullout couch in the sitting room. The upstairs guest rooms had been taken by the Blakes and the Secret Service guys, who didn't want us upstairs for some reason. As tired and drained as we both had been, Susan and I made love with the knowledge that this could be the last time.

I had my scrambled eggs in the breakfast room with Susan. Only Anne Quinn had been there, and she explained that the Blakes and the Ambassador had gone early to the embassy, and she was just on her way to join them. Susan and I expressed our regrets that we'd missed them, and Anne said she'd pass on our good-byes. We thanked her for her hospitality and a great party, and she left without extending another invitation. I think she knew something was up.

Susan and I stood now in the diplomatic lounge, looking out through a big picture window at the runways and the gray, heavy sky. There seemed to be more takeoffs than landings, like at a resort whose season was ending, though in this case, I thought it was probably the Viet diaspora, here for Tet, returning to the countries of their exile.

I was booked on an Air France flight to Paris, where someone would meet me and give me a ticket to Dulles International. This wasn't the shortest route home, but it was the first available flight out of Hanoi, and I'd overstayed my welcome.

From Dulles, where this journey had begun, to my house in Falls Church would be a short taxi ride, or more probably I'd be met by people who wanted to take care of me. In any case, the journey home had begun, and like the last two times here, I didn't know how I was feeling at the moment.

I'd insisted that Susan come with me, but it was Susan herself who wanted to stay in Hanoi; she'd been in Vietnam a long time, and there were many loose ends to tie up with her life, her job, and, I suppose, this mission. As for me, like the last two times, I didn't need much notice or convincing to get out of Vietnam fast.

In the diplomatic lounge was a white door that led, according to Susan, directly out to the tarmac where a waiting vehicle would take me to the aircraft. The flight left in twenty minutes.

Susan and I didn't sit, nor did we have a drink or coffee; we just stood there, near the white door that led to Falls Church, Virginia.

Susan said, "We have about ten minutes. Someone will let you know."

I nodded.

She said, "I'm not going to cry."

Again, I nodded.

We looked at each other, and neither of us knew what to say, but the time was short.

Finally, she smiled and said, "Well, we had a hell of a two weeks, didn't we?"

I smiled.

She suggested, "We should do it again someday."

"It's never as much fun the second time."

"Maybe not. But we don't have a single photograph." She smiled. "Not even Pyramide Island."

I didn't reply.

Muzak was being piped into the lounge, and they were playing tinkly piano music. We stood in silence listening to "Let It Be."

I said to her, "Thanks for Sunday in Saigon."

"Hey, you owe me a tour of Washington."

"Anytime."

She nodded and looked at me. "I should be out of here in a week or so . . ."

"Where will you go?"

She shrugged. "Lenox, I guess. Then to New York to see if I still have a job with AAIC. Then . . . I think I'd like another overseas job. I think I was born to be an expat."

"Pick someplace nice this time."

"I still have my book of worst places to live."

I smiled and asked her, "Will you miss this place?"

"Terribly. But it's time to move on."

"It is."

She nodded. "You know, Paul . . . in the Apocalypse Now lounge . . . when I got teary . . . you remember that?"

"Yes."

"I was feeling awful about everything . . . I had a sudden case of homesickness, and I think it was you that brought that on in some way . . . and I was also thinking ahead to . . . to what I had to do . . . I had trouble lying to you from the minute I met you . . ."

"I know. I could see that."

"Could you? Good."

"Let's forget that part of the trip. Interesting as it was."

She laughed, then got a little misty and said again, "I'm not going to cry. You don't like that."

I didn't know what to say, so I changed the subject. "Maybe your friends in Langley can use your knowledge of Vietnamese there." And it's not far from Falls Church.

She shook her head. "I think I've lost that job, too."

"You did a good job. You're a natural."

She ignored that and asked, "How about you? What are you going to do?"

"Well . . . as I said . . . I need to take care of some personal business . . . see how that stands . . ."

She nodded. "You need to do that."

I didn't reply.

"Then what?"

"I think that depends on my mission report."

She nodded. "What are you going to do about that?"

"I'm not sure. Maybe I don't have to do anything. Maybe I won't be able to do anything."

"Just be careful, Paul. I mean really careful."

"I know."

"You say you know, but from what I saw, Mr. Brenner, you have more balls than brains."

I smiled. "Sometimes that's enough."

"For here, but not for Washington." She looked at me. "I'm still on your side. And available."

"I'll let you know."

She informed me, "I'm going to speak to Karl. He needs to get on the right side."

"Karl disappointed me. But I guess when your lifelong dream is in your grasp, you'll do almost anything."

She looked into my eyes. "But you have to be able to live with yourself afterward. Sometimes you just have to wait to see if your hopes and dreams come true . . . like the fairy on Nui Co Tien Mountain."

"That didn't end too well."

"It did. She waited for her lover, and he returned as soon as he was able . . . now, they're together for eternity."

"Yeah . . . look . . . Susan . . ."

A young Viet guy came through the white door with a piece of cardboard on which was written *Brenner Paul*. Susan said, "Well, Mr. Paul, you are being paged."

"Yeah . . ." I tried a smile. "Well, Ms. Susan . . ."

She said, "I am *not* going to cry." She took a deep breath. "Take care of yourself. Have a good flight, and . . ." Tears started to form in her eyes.

I put my arms around her, and we kissed. I said, "Susan . . . I need to do this clean."

"I know. This was too intense. We need a few months to see . . ."

The guy with the sign was holding it up, and he was looking at me anxiously. One of the embassy security guys was signaling me to wrap it up.

Susan said something to the young Viet, then said to me, "Don't miss your freedom flight, soldier."

We hugged again and kissed. She said, "Call me . . . whenever."

"I will. Maybe in a few weeks."

"Whenever. You have to go."

"Okay . . ." I moved toward the open door, and Susan didn't come with me. I turned back to her and asked, "Lenox?"

"Yes. I'll wait for your call."

"Wait for a knock on the door."

She smiled.

I turned and followed the young man through the door.

We descended a flight of stairs, got into an open electric cart, and drove toward the boarding gate and the aircraft.

A yellow police jeep was parked near the aircraft, and as we approached, a man in uniform stepped out of the jeep. It was, unfortunately, Colonel Mang.

He put up his hand, and the driver stopped.

I didn't get out, and I sat there waiting for Nguyen Qui Mang, Colonel, Section A of the Ministry of Public Security. He wore his sidearm, which didn't bother me; it was mine if I wanted it. But he also carried his attaché case, which always makes me more nervous than a gun.

Behind the approaching Colonel Mang was my Air France 747 with the stairs still in place, and I could see that the last passengers were boarding. A gate agent stood nearby looking at his watch.

Colonel Mang stopped beside the cart and asked me, "Where are you going, Mr. Brenner?"

"I'm going home, Colonel. You should do the same."

"Yes? And how was your diplomatic reception? Did you meet your Vice President?"

"I did."

"And was he delighted to make your acquaintance?"

"He was. We swapped war stories."

I could see that the ground crew was about to roll away the stairs. I said, "I'd love to chat awhile, but I'm going to miss my flight. So if you'll excuse me."

"I have instructed them to wait for you."

"It doesn't look that way."

"Where is Miss Weber?"

"She's staying awhile. She likes it here."

"Yes? And you? Do you like it here?"

"I have mixed emotions."

"Ah. And was your parting with Miss Weber a sad one?"

"It was not as happy as our parting is going to be. And by the way, the lady would like her film back."

"Perhaps. I first need to see the photographs you took."

"Speaking of which, if you send those photographs of Pyramide Island to one more person, you will be sorry you did."

"Are you threatening me?"

"I'm telling you."

"Did Mr. Stanley not enjoy the photographs?"

I wasn't going to give him the satisfaction of a response, and I said, "Okay, thanks for seeing me off. Gotta go."

"In a moment. So, do you think this man Blake will be your new president?"

I answered his question with a question. "What do you think?"

"I had an interesting conversation with Tran Van Vinh last night. I must think about this."

"You do that." I could see the ground crew looking my way.

Mang said to me, "You have a diplomatic pass, and you have not even mentioned it."

"I don't need anything but a ticket to get on that plane."

"Perhaps you enjoy my company."

"No, I don't. But I find you interesting."

We looked at each other, and for the first time since I'd had the misfortune of making his acquaintance, I saw no malice in his eyes. He said, "I have something for you." He reached into his attaché case and handed me the snow globe. I took it and looked at the snow falling on the Wall.

He said, "Your other personal effects will be returned through your embassy. I do not take what is not mine."

I didn't reply.

He said to me, "You and I, Mr. Brenner, will never be friends, but I will tell you that I respect your courage. So, for that reason only, I wish you a safe trip home."

I handed the globe back to him and said, "Something to remember me by."

"That is very thoughtful. And will I see you again?"

"You should hope not."

"And you as well."

"Go easy on this country, Colonel. The people have suffered enough."

He didn't reply and said something to the driver, who accelerated off toward the aircraft.

As we reached the stairs, I glanced back over my shoulder, but Colonel Mang was gone.

I looked off into the distance at the white door of the diplomatic lounge and saw Susan in the jade green dress watching me. She waved, and I waved in return.

Vietnam, third tour, had ended, and once again, I was going home sitting up.

I climbed the stairs to the aircraft and at the top, a flight attendant took my ticket, looked at it, and said in a nice French accent, "Ah, Mr. Brenner, we have been waiting for you."

"I'm here." I turned around, and as I'd done so many years ago, I surveyed the expanse of rice paddies and villages that now, as then, appeared misty through my eyes.

I looked again at the door where I'd last seen Susan, and she was still standing there.

We waved again. I took a final look at her, turned, and boarded the aircraft.

The journey home is never a direct route; it is, in fact, always circuitous, and somewhere along the way, we discover that the journey is more significant than the destination, and that the people we meet along the way will be the traveling companions of our memories forever.

★

Acknowledgments
And Other Matters

When I returned to Vietnam in January 1997, I went with two good friends: One was Dan Barbiero, a childhood friend, and former marine lieutenant with the Third Marine Division. Dan served in Vietnam at almost the same time and place I did—Quang Tri Province, November 1967 to December 1968. We tried to get together when we were there, but the war put time-consuming demands on our calendars.

The other friend who accompanied me in 1997 was Cal Kleinman. Cal served as a medic with the Eleventh Armored Cavalry, also in that memorable year of 1968. Cal is a fellow Long Islander, and we grew up in adjoining towns with rival high school football teams, but we're both on the same team now.

Cal and Dan knew I was contemplating a novel set in contemporary Vietnam, and they lent extra eyes and ears to my research, and also took good notes and interesting photographs. More important, we were able to discuss and digest what we'd seen and felt each night over a few drinks after sometimes emotionally draining days in places we thought we'd never see again. Thanks, guys, and welcome home.

Special thanks go to a fellow Long Islander, Al DeMatteis, Director of Operations, DeMatteis Vietnam, and President of DeMatteis International Group. Al has lived and worked in Vietnam for many years, and was kind enough to show me the real Hanoi, for which I am indebted to him. He's a great host, and a wonderful unofficial ambassador of goodwill to Vietnam. It's American men and women like Al DeMatteis, living and working in Vietnam, who will ultimately bring the two countries together in a way that the politicians can only begin to do.

Also in Hanoi, Dan, Cal, and I were fortunate to be introduced to an American resident of that city, Mattie Genovese, and I thank her for all her insights into the life of an American businesswoman in Vietnam. My fictional character of Susan Weber would not have been possible without the real Mattie Genovese.

I'd like to thank Lieutenant John Kennedy, Deputy Police Commissioner of Nassau County, for his close readings and suggestions, especially regarding the army Criminal Investigation Division. John has worked with CID men and women and has shared with me some astute observations and facts. John was a big help on *Plum Island* and *The Lion's Game* and has an astounding amount of knowledge about criminal justice.

This is a good time and place to thank an old friend, Patricia Burke, who has a unique job. Patricia is Vice President of Literary Affairs for Paramount Pictures and was instrumental in bringing my novel *The General's Daughter* to the attention of Paramount, which led to the motion picture of the same name. Patricia is one of the best read people in the universe, so when I was contemplating this sequel to *The General's Daughter*, I took the unusual step of pulling her into the editorial process. I never knew if she was flattered or annoyed, but she produced a cogent and coherent memo that served as a good guide for this story. Patricia also recommended *Up Country* to Paramount, which is now in development as a motion picture.

An author should always thank his or her editor, and I've been blessed by many editors. First, my editor and publisher, Jamie Raab of Warner Books, and also my editor, friend, and Chairman of AOL Time Warner Book Group, Larry Kirshbaum, and, of course, my longtime editor and wife, Ginny DeMille, who's still trying to teach me the parts of speech. And last but not least, my assistants, Dianne Francis and Patricia Chichester, who are the first to read, type, correct, and comment on the manuscript. These two ladies are my frontline editors, and if it's true that no gentleman is a hero to his valet, then certainly no writer is a genius to his typists.

Rather than thank my agent, Nick Ellison, again, I'll thank his excellent staff. First, his assistant, Megan Rickman, a California girl with a New York attitude. Also, Alicka Pistek, who is Director of Foreign Rights, a talented, multilingual lady who has done a wonderful job of introducing my novels to the rest of the world.

I'd like to thank, once again, Martin Bowe and Laura Flanagan of the Garden City Public Library, and Dan Starer of Research for Writers, New York City. Research becomes the reality around which all good fiction is built.

Last, but really first, I want to thank the early readers of the manuscript. Someone once said that an author who shows early drafts of his manuscript is like someone passing around samples of his sputum. True enough, but someone's got to look at the stuff that's coughed up first. Aside from my wife and my two assistants, I've shown my early drafts to Tom Block, childhood friend, novelist, retired US Airways pilot, and co-author with me of *Mayday*, and his wife, Sharon Block, retired US Airways flight attendant and excellent reader.

Finally, I gave the manuscript to Rolf Zetter-sten, Vice President, Warner Books, who has a reputation of being tough, honest, and thorough—an author's dream, or nightmare. I thank Rolf for his very close reading and excellent suggestions.

The germ of the idea for this novel came from my association with Vietnam Veterans of America. VVA has a program called the Veterans Initiative, whose purpose it is to assist the Vietnamese government in locating their missing soldiers. VVA was most helpful in bringing this program to my attention, and I especially want to thank Marc Leepson, Arts Editor and columnist for *The VVA Veteran*, for providing me specifics on this program.

Regarding the Veterans Initiative program, if anyone reading this has any sort of hard information regarding the fate of a former enemy soldier in Vietnam—letters, identification cards, maps, or similar documents with a name on it—please send it to Vietnam Veterans of America, Inc., Suite 400, 8605 Cameron Street, Silver Spring, MD 20910. Include a brief description of when, where, and how the item was found, and the fate of the individual, i.e., POW, MIA, KIA. VVA will forward this information to Hanoi to assist them in their efforts to locate their 300,000 missing servicemen and women; this will, in turn, encourage Vietnam to continue as-sisting us in locating the remains of our 2,000 missing in action.

I did, in fact, find a letter on the body of a North Vietnamese soldier in the A Shau Valley in May 1968, and turned it over to VVA some years ago for forwarding to Hanoi. Hopefully, a family in Vietnam has learned the fate of a missing son, husband, or brother.

Several people have made generous contribu-tions to charities in return for having their names used as characters in this novel. They are: Rita Chang (contributor to the Boys and Girls Club of East Norwich–Oyster Bay), John Eagan Jr. (Great South Bay YMCA), Earl E. Ellis (Tilles Center for the Performing Arts), Marc Goodman (Diabetes Research Institute Foundation), Lisa Klose (C. W. Post/Long Island University), Victor Ort (Boys and Girls Club of East Norwich–Oyster Bay), and Janice Stanton (Muscular Dystrophy Association). I hope these men and women en-joy their fictitious alter egos and that they con-tinue their good work for worthy causes.

★

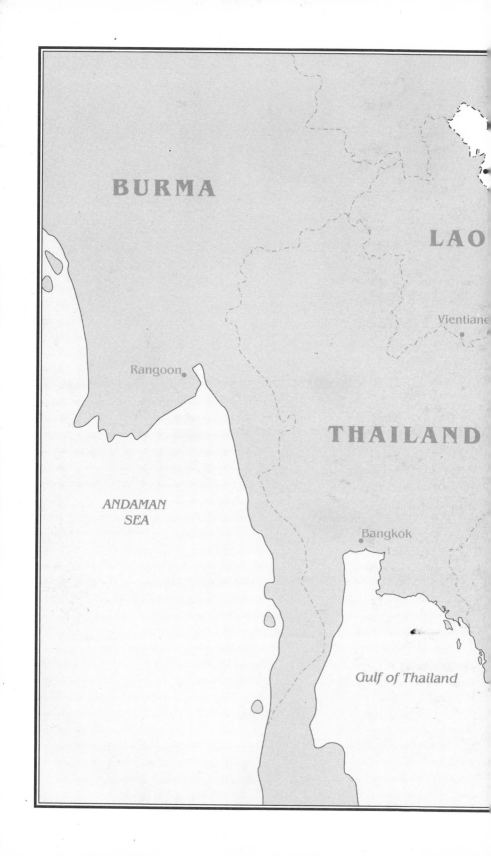